T4-ALA-620

THE CASTLE OF FRATTA

THE CASTLE OF FRATTA

By

IPPOLITO NIEVO

Translated by LOVETT F. EDWARDS

The Riverside Press Cambridge

HOUGHTON MIFFLIN COMPANY BOSTON

1958

IPPOLITO NIEVO

Born: 30 November 1831, Padua

Died at sea: March 1861

First published as

Le Confessioni di un ottuagenario, Florence, 1867

Library of Congress Catalog Card Number: 57-13458

First printing

The Riverside Press

Cambridge • Massachusetts

Printed in the U.S.A.

CONTENTS

TRANSLATOR'S FOREWORD

I FIRST read *The Castle of Fratta* in the Castle of Montechiarugolo, where I was a prisoner of war. I knew nothing of the book or of the author. It was in the camp library that I came upon the two-volume edition by Le Monnier, published posthumously under the forbidding title: *Confessions of an Octogenarian*. It was only in a concentration camp that I should have considered so formidable an undertaking as to read it. But, once tasted, I was carried away by the sweep of the story and the vigour of the language, so different from the arid classicism of earlier Italian novels and the banal puerilities of most later ones—or, at least, of those available to me. I determined to find out if it had been translated and, if not, to translate it myself.

Nievo's style has the vigorous, and somewhat careless, sweep of a great writer who has something to say and very little time in which to say it. Its key may be found in an aside by the author himself: 'Our great authors', he writes, 'I have guessed at rather than understood, loved rather than studied, and I must admit that the greater number of them have set my teeth on edge. I am aware that the fault must have been mine alone, but none the less I flatter myself that in the future he who writes will remember how he used to speak and that the aim of speaking is precisely to make oneself understood. Is it not far better to make oneself understood by the many than by the few? . . . Amongst us in Italy there are three or four vocabularies and the learned have the habit of employing the least used of them. As for logic, they use it as a springboard to make continuous leaps . . . those who are accustomed to ascend step by step remain a good half-mile behind and, having lost their guide from view, sit down contentedly to wait for another who may never come. I speak ill of no one, but in writing think that many will have to read. In this way we shall see if our literature may perhaps afford an assistance greater than it has so far given to our national renaissance.'

Nievo worked from life; and this live material is filled with humour about the customs, the society and the history of the times. Giuseppe Ravegnani, a leading critic, writes: 'It is the picture of an ancient and noble family of the past, anchored in times that have gone and defended from the outer world by a drawbridge that no longer serves any purpose. This little world has as its epicentre the kitchen, immense and mysterious, of Fratta, dominated by the autocratic and formalist figure of the old Count, seated with his rusty sword and spurs, rigid in his great armchair. It has the charm of the most beautiful pages that can be found among the few great novels of Italian literature . . .'

The opening of this vast epic is a story of childhood and of decay; the decay of a feudal society, drawn with swift touches of malignant wit, saved from caricature by deep feeling for the pitiful and the absurd. The ancient feudal family of Fratta is dying in a shabby aura of magnificence, while in the grass-covered courts and beneath the mouldering towers of its fantastic castle is growing up the new generation that is to supplant it. Even as children the basic character of the main protagonists becomes clear. Carlo, a blend of the author himself and of his noble grandfather Carlo Marin; Lucilio, only to be seen in the round as the story develops, but clearly based upon Mazzini; and the Pisana: 'creature of love and ardour, exuberant in fancy yet in essentials sound, unstable and capricious yet faithful to a single great love, sinner and heroine, the Pisana is a remarkable woman and certainly among the most original and complete female figures in our literature.'

The first part of the book contains an exquisite account of the childish loves of Carlo and the Pisana, thrown into greater relief by the stormy secondary love affair of Clara and Lucilio. But the many subsidiary characters live in their own right and are described with malicious humour that makes them live in the memory: the braggart Captain Sandracca, the otiose and gourmand Monsignor Orlando, the primitive country doctor Sperandio and the arrogant feudal lord of Venchieredo among many others.

As the long story develops, other characters take their part in its events, while some of those who have hitherto been subsidiary come to the fore. Despite the biting humour of some of his early descriptions, Nievo's characters are never caricatures or lay figures; they progress or deteriorate under the pressure of the stormy times in which they lived. During the eighty years of which Nievo writes there are too many persons in the story to mention all of them; but amongst the most vivid are the old Countess, degraded by poverty and lust for gaming to a sorry parody of her earlier patrician pride; the half-oriental father of Carlino, who hopes by the power of his *zecchini* to achieve political eminence, the tortuous Jesuit Father Pendola and his jackal, the shyster lawyer Ormenta, the swashbuckling bravo Partistagno, the whole Apostulos family, the chivalric condottiere Ettore Carafa and Napoleon himself.

It has been said that some of Nievo's characters are modelled on men and women of his own time. It is a statement difficult to sustain. His vigorous imagination far surpassed the narrow bounds of biography. But certain of them clearly owe some of their characteristics to men and women whom Nievo knew or admired during the *risorgimento*, the historical sequel to the Napoleonic ferment of which he writes. Lucilio, for example, has much to remind one of Mazzini; Carlo has much of the author himself and of his grandfather Carlo Marin; the Pisana of his cousin Bice Melzi.

Some of the minor characters are, in name and action, real persons in the literature or politics of the time. Ugo Foscolo for one, and Ettore Carafa, whose exploits have only been lightly modified by Nievo.

One of the main protagonists in the drama is the city of Venice itself, in decadence, shame and eventual hope of renascence in a united Italy. Throughout the whole book the love interest is parallel to, and intertwined with, the political interest which is indicated in its first sentence: 'I was born a Venetian on the 18th of September 1775, the Day of St Luke the Evangelist, and I shall die, by the Grace of God, an Italian, whenever the Providence that mysteriously controls our world shall so ordain.'

My decision to translate Nievo's book was taken more than ten years ago. But the many distractions of an active life kept postponing its completion and the difficulty of finding a publisher courageous enough to publish a novel which, in the original, is almost half a million words long, delayed publication even longer. The present translation has been cut to about three-quarters of its original length.

The greater part of this enormous manuscript was never revised by the author. This is evident both in manner and in matter. Rather less than half the book, judging from internal evidence, was revised by Nievo himself. The second half is not only more loosely written, but the plot, hitherto close-knit, ravels off into digressions that have little to do with the main story. The 'labour of the file' was still to do. Herein lies the main justification of a translator who has dared to apply this labour and who hopes that, in nearly ten years of close spiritual harmony with the author, he has acquired some insight of his intentions.

In his original and uncorrected manuscript, Nievo had begun to carry his story onward to the second generation. This greatly weakens the book, and is more didactic than artistic in intention. It has therefore been cut, and the last three chapters condensed to a short epilogue. The real story ends with the death of the Pisana, leaving for the epilogue the nostalgic return to Fratta in old age and the magnificent peroration with which the whole work ends.

This is the principal cut and one which, I am sure, Nievo himself would have made had he lived to do so. Other larger cuts involve the shortening of certain conversations, the omission of a passage in which Carlino in a moment of adolescent altruism renounces his love for the Pisana in favour of Giulio del Ponte, a long passage of moralizing after the death of Martino and some episodes during the siege of Genoa.

It was inevitable, in such case, that some of Nievo's characters should suffer by this foreshortening; but I feel that only one has done so. He is Giulio del Ponte who is, throughout the book, rather a foil to the emotions of Carlino than a person in his own right. Of the brilliant series of pictures that Nievo evokes, ranging from near caricature to the tenderest evocations of love, heroism and honour, I have felt that Giulio del Ponte was the most easily spared. Other cuts are minor, being mainly to avoid allusion to those episodes already omitted.

For the benefit of those who wish to read the Confessions in the original—Nievo's original title for the book was *The Confessions of an Italian*—I mention that there are some divergences between various editions. I have used sometimes one and sometimes another. Those who cannot obtain—or afford—the magnificent centenary edition will find the last, best and presumably definitive text in *La Letteratura Italiana*, Vol. 57, *Ippolito Nievo: Opere*, published by Riccardo Ricciardi of Milan.

* * * * *

Born in Padua in 1831, Ippolito Nievo was one of those many-sided and colourful personalities so often considered typical of the Italian renaissance, but who were to spring up again in the stormy times of the *risorgimento*. Poet, philosopher, dreamer, conspirator and soldier, he crowded as much incident into the brief thirty years of his life as into the vast canvas of his book.

His grandfather was the Venetian patrician, Carlo Marin, from whom he learnt, while still a boy, during the long winter vigils at the ancestral castle of Colloredo in the Friuli, the events of the fall of Venice and the Napoleonic whirlwind that he was to evoke in *The Castle of Fratta*. It was near Portogruaro that he saw the ruins of that castle which he was to make live again in his masterpiece. Today only the site remains.

In 1847 Nievo was sent to the *liceo* of Mantua, where there was a considerable amount of clandestine student politics which, in those days, was equivalent to conspiracy. It seems that, while only seventeen, he joined the Mantuan Civil Guard. But Mantua did not attain even the ephemeral liberty of Venice or Milan, and the young poet, bitter and disillusioned, was sent by his father to Pisa on the pretext of learning a purer Italian, but with the evident intention of keeping him away from the Po Valley where there were too many rumours of revolt.

At Pisa he saw the last embers of the Italian revolution stamped out. It was there that he heard the news of 'fatal Novara' that led to that 'decade of grievous and disillusioned truce' that was for Nievo a period of intense spiritual and artistic ferment. 'The catastrophe of Novara, the downfall of the hopes placed in Pius IX, and later the gallows of Belfiore, seemed to close a cycle of history nor could any hopes be seen for the morrow.'

In the summer of 1849 he returned to Mantua and later went on to the University of Padua, where he obtained his degree in 1855. By this time he had already written some books of verse of a fiercely patriotic nature as well as a number of stories based on the life of the country people of his beloved Friuli. In one of these the description of a requisition by the local police brought him into conflict with the Austrian authorities. The charge was of so absurd a nature that even the judges did not take it seriously. None the less, pressure from Vienna assured his conviction and he was sentenced to prison. Nievo appealed and the case dragged on through court after court, till his sentence was finally and ignominiously commuted for a fine of twenty-five florins. In a letter to a friend Nievo wrote contemptuously: 'To tell you the truth I felt very little desire to pay and preferred to be committed for contempt of court. But it seemed to me that I should have bought martyrdom at too cheap a price.'

Towards the end of 1857 Nievo went to Milan for another hearing of his trial. He remained there, not out of any great affection for that city, but because of his cousin, the Countess Bice Melzi, whose features and character he immortalized in those of the Pisana. (Her essentially Venetian name, however, he borrowed from that of another friend, Pisana di Prampero, of San Martino in the Friuli.)

By combining a number of accounts we can get a picture of Nievo at the time when he first met Bice Melzi. Fairly tall, slim and spare, he was dark in complexion, with black hair and very black eyes. His whole being displayed physical vigour and it was clear to all who came into contact with him that he had grown up in the most perfect balance of body and spirit. Long experience of the countryside and the open air, rare in Italians of his time and class, had bronzed his skin, hardened his muscles and helped to form his gay and open nature. In life, as in art, he preferred the simplest forms, clear and precise. He never let an opportunity pass of showing his aversion to 'rationalist utopias, declamations and heroic pomposities' or of poking fun at the faint-hearted liberals of his time whom he lampooned as 'penny-a-dozen Robespierres'. He loved to live dangerously but detested shams. When discussing with a friend a project of going to the Balkans to fight the Turks, he begged that his gesture should not be interpreted as a Byronic pose.

The Castle of Fratta was written in a fury of creative effort in only eight months, between December 1857 and August 1858, in the midst of patriotic anxieties, amorous distractions and journalistic effort. It remained for some years without a publisher, largely due to the preoccupations of the author, and was only published in 1867, some years after his death. 'Even as it has come down to us, however,' writes a leading Italian critic, 'Nievo's book is one of the greatest and most significant in our literature; ours above all for its absolute character of *italianità*, which makes it worthy of being compared, alone among Italian novels, to *The Betrothed*.'

A year after he had completed his book and laid down his pen, the young author took up the sword. The hour had come for that action of which he himself had stressed the necessity. He who had said the first word must complete the last action.

On 28 April 1859 the Emperor of Austria declared war on Piedmont. On 5 May Nievo crossed the frontier to enlist in the Sardinian army. On the 12th he was enrolled in the Guides and later passed to the mounted *Cacciatori* of Garibaldi. On his departure for the front, he commenced another volume of verse, left unfinished, his *Amori Garibaldini*.

In the reorganization of Garibaldi's armies, Nievo became one of 'the Thousand'. Abba, in his *Noterelle* of Garibaldi's campaigns, writes: 'The Ministry of War is a broken down cart that follows us, carrying the administration, the maps and the pay chest amounting, as far as we know, to thirty thousand francs. But in this cart we have two treasures; the heart of Acerbi and the intellect of Ippolito Nievo. Nievo is a Venetian poet, who at twenty-eight has written novels, ballads, tragedies. He will be the poet-soldier of our enterprise. I saw him squatting in the bottom of the cart; sharp profile, soft eye, genius shining on his brow . . . a fine soldier . . .'

Nievo was indeed a fine soldier, though not so enthusiastic about the administrative duties assigned to him. He wanted to live dangerously, to be in the forefront of the battle, and indeed he is reported to have shielded Garibaldi with his own body at the battle of Calatafimi. He intended to become the poet-soldier of the campaign for, after the entry into Palermo, he added to the *Amori Garibaldini* the first pages of his *Journal of the First Expedition of Sicily* which also, alas, remained unfinished. However, in the few pages that remain, he has left us a portrait of himself at that time: 'We have the compensation of being regarded as heroes; and this advantage, with a couple of spans of red blouse and seventy centimetres of scimetar, makes us the happiest men on earth. . . . I was dressed as when I left Milan, and carried a huge musket that needed four caps to fire a shot; in compensation I have a loaf of bread spiked on my bayonet, a fine aloe flower in my hat and a magnificent bedcover on my back. I confess that I cut a fine figure! The General (Garibaldi) too was stupendous. He was always in his shirt-sleeves and had the sole advantage over me that his boots, instead of being full of holes, had been repaired. . . .' After the formal wars of a hundred years, it has been left to men of our own generation to appreciate the vigour, and the valour, of such irregular, partisan troops.

When 'the Thousand' left Sicily, Nievo was left at Palermo to look after details of the administration. This duty finished, he made a rapid trip to northern Italy to see Bice Melzi and try to find, in vain, a publisher for his book. In February 1861, while he was at Naples with the duties of chief of the administration of the Southern Army, he received orders to go once more to Palermo. By the end of the month everything at Palermo was completed, and Nievo was eager to return. He was advised to leave on the *Elettrico*, the only sound ship then plying between Palermo and the mainland. But the ramshackle *Ercole* was leaving three days earlier and Ippolito, deaf to the remonstrances of his friends, decided to leave on her.

There were about eighty persons on the *Ercole* and a certain quantity of military stores. She left Palermo on 4 March.

What happened on the voyage is not exactly known. Certainly the *Ercole* was never seen again. According to one account, the old ship foundered in a violent gale some twenty miles from Capri. The Ministry of War, on the other hand, said that a fire broke out during the journey. No wreckage and no bodies were ever certainly found. Nievo perished, only thirty years old and his work but just begun. He lost his life trying to anticipate by three days the joy of seeing once more Bice Melzi, whose character and features he has made live for ever in those of the Pisana.

LOVETT F. EDWARDS

CHAPTER I

I WAS born a Venetian 18 September 1775, the Day of St Luke the Evangelist and I shall die, by the Grace of God, an Italian, whenever the Providence that mysteriously controls our world shall so ordain.

That is the lesson of my life. But in so far as this lesson was due not to myself but to the times in which I lived, it has occurred to me that a simple account of the influence of those times upon the life of one man could be of some use to those who, in later days, are destined to feel the less imperfect consequences of what has already been achieved.

In this Year of our Lord 1858 I am now aged more than eighty years, though still young in heart, perhaps more so than in the days of youthful struggle and overtaxed manhood. I have lived and suffered much, but am not less rich in those consolations that, for the most part, remain unrecognized among the tribulations that always owe overmuch to human intolerance and weakness, but none the less uplift the soul to a serenity of peace and hope, when they are recalled to memory as they really were, invincible talismans against every adverse fortune. I mean those feelings and opinions which, even though they are moulded by external events, yet victoriously command them and make of them the fields of active struggle. My nature, my talent, my early education and the progress of my destiny were, as all things human, a mingling of good and of bad; were it not an indiscreet quirk of modesty I could also add that, in my own case, the bad was rather more abundant than the good.

Nothing of all this would be unusual or worth the telling, were it not that my life was passed astride those two centuries which will always remain a memorable epoch, more especially in the history of Italy. Then could be seen the first ripening of the fruit of those political speculations that from the fourteenth to the eighteenth centuries were evident in the works of Dante, of Machiavelli, of Filicaia, of Vico and of so many others whose names my mediocre culture and almost complete literary ignorance can no longer recall. The chance, some might say the mischance, of having lived in those years has therefore led me to this task of writing what I have seen, felt, done and experienced from early childhood to the advent of old age, when the infirmities of age, forbearance to those younger, the temperance of mature opinions and, let me say also, the experience of many misfortunes in these recent years, have driven me to this country dwelling whence I have taken part in the last and most ridiculous episode of the great feudal drama. Nor has my simple account any more importance to history than would be a note added by an unknown but contemporary hand to the revelations of an ancient codex. The private activities of a man who was neither so petty as to withdraw himself from the common miseries, nor so stoical as to opposte them deliberately, nor indeed so wise or so proud as to pass them by disdainfully, should, it seems to me, in some way reflect the communal and national activity that absorbed them, even as the fall of a drop of water indicates the direction of the rain.

Thus an account of my experiences will serve as an example of those countless individual destinies that, from the breaking up of the old political orders to the refashioning of the present one, together compose the great national destiny of Italy. Perhaps I deceive myself, but I feel that, in thinking them over, some young men may be able to avoid being disheartened by dangerous allurements and others filled with enthusiasm for the work so slowly but lastingly accomplished, while many may be able to fix securely those wayward aspirations that lead them to try a hundred ways before finding that one which leads them into the true practice of civil ministry. So at least it has appeared to me in the nine years which, by fits and starts and as memory and inspiration have suggested, I have spent in writing these notes. I began them with unwavering faith on the eve of a great defeat and brought them to an end through a long expiation in these years of renewed effort, and they have in some measure helped to persuade me of the greater energy and more legitimate hopes of the present in comparison with the spectacle of the weaknesses and wickednesses of the past.

And now, before setting down to transcribe them, I have wished, in these few lines of prelude, to define and better to justify that idea that has led me, in my old age and without literary art, to try, perhaps in vain, to learn the difficult art of writing. Let the clarity of ideas, the simplicity of sentiments and the truth of history be my excuse and a compensation for my lack of rhetoric. The sympathy of kind readers rather than the desire of reputation will sustain me.

In the shadow of the tomb, already long alone in the world, abandoned both by friends and enemies, without fears and without hopes that are not of eternity, freed by age from those passions which only too often caused my judgements to deviate from the true path, and from the transient hopes of my not overbold ambition, I have garnered in my life one fruit alone, peace of soul. In this I live content, in this I place my trust; this I hand on to my younger brothers as the most enviable of treasures, as the unique shield to defend one against the lure of false friends, the deceptions of the vile and the extravagances of the powerful. Yet one more thing I must say, a thing to which the experience of an octogenarian may perhaps add some authority, and that is, that life as I experienced it was on the whole good, whenever humility allows us to consider ourselves merely the infinitesimal creations of human life, and whenever uprightness of soul accustoms us to look on the good of others as in great measure superior to the good of ourselves alone.

My earthly existence at last is coming to its end; content with the good that I have done and sure that I have repaired, as far as in me lies, the evil that I have committed, I have no other hope and no other faith save to flow into and become one with the great sea of existence. The peace that I now enjoy is like that mysterious gulf at the end of which the bold navigator finds a passage to the infinite calm of the Ocean of Eternity. But my thought, before plunging into that time when time exists no more, leaps forward once again into the future of men; to them I confidently bequeath my own faults to be discerned, my own hopes to be accomplished, my own vows to be fulfilled.

I passed my early years in the Castle of Fratta, which is now no more than a heap of ruins whence the peasants take at their pleasure stones and rubble for draining the subsoil of their mulberry trees. But at that time it was a huge block of buildings with towers and pepper-pots, a great drawbridge rickety with age, and the finest Gothic windows to be found between the Lemene and the Tagliamento. In all my travels I have never encountered any buildings that made so bizarre a spectacle on the landscape, nor which had angles, cornices, embrasures and bastions sufficient to content all the quarters and sub-quarters of the wind-rose. These angles were combined with such daring fantasy that there was not one that matched its companion. I do not know whether or not the T-square had ever been used in their construction, or whether all those that lumber up the studios of engineers had become exhausted in the process.

The castle stood firmly between extremely deep moats where sheep pastured whenever the frogs were not croaking there; but the slow growth of the ivy had gradually invested it by the counterscarps and, sprouting here and climbing there, had finished by creating such draperies of festoons and arabesques that the reddish colour of the stone could no longer be seen. Nobody ever dreamed of laying a hand upon this venerable covering of the ancient signorial dwelling, and even the shutters torn down by the north wind hardly dared to break off some hanging fringe. Another anomaly of this building was the multitude of chimneys, which from a distance gave it the appearance of a chess-board spread with a still unfinished game. Certain it is that if its ancient lords could have counted one retainer per chimney it would have been the best guarded castle of all Christendom.

Its high portalled courtyards, filled with mud and hen-roosts, fulfilled with their internal disorder the promise of the façade; even the campanile of the chapel was cracked here and there by the repeated salutations of the lightning. But its perseverance was in some way justified, since there never howled a *temporale* that its cracked bell did not make welcome, so it became almost a duty to return the courtesy with a thunderbolt or two. Some gave the merit of these meteorological jests to the age-old poplars that shaded the countryside around the castle, while the peasants said that, since the devil inhabited it, it was natural that from time to time it should be visited by some of his good companions. The gentry, used to seeing only the campanile struck, were accustomed to regard it as a sort of lightning rod and willingly abandoned it to the celestial anger, if only thereby the roofs of the barns and the great cowl of the kitchen chimney remained unharmed.

But we have now reached a point which requires a fairly long digression. Suffice it to say that, for me who have not seen either the Colossus of Rhodes or the Pyramids of Egypt, the kitchen of Fratta and its hearth were the most awe-inspiring monuments that ever burdened the surface of the earth. The Cathedral of Milan and the Church of St Peter are indeed something, but they do not by a long way give an equal impression of immensity and solidity. Nothing similar can I recollect ever having seen save Hadrian's Mole, although since it has been transformed in the Castel Sant Angelo it seems today much diminished.

The kitchen of Fratta was a vast place, with an indefinite number of walls very varied in size, which rose towards the heavens like a cupola and delved under the earth deeper than an abyss; obscure, even black, with a secular layer of soot, whence shone like so many huge diabolical eyes the shining bottoms of saucepans, dripping pans and flasks, cumbered in every direction with immense sideboards, colossal dressers and endless tables, it was haunted at all hours of the day or night by an unknown number of black and grey cats, which gave it the appearance of a witches' laboratory—so much for the kitchen. But in the deepest and darkest of its chasms yawned an acherontic gulf, a cavern still more grim and terrifying, where the darkness was broken by the crackling flicker of embers and the greenish light of two window-slits with double iron grilles. There, there was a dense curling of smoke, an eternal bubbling of beans in monstrous cauldrons. There, sitting in rows on creaking and smoke-blackened benches, was a grave sanhedrin of fateful and somnolent figures. This was the hearth and the domestic Curia of the castellans of Fratta. But hardly had the evening Ave Maria sounded and the echo of the Angelus Domini ceased, than the scene changed in a moment and for that little world of shadows commenced the hours of light. The old cook lit four lamps with a single taper, two under the chimney shaft of the hearth and one on either side of the Madonna of Loreto. Then she dragged together the embers with an enormous poker and threw on them an armful of thorns and juniper. The lamps reflected a calm yellowish light, the fire crackled into smoke which rose in curling spirals right up to the crossbar of the two gigantic andirons bossed with bronze, and the evening inhabitants of the kitchen revealed their varied faces to the light.

The Count of Fratta was a man of more than sixty, who seemed as if he had just that moment stepped out of his armour, so rigid and pokerlike he sat in his great armchair. But his wig, his purse, his ash-coloured surcoat piped with scarlet and the boxwood snuffbox always in his hands were a trifle out of keeping with this military attitude. It is true that he held between his legs a slender sword, but its sheath was so rusty that it could well have been exchanged for one of the spits and, furthermore, I could not assure you that there was really a steel blade concealed in that sheath, and the Count himself had probably never taken the trouble to convince himself of the fact.

The Count was always shaved with such care that he looked as if he had just come from the hands of the barber; from morn till eve he always carried a blue kerchief under his armpit and, though he seldom went out on foot and never on horseback, he wore jackboots and spurs that would not have disgraced a courtier of Frederick II. This was a tacit declaration of sympathy with the Prussian party, and though the wars in Germany had long been over, he had not ceased to menace the imperial faction with the disfavour of his spurs.

When the Count spoke, everyone agreed with him, either aloud or with a nod of the head; when he laughed, everyone hastened to laugh too; when he sneezed after snuff, eight or nine voices competed with: 'Long live the Count', 'Good health' or 'God preserve the Signor Count'; and when he rose, all rose. When he left the kitchen, all, even including the cats, breathed deeply with both lungs as if a millstone had been taken from their chests. But more profoundly than all the rest breathed the Chancellor, if the Count did not make a sign to him to follow, and mercifully permitted him to remain in the quiet ease of the hearth. It must, however, be added that this miracle occurred but seldom. They rose together and sat together, and their legs alternated in so true a measure that they seemed to be keeping time with the beating of drums. When these habits were first being formed, the frequent desertions of his shadow had made the Count turn around every three paces to see if he were being followed according to his desire. But by now the Chancellor had become resigned to his destiny, and occupied the second half of his day in picking up his patron's kerchief, wishing him good health at every sneeze, approving his every observation and telling him whatever he felt would be received with favour in all matters concerning the local administration of justice. For example, if a peasant accused of stealing the first-fruits of the signorial garden replied to the reprimands of the Chancellor by flattering him or perhaps by slipping a half-ducat into his hand, the Chancellor would tell the magistrate that such and such a one, terrified by the severe justice of His Excellency, had asked for mercy, had repented of his misdeeds and was disposed to make amends with whatever fine might be considered adequate. The Count then breathed in enough air to have sustained Goliath for a week and replied that the clemency of Titus should be mingled with the justice of the tribunals and that he for his part would pardon anyone who genuinely repented.

The Chancellor, perhaps for modesty's sake, was as humble and disorderly in his appearance as his principal was pompous and splendid. But nature had counselled him to such modesty, since a more miserable and afflicted manikin it would have been hard to find. It was sometimes said that he squinted as a matter of habit; but the fact was that few squinters had as much right to the title as he. His nose, aquiline, hooked and snub at the same time, was a Gordian knot of noses aborted together; and his mouth yawned beneath it so menacingly that the poor nose used to draw itself up for fear of falling into it. His legs, gaitered in leather, were splayed out on either side of him to give the maximum support to a figure which it seemed must collapse before every puff of wind. Without wishing to joke, I believe that if you had taken away the wig, the clothes and the sword, the weight of the Chancellor of Fratta would not have surpassed a bare twenty pounds, counting therein for a full four the goitre which he sought to hide behind an immense starched ruff. Ugly as he was, he had the happy illusion of thinking himself anything but unappetizing and he would talk on no subject so willingly as on beautiful women and gallantry.

How content Madame Justice was to find herself in his hands I could not in all conscience tell you. But I remember to have seen more downcast than contented faces descend the open staircase of the Chancellery. There was much trumpeting in his anteroom on audience days, and those who had big fists and loud voices and used them alternately, and who in addition had silver in their pockets, easily obtained the fruits of justice before his tribunal. What I can say is that on two occasions I happened to witness floggings in the courtyard of the castle, and on both occasions this ceremony involved two poor devils who certainly had not deserved it. It was as well for them that the Serjeant empowered with the execution of justice high and low was a man of judgement and flourished the rope's end with such skill that the weals healed at the worst on the seventh day. Therefore Marchetto, nicknamed the Bonebreaker, was as loved by the common people as the Chancellor was hated. As for the Count, concealed as was Destiny in ancient times in the high clouds of Olympus, he escaped both the hatred and the love of his vassals. They took off their hats to him as to the image of some foreign saint in whom they had small confidence, and drove their carts into the ditch when the postillion on the roof of his bombay shouted to them to make way while still a good half mile distant.

The Count had a brother who in no way resembled him and was an honorary canon of the Cathedral at Portogruaro, the roundest, smoothest and most mellifluous canon in the whole diocese, a real man of peace who divided his time wisely between the breviary and the table without letting his greater predilection for the one or for the other be revealed. Monsignor Orlando was not begotten by milord his father with any idea of dedicating him to Mother Church; his baptismal name was witness for this. The genealogical tree of the Counts of Fratta had always boasted some military glory in every generation, and he had been destined to perpetuate the family tradition. But man proposes and God disposes; this time at least the great proverb was not wrong. The future General began his life by demonstrating an extraordinary affection for his wet-nurse, so that it was not possible to wean him before the age of two. Even at that time it was still uncertain whether the one word he could utter was 'pap' or 'papa'.

When he was at last able to walk, they began putting wooden swords and cardboard helmets in his hands; but hardly had they done so before he escaped into the chapel to play with the sacristan's broom. As for trying to accustom him to real weapons, he showed from the first an instinctive revulsion against table knives and wanted at all costs to cut his meat up with a spoon. His father tried to vanquish this accursed repugnance by making him sit on the knee of one of his buli (feudal retainers); but the little Orlando was so terrified that they had to transfer him to the cook's lap lest he should die of fright. After the wet-nurse, the cook was his second love; it was not for nothing that he made clear his vocation. The Chancellor held that the captains of old time always ate so much that the little master would indeed in course of time become a famous captain.

The old Count was not reassured by these hopes, and sighed as his eyes wandered from the puffy and bewildered face of his second-born to the proud and hirsute moustachios of the old family portraits. He had dedicated the last powers of his generative faculties to the ambitious task of inscribing in the future annals of the family a Grand Master of the Order of Malta or an Admiral of the Most Serene Republic, and it galled him to have employed them merely to have at his table the terrific appetite of a Captain of the Cernide (local militia). Therefore he redoubled his zeal to awaken and stir up the bellicose spirit of Orlando; but the effect did not justify his efforts. Orlando built little altars in every corner of the castle, sang Mass, high, low and ceremonial, with the sacristan's brats and whenever he saw a musket, flattened himself under one of the kitchen sideboards. Then they tried other means of persuasion, forbidding him to play in the sacristy and to sing vespers through his nose as he had heard the choirboys of the parish do. But his mother was scandalized by such violence and began, on her side, secretly to take up the defence of her son. Orlando found it much to his taste to act the part of a little martyr; and since his mother's sweetmeats amply consoled him for his father's rebuffs, the profession of priest seemed to him more than ever preferable to that of a soldier. The cook and the house-servants sniffed around him an odour of sanctity and thenceforward he began to grow fat with contentment and to show an even more exaggerated devotion in order to maintain the adoration of the womenfolk. So that finally his august father, with his military ambitions, had against him the opinion of the whole family. Even the buli, who always supported the cook's party when their feudal master was out of hearing, deplored the sacrilege of obstinately trying to turn a St Louis from the true path. But the feudal master was obstinate and only after twelve years of vain assault decided to lift the siege and to put away in the storehouse of vanished dreams the future military laurels of Orlando. One fine morning Orlando was called with imposing solemnity before his father who, however much he outwardly assumed the authoritative frown of the absolute master, yet felt within him the vacillating and contrite feelings of a general about to capitulate.

'My son,' he began, 'the profession of arms is a noble profession.'

'So I believe,' replied the boy with a saintly expression, a little marred by a sly glance secretly directed towards his mother.

'You bear a proud name,' continued the old Count, sighing, 'Orlando, as you must have learnt from the poem of Ariosto which I have so much recommended you to study . . .'

'I read the Offices of the Madonna,' interrupted the boy, humbly.

'Excellent,' continued the old man, adjusting the wig on his forehead, but 'Ariosto is also worthy of being read. Orlando was a great paladin who liberated from the Moors the fair realm of France. And even more, if you have glanced through *Gerusalemme Liberata*, you would know that it was not with the Offices of the Madonna, but with great strokes of the sword and thrusts of the lance that the good Geoffrey wrested from the hands of the Saracens the Sepulchre of Christ.'

'May God be praised,' exclaimed the boy. 'Then there remains nothing more to be done!'

'Nothing more, indeed!' burst out the old man. 'Know then, wretched boy, that the infidels reconquered the Holy Land and that now, even as we are speaking, a Pasha of the Sultan governs Jerusalem to the shame of all Christendom!'

'I will pray the good Lord that such shame should cease,' put in Orlando.

'Prayers, indeed! It is deeds that are needed,' shouted the old Count.

'Your pardon,' interrupted the Countess, 'but you surely do not pretend that our baby should carry out a crusade all by himself.'

'Bah! He is no longer a baby,' replied the Count. 'He has just completed his twelfth year.'

'Even had he completed his hundredth,' went on the Countess, 'it is certainly not necessary to fill his head with the conquest of Palestine.'

'We shall never conquer it as long as we teach our children to play the woman with a rosary,' exclaimed the old man, purple with anger.

'It only wanted that sort of blasphemy!' the Countess went on patiently. 'Since the Good Lord has granted us a son who has the idea of being good, let us show ourselves grateful indeed by refusing to recognize his gifts!'

'Fine gifts, fine gifts!' muttered the count, '. . . a gluttonous little saintling . . . half fox and half rabbit . . .'

'At least he never said anything like that,' added the lady. 'All he said was that he would pray to God to grant that the places of His passion and His death return to the hands of the Christians. That is the best thing to do now, since the Christians of today are occupied in cutting one another's throats and the profession of soldier has become a mere school of cut-throats and butchers.'

'Body of the Serenissima!' thundered the Count. 'If Sparta had had mothers like you, Xerxes would have passed Thermopylae with three hundred hogsheads.'

'Even had things been as you say, I should not have worried overmuch,' replied the Countess.

'What!' roared the old man. 'Have you reached the point of denying even the heroism of Leonidas and the virtue of the Spartan mothers?'

'Bah! Now we know where we are,' the lady said quietly. 'I know little enough of Leonidas and the Spartan mothers, though I have heard them mentioned only too often; furthermore, I am quite prepared to believe blindly that they were very fine fellows. But recall that we have summoned before us our son Orlando to throw some light on his true vocation and not to squabble in his presence about these rancid fairy-tales.'

'Women, women! . . . Born to educate hens!' muttered the Count.

'Husband mine! I am a Badoera!' said the Countess, drawing herself up. 'You will allow, I hope, that the hens in my family are not more numerous than the capons in yours!'

Orlando, who had been holding his sides for some time past, now broke into a laugh at this fine compliment of Madame his mother but was quelled instantly like a wet chicken at the severe glance she turned on him.

'You see,' she went on, speaking to her husband, 'we will end up by losing both goat and cabbages. Put a rein on your caprices till God makes you understand He cannot be thwarted for nothing, and ask yourself instead, as becomes a good father of a family, about the soul of this boy.'

The old impenitent bit his lip and turned to his son with an expression on his face so terrifying that the boy was scared out of his wits and ran to hide his head in his mother's lap.

'So,' the old Count began, without looking at him, since he felt that if he did so his anger would rise again. 'So, my son, you do not want to make your appearance on a fine horse, with trappings of gold and red velvet, with a long flaming sword in your hand and behind you six regiments of Slavs, all six feet high, who only wait an order from you to rush to their death on the Turkish scimitars?'

'I want to sing Masses, I do!' whimpered the boy from under his mother's apron.

The Count, hearing this whining voice half suffocated by the folds of the garment whence it issued, turned to see what was the matter, and seeing his son with his head wrapped up like a pheasant in its hide, could no longer control his anger.

'Go to the seminary then, bastard!' he shouted, rushing out of the room.

The little wretch began to sob and tear his hair and beat his head against his mother's lap, quite sure that he could not do himself any harm. But she took him in her arms and consoled him with caresses, saying:

'Yes, heart of mine, don't be afraid; we will make a priest of you. You will sing Mass. You are not made, indeed, to spill the blood of your brothers like Cain.'

'Ee, ee, ee! I want to sing in the choir! I want to become a saint!' howled Orlando.

'Yes, yes . . . you will sing in the choir; we shall make a canon of you. You shall have your cloak and your fine red stockings. Don't cry, my treasure. These are trials which we must bear for the Good Lord's sake, to make ourselves more worthy of him,' went on his mother.

The boy consoled himself with these promises, and therefore the Count Orlando, despite his baptismal name, and in opposition to his father's views, became Monsignor Orlando. But however much the Curia was disposed to favour the devout ambition of the Countess none the less, Orlando was no eagle, so that it took no less than twelve years in the seminary and another thirty as a postulant to help him to reach even the half of his aspirations; and the Count had the triumph, and the Countess the mortification, of dying many years before the red flakes began to snow down upon his head. None the less, it could not be said that our priest entirely wasted all this time of waiting. He acquired a respectable knowledge of the missal; and his shirt-front developed to such an extent that it would rival the softest and most elaborate of any of his colleagues.

A castle which sheltered within its walls two such dignitaries, forensic and clerical, as the Chancellor and Monsignor Orlando, could not be without its military celebrity also. The Captain Sandracca wanted to be a Slav at all costs, though it was rumoured that he had been born at Ponte di Piave. Certainly he was the tallest man in the whole neighbourhood and the goddesses of grace and beauty had not presided at his birth. But none the less he spent a good hour every day in making himself three times as ugly as he was already and was always studying some new way of glowering or some new embellishment of his moustaches to make himself still more formidable.

To listen to him when he had emptied his fourth glass, there was no war from the siege of Troy to that of Belgrade where he had not fought like a lion. But once the fumes of the wine had a little chilled, his pretensions were reduced to more honest proportions. He contented himself then with recounting how he had received twelve wounds in the war of Candia, offering on every occasion to take down his breeches and let you count them. And God alone knew how these wounds could have been made, since now, on thinking it over, it does not appear to me likely that, with the fifty years which he then admitted to, he could have taken part in a war fought sixty years before. Perhaps his memory deceived him and made him believe the exploits of some braggart which he had heard recounted by the storytellers of the Piazza San Marco to be his own. Indeed, the good Captain got confused easily enough with his dates. But he never forgot the first of each month to make sure he was paid by the factor his twenty ducats of salary as Captain of the Cernide (militia). That day was his festa.

At crack of dawn he sent out two drummers who hammered away until noon in all the four cantons of the jurisdiction. Then, in the afternoon, when the militia was assembled in the courtyard of the castle, he would come out of his room looking so ugly, so very ugly, that his appearance alone was enough to throw his little army into confusion. He wielded a great sword, so long that it would have sufficed to mark the pace of an entire column. And since at the slightest mistake he used mercilessly to beat with it the paunches of the front rank, as soon as he appeared to lower it the front rank withdrew upon the second, the second upon the third, and thus created such confusion that the approach of the Turkish army itself could not have caused more. The Captain smiled with content and reassembled his troop, raising his sword. Then those twenty or thirty ragged peasants, with their muskets over their shoulders like so many mattocks, recommenced their march towards the square, to the beating of drums. But as the Captain marched ahead on legs so much longer than the longest in his company, he always arrived alone upon the square. Then he would turn furiously to rain blows upon this indolent rabble; but none of them was stupid enough to await them. Some took to their heels, others leapt over ditches, others squeezed behind doors and others hid in the hayricks. The drummers defended themselves with their drums. So almost always ended the monthly review of the militia in the jurisdiction of Fratta. The captain sent in a long report, the Chancellor put it in the archives and nothing more was said on the subject until the next month.

It may seem very remarkable to read today of such political and military goings-on, which appear to be mere buffoonery. But matters were exactly as I have described. The district of Portogruaro, to which the commune of Teglio, which included the parish of Fratta, belonged, now forms the eastern march of the Venetian Province, which covers the whole plain from the lower Adige in the Polesine and the steep banks of the Tagliamento down to the edge of the lagoons. In the time of which I write, matters remained as nature had made them and Attila had left them. The Friuli obeyed some sixty or seventy families, by origin from across the Alps but assimilated in the country by a century-old residence, to whom was entrusted local and absolute authority in the jurisdiction of their several dominions; and their votes, with those of the Free Communes and the Counties, formed the Parliament of the Fatherland that met once every year as a consultative body in association with the Viceroy sent to Udine from Venice.

I have few sins of omission upon my conscience, but amongst them the most serious and the one that causes me the most regret is that I was never present at one of these Parliaments. To have been there must really have been a most entertaining experience. Few of the Magistrates knew how to read; and the deputies of the countryside can hardly have known more than they. That all understood Tuscan I do not believe; that none spoke it is sufficiently shown by their decrees and the resolutions adopted, wherein, after a short preamble in Latin, they rushed headlong into a mishmash of Italian, Friuli and Venetian that was not without its beauty for those who liked a good laugh. Everything therefore combined to assure that when the Magnificent General Parliament of the Fatherland petitioned His Serenity the Doge for leave to legislate upon a given subject, the tenor of those laws should already have been concerted down to the smallest detail between His Excellency the Viceroy and the Most Excellent Council of Ten. The fact was that, once permission had been obtained to make suggestions on any given matter, the Magnificent General Parliament proposed, discussed and approved everything in a single day, more precisely on the 11th of August. The reason for this haste and for the choice of this, rather than any other day, was that precisely at this time the Fair of Saint Lorenzo was held, which afforded an opportunity for all the members of the Parliament to meet at Udine. But since, during the Fair, few had any inclination to neglect their own affairs for those of the public, the period of twenty-four hours was considered amply sufficient to relieve them of the latter cares. The Magnificent General Parliament then implored the dominant Most Serene Republic for confirmation of all that had been discussed, proposed and approved; and once this confirmation had been received, the town crier announced to all and sundry, to the sound of the trumpet, on the feast day, all the resolutions taken by the Magnificent General Parliament. It did not follow that all the laws promulgated by this method must therefore have been unjust or ridiculous; since, as says the editor of the Friulian Statutes, 'these laws are an embodiment of justice, maturity and experience and have always in view commendable and salutary objects'; but there might well be considerable doubt about the merit which the magnificent deputies of the Fatherland could claim for themselves.

One amongst their many laws that merits especial praise is that of 1770 which occupied itself with the reorganization of the Cernide, or local militia, raised by the communes and the Feudal Lords to maintain order in their respective jurisdictions. 'The Signor Syndics and Inquisitors hereby permit the Cernide, the Corporals and the Heads of Hundreds (Captain Sandracca was a Head of a Hundred, or perhaps fifty or twenty according to the good will of his subalterns, but arrogated to himself the title of Captain in view of his past glories), permit them, I repeat, to carry freely their muskets unloaded in the cities and cultivated areas while in transit or on duty, but never in church, at feasts or markets or while accompanying citizens.' 'They can furthermore'—thus the Most Illustrious Syndics—'on occasions of parades, reviews, inspections and patrols, be armed other than with firearms with a bayonet; but with entire prohibition of the dagger, forbidden also in the territory of the old republic, but now also applied to the impudent use of knives, arms that are abominable to all classes of militia and condemned by all the laws.'

This paragraph affected, more than the Cernide, the insolent castellans who used to recruit the famous buli, who were armed to the teeth, and whom they kept as retainers for their usual exactions. It is, however, right to add, in praise of the Counts of Fratta, that their buli were famous in the whole area for an exemplary meekness and that they kept them more out of custom than for any kind of arrogance.

Captain Sandracca, the ancient hero of Candia, looked with horror upon this rabble of vagabonds, as he used to term them, and had so influenced the Count that he had relegated them to a tiny room close to the stables while Marchetto, the serjeant, who on occasion was their leader, was not allowed to enter the kitchen without first leaving his pistol and his knife in the entry. As a reason for this horror of knives, the Captain gave the same motive as the Syndics, namely that such arms are abominable to all types of militia. He said, moreover, that he was more afraid of a knife than of a cannon; and this may well have been true at Fratta where a cannon had never yet been seen.

But the control of arms was no easy matter in a province divided and subdivided into a hundred different authorities, superimposed and interdependent, and with common frontiers with many foreign countries such as the Tyrol and the County of Gorizia, and furrowed at every step with rivers and torrents whereon not merely bridges but even ferries were very rare, and made ten times larger than it is today by roads badly made, deep in mud, infamous to a degree and more likely to hinder than to assist travellers. I can remember that, up to twenty years ago, to go from Colloredo to Collalto, a distance of four miles, two mettlesome and powerful horses sweated for three hours to drag any coach sufficiently well made to withstand the lurches due to the holes and rocks that it encountered. More than that, there was a good mile where the road ran in a ditch or torrent; and to overcome this, the assistance of a pair of bullocks was considered indispensable. The carriage roads in the rest of the province were no better, and anyone can work out for himself what must have been the executive power of the authorities over persons assisted on every side with so many natural obstacles.

Amongst such obstacles I would like to be able to omit the idleness and venal complicity of the officials, the serjeants and even the Chancellors, who were almost compelled to such compromises to remedy the excessive moderation of the tariffs and the proverbial avarice of their principals. There were some, for example, who instead of rewarding their Chancellors or notaries with a sufficient wage, aimed at sharing with them the dues they collected, and I can recall one such notary who was compelled to condemn persons to twice what should have been due in order to satisfy the greed of the magistrate and, at the same time, extract from them something on which to live himself. Another castellan, when he was hard up, used to denounce to his own Chancellery some imagined crime in order to pocket his share of the charges due to the official over the trial of the person condemned.

The Magistrate and the Chancellor of Fratta were not of such sentiments; but I none the less cannot recall ever having heard their justice exalted to the skies. Instead, the Chancellor, whenever he was relieved of his ministry as shadow to the Signor Count and was not wasting his time chattering about loose ladies and gay intrigues, would break into interminable laments about the meanness of the legal tariffs, which, according to him, absolutely prohibited the entry into Paradise of any officer of justice who could not prove categorically to St Peter that he had died of hunger. With what right he complained, I do not wish to judge; I know, however, that the investigation of one or more culprits was rewarded according to the tariff by one lire, equivalent to fifty centisimi of stamp duty. I believe it would not be possible to assure justice to the citizens at a cheaper rate; but it is with justice as it is with other things, that he who spends more spends less; and proverbs are seldom wrong.

It was the same thing with letters, where the postal charges within the borders of Fratta were three soldi a letter. But delivery was a mere matter of chance with those infernal roads; and what did so cheap a charge serve when one had to write ten letters in order to assure the arrival of one and even that one only arrived by chance and in many cases was quite useless because of the delay?

Certainly, for those who had inherited many rights and few duties, and intended to continue their usage, St Mark was a most commendable master. No conservative was more conservative than he, not even Metternich or Chateaubriand. As the Friuli had at one time been attached to the Patriarchs of Aquileia, it had kept its jurisdictions, its statutes and its Parliaments. Phantasms of public life, they perhaps harboured a germ of vitality, but under the wings of the Lion they finally did no more than to conceal a profound indifference, or a tired resignation to the old-fashioned ordinances of the Republic. The casual forays of the Turks towards the end of the fifteenth century had imbued this frontier province of Italy with an immeasurable, almost superstitious, fear; so that its present attachment to Venice, as the old-time victor over the Ottoman power, seemed a stroke of good fortune. But the astute old trader knew that to maintain her power without force in this new dominion, she had need of the strong arms of the castellans, now risen to a height of insolent power after the need that the countryside had had for them during the last invasions of the Turks. Hence the tolerance of the old feudal ordinances; which were perpetuated, even as everything was perpetuated in the body, crumbling and already weakened, of the Republic.

The nobles went on living in castles three centuries after their colleagues and compatriots elsewhere had already become citizens, and the virtues of ancient times had already in part become vices, as the general change of conditions took from them the air in which they breathed. Valour became ferocity, pride became arrogance, and hospitality changed little by little into a proud and illegal protection of the worst types of gallows birds. St Mark drowsed; and, when he watched and punished, his justice was done in darkness, atrocious in its mystery and useless as an example.

Meanwhile, the Friuli patricians began to split into two factions; the one peasant, rough, wild and little propitious to the domination of the Venetian curias; the other Venetianized, town-dwelling, softened by long consorting with the nobles of the Dominant City. Ancient family traditions and the proximity of the lands of the Empire drew the former to the Imperial party; the latter, by similarity of customs, turned to a sheeplike obedience to their rulers; rebels the first by instinct, sheeplike the second by worthlessness, both were more than useless, indeed were harmful, to the good of their country. Thus one could see many patrician houses in the service of the Court of Vienna for many generations, while others, allied by kinship with the nobles of the Canalazzo, were honoured in the Republic by exalted positions. But the two parties had divided between them the customs and the favours in a somewhat promiscuous manner. Thus some amongst the most turbulent castellans were sometimes seen to go to Venice to make amends for their misdeeds and to buy forgetfulness from the senators with long purses of *zecchini*. There were also some petty lords, Venetianized in the city for the three months of winter, who, once returned behind their own battlements, became more ferocious than ever, though their bragging often seemed more knavery than violence, and even before committing their misdemeanours they had usually assured impunity for their actions.

As for justice, it was a cat and dog affair, that is, none considered it seriously save for a few timorous Godfearers who used to blunder into punishment through ignorance. This was the kingdom of knaves; and it was only with knavery that the common people could find the way to recompense themselves for the arrogances that they suffered. In the forensic transactions of the Friuli the astuteness of the administered took the place of the *equitas* of the Roman law, while the greed and pride of the officials and their patrons marked the limits of the *strictum jus*.

Howsoever it was, it chanced that on this side of the Tagliamento the castellans were largely of the Venetian party, to which the Counts of Fratta boasted that they had belonged from time immemorial; whilst on the other side the Imperial faction lorded it openly; the former were the more popular and the richer, the latter far superior in activity and audacity. However, even amongst these there were some who blew now hot now cold and some who remained lukewarm and these last always among the most useless and the worst. The summary justice executed by the Council of Ten on occasional imprudent ones accused of conspiring in favour of the imperialists and to the detriment of the Republic, was not of a sort to encourage the plots of the seditious. But such outbreaks were too rare for the terror of them to endure for long, and the plots continued more and more frivolous and innocuous as the times became unpropitious and the common people indifferent to these artificial and unsought innovations.

In the days of Maria Theresa three castellans of the Piedemonte, a Franzi, a Tarcentini and a Partistagno, were accused of stirring up unrest and of trying to influence the country in favour of the Empress. The Council of Ten spied on them carefully and it might well have been that the accusations were not false. More than all the rest, the Partistagno, with his castle almost on the Illyrian frontier, took open part for the imperialists, mocked at St Mark and at the head of his long table drank to the day when the Signor Viceroy—I repeat the words of his toast—and all the other *caca in aqua* would be kicked in the pants to the other side of the Tagliamento.

Everyone laughed at these fine words and the boldness of the feudal lord was admired and even imitated, as far as they dared, by the vassals and castellans of the neighbourhood. At Venice a Secret Council was held and it was decided that these three turbulent lords should be cited to appear in Venice to justify themselves; everyone knew that such justification was the surest step to the famous prison of 'The Leads'.

The redoubtable Messer Grande was therefore sent to the Friuli with three sealed letters, each of which was to be unsealed and read in the presence of the respective culprit, and which contained the order to come in person to Venice to reply to the questions of the Most Excellent Council of Ten. Such injunctions were usually blindly obeyed; the power of the Lion still appeared so formidable to those distant and ignorant that it was considered useless to try to escape it. Messer Grande therefore came in solemn embassy to the Franzi and the Tarcentini, both of whom bowed their heads and went voluntarily to put themselves in the dungeons of the Inquisitors. Thence he passed with the third letter to the castle of the Partistagno, who had already heard of the submission of his companions and awaited him respectfully in the great hall of his castle. Messer Grande entered with his great red robe sweeping up the dust and with due solemnity drew the letter from his breast and began to read the contents. He read with a nasal voice that the noble and exalted Signor Gherardo di Partistagno should be requested within seven days to present himself before the Most Excellent Council of Ten, etc., etc.' The noble and exalted Signor Gherardo di Partistagno stood before him, trembling and with bowed head, as if listening to a sentence of death. At the sight of this attitude of submission, the voice of Messer Grande became ever more menacing and finally, when he read the signatures, it seemed that through his nostrils breathed all the terrors of the Inquisitorial Council. The Partistagno with trembling voice assured him that he would incontinently obey and made a sign with the hand which had been supporting him on a table, as if to command a horse or a litter. Messer Grande, proud of having fulminated according to his usual custom against the proud feudatory, turned on his heel to leave the hall, head erect. But he had not moved a step before seven or eight buli, brought specially the day before from a castle of the Partistagno in Illyria, leapt on him and striking him here and pounding him there, gave him such a beating that in a very short time poor Messer Grande had not enough breath in his body to shout. The Partistagno encouraged the scoundrels, shouting:

'Yes, indeed! I am ready to obey. Give it him hot, Natale! Down, down with this parchment nose! To dare to come here, to my own castle, with such a message! Clever, indeed! A rogue, by Diana. . . . What a state you are in, Messer! Bravo, my sons! Now, enough, enough; give him breath enough to get back to Venice to tell the news to these good signors. . . .'

'Ay, ay, treason! mercy! I am dead!' groaned Messer Grande, quivering on the floor and trying to put himself to rights.

'No, you are not dead,' replied the Partistagno. 'You see? . . . You can still stand well enough, and with a little mending of your fine red clothes there won't be a sign of this unpleasant incident to be seen. Now go. . . .' So saying, he led him to the door of the hall. 'Go and tell your masters that the head of the Partistagno takes orders from nobody, and as they have invited me, so I invite them to come and find me in my castle of Caporetto above Gorizia, where they will get a triple dose of what you have got.'

With these words he led him tottering to the castle threshold where he gave him a push that sent him headlong out about ten paces, amid the guffaws of the bystanders. And then, while Messer Grande, still feeling his bones and gently touching his nose, went towards Udine in a hand-barrow requisitioned along the road, the Partistagno and his buli made all speed for Caporetto, whence he was not again seen on the lands of the Most Serene Republic. Old persons say that of his two companions lodged in the dungeons no word was ever heard again.

These trifling incidents took place in the Friuli about a hundred years ago and seem like stories dug out of Sacchetti. Such was the temper of the mountain lands, that for long the memory of ancient times was preserved among their granite peaks; but since the Friuli is a little compendium of the universe, mountainous, level and marshy by turns within its sixty miles from east to west, so one found there also the other side of the medal. In fact at the Castle of Fratta during my childhood they always spoke of the castellans of 'up there' with horror, so deeply had venetianism entered the blood of those good Counts. And I am sure that they were even more scandalized than the inquisitors themselves at the entertainment afforded to Messer Grande by the Partistagno.

But the justice, high, low, public, private, legislative and executive, of the Fatherland of Friuli has driven from my mind the great hearth, around which in the light of two tiny lamps and the flickering flames of the juniper, I was recalling the figures who used to sit there in the long winter afternoons in the days of my childhood: the Count with his shadow, Monsignor Orlando, Captain Sandracca, Marchetto the serjeant and Ser Antonio, the leading figure of the commune of Fratta. I have not yet spoken of this last personage and it would need a long disquisition to give any idea of what was the precise standing of this half-countryman, half-gentleman, midway between the signori and the peasants. What he was in truth would be too intricate to try and understand, but what he tried to appear to be I could say in a few strokes of the pen. He wanted to appear the most humble servant of the castle and the confidant of the castellan and therefore the second patron of the countryside. Those who had good character turned this singular ambition to the good, but those on the other hand who were by nature sordid swindlers became in this office the lowest and most evil of the whole gang. Ser Antonio was among the former; although he was prudent and talkative, he was at heart one of the best fellows in the world and would not have pulled the wings off a wasp even after being stung. The servants, the grooms, the town-crier, the scullions and the cook were bread and cheese with him and when he was not taken up with the Count, he used to joke with them and help the bailiff's small son to pluck little birds for the spit. But as soon as the Count chanced to appear, he pulled himself together and paid attention only to him, as if it were sacrilege to attend to anything else when one had the good fortune of basking in the effulgence of a magistrate. And according to His Excellency's probable desires, he was the first to laugh, to say yes, to say no, and even indeed to contradict himself rapidly when his first thrust had gone awry.

There was also a certain Martino, a former valet to the father of His Excellency, who was always pottering about the kitchen like an old hunting dog long retired, and wanting to poke his nose into cupboards and casseroles to the great desperation of the cook, always grumbling about the cats which got between his legs. But being deaf and not much inclined to chatter, he did not join in the conversation. His one task was to grate the cheese. It is true that with his naturally phlegmatic nature made more so by age, and with the extraordinary quantity of minestra consumed in the kitchen, this task kept him occupied for many hours a day. I can still hear the monotonous sound of the rinds being drawn up and down the grater with the minimum respect for his nails, and in proof of his parsimony old Martino always had the tips of his fingers torn and plastered with cobwebs.

But it is not for me to make fun of him. He was, if I may say so, my first friend and if I wasted a good deal of breath trying to penetrate his eardrums with my words, I had for him through all the years that we lived together a tender affection. It was he who would come to look for me, when some impertinance committed had put me in Coventry with the family; he would make excuses for me to Monsignor when, instead of serving him, I had escaped into the vegetable garden to look for birds' nests; he bore witness to my illnesses when the Rector was hunting for me to give me my lesson in catechism and if they sent me off to bed, he was even capable of swallowing the oil and jalap in my stead. In fact, Martino and I were as hand and glove, and if on entering the kitchen I was unable to see him in the deep shadows that reigned there during the daytime, some inner sentiment would warn me if he were there and lead me directly to him, to pull his wig or ride horseback on his knees. If Martino was not there, everyone would ridicule me because I remained so quiet and timid like a chicken far from the hen; and in the end I would take to my heels, unless a rasp of the Signor Count held me rooted to the floor. Then I would stand so deathly still that not even the Epiphany witch could have made me move, and only after he had gone out did I recover freedom of thought and movement. I never knew the reason of this strange effect produced on me by the tall and rigid old man; but I believe that his scarlet trappings used to hypnotize me like a chicken.

Another of my great friendships was the Serjeant who sometimes placed me on the crupper behind him on his pleasure trips for the sticking of eviction notices and similar duties. But I did not have a hatred for knives and pistols like Captain Sandracca and on the way used to forage in Marchetto's pockets to try and steal his dagger and make a thousand childish defiances at the peasants whom we met.

On one of these jaunts to Ramuscello to carry a summons to the local castellan, the Serjeant had taken his pistols with him. I was rummaging in his pockets despite the slap he had given me a while earlier, and pulled the trigger, so that I injured one of my fingers: it is still a little curved and maimed in the top joint in memory of my praetorial excursions. This punishment, however, in no way cured me of my passion for arms, and Marchetto asserted that I should turn out to be a good soldier, and said that it was a pity I had not been brought up in one of the districts 'up there' where young people were taught to be accustomed to arms and not to chase peasants or play cards with priests and old women.

Martino, on the other hand, was not at all pleased at my escapades. The country people, though not turbulent and quarrelsome like those of Piedemonte, were likely enough to revolt now and again at the sentences of the Chancellor and to look askance at the Serjeant who enforced them. And with Marchetto's hot blood, who knew what might happen? Marchetto, however, claimed that my presence made him restrain himself and prevented him from doing anything rash; for my part, I used to boast that in an emergency I would have given him a hand reloading his pistols or striking desperate blows with my pruning-knife and, morsel that I was, felt offended that others should laugh at these vaunts. Martino bent his head, understanding little enough of our talk, but went on muttering that it was not prudent to expose a boy to the reprisals that might be taken against a serjeant going to levy charges or affix notices of taxes and confiscations. In truth, those very peasants who cut so poor a figure in the Cernide and trembled in the Chancellery at an official glance, knew well enough how to handle a gun or an axe in their own houses or in the countryside.

As for me, though at first I used to marvel at these inconsistencies, I now feel that I have found the true reason. We Italians have always a natural antipathy for jacks in office, and we laugh at those who set themselves up above us, to whom we should raise our hats. Now this troop of men, herded together like sheep, marshalled into ranks to the sound of a kettledrum and animated with squeaks of the fife, whose valour was regulated by some curt word from their commander, always seemed to them a famous company of marionettes; the more so since their appearance was almost always unfavourable and only very rarely to advantage. Thus the idea of entering such a troop and looking like a doll, so disgusted them that every wish to do well and every feeling of dignity entirely disappeared.

I am speaking, be it understood, of times past; now the consciousness of a great aim may have improved them in this respect. But even now, philosophically speaking, it would not perhaps be wrong to think as one thought at that time; and the wrong lies in the fact that it is always rash to be wise and act according to the tenets of wisdom when all others are mad and behave according to their madness. It has been said and said again a hundred times, and proved up to the hilt, that one of us can stand firm and make any of the bravest of other nations turn tail. But on the other hand there is certainly no nation where it is more difficult to recruit an army and make it sound and disciplined as the military art today demands. Napoleon, indeed, showed the world, once and for all, that we have no lack of military valour, but only the desire and the constancy of leaders. Furthermore, our perverseness in refusing to abdicate our freedom of choice, and our independent and rational temperament, is perhaps excused by our complete lack of military traditions. But enough of that as regards the people of Fratta; and as for their tremors in face of authority, it is not out of place to add that it was not so much the result of cowardice as of centuries-old reverence, and the fear always shown by illiterate persons for those who know more than they. A Chancellor who with a few strokes of the pen can at his caprice expel two, three or twenty families from their houses in misery and hunger must have seemed to these poor devils little less than a wizard. Today, when public affairs move more surely, even the ignorant look upon justice with a more favourable eye and are not frightened by it as if it were the sister of the gallows.

In company with the various persons whom I have so far mentioned, the Rector of Teglio, my master in catechism and calligraphy, used to pass long hours in the inglenook of the great hearth, facing the Signor Count and making him deep bows whenever he was vouchsafed a word. He was a good priest from the mountains, and incidentally no friend of the town clergy, and so pitted with the smallpox that his cheeks always put me in mind of a stracchino cheese, when, as the gourmands say, it is very fat and full of eyes. He walked very slowly, spoke even more slowly, never omitting to divide every sentence into three parts; and this habit had become so much a part of his being that when eating, coughing or sighing it always seemed that he divided his eating, coughing or sighing into three parts also. All his movements were so ponderous that if he ever had happened to commit some sin, despite his usually quiet and evangelical life, I doubt if the Good Lord could have been induced to pardon him for it. Even his glances were not given without some weighty motive and seemed only with difficulty to penetrate the two hedges of eyebrows that protected them. He was the very ideal of premeditation, descended to become incarnate in the body of a mountaineer from Clausedo; tonsured by the Bishop of Porto, he wore the longest hair doublet that had ever competed with a priest's calves. His hands used to tremble a little, which somewhat hindered him in his role of a calligrapher, but it did not prevent his leaning firmly on his malacca cane with a real horn handle. Concerning his moral qualities, even though he was born in the eighteenth century, he was a model of ecclesiastical independence. The exceedingly deep bows that he made to the Count did not prevent his carrying on his cure of souls in his own manner, and were perhaps equivalent to saying: 'Most Illustrious Signor Count, I venerate and respect you; but in my own house, it is I who am master.'

The Chaplain of Fratta, on the other hand, was a scared and pusillanimous little grasshopper who would have given the benediction with a kitchen ladle had the Count had the whim to ask him to do so. Not for lack of religion, but because the poor devil became so flustered when faced with the gentry that he really did not know what he was doing. Whenever he had to stay in the castle, he seemed to be on thorns; and I believe that, now he is dead, had God desired to give him a real Purgatory, he could have imagined nothing better than to allow him another life in the person of a house-steward. There was no one more able than he to remain seated for hours and hours without ever lifting his eyes or moving a finger when others were watching; but he possessed an equally miraculous art of disappearing without being seen, even from a company of ten persons. Only when he followed the Rector of Teglio did some flash of clerical dignity illuminate his countenance, but it was clearly to be seen that on such occasions it was an effort for him to keep behind his superior and he was so occupied in bearing in mind the part he had to play that he neither heard nor saw anything and was capable of putting live coals instead of hazelnuts into his mouth, as the factor had once tried this experiment on him for a bet. Signor Ambrogio Traversini, factor and valuer for the castle, was the poor chaplain's cross. Between those two there were always jokes and larks so in fashion in past times and which, in country gatherings, took the place of reading the newspapers. The Chaplain, as if in duty bound, was always the butt of these jests, and was rewarded by an occasional invitation to lunch, a reward more cruel than the misadventure itself. In the greater number of such cases, his obsession with these invitations gave him a double quartan fever so that he had no need of lies in order to excuse himself.

Once, however, he was able to set foot on the farther side of the drawbridge, no man, I believe, felt happier than he, and that was the recompense for his martyrdom. He leapt, he ran, he rubbed his hands, his nose, his knees, took snuff, whispered ejaculations, passed his stick from one arm to the other, talked, laughed and joked with everyone and caressed everyone he found to hand, were it a boy, an old woman, a dog or a young cow.

I first had the glory and the malice to reveal the strange jubilation of the Chaplain at every escape from the castle, and once I had made the discovery, everyone, as soon as he left, rushed to the windows of the dining-hall to enjoy the spectacle. The factor swore that, some time or another, he would have leapt into the fishpond for excess of consolation; but it must be said in praise of the poor priest that this accident never once happened.

The greatest sign of joy that he ever gave was once when he joined the local urchins behind the church in ringing the festival bells. But that day he had really had a lucky escape. There had come to the castle a prelate of Porto, known as the Canon of St Andrea, a great theologian and little tolerant of others' ignorance, who had honoured in the past and continued to honour the Countess with his spiritual ministrations. With Monsignor Orlando and the Rector, he had taken his place on a bench near the hearth and begun to dogmatize about morals. The chaplain who had come to make his usual inquiry about the digestion of the Signor Count, as he did every afternoon, nearly fell into the snare; but half-way into the kitchen he had overheard the voice of the theologian, and protected by the shadows, had taken to his heels, thanking all the saints in the calendar. Judge for yourself, if he had not every right to ring the bells for joy!

Besides these two priests, and the other clergy from the city, who frequently came to visit Monsignor di Fratta, the castle was frequented by all the lesser gentry and castellans of the neighbourhood, a mixed bag of tipplers, idlers, rogues and agreeable fellows who wasted their time in hunting, in disputes, in flirtations and in endless suppers, and pandered to the aristocratic pretensions of the Signor Count. When they came it was a day of turmoil. The best casks were broached, and many flasks of Picolit and Refosco lost their necks; and the young assistants of the cook took refuge in the scullery. Then the cook knew neither friends nor enemies; she ran hither and thither, sticking her elbows into Martino's stomach, trampling on Monsignor's feet, plucking ducks and eviscerating capons. Her activity was only surpassed by the turnspit, who shouted and dripped oil on all the pulleys in his task of turning three or four spits, loaded with hares and game. The tables in the hall and in two or three adjacent rooms were put together, and the fire in the great gallery fireplace was lit, which was so large that to keep it filled needed a good half standard of wood. It was noticeable that after the first outburst of the flames, the company had to take refuge behind the most distant walls or in far corners to avoid being roasted.

The gentlemen used to make the most infernal uproar, but for the most part the witty sallies were confined to some petty doctor or another, some minor priest or some poet from Portogruaro, none of whom ever failed to rush to the odours of the feast. At the end of the long tables some sonnet used to be improvised, though the rough draft, with corrections, was doubtless at home. But if memory failed, the usual round of congratulations and excuses for the liberty never lacked and the company 'if it were permitted' hastened to drink wine and to praise the infinite merits of the Count and Countess.

The most frequent of such visitors was an elegant and powdered advocate who in his youth had paid court to many Venetian ladies and was then living on memories in the company of his housekeeper. A youth called Giulio Del Ponte always arrived with him, prided himself on competing with the most subtle verses and used to enjoy making him lose his senses by emptying his glass once too often. The comedy finished in the kitchen with great guffaws behind the doctor's back, but the young man, who had been at Padua, behaved so well that he remained in better grace than ever.

This one, and a pale, taciturn young man from Fossalta, Signor Lucilio Vianello, were the only ones of that semi-plebeian rabble to have remained in my memory. Amongst the gentry, I can still remember a Partistagno, perhaps a kinsman of he who had received Messer Grande, tall, bold and strong, and with a certain haughty reserve of manner which contrasted strikingly enough with the fuddled licence of the mob. And from then onwards I remember to have noticed certain hostile glances pass between him and Vianello which certainly did not denote any good feeling between them. In truth, it was just these two who should have been able to get on together, since all the rest were a common scum of rogues and nitwits.

When I began to think for myself and was already able to scare the hens in the courtyard of Fratta, the only son of the Count had already been a year in Venice with the Somaschi Fathers, where his father had been educated before him; therefore I remember nothing of him, save an occasional slap he had given me before leaving to prove that he was the master; and at that time I was still a baby hardly able to gnaw a crust. Old Martino had then undertaken my defence, and I can still recall a good ear-pulling given by him to the young master, who rushed away screaming to the rafters; and Martino got a good dressing down for it from the Count. Luckily for him he was deaf!

As for the Countess she only appeared in the kitchen twice a day, in her role as controller of household affairs; the first in the morning to distribute the flour, butter, meat and other needs of the day, the second after the last lunch session to control the division of the food sent down from the patronal table to the servants, and to rearrange the rest in smaller plates for supper.

She was a Navagero of Venice, a tall gruff noblewoman, curt of speech, who snuffed tobacco in one nostril after another and never moved without the tinkle of the key at her belt. She always wore on her head a white lace cap flecked with rose at the temples like that of a young bride; but I believe that she did not wear it from vanity but simply out of habit. A necklace of gold coins hung round her neck over a black silk kerchief, whence dangled a little diamond cross which, to quote the cook, would have furnished a dowry for all the girls of the district. On her breast, set in a gold brooch, she wore the portrait of a handsome man in a flowing wig, which was certainly not that of her husband; since he had a huge and malproportioned nose, while the man in the portrait on the other hand had a most delicate little nose, a real toy for smelling rosewater or Naples essence.

To put briefly what I came to know later, the noble lady had most half-heartedly been constrained to this marriage with a castellan of the *terraferma*, and it seemed to her that she had fallen into the hands of the barbarians, accustomed as she was to the refinements and pastimes of the Venetian damsels. But forced to make a virtue of necessity, she had done her best to remedy this misfortune by dragging her husband with her from time to time to Venice and had there made up for her provincial retirement with luxuries, gallantries and being courted by all the most famous dandies. The portrait that she wore on her breast might well have been of one of the boldest of these; it was said that he had died of a chill from the night air, caught while he was with her in a gondola, and after that she would not ever hear of Venice and had retired to Fratta, to the great complacency of the Signor Count. At the time this terrible affair happened, the lady was close to her forties. Otherwise, the Countess passed long hours at her prie-dieu and whenever she encountered me, either at the door of the kitchen or on the stairs, she would give a little tug to the hairs on the nape of my neck, the sole gentleness that I ever recall having received from her. A quarter of an hour a day she employed in assigning her duties to the chambermaid, and the balance of her time she passed in one of the small salons with her mother-in-law and her daughters, knitting stockings and reading the life of the saint of the day.

The old mother of the Count, the former Lady Badoer, was still living at that time; but I only saw her four or five times, for she was relegated to the wheel-chair of age and I was forbidden to enter any room save the one in which I slept with the second chambermaid or, as they used to call her, the children's woman.

The old Countess Badoer was an old woman of almost ninety, still fairly plump and with an expression showing goodness and common sense. Her voice, sweet and quiet, despite her years, had such a charm for me that I often risked getting a few slaps to go and listen to it, with my ear at the keyhole of her door. Once, when the chambermaid suddenly opened the door when I was in this position, she noticed me and beckoned to me. I think my heart was ready to leap out of my breast with relief when she put her hand on my head and asked me sternly, but without a trace of harshness, what I was doing there. I answered simply, yet trembling with emotion, that I was there because I liked to hear her talking and that her voice pleased me very much and seemed to me like what I should have wished my mother's to have been.

'Good, Carlino,' she replied, 'I will always talk to you with kindness so long as you deserve to be well treated for your good behaviour; but it is not good for anyone, and least of all for little boys, to listen behind doors. When you want to talk to me, you must come into the room and sit near me, and I will teach you, as well as I can, to pray to God to make you a good boy.'

When I heard those words, poor little wretch that I was, the tears came running down my cheeks. It was the first time that anyone had spoken to me from their heart; it was the first time that anyone had made me the gift of a kind word and a caress; and that gift was from an old woman who had seen Louis XIV! I say seen, really seen, for the husband of the noble Lady Badoer, that old Count so covetous of grand-masters and admirals, had gone a few months after his marriage to France as Ambassador of the Most Serene Republic and had taken with him his wife, who for two years had been the jewel of the Court.

This same lady had then returned to Fratta where she had retained the same graces of manner and of speech, the same rectitude of conscience and the same spirit of moderation and charity, so that, although she had lost the flower of her beauty, she had continued to enchant the hearts of her vassals and the inhabitants of the castle as she had previously so enchanted the hearts of the courtiers of Versailles. So true is it that real dignity is admirable and admired everywhere and neither becomes, nor is considered, less whatever may be the changes of its dwelling.

I wept copiously, pressing and kissing the hands of this venerable woman and promising in my heart to make frequent use of the largesse granted me to go and talk with her, when the real Countess, she of the keys, entered and gave a little start of indignation on seeing me in the little salon against her express orders. This time the tug at the nape of my neck was longer than usual and accompanied by a solemn rebuke and an eternal prohibition ever to enter these rooms again unless called for. As I went down the stairs, scratching the back of my neck and weeping this time more from rage than from grief, I could still hear the voice of the old woman, which seemed to become even sweeter as she interceded in my favour, but a scream from the Countess and a violent banging of the door, which was locked behind me, prevented me hearing the end of the scene. So I went down, one foot slowly after the other, to find consolation with Martino in the kitchen.

This friendship of mine with Martino was also not to the liking of the Countess or the factor, who was her right-hand man; according to him my teacher ought to have been a certain Fulgenzio, half sacristan and half writer in the Chancellery, who enjoyed within the castle the reputation of a spy. For my part, I could not stand this Fulgenzio and played him several tricks which must have made me insupportable to him also.

Once for example, though this happened later, I was in the choir behind him during matins on Holy Wednesday, and seized the opportunity of his meditations to remove the taper from the cane with which he used to light the candles, and which was already lit, and to attach it to his coat-tail. When the taper was almost consumed, the fire caught his coat-tail and thence extended to the tow of his wig, and Fulgenzio began leaping about the choir and the boys who held the lutes began running round him shouting: water, water! In this commotion the luteboys rushed around and created such an uproar that the ceremony had to be postponed for a good half-hour. Nobody knew exactly what had been the cause of the scandal and I, who was suspected of being its author, had sense enough to play the Indian: but for all that I earned the fee of a day in my room on bread and water, which certainly did not put Fulgenzio any the more in my good graces, even as the conflagration in his wig had certainly not contributed to put me in his.

I have already said that the Countess spent the greater part of her spare time knitting stockings in the little salon in the company of her daughters. The last of these, in the years I am now recalling, was still quite a baby, younger than I by some years, and who slept in my room with the 'children's woman', who was called Faustina.

The Pisana was a lively baby, restless and petulant, with lovely brown eyes and very long hair, who already at three years old knew all the arts of a little woman and would have justified those who hold that women are never children, but are born full blown with all the elements of their attractions and their malice. There was not an evening before I went to bed that I did not bend over the cradle of the little girl and look long at her; she lay there with her big eyes closed, one tiny arm out of the bedclothes and the other curved over her forehead like a little angel asleep. But while I was enjoying her beauty, she would suddenly open her eyes and, overjoyed to have taken me in with her pretence of sleep, jump up in bed, giving me great slaps. This used to happen when Faustina was looking the other way, or when she had forgotten the instructions given her, for the Countess had told her to keep me at a respectful distance from her little angel and not allow me to get too intimate with her. For me, there were the sons of Fulgenzio, who seemed to me even more abominable than their father, and I never let pass an opportunity of making trouble for them, especially when they went piping to their father that they had seen me give a kiss to the little Countess, or had carried her in my arms from the sheep-pond to the edge of the fishpond. But the little girl paid as little attention as I to others' remarks and continued to love me and try to make every possible use of me in her childish affairs, rather than of Faustina or Rosa, the other chambermaid, or 'the woman with the keys', whom we should today call the wardrobe-mistress.

I was happy and proud to have at last found a creature who believed me to be of use, and took a certain air of importance when I told Martino: 'Give me a good piece of string to take to the Pisana.' It was so I called her to him, though with all the others I dared not call her anything but 'the little Countess'. But these joys were not without their torments, since, alas, it is as true in childhood as in all other ages that there is no rose without thorns. Whenever the gentry of the neighbourhood arrived at the castle, with their well dressed and tidy children, with their starched collars and plumed hats, the Pisana left me at once to coquet with them and my nose was quite put out of joint in watching her make dainty little steps, twisting her neck like a swan and enchanting them with her sweet and ingenuous chatter. I would run to Faustina's mirror to make myself beautiful too; but, alas, I very quickly saw that I could not succeed. My skin was dark and smoked like a herring, my shoulders were badly set, my nose covered with spots and scratches and my untrimmed tangled hair stuck out around my head like the bristles on a hedgehog, while my trousers were torn and rumpled like the tail of a blackbird escaped from the limed twigs. It was to no purpose that I martyred my scalp with combs, sticking out my tongue with the intense effort I put into it; that unruly hair was even more tangled than ever.

Once I had the idea of putting oil on it as I had seen Faustina do; but fate ordained that I should mistake the phial and instead of oil I poured on my head a little bottle of ammoniac that she kept in case of convulsions and which gave me for a whole week the aroma of a compost-heap strong enough to turn one's stomach. In short, I was most unlucky in my first vanities and even while I tried to make myself more agreeable to the little one and wean her away from her new guests, I afforded her and them fresh material for laughter and myself yet another reason for fury and degradation.

It is true that once the strangers had departed, the Pisana returned to amuse herself by playing the mistress over me, but the ill humour of such infidelities was slow to dissipate and, without knowing how to liberate myself, I began to find her caprices too various and her tyranny a little hard. But she, the little devil, paid no heed. Perhaps she had guessed the stuff of which I was made and redoubled her oppressions, and I, for my part, my submission and affection, since in some natures devotion to those who torment them is even greater than gratitude to those who make them happy. I do not know if such beings are good or bad, wise or stupid; I only know that I was an example of them and that my fate has been such for all these long years of life. My conscience is not ill at ease either with the means or the results; and that contented, all is contented, at least in my own case.

I must however confess, in honour of the truth, that however talkative, flirtatious and cruel the Pisana showed herself even from the tenderest age, she never lacked a certain generosity, the generosity of a queen who, after having buffeted and reviled some too ardent suitor, would intercede in his favour to the king, her husband. Sometimes she would kiss me repeatedly like a lapdog and enter into the most intimate confidence with me, but a little later she would make me act as her horse and strike me with a switch with little regard for my neck or my cheeks; but when Rosa or the factor appeared on the scene to interrupt our games together, which were, as I have said, contrary to the Countess' instructions, she would shriek and stamp her feet and shout that she loved me more than all the rest and that she wanted to stay with me and so on and so on, until, struggling and screaming in the arms of whoever took her away, her shouts passed into silence before the dressing-table of her mother.

These frenzies, I confess, were the sole reward of my abnegation and later I thought many times that they were more due to her pride and obstinacy than to any love for me. But we should not mix the bold judgements of a more mature age with the purest illusions of childhood. I did not feel the blows which I often got for my arrogance in wanting to join the Contessina's games and went back, happy and content, to the kitchen to watch Martino grate the cheese.

The other daughter of the Countess, named Clara, was already a young woman when I first opened my eyes to the things of this world. She was their first born, a tall, blonde girl, pale and melancholy, like the heroine of a ballad or the Ophelia of Shakespeare; though she had never read a ballad and certainly did not know *Hamlet*, even by name. It seemed that long association with her aged grandmother had reflected in her face the calm splendour of that serene and venerable old woman. Certainly there was no daughter who ever watched over a mother with greater care than she in divining every wish of her grandmother; and she always divined them, since the continual company between them had accustomed her to understand them at a single glance. The Countess Clara was beautiful as a seraph would be who passed among men without even grazing the filth of this earth and without understanding its impurity and grossness. But to the eyes of many she might have appeared cold and this coldness could change into an aristocratic hauteur. However, there was never soul more modest and candid than hers, so that the servants quoted her as a model of sweetness and goodness; and everyone knows that when it is a question of the master's praises the vote of two servants is equivalent in itself to a whole volume of sworn testimonies. When her grandmother wanted a coffee or a chocolate and there was no one in the room, she would not ring the bell, but herself descended to the kitchen to give the order to the cook; and while the cook was getting everything ready, she would stand patiently leaning on the step before the hearth and even give a hand in taking the pan off the fire. When I saw her standing like that the kitchen seemed to be bathed in a heavenly light and no longer that sad and darksome place of every day.

People may ask me why, in my descriptions, I always return to the kitchen and why in it, and not in the dining-hall or on the staircase, I have introduced my personages. But the reply is very easy and very natural! The kitchen was the habitual residence of my friend Martino and the one place in which I could stay without being scolded (perhaps because of the darkness which prevented my attracting general attention); it was the commonest recollection of my infancy; so that even as the townsman recalls with pleasure the public ways in which he played his first games, I for my part have my first memories interwoven with the smoke and the darkness of the kitchen at Fratta. It was there that I first saw and knew men; it was there that I experienced and reflected upon my first loves, my first sorrows, my first judgements.

So it happens that, as my life runs on like that of other men in many lands, in many rooms, in different dwellings, my dreams lead me almost always to a kitchen. It is, I know, an ambience of but little poetry, but I write to tell the truth and not to entertain people with poetical fantasies. The Pisana had so much horror of this dark abode, deep and badly paved, and of the cats that inhabited it, that she would seldom set foot there save to pursue me with strokes of a switch. But the Contessina Clara, on the other hand, showed no such disgust, and came there whenever she needed, without twisting her lips or pulling up her skirts as did, indeed, the more disdainful of the maids. Therefore I leapt with joy to see her there; and if she asked for a glass of water, I was happy to offer her one and to hear her say graciously: 'Thank you, Carlino!' Then I would go back to my den in a corner, thinking 'Oh, how beautiful are those three words: Thank you, Carlino!'

A pity that the Pisana had never said them to me with so sweet and caressing a voice!

CHAPTER II

THE principal effect produced upon readers of my first pages will certainly have been curiosity to know at last who was this Carlino. It was, indeed, a real miracle on my part, or if you will, a solemn fraud to lead you sauntering through a whole chapter of my life, speaking always about myself, without first saying who I was. But since I must, sooner or later, tell you, know then that I was born the son of a sister of the Countess of Fratta, and was therefore first cousin to the Contessina Clara and the Pisana. My mother had made, as I would call it, a runaway match with the most illustrious Signor Todero Altoviti, gentleman of Torcello; she had fled with him on a galley going to the Levant, and they had been married at Corfu. But it seemed that the taste for travel had quickly passed, because four months later she had returned without her husband, bronzed by the suns of Smyrna and, in addition, quick with child. When she was delivered, I was at once sent without formality to Fratta in a hamper; and so I became a guest of my aunt on the eighth day after my birth. How welcome I was can easily be guessed from the manner in which I arrived. Meanwhile my mother, poor thing, was expelled from Venice at the demand of her family and had set up house in Parma with a Swiss captain. Thence she returned to Venice to ask forgiveness of my aunt and died in the hospital without so much as a dog to mourn her fate.

These things were told me by Martino and his telling of them made me cry; but I had never discovered how he came to know them. As for my father, they said that he had died at Smyrna shortly after the flight of his wife, some said of a broken heart for this desertion, others because of desperation for his debts, yet others of a flux brought on by drinking too much Cyprus wine. But the real story was not yet known, and there was also current a vague rumour among the Levantine merchants that before dying he had become a Turk. Whether Turk or not, they had baptized me at Fratta, being in doubt whether this had been done in Venice, and since the task of finding me a name had been left to the Rector, he saddled me with the name of the saint of the day, who happened to be San Carlo. The good priest had no predilections for any of the Saints of Paradise and no desire to cudgel his brains to find any unusual name for me, and I am grateful to him, for experience has shown me that San Carlo was in no way less worthy than any of the others.

The Countess had only abandoned her brilliant life in Venice a few months before my hamper arrived; therefore you can understand that she looked on its contents with some little annoyance! With all the trials and tribulations that she had had, she had now to add to them a baby to put out to nurse—and furthermore the baby of a sister who had dishonoured both herself and her family and had so bungled her marriage with a semi-gaolbird of Torcello that even now no one had been able to get at the whole truth of the affair.

The Signora Contessa therefore, from the first glance she cast at me, felt for me the most sincere hatred and it was not long before I was called on to feel the consequences. Firstly, it was considered unnecessary to bring a wet-nurse into the house for a little serpent issued from no one knew where. I was therefore consigned to the cares of Providence and circulated from house to house, wherever there were breasts to suck, like St. Antony's piglet or the Child of the Commune. I am milk-brother of all the children, all the calves and all the kids born at that time in the jurisdiction of Fratta and had, as nurse, in addition to all the mothers, the goats and the cows, all the old women and even men of the neighbourhood. Martino indeed told me how, seeing me sometimes doubled up with hunger, he had had to prepare for me a sort of paste of water, butter, sugar and flour with which he used to stuff me until the food reached my throat and stopped me from crying. And the same thing happened to me in many houses, when the breasts charged to feed me that day had already been drained dry by some hungry infant of eighteen months.

Having survived those early days by a real miracle, the porter of the castle, who was also the winder of the tower clock and the armourer of the district, shared with Martino in the glory of seeing me make my first steps. He was a certain Mastro Germano, an old bulo of the past generation, with perhaps several murders on his soul, but who had certainly found a way to make his peace with the Lord God, since he used to sing from morning till eve as he collected droppings along the roads in a little cart in order to manure a tiny field that he had leased from the master. In the inn he drank his flasks of ribolla with a truly patriarchal serenity. To look at him, one would think he had the easiest conscience of the parish. And my recollections of him have led me to conclude that the conscience of each one of us is adjusted to his own degree, so that what for one may be merely sucking an egg is for another a most grave offence.

Mastro Germano in the days of his youth had killed quite a number of persons in the service of the castellan of Venchieredo; but that account he thought was up to his master to clear with God and, as far as he was concerned, once his Easter confession had been made, he felt himself as pure as the water of the fountain. This was not a mere quibble to quiet his remorse, but a general maxim that had armed his soul with a triple cuirass against every melancholy. Once he had passed on to the pay-roll of the castellans of Fratta as chief of the cut-throats, he had taken to telling his beads, which was the chief occupation of his new subordinates, and had thus finally purged himself of the old leaven.

Now that he had passed his seventieth year, they had finally completed his satisfaction by granting him custody of the portal and superintendence of the clocks and he believed firmly that the way he had chosen was that which led surely to the Papacy. One may well believe that he and Martino were not always of the same opinion. The one was born to become the Black Cap of some Rialto patrician, the other educated in all the villainies and outrages of the Zaffi of that time; one had been with the diplomatic servant of a powdered magistrate, the other was the broken lance of the most intolerant of the lowland castellans. And whenever there was some dispute between them, I was always involved, each wanting to take me away from his adversary and boasting greater rights in my person. But for the most part they were in accord, with a tacit tolerance, and enjoyed in common the progress made by my little legs, and, one on each side of the castle drawbridge, they made me toddle from the arms of one to those of the other.

When the Countess, going out for her afternoon walk with the Rector of Teglio or some guest from Portogruaro, surprised them in these exercises of pedagogy, she would turn aside to give them a glance of excommunication, and if I stumbled against her she never failed to favour me with that tweak at the back of the neck. Then I, trembling with fright, took refuge in the arms of Martino, and the Countess went onward, grumbling at the childishness of 'those two old fools' as my mentors were known to the people of the kitchen. However that may be, I owe it to the efforts of 'those two old fools' that I became steady on my feet and even able to escape under the parish linden whenever I saw appear at the end of the avenue the white cap of my lady aunt. I call her aunt, now that the poor thing has been dead for a good half century, but then, as soon as I was able to pronounce a word, they taught me at her command to call her the Signora Contessa, and so it always remained, our kinship being forgotten by common accord.

It was at this time that, having grown a big boy, and since it displeased the Countess to see me on the bridge, that they decided to hand me over to Fulgenzio the sacristan, of whom you already know my opinion. The lady thus believed that she would keep me away from her Pisana, but that instinct of contradiction, which boys also have, against those who command them without good reason, made me remain even more attached to my exigent little lady.

It is true that, as we grew up, and found that we two alone were not enough for our games, we collected together all the urchins of the neighbourhood, to the great scandal of the maids, who, for fear of their mistress, took the Pisana away as soon as they were aware of what was going on. This, however, did not worry us in the least; and since both Faustina and Rosa could think of little save their suitors, there was no lack of opportunity of their charge escaping them and returning to join us. As the band grew, there grew in her the ambition to hold court, and as she was a little girl, as I have said, rather too advanced for her years, it pleased her to play the little lady and there began childish love affairs, weddings, divorces, reconciliations; all childish games, be it understood, but which none the less showed the trend of her nature. But I do not want to imply that everything was as childish as one would believe, and I wonder how they allowed the Contessina to roll in the hay and play piggy-back with this one and that one, marrying in jest and making pretence of sleeping with her husband and displaying, in these delicate circumstances, the most realistic actions.

Who could have taught her such things? I could not say for certain, but I at least believe that she was born with an innate knowledge of such matters. What was still more remarkable was that she never stayed with the same lover or the same husband, but changed them with the moon. And the village boys, who shamefacedly and more out of respect and submission than anything else took part in such comedies, paid no attention at all. But I, with my fixed idea, felt a bitterness and an indescribable pang at the heart when I saw myself deserted and it was my turn to leave her alone with the little son of the bailiff or the son of the apothecary of Fossalta. For she was not very particular in her choice. It was enough for her to change, though it is true that she wearied more rapidly of the more dirty or unmannerly of them than of the others.

Now that I can think coolly of these things (they are matters of eighty years ago, or maybe a little less), I see that I ought to have felt proud, that I alone was sometimes able to boast of enjoying her favours for a full three days running and that while the turn of the other little boys fell only once a month, mine came round almost every week. Weathercock as she was and arrogant in her dismissals, she was flattering and imperious in her demands. She had to be obeyed at all costs and loved as she desired; and she insisted too that we must laugh with her, for if she found her husband sulky she would get angry and strike him. I believe that no Court of Love was ever governed by any woman with so much tyranny.

If I dwell so long over these childish affairs it is because I have my own reasons and mainly because they do not seem to me so childish as they would to the common run of moralists. Leaving aside the fact that, as I have said a while back, even children have their own vices, this childish liberty does not seem to me in any way becoming or profitable, since the senses become stimulated before the sentiments, with great danger to the symmetry of a whole life. How many men and women of great judgement have inherited the shameful necessity of libertinism from the habits of childhood? Let us talk openly. The metaphor of likening man to a young and tender plant which bends or stands erect according to the skill of the cultivator has been often enough used for me also to use it as a comparison. But better than such a metaphor to explain my idea is the image of the cautery that, once open, can no longer be closed; the humours run together to this part and it is best to let them run or risk spoiling the whole organism. Given that the senses have awakened as far as they can in the years of ignorance, it may well happen that reason will be ashamed of them or will lament their sordid mastery; but whence will come the force to war against them and thrust them back to their role as subjects? Their development follows the trend given them in the beginning despite the dictates of reason and the blush that it may occasion; and so are formed those beings wherein depravity is united to the height of intellect and, up to a point, the height of feeling. Sappho and Aspasia belong to the history, not the mythology, of the Greeks, and are two types of those souls capable of great passions but not of great affections, as so many in our days, through the sensual licence that prevents children from being innocent even before they are capable of becoming guilty. It will be said that Christian education destroys the pernicious effects of these first habits. But setting aside that the time spent in destroying their effects, which could better have been employed in building up the character, is time lost, I believe that such religious education serves rather to conceal than to extirpate the evil. All know with what torments St Augustine and St Anthony tamed the desires of the flesh and conquered their temptations; but today few can pretend to be such saints as they, and how many will you find who practise equal abstinences to obtain equal results? It is a sign of the times that all are content to take things as they are, content to save the decencies with the cunning of the cat which, as says and counsels Ariosto, covers its own ordures.

I who have by nature a temperament rather far from tepid owe perhaps to this circumstance the fact that I emerged exempt from the disorders derived in our moral state from the precocity of the senses. As well as I can recall, the battles of the spirit awoke in me before those of the flesh and I learnt, by good fortune, to love before I learnt to desire. But the merit was not mine, as it was not the fault of the Pisana if her childish stubbornness, her arrogance and her unrecognized vices had developed her impetuous, variable and restless nature and her petulant, vehement and faithless instincts. From the sort of life that they let her lead as a baby and a young girl, there emerge heroines, but never prudent and temperate women; not good mothers, not chaste wives nor true and patient friends; there emerge creatures who today would sacrifice their lives for a cause for which the next day they would not give a button. It is, more or less, the school wherein are tempered momentary and very great virtues and also great and lasting vices, the school of ballerinas, of singers, of actresses and of adventuresses.

Ever since she was a little girl, the Pisana displayed a rare intelligence, but it was vitiated by the frivolities and vanities to which she was abandoned. The wife of Captain Sandracca, Signora Veronica, who acted as her governess, had to exercise an exemplary patience to concentrate her little brain for a quarter of an hour on the task she had to complete. Certain of learning everything with the greatest of ease, the little girl would study the first part of her lesson and leave all the rest; but even so, as she fortified her facility of learning, so she generated that of forgetting. Praise would sometimes spur her on to show herself worthy, but a moment later some caprice would make her forget her brief ambition. Used to conduct herself solely according to the rules of her own temperament, she wanted to change amusements and occupations every moment, not knowing that this is the best method of becoming bored with everything and to find in life neither repose nor content and to end up by never feeling happy, for the very reason of wishing to be so in a hundred different ways.

The science of happiness is the art of moderation; but the little girl could not see this and gave way to her whims in this way because it was in her power to do so. Wanting always to command and to be the first in everything, it is not strange that she tried to set everything right with lies, when she did not know how to make others hold the very high opinion that she wished them to have of her. Since everybody flattered her and pretended to believe them, she accepted this good-humoured simplicity seriously and did not even try to make her fables credible. It often happened that to set one lie right she had to invent two more, and then four to justify those two, and so on indefinitely. But she was of a prodigious imagination and quickness. Without ever showing the least embarrassment or fear lest others should not believe, she paid no attention to the complications which might arise from her fancies. I believe they so much encouraged her that little by little she was not even able to discern herself the true from the false.

I, however, often had to hold the bag, but I held it with such awkwardness that the cat soon escaped, and she never showed the slightest scorn or regret; it seemed that she did not expect anything better of me, or perhaps considered herself so superior that her assertions ought never to be doubted for the contrary testimony of another. It is true that the punishments all fell on me, and that, from that viewpoint at least, her imperturbability was in no way meritorious. These punishments, moreover, touched me very frequently, for my daily games with her were a continual infraction of the orders of the Countess and without troubling who was to blame, the crime first to be punished was mine, since my back-sliding was the more obvious. In any case, no one would have dared to punish the Contessina except her mother, and she as a rule gave no more thought to her than she would to someone else's daughter. For the Pisana there was the 'children's woman', and up to the time when she was ten years old maternal vigilance was limited to paying two ducats a month to Faustina.

From ten years old to twenty the convent, and from twenty onwards Providence; that was the type of education that the Countess considered should free her of every obligation towards her female offspring. Clara, it is true, had left the convent while still very young to act as nurse to her grandmother; but her grandmother's room was in fact even stricter than a convent and the difference was only in name.

That dear Countess, abandoned by her youth and by the passions that had given her a hint of something that was not entirely selfish, was now so wrapped up in herself and in the care of her own health, temporal and eternal, that, save for her rosary and a good digestion, she found no other occupation that suited her. If she knitted stockings it was mainly from habit or because no one else had so light a hand to make woollens delicate enough for her fine skin. As regards the surveillance of the household, she kept a firm hand on it, because she guessed that by shutting her eyes she would have made her family too happy, and the joy of others did not please her, since she herself had had so little. Envy is the sin or the punishment of niggardly souls, and I fear that the nape of my neck owed its daily martyrdom to the rage of the Countess at knowing herself old while I was still a young boy. For that reason also she loathed Monsignor Orlando as much as I did. The sight of a heart at peace and of those hands crossed over his paunch as if to hold in a superfluity of beatitude, gave her a twinge of anger, and she could not understand how it was possible to grow old so contentedly. But there was good reason for the difference! Monsignor Orlando had centred all his complacency in the contentment of his stomach, which is a passion that can be contented, perhaps even better, at an advanced age. While she on the contrary . . . but what will you? I do not want to say more, now that her skeleton will have been purified by fifty years of burial.

Meanwhile, we began to grow up and our temperaments to become better defined; caprices to become passions and the mind able to reason about them. Already the horizon of my desires had widened, for the kitchen, the courtyard, the hayloft, the bridge and the square no longer seemed to me greater than a universe. I wanted to see what there was beyond and, left to my own resources, every pace that I made outside my usual circle brought me the same joys as Columbus experienced in discovering America. I rose very early in the morning and while Faustina was still occupied with her household cares or in the rooms of the masters, I used to slip out with the Pisana into the vegetable garden or to the edge of the fishpond. These were our happiest hours, when the little chatterbox importuned me less and rewarded my servitude more amicably.

I have often noticed that the morning is more apt for peace of soul and that then even the most artificial natures find some breath of simplicity or rectitude. But as the day wears on, daily habits and considerations begin to assert themselves more and more, till towards evening or after nightfall we can observe the most grotesque affectations, the grossest lies and the most irresistible outbursts of passion. Perhaps it is also because the hours of the day are usually spent in the open air, where men feel less the slaves of their own passions and more obedient to the universal laws of nature, which are never the worst. I will not say, however, that the Pisana changed her behaviour or manner of speaking when she was alone with me. I understood very well that she was more appreciative of my admiration than of my friendship or my confidence, and for that reason I never ceased to be for her pantomimes a sort of audience, however restricted and familiar. However, I must write what I now realize and not what I realized at the time. Then, I enjoyed these sweet interludes, believing that the Pisana who was so eager to please me was the real Pisana, and that the changes in manner that took place during the day were the effect of those around her.

At the hour of Mass (it was Monsignor Orlando who celebrated it in the castle chapel) the whole family, masters, servants, bailiffs, estate employees and guests, collected along the benches reserved for each class of persons. The Signor Count knelt alone at a prie-dieu in the choir facing the celebrant, and there acknowledged with much dignity the greetings of Monsignor as he went in and out, as well as the three swings of the censer as the Mass was sung. In the solemn benediction and in the Oremus the celebrant never omitted to bless by name, with a profound bow, the most excellent and most powerful Patron and magistrate, who then turned upon the whole assembly a haughty glance which seemed to indicate the exceeding height that divided him from the flock of his vassals. The Chancellor, the bailiff, the Captain, the gatekeeper and even the maids and the cook absorbed as much of that glance as was their due and then addressed similar glances at those who occupied places in the chapel inferior to them; the Captain would preen his moustaches and place his hand noisily on the hilt of his sword.

The ceremony over, all remained with bowed heads in meditation and turned towards the Altar of the Rosary if the ceremony had been at the High Altar, or vice versa, until the Signor Count rose, sighed deeply as he made the sign of the cross, replaced in his pocket his missal, his kerchief and his snuffbox, and moved gravely and stiffly towards the holy water stoup. Then, crossing himself again, he left the chapel after saluting the High Altar with a brief nod. After him came the Countess with her daughters, the kinsmen and guests, who bowed a little deeper, then the servants and estate employees, who bent one knee, and lastly the peasants and country people, who bent both.

Now that the Lord seems to us very very far away, He seems also equally distant from all the social grades, even as the sun does not warm the summit of a campanile more than the base. But then, when He was held to reside a good deal nearer, greater or less distances were more easily discernible, and a feudal lord considered himself so much nearer than all the rest, that he might permit himself a greater degree of confidence.

Usually for half an hour before the daily Mass they looked for me to serve Monsignor, who intended thereby to grant me a sign of his especial favour over the sons of Fulgenzio. But I did not feel in any way grateful for this distinction and knew how to take my own precautions, so that more often than not whoever was sent to hunt for me returned with empty hands. As a rule I took refuge with Mastro Germano and did not emerge from his hole until the last bell had already sounded. In the meantime they would already have put the surplice on Noni or Manichetto, who with their wooden pattens always ran the risk of breaking their noses on the altar steps when changing positions during the Mass, and I only entered the church when I was sure that all danger was past. However, my tricks were quickly discovered, so that I received many rebukes from Monsignor before the kitchen hearth; but I always excused myself by saying that I did not know the Confiteor. And in fact, to justify this excuse of mine on the few occasions when I was trapped, I had always the prudence to halt and begin again as soon as I reached the *mea culpa*, and then repeated the manoeuvre two, three or four times, until Monsignor lost patience and finished it himself.

On these unlucky days, I had afterwards the pleasure of remaining shut up in a little room under the dove-cote with the missal, a glass of water and a greyish loaf until an hour before vespers. I used to amuse myself by dipping the book into the water and crumbling up the bread for the pigeons; and later, when Gregorio, Monsignor's valet, came to let me out, I ran at once to Martino, who was always certain to have kept some lunch for me. During these hours I had the chagrin of hearing the voice of the Pisana playing with the other little boys without any apparent regret at my incarceration; and I then took such a dislike to the Confiteor that I rolled it into pellets and threw them down into the courtyard on those chatterboxes, together with whatever small stones and bits of mortar I could find in the corners, or scratch out of the walls with my nails. Sometimes I would shake the door with all my force and throw myself against it, battering at it with my elbows, feet and head until after half an hour of this uproar the bailiff never failed to come up and reward me with four strokes of his stirrup-leather. And this dose was repeated in the evening when they found that I had completely soaked and torn up my missal.

On ordinary days after Mass, everyone went about his own affairs until the hour for lunch; I, however, had plenty to do to defend myself against the Rector's manservant who came to look for me to take me to my lessons. Running here and there, I in front and he behind, I always ended by being caught, half dead with anger and fatigue, and then had to go with him at a trot for the mile between Fratta and Teglio to make up for lost time.

When I arrived at the Rectory, I would waste time each day in looking at certain pictures of Udine which adorned the walls of the entrance hall and then only with great difficulty were they able to shut me up in a small study where, after the first day's experience, everything was kept rigorously under lock and key for fear of my misdoings. I would amuse myself drawing on the walls faces of the Rector, with two bushy eyebrows, and a certain cap on his head which left the satiric intentions of the artist in no doubt. Often, during these artistic exercises, I would hear in the hall the stealthy step of Maria, the Rector's housekeeper, who came to the keyhole to see what I was doing. Then I would leap to the writing desk and with elbows well spread out and head low on the paper, rounded certain A's and certain O's, which took up half a page each and which, with the addition of another four or five clumsy letters, still more Arabic, ostensibly completed my daily task. Or I used to shout B-a Ba, B-e Be, B-o Bo, with so demoniacal a voice that the poor woman fled, half deafened, to her kitchen.

At half past ten the Rector arrived, gave me some slaps for the unseemly scrawls that he saw on the walls, added others for my atrocious writing and then administered a third dose for the great lack of attention that I gave to his finger in reading my A. B. C. I remember that I often used to look away at some little red books in a bookcase near by and then, instead of applying myself to the next line, would always jump to the line V-a Va, V-e Ve, V-o Vo. . . . It was at this point that I would be interrupted by the third correction administered from behind, and I have never been able to realize the reason for the preference my memory demonstrated for the letter V, if not perhaps that it is one of the last ones of the alphabet.

My mistakes and my fidgeting and the doggerel that I wrote during my lessons have always remained in my mind as a sign of my bad behaviour and of the exemplary patience of the Rector. If ever I had to teach a little pig such as I was then to read, I am sure that by the first two lessons I would have pulled both its ears off, but I experienced no other inconvenience than to take them back home again somewhat lengthened. But this inconvenience, which continued and increased for four years, between the ages of six and ten, procured me the advantage of being able to read all printed letters, and to write sufficiently fluently so long as capitals were not in question.

The thrift that I have afterwards had all my life for full stops and commas I owe entirely to the continuous and liberal instruction of the excellent Rector. Even now, in proceeding with this story, I have had to refer for the punctuation to a friend, a writer to the Prefecture, or otherwise it would be from beginning to end one single long sentence and there would be no preacher alive whose voice would be capable of intoning it.

When I returned to Fratta and did not lose myself by the way in chasing dragonflies or salamanders, I would arrive just at the moment when the family sat down to table. The dining-hall was divided from the kitchen by a long corridor which rose gradually for a couple of yards, so that it was sufficiently high to be able to tell from the windows in the hours of sunlight that it was still day. It was a vast square room, a good half of it occupied by a table covered with a green cloth and as big as two billiard tables. Between two embrasures looking on to the moat there was a huge chimney-place; opposite, between two windows giving on to the courtyard, was a walnut dresser and in the four corners were four smaller tables with candlesticks prepared for the evening's games. The rough chairs certainly weighed fifty pounds apiece and were all the same, very wide in the seat, bolt upright from feet to headrest and covered with black morocco leather, stuffed with nails, or so at least one might have judged from their softness.

The table was usually laid for twelve covers, four each on the two long sides, three on the side next to the corridor for the bailiff, the surveyor and the Chaplain, and a side free for the Signor Count. His lady consort, with the Contessina Clara, sat on his right, the Monsignor and the Chancellor on his left; the places between these and the other sides of the table were occupied by the Captain, his wife and the guests. If there were no guests, their places remained unoccupied and if they exceeded two, the Captain and his wife sought refuge in the spaces between the bailiff, the surveyor and the Chaplain. The latter, however, as I have said, almost always wriggled out of the honours of the patronal table, so that his plate, more often than not, returned clean to the kitchen. Agostino, the butler, served the places near to the Signor Count, and he from his high chair (he alone had a sort of throne that almost lifted his knees to the level of the table) gave him the sign to carve. When he had finished, the Signor Count chose the best tit-bits and then with a gesture motioned the platter to his wife, but while he was doing this with his right hand, his left was already occupied with eating.

The coachman and Gregorio helped in the service, but they were of very little assistance, because they were too occupied in pouring out for Monsignor, unlacing his napkin or giving him great slaps on the back when a mouthful threatened to go down the wrong way. The Pisana, naturally, did not dine at the high table, which was an honour reserved for girls only after their years in a convent. She ate in a pantry between the dining-hall and the kitchen, with the maids. As for me, I gnawed the bones in the kitchen with the dogs, the cats and Martino. No one had ever dreamed of telling me where was my place or which my cover, so that my place was wherever I could find one, and instead of knife and fork, I used my fingers. But I deceive myself. To eat my soup, the cook had given me a certain ladle, which had the advantage of widening my mouth by a good two fingers. But they tell me that because of this my smile had assumed a pleasanter expression, and since I have always had white and healthy teeth, I do not want to complain. Thus Martino and I did not come into account either among the gentry who dined in the hall or among the servants, to whom the Countess after the meal gave their portions, so that we were left the privilege of scraping the plates, the frying-pans and the saucepans; and from those made up our meal. There was also in the kitchen a basket full of polenta hung on a hook; and when the scraps were not enough to satisfy me, it was enough for me to point to the polenta. Martino understood me; he would roast me a slice and then good-bye all my miseries!

The Serjeant and the sacristan, who had wives and children, did not as a rule eat at the high table; so too Mastro Germano, who cooked for himself and concocted certain mixtures of his own that I have never been able to understand how human palate could support. It was by no means rare that he would catch one of the multitudinous cats who populated the Count's kitchen and make of it a ragout and a roast to last him for a week. Therefore, although he often invited me to lunch, I always took good care not to accept. He held that the cat has a most exquisite flesh and that it is the best remedy against many diseases; but he never said these things in the presence of Martino and therefore I fear that he wanted to impose on me.

After lunch and before the Countess appeared in the kitchen, I used to rush out to meet the crowd of urchins who gathered at that time in the forecourt of the castle; and many of them followed me into the courtyard, where the Pisana joined us a little later to indulge in those prodigies of coquetry of which I told you a while back. You will certainly ask why it was that I myself went to call my rivals, who were later to give me so much annoyance. But the Contessina was so barefaced that she was quite capable of calling them herself if I did not do so; and this led me to pretend to do of my own accord what, with a double shame, I should be forced in any case to endure.

The tranquil digestion of the Countess and the affairs that occupied the women all afternoon left us free for our games; and if perchance the old grandmother asked in those hours to see her little granddaughter, the Pisana behaved so badly in her room that the Countess ended by sending her away as a dangerous disturber of her digestive processes. We had, therefore, full liberty to run, to shout, to pull one another's hair, in the vegetable garden and in the precincts of the castle. Only one terrace, overlooked by the windows of the Count and Monsignor, was forbidden us by the incorruptible vigilance of Gregorio. Once when some of the boldest tried to evade this prohibition, the valet had emerged from the little doorway of a secondary staircase with a broom-handle and had so belaboured those disturbers of the peace that we all understood that there could be no joking with that question. The Count used to say that he occupied himself during those hours with the affairs of the Chancellery, but if this were the case, he must have enjoyed a most extraordinary sense of sight, since his windows always remained firmly shuttered until six.

As far as Monsignor was concerned, he slept and he said that he slept, but even had he wished to deny it, he snored so loudly that no one in any of the infinite corners of the castle would have believed him. Between six and half past, when the weather permitted, the Countess went out for a walk; and the Count and Monsignor usually went out to meet her half an hour later. They had no fear of not meeting her because she invariably walked at the same pace every evening as far as the first house of Fossalta and then turned back at the same pace, occupying in the whole walk exactly seventy-five minutes, save for unforeseen incidents.

It is hardly necessary for me to say that the Chancellor went out with the Count; he used to walk a pace behind his master, amusing himself by kicking the pebbles on the pathway into the ditch when he was not honoured by any questions. But more often the Count would ask him about the morning's doings and he regaled him with accounts of the examinations that he had made and of the legal cases, the reports of which he spread out before His Excellency. These reports were, in fact, so many sentences to which His Excellency deigned to append his signature, putting on for that purpose a double pair of spectacles and using all the sweat of his calligraphic knowledge. While the two magistrates were discussing the affairs of this world, Monsignor Orlando would saunter on, passing his tongue over his teeth and caressing his paunch. The two companies met at the stepping stones on the old road at the border of the two districts. The Chancellor halted with his hat lowered to the ground, Monsignor made way with a wave of his hand, and the Count advanced half-way across the stepping stones to give his hand to the Countess. After them passed the Contessina Clara, though she often used to remain at home to look after her grandmother, and finally the Rector, the Chaplain, Signor Andreini or Rosa or whoever else of the band happened to be with them. They returned thus in company to the castle, walking two by two, or more frequently in single file because of the atrocious state of the road.

As soon as they arrived, Agostino ran to light the lamp in the dining-hall, a great silver lamp on which was blazoned, in place of the handle, the arms of the family: a wild boar between two trees with a Count's coronet above. The boar was larger than the trees and the coronet larger than both. Although the Count attached great value to this work, one could see at first glance that Benvenuto Cellini had had no hand in it. In the meantime, the cook put a great pan of coffee on the fire and the company waited in the dining-hall, continuing the conversation begun during the walk. But the afternoon was only passed thus during the fine months and when the weather was dry. At other times, neither the Signor Count nor Monsignor ever left their rooms save to take a bench by the kitchen fire, and it was there that the family gathered until the hour for cards. At these times they would take their coffee at the hearth and then move together to the dining-hall, where the small tables had already been prepared and the whole company would follow them, walking on tip-toe. The Countess alone was there to welcome them, for the Contessina Clara did not come down until later, after she had seen her grandmother to bed.

Sometimes the Captain's wife had the good fortune to take coffee with the Countess and this was a sign that the affairs of the day could not have gone better. The Signora Veronica showed herself very haughty at this honour and looked her husband up and down when he stood before her, as was his usual custom, to preen his moustaches before sitting down. When the gathering was made up only of the family, two small tables of 'three-seven' were sufficient;

but if there were visitors or guests, a thing that never failed to happen every autumn evening and on every Sunday during the rest of the year, the high table was invaded with 'merchant at the fair', or with a tombola. The puritans like Monsignor, and the Chancellor, who did not like games of chance, retired into a corner to play 'three-seven', while the Captain, who declared that luck was always against him, went into the kitchen to play 'goose' with the Serjeant or Fulgenzio. The truth of the matter was, I believe, that the stake of three soldi, which was customary in the dining-hall, was too risky for him and he felt more at ease with the halfpennies or farthings of the kitchen.

I, however, after having played with the Pisana until sunset, when Faustina took her away to put her to bed, found myself a corner in the inglenook and made Martino or Marchetto tell me stories. So the evening passed until my head began to droop on my breast, when Martino took my arm and crossed the courtyard, so as not to pass through the dining-hall and up the stairs to Faustina's door. There I would enter, groping and rubbing my eyes, and having unbuttoned my trousers was already fully undressed and ready for bed, with a single wriggle, for neither shoes, nor waistcoat, nor stockings, nor drawers, nor neckwear of any kind ever complicated my toilet until the age of ten; a jacket and a pair of trousers of peasant homespun that was woven in the castle for the servants, together with a piece of cord to hold up my trousers, comprised all my personal attire. I had also one or two shirts, which compensated with their superabundance of material for all their other defects, since it was Monsignor who handed his on to me when they were worn out, and no one ever took the trouble to make them fit me save by shortening a little the tail and sleeves. As for my head, one winter when it was freezing hard, Mastro Germano had provided me with a huge fur cap which he had worn from the time when he was a bulo at Ramuscello. This cap would easily have slipped down to my chin if the Rector had not previously prepared my ears to prevent it ceding to the force of gravity, and Martino used to say that when I had that thing on my head I looked to him like an angry cat. But he said it perhaps to annoy Germano and I am grateful to him and his big cap, thanks to which I was saved from many a chill. Certain it is that I still had it when I became a young man and even saved it to wear at festas because my head, being thus made so much larger, seemed to suit me wonderfully and to give me a terrifying appearance.

One day, when I was at the fair of Ravignano beyond the Tagliamento, and they were dancing on the platform in the square, I took it into my head to make fun of some Cernide of the Savorgnani who had come to maintain order in the fair, with their muskets in one hand and napkins in the other filled with eggs, butter and salami to make what they called a 'scabby omelette'.

These Cernide with their wooden sandals, their jackets of threadbare homespun and their faces that radiated grossness a mile off, made me die with laughing, therefore I and one or two other louts from Teglio and the neighbourhood began to make horns at them and ask them if they were clever enough to turn their omelettes and if they intended to cook them with their wooden sandals. One of them retorted that we would do better to go and dance, so I jumped in front of him and said that I would begin with him. In fact I did so and taking him by his arms, just as he was, with his musket still on his shoulder, led him around in the strangest furlana that was ever seen. But since he had put his provisions on the ground, it chanced that in our gyrations we stepped on the eggs and thus made his omelette before it was due. Then these valorous soldiers, who had not moved an eyelid to see their comrade thus derided, suddenly became much concerned at the destruction of the eggs and wanted to attack me with their bayonets. But I, taking my pistols from my pockets and pushing my ballerino flat on the ground, began to scream that the first man to touch me would be killed. In a moment my companions gathered round to defend me, one with an unsheathed knife and another with pistols like my own. There was a moment of suspense, and then commenced an uproar in which, I don't know how, we all found ourselves one on top of the other without either firing our pistols or using any other weapons save our fists, and indeed the occasion was not worth it. Beaten on this side and trampled on that, those poor Cernide emerged much the worse for wear, and their eggs the same, till their Captain of a Hundred arrived with the rest of the band and leapt into the fray, forcing them with dire threats to end this fracas; if not, he said, he would give the order to fire without regard to friend or foe.

Witnesses were then summoned to find out the culprits, but they, as always, backed us up and blamed the Cernide, so that we were let go without further trouble. But just as I was withdrawing, bragging to my companions at this triumph, the Cernida who had danced the furlana with me shouted after me that I ought to take great care not to lose my fur cap and that he would use it as a trophy to put on the head of his ass on the second day of the fair. I replied with a rude gesture from the square that he and his ass would make a pretty pair but that he would never lay hands on my crest. Here the Captain of the Hundred cut us short, and we went away to dance with the prettiest girls of the fair, while the Cernide lit their fires to make their omelettes with the few eggs that remained to them.

That evening I stayed on at the festa longer than I had intended on my arrival, to see what the rogue who had taunted me intended to do; and so also did some of my companions. Then, at an hour of night when it was blacker than hell itself, we moved off towards the Mendrisio ferry where, on the farther side, the bailiff's cart was waiting for me.

The road was low and winding, through a countryside thick with trees and in some places so narrow that four persons could scarcely walk abreast, but since every one of us, due to the abundant draughts of *ribolla* we had taken, needed room enough for four, there was always a good chance of someone falling into the ditch. We were laughing together and singing as well as we could with the wine gurgling almost to our throats, when at a turn of the road I saw something like a dark figure that leapt quickly over the ditch and flung itself on me like a bomb. I jumped back when a voice said: 'So it's you!' and I felt a heavy blow on the back that sent me rolling in the puddles like a sack of salt pork. As I was raising myself on my elbows I saw the same figure leap back over the ditch and disappear into the darkness of the countryside. It was only then that I realized that I had lost my hat and crawled along the road looking for it; but it must have been either that one could see the road from the surrounding country more easily, or that the darkness was in my own eyes, for he who had jumped the ditch saw me bending over to look for it and from a distance called out to me to set my heart at ease, because he had taken my crest to beautify his ass on the following day.

On hearing the words, I recollected the Cernida and the spirit returned to my companions, since to their eyes this apparition had all the appearance of a devil. But once known for what it was, they all wanted to have revenge at all costs; but the ditch was wide and no one sure enough of his legs to try and jump, which was a sign that we still possessed a glimmer of sense. So we went our way, promising to return the next day. Thus it was that we all finally decided to spend the night at Mendrisio, and the next day returned to the fair, examining all the Cernide and all the asses that we came across. When we came on one that had between its ears my fur cap glued to its forehead with pitch, we gave such a drubbing to its master that he had afterwards to be loaded on to his own ass and sent home; and my cap, since it could no longer be worn, was glued on to his face, saying we would leave it to him as a souvenir.

That was the end of Mastro Germano's present that had given me such good service for so many years; and from that incident was later born a complaint which kept me pretty busy, as I shall tell you in its proper place. Meanwhile, I beg you not to lose your good opinion of me if you find me for once in my life creating an uproar and associating with peasants and pot-house brawlers. I promise that you will see me, more suitably, as a man of importance and, in the meantime, I return to being once again a small boy, in order to tell my story in the proper order.

I have told you that I used to go to bed while they were still playing cards in the dining-hall; but the game did not go on for very long, for at half past eight exactly it was interrupted to chant the Rosary and at nine the company sat down to supper, and at ten the Signor Count gave Agostino a sign to light his lantern. The company then filed to the door that led to the great staircase, on the far side of the room to that which led to the kitchen. I say great staircase in a manner of speaking, for it was an ordinary staircase like all the others; on the first landing the Signor Count always used to stop in order to make his prognostications for the next day by feeling the wall. If it were moist, the Signor Count would say: 'Tomorrow will be bad weather,' and the Chancellor behind him repeated: 'Bad weather,' while all the others added with solemn faces: 'Bad!' If on the other hand he found it dry, the Count exclaimed: 'We shall have a most beautiful day tomorrow,' and the Chancellor also: 'A most beautiful day,' and the others, down to the lowest step: 'Most beautiful!' During this ceremony the procession halted on the staircase, to the great distress of the Countess, who was afraid of getting sciatica amongst all those draughts. Monsignor, indeed, had time to drop into his first sleep and it fell to Gregorio to hold him up and shake him, otherwise every evening he would have rolled down on Signora Veronica who was behind him.

As soon as the whole band had reached the hall, the function of saying good night began, after which they separated each in search of his room; and some of these were so far away that there was plenty of time to recite three Paters, three Ave Marias and three Glorias before reaching them. So at least Martino used to say, who had been assigned a tiny room on the second floor next to the tower and close to the room destined to house any friars who might come to the castle on a mission.

The Signor Count and his lady occupied the room that from time immemorial all the heads of the most noble family of Fratta had inhabited. It was a large, very high room with a terrace that in winter gave one cold shivers even to look at, and with a ceiling of cross beams painted with yellow and blue arabesques. Terrace, walls and ceiling were all covered with boars, trees and coronets, so that one could not glance around without meeting a boar's ear, the branch of a tree or the point of a coronet. The Signor Count and the Signora Contessa, in their immense wedding bed, were literally invested by a phantasmagoria of family coats of arms and crests, and this glorious spectacle imprinted on the imagination before dowsing the light could not but instil an aristocratic character even to the most dark and secret functions of their matrimony. Certainly if the flocks of Jacob brought forth speckled lambs because of the withies that they saw at the watering place, then the Signora Contessa could only have conceived children convinced and blessed by the illustrious excellence of their line. That later events did not always justify this hypothesis could well have been more the fault of the Signor Count than of his lady.

The Contessina Clara slept near her grandmother in an apartment that opened into the hall opposite to her parents' room. She had a little room that resembled a nun's cell; and the only boar, which was engraved on the stucco of the fireguard, she had, perhaps without noticing, covered with a pile of books. These were the remnants of a library allowed to rot in a basement through lack of interest of the castellans and the combined assaults of worms, mice and damp. The Contessina, who in the three years spent in the convent had taken refuge in reading from the tedium and the gossip of the nuns, had remembered this room lumbered with torn volumes and vellums and set herself to fish about for the little of value that remained. A few volumes of memoirs translated from the French, some stories by those old Italians who wrote without exaggeration of household affairs, Tasso, Ariosto, the *Pastor Fido* of Guarini and almost all the comedies of Goldoni, printed only a few years before; that was all her spoils amounted to. Add to these an office of the Madonna and a few devotional works and you have the library behind which, in Clara's room, the family boar was hidden.

After she had gone to her grandmother's bed on tip-toe to make sure that nothing disturbed the placidity of her dreams, holding her hand in front of the lantern to lessen the reflection from the walls, she would withdraw into her little cell to pore over some of these books. Often all the other inhabitants of the castle were already sleeping soundly while the light of her lamp was still shining from the cracks of her balcony; and when at last she took up either the *Gerusalemme Liberata* or the *Orlando Furioso* (the identical volumes that had not been able to decide the military vocation of Monsignor her uncle) the oil failed in her lamp before the will to read from the eyes of the young girl. She lost herself with Erminia in the shady groves or followed her in the quiet dwellings of the shepherds; she passed her time with Angelica or Medoro in writing love songs on the mossy walls of the grottoes and raved with the mad Orlando and wept with compassion for him. But above all her soul was filled with pity for the end of Brandimante when the fatal hour cut short upon his lips the name of his loved one and it seemed that his soul passed onwards to finish and repeat it continuously in the happy eternity of love.

When she dropped off to sleep after such reading, she sometimes in dreams thought herself the widow Fiordiligi. A black veil fell from her forehead over her eyes as if to seal off from the vulgar gaze the sanctity of her inconsolable grief; a sweet, melancholy, eternal sorrow expanded in her heart like the distant echo of weeping harmonies and from the purest substance of that grief there emanated a spirit of hope that, too delicate and ethereal to wander on the earth, flew upwards to highest heaven. She did not know it, but the affections of that Fiordiligi of her dreams corresponded exactly to the sentiments of the Contessina Clara.

A soul impervious to the impressions of this world, she was preserved as God had made her, among the frivolities, scandals and vainglories that surrounded her. And the devout beliefs and gentle habits of her grandmother, purified by the serene meditations of old age, were renewed in her with all the spontaneity and perfume of her virginal years. In her early infancy she had always remained at Fratta, the faithful companion of the infirm old woman. She seemed the young chestnut shoot that rises from the old stump, instinct with exuberant life.

This solitary existence had preserved her from the vicious company of the maids and from the lessons that she might have learnt from the example of her mother. She lived in the castle simply, tranquilly and innocently, like the swallow that conceals its nest under the rafters of the granary. Her beauty increased with her years as if the air and the sun in which she steeped herself from morning till eve, with the robust carelessness of a country girl, had mingled within her to develop and illuminate her. But it was a good growth and a light modest and pleasant like that of the moon, not the garish and glittering flicker of the lamp. Her appearance seemed to spread about her a devout and almost celestial peace; one scarcely understood, seeing her, that beneath this gentle and harmonious exterior the fervour of devotion was mingled with the poetry of a pure imagination, hidden and active, and with the utmost delicacy of sentiment. She was the fire of the South reflected on the pure and shining ice-fields of the North.

The simple peasant women of the surroundings called her 'the Saint', and remembered with veneration the day of her first communion when, as soon as she had received the mystic bread, she had fainted from delight, from fear and from humility; and they said indeed that God had called her in an ecstasy as worthy of a still closer marriage with him. Clara too recalled, with joy mixed with terror, that celestial day, always relishing in memory that sublime rapture of the soul invited to participate for the first time in the highest and sweetest mystery of her religion.

The Contessina Clara, as well as being a believer, was devout and fervent, since to her faith was not enough, and she wanted love also. Her reputation for sanctity was not due merely to the fervour and frequency of her religious practices, but even more to her continual and active deeds of the most holy virtue. Her manner did not reveal the humility of the kitchen maid or the housekeeper, but that of the Countess who accepts from God the inequalities of society and who feels before Him no higher than the most abject of the human family. She had what they used to call the gift of second sight to sense the afflictions of others and that of simplicity to become by common consent their counsellor and consoler. To wealth she gave that value that it assumes from the needs of the poor, its real value, as it should be established in a sane economy, to become blessed of humanity. People used to say that money slipped through her fingers; and it was true, but she paid no attention to it, regarding it as a duty to be done, even as we do not notice the blood that circulates in our veins or the lungs with which we breathe. She was completely incapable of hate, even against the bad, since she did not despair of their repentance.

All created things were her friends and nature never had a daughter more grateful and loving. She went so far that she could not see mousetraps in the house and when walking in a meadow went out of her way not to tread down some flower or fresh tuft of green grass. Without poetic exaggeration, she had so light a step that the flower would bend only for a moment under her heel and the grass was scarcely aware that it had been trodden. If she kept little birds in a cage, it was only to set them free again at the coming of spring, and sometimes she became so familiar with these charming songsters that it pained her to have to separate from them. But what was her own pain to Clara when the good of others was concerned? She would open the door of the cage with a smile made more beautiful by tears, and sometimes the little birds would come back to peck at her fingers before flying away, and even remained a day or two in the vicinity of the castle, visiting with confidence the window where they had lived as happy prisoners throughout the evil season. Clara used to recognize them and knew the degree of affectionate remembrance they preserved. She thought then that the things of this world are good and that men could not be bad, if goldfinches and tomtits showed themselves so grateful and loving.

Her grandmother smiled at her from her armchair, watching these tender and moving girlish fancies of her granddaughter. And she took good care not to laugh at her, for the good old woman knew from experience that these delicate virginal feelings were preparing for her later age an inexhaustible source of pure and modest joys that were neither frail nor grudging. In the three years that she had lived in the Salesian Convent of San Vito, the girl had been ridiculed enough for her fancies, but she had the goodness of heart not to be ashamed of them and the constancy not to deny them. So that, when she went out again to take up once more by her grandmother's bed her duties of nurse, she was still the same Clara, modest and willing, quick to laugh and quick to tears for whatever affliction was not her own. The Countess, having only recently transplanted herself from Venice to Fratta, had found her still a little uncouth and had thought to correct her by the usual ten years in a convent, but after three years she began to say that Clara, being by nature clever, must have had enough of it. The truth was that the care of her mother-in-law weighed too heavily on her and in order not to have to sacrifice the services of a waiting woman for a whole year, it seemed a double saving to bring her daughter home again.

On the other hand her extravagances in Venice had somewhat unbalanced the family budget and being then concerned with providing for the education of her son, she wanted to curtail her expenses for her daughters. There were already two of them, for the Countess was carrying the Pisana when she decided to remove Clara from the convent, and never doubted for a moment that she would deliver a girl, for whom, indeed, she had already chosen a name in honour of her mother, who was a Pisani.

So it was while I was sucking breasts and swallowing pap in all the houses of Fratta; but when I was nine and the Pisana seven, and the young Count Rinaldo was finishing his course of rhetoric with the Reverend Fathers Somaschi, the Contessina had already grown up into the perfect comeliness of a young woman. I believe she was then roughly in her nineteenth year, though she did not seem so old because of the delicacy of her complexion which always preserved the glow of youth. Her mind had been enriched by good examples from the books that she had been reading and with the finest thoughts in the tranquil development of a compassionate and meditative nature; her affections kept her busy with the help that she gave to the poor women of the countryside while losing nothing of her childish graces. She still loved flowers and birds, though she now thought less about them since she had more important cares, but her serenity remained the same, made even more charming by an almost celestial assurance.

When, after having helped her grandmother to undress, she entered the dining-hall and sat down close to the little table where her mother was playing cards, with her white embroidery in one hand and her needle in the other, her presence drew all eyes and sufficed to moderate for a while the voices and the comments of the players. The Countess, who had wit enough to see this, noticed the effect produced by her daughter and was even mildly jealous of it; despite her white lace cap and all the pride of the Navagero house stamped on her features, she had never been able to achieve as much. When the chatter, often coarse and slanderous, of the company moderated, the momentary respite displeased her and she was the first to stimulate the Captain or Signor Andreini to continue and say their piece. The Signor Count stared in astonishment to hear his wife taking pleasure in the castle gossip and Monsignor glanced sharply at his kinswoman, not understanding the reason for these fits of affability, which were really unusual and perhaps a little shamefaced.

I was then still very small, but none the less from the keyhole whence I was sometimes a spectator of the play, I understood very well the anger or the good humour of the Countess; I also understood Clara, for I still remember that when the Captain or Andreini replied somewhat crudely to the invitations of the most illustrious lady, a delicate blush coloured her cheeks. It seems to me that I can still see that angel of a girl redouble her attention to her embroidery and, in her confusion, get her fingers tangled in the threads. I am quite sure that that blush was more due to timidity than anything else and that the thoughts that crossed her mind at those moments were not of unmixed pride. But how could Monsignor have been expected to understand or even suspect that? I repeat; I was nine years old and he over sixty; he was a canon with a long cloak and scarlet stockings, I almost a foundling, shirtless and barefoot. Yet, despite the fact that he was called Orlando and I Carlino, I knew more of the world and of morality than he did. He was the simplest theologian of the whole Catholic Church; I would put my hand in the fire for that!

About that time, the visits to the Castle of Fratta, for the most part by the youths of Portogruaro and the neighbourhood, greatly increased. It was no longer the privilege of Sundays or the evenings of harvest time, but all the year round, even in the hardest and most snowy winters, some courageous visitor arrived on foot or on horseback, with arquebus on shoulder and lantern slung high. I do not know whether the Countess claimed the honour of attracting these visits; certainly she used to take much trouble in making herself lively and gracious. But despite the attractions of her respectable and more than mature years, the eyes of these signorini used to wander here and there until they finally rested on the charming little face of Clara. Lucilio Vianello of Fossalta, being the nearest, was also the most assiduous; but the Partistagno was not far behind him, though his Castle of Lugugnana was on the seashore at the edge of the pine-woods, seven good miles from Fratta. This distance perhaps gave him the right to come rather earlier, and it happened many times that he arrived just at the moment when Clara went out to meet her mother on her walks. He would then ask for the honour of accompanying her and Clara would agree courteously, although the harsh and bold manners of the young cavalier were not much to her taste.

When they had finished playing cards, the Countess never failed to invite the Partistagno to spend the night at Fratta, always lamenting the dangers, the darkness and the length of his journey, but he would decline the invitation with a brief 'thanks' and, shooting a glance at Clara which was seldom, and then only by chance, returned, he would go to the stables and saddle his strong Furlana racer. Wrapping himself well in his cloak and settling the shoulder strap of his musket with the indispensable lantern on it, he would leap into the saddle and go out over the drawbridge at a sharp trot, assuring himself with one hand that his pistols were still in the side pockets of his saddlebags. He would then pass away like a ghost along those dark roads with their deep ditches, but for the most part would stop to sleep at San Mauro, about two miles away, where for greater comfort he had arranged for himself four rooms in a farmer's house on one of his properties.

The people of the district had a most wholesome respect for the Partistagno, for his musket and for his pistols, as also for his fists, should he be unarmed; for these fists were so heavy that after a couple of blows from them in the stomach, there was no need of shot or bullets to send a man to his creator.

Lucilio, however, came and went every evening on foot, with a small lantern attached to his stick stretched out in front of him like the sacristan's collection bag during the intervals of the sermon. He appeared to be unarmed; though perhaps had you searched his pockets you would have found an excellent double-barrelled pistol, an arm not too common at that time. But, being the son of the Fossalta doctor, he had his share of the paternal invulnerability and nobody would have dared to molest him. Doctors at that time counted, in popular opinion, in the category of wizards and no one felt bold enough to provoke their revenge. There are plenty of vendettas, still unknown, at the present day; in the last century there were three times as many and you may judge for yourself how many were carefully planned! The common people were almost able to believe that a doctor could bring the plague to an entire province and I know one patriarchal family of that district where, before calling in the doctor, they would recite several orations to the Madonna to pray that his visit should be accompanied by good fortune.

Doctor Sperandio (a good name for a doctor and which in itself gave good counsel to his patients) had nothing in his appearance to give the lie to the reputation of witchcraft with which he and his colleagues were honoured. He used to wear a huge fleece and horse-hair wig, as black as ink, which well protected his forehead, his ears and his neck against the wind, as well as an enormous three-cornered hat, equally black and as big as a thunder-cloud. To see him from a distance on his bony and exhausted nag, ash-coloured like a donkey, he seemed more like a grave-digger than a doctor. But when he dismounted and put on his spectacles by a sick-bed to look at a tongue, he seemed more like a lawyer preparing to draw up a will. Generally, he spoke half Latin and half Friuli; but by the afternoon Latin had taken up three-quarters of his conversation and towards night, after having drunk the decanter of the Ave Maria, he would give himself up entirely to Cicero. So also, if in the morning he would order a lenitive, in the evening he used drastic remedies only; and the leeches of the afternoon changed in the hours of the night to blood-letting. His courage increased with the hours and after supper he would have removed the brain of a madman in the hope that the operation might be successful.

No doctor of physics, no surgeon, no phlebotomist ever had lancets longer or more rusty than he. I believe that they were really lancets of the Huns or the Visigoths excavated in the ruins of Concordia; but he used them with singular skill so that in his long career he had only mutilated the arm of a paralytic, and his sole difficulty, though a frequent one, was that of stemming the blood, so large were the wounds he made. If the blood did not stop running with 'dragon's powder' he had recourse to the simple expedient of letting it flow, citing in Latin an axiom all his own: that no peasant had ever died unconscious. Seneca, however, was not a peasant but a philosopher.

Doctor Sperandio held the art of Hippocrates and of Galen in the highest esteem. And, indeed, he was quite right to do so; for, in addition to furnishing him with a living, he had made enough out of it to be able to buy a small house and a small estate near it in Fossalta. He had completed his studies at Padua, but named with a greater veneration the School of Salerno and the University of Montpellier; and in his prescriptions he paid great heed to simples which he found growing wild in the marshes and along the hedges, a most anti-Christian method that often put him at loggerheads with the apothecary of the district. But the doctor was a man of conscience, and since he knew that the apothecary himself extracted even foreign medicines from the local flowers, he revealed the fraud with the abominable simplicity of his remedies.

As regards social theories, he was a trifle Egyptian. Let me explain myself. He stood for the tradition of a profession in a family, and wished at all costs that his son should inherit his clients and his lancets. Signor Lucilio did not share this opinion, replying that the deluge would have been of no avail had it not washed away those mouldy doctrines of hereditary tyranny. However, he bent himself to obedience and studied his five years in the most learned and ancient University of Padua. He was a scholar most notable for his idleness, who never made an appearance at the rare lectures, who was continually fighting with the gentlemen and policemen of the town and who at every snowfall always ran first of all to announce the fact at the Parlatorium of the Nuns of St Croce. It was well known that whoever succeeded in this priority used to receive from the hands of the Reverend Mother the gift of a basket of fine pastries. Lucilio Vianello had emptied many of these baskets before obtaining his laureate.

But now arose the eternal question between father and son. There was no way in which the former could induce him to obtain this blessed laureate. Money for the trip there and back was put in his pockets, together with enough for a month's residence and the fee for the first examination. Lucilio embarked at Portogruaro on the postal boat for Venice; but he left, he stayed, he returned without money and without having taken his examinations. Seven times in two years was he absent in this way, sometimes for a month, sometimes for two, and the Professors of the Medical Faculty had not yet smelled their first fees. But what did he do in these absences? That was what Doctor Sperandio stubbornly set himself to discover, but to no result. After the seventh trip, he finally discovered that his noble son did not even take the trouble to reach Padua and that once in Venice he found himself so comfortable there that he did not dream of having to go farther to spend his father's money. This the doctor eventually learnt from one of his patrons, a Senator, a certain nobleman Frumier, kinsman of the Count of Fratta, who spent the summer months at Portogruaro, and who also warned him of the suspicious behaviour of Lucilio at Venice and that the Inquisitors were keeping a paternal eye on him. Ipecacuanha! What more! Doctor Sperandio burnt the letter, stirred up the ashes with a spatula and looked askance at Lucilio who was sitting opposite him wiping some buffalo horns; but for a long time he spoke no more of the laureate. However, he took his son with him into his practice to try and discover the extent of his knowledge of the science of Aesculapius; and as he found himself satisfied with the results, began to send him about to look at the tongues and the urine of the various peasants he had visited in the morning.

Lucilio opened a little notebook for the cases of Giacomo, Toni or Matteo, with a triple rubric for pulse, tongue and urine and, one after the other, as he made his visits, he filled these tables with requisite indications and reported in good order to his father, who was sometimes astonished at the violent changes and unexpected crises not usually associated with the maladies of ploughmen.

'What! Matteo's tongue clear and moist? Yesterday he was in bed with fever complicated by the putrid evil! *Putridum autem septimo aut quattuordecimo tantumque die in sudorem aut flexum ventris per purgationes resolvitur.* Clean and moist indeed! But this morning it was dry as tinder and coated two fingers deep. . . . Come, come . . . the Gaetana with a convulsive pulse! But only today I counted fifty-two beats to the minute and ordered her a potion *vinum tantummodo pepatum et infusione canellae oblungatum.* What does this mean? . . . Well, we'll see to-morrow! *Nemo humanae naturae pars qua nervis praestet in faenominali mutatione ac subitaneitate.*'

On the next day he would go and find Matteo with his tongue furred and the Gaetana with her pulse feeble, despite the pepper, the cinnamon and the wine. The cause of these miracles was that, on this occasion, Lucilio, not feeling inclined to make his round of visits, had compiled his own indications and filled in his rubric by guesswork in the shade of a mulberry tree. He had then handed it to his father to make him despair of his theories *de qualitate et sintomatic morborum.*

There were certain other occasions, however, when it was not so displeasing to the young man to have studied medicine at the University of Padua; when, for example, as soon as he arrived, Rosa prayed him to come upstairs to the old Countess, who was subject to nervous fits, and wanted to get from him a potion of laudanum and distilled water to calm her. Lucilio had for this almost centenarian old woman a reverent feeling compounded of love and veneration, and he could not give medicine and attention enough to maintain so worthy and precious a life. He would often stand and listen to her with an attention bordering on wonder, filled with delight at the words she spoke. Although of a secretive and reserved temperament, when talking with her he would warm to an involuntary candour and was not unwilling to speak to her about himself and his affairs as to a mother. Nobody, if he were to be believed, suffered as he did in being an orphan since the wife of Doctor Sperandio had died of childbed fever after bearing him, her only child; and he seemed to seek comfort in his loneliness in the feeling, almost as for a mother, inspired in him by Clara's grandmother. Little by little the old woman grew accustomed to him; she had him called even when she had no need of a doctor and listened to him telling her the news of the day with pleasure, finding him quite different from the other young men who frequented the castle.

Lucilio, indeed, merited this distinction; he had read much and had a great liking for history, and since he knew that every day is a page in the annals of the peoples, he followed with eager attention those first signs of disorder that were then to be seen on the European horizon. The English were at that time not too well regarded by the Venetian patricians; perhaps for the same reason that the bankrupt cannot regard with a kindly eye the new masters of his property. Therefore they always glorified the exploits of the Americans and the civil greatness of Washington who had liberated from subjection to the Lords a whole new world. The infirm old woman listened eagerly to his talk of events and of battles that always turned to the disadvantage of the English, and joined with him in a warm enthusiasm for that federal pact that had taken from them for ever the possession of the American colonies. When he spoke with pursed lips of the affairs of France, of the king's ministers who were being ousted one after the other, of the king himself who no longer knew on what party to rely and of the plots of the germanized queen, she interrupted to tell him of the events of the times she had known: of the splendours of the court, the servility of the courtiers and of the proud and almost lugubrious solitude of the great king, who had outlived the glory with which his contemporaries had surrounded him, only to assist in the frivolities and immoralities of his grandsons. She spoke with horror of the openly lewd customs which the new generation had begun to introduce, and thanked heaven that had protected the Republic of San Marco from the onset of this pestilence.

Once having left the Court of France for the Castle of Fratta she remembered Venice as it had been at the beginning of the Settecento, not yet unworthy of a place in the great council of European states; she could not know how much had happened in the meantime and with what flattering tinsel of elegance the indecencies of Versailles were now eagerly copied at the Rialto and in the palaces of the Grand Canal. When Clara read her some of the comedies of Goldoni she was scandalized and made her skip several pages; some volumes she had thought to take away and lock up. She could not have understood that what to her seemed barefaced impropriety of speech and licence of thought, created, in the theatres of San Benedetto or Sant' Angelo, the effect of a whiplash on customs even more impudent and corrupt.

Sometimes, too, she would touch on the reforms already begun by Joseph II, especially in ecclesiastical affairs; but the devout old woman did not know whether she should grieve at the humiliation of religion or console herself at seeing it carried out by such an enemy and antagonist of the Republic that he would surely be punished later by the hand of God. The Venetians had long felt, especially in the Friuli, the pressure of the Empire; and they had resisted it with force in the time of their military greatness and with prudent policy in the time of their continued civic wisdom, but now that both one and the other had been lost in universal indolence the more thoughtful contented themselves with relying upon Providence. That was reasonable for an old lady, but not for a governing Senate. Everyone knows that Providence matures her designs through our own thoughts, our own sentiments and our own works; and to hope to receive from her food already cooked was either a dream of the desperate or the flattery worthy only of street women.

Therefore when the Badoer fell into this childish hope, Lucilio could only shake his head; but as he did so, he bit his lips to hold back a smile that flickered at the corners of his mouth from under a pair of delicate and very black moustaches. I can wager that the reforms of the Emperor and the perdition of St Mark did not displease him as much as he wanted to show.

The talk did not always concern such exalted topics; very often, indeed, it dealt with much nearer matters. In those times, steamships, telegraphs and metalled roads had not yet realized the great moral dogma of human unity, and every little group left to itself by the great difficulty of communications and almost complete judicial independence occupied itself almost exclusively with its own affairs, paying little heed to the rest of the world save as a subject for idle curiosity. The molecules had been divided from chaos, but there was not yet any centripetal force to weld them into other systems, interdependent upon one another and with reciprocal influences, both active and passive. Thus the inhabitants of Fratta lived, like the gods of Epicurus, in an enormous conception of their own importance, and only when some respite in their business or their pleasure allowed did they throw a curious or indifferent glance to right or left as occasion demanded. This explains why in the century just past there was such a lack of statistical information, why geography lost its way in accounts of strange customs and travellers' tales rather than revealing the real conditions of the world. This was the result of the capacity of the readers rather than the imperfection of means or the ignorance of the writers. The world for them was not a market-place but a theatre.

Frequently, therefore, these two would talk over the gossip of the neighbourhood; how such and such a commune had usurped the rights of such and such a feudal lord; how such a dispute was being argued before the Most Excellent Viceroy, what sentence had been given, or what soldiers or cavalry had been sent as a punishment to the said commune to eat up all its revenue. Future marriages were forecast and sometimes there was even a murmur of comment about those already established; and as a rule, the disputes, the oppressions and the discords of the signor castellans took up a good part of their discourse.

The old woman spoke of everything with sweetness and tranquil self-assurance, as if she judged from the standpoint of her great age and station; but this way of thinking was not always maintained and a good dose of simplicity and Christian modesty mingled with it. Lucilio played the part of a young man who enjoys learning from whoever knows more than he, and with such discretion in a young wiseacre already seasoned with study, that he won more and more the esteem and affection of the old grandmother. Anyone who could have seen him adapt himself to her wishes and strive to render her every little service that she required, would have said that he was a real son to her, or was at least bound to her by the ties of some great benefit received. But this was not the case; it was indeed the effect of a good heart, of good breeding . . . and of design. For can you not guess? . . . I will explain in a few words.

When Lucilio took leave of the old woman to go down to the dining-hall or to return to Fossalta, she remained alone with Clara and never tired of praising the excellent manners, polite and educated spirit and wise discourse of this young man. Indeed his actions gave her material enough to sing his praises, like a mirror that seemed to reflect his inner excellences.

Simple and good-natured old women, when they take a liking to a person are wont to find in this one being all the tenderness, the care and even the illusions of all the loves that have been left alive in the fibre of their hearts. So I could not tell you whether a lover, a sister, a wife, a mother or a grandmother could have been bound to a man with stronger ties than the old Countess to Lucilio. Day after day he had known how to rekindle a flame in that aged soul, drowsy but not yet moribund, and finally she had come to love him, so that not a day passed without her wanting to see him and calling on him to keep her company.

Clara, for whom the wishes of her grandmother had the force of law, had begun to want him also, and the arrival of the young man was for the two women a great occasion. The Countess did not even suspect that the young man could think of anything else save to be kind to her, or perhaps to find pleasure in their conversation after the empty uproar of the dining-hall; Lucilio was the son of Doctor Sperandio and Clara the first-born of her first-born. If any suspicion had ever crossed her mind in this matter, she would have rejected it as a rash judgement and a dishonest and culpable thought, quite without justification for this pearl among young men. Let us say simply that she was too good and too aristocratic to harbour even the shadow of such a fear. Her affection for Lucilio was a real weakness and she became, as far as he was concerned, what she had once been for the little Orlando, when she had defended the liberty of his vocation. That she was not aware of the snare that had imprisoned the hearts of the two young people from the habit of seeing and talking to each other so frequently was not to be wondered at. Clara herself was not aware of it, and Lucilio used every art to conceal it. Do you understand me? He had sought the blind alliance of the old woman in order to conquer the young one.

I should be much embarrassed to guide you surely in the labyrinth of the soul of this young man and to say what portion in it was a virtue or a defect. His was one of those vigorous and fiery natures that have in them the seeds of all the qualities, good and bad, with the ever smouldering tinder of imagination ready to set them alight and the invincible reserve of an iron and calculating will to guide and correct them. At the same time more slave and more master of his own passions than other men, he was bold and patient, as one who esteems highly his own powers, but does not want to let them dissipate in vain; an egoist, generous or cruel according to need, who despised in others obedience to those passions of which he felt himself master and who believed that the lesser must always by Nature's law cede to the greater and the weak subject themselves to the strong, the coward to the brave, the simple to the cunning. Superiority, force, greatness of soul, shrewdness, he concealed them all in his knowledge of how to desire tenaciously, and to profit by all and dare all for the satisfaction of his desire. Of such a temper are those who do great deeds, whether good or evil. But how had he come to have, in his humble and circumscribed position, a nature so strong and tenacious, even if not in everything distinguished and perfect? I could not tell you certainly. Perhaps the reading of old historians and modern philosophers and the observation of society in the various communities where he had lived, had created in him a profound and haughty conviction. He believed that all men, great or small, must think in this way if they claimed the right to be called men. Great, such a temperament would have led him to command; small, it led him to despise others; two different sorts of pride of which I know not which would better suit the ambition of Lucifer. Everyone will agree that, if his spirit was lacking in that sensitive and almost feminine element wherein grows true kindness and pity, none the less a powerful intellect sustained him as he was, far superior to the humble destiny which seemed prepared for him by the circumstances of his birth and his more than modest condition.

His forehead, vast repository of great thoughts, seemed to rise even beyond the fine hairs that shaded its summit; his deep-set brilliant eyes searched the souls and the hearts, rather than the faces, of men; his nose was straight and delicate and his mouth, firm and very mobile, denoted strong intention and secret and continuous internal activity. His stature was on the small side, as in the majority of great men, and his muscles, firm and elastic, served a body suited to his turbulent and active spirit. In all, he could have been called a good-looking youth, but the mass would have been able to find a thousand more handsome than he, or at least would not have picked him among the first.

A certain elegance, almost a foretaste of that English simplicity that was soon to take the place of fripperies and powder, regulated his manner of dressing; and that should have compensated for the lack of the prevailing fashion to make him conspicuous. He never wore a wig or used powder, even on gala days; he wore a round Quaker hat, knee breeches and highboots in the Prussian style, a doublet without ornament or enamelled buttons and a waistcoat in simple colours, either greenish or beige, not more than four fingers below his waist. These fashions he had brought with him from Padua and he said that they pleased him, as being more suitable to the country, as indeed was true. We, however, who were accustomed to fripperies in the manner of Pantaloon, used to laugh at this simple and severe form of dress, without gold trimmings, fringes or bright colours.

The Pisana used to call Lucilio Mr. Blackbird, and when he appeared the urchins of Fratta crowded around him shouting this nickname in order to annoy him. He did not smile, like one who takes pleasure in the malice of children, nor did he get angry like a fool who takes account of it; he merely passed on his way, occupied with other matters. That was why we were so angry with him, and I believe that this air of indifference made him antipathetic to us, as his dress made him seem ridiculous. When, finding the Pisana, or even me, at the castle, he would smile at us and caress us, we enjoyed showing him that all his wheedling merely irritated us, and would run away, never failing to throw ourselves into the arms of whoever else happened to be there, or would begin playing with the Captain's hunting dog. Childish reprisals! But, while we avenged ourselves in this way, he would go on looking at us, and I still remember the impression and even the flavour of those looks. It seemed as if they were trying to say: 'My children, if I thought it worth my while to make you like me, I would do it in an hour.'

Indeed whenever he set his mind on anything, he succeeded every time. When I think back over the long way he travelled so constantly to get himself received into Clara's heart by means of the love and the praises of her grandmother, I cannot but be astonished. But he was always so; and I do not remember any enterprise whether large or small, on which he embarked, without proceeding therein with equal constancy, fair wind or foul.

The robust temper of this man, which did not at first invite my sympathy, ended by imposing on me that admiration which strong things merit in these times of universal flaccidity. More than that, his love for Clara, born and nurtured through long years of silence, protected by a thousand wiles of prudence and with all the internal fire of an invincible passion, had such an impression of sincerity that it redeemed other and less attractive sentiments of his soul. He always used shrewdness in his methods and perseverance in his ends, and if this was egoism it was the egoism of a Titan.

The old Countess, however, who saw in him nothing save what he thought suitable to show her, became more and more enamoured of him. The few other visits that she received during the day were not such as to diminish the pleasure of this one. The Signor Count, who used to come about eleven o'clock in the morning to ask how she had passed the night, before going to the Chancellery to sign everything the Chancellor put before him; Monsignor Orlando who, between eleven and noon, made a fourth with her kinswoman and her granddaughter, yawning widely in his desire for lunch; her daughter-in-law who sat by her for long hours, mute and rigid, knitting and never opening her mouth save to bewail the good old days; Martino her late husband's major-domo, who kept her company in his own way, speaking little and never replying to the point, while Clara went out for her brief afternoon walk; the Pisana, who now and again was brought, with screams and scratchings, in Faustina's arms; these were the persons who passed before her every day with the monotonous satiety of characters on a magic lantern. It was not, therefore, strange that she awaited with impatience the afternoons when Lucilio came to make her laugh with his banter and to light up with a flash of gaiety the serene and grave countenance of Clara. When Lucilio perceived that the good humour which he instilled into the old woman passed also to the girl, and that she became accustomed to answer his smiles with others of her own, his patience began to hope that his reward was near.

Two persons who find pleasure in one another's company are very apt to fall in love; the sympathy of two melancholy persons passes through smiles to the fervour of love and this joy has its own reason in the similarity that it reveals between our sentiments and those of another. Passion is in great measure formed of compassion. Lucilio knew that and more. Month by month, day by day, hour by hour, smile by smile, he followed with eager eye, enamoured but none the less tranquil, patient and sure, the increase in that affection that he was instilling into Clara's soul. He loved, but only looked; a new miracle of love. He saw the sympathy for the pleasure enjoyed by her grandmother in his company change into gratitude to him and thence into agreement for the praises which must always have been buzzing in her ears of his rare and brilliant gifts. Sympathy generated confidence and so desire, the pleasure of seeing him and speaking always of him.

So Clara began to smile of her own accord, as soon as the young man entered to ask the old lady about the state of her nerves and to take off his gloves to feel her pulse. This, as we have said, was for him the true beginning of hope, and he saw that the seeds had ripened and the young shoot was beginning to bud. At his first visits, too, Clara had smiled at him, but these smiles were different. Lucilio had a doctor's eye for souls rather than for bodies. For him the vocabulary of glances, of gestures, of accents, of smiles, had as many words as that of any other language, and he seldom erred in interpreting them. The girl was not aware of feeling in his presence any greater pleasure than she had felt at first but now he could always, without fear of error, send her a glance that could have said: 'You love me!' But he did not adventure such a glance while she was still unprepared. His will was master over him and backed by reason; passion, though powerful and tyrannical at its first onslaught, had still sense enough to confess itself blind and rely for its methods on these eloquent glances. Clara was devout; she must not be alarmed. Clara was the daughter of Counts and Countesses; one must not grope in her soul before having expelled all pride of birth. Therefore Lucilio halted at his first triumph, like Fabius Cunctator; perhaps also, since he was very subtle in human relations, he enjoyed remaining for a while in that enchanting stage of love that has discovered that it is returned.

None the less, when coming sometimes from Fossalta he encountered the Fratta company returning from their daily walk and seeing Clara on the road, his cheeks would pale slightly. Not infrequently it chanced that the Partistagno was with her, proud of the honour, and while conversing with the others did not fail to turn upon the little Fossalta doctor a look of almost haughty disdain. Lucilio bore this look as he did the ridicule of the children, with an indifference even more proud and contemptuous. But that indifference showed only on his face; a hymn of victory sang in his heart. Clara's face, clouded at the sincere but crude gallantries of the young castellan, shone with a splendour of content when she saw from afar the grave and contemplative figure of her grandmother's adopted son. The Partistagno looked at her with a long glance of admiration. Lucilio scarcely glanced at her in passing. But both were intoxicated, the one with a vain hope, the other with a reasoned certainty of success.

As to the Signor Count, the Lady Countess and the good Monsignor, they were too involved in their thoughts or too occupied with their own greatness to pay any attention to such trifles. The rest of the company dared not lift their eyes so high, so these incidents went on between the three young people without incurring any profane or inopportune glances. Martino sometimes asked 'Have you seen Dr. Lucilio today?' (He called him doctor even though he had no diploma, since he had looked at many tongues and felt many pulses in the village.) I would reply, shouting at the top of my voice: 'No, I haven't.' This dialogue always took place when Clara, either alone or accompanied by the Partistagno, went out in the afternoon, less serene and joyful than usual. Martino perhaps saw more than anyone else, but he never gave any other indication than this.

As for the Pisana, she often said to me: 'If I were my sister, I would marry that handsome young man who has so many lovely ribbons on his doublet and so fine a horse with a gold-embroidered saddle-cloth; as for Mr. Blackbird, I would put him in a little cage and give him to Grandmother as a present on the day of the wedding.'

CHAPTER III

THE first time that I escaped from the kitchen of Fratta to wander in the outside world, it seemed to me beautiful beyond all measure. Comparisons are always odious; but I cannot therefore help making them, if not with my mind, at least with my eyes; and I must confess that, between the kitchen of Fratta and the outside world, I did not hesitate a moment to give the palm to the latter.

In the first place, Nature prefers light to darkness and the sun in heaven to flames in a chimney-place; secondly, in this world of grass, of flowers, of jumping and somersaults, there were neither the formidable scarlet trappings of the Signor Count nor the rebukes of Monsignor about the Confiteor, nor the persecutions of Fulgenzio, nor the little-welcomed caresses of the Countess, nor the cuffings of the chamber-maid. Finally, though I lived in the kitchen as a vassal, two paces outside and I felt myself master and could breathe at my ease, even sneeze and say to myself: 'Your health, Excellency,' and reply: 'Thank you,' without anyone finding so much ceremony unseemly. The compliments received by the Count on the momentous occasions of his sneezes had always been a source of envy to me since I was a very little boy; for it seemed to me that a person who was wished so many good things must be of great importance and infinite merit. As I advanced in life, I corrected this unusual opinion; but so far as the feeling is concerned, I cannot even now sneeze in peace but there swarm within me desires to hear myself wished long life and happiness by a chorus of voices. Reason becomes mature and grows old; but the heart remains boyish and must be schooled with boxes on the ear in the patriarchal manner of the Rector of Teglio. As for the education that has now become the fashion, our hearts have very little to gain and much to lose in the exchange of sentimental banknotes that are now currency, for the true ring of the metal of times past. It is an education of artifice and fraud, with no advantage to the cause of good since, according to the old saying, the greater always includes the less. But to return to the world which, as I have said, had at first acquaintance seemed so beautiful to me, I can assure you that it was, after all, no terrestial Paradise.

A small wooden bridge over the moat behind the castle led from the small courtyard of the stables into the vegetable garden, where two pergolas of knotted vines, laden in autumn with lovely golden clusters, were courted by all the wasps of the neighbourhood. Beyond were green waving fields of beet and maize which ended finally at a low surrounding wall, battered and tumbledown, and beyond this again vast rolling meadows filled with silver rivulets, flowers and crickets! Such was the world behind the Castle of Fratta. As to what extended in front of the castle, or on either side, I had to content myself with making its acquaintance at a later date; they kept me so tight on the chain with their Fulgenzio, their Rector and their spit that I had to enter the world of fresh air, the great temple of Nature, by escaping down the back stairs. But now a digression with regard to the spit, which has been for some time a load upon my conscience.

In the Castle of Fratta everyone had his daily task, save for the turnspit, who only carried out his on solemn occasions. It was not considered seemly to disturb him for the customary two chickens. So, while His Excellency the Turnspit enjoyed his silent and dusty ease, I was the turnspit. . . . The cook placed the two chickens on the spit, passed one end of it into a hole in the andirons and then gave me the handle, so that I should turn it with close attention and isochronous constancy until the victims had turned a rich golden brown. The sons of Adam, perhaps even Adam himself, had often done so; and I, as a son of Adam, had no right to complain of the duties entrusted to me. But how many things are done, said and thought without due consideration of one's rights! At least, so it used to seem to me for, since there was an enormous roasting-jack on the hearth, it was a bitter wrong to turn me into a roasting-jack. Was it not a sufficient martyrdom for my teeth that of all this infernal roast I was only permitted, later, to chew and lick the bones, without also making me scorch my face, turning this way and that, this way and that, in an infinity of boredom?

Sometimes I had to turn a spit laden with tiny birds which, when their feet turned upwards, at every turn drooped over the coals their tiny flayed and bloodstained heads. My own head nodded in rhythm with theirs, and I believe that I would have liked to change places with one of those chaffinches, so as to have my revenge on my tormentors by sticking in the throat of whoever was destined to eat me. While these sad little whimseys rasped my heart, I would laugh with a malicious joy and begin to turn the spit in greater haste than ever. But the cook would come clattering up and, pounding my hands, cry out: 'Slowly, Carlino, slowly. Small birds must be treated with care.' If anger and fear had allowed me to speak, I would have asked this greasy old woman why Carlino too should not be treated as least as well as a chaffinch.

The Pisana, whenever she knew that I was on duty as a roasting-jack, conquered her dislike of the kitchen and came to enjoy my rage and humiliation. Ah, what would I not have given this brazen little coquette for each one of her sneers! But none the less I had to swallow some bitter mouthfuls, and turn my spit, while an almost malevolent fury filled my heart and made me grind my teeth. Martino would sometimes, I believe, have relieved me, but the cook would not allow it, and indeed the good fellow had enough to do with his crusts of cheese and his grater. Moreover, when the soup began to boil, I had finally to endure the consolations of Monsignor who, angered at seeing me with tearful or drowsy eyes, suggested in his mellifluous voice that I should stop playing the clown or the naughty boy, and instead commit to memory the last part of the Confiteor until I understood it perfectly. But enough of all that; only to think of it, I still feel running down my back the juicy sweat of all those roasts, and as far as Monsignor is concerned, I would willingly send him where he has already been for some time, had I not greater respect for the memory of his quondam red stockings.

The world, however, had for me this last and most striking

advantage over the kitchen of Fratta, that there I was not condemned to the martyrdom of the spit. When I was alone, I leapt, I sang, I talked to myself and laughed with the joy of feeling myself free, and began to study some fine gesture to the taste of the Pisana in order, later, to find favour with her. When I succeeded in dragging my enchantress with me over the furrows and through the thickets, it seemed to me that I had all that I could desire or that she could have desired. There was nothing that I did not consider to be mine or which I did not think I could get to content her; she was mistress and lady in the castle, but here in the countryside it was I who felt myself master and did the honours as if it were my patrimony.

From time to time, to make me conscious of my rags, she would say with a serious little frown: 'These fields are mine and that meadow is mine.' But to such childish assumptions of feudal rights I paid no attention whatever. I knew and felt that I had a mastery over nature not conceded to her: the mastery of love. I felt the same indifference as Lucilio felt for the haughty glances of the Partistagno and the ridicule of the village brats for these regal airs of the Pisana. Once far from the battlements and the smells of the Chancellery, there boiled up in my heart that feeling of equality with which a sincere and courageous nature can look down upon even the heads of kings. I was the fish put back into the water, the bird escaped from its cage, the exile restored to his homeland. I felt such richness of joy that I looked for the chance of sharing it; and in default of friends, I could have made a present of it even to strangers or to those who wished me ill. Fulgenzio, the cook and even the Countess could have had their share of air, of sun, had they come to ask it of me nicely, without trampling my hands or tanning my backside. The Pisana followed me on my country escapades willingly enough when she could not find in the castle her little troup of retainers whom she could force to obey her.

In such cases she had to content herself with me and since she had often shown me the pictures in Clara's Ariosto, it did not displease her to be either Angelica followed by Rinaldo, or Marfissa the unstained virgin, or even Alcina who enchanted and ensorcelled the captain of the island. For my part, I chose the role of Rinaldo with resignation enough, and fought fierce battles against rows of poplars which became dragons, or countered the desperate feats of some treacherous magician, bearing my ladylove behind me as if on the crupper of a horse. Sometimes we pretended to be taking long voyages, to the Kingdom of Cathay or the Republic of Samarcand; but we created terrible obstacles to be overcome, some hedge that must be a forest, some dyke that was a mountain, some brook that became a river or torrent. Then we used to comfort one another with brave gestures or took counsel with hushed voices, wary eyes and bated, half-stopped breath. At last we would decide to try our fortunes; down, therefore, at breakneck speed through puddles and ditches, leaping and shouting like two demons. The obstacles were not insuperable, but not seldom the little girl's clothes suffered some damage or she got her feet soaked paddling in the water in her little brown leather shoes. As for me, my jacket was an old familiar of the thorns, and I could have stayed in the water for a hundred years before the damp seeped through the calloused soles of my feet. It was therefore my part to console her, to repair the damage and to dry her when she got a little sulky after such misfortunes; whenever she did not begin to cry, or to start scratching me, I would make her laugh by taking her on my shoulders and leaping with her over ditches and brooks. I was as strong as a young bull and the pleasure I felt when she leant her face against my neck in order to have her hands free to sport with greater ease, would have given me wind enough to have reached, with this precious burden, if not Cathay, or Samarcand, at least beyond Fossalta.

Wasting in this way the early hours of the afternoon, we began to range farther and farther from the immediate vicinity of the castle and to become familiar with other roads and paths and more distant retreats. The downland meadows where our first excursions took place sloped westward towards a fine stream of water which meandered over the plain under great rows of poplars, alders and willows, like some peasant girl who has time to waste and little will to work. Under them there was always the sound of the perpetual twittering of little birds; the grass grew thick and very high like the carpet in the most secret chamber of some lady of fashion. The winding tendrils of creepers surrounded us amongst the thorny bushes and perfumed shrubs, and seemed to prepare for us the shadiest of retreats and the softest of couches for the games of innocence and the colloquies of love. The murmur of the water made more harmonious the silence and redoubled the enchantment of pure, fresh and silvery voices.

When we sat down on the greenest slopes to recover our breath, some green lizard would scuttle to the edge of a nearby thicket whence it would turn to look at us as if wishing to ask us something or to spy out our doings. For these pleasant respites we nearly always chose a bank of the river where, after a labyrinth of murmurous and capricious windings, it ran straight for a while, still and silent, like some madcap who all of a sudden had become a nun. The gentleness of the slope calmed its violent course, but the Pisana used to say that the stream, like her, was tired of using its legs and that we should imitate it and sit down for a while. But you will scarcely believe that the little coquette could remain quiet for long. After giving me a few caresses or taking part for a while in my games, according to her mood, she would rise to her feet, unheeding and forgetful of me as if she had never known me, and lean out over the water to look at her reflection, or splash in it with her arms, or search the bushes for snail shells to make herself bracelets and collars, without heeding whether her sleeves or scarf trailed in the water. I would call her and tell her to be careful, more for the delight of having her once more playing beside me than out of respect for her clothes, but she would not even give herself the trouble to reply. Capable of falling into despair if a fold of her little collar was crushed when she condescended to join in the caprices of others, she would have broken or torn anything, even to her beautiful long black hair, her round and rosy cheeks or her plump little hands, if the caprices to be satisfied were her own.

Sometimes, for the whole of the rest of our ramble, I could not succeed in rousing her from her grave, solitary and endless games. She would insist for a whole half hour in trying to make a hole with her teeth or nails in a snail shell in order to hang it on her ear, and if I made a move to try and help her, she would protest vigorously, stamping her feet, almost weeping and hitting me in the stomach with great strokes of her elbows. It seemed as if I had done her some great wrong, but it was all a caprice of her humour. Volatile as a butterfly which cannot remain for two seconds on the corolla of a flower without beating its wings to search out another, she passed in a single moment from gentleness to moroseness, from the noisiest chatter to an obstinate silence, from gaiety to anger, even to cruelty. The truth was that in all the phases of her moods her temperament never changed; she remained always the little tyrant of Fratta, capable of giving joy to some at one moment in order to try her powers and at the next to anger another, and make him cry, in some other experiment.

In sudden and sensual natures, caprice becomes a law and egoism a system, if they have not been chilled by a careful preventive education that arms the reason against the continual effort of their excesses and diminishes the sensibility with a barrier of good habits that acts as a refuge against the surprises of instinct. Otherwise, however many excellent qualities are innate in such natures, no one will rely upon them and they remain the slaves of sensual insolence. The Pisana was at that time a little girl, but what are girls but the buds of women? Whether painted in oils or on a miniature the features of a portrait remain ever the same.

But the new horizons now opening before my spirit afforded it a refuge against the petty tyranny of these first childish griefs. I found peace in the great bosom of Nature and her beauties diverted me from the melancholy company of my angry thoughts. That vast countryside where I then wandered was very different from the narrow limits of the vegetable garden and the fishpond that from the age of six up to that of eight had given me so much pleasure. If the Pisana deserted me to caress or torment other small boys, or if she ran off halfway through one of our trips in the hope that in the meantime something had happened in the castle, I no longer ran after her to make a show of my miserable face and bowed shoulders; I went instead to forget my cares in the freshness of the fields or on the banks of the rivulet.

At every step there were new prospects and new marvels. I found a spot where the water widened out almost into a little lake, limpid and silvery as the face of a mirror. The lovely tresses of the water weeds mingled in it as though caressed by a magic zephyr; and the pebbles at the bottom shone white and polished like pearls that had escaped from their shells. The ducks and geese fluttered on the banks or suddenly all leaped tumultuously into the water and, after a momentary disturbance, swam in calm and intricate order like a fleet manoeuvring. It was a delight to see them advance, recede, turn hither and thither, without the transparency of the water being disturbed by more than a faint ripple, which died away at the water's edge in a still lighter caress. All around were dense thickets of trees on whose trunks the wild grape-vine wove countless green and capricious decorations; it would crown the summit of some elm and then abandon itself to the support of an oak, embracing it on all sides and falling in delicate festoons; from branch to branch, from tree to tree, it wove its way as if dancing and its tiny black clusters invited the starlings to a feast and the doves to quarrel with them for their share.

Just above this open space, where the little lake became a stream, two or three mills had been built, whose wheels appeared to run backwards, wildly splashing the water in every direction. I would stay there for hours watching it and throwing pebbles into the cascades of water, to see them bounce back once more and disappear under the giddy turning of the wheels. One could hear from within the rumble of the millstones and the singing of the millers, the shouting of the boys and finally the rattle of the chain on the hearth as they were stirring the polenta. I used to watch the smoke that began to plume upwards from the chimneys of the house and always preceded the entry of this new sound into the universal orchestra.

On the flat space before the mills was a continual piling up of sacks and confusion of flour-covered figures. The good wives from all around used to gather there and chatter with the women of the mills while their grain was being ground. In the meantime, the little donkeys, freed from their pack-saddles, fell gluttonously on the bran which was kept for them as a reward for their trip to the mills; when they had finished they used to bray with joy, stretching their long ears and legs; the millers' dogs barked at them and ran round them making a thousand feints of attack and of derision. It was a very animated scene and I at least wanted nothing better, since in my whole life I knew nothing else save what had come my way in the tales of Martino, master Germano or Marchetto. Now, however, I was beginning to see with my own eyes, to reason and to learn with my own mind; to know what work and trade meant; to distinguish the various duties of the housewives, the peasant women, the millers and the donkeys. These things occupied me and entertained me; and I turned towards Fratta with my head in the clouds, watching the beautiful colours which varied according to the shifting mastery of the light.

My wanderings became ever longer and longer, and longer and more daring my desertions from the custody of Fulgenzio and from the Rector's school. When I had gone around on horseback with Marchetto, I had been too small to be able to imprint on my memory what I saw; and when I grew bigger, he did not want to risk taking me on the crupper of a nag who was too old in intelligence to be strong in the legs. So everything seemed to me new and unusual; not only the mills and the millers, but the fishermen with their nets, the peasants at their ploughing, the shepherds with their flocks of sheep and goats, and all, all gave me material for wonder and delight. Finally the day came when I thought I had lost my head or had fallen into the moon, so marvellous and incredible seemed to me the things I had before my eyes. I want to speak of it, for that adventure confirmed for me, perhaps for ever, that simple and poetic religion of Nature which has since consoled me in every human sorrow with the sweet and never changing quietude of its joys.

One afternoon the Pisana was expecting a visit from three of her cousins, children of one of the Count's sisters, married to an up-country castellan. That afternoon, therefore, she slighted me so often and exposed me with such barbarity to the scorn of her cousins that she made me run away in a state of extreme fury, my only wish being to put as great a distance as possible between her and myself. I went out by the little bridge near the stables and off hotfoot across the sown fields, with anger at my humiliation riding at my back. I walked and walked with my eyes in the soles of my feet, heedless of everything, and when at last I came to raise them, I found myself in a place entirely unknown to me. I stood for a moment without being able to think, or better without being able to free myself from those thoughts that had up till then been hammering in my mind.

'Is it possible,' I thought when I had finally managed to shake them off, 'is it possible that I could have walked so far?' I was quite certain that the place where I now was did not belong to the usual circle of my wanderings; step by step I went back over all the territory that stretched for two miles behind the castle, sure that I had made no mistake. This, however, was a sandy and deserted spot, that sloped down into a canal, muddy and stagnant; on one side a meadow invaded by rushes stretched as far as the eye could see, and on the other sloped a badly cultivated countryside, in which the lack of order and apparent sterility contrasted sharply with the rank exuberance of a few large trees in irregular rows. I looked around me and could see no familiar landmark.

'*Capperi!* This is new!' I said to myself, with the satisfaction of a miser who discovers a treasure. 'Let's go on a bit and see.'

But there was a difficulty to be overcome in going forward, the wide canal, marshy and entirely covered with a lovely carpet of weeds and rushes. The vast meadow, with the unknown and the infinite, stretched away on the further side; on this side there was nothing but the arid and abandoned countryside, which did not attract me in the least. I was too spurred by curiosity to go back and too heedless to fear that the canal might be deeper than I thought. I rolled up my breeches to my thighs and descended into the water, using my hands and feet to clear the reeds and water lilies that encumbered it. Pushing on this side and pulling on that, I made my way through this floating forest, but the way sloped always downwards and the soles of my feet slithered over mud slippery as ice. When God wills, the bottom will commence to rise, I thought, and banished all fear from my mind; but I believe that I was so eager to go on that I would not have been able to turn back even had I drowned. Once I set foot on the grass I seemed to fly like a bird; the meadow rose slowly and it was already late when I had reached the highest spot whence I could look out over all my great conquest. I reached it at last, but so out of breath that I felt like a dog after coursing a hare.

As I looked around, I will always remember my astonishing pleasure, almost my bewilderment, at the marvels that I saw. In front of me was a vast, grassy, flowery plain, intersected by great canals similar to the one I had already crossed, but even wider and deeper. They went on until they lost themselves in a stretch of water considerably larger still; and beyond this rose here and there a number of hummocks, some of them crowned by campaniles. But further yet my eye could not divine; what was that infinite stretch of blue, which seemed like a piece of the sky that had fallen and shattered upon the earth; a transparent blue, variegated with streaks of silver, which merged far, far away in the distance into a blue paler than the sky?

It was the last hour of the day; from that I understood that I must have walked very far. The sun at that moment, as the peasants say, turned backward, that is, after having declined behind a dense cloudbank, found close to the horizon a space whence to send to the earth a last glance, the glance of a dying man from under a lowered eyelid. Suddenly the great canals and the great lake into which they ran became a sea of fire, and that distant mysterious azure changed into an immense flashing mass with an infinity of varied and vivid colours. The flaming sky shone reflected in this mirror and every moment the spectacle grew in intensity, became more beautiful before my eyes, and assumed the ideal and almost impossible appearance of a dream.

I fell on my knees, as Voltaire on the Grütli when he avowed before God the sole article of his creed. God came into my mind also: the great and good God that is in nature, father of all and for all. I adored, I wept, I prayed; and I must confess that my soul, when later ravaged by greater tempests, often took refuge in the childhood memory of that moment in order to attain some ray of hope. No, it was not the repetition of the Act of Faith taught me by dint of much ear pulling by the Rector of Teglio; it was a fresh impulse, spontaneous and with all the vigour of a new faith which had been sleeping quietly, quietly, within my heart and which now suddenly awoke at the invitation of nature! In that universal beauty, I experienced a foretaste of the sentiment of universal good; I believed thenceforward that, even as the spring storms could not spoil the universal harmony of creation, so human passions would never be able to obscure the wondrous serenity of eternal justice. That justice is around us, above us, within us. It punishes us and rewards us, it alone is the great unifier of all those things that assure the happiness of the soul within the greater soul of humanity. Ill-defined sentiments that may at some time become ideas; but from the hearts wherein they are born illuminate the souls of men, and mine also; poetic sentiments indeed, but of that poetry that lives and becomes incarnate, line by line, in the annals of history; sentiments of a soul tried by the hazards of life, but which lie dormant in that sense of happiness and of religion, made me, a boy, bend my knee before the majesty of the universe.

Alas for me, if I had then thought of these high and almost inexpressible matters! I would have racked my brains with philosophy and certainly would not have returned to Fratta that night. Instead, when darkness began to fall and the marvellous spectacle grew dark before me, I became once more of a sudden a boy, and almost burst into tears, fearing that I would not be able to find my way back to Fratta. I had run in coming; in returning, I ran even faster till I had reached the passage over the canal on which the sun still shone. But when I tried to make my way back over the countryside, the situation had greatly changed; night had already fallen, misty and very dark, and I who had come so thoughtlessly no longer knew how to find my way. I began to feel a feverish trembling and an impulse to run in order to arrive I knew not where. It seemed to me that however much I might have strayed on my way thither, I should have been able to return more rapidly by running than by my slow approach; but my calculations were at fault since my haste made me overlook those landmarks which could at least have assisted me not to lose my sense of direction. Also fatigue slowed my steps and I was too obsessed with the thought of not being able to reach home to persuade my legs to bear me onward.

It was mere luck that I moved sufficiently straight not to wander into the marshes where I should certainly have been drowned; and finally I came upon a road. But what a road! My God! Today one would no longer dignify it with such a name. One would call it a deathtrap or worse. None the less I thanked Providence for it, and was able to walk more calmly, guessing reasonably enough that I should be able to ask my way at the first house I came to. But who could have been stupid enough to build a house in these marshy hollows? But I was confident and went on. The first houses would appear, sooner or later. I had not walked along this road for half a mile before I heard behind me the sound of a horse approaching at a gallop. I made the sign of the cross and huddled into the ditch as much as I could; but its pace was very fast and the horse, sensing that I was there in the shadows, shied violently, bringing from its rider a fine string of blasphemies.

'Who's there? Make way, scoundrel!' he shouted in a rough voice that froze the blood in my veins.

'Have pity on me! I am only a boy who has lost his way, and I don't know where this road goes,' I just found voice enough to say. My childish pleading voice must certainly have touched the horseman, for he reined up, even though he had just been spurring his horse on to ride me down.

'Ah, so you are a boy?' he said, leaning over towards me, and revealing a huge, dark figure wrapped in the folds of a great cloak, worthy of a smuggler or a wizard, 'Yes, so you are. Where are you going?'

'I am going to Fratta, if God wills,' I said drawing back a little, fearful of this apparition.

'But what are you doing in these parts, where no living soul ever goes by night?' the unknown asked with some suspicion.

'I ran away from home,' I replied, 'and have been walking and walking, till I found myself in a wonderful place where I saw a lot of water and a lot of sun and many other beautiful things, though I don't know what they are; and coming back I got into difficulties because it was so dark and I did not remember the way, and now after running wildly, you see me here, and I don't know where here is.'

'You are behind San Mauro, near the pinewoods, son,' the man replied, 'and you are a good four miles from Fratta.'

'Signore, you are so good,' I began again, with more confidence, 'perhaps you could tell me how to get home by the shortest way?'

'Ah, so you think I am good?' said the horseman in a rather mocking tone. 'Well, perhaps you are right, and I will prove it. Get up behind me and, since I must pass that way anyhow, I will put you down at the castle.'

'I live in the castle,' I replied, not knowing if I should confide myself to the care of this unknown man.

'In the castle?' he exclaimed with surprise and displeasure. 'And to whom in the castle do you belong?'

'To no one! I am Carlino, who turns the spit and goes to school at the Rector's.'

'Not so bad; if that is so, jump up, I tell you; the horse is strong and won't even notice.'

Trembling a little and trying to reassure myself, I climbed on to the beast's back. The man helped me with one hand, saying that I should not be afraid of falling. In those districts one was almost born on horseback and one could say to any boy: get up on that colt! as one might say: sit on that rail. Therefore, when I had seated myself, he forced the animal to a frantic gallop that on such a road had all the dangers of a continual precipice. I held on with both hands to the chest of the horseman and felt the hairs of a very long beard gently tickling my fingers.

'Perhaps he is the devil,' I thought. 'He might well be!' And I made a rapid examination of my conscience, in which it seemed to me notable that I must have sinned more than usual to give him the right to carry me away on his horse. But I recollected in good time that the horse had been frightened of my shadow and since the devil's horses, according to me, should not have the weaknesses of ours, I gave myself a little peace on this score. But if it were not the devil himself, perhaps it was one of his lieutenants, some thief or assassin or who knows what else? But I had no fear of this. I had no money and felt that this was the best possible arm against any theft. So after having thought out what he was not, I began to consider what my nocturnal protector could be. Worse and worse! I defy the imagination of a Neapolitan to come to any more certain conclusions than mine and I had in the end to decide that I knew nothing. Suddenly the black subject of these fantasies turned his great beard towards me and asked in his usual and not very pleasant voice:

'Is Mastro Germano still at Fratta?'

'Yes, sir!' I replied with a start of surprise at this unexpected voice. 'He winds the tower clock every day, opens and closes the great gate and also brushes the courtyard in front of the Chancellery. He is very good to me and has often taken me to see the wheels of the clock with the Pisana, who is the daughter of the Signora Contessa.'

'Does Monsignor de Sant'Andrea often come to visit you?' he asked me again with a laugh.

'He is the confessor of the Signora Contessa,' I said. 'But it is some time since I have seen him because now, after I have begun to see the world, I stay in the kitchen as little as possible.'

'Bravo! Bravo! The kitchen is for the clergy,' he went on. 'Now you can get down, squirrel. We are at Fratta. You are the best horseman in the district. I congratulate you.'

'Surely,' I said, leaping to the ground. 'We always used to go on horseback, I behind Marchetto.'

'Oh, so you are that little parrot who used to ride behind him a few years ago,' he replied chuckling. 'Take this,' and he gave me a sharp blow on the neck, 'and give it on my account to the Serjeant; but since you are a friend of his, don't tell him you have seen me in these parts; don't tell either him or anyone else.'

As he said this, the man with the big beard forced his horse at full speed into a gallop down the side road that led to Ramuscello, and I remained where I was with wide open mouth listening to his horse's hooves growing fainter in the distance. When they had become only a faint murmur, I walked around to the moat and on the castle bridge saw Germano, who was looking around as though expecting someone.

'Ah, you little wretch! Ah, you rascal! Wandering about at such an hour! Coming home so late! Who taught you such tricks? Now, I'll teach you. . . .'

That was the manner in which Germano welcomed me; but the warmest part of his oration I cannot translate into words. The good Germano drove me in front of him with blows, from the gate of the castle to the door of the kitchen. There Martino jumped out at me:

'Little wretch! Gadabout! You won't do that a second time, I promise you. How dare you go out of the house at night and in such darkness . . .'

Here too words were the least part of my welcome, the most was the slaps that accompanied them. If I got this from my friends, you can well imagine what I might expect from the others! . . . The Captain, who was playing 'goose' with Marchetto, contented himself with giving me a heavy blow on the back, saying it was all due to idleness and that they should hand me over to him to get good results out of me. Marchetto pulled my ears amiably; Signora Veronica, who was warming herself by the fire, turned to cap the blows of Germano, and that greasy old woman, the cook, gave me a kick in the seat with such skill that I ended up with my nose on the roasting-jack that was turning.

'Just at the right moment! You are back in time!' the old witch cried. 'I have just had to put the roasting-jack into use, but now that you are here, there is no longer any need.'

With these words, she took the cord off the pulleys and put the spit in my hands after having taken it out of the jaws of the jack. I began to turn and turn again, not without being assailed and sniped at by the servants and maids as they came into the kitchen; and turning and turning once more, I thought of Gregorio, of Monsignor, of the Confiteor, of the Signor Count, of the Signora Contessa and of the nape of my neck. That evening if they had spitted me from end to end it would have done no more than diminish for me the martyrdom of fear. Certainly I would have preferred to see the nape of my neck well roasted rather than submit it to the hands of the Countess, and as regards tanning, I found that in my view St Lawrence was more fortunate than St Bartholomew. Since all were waiting to punish me, no one had been able to ask me what I had been doing during my long absence; but once I was pinned to the spit they commenced to bombard me with every manner of demand and question until, after having long stood firm under their battery, I finally broke into a flood of tears.

'But what's the matter with you, bursting into tears like that?' Martino asked me. 'Wouldn't it be better to reply to their questions?'

'I was down in the meadow by the mills; I stayed there near the water to catch crickets. I was . . . oh, oh, oh . . . it grew dark . . . and then I was late. . . .'

'And where are those crickets?' the Captain asked me. He had sometimes taken part in the criminal interrogations in the Chancellery and had picked up some of the tricks of the trade.

'I . . .' I added in an even more tearful voice, 'I don't know. They must have escaped from my pockets! I don't know anything,

I don't . . . I was down near the water catching crickets . . . I was . . . ih, ih, ih . . .'

'Attend to that spit, impostor,' shouted the cook, 'or I'll tan you . . .'

'Don't scare him too much, Orsola,' Martino intervened, since he had guessed the meaning of her words from that old witch's face.

'Body of Pancrazio!' shouted the Captain, beating his hands on the table so that all the dishes laid for supper danced. 'Three times running those infernal dice must turn up a nine! . . . That has never happened to me before! . . . The game is ruined! . . . That's enough; bear in mind, Marchetto! . . . That's three bezzi I owe you from Sunday and two and a half today.'

'There are also seven from last week,' the Serjeant added cautiously.

'Ah yes, yes! Seven and five, twelve and a half,' replied the Captain, stroking his disordered hair, 'Just half a bezzo short of six soldi. I'll pay you tomorrow.'

'At your convenience,' said Marchetto with a sigh.

'As for you,' went on the Captain, turning to me in order to change the subject, 'as for you, little hypocrite of a turnspit, I'll soon deal with you. Isn't it true, Veronica, that I am famous at dealing with people?'

'Don't be silly! Do you want to send him quite crazy?' replied his wife, leaving the hearth and making her way towards the dining-hall. 'I shall go to the Signora Contessa and tell her not to worry any longer, since Carlino has returned.'

I did not have a mirror near me; but none the less I could swear that at this announcement my hair stood upright on my head like so many lightning rods. But I was soon brought to my senses by a fresh exhortation from the cook to get on with turning the spit and I stayed where I was, more stunned than ever, to await developments. Indeed, I had not to wait for long. From the one side the Countess broke her daily rule and appeared for the third time that day in the kitchen with the Signora Veronica by her side, and from the other entered Fulgenzio, with his fat, smug face buried even more deeply than usual in the collar of his jacket. Never did the simile of Christ between the two thieves seem to me so appropriate as then; but at the moment I had no time to jest, since I knew very well that neither of those two thieves would have repented. The Countess advanced, tugging even more than usual at the hem of her coat, and stood directly in front of me; the hearth-fire made her eyes glow like two coals and the drop that only too often hung at the end of her hooked nose shone like a carbuncle.

'So,' she said, stretching out a hand towards me that made me shudder all over at the tremors that ran up and down my spine, 'so, ugly little toad, you repay the kindness of those who took you in, brought you up and even taught you how to read and write and to serve Mass? . . . I am sorry for you . . . I can see that your bad behaviour will drag you to perdition, that you will live an evil life, like your father, and that you will end up on the gallows, for in truth up till now you have always shown the right disposition for it.'

At this point I believed that I could already feel the tightening of the noose on my neck. But no! It was the fingers of the Signora Contessa which had fastened on their usual hold. I let out two screams so shrill that the Rector, the Chancellor, Clara, Signor Lucilio, the Partistagno and even, a moment later, the Signor Count and Monsignor came running out of the dining-hall. All these persons, together with those already in the kitchen, made up a very fine retinue of assistants at my passion. The spit remained still and the cook intervened to take my hands from the back of my head and set them to work again; but I was far too distracted at the furious actions of the Countess to pay any attention to any other matter.

'Tell me what you were doing, wandering about till all hours of the night,' she went on, putting, to my immense relief, both hands on her hips. 'I want to know everything, the truth, the whole truth and don't tell me any more of your stories about crickets and don't blubber!'

The Signora Veronica grinned, as only wicked old women and the devil himself know how to grin; I for my part threw a glance at her that was worth a hundred curses.

'Speak up, little gaolbird,' shouted the Countess, waving her crooked paws over my head like the claws of a cat.

'I went up to a place where there was a lot of water, and a lot of sun. And then . . .' I paused.

'And then?' asked the Countess.

'Then I came back.'

'Ah, then you came back and at what a time!' went on the Countess. 'I will show you whether or not you will have to tell me; but if you don't want to tell me what you were doing all those hours, I promise you on the word of a noblewoman that you will not taste the savour of salt again! . . .'

I remained silent; then screamed again because of another tweak at my neck from those monkey fingers of hers. Then I was silent and began to turn the spit sullenly, since the cook had put the handle into my hands again.

'I can tell you, Signora Contessa, what this fine fellow has been doing,' Fulgenzio took it on himself to say. 'I was in the sacristy a few minutes ago cleaning the vases and the ampullas for Easter which is drawing near, and having gone out to the moat to get a little water, I saw coming from the direction of San Mauro a man on horseback who put down the signorino here and then said something to him which I did not quite understand. Then the man and his horse went on towards Ramuscello and the signorino went round the moat to come in at the main gate. That was how it was!'

'And who was this man on horseback? Was it you, Marchetto?' asked the Countess.

'Marchetto was with me all the afternoon,' broke in the Captain.

'Who was this man, then?' repeated the Countess, turning to me.

'It was . . . it was . . . nobody . . .' I stammered, recalling the service rendered me and the warning given me by the unknown.

'Nobody, nobody,' grumbled the Countess. 'We will find out soon enough who this nobody was! Faustina,' she added, speaking to the 'children's woman', 'take Carlino's bed immediately into the little dark room between Martino's and the friars' guest-room and take him there as soon as the roast is finished. Out of there, my dear,' she went on, turning to me, 'you will not come until you have told us who this man on a horse was with whom you came as far as the Ramuscello crossroads.'

Faustina had picked up a light but had not yet gone to transport my mattress.

'Will you tell us who this man was?' asked the Countess.

I turned to look at Faustina and felt my heart breaking to think that, before going to bed, I would no longer be able to gaze at the Pisana, and even risk a kiss on the closed eyelids and dewy mouth. I thought perhaps that Faustina would not go.

'No, I saw nobody! I came with nobody! . . .' I replied suddenly with greater boldness than I had so far shown.

'Very well,' said the Countess, turning back to the dining-hall after making a sign to Faustina to tell her to go about the execution of her orders, 'let it be as you wish.'

She put her hands in her pockets and marched out, dragging behind her the whole band, like a retinue; but each of them before following her turned his eyes on me, sanctioning the just sentence of the lady castellan. The Count even exorcised me with a gesture that meant 'he has the devil in him'; Monsignor went on shaking his head as if he despaired of the rest of the Confiteor; the Rector pursed his lips as if to say: 'I understand nothing of all this'; and the Partistagno turned away gaily since he was bored with the whole affair. There remained the Contessina Clara, who despite the scowls of the Signora Veronica, of Fulgenzio and of the Captain, came up to me kindly and asked me if I had really told the truth. I looked around me and then answered yes, letting my chin fall on my breast. She then patted me kindly on the head and went out with the others; but before she left, the Signor Lucilio came up close to me and whispered in my ear that I should stay in bed the next day and ask for him to be called in, and that in this way we should be able to settle the whole matter with little damage. I looked up to see if it were really he who was speaking to me with so much kindness; but he had already moved away, pretending not to notice a glance almost of complicity that Clara turned on him before moving towards the door.

'What did you say to that poor child?' she asked.

'I told him so and so,' replied Lucilio.

The young woman smiled and they returned together to the dining-hall since the hour for supper was approaching. They were followed by the Captain and his wife. There remained only Fulgenzio and the cook; but Marchetto and Martino liberated me from them, after making sure that the roast was finished, and advised me to go and sleep. Indeed Marchetto picked up a lamp and took me to my new abode by such long mazes of stairways and corridors that they seemed to me that evening to be unending. He arranged my pallet in a corner of the little room that was no more than a cupboard under the stairs, helped me to undress, and tucked the covers up to my neck so that I should not catch cold. I let him do all this, as if I were a corpse; and when he had left me and by the light of the little lamp left by him on a box I saw the battered walls and sloping ceiling of that cats' hole, desperation at no longer being in the gay, white room of the Pisana seized me so violently that I beat with fists and nails at my forehead and was not still until I saw my hands red with blood. In the midst of this frenzy I heard a soft scratching at the door and, most natural in a boy, my desperation gave place in a moment to fear.

'Who is it?' I said in a trembling voice through the sobs that still racked my breast.

The door opened and the Pisana, half naked in her little night-gown and with bare feet, trembling with cold, jumped suddenly on to my bed.

'You? . . . What are you doing here? . . . Why have you come?' I said, not yet recovered from my surprise.

'I came to find you and to kiss you, because I love you,' the little girl replied. 'I woke up when Faustina was taking away your bed and when I knew that they wouldn't let you sleep in our room any more, and that they had put you with Martino, I came to see how you were and to ask why you ran away today and nobody saw you again.'

'Oh my dear Pisana, my dear Pisana!' I began to cry out, holding her with all my strength to my heart.

'Don't make such a noise or they will hear us in the kitchen,' she replied, stroking my forehead. 'What's the matter?' she added, feeling her hand wet and looking at it in the moonlight. 'Blood, blood, you are covered in blood. . . . You've got a wound here on your forehead and it is pouring out! . . . What have you done? Did you fall or run into something sharp?'

'No, it is nothing . . . it was against the edge of the door,' I replied.

'Very well, so be it; whatever it was, let me heal it,' went on the Pisana.

And she put her lips to the wound, kissing and sucking it, as did the good Sisters of olden times to the breasts of their crusader brothers, and I went on saying:

'Enough, enough, Pisana; I am quite all right now. I can't feel that I ever hurt myself.'

'No, there is still a little blood coming out,' she replied, and again pressed her mouth to my forehead with such force as seemed impossible in an eight-year-old child. At last the blood was staunched and the vain little thing preened herself on seeing me so happy after her caresses.

'I came here in the dark, feeling my way along the walls,' she said to me, 'but down there they are at supper and I wasn't afraid that they would catch me. Now that I have cured you, I must go back again in case they find me on the stairs.'

'And if they do find you?'

'I will pretend to be walking in my sleep.'

'Yes, all right. But I am sorry that you are in danger of being punished by your mother.'

'If you are sorry, that makes no difference to me; it even pleases me,' she replied with a gesture of gratified pride, tossing her head to throw back from her forehead the loose hair that had fallen across it.

'You see that I like you more than all the others and when you have not got that filthy jacket on, as now, my Carlino, now that I can see you as you really are, I like you three times as much! Why don't they dress you in pretty clothes like my cousin Augusto had on today? . . .'

'Oh, I will get some nice clothes,' I exclaimed, 'I want them more than anything else!'

'And where will you get them?' she asked me in return.

'Where? Where? . . . I will work and make money and with money Germano says you can have everything . . .'

'Yes, yes! Work, work! . . .' said the Pisana. 'Then I will like you even more! But why aren't you laughing? . . . You were so gay just now.'

'Look and see if I am laughing,' I said with my lips on hers.

'No, I can't see you like that! . . . Farther away! Let me see. I want to see if you are laughing! Don't you understand, I want to see you?'

I obeyed her and made a show of laughing with my lips, but in my heart I was thinking how much she would love me as soon as I could get those fine clothes.

'You are a dear and I like you,' replied the Pisana, murmuring in that little voice of hers that I still seem to hear and which still delights my ears in memory. 'Good-bye, Carlino, I kiss you and am going down now before Faustina comes back.'

'I must give you a light.'

'No, no,' she said, jumping off the bed and preventing me from doing likewise with one of her hands. 'I came in the dark and I will go back the same way as I came.'

'But I am afraid you will hurt yourself and will light you as far as the stairs.'

'Don't dare to move!' she said, changing her tone and leaving me free, as if sure that her gesture would have been enough to keep me still. 'Otherwise I shall be angry; I tell you I want to go down in the dark! I am brave and fear nothing! I want to go and I will go.'

And if you fall or lose your way in the corridors?'

'If I fall or lose my way? . . . Are you mad? Or do you think I was born yesterday? . . . Good-bye, Carlino. Thank me for being good and coming here to find you.'

'Oh yes, I thank you, I thank you,' I told her, my heart swelling with gratitude.

'Let me thank you too,' she went on, kneeling down beside me and covering my hand with kisses, 'since you go on loving me even when I am bad. Oh yes! You are really the best and nicest boy of all and I don't understand why you never punish me for all the nasty things I do sometimes.'

'Punish you. What for, Pisana?' I said. 'Get up now and let me give you a light. You will get ill in this cold.'

'What?' exclaimed the little girl. 'You know very well that I never get ill. Before I go, I want you to punish me. You must pull out a big tuft of my hair for all the times I have been naughty to you.'

And she took my hands and put them on her little head.

'Oh no,' I said, 'I would rather kiss you.'

'But I want you to pull out my hair.'

'And I don't want to!' I replied.

'What do you mean, don't want to? I tell you to do it . . .' she began to shout 'Pull out my hair, pull out my hair; if you don't I shall scream so loud that they will come upstairs and I shall get a whipping from mama.'

To quieten her, I took a lock of her hair in two of my fingers and twisted it round my hand, playing with it.

'Pull! Pull out my hair!' she said angrily, drawing back her head in such a way that I had to let my hand go with it for fear of hurting her.

'I tell you I want to be punished!' she went on, stamping her feet and pounding her knees on the stone floor which was all rough and uneven.

'Don't do that, Pisana, you will hurt yourself.'

'Come on then, pull out my hair!'

I tugged very gently at the lock I held in my fingers.

'Harder, harder!' said the crazy little thing.

'Like this, then,' I said, tugging a little harder.

'No, not like that. Harder still,' she replied furiously. And while I still did not know what to do, she jerked away her head with such force that the lock of hair remained in my fingers. 'Do you see?' she added. And then, quite satisfied, 'That's the way I want to be punished when I need to be! . . . And now, till to-morrow, Carlino, and don't you dare to move or I won't go out with you any more.'

I stayed, astonished and motionless, with the lock between my fingers, while she slipped out of the door and closed it behind her; then I leapt up to follow her, but she had already disappeared down the corridor. I was certain that if her mother had torn out such a lock when punishing her, the child would have made noise enough to turn the whole castle upside down, and even to-day I marvel that she should have borne the pain without even blinking; so strong in her was her will and her fancy even from childhood. I do not know if those moments brought me more pleasure or regret. The courage of the Pisana in coming to find me through that dark labyrinth of the gloomy castle, despite the punishment that she might have received, had raised me to the seventh heaven; later her stubbornness had intervened to clip my wings, since I felt (I say felt, since at nine or ten years of age certain things could not yet be understood), I felt, I repeat, that the vainglory and vanity of displaying her prowess counted for more than affection in this proof of courage. I was therefore more than a little downcast after my first fervour of enthusiasm; and the lock of hair that remained with me remained rather as a proof of my servitude than of her good intentions towards me.

However, from my boyhood, the material signs of my joys, my sorrows and my various experiences were always very dear to me; and I would not have given up that lock of hair for all the fine gold and mosaic buttons and other extravagances that decorated the person of the Signor Count on ceremonial occasions. For me, memory has always been a book, and the objects that recall it at certain moments in my annals seem to me like those ribbons that one uses to mark the more notable pages. They fall immediately under one's eye and one has only to rely on them to find that point in the recital or that particular sentence that struck one, without needing to turn over the pages. I have always carried about with me for long, long years a little museum of trifles, of hair, of pebbles, of dried flowers, of knicknacks, broken rings, pieces of paper and other scraps that represent so many incidents, gay or serious, sweet or painful, but always memorable, of my life. This museum is always increasing and I preserve it with as much devotion as an antiquarian a rare medallion. If you, my readers, had lived as I have lived, I would only have to refer you to this long series of trifles and relics to recall to mind the whole story of my life, in the manner of the Egyptian hieroglyphs.

That lock of hair, uneven and tangled, that still preserves the marks of its tearing out, was like the first cross marked up to signify the passing of a day in the domestic shrine of memory. And it often later came into my mind to pray, to meditate, to laugh or to cry before this cross, from whose significance mixed of joy and anguish, one could perhaps even then have prophesied the course of those events, sharp, confused and convulsive, that would later consume my soul and happily renew it. That lock of hair remains the A of my alphabet, the first mystery of my Via Crucis, the first relic of my happiness, the first record of my life, as varied and inexplicable as is that of all of us. Certainly, from the first moment, I realized its importance since it seemed to me then that I had no hiding-place secure enough in which to conceal it. I wrapped it up in a blank page of my missal and put it between my bedcovers and my mattress. A strange thing! So great seemed to me the inestimable value of those few hairs that they seemed to burn my fingers. I do not know if it were fear of losing them or of having them taken from me, or an instinctive perception of the tremendous promise that they later signified. . . .

I had already hidden them and lay very quietly pretending to be asleep when Martino arrived. Seeing me asleep, he took the light for himself and went into his own room. Then little by little the pretence of sleeping became a real sleep and this in turn became a fantasy of dreams, of phantasmagoria and transfigurations, which left me the impression of a whole life in that single night. Time is not to be measured as it would seem, by the swinging of a pendulum, but by the number of sensations. It could be so; and it could equally be that such a question is merely a juggling with words. I have sometimes in a dream lived long years and it seems to me that to explain this phenomenon one must compare time to distance and a dream to a steamship. Things seen are the same but they pass more quickly; distance is not so much diminished as devoured.

The next day I awoke with such a serious mien that I almost felt myself a fully-grown man, so long a time seemed to have been condensed into the last twenty-four hours that I had lived; and the memories of the previous day passed before me clear, ordered and vivid, like the chapters of a great romance. The scorn of the Pisana, the sneers of my pretty cousins, my humiliation, my flight, my re-awakening on the edge of the canal, the perilous fording of that canal, the great prairie, my mounting on the hillock, the marvel of that stupendous scene of grandeur, splendour and mystery, the falling of darkness, my fears and my rush across the countryside, the noise of the horse's hooves behind me and the man with the great beard who had taken me on his crupper, the wild gallop through the darkness and the mist, Germano's whipping on my first arrival at Fratta, those other martyrdoms in the kitchen, the spitefulness of the Countess and my firmness, despite the dreadful punishment hanging over me, in not wishing to disobey the wishes of one who had rendered me a service, the caresses of Clara and the words of Signor Lucilio, my frenzy and the despair in which I went to bed, and the appearance in the midst of it all of the Pisana, a Pisana humble yet proud, kind yet cruel, thoughtless, capricious and yet very lovely as was her wont; does it not seem that all this would be too much for the brain of a child? And there in a sheet of paper under my pallet I had a talisman that during my whole life would recall at my pleasure all that day so long and varied. Then recollecting the words of Signor Lucilio, I decided to profit by them and began to call Martino with all the voice I had. But the old man would have made me tear my throat to pieces before his eardrums would resolve to warn him of my cries so I leapt out of bed and went into his room where he was just finishing dressing and told him I had a headache, that I had not closed an eye the whole of the night and that he should call the doctor as I was very much afraid I was going to die.

Martino told me that I was mad and that I should go quietly back to bed and that he would meanwhile go for the doctor; but first he went down to the kitchen to steal a little soup for me, an enterprise in which, protected by the darkness of the place, he succeeded admirably. I drank the soup with great difficulty since I had a burning desire for bread, and then retreated slowly under the bedclothes, promising that I would try and sweat. I believe that between the blows on my head, the exhaustion of fatigue and fasting and the sweat produced in me by that hot soup, I succeeded in achieving a magnificent fever; so much so that when Signor Lucilio arrived in about an hour my hunger had passed and an intense thirst had taken its place. He felt my pulse, looked at my tongue and while he asked me about those scratches that disfigured my forehead, he smiled on me more kindly than at first, hearing in the corridor the rustling of a skirt. Clara then entered my mousehole to hear from the doctor the reasons for my illness and to comfort me by saying that the Countess, in view of my illness, did not insist on punishing me so severely and provided that I would tell her the truth about the evening before, she would even forgive me. I said that I had already told the truth and would have gone on repeating it; and if it seemed strange to them that I had wandered off in that way without knowing where I had passed almost an entire day, it seemed equally strange to me and I did not know what to do about it.

Clara then asked me about that place which was so marvellous and so full of light and sun and colour, where I said I had been; and when I repeated the description of it to her with all the emphasis that I could, she said that perhaps Marchetto had been right and that I might have been at the Bastion of Attila, which was a height near the Lugugnana sea-coast, where the country tradition had it that, on coming from Aquileia, the King of the Huns had pitched his camp before being met by Pope Leo. However, from there to Fratta was seven good miles the shortest way and she could not understand how I had not lost my way on my return. And she went on to tell me that that most beautiful thing, immense, blue and of all colours, in which the sky was reflected, was certainly the sea.

'The sea,' I exclaimed. 'Oh, what happiness to pass one's life on the sea!'

'Indeed!' said Signor Lucilio. 'I have a cousin who has enjoyed this happiness for many years and is by no means so pleased with it. He says that water was made for fish, and that it was very foolish of the old Venetians to settle down in the middle of it.'

'It would be stupid now; but it wasn't at one time,' said Clara, 'when on the other side of the sea we had Candia, the Morea, Cyprus and all the Levant.'

'Oh, as far as I am concerned,' I replied, 'I would like to be always on the sea without bothering myself what might be on the other side of it.'

'But in the meantime, see that you keep well covered up and get well, little demon,' said Lucilio. 'Martino will bring you a little bottle from the apothecary's, as nice as jam, and you will take a spoonful every half-hour; do you understand?'

'In the meantime we will arrange matters with Mama as well as we can,' went on Clara, 'and since you have repeated that it was the truth that you told yesterday evening, I hope that she will forgive you.'

Lucilio and Clara went out and Martino with them, to go to the apothecary's; I remained with my sweat, with my thirst and with an overwhelming desire to see the Pisana, and it did not matter to me in the least then whether they forgave me or not. But the little girl did not appear and only in the courtyard I heard her voice and those of the other children twittering over their games. And though I was afraid of being seen or prevented by Martino, I did not dare to get dressed and go down into the courtyard, much as I wanted to; I stood with ears strained and my heart in such a tumult that I could scarcely hear, till, about an hour later, I heard the Pisana shout up at the top of her voice:

'Martino, Martino, how is Carlino?'

Martino must have understood her and even replied to her, but I understood nothing; but I saw him come in a little later with the bottle of medicine, and he told me that he had met the Countess on the stairs and she had asked him if it were true that I had split my forehead against the wall for desperation.

'Was it true?' asked the good Martino.

'I don't know,' I replied, 'but yesterday evening I was so wrought up that I might have done all sorts of foolish things without remembering anything about them later.'

'You don't remember?' said Martino who had understood very little.

'No, no, I don't remember,' I replied.

He was not at all satisfied with such a reply, since it seemed to him that after having injured my face in such a way, I should have had the best possible recollection of it.

The medicine had its effect, however, perhaps better and more rapidly than anyone had anticipated, for I got up the same day; and as for the punishment threatened by the Countess, nothing more was heard of it. It was true, however, that there was no question of sending me back to Faustina's room and that my kennel remained permanently next to Martino's room. As may be imagined, my desire to see the Pisana again, after the incidents of the previous night, played a major part in my unexpected recovery; and when I went down to the kitchen, my first thought was to look for her.

The family had only just finished lunch, and Monsignor, meeting me on the staircase, chucked me under the chin, contrary to his usual custom, and looked at the scars on my forehead, which by this time were no great matter. He said that I could not be the pest they believed me to be if the shame of being thought a liar had made me do such violence to myself; but he advised me to use more discretion in the future, to lay my sorrows before God, and to learn the second part of the Confiteor. In the benign words of Monsignor I recognized the good offices of Clara, who had given the most edifying reasons for my folly, and thus, if not completely forgiven, I was at least conceded a complete oblivion. I learnt later from Marchetto that Signor Lucilio had described me as a very timid and moody boy, easily depressed in strength and health by any displeasure, and between him and Clara they gave such surety for my sincerity that the Countess did not like to accuse me of duplicity. Furthermore, she did not bother about interrogating Germano; but he, perhaps primed by Martino, volunteered that he had certainly heard the sound of a horse's hooves the night before, but some little time after my return to Fratta, so that it was quite possible that the horse had not brought me. So the testimony of Fulgenzio was left in peace and I too remained in peace and no longer had to tell lies owing to my scruples of conscience. None the less, I must add that what may appear to some to be the frivolous and determined obstinacy of a boy seemed to me then, and still seems to me, a good proof of fidelity and gratitude.

That was the first time my spirit had to struggle between pleasure and duty; nor did I waver a moment to hold to the latter. If the duty in this case was not very stringent, since neither had the request of the unknown been given very stringently, nor had I promised anything nor had I done any good by keeping silent about a fact so usual as the passage of a horseman by night, yet all that proves thricefold the rectitude of my sentiments. Perhaps also my first sacrifice, which I accepted voluntarily and for so idle a motive, gave to my nature a twist that I have not ceased to follow almost always in graver and more serious circumstances.

That afternoon, as I have said, my first care was to go in search of the Pisana, but to my chagrin I was unable to find her anywhere. I asked the maids who, as if caught in default for their carelessness about the little girl, were irritated by my insistence. Germano, Gregorio and Martino, whom I also asked, could not tell me anything and finally in a fury I went to the back of the stables and asked the gardener if he had seen her go out somewhere. He replied that he had seen her go off into the countryside with the son of the apothecary, but that was already two hours ago and the little Countess must by now have returned since the sun was already high and scorching and she did not like to get sunburnt. I, however, knowing the crazy humour of the girl, did not believe this and went out too into the fields. The sun shone down scorching on my head and the ground crackled under my feet because of the heat, but I did not notice it because of the great mission that drove me on. At the edge of a ditch I found a pair of shoe-laces. They were the Pisana's and I followed the trail convinced that my great desire would lead me to find her somewhere or other. I looked into the thickets and along the brooks and in the shade where we used to rest during our walks; I hunted everywhere, driven by jealousy, and if the little son of the apothecary had then fallen into my hands I would have given him a good beating without giving him a chance to ask why.

As for the Pisana, I knew her through and through and was foolishly inured to her ways. I had commenced to love her even because of her faults. just as a good trainer prefers amongst all his horses the one who rears and kicks the most and resists the spurs and the reins. There is no quality that makes a thing so dear and precious to us as that of realizing that it is always ready to escape us; and if such an attitude of fear and effort wearies weak spirits, it arms and strengthens the constant ones. It might be said that the Pisana had bewitched me if I could not read clearly enough the reason for this spell in the pride continually stimulated in me by my superiority over all her other pretenders. I saw myself preferred most frequently and above all the others, but I wanted to be so always.

As for the sentiment that made me want this, it was the purest and most unmixed love; love that later increased, that was for ever changing temper and colour, but which filled my soul with all its madness. And love at ten years old is so excessive, as is every other wish at that age of trust that does not yet know what impossible means. Here the paucity of words makes me say love in place of that other word, whatever it may be, that should be used. Because a passion so varied, that embraces the highest culmination of the soul and the lowest bodily impulses, that knows how to bow on the one hand in assent and to rise to the heights on the other, and confound them all sometimes in an ecstasy almost divine and yet sometimes almost bestial, should have twenty different names instead of a single generic one, devoted to good or to ill according to the occasion and chosen one might say on purpose to alarm the modest and excuse the unworthy. I therefore say love, and could not say otherwise; but every now and then when I have to use such a word in the course of my story, I feel obliged to add a line of comment to supplement our vocabulary.

At that time, therefore, I loved the Pisana as the companion of my childish games; and since at that age games are all-important, that means to say that I loved her completely; which, if it does not constitute that pure unmixed love which I have referred to above, you must take it up with the dictionary makers. Despite my frenzied search for her that afternoon she did not allow herself to be found, and searching here and looking there, I took without being aware of it the way that had led me so far afield the day before. When I noticed this I found myself at a country crossroads where on a low, rough stone wall a poor San Rocco showed the wound on his leg to the devout passers-by. The faithful dog stood by his side with drooping tail and his nose raised as if to see what his master was doing. All this I saw when I first raised my eyes; but on looking round, I also noticed an old bent beggar-woman who was praying with great fervour before that San Rocco.

It appeared that she was the Martinella, a poor beggar-woman so called in the district, who used to stop and take her alms from Germano's box whenever she passed by the Fratta bridge. I spoke to her with a certain hesitation, since Marchetto's tales had made me suspicious of witchcraft in all old women; but the strength of my need pressed me on. She turned an angry face towards me, though she was usually the most patient and amiable of all the old women in the neighbourhood; and mumbled questions as to what I was doing in that place and at that hour. I replied that I was looking for the Pisana, the little daughter of the Contessa, and that I was just going to ask if she had seen her pass with the apothecary's little boy.

'No, no, Carlino, I haven't seen her,' the old woman replied hastily and with irritation, though I had tried to show her every consideration. 'While you were looking for her she had already gone back to the castle another way. Go, go back to the castle. I am sure you will find her there.'

'But no,' I said, 'she only finished lunch just an hour ago.'

'I tell you that if you go there you cannot fail to find her,' the old woman interrupted me, 'only five minutes ago, now I remember, I must have seen her as she went back by the Montagnesi fields.'

'But I passed that way five minutes ago,' I persisted in my turn.

'But I tell you I saw her.'

'No, you can't have done.'

While I was reasoning with her and the old woman was doing her best to make me go back, we suddenly heard the sound of a horse galloping down one of the side roads. The Martinella left me standing there and with a shrug of her shoulders moved off to meet the horseman, as if to beg from him. The next moment the horse plunged out of the sunken ditch of the side road. It was a strong fiery colt with quivering nostrils and mouth flecked with foam. On it was a man, large and ragged with a huge grey beard blown to the four winds and a great hat, faded from the rains, over his nose. He had neither stirrups, saddle nor bridle and only controlled his mount with the ends of a halter which he used as a whip to make it increase its pace. At first glance he reminded me of the bearded man who had brought me home the evening before; and the suspicion became a certainty when he replied in a harsh and grating voice to the salutations of the beggar-woman. She turned, glancing towards me, and he, having pulled up the colt near the old woman, leant down and muttered a few words in her ear. The Martinella at once brightened up, lifted her arms to the sky and then said aloud:

'God and San Rocco will reward you for your good action. And as for charity, I will look to it and will remember you at the end of the week.'

'Yes, yes, Martinella, don't fail me,' said the man, pressing his legs against the colt's flanks and dashed off at full speed on the road to the lagoons. When some distance away, he turned back to the old woman and made a sign towards the road from which he had just come; then horse and rider disappeared in the dust raised by its hooves.

I stood intent on this scene when, looking away from the spot where the horse had disappeared towards the countryside opposite, I saw the Pisana herself and the apothecary's boy who were running towards me in a great fright. I began to go towards them when the Martinella shouted to me: 'Where are you going, Carlino?' I called back: 'There, there she is, the Pisana! Don't you see her?' I soon reached the little girl, but she was so pale and terror-stricken that she moved me to pity.

'But, Pisana, what is the matter? Are you ill?' I asked, taking her by the arm.

'What a fright I have had . . . what a rush . . . they are over there with their muskets . . . they want to cross the stream,' replied the little girl, panting for breath.

'Who are you talking about—who wants to cross?'

'There they are!' Donato, the apothecary's son, burst out in reply, recovering a little from his fright. . . . 'There they are . . . we were playing near the mill stream when four or five men suddenly appeared on the far bank with pistols in their hands—enough to frighten anyone—and they seemed to be looking for something and getting ready to wade across. And the Pisana ran away and I ran after her as fast as I could; but some of them started shouting: "Have you seen a man on horseback over there?" The Pisana didn't answer and neither did I and we went on running, and here we are; but the men will surely come here for, even though the water is deep, the mill bridge is not far away.'

'Let's get away! Let's get away!' shouted the little girl, panic-stricken.

'Have courage, Signorina!' interrupted the old woman, who had been listening to all this. 'These Cernide are not looking for you but for a man on horseback; and when they come here Carlino and I will tell them that we have seen no man on horseback except the guard from Lugugnana going to look at the hay at Portovecchio.'

'No, no, I want to go away. I am afraid!' shrieked the little girl.

But there was no time to run away for four buli suddenly appeared and after looking down the four side roads turned to the old woman with the same question that they had just asked the two children.

'We only saw the guard from Lugugnana who was going to Portovecchio,' the old Martinella replied.

'Eh, what guard from Lugugnana? That must have been him!' said one of the band.

'Listen, Martinella,' asked another of them, 'don't you know the Spaccafumo?'

'The Spaccafumo!' exclaimed the old woman with horror in her eyes. 'That ruffian, that bandit, who fears neither God nor the law, as bad as a Turk! No, thanks be to God, I don't know him; but I saw him one Sunday in the pillory at Venchieredo about two years back.'

'And you haven't seen him anywhere around today?' asked the man who had spoken first.

'How could I have seen him today? They say he was drowned at the end of last year!' replied the old woman. 'And I must admit to you gentlemen that I suffer a little with my eyes.'

'Listen to that! Of course it was he!' exclaimed the man. 'Why didn't you say at first that you are as blind as a mule, old hag? Come on, don't waste any more time. To Portovecchio, brothers!' he added, turning to his men.

And all four set off by the road to Portovecchio which was in the opposite direction to that taken by the bearded man a quarter of an hour before.

'But they have made a mistake . . .' I began to say.

'Quiet!' whispered the Martinella, 'let those ruffians go away and we will say a Pater Noster to San Rocco who has rid us of them instead.'

The Pisana during the talk with the men had recovered all her courage and now seemed surer of herself than any of us.

'No, no,' she cried, 'before praying we must run to Fratta and warn the Chancellor and Marchetto about these horrible men that we have seen. Isn't it the Chancellor's duty to keep all evil-doers off papa's lands?'

'Yes, certainly,' I replied, 'and also to put them in prison if he thinks fit.'

'Then let's go and have those four nasty men put in prison,' she went on, dragging me towards Fratta, 'I won't, I simply won't have them frightening me again!'

Donato followed behind, left completely out in the cold by the capricious little girl; and the Martinella remained on her knees before San Rocco as if nothing out of the way had happened.

CHAPTER IV

THE Spaccafumo was a baker from Cordovado, a picturesque little district between Teglio and Venchieredo, who, having entered into open war with the local authorities, had won the award of such a nickname from the prodigious hue and cry that they made in pursuit of him. (Spaccafumo, in the somewhat Venetianized dialect of the Friuli at that time, was equivalent to 'dust-raiser'—*sbattipolvere*—but if I translated his name so, it would almost seem as if I debaptized him; I do not remember ever having heard his real name.) His first venture was against the agents of the customs and excise, who wanted to confiscate a certain bag of salt that they found at an old woman's who lived in the house next to his. I seem to remember that the old woman was the Martinella herself who at that time, since she was still able to work, had not yet begun to beg. Condemned to two years' banishment, the Mayor of the commune, Signor Antonio Provedoni, had compounded his punishment for a fine of twenty ducats. But after this brush with customs officials over the bag of salt, he had got involved in another with the Vice-captain of the prisons, who wanted to imprison a cousin of his for having been found at the Venchieredo festa bearing arms. He was then condemned to three days in the pillory on the village square, with two months' imprisonment and banishment from the district for twenty-eight months. He then stopped making bread; but that was all his obedience to the decrees of the Criminal Chancellery of Venchieredo amounted to. He went on living here and there in the countryside and exercising his ministry of private justice for the good of the public.

The posse of Portogruaro had been unleased upon him twice; but he beat the dust at such speed and knew so well all the hiding places and byways of the country that they had done nothing at all towards catching him. As to surprising him in his lair, that was a still more difficult enterprise; all the peasants were on his side, and nobody could say where he used to sleep or take refuge in bad weather. Furthermore, if the posse of Portogruaro moved with too great solemnity ever to catch him unawares, the bravos and militia of the local magistrates were on much too good terms with the local peasants ever to try and pursue him seriously.

Sometimes, after nothing had been heard of him for weeks and weeks, he would appear quite calmly at the parish Mass of Cordovado; but he listened to the Mass with one ear only; the other he kept well cocked towards the main door, and was ready to escape by the side one if he should chance to hear the heavy measured tramp of a patrol. That they should ever be cunning enough to station themselves at both doors was not to be thought of, granting the perfect good faith of that militia. After Mass he would join some old cronies on the square, and at lunch-time went directly and openly to the Provedoni house, which was the last house in the village in the direction of Teglio.

Signor Antonio, the Mayor of the commune, closed an eye; and the rest of the family used to gather round him in the kitchen with great pleasure to hear him tell of his prowess and to laugh at the jests with which he enlivened his tales. He had been on good neighbourly terms with that family since boyhood and he continued to be so, as if nothing had happened; so much so that to see him go there every so often to eat his bowl of *brovada* in front of the fire had become a matter of habit with all of them.

The Provedoni family was of some importance in the country for its age and reputation. I myself remember having read the name of Ser Giacomo della Provedona in the records of a district gathering held in 1400, and from then on it had remained the leading family in the commune. But if the fate of the poor communes was not very gay in the midst of the castellans' jurisdictions, even shabbier was the standing of their leaders in the face of the feudatories.

San Marco was popular, but at a distance, and mainly for show; at heart it was too wishful to retain, more especially in the Friuli, the homage of the nobility to want to raise up against them that scarecrow of the communal jurisdictions. They patiently put up with those already in existence, which were excusable so long as they did not give reason for being abolished by some too haughty insistence on their strict rights, but kept them in holy humility with a thousand restrictions and a thousand fetters; while as to establishing new ones, they never even dreamed of it. If a juridical office, for reasons of extinction, of sentence or of felony, reverted to the Republic, rather than reconstitute it as a commune, it was the custom to invest its powers in some feudal magistrature, or as it was then termed, some provincial office. Thus there was achieved, without undue fuss, the double aim of restricting the number of castellans, whose support was a necessity not always altogether desired, and of maintaining the population in their usual blind servitude, divorced as much as possible from public affairs. Moreover, if the communes in their disputes with the castellans were often in the wrong according to the letter of the law, they were always so before the courts; and that, incidentally, by the private connivance of the patrician magistrates sent year after year from the Serene Dominant to judge in the Supreme Assizes of the Terraferma. There was, however, one method to make all ranks equal before the sacred impartiality of the tribunals; and that was money. But if one considers the Italian love of litigation that clashed in the communes with the very prudent Friuli economy, it was easy to understand how very rarely they were disposed to look for and obtain justice by such means. The castellan had already paid his *zecchino* while the commune was still arguing about its farthing; these had already a favourable judgement in their hands while those were still squabbling about a clause in the reply or the duplicate.

Signor Antonio Provedoni was respectful to the nobility by sentiment, not servile by worthlessness. His family had always behaved in this way and he did not intend to change its ways. But this respect of his, sufficient but not profuse, made him looked on with a favourable eye; as things were then, not to make a show of cowardice was reputed as great valour of spirit. By that, I do not mean to say that he would resist the arrogance of the neighbouring castellans; he merely did not go to meet them with gifts, and that was much. He would, however, grumble to himself about this arrogance, a sign to his mind that the old nobility, a mingling of grandeur and courtesy, was tumbling into the abyss; in greed and oppression they were now almost comparable to the police. But never did one of these laments emerge from that silent and prudent mouth; he contented himself with remaining silent and bowing his head as the peasants do when providence sends them hail. The sun, the moon and the stars, he and his forbears had always seen them turning in the one way, whether the year was wet, dry or snowy. After a bad year had come many good ones and after a good year many bad ones; and a similar reasoning he applied to the things of the world. They were prosperous or adverse in their turn; he had lighted on a bad one, that was all. But he had great faith that matters would be better for his sons and grandsons; it was enough for him to have engendered them in good time, so that the family should not be defrauded of its share of happiness. Only the second-born of his numerous children, on whom he had been pleased to impose the name of Leopardo, gave him some cause for bitterness. But how could anyone be tame and docile with a name like that?

The good Mayor of Cordovado had behaved in this matter with somewhat insufficient circumspection; the names of his sons were all more or less ferocious and animal, far indeed from instilling in them the practice of those virtues of tolerance, silence and compliance that he knew were most suitable to men of their rank. The first was called Leone; the second, as we have said, Leopardo; the others were in order: Bruto, Bradamante, Grifone, Mastino and Aquilina. Indeed, a real menagerie, and Signor Antonio could not understand that, saddled with such names, the usual peasant good-humour became burlesque and impossible. If at that time, as in that of the Latins, they had dared to adopt the Christian name of Bestia, certainly his first-born would have received it in gift, so enthusiastic was he for zoology. But granted the impossibility of putting into operation this generic name, he had replaced it with the even prouder and more menacing one of the King of the Beasts, according to Aesop. Leone, however, did not show himself less sheeplike than the times, or at least his paternal example, required. He had gone his way, supporting much, and sighing from time to time, and then, like his father, had taken a wife and begotten sons, of whom he had already half a dozen, at the time when Leopardo first began to take an interest in women. This is the point where we shall begin to treat of the family dissensions between Signor Antonio and Leopardo.

Leopardo was a young man of few words and many deeds; that is to say, of few deeds too, but in those few he was so obstinate that there was no means to dissuade him. Whenever anyone rebuked him, he would turn on them with a kind of roar deep down in his throat and with two eyes so baleful that the rebuker as a rule never got beyond his exordium. Otherwise he was as good as bread and as useful as five fingers.

He worked in his own way for two hours every day and in those hours he would have defied the devil himself to employ him otherwise; the remaining twenty-two they could put him to cutting wood or planting cabbages or even turning the spit as I did and he would not even give a sign of annoyance. He was on these occasions the tamest leopard that ever existed. Intent on his own duties and assiduous in all that he did and at his rosary, he was in short a good Christian, as was usual in those times, and furthermore educated and learned beyond all custom of his contemporaries. But as regards logic, I have every reason to believe that he was a trifle obstinate. A racial merit, perhaps, but while the obstinacy of others was often hidden away in their conscience, leaving the rest free to outward compliance, he was indeed, so to speak, a mule inside and out and would have kicked in the face, I believe, even the Most Serene Doge himself if he had dreamed of opposing him in his fixed ideas. Laborious and vehement in all his actions, when inactive he became inert and leaden, like the wheel in a workshop when the strap has been cut. His strap was his conviction, without which he would not advance even at a snail's pace, and as for allowing himself to be convinced, Leopardo had all the flexibility of a fanatical Turk. The reason for so much tenacity was perhaps that he had grown up in solitude and silence; the thoughts in his brain were not stiffened with the fragile joining of a graft but with the thousand tendrils of an oak root, that grows slowly before breaking into bud and bearing fruit. Over an exhausted and sterile graft another graft may grow, but roots cannot be uprooted, or if uprooted, wither; and Leopardo had his head formed in such a way that it could not be planted on the neck of any save a great man or a madman. Either just so or nothing at all. That was the formal significance, the heraldic motto, of his nature.

Leopardo had lived happily up to the age of twenty-three without questioning or suffering questioning from anyone. The precepts of his parents and masters had agreed so exactly with his own views that he found no need to ask anything of them or they to demand anything from him. But the source of all his troubles was the spring of Venchieredo.

After he had begun to drink of the waters of that spring there ensued a hailstorm of questions, of counsels and of reproofs from his father. However, since all these discourses in no way corresponded with Leopardo's views, he for his part took to roaring and scowling. Then, as Sterne would say, the bestial influence of his name took the lead; and if this were so, Signor Antonio's passion for beasts must have cost him dear.

Let us make this riddle a little clearer.

Between Cordovado and Venchieredo, about a mile from each of them, was a large and limpid spring which had the reputation of containing in its waters many salutary qualities. But the nymph of the spring did not rely solely on the virtues of her waters to allure her worshippers, but had surrounded herself with such a beautiful horizon of meadows, woods and skies and with such a hospitable shade of alders and willows that it was in truth a retreat worthy of the pen of Virgil. Hidden and winding bypaths, the murmuring of many brooks, sweet and mossy banks, nothing was lacking in the surroundings. It was really the mirror of a magician, that clear blue water that bubbled out from amid tiny pebbles and rose to reflect upon its bosom a scene so pastoral and picturesque.

There are places that make us think of the inhabitants of Eden before the fall and even make us think without rebuke of that sin itself now that we are no more inhabitants of Eden. Therefore, around that spring the gay young girls of Cordovado, of Venchieredo and even of Teglio, Fratta, Morsano, Cintello, Bagnarola and other villages around had been in the habit of gathering on festa evenings from time immemorial. And here they would remain for long, singing, talking, laughing, having picnics until their mothers, their lovers or the moon sent them home again. I do not need to tell you that with the girls there gathered also the young men; since that you could imagine for yourself. But what I want to point out is that when all accounts were closed at the year's end, I believe and affirm that more came to the spring of Venchieredo to make love than to drink their fill; and moreover that more wine than water was drunk there. Naturally, in such cases, one must rather obey the compulsion of the ham and sausages than the superstition of running water.

I myself was many times at this enchanting spring, but once, and once only, did I dare to profane with my hand the virgin crystal of its surface. Hunting had brought me thither, broken with fatigue and burning with thirst; and moreover my flask of white wine had refused to shed any more tears for me. If I were to return there now perhaps I would drink deep draughts in order to make myself young again; but the hydropathic taste of old age would not make me forget the joyous and turbulent mouthfuls of good wine of former times.

As it happened, some years before me, Leopardo Provedoni had acquired a familiarity with the spring of Venchieredo. This solitary, calm, remote spot suited his mood as a well-made suit fits the person. Every thought of his found there its natural corollary; or at least none of the willows intervened to say no to whatever he was thinking. He embellished, coloured and peopled in his own way the deserted landscape; and so, without being as yet at war with anyone in the world, he still felt himself different from others and it seemed to him that there he lived more happily than elsewhere for the simple reason that there he was free and alone. This feeling which Leopardo had for the spring of Venchieredo was the first 'fact' of which he would not admit contradiction; the second was the love he bore, even more than for the spring, for a beautiful girl who often went there and whom he met alone there one lovely May morning. To hear him tell of this scene seemed to me like listening to a reading from the *Aminta*, but Tasso wrote his verses first and read them over afterwards; Leopardo remembered and, in remembering, improvised, so that to see and hear him was to feel on one's brow the cool dews of poetry.

He had left his house one fine sunny May day with his gun over his shoulder more to satisfy the curiosity of the passers-by than with any hostile intent towards the snipe and partridges. Step by step, with his head in the clouds, he found himself at the edge of the wood that surrounded the spring on two sides, and strained his ears for the usual salutation of a nightingale. The nightingale had indeed awaited his arrival and trilled its usual song, but not from the usual tree;

that day the sound came, timid and subdued, from a more hidden branch and it seemed that his greeting was a little diffident because of the weapon his friend was carrying on his shoulder. Leopardo listened among the branches to spy out the new refuge of his harmonious host but, turning here and there, his glances suddenly succeeded in finding even more than they sought.

Oh, why was it not I who was enamoured of Doretta? Old as I am, I could write a page to bewilder my readers and take by assault the highest seats of poesy! I would that youth could mark the outlines, the heart lay on the colours and that youth and heart together could shine through every part of the picture with such magic that the good for tenderness and the bad for envy should take up the book again. Poor Leopardo! You alone could do much, you who for all your life carried painted in your eyes and graven upon your heart that spectacle of love. And even now the uncertain memory of your words shines through me to thoughts so amorous and innocent that I cannot without tears trace these lines.

He sought, therefore, the nightingale and saw instead, seated on the bank of the stream that bubbled out of the spring, a young girl, who was dangling one foot in the water and with the other, bare and white as ivory, was tracing circles and curves among the little fish that darted on its surface. She smiled and clapped her hands from time to time when she succeeded in touching one of them with her foot and tossing it out of the water. Then the scarf which floated disordered on her breast opened to reveal the whiteness of her shoulders, half uncovered, and her cheeks flushed with pleasure without losing the radiance of innocence. The little fish did not cease their play except to return again after a brief fright, for in her hands she held the secret of this familiarity. A moment later she dipped her little foot in again very gently and having taken from under her apron a small piece of bread, she began to crumble it into pieces for her playmates. Then there was a coming and going, a rushing and darting, a competing and robbing of one another in this little family of living silver; and the young girl bent over them as if to receive their thanks. And then when the feast was at its height, she stirred the water with her feet, amused at their greed, which although they were terrified for the moment, soon made them recover their daring so as not to lose the choicest mouthfuls. This shuffling of her little feet showed a glimpse of the delicate shape of a rounded and well-formed leg; and the ends of her scarf became quite disordered on her shoulders and her breast seemed scarcely to be confined to her linen bodice, so much did merriment swell and agitate it.

Leopardo, at first all ears to listen to the nightingale, was now all eyes, without even being aware of the metamorphosis. This innocent girl, simple and gay, this joyous ignorance and unself-consciousness, this still girlish immodesty which recalled the nakedness of the cherubs that sported in Pordenone's pictures, the thousand charms of a slim and delicate figure, that hair, golden-chestnut, curling over her temples like a boy's, that fresh and candid smile, made as if specially to enhance two rows of shining teeth as small and even as the beads of a crystal rosary; all these things, I say, were depicted with the colours of wonder in the young man's eyes. He would have given anything demanded of him to be one of those little fish, so familiar with her; he would have been content to remain there all his life only to watch her. But he was somewhat delicate in conscience, and these pleasures enjoyed by stealth, even in the rapture of ecstasy, filled him with a sort of remorse. He therefore began to whistle some tune or other, with what correctness you can well imagine, who know by experience the effect produced on the voice and lips by the first stimulus of love.

Whistling tonelessly and tunelessly and bending back the branches that were in his way, he arrived, reeling like a drunken man, at the edge of the spring. The young girl arranged the kerchief on her shoulders but had no time to take her feet out of the water and so remained a little bashful and a little astonished at this unexpected visit.

Leopardo was a handsome youth; of that beauty that is made up of comeliness of form combined with strength and composure, the greatest attraction to the eye and which best reflects the ideal of divine perfection. He had something childlike in his expression, something of the philosopher in his brow and of the athlete in his figure; but his modest way of dressing in the peasant fashion greatly diminished the impression of this aspect. Therefore at first the girl was not so embarrassed as if it had been a gentleman who had thus appeared, and she became more reassured on raising her eyes to his face and recognizing him. She murmured in a voice almost of satisfaction: 'Ah, so it is the Signor Leopardo!'

The young man heard this quiet exclamation and for the first time his name seemed to him not sufficiently gracious and delicate to rest worthily on such lovely lips. But it overjoyed him to be already known to the girl and thus find himself freed from the necessity of having to introduce himself.

'And who are you, beautiful one?' he asked, stammering and looking at the reflection in the water, since he had not yet courage enough to look at the original.

'I am Doretta, the daughter of the Chancellor of Venchieredo,' replied the girl.

'Ah, so you are the Signora Doretta!' exclaimed Leopardo, who despite his doubled desire to look at her, found himself greatly hindered by his confusion at having first treated her with so little respect.

The girl looked up as if meaning: 'Yes, it is most certainly I, and I do not see why you should be so surprised.' Leopardo gathered together all his reserves of courage to return to the charge, but he was so much a novice in the art of questioning that it was not strange that, on this first occasion, he cut a very mediocre figure.

'Don't you think it is very hot to-day?' he ventured.

'Enough to kill one,' replied Doretta.

'Do you think it will continue?' asked the other.

'That depends on your almanack,' said the girl maliciously, 'Schieson says yes and Strolich promises no.'

'And you, what do you think?' went on Leopardo, going from bad to worse.

'It is all one to me,' replied the girl, who was beginning to be amused at this dialogue. 'The Rector of Venchieredo calls for three-day rogations equally for drought or frost, and as far as I am concerned, praying for either one or the other does not make the slightest difference.'

'How lively and pleasant she is,' thought Leopardo; and this thought relieved his mind from that trying interrogation that had succeeded so well up till then.

'Have you had good hunting?' Doretta decided to ask, seeing him fall silent and not wanting to forgo so exquisite a chance to amuse herself.

'Oh!' exclaimed the young man, as if he had only just become aware of the gun slung over his shoulder.

'I bet you have forgotten the flint at home,' she went on, teasing him, 'or perhaps it is some new kind of gun?'

Leopardo's arquebus dated back to the first generation of firearms and it was enough to look at it to realize all the malice of that pretended ingenuousness.

'It is a family heirloom,' the young man replied seriously, since he had thought on this subject often enough and knew its birth, life and miracles by family tradition. 'It fought in the Morea with my great-great-great-grandfather; my grandfather once killed with this very weapon twenty-two snipe in a single day, a thing that till then would have been thought impossible when one considers that it needs ten full minutes to load it and that after the firing of the powder in the touch-hole it needs another good half-minute before the discharge. However, my father has never succeeded in hitting more than ten, and up to the present, I have never exceeded six. But the snipe have begun to learn cunning and in that half-minute that it takes to fire, they have already flown half a mile away. The time will come when I have to run after them with the ramrod. However, I do the best I can with this old musket; but the trouble is that the catch no longer holds firm and at times I take aim and pull the trigger but after half a minute, when the explosion should take place, I find instead that the flint has fallen out. Then I must take it to Fratta, to Mastro Germano, to be mended. It is true that I could ask papa to get a new one, but I am sure that he would reply that I should not try to introduce novelties into the family. Indeed, that is also my own view. If the musket is a little out of sorts, after having gone through the Morea campaign and having killed twenty-two snipe in one day, one must really sympathize with it. None the less, as I say, I will take it to Mastro Germano to be repaired. Don't you think I am right, Signora Doretta?'

'Yes, certainly,' replied the girl, withdrawing her feet from the stream and wiping them on the grass, 'the snipe at least will say that you are right a thousand times.'

Leopardo meanwhile looked lovingly at the musket and polished its barrel with the sleeve of his jacket.

'For the moment we will repair it so,' he went on, taking a handful of flints out of his pocket and choosing the sharpest of them to put in the catch, 'You see, Signora Doretta, how I prepare for the unforeseen? I must always carry with me a bag full of flints, but it is not the fault of the musket if old age has blunted its teeth. One has to carry a powder-horn and a ramrod and bullets, anyway; one can very well carry some flints too.'

'Surely. You are strong and that should not worry you,' added Doretta.

'You think so? For four little flints? I don't even feel I am carrying them,' replied the youth, putting them back in his pocket. 'I could even carry you as well as far as Venchieredo and would no more be out of breath than the barrel of my musket. I have good legs, excellent lungs and can walk to and from the Lugugnana marshes in a single morning.'

'*Caspita*, what a rush!' exclaimed the girl. 'When the Signor Count goes down there to hunt he goes only on horseback and stays away three days.'

'But I am quicker; I go and come back in a flash.'

'But without shooting anything?'

'How, without shooting anything? The ducks, fortunately, have not yet learnt the cunning of the snipe, and would await the convenience of my gun not for half a minute but for half an hour; I never come back from there save with a full bag. It is true that I go to hunt the game where it lives and am not afraid of plunging into the marshes up to my waist.'

'Mercy!' cried Doretta, 'aren't you afraid of getting drowned there?'

'I am only afraid of ills that have actually taken place,' replied Leopardo, 'and even to those I do not pay much attention. I don't even think of the others and, since up to now I am not dead, I would not have the slightest fear of dying even though I found myself facing a whole file of muskets! It would be a fine thing to be afraid of an ill that one doesn't even know!'

Doretta, who up till then had been jesting at the simplicity of this youth, now began to look at him with a certain respect. Furthermore, Leopardo, now that he had surmounted the first obstacle, felt quite ready to open his heart, perhaps for the first time, and the confessions that rose spontaneously and sincerely to his lips aroused his own curiosity as much as that of the girl. He had never before troubled to make a judgement on himself; and therefore listened to his own words as so many interesting novelties.

'Tell me the truth,' he went on, sitting down opposite the girl, who stopped glancing here and there for her sandals, 'tell me the truth; who taught you to love the spring of Venchieredo so well?'

The question distressed Doretta a little and it was her turn to be embarrassed. Chattering and joking she was expert enough in, perhaps more than was needful, but she was unable to give an account of anything without the greatest effort of gravity and concentration. None the less, strangely enough, when confronted with that good fellow, Leopardo, she could not succeed in turning the question aside with a joke and had to reply, stammering, that the nearness of the spring to her father's property had accustomed her from girlhood to play there and that, the habit once formed, she had gone on doing so.

'Very good,' replied Leopardo, who was too simple to have noticed her embarrassment as he had been too good-hearted to have noticed her earlier mockery, 'but aren't you afraid to play tricks with the waters of the brook?'

'Afraid?' said the girl, blushing, 'why should I be?'

'Because if you slipped in you might drown yourself.'

'I never even thought of such danger,' said Doretta.

'Nor do I think of it or of any others,' replied the young man, fixing his large tranquil blue eyes on the little sparkling ones of the girl. 'The world simply goes on with me and could very well go on without me. That is my comfort, and for the rest the good Lord will provide. But you, do you often come here to the spring?'

'Oh, very often,' replied Doretta, 'especially when it is hot.'

Leopardo thought that, as they had met just then, they could meet again many more times; but such a thought seemed to him too daring and he confined himself to a long look of hope and longing. However, with his lips he began talking of the heat and the time of year and said that, for him, winter and spring were all one. He would not even notice the difference save for the leaves turning brown and falling.

'I love the spring best of all!' put in Doretta.

'I also,' exclaimed Leopardo.

'But surely . . . are they not all the same to you?' said the girl.

'That's true. It seems to me . . . but . . . today is such a lovely day that it makes me give the palm to this season of the year above all. I meant, when I said they were all one to me, only as regards the heat and the cold. As regards the pleasure of the eyes, I am sure that the spring comes first of all!'

'And yet that scoundrel of a Gaetano at Venchieredo always defends the winter,' went on the girl.

'That Gaetano is really a scoundrel,' replied the other.

'Oh, so you know him too?' asked Doretta.

'Yes . . . that is . . . isn't he the gatekeeper?' stammered Leopardo. 'I have a vague idea that I have heard his name.'

'No, he is not the gatekeeper, he is the Serjeant,' said the girl, 'with him it is always a question of going to extremes over a trifle. I never want to hear winter spoken of, and he always praises it to the skies just to spite me.'

'Oh, I'll make him hold his tongue,' exclaimed Leopardo.

'You will? . . . Then you must come some time or another,' replied Doretta, rising to her feet and putting on her sandals. 'But be sure and bring a good dose of patience with you, for that Gaetano is as stubborn as a donkey.'

'I'll come all right,' said Leopardo, 'but I shall see you again at the spring, shan't I?'

'Yes, certainly; when the whim takes me,' replied the girl, 'and on festas I am always here with the other girls of the district.'

'On festas, on festas,' murmured the young man.

'Oh, you must come,' broke in the girl, 'and you will see what a paradise we have here all around.'

Leopardo followed Doretta, who was returning to Venchieredo, like a dog that follows its master after having been chased away. Doretta turned around from time to time to look at him smilingly; he too smiled but his heart was pounding so heavily that it made him tremble. So at last they reached the gateway to the village.

'Goodbye, Signor Leopardo!' the girl cried to him from a distance.

'Good-bye, Signora Doretta,' replied the young man with a look so intent and prolonged that it seemed he would send his soul with it, and bent, blushing, to pick up some flowers that she had mischievously dropped. Then, when the leafy pergola of the vines had hidden from his sight the slim graceful form of Doretta, who was hurrying towards the castle, his look fell to the ground so gravely, so seriously, that it seemed as if seeking eternal burial there. Some moments later he looked up with a sigh and went his way homewards with his head filled, if not with new thoughts, certainly with very new and strange ideas. Those few little flowers he put next his heart and kept them for ever after.

Leopardo had fallen in love with the girl; that was all. But how and why had he fallen in love? The how was certainly by looking at her and listening to her; the why nobody will ever know; as one can never know why sky blue appeals to one, scarlet to others and orange to others still. Girls as pretty as Doretta, or even three times prettier, he had seen at Cordovado, at Fossalta and at Portogruaro, and indeed the daughter of the Chancellor of Venchieredo was too slim for real perfection; yet he had never shown any interest in these, though he had had every chance of being with them and talking with them, but on the other hand was well cooked at the first sight of this one.

Perhaps familiarity takes away from rather than adds to the force of feminine charm? I do not say so; it would be too unfair to women. Among them there are many who do not impress at first glance but who, when familiar by long habit, gradually warm the heart until at last they create a conflagration that may not be extinguished. There are others who consume us in their flame at the mere sight, but often of the flame thus kindled there soon remains only ashes. But as there are men of straw who, even slowly warmed, end in nothing, so also there can be found hearts of iron which become red-hot in a moment and do not cool again. Love is a universal law, which has as many various corollaries as have the souls subject to it. To dictate a complete and practical treatise on it, one would need to create a library wherein every man and woman should deposit a volume of their own observations. One would read therein the noblest and the vilest things, the most celestial and the most bestial that the imagination of a novelist might conceive. But the difficulty would be that such writings should obey the first impulse of sincerity; since many enter into love with preconceived ideas, and desire according to them and not according to the force of their sentiments. Thence comes the abuse of those terrible words 'for ever' which are often spoken so light-heartedly in conversations and lovers' vows.

Doretta of Venchieredo certainly did not seem created to satisfy the grave, warm-hearted and concentrated spirit of Leopardo. None the less, she was the first who commanded his heart to live and to live completely and for ever in her. Another mystery, no less obscure and sorrowful than the others, since the one who might have satisfied him better did not move in his spirit any of those desires that compose or lead to love. Would it be, perhaps, so ordained in the mortal scheme that like avoids like, while opposites search each other out? But not even this could I affirm in the face of so many examples that contradict it. One can only suspect that if material things wandering confusedly in space have been subjected for centuries to a regulating force, so the spiritual and inner world still perhaps awaits in a state of chaos that virtue that co-ordinates it.

Meanwhile it is a contrast of sentiments, of forces, of judgements; an unformed and tumultuous medley of passions, of nobility and of vileness, a real chaos of spirit not yet developed from matter, and of matter urging disorder upon the spirit. Everything is agitated, is moving, is changing; but, I once more repeat it, the kernel of this future order is already existent and every day gathers around itself new elements, as those nebulae that in turning grow larger, grow denser or thinner in the atmosphere of atoms that surrounds them. How many centuries are necessary for this nebula to grow from an atom to a star? The astronomers will tell you. How many centuries does it need for human sentiment to crystallize into conscience? The anthropologists will tell you. But as the star matures, perhaps at the last and disordered ends of the universe, into another solar system, so conscience promises to the internal disorder of the sentiments a stable and truly moral harmony. There are spaces of time which are confounded with eternity in the thought of man; but what is denied to thought is not forbidden to hope. The spirit of man can hope for long and await with patience.

But even poor Leopardo, though he had not to look forward to a life of centuries, had to await with patience for Doretta first to show herself aware of his intentions and then to judge him acceptable to her. But, first of all, Leopardo was handsome, then he was one of the best matches in the district and finally he gave her so many proofs of a devoted love that it would have been sheer foolishness not to take advantage of them. Further, though he often amused her by his simplicity, he often also fascinated her by the outlook of his valiant and serene soul. She was aware that, though he was peaceable and tolerant with women even when they made game of him, he was by no means so with the young men around him. A glance from him was enough to make them fold their wings and it was no small glory for her to have always attentive to her nods one who so easily curbed the insistence of others.

Doretta therefore allowed herself to be found often enough at the spring and behaved even more kindly towards Leopardo at the festa gatherings; though from accepting his courtesies to returning them the road was long enough, yet one step after another, at last it came to an end. Then Leopardo no longer contented himself with seeing her on those mornings when she chanced to appear, or at the festas, among the throng, but went every evening to Venchieredo and there, either walking in the village or on the staircase of the Chancellery, would remain with her until the hour for supper. Then he saluted her again, more with the heart than with the lips, and made his way back to Cordovado, whistling his accustomed tune with greater assurance.

So the two young people arranged their life between them. As to their elders, it was a different story. The most illustrious Dr. Natalino, Chancellor of Venchieredo, let matters take their course, since he had seen so many flies buzzing around his Doretta that one more or less did not disturb him in the least. Signor Antonio, however, as soon as he noticed the affair began to stick his nose in the air and to give a hundred other signs of ill-humour. He was of peasant stock and a peasant through and through and could not be pleased that his son should move in another sphere. He therefore began to put his nose in the air, a manoeuvre that left Leopardo quite unruffled; so seeing that was not enough, he adopted sterner measures, began to scold him and to speak to him with a certain gravity that seemed to say: 'I am not quite satisfied with you.' But Leopardo was very satisfied with himself and believed that he was giving an example of Christian patience in putting up with the ill-humour of his father. But when Signor Antonio came, as they say, to breaking the ice and speaking openly and explaining fairly and squarely the reasons for his upturned nose, then Leopardo also felt himself obliged to explain fairly and squarely in return his unshakable determination to continue on his present course.

'Aren't you ashamed of yourself, going sniffing after all those fine feathers? What will they think of it in the district? Haven't you seen that even the Venchieredo buli are laughing at you? And how do you think this fine game of yours is going to end? Aren't you afraid that some time or other the castellan will get his servants to throw you out? Perhaps you like putting me into bad odour with that gentleman, who you know is already pretty hard to please? . . .' With these and similar complaints the prudent Mayor went on attacking and striking at his Absalom, but Leopardo paid no attention to such nonsense, as he called it. He replied that he too was a man like any other and that if he loved Doretta it was certainly not a matter to laugh at or to forgo at the banter of the first newcomer. Signor Antonio raised his voice, Leopardo shrugged his shoulders, and each stuck to his own views, and I believe too that these arguments still further excited the already inflamed spirit of the young man.

However, it soon became evident that the old man's misgivings might not have been misplaced. If Doretta always welcomed her suitor warmly, all the other inhabitants of Venchieredo did not show an equal complacence. Amongst these was that Gaetano, who was captain of the castellan's buli and who perhaps himself boasted some pretensions to the young lady and could not stomach the thought of the handsome youth from Cordovado and his daily visits. They began with jests, advanced to arguments and at one time ended up by exchanging a few blows. But Leopardo was so calm, so deliberate, that the bulo had to slink away with his tail between his legs; and this defeat on the public square in no way helped to lessen his hostility.

It must be added that Doretta, more vainglorious for herself than enamoured of Leopardo, enjoyed the war that had broken out about her and certainly did nothing to calm it. Gaetano whispered so much in the ear of his patron about the arrogance of the young Provedoni and his lack of respect for persons of high rank and in particular for the Signor Magistrate, that to satisfy him, he ended by regarding Leopardo with an even more hostile eye than he did the majority of men. His attitude seemed to say 'Keep clear of my feet!' and it was well understood for ten good miles around that such a hostile look from the castellan of Venchieredo was equivalent to a sentence of banishment for at least two months.

Leopardo, however, was looked at, looked in his turn and went quietly on his way. Gaetano asked no more, for he knew very well that this tacit defiance would have counted for a hundred crimes in the opinion of his haughty castellan. Indeed the latter was very much irritated to see Leopardo take so little heed of his glances and after having encountered him two, three or four times in the courtyard of the castle, he once stopped him and said resentfully that Leopardo had too much time to waste and that all this walking from Cordovado to Venchieredo might give him a pain in the loins. Leopardo bowed and did not understand, or pretended not to understand, and went on walking as before without fear of endangering his health.

The Signor then began, as they say, to find Leopardo really getting on his nerves and seeing that he had accomplished nothing by half-measures, one afternoon had Leopardo summoned and told him clearly that he did not maintain his castle for the convenience of the young gentlemen of Cordovado and that, if he needed love, he should try his fortune with other girls, and not with those of Venchieredo, but that if he wanted a good beating he should come that evening to his usual tryst and he would be served as well as he could wish.

Leopardo bowed again but did not say a word; but the same evening he did not fail to go to Doretta who, be it said, was proud to see him defy such a storm for her sake and rewarded him with redoubled tenderness. Gaetano fumed, the castellan looked askance even at his dogs and all of them gave every indication that they were concocting some dirty trick among themselves. Indeed, one fine night (that very night on which I received a nocturnal visit from the Pisana after having returned to Fratta on the crupper of the unknown, bearded cavalier), when Leopardo had just taken leave of his adored one and was scrambling over the village fence to return to Cordovado, three villainous rogues leapt on him and began to set about him so vigorously that he, overcome by their sudden attack, was thrown to the ground and was in a bad way. But at that moment a wild dark figure leapt out of the hedge and commenced to batter the three ruffians with the butt of his musket and to set about them with such a will that it was their turn to defend themselves and Leopardo, having recovered from his first surprise, set about them in his turn.

'Dogs! I'll let you have it!' shouted the new arrival, rushing after the three bravos, who were flying towards the castle bridge.

But they, avoiding the blows of the two demons behind them, ran so quickly that their assailants were unable to catch them up save at the very gates. Fortunately these were barred so that, however loudly they shouted for them to be opened, and opened at once, there was plenty of time to get in a few blows. Scarcely had the gatekeeper opened the wicket than they rushed inside as though escaping from the clutches of the devil.

'Ho, there! I know you!' one of them, Gaetano himself, said, turning round. 'You are the Spaccafumo and you'll pay dearly for your insolence and for daring to meddle in what doesn't concern you!'

'Yes, yes, I am the Spaccafumo,' shouted the one outside, 'and I'm not afraid of you or your ill-born patron or thousands like you.'

'Did you hear? Did you hear?' shouted Gaetano as he secured the gate with stout chains. 'As God lives, the patron will have him hanged!'

'Perhaps. But first I shall hang you!' shouted the Spaccafumo in reply, departing with Leopardo, who retreated unwillingly from that gate closed in his face.

The smuggler retired behind the hedge, mounted his horse and wanted to escort the young man back to Cordovado.

'How did you happen to arrive so opportunely?' Leopardo asked him, feeling more shame than pleasure at another's help in his own predicament.

'I got wind of what was going to happen and was waiting there on purpose,' replied the Spaccafumo.

'Rogues! Villains! Traitors!' cursed the young man.

'Quiet! That's their job,' said the Spaccafumo. 'Let us talk of other things. What do you think of me today as a horseman? You know that a short time ago I decided to give my legs a rest, since they are no longer as young as they were, and I thought the legs of the colts that pasture in the lagoons should take their turn. Today the lot fell on this one and I have come here from down Lugugnana way in less than an hour and also gave a lift on my crupper as far as Fratta to a boy who had lost his way in the marshes.'

'But tell me how you came to know of the plot,' interrupted Leopardo, who was still thinking over the dirty trick that had been played him.

'No, I am not going to tell you,' replied the Spaccafumo, 'and now that you are at your own door, I will say a cordial good night. We shall meet again soon.'

'But why? Won't you come in and sleep at our house?'

'No, no, the air there is not good for my lungs.'

As he said this, the Spaccafumo was already on his way and I could not tell you where he spent the night. Certainly at noon the next day he was seen to enter the house of the Chaplain of Fratta, who was his spiritual father and was said to receive him with great respect owing to the fear he had of him. But a little later there came to Fratta four assassins from Venchieredo who, having learnt that the Spaccafumo was with the Chaplain, went openly to the parsonage. They knocked and knocked again, called and called again, until at last the Chaplain, all drowsy and feigning ignorance of what they wanted, came to open the door and ask them their business.

'What do we want, indeed!' replied Gaetano furiously, rushing off towards the fields behind the parsonage where he could see a man on horseback at full gallop. 'That's who we want! Come on, come on, all of you! The Signor Chaplain will pay for his part in this later.'

The poor priest fell back in an armchair, fainting with fright, while the four buli began to run across the furrows, hoping that the thickets and ditches would cut down the speed of the fugitive. But the peasants were of the opinion that if the Spaccafumo had never allowed himself to be caught when he was on foot, it was even less likely that this misfortune should occur now that he was mounted. The Signori buli would merely have wasted their breath to no avail.

These matters were already known in the Castle of Fratta and were being discussed as grave and mysterious events, when we three, the Pisana, myself and the apothecary's son, returned. The Count and the Chancellor were running around looking for Marchetto and the Captain. Fulgenzio had flown to the bell-tower and was ringing the bells as if the hayloft were on fire; Monsignor Orlando, rubbing his eyes, was asking what had happened and the Countess busied herself in ordering the doors and windows to be barred and the fortress put in a state of defence. When God willed, the Captain managed to recruit three men who, with two muskets and a blunderbuss, were drawn up in the courtyard to await the orders of His Excellency. His Excellency ordered them to go to the piazza and see if public order had been disturbed and give their armed support to the authorities against all evil-doers and especially against the said Spaccafumo. Germano lowered the drawbridge with many grumbles and the valiant soldiers went out.

The Spaccafumo had, however, no intention of letting himself be seen that day on the piazza of Fratta; and however much the Captain displayed his ugliest face and brushed up his moustaches at the door of the inn, nobody appeared who dared to defy so menacing a frown. This was a great satisfaction for the Captain, and when the Venchieredo buli returned towards evening from their useless chase, tired and panting like so many hounds, he did not fail to complain about them. Gaetano sneered at him to his face with scant show of politeness, so much so indeed that the three Fratta Cernide were panic-stricken and dived into the inn, abandoning their leader. But the Captain was a man of the sword and the toga; and did not find it hard to defend himself decorously against Gaetano's sneers. He pretended to be aware, only then, that the Spaccafumo had fled on horseback across the fields. To listen to him, one would have thought he was only waiting for the villain to emerge from his hiding-place at any moment and then would make him pay dearly for the affront shown to the authority of the noble magistrate of Venchieredo. Gaetano replied to these overbearing remarks that his patron was more than capable of exacting payment himself and that furthermore the Chaplain should be told that they would think over how to settle accounts with him for the night's shelter that he had given the Spaccafumo.

That afternoon nobody dreamed of going outside the castle; the Pisana and I spent a dull and irritating day squabbling in the courtyard with the sons of Fulgenzio and the bailiff. And in the evening Germano, from his gate-room, questioned every visitor who arrived and only when he had received assurances from without, lowered the drawbridge so that they could enter. The rusty chains squealed on the pulleys as if in protest at having been set to work again after so many years of tranquil ease; and no one passed over the uneven planking without first glancing with little confidence at the cracks that opened beneath them.

Lucilio and the Partistagno remained that evening in the castle later than usual; but their laughter was hardly enough to calm the nerves of the Countess who saw the whole jurisdiction of Fratta already in flames as a result of this enmity between the Spaccafumo and the Count of Venchieredo.

The next day, which was Sunday, there was fresh news in the countryside. At half past seven, when the people were returning from the first Mass at Teglio, a great clattering of horses' hooves was heard and a little later the Lord of Venchieredo with three of his buli appeared in the market-place. He was a man of middle age, florid and sturdy, in whose eyes one could not say whether cunning or ferocity was the more evident, but proud and arrogant above all others, as could be judged from his voice and bearing. He drew up his horse abruptly and asked harshly which was the house of the Most Reverend Chaplain of Fratta. The parsonage was pointed out to him and he entered there with the air of a master, after handing his reins to Gaetano, who had accompanied him.

The Chaplain had only just been shaved and was at that moment under the orders of the servant-girl who was finishing his tonsure. Their laboratory was the kitchen and the little priest, who had somewhat recovered from his fright of the day before, was joking with Giustina, telling her to cut his crown properly and not as at the last festa when the whole church had burst out laughing as soon as he had lifted his biretta. Giustina for her part was studying her problem so intently that she had no time to reply to these sallies; but, shorn here and shaven there, the tonsure grew larger, like a splash of oil on the poor priest's head, and though he had given her orders not to make it larger than a half-ducat there was already no coin in existence big enough to cover it.

'Ah, Giustina, Giustina,' sighed the Chaplain, feeling the extent of his new tonsure with his hand, 'it seems that we have gone a little too close to this ear.'

'No doubt about it,' replied Giustina, who was a good-natured and clumsy peasant woman in her thirties, though she looked about forty-five, 'but if we are too near this ear we shall have to go a little farther from that.'

'*Cospetto!* Do you want to pluck me like a friar?' exclaimed the patient.

'No, no, I have never plucked you,' said the woman, 'and I won't pluck you today, either.'

'No, no, I tell you . . . let it alone . . . enough!'

'On the contrary . . . let me finish . . . keep still and don't move for a moment. . . .'

'Eh, you women are the devil!' murmured the Chaplain. 'If it were a question of fashion, you would even allow yourselves to be tonsured . . .'

Who knows what he might have added to the word 'tonsured' if he had not stopped, hearing a noise at the door like the rattling of spurs. He leapt to his feet, pushed Giustina aside, snatched the towel from around his neck and, turning round, found himself face to face with the Lord of Venchieredo. What a grimace, what eyes, what an appearance the poor priest then made may be left to the imagination! He remained in that uncertain attitude of wonder, of fear, of curiosity in which he had first become aware of the menacing appearance of the castellan. His mantle fell to the ground and between the folds of his doublet he moved his hands weakly as if to say: 'Now we are in the soup!'

'Oh, most beloved Chaplain, how is your health?' the feudatory began.

'Well . . . I really don't know . . . that is . . . take a seat . . . the pleasure is mine . . .' stammered the priest.

'It doesn't seem to be so great a pleasure,' went on the castellan. 'You have the most terror-stricken expression, Your reverence. Oh perhaps,' he went on, turning a mocking eye on Giustina, 'I have interrupted some canonical labour?'

'Oh no, no,' murmured the Chaplain, 'I was . . . Giustina, put on water for coffee or chocolate. Would you like chocolate, Signor Count . . . Your Excellency?'

'Go and feed the hens. I want to talk to His Reverence alone,' replied the castellan, turning to Giustina.

She did not wait to be told twice and wriggled her way into the courtyard, still holding the razor in her hand. The castellan then addressed the Chaplain and, taking him by the arm, drew him towards the fireplace where, before he knew what was happening, the priest found himself seated on a bench.

'Now to our affairs,' said the castellan, seating himself opposite. 'A fire freshly kindled does not spoil the skin even in summer, they say. But tell me truthfully, Your Reverence, are you a priest or a smuggler?'

The poor wretch quivered all over and made so many grimaces that, however often he resettled his collar or twisted his lips, he was unable to resume his normal expression for the whole of the subsequent conversation.

'They are both occupations and I don't want to make any comparisons,' went on the Count, 'I am only asking for my own information which you intend to exercise. For priests, there are alms, capons and tithes; for smugglers, musket-shots, prison and the noose. Everyone is free to choose; and in such a case I do not say that I would choose the priest. Only it seems to me that the canons should forbid a mingling of these two professions. What do you say, Your Reverence?'

'Yes, Signor, Your Excellency . . . I am quite of your opinion,' stammered the priest.

'Well then, reply,' said the Venchieredo. 'Are you a priest or a smuggler?'

'Your Excellency . . . is joking.'

'Joking! I? Oh no, Your Reverence! . . . I got up at dawn, and when I do that I am in no mood for joking! . . . I have come to tell you, fairly and squarely, that if the Signor Count of Fratta is not able to safeguard the interests of the Most Serene Republic, I am not far away and feel myself quite capable of doing so. You receive in your house smugglers and contraband. No, no, Your Reverence, it is no good shaking your head . . . we have witnesses and at need could bring them forward in perfect accord with the Courts. . . .'

'Mercy!' exclaimed the Chaplain.

'However,' continued the feudatory, 'since it is in no way pleasant to me to have such bands as neighbours, I will ask you to take a change of air at your discretion, before I am compelled to make you change it by force.'

'A change of air? What do you mean? To change air, me? How? Please explain, Your Excellency!'

'I mean to say that if you could obtain a parish in the mountains you would be showing real finesse.'

'In the mountains?' said the Chaplain, even more astounded. 'I, in the mountains? It is impossible, Your Excellency. Why, I don't even know where the mountains are.'

'They are there,' remarked the castellan, with a gesture towards the window.

But the castellan had reckoned without the excessive timidity of the priest. In certain beings, rough, simple, modest but individual and primitive, timidity may sometimes take the place of courage; and to the Chaplain the necessity of commencing a new life in a new country, with people unknown to him, seemed a burden even heavier and more formidable than to die. He had been born in Fratta, had his roots there and felt that if he were uprooted from this place he would never survive it.

'No, Your Excellency,' he replied, with more assurance than he had shown hitherto, 'I must die at Fratta, as I have lived; and as for the mountains, if I were to be sent there, I doubt if I should reach them alive.'

'Very well then,' said the petty tyrant, rising, 'you will reach them dead, but in one way or another, I assure you that the accomplice of Spaccafumo will not remain Chaplain of Fratta. Bear that well in mind.'

Saying this, the nobleman gave a great rattling of spurs on the step of the hearth and went out of the parsonage followed by the priest with hanging head. The latter made one last bow as he saw the Count mount and then returned to talk things over with Giustina, who had been listening to the whole conversation from behind the courtyard door.

'Oh no, no, they must not bundle you off to the mountains!' whimpered the woman. 'Surely some evil would overtake you if you went so far! . . . and then, aren't your own people here? . . . What should we say to the Good Lord when he decided to take account of us?'

'Put that razor away, my daughter,' replied the priest. 'You can be quite sure that I shall not go to the mountains! . . . They can put me in the stocks, but in another parish, no, certainly not! . . . Can you imagine me at the tender age of forty finding myself among new faces and having to begin again from the beginning all that drudgery which I have gone through since childhood? No, Giustina! . . . I have said it and I repeat it: I will die in Fratta. But for all that it is a heavy cross that now weighs upon my neck; but I must bear it in holy peace. Ufff! . . . that Signor Magistrate! What an ugly snout he showed me! . . . But rather than move, I can put up with anything; and if he should play me some other dirty trick, what can I do about it? Better to be at odds with his buli than with someone else's. . . . At least I know them and will mind less being beaten by them.'

'But what are you saying?' said the servant. 'Even the buli should be submissive to you. How does it seem to you that a priest should be like the head of a nail to be driven here and there?'

'Little more, little more, my daughter, in these days. We must be patient!'

At this the sacristan entered to warn him that the people were waiting for him to say Mass; and the poor man, recollecting that he was already late, rushed out to fulfil his duties with his tonsure only half finished. In vain Giustina ran after him with the razor in her hand as far as the piazza; and the ragged tonsure of the Chaplain and the sight of the Signor of Venchieredo, added to the events of the previous day, gave rise to the most singular comments.

The next day an imposing letter from the Lord of Venchieredo arrived for the Count of Fratta in which, without beating about the bush, he prayed his illustrious colleague to evict the Chaplain in the shortest possible time, accusing him of a thousand villainies, including that of assisting to defraud the Customs of the Most Serene

Republic and of being an accomplice of the most desperate smugglers of the lagoons. 'And since such a crime must be hateful to the Most Excellent Signoria,' so ran the letter, 'how great is the merit of whoever hastens to punish it and how capital the danger to those ill-advised persons who for private reasons leave it unpunished, you, Most Illustrious Signor Magistrate, must know as well as any. The statutes and the proclamations speak clearly; and one's head may well be in question since monies are the life-blood of the state and he who by his negligence conspires to drain it of this truly vital fluid is guilty of a crime against the state.' As can be seen, the castellan had found the right road, and the Count of Fratta, on hearing this antiphonal read to him by the Chancellor, wriggled so much on his armchair that his customary majesty was much impaired. He had hoped to keep the facts of the matter secret; but the summoning of the Chaplain, the visit received by him the previous morning, his bewilderment, his gossiping with Giustina had all revealed to the entire countryside what had happened and had resulted in an uproar.

The Chaplain was loved by all as a good spiritual father; and further, the people of Fratta, accustomed to the patriarchal Venetian type of government by its magistrates, had the trait of not liking to allow anyone to put a foot upon their necks. There was much murmuring against the insolence of the castellan of Venchieredo and to the dismay of the Signor Count, the very inmates of the castle, by their stubborn and imprudent bearing, showed that they too wanted to bring down this ugly storm upon his head.

I had never seen the Count and his Chancellor so indivisible as in those days; they resembled two weather-beaten rafters which leant one upon the other in order to stand up against a high wind; if one moved, the other immediately felt that he was falling and followed the movements of the first so as to keep in balance. Many arguments were put forward to curb the dangerous agitation of spirits, but the remedies were usually worse than the disease. They bit with greater gusto into the forbidden fruit; and tongues, bridled in the kitchen, broke out the more violently in the piazza or at the inn.

More than anyone else, Mastro Germano stormed against the arrogance of his former master. By the virulence of his philippics and the daring with which he defended the Chaplain, he became practically the ringleader of the disorder. Every evening, seated on an alehouse bench, he held forth in a loud voice on the necessity of not allowing this sole representative of the poor, their village priest, to be taken from them. Let the arrogant ones stir up trouble, he said, but there was justice for all and certain past sins might come to light which would send the judges to prison and leave the accused triumphant. Fulgenzio, the sacristan, navigated wisely through all this confusion; and although he had within the castle an official position of trust, outside it he never wearied of trying to pry out of Germano with every circumspection what truth there might be in these menacing hints.

One evening, when the gatekeeper had drunk more than he should have, Fulgenzio pestered him to such an extent that he quite let down his guard and sang and shouted to the four winds that the Signor castellan of Venchieredo would have had him put out of the way, had not he, poor brushwielder, been in a position to publish certain old tales that would have given the noble lord a very bad Eastertide.

Fulgenzio asked for no more. He did his best to change the subject and tried to show that the words of the old toper were either of no importance or the ravings of a drunkard. He then returned to his home to say the Rosary with his wife and children. But the next day, being market-day in Portogruaro, he went there early in the morning and returned even later than usual. He was seen, when there, to enter the house of the Vice-captain of Justice, but being, as I have said, a sort of unofficial writer to the Chancellery, the fact aroused no particular comment. But a week later, just as the case for sending the Chaplain to breathe the air of the mountains was about to come before the Courts, the Chancellery of Fratta received from Venice a formal order to desist from all further action in the matter and to institute instead an inquisitorial and secret investigation on the person of Mastro Germano concerning revelations of great importance to the Signoria which he could and must make regarding the past life of the Most Illustrious Magistrate of Venchieredo.

A meteorite fallen from the moon to interrupt the revels of a band of bon-viveurs could not have caused greater astonishment and consternation than that decree. The Count and the Chancellor completely lost their heads and felt ready to sink into the earth; and since in their first bewilderment, they had failed to take shelter behind their usual reserve, the fears of the Countess and of Monsignor and the joy of the rest of the family showed itself in a thousand ways at the news and made their state of mind still more deplorable.

The position was indeed critical; on the one side was the imminent and proved insolence of a feudatory accustomed to scorn every law, human and divine; on the other the imperious, inexorable, secret tribunals of the Venetian Inquisition. Here the perils of a ferocious vendetta, there the terrifying spectre of a punishment, secret, terrible and inevitable. On the right hand, a fearful vision of buli armed to the teeth, of blunderbusses ambushed behind hedges; on the left, the sinister apparition of Messer Grande, of deep dungeons, glowing irons, nooses, pincers and axes. The two illustrious magistrates felt their heads swimming for forty-eight hours; but, as was to be foreseen, in the end they decided to offer the cake to the largest dog, since to reconcile the two of them was an enterprise not even to be attempted.

I cannot, however, conceal that the encouragements of the Partistagno and the wise counsels of Lucilio Vianello helped considerably to tip the balance to this side; and the Signor Count felt a little more secure at finding himself flanked by persons so valorous and so wise. This, however, in no way altered the fact that the investigation of Germano remained wrapped in the most impenetrable shades of mystery; but those shades were not so impenetrable as to prevent prying eyes wanting to see beyond at all costs. Indeed, there was so much whispering that the old bulo of Venchieredo, terror-stricken by the decree of the inquisitors, had produced as evidence against his former master certain writings of ancient date, which strongly reflected upon his fidelity to the government of the Most Serene Republic, and that if on these hypotheses (let it be well understood that they were no more than hypotheses, because after the interrogation had been opened, the Count, the Chancellor and Mastro Germano, who alone were taking part in it, had become like deaf-mutes), if on these hypotheses, I say, some very fanciful structures were built, I leave it to you to imagine.

As might well be believed, one of the first to get wind of what was happening was the castellan of Venchieredo himself and it was obvious that he did not feel his conscience entirely clear, since at first he showed that he was more worried about the affair than he later wished to admit. He thought, observed, weighed and thought again and finally, one fine day, when they had just risen from the table at Fratta, his visit was announced to the Signor Count.

The Chaplain, who was in the kitchen, believed that at the announcement of that name he would faint then and there; as for the Signor Count, after having sought counsel from the eyes of those at table with him, no less amazed and uncertain than his own, he told the servant, stammering, to show the visitor into the room above and to say that he and the Chancellor would come up immediately. There were too many menaces, risks and dangers connected with this visit to be able to hope for any preliminary discussion, and, furthermore, the two worthies were not such eagles as to finish such a deliberation in a couple of minutes. Therefore they put their heads into the sack with resignation and went upstairs to meet the dreaded arrogance and the no less dreaded cunning of the haughty castellan. The family remained in the dining-hall with their hearts beating as must those of the family of Regulus when the question was being debated in the Senate whether he should be kept in Rome or sent back to Carthage.

'Your Lordship's servant!' began Venchieredo quickly, as soon as the Count and his shadow set foot in the room. And he turned on that shadow a glance that made him three times more livid and obscure than before.

'Your Excellency's most humble servant!' replied the Count, without raising his eyes from the floor where he seemed to be seeking an inspiration to get him out of this encounter. But since no inspiration came, he turned to ask counsel of the Chancellor and felt most uneasy at seeing that he had withdrawn to the far wall. 'Signor Chancellor . . .' he managed to mutter.

But the Venchieredo cut his words short.

'It is useless,' he said, 'it is useless for the Signor Chancellor to be kept from his usual duties to waste time listening to our chatter. It is well known that he has in hand many most important cases which require careful treatment and the most diligent examination. The good of the Most Serene Signoria must come first! Is it not so, Signor Chancellor? Moreover you can safely leave us here together since our conversation is in no way concerned with legal matters and we can settle everything between ourselves.'

The Chancellor could hardly find the strength necessary to drag his feet out of the room, and his squint was at that moment so marked that he hit his nose against the jamb of the door. The Count made towards him a silent and impotent gesture of fear, entreaty and desperation, such a gesture as the arms of a drowning man, gasping for air, might make before he abandoned himself to the stream. Then, when the door had closed, he settled his lace waistcoat and lifted his eyes timidly, as if to say: 'Let us conduct ourselves with dignity!'

'I am pleased that you have received me with so much confidence,' declared the Venchieredo, 'that shows that we shall end by coming to an understanding. After all, you have done rightly, since I must discuss with you a most confidential matter. We shall come to an understanding, Signor Count, shall we not?' added the old fox, coming close to the other to shake his hand craftily.

The Signor Count was somewhat relieved by this sign of friendliness; he let his hand be shaken with a slight hesitation and felt a sense of constraint until he had concealed it hastily in a pocket of his cloak. I believe he chose the first possible moment to go and wash it, lest the Vice-captain of Portogruaro might sense upon it the odour of that greeting.

'Yes, Signor,' he replied, summoning up a little smile, an effort which brought tears to his eyes. 'Yes, Signor, I believe . . . that is . . . we have always been in agreement!'

'Well said, by God!' said the other, sitting down beside him in an armchair. 'We have always been in agreement and we shall be in complete agreement this time also. The nobility, however varied in customs, temperament and affinities, have none the less common interests. A wrong done to one of its members affects all the others. So it is necessary to stand firmly united and support one another and to assist whenever possible to maintain our privileges inviolate. Justice is good, indeed very good . . . for those who have need of it. For my part I feel that I have all the justice I need in my own house and those who try to use it against me cause me a great deal of trouble. Is it not true, Signor Count, that for you too all these pretensions by certain persons who want to meddle in our affairs are by no means pleasant?'

'Eh? . . . Just so . . . that is quite clear . . .' stammered the Count, who had also sat down automatically and of all those words had heard no more than a confused murmur and a sort of droning like a machine turning in his ear.

'And more,' went on the Venchieredo, 'the justice of such persons is not always the most expeditious or the best served; whoever wishes to obey it like a child can easily find himself at loggerheads with those who hold different views and have at their command another justice, rapid and effective.'

These phrases, pronounced one by one and, so to speak, underlined by the firm and curt accents of the speaker, deeply shocked the Count and made him raise a face I know not whether more scandalized or terrified as he grasped their meaning. But since to show indignation might expose him to some unpleasant explanations, he was sufficiently diplomatic to have recourse a second time to his usual smile, which this time obeyed his summons rather more tardily than the first.

'I see that you have understood me,' the other went on, 'and that you are able to weigh the force of my arguments, and that the favour I have come to ask of you will seem neither strange nor excessive.'

The Count opened his eyes very wide and took his hand out of his pocket to place it on his heart.

'Some evil tongue, some slanderous and lying scoundrel whom I will punish with a whipping, have no doubt about that,' continued the Venchieredo, 'has done me the favour of putting me in bad odour with the Signoria for I know not what trifles of long ago which are not even worth recalling. These are mere stupidities, mere fatuousness, everyone agrees; but in Venice they have to take account of these matters so as not to do wrong to their code. Your Excellency understands me; if they pass over frivolous denunciations in silence, they will fail in their duty over important ones, and once a principle is established its consequences must be accepted. However, I know for certain that down there they have only commanded the institution of this examination half-heartedly . . . you understand me . . . that secret protocol . . . concerning Mastro Germano.'

'If only the Chancellor were here . . .' murmured the Count of Fratta, a ray of hope lighting up his face.

'No, no. I don't wish, nor do I wish you, to talk openly of this examination,' broke in the Venchieredo. 'It is enough for me to have reminded you, and to have proved to you, that it was not for suspicion against me, nor for the matter in itself, but simply as a principle of good government, that this decree was issued. . . . There is no longer any use in dragging this matter on. In fact, even at Venice they will not be displeased to see the whole thing cut short; it always happens that in actual application it is better to sóften and smooth what seems too rough and too general in the maxims of state. Now, Signor Count, it is up to us, as between good friends, to interpret the hidden intentions of the Most Serene Inquisitors. The spirit, as you know even better than I, goes beyond the letter; and I assure you that even if the letter commands us to go on, the spirit counsels us to put a stop to all this. In confidence, I have even had communications from Venice to this effect and you may already guess the means . . . by an honest compromise . . . by some good half-measure, if needs be. . . .'

The Count opened his eyes still wider and tugged with his fingers at the lace of his shirt; at this point all the breath that he had kept bottled up in his chest because of his great agitation rushed out noisily in a great snort.

'Oh, don't upset yourself for that!' went on the other. 'The matter is easier than you think. And even were it very difficult, one would have to try and obey the spirit of the Most Serene Council of Ten. The spirit, remember well, not the letter! . . . Since the justice of the Most Serene Republic cannot desire that a most excellent Signor, such as you, should find himself in grave embarrassment because he felt too much bound by the apparent meaning of a decree. Think of it! To put a magistrate at loggerheads with all his colleagues! . . . It would be ingratitude, it would be unpardonable wickedness towards you.'

The poor magistrate understood, with the acumen of fear, only too well what all this was aiming at, and the cold sweat began to form on his temples like the drops from a taper on processional days. The necessity of replying, of saying either yes or no, was such a torture for him that he would have preferred to cede all his rights of jurisdiction to be released from it. But at last it seemed to him that he had found the best way of extricating himself! Imagine what talent! . . . Really he had hit upon a great novelty!

'But . . . in time . . . we shall see . . . we shall arrange something!'

'Egyptian darkness!' the Venchieredo leapt up in a fine fury. 'Who has time needs not wait for time, dearest Count! I, for example, if I were you, would say at once and for my own good reasons: "To-morrow there shall be no more talk of this examination!" '

'But how? How is that possible?' exclaimed the Count of Fratta.

'Ah, I see we are beginning to understand one another again,' said the other. 'He who looks for means is already persuaded of the greatest. And the means are already to hand. Everything is in order, Signor Count, for you to be disposed to satisfy, as is your need, the secret desires of the Council of Ten and mine also.'

That *mine* was pronounced in a way that reminded one of the discharge of a blunderbuss.

'But surely . . . I am very well disposed to . . .' stammered the poor man. 'When you assure me that even those above us so desire. . . .'

'Certainly, for the lesser evil,' went on the Venchieredo. 'It being always understood that everything must take place as if by chance. That is the knot in the skein. One good word to Germano, you understand me! . . . And a touch of hot steel on those papers, and that is the last that we shall hear of it. . . .'

'But the Chancellor . . . ?'

'He will not speak, be easy on that score! I have a word for him also. Thus it is desired by those who stand high, and thus too I desire it; not that the matter could have any consequences to harm me; but I should grieve to have to make reprisals against a man of his merit. The castellan of Venchieredo to undergo a trial instituted by one of his peers! Imagine it! I should myself insist that such a trial be held elsewhere; at Udine, at Venice, where you will, then I should clear myself, then I should defend myself. Here, as you can see well, it would be impossible; I cannot allow it at the cost of killing not one but a thousand.'

The Count of Fratta trembled from head to foot, but by this time he was getting accustomed to these sudden assaults and found breath to remark:

'Very well, Your Excellency, and if it should not be found possible to send these inconclusive papers to Venice?'

'Bah!' the Venchieredo hastened to interrupt him. 'Have I not told you that, being inconclusive, there is no need to worry the postal authorities about them?'

'Since that is so,' replied the Count in a low tone, 'since that is so, let us burn them . . . tomorrow . . .'

'We will burn them at once,' broke in the castellan, rising.

'At once? . . . At once, you say? . . .' The Count raised his eyes, since he did not at that moment feel the least desire to get out of his chair. But one must suppose that the face of his interlocutor must have been very expressive, since he added immediately: 'Yes, yes, you are right! . . . They shall be burnt at once, at once!'

With a great effort he rose to his feet and moved towards the door, no longer even conscious of the world around him. But as his hand was on the latch a modest and whining voice was heard asking: 'With permission?' and the humble Fulgenzio entered the room with a paper in his hand.

'What is it? What do you want? Who told you to come in?' asked his patron, trembling all over.

'The Serjeant has brought this most urgent message from Portogruaro, from the Most Serene Signoria,' replied Fulgenzio.

'Leave it. Leave it till to-morrow!' replied the Venchieredo, who had gone a little pale and had moved towards the threshold.

'Your Excellency will excuse me,' replied Fulgenzio. 'The order is peremptory. It must be read at once.'

'Alas, yes . . . I will read it immediately,' said the Count, putting on his spectacles and unsealing the message. But hardly had he set eyes on it than such a tremor ran through his person that he had to support himself by a chair in order to maintain control of his legs. At the same time the Venchieredo scanned the piece of parchment and got a hint of its contents.

'I see that we shall not come to an understanding to-day, Signor Count!' he said with all his usual arrogance. 'I recommend you to the protection of the Council of Ten and of St. Anthony. I remain with the pleasure of having made my bow to you.'

Saying which, he went down the stairs, leaving the Magistrate of Fratta quite bemused.

'Ah, so? . . . You are going?' said the Count when he had recovered from his bewilderment.

'Yes, Excellency! He has gone,' replied Fulgenzio.

'Look, just look what they have written to me!' the Count went on, handing the message to the sacristan.

Fulgenzio read without surprise a formal order to arrest the Signor of Venchieredo whenever occasion offered to do so without causing an uproar.

'Now he has gone, he has really gone, and it is not my fault that I did not stop him,' said the Count. 'You are witness that he had gone before I was able to understand the meaning of the message.'

'Your Excellency, I will be witness of whatever you command!'

'It would perhaps have been better if the Serjeant had delayed another half-hour!'

Fulgenzio smiled to himself; and the Count went in search of the Chancellor to share with him this new and even more terrible complication in which they were now embroiled.

Who Fulgenzio was and what was his office, you can imagine as well as I can; there were frequent similar cases, in which the Signoria of Venice made use of the most abject servants to watch over the fidelity and zeal of their masters. As to Venchieredo, despite his apparent arrogance, he had had a great shock as he read that message. He had at once understood that they were going to settle with him mercilessly, since the arguments of fear are ever victorious. But a little after, he regained confidence in his own wiliness, in his exalted relations and in the weakness of the government, and again thought of attempting to escape. His first plan was to slip over into Illyria; and we shall see later whether he would have been right or not in that decision. Then he reflected that it would not be easy to capture him without causing a great uproar and, at the worst, he would be able to slip across the Isonzo at any time it seemed expedient to him. The desire to revenge himself by a single blow on Fulgenzio, the Chaplain, the Spaccafumo, the Count and even to make the Most Supreme Signoria come to their senses, finally decided this ferocious and turbulent spirit. He remained, therefore, constrained by fear to an even greater temerity.

CHAPTER V

It is with the story of my life as I believe it is with that of others. It departs solitary from the cradle, only later to become involved with, wander among, and be confounded with the infinite multitude of human affairs, to return solitary and rich only in sorrows and memories to the peace of the grave. Thus the irrigation channels of well-watered Lombardy emerge from some Alpine lake or some river of the plain, to divide, sub-divide and break into a hundred brooks, a thousand runnels and streams; further down, the waters meet again in a single slow-moving stream, pale and silent, which breaks into the Po.

Is it a merit or a fault? Modesty would that I should call it merit: since my affairs would be very unimportant and my opinions and changes and conversations unworthy of study were they not interwoven with the stories of other men who found themselves in the same path and with whom I was for a time a fellow traveller in this world's pilgrimage. But would these then be my confessions? Or shall I not seem rather like the village flirt who, instead of her own sins, tells the priest those of her husband or sister-in-law, or the gossip of the countryside? Patience! Man is so bound to the century in which he lives that he cannot declare his own soul without examining also the husks of the generation that enfolds him. As the thoughts of time and space are lost in the infinite, so man is lost on every side in the tide of humanity. The barriers of egoism, of interest and of religion are not enough; our philosophy may be right in practice, but the inexorable wisdom of primitive India takes revenge upon our arrogant little systems in the full truth of the eternal metaphysic.

Meanwhile, you will have noticed that in this account of my childhood my personages have so multiplied about me as to cause real alarm. I am myself dismayed by them, like that witch who was frightened by the devils she had so imprudently invoked. It is a real phalanx that pretends to walk with me and much hinders with its noise and chatter my haste to press onward. But do not doubt; life is not a pitched battle but rather a continuous development of skirmishes and daily forays. The phalanx does not fall in ranks as under the fire of cannon, but is broken and decimated by desertion, by ambush and by epidemic. The companions of our youth leave us one by one and abandon us to the new friendships, infrequent, cautious and self-interested, of maturity. From thence to the desert of old age is but a short step filled with lamentations and with tears. Give time to time, my sons! After having passed with me through the gay, varied and populous labyrinth of my green years, you will end by sitting in an armchair whence the poor old man can only just move and confides himself, by the aid of courage and meditation, to the future that extends beyond the tomb. But for the moment, let me show you the old world; that world that went its childish way at the end of last century, before the magic breath of the French revolution rejuvenated it in body and in spirit. The men of that time were not as those of to-day; look well at them and see in them a mirror to imitate their little good and to correct their much evil. I, the relict of that covey, have the right to speak clearly; you have the right of judgement and you will use it after I have spoken.

I no longer recall how many, but certainly very few, days after the meeting of the castellan of Venchieredo with the Count, the district of Fratta was disturbed towards evening by an unexpected invasion. They were rustics and smugglers who were running away pell-mell and after them Cernide, buli and a posse of serjeants, bullying the peasants whom they met and creating the greatest uproar that could be imagined. At the first sound of this rabble, the Countess, who had gone out with Monsignor de Sant'Andrea and Rosa for her afternoon walk, hastened to shut herself up in the castle and caused her husband to be woken up to find out what this new development was.

The Count, who for the past week had only been able to sleep with one eye shut, descended precipitously to the kitchen and in a short time the Chancellor, Monsignor Orlando, Marchetto, Fulgenzio, the bailiff and the Captain had gathered about him with the most dismayed faces in the world. By now each of them had understood that they could not so easily recover their one-time calm, and at every new sign of commotion their fears redoubled, as the symptoms of a relapse redouble in the soul of a convalescent. That evening it was up to Captain Sandracca and three of his assistants to show their lion hearts and go out into the open. But not five minutes had passed before they returned with their tails between their legs and with no desire to repeat the experiment.

The rabble that was rioting in the public square was made up of the posse of Venchieredo and showed no disposition to withdraw. Gaetano, at the staff headquarters of the inn, swore and forswore that he would tear the smugglers into pieces and that those who had taken refuge in the castle would pay even more heavily than the others. He pretended that here in the district there was a confederation to defraud the revenue and that the Chancellor and the Count were its ringleaders. The moment had come, he said, to exterminate this band, and if he who was supposed to be the guardian of the laws had become their most open enemy, it was their duty to carry out the decrees of the Most Serene Signoria and acquire great merit by this enterprise.

'Germano! Germano! Pull up the drawbridge and bar the doors well!' screamed the Count after he had heard all this long-winded talk of insults and fables.

'I have already lifted the drawbridge, Your Excellency,' replied the Captain, 'and for greater security I have had it thrown into the moat by three of my men, because the pulleys would not work.'

'Excellent, excellent! Bar the windows and put padlocks on all the exits,' added the Count. 'Nobody must dare to stir a foot outside the castle. . . .'

'I defy anyone to move now that the bridge has been destroyed,' observed the Serjeant.

'It seems to me that the small bridge by the stables would assure a sortie in case of necessity,' the Captain added sagaciously.

'No, no, I want no sorties!' the Count shouted. 'Throw down the little bridge by the stables as well, at once; from now on, I put my castle in a state of siege and of defence.'

'I would like to observe to Your Excellency that once this bridge has been destroyed, there will be no way to get out to collect the daily provisions,' objected the bailiff with a deep bow.

'No matter! My husband is right,' replied the Countess, who was the most frightened of all. 'Your place is to obey and to demolish the bridge by the stables immediately; there is no time to lose! We might be assassinated at any moment!'

The bailiff bowed even more deeply and went to carry out the task assigned to him. A quarter of an hour later all communications between the Castle of Fratta and the rest of the world had been completely cut off and the Count and Countess breathed more freely. Only Monsignor Orlando, who was certainly no hero, risked showing a little anxiety about the difficulty of obtaining the usual quantity of beef and veal for the morrow. The Signor Count, hearing the remonstrances of his brother, now had the chance to show his acumen and the readiness of his administrative genius.

'Fulgenzio,' he said in a solemn voice, 'how many little ones has your sow in her litter?'

'Ten, Excellency,' replied the sacristan.

'Then we are provided for a whole week,' replied the Count, 'since the fishpond will provide us for the two fast days.'

Monsignor Orlando sighed, sorrowfully recalling the fine oradas of Marano and the succulent eels of Caorle. Alas, what in comparison with these were the muddy carp and the frogs of the fishpond?

'Fulgenzio,' the Count meanwhile went on, 'have two of your piglets killed, one for boiling and one for roasting; have you understood, Margherita?'

Fulgenzio and the cook bowed; but it was now the turn of Monsignor de Sant'Andrea, who because of an intestinal complaint was unable to digest pork, and the perspective of a week of siege with such a régime did not suit him at all. However, the Countess, who had read the discontent in his face, hastened to assure him that a pullet would be set aside to boil for him. The features of the canon cleared to a holy tranquillity, for with a good pullet even a week of siege seemed to him a very moderate purgatory.

After the orders had been given to the kitchen staff, the garrison dispersed to put the castle in a state of defence. Some old muskets were placed in the loop-holes and two long-disused saluting pieces were dragged into the first courtyard; the doors and balconies were barred. Finally the bell was rung for the Rosary and none of them ever said it with greater devotion than on that evening. The Countess meanwhile had been too distracted to pay attention to anyone save herself, but her mother-in-law, as soon as it began to grow dark, asked about Clara, for she was so late in bringing her bread and milk. Faustina, the Pisana and I set ourselves immediately to look for her; calling here, running there, we could find her nowhere. The gardener told us he had seen her go out by way of the stables a couple of hours before, but he knew nothing more and believed that she had returned, as usual, with the Signora Contessa.

She certainly would not now have been able to return the way she went, for the bailiff had carried out his orders with such despatch that not a trace remained of the little bridge.

Besides, night had already fallen; it was very dark and not to be thought that she was still walking around outside.

We began looking for her all over again and only after another hour of close and fruitless search Faustina decided to go back to the kitchen and tell her masters the sad news of the disappearance of the Contessina.

'*Giurabacco!*' exclaimed the Count, 'those scoundrels have certainly carried her off!'

The Countess tried to show great distress, but her anxiety about herself kept her too preoccupied to succeed.

'Just think,' went on her husband, 'just think what those wretches are capable of doing, since they dare to call me a smuggler and to put the whole countryside in disorder. But they'll pay me for this, they'll pay me for this!' he added in a low voice in fear lest someone outside his little circle should hear him.

'Talk, talk!' broke in the Countess. 'It's all very well for you to talk and meanwhile it is we who are being fried! Here we are already three hours in this net and you haven't even thought of any way to get us out of the mess. They carry off our daughter and you waste your breath in saying that they will pay you for it! . . . For all that's worth, you could claim little enough!'

'But, wife! . . . For all that's worth? . . . What do you mean?'

'Eh, if you don't understand me, sharpen your wits. I mean to say that you have been thinking about our children, about me myself and about our salvation, about as much as straightening the bell-tower.' Here the Countess angrily took a pinch of snuff. 'Let us see. What have you thought about getting us out of this mess? How do you intend to go and look for Clara?'

'Be reasonable, *diamine*! . . . Clara! Clara! There is no reason to go up in the air like that. You know how quiet and well bred she is. Even if she does sleep a night outside the castle, I don't see why any harm should come to her. As for us, I hope you don't want it to come to shooting.' The Countess made a gesture of fright and impatience. 'Well,' went on her husband, 'we shall try to parley.'

'To parley with thieves! A good idea, indeed!'

'Thieves! . . . Who said they were thieves? . . . They are organs of justice, a little over-hasty, a little drunk, if you like, but none the less invested with a legal authority, and once their madness has passed they will listen to reason. They have become rather over-eager in hunting down one or two smugglers, the wine has gone to their heads and they have got the idea that the fugitives have taken refuge at Fratta. What is there strange in that? . . . If we persuade them there are no smugglers here, nor ever have been, they will go back home as quiet as lambs.'

'Excellency, you are forgetting one thing,' interrupted Monsignor de Sant'Andrea. 'It seems that these fugitives are assassins disguised as smugglers and are being hunted merely as a pretext to create this disorder. Germano says that he has recognized amongst them some of the moustachioed bravos of Venchieredo.'

'But how do I come into all this? What has it to do with me?' the poor Count exclaimed in despair.

'One might send someone out secretly to try and see how things are and look for news of the Contessina,' advised the Serjeant.

'Oh, oh!' replied the Countess, feebly. 'That would be a great imprudence, since we are so short of men in the castle. This is not the time to send any of the best of them away.'

The Pisana, who was squatting with me between Martino's knees, advanced boldly towards the hearth and offered to go and look for her sister; but they were all so terrified that nobody but Marchetto seemed to take any notice of this childish and moving temerity. But her offer was not without result as, after the Pisana, I too offered to go out and look for the Contessina. This time the suggestion had the good fortune to attract someone's attention.

'Would you really take the risk of going out to have a look around?' the bailiff asked me.

'Yes, certainly,' I said, raising my head and looking proudly at the Pisana.

'Let's go together,' said the little girl, who did not want to appear less daring than I.

'Oh no, these are not matters for little girls,' said the bailiff, 'but Carlino here would wriggle easily out of any difficulty. Isn't it true, Signora Contessa? The idea is quite a good one.'

'For lack of a better, I won't deny it,' replied the Countess. 'Here, inside, a boy would be of little use to us, but outside he would not be suspected and could push his nose in anywhere. Also he can be as malicious and bold as the devil himself, as we already know.'

'But I want to go too! I want to go and look for Clara too!' the Pisana began to scream.

'You, miss, will go to bed at once,' replied the Countess and motioned to Faustina to put the command into immediate effect.

Then there was a little battle of howls, scratches and bites, but the maid won, and the desperate little being was taken fairly and squarely to bed.

'What must I tell the old Countess about the Contessina Clara?' the woman asked as she was going away with the Pisana in her arms.

'Say she is lost, that she cannot be found, that she will be back tomorrow!' replied the Countess.

'If I may be permitted to advise, it would be better to say that her aunt from Cisterna has come to take her away,' suggested the bailiff.

'Yes, yes, make her believe some story or other!' exclaimed the Countess, 'not to worry her, since we have quite enough troubles already.'

Faustina went out, and the cries of the Pisana could be heard diminishing along the corridor.

'Now attend to me, little serpent,' said the bailiff, taking me roughly by the ear. 'Let us hear. What good will you be to us once you are outside the castle?'

'I . . . I will just take a walk round the countryside a little,' I suggested, 'and then, as if there was nothing the matter, I would drop in at the inn, where all these gentry are, to weep and complain that I can't get back again into the castle. I will say that I went out with the Contessina Clara and then lost my way chasing butterflies and wasn't able to find her again. Then, if any of them knows anything about her, they will surely tell me and I will come back here and whistle behind the stables. The gardener will push a table across to me and I will come back across the moat in the same way as I went out.'

'Wonderful! You are a real paladin,' replied the bailiff.

'What is all this about?' Martino asked me. He was quite confused by all this talking that he saw me doing without being able to understand a word of it.

'I am going out to look for the Contessina, who has not yet come back,' I shouted at the top of my voice.

'Yes, yes, you are doing very well,' said the old man, 'but be very careful.'

'And don't compromise us . . .' continued the Countess.

'It would be a good thing if you could overhear something of what these assassins are saying at the inn, so that we can know their intentions.' Added the Count. 'In that way we shall know what to do later.'

'Yes, yes, and come back quickly, little one,' went on the Countess, caressing me by that unfortunate lock of hair that had so many times experienced a different fate. 'Go, look, observe and tell us faithfully all about it! The Good Lord has made you so cunning and resolute for our greater good! . . . Go, and may the Lord bless you! And remember that we are all waiting for you here with anxious hearts.'

'I will come back as soon as I have smelt out something,' I replied with an air of importance, since I felt myself the only man in that warren of rabbits.

Marchetto, the bailiff and Martino came to me, encouraging me and recommending me to be prudent, wary and careful. A table was pushed into the moat and I, who was skilful enough in this manner of navigation, reached the further bank successfully and with a push sent my vessel back to them. Thence, while on the advice of Monsignor Orlando, a second Rosary was intoned in the castle, I set out among the deep shadows of the night on my courageous expedition.

Clara, meanwhile, had gone out by the postern before vespers, as the gardener had said, and had not returned. She had expected to meet her mother along the Fossalta road and so, step by step, had reached that village without coming across anyone. Then she thought that it must be later than usual and that the band from the castle must have turned back while she was making the detour round the vegetable garden to the road. Therefore she too turned hastily back to return to the castle, but she had not walked more than a stone's throw when the sound of footsteps made her turn round. It was Lucilio; Lucilio calm and pensive as ever, but irradiated at that moment by an ill-concealed joy that perhaps he did not even try to conceal.

Nothing will ever satisfy the speed of thought; the steamship seems too slow and one day even electricity will seem more idle and tedious than a carriage horse. Believe me, it will be so, and in the final analysis the proportions will remain the same, though as if in the magnified circle of a spy-glass. The mind divines about itself a world very high, distant and inaccessible, and every turn, every step, every spiral that moves or stirs without approaching that dreamed-of Paradise will not seem like motion, but torpor and tedium. What use is it to go from Milan to Paris in thirty-six hours rather than two hundred? What use is it to be able to see the four quarters of the world ten times in forty years rather than once? Neither the world grows larger nor life longer for that, and whoever thinks much will always run beyond those limits into the infinite, into the mystery without light.

To Clara and Lucilio this moment that they were one beside the other seemed very long, while the time from their meeting as they walked together to the first houses of Fratta passed in a flash. Though their feet advanced lingeringly, even without noticing it, they stopped many times along the way, talking of the old Countess, of the castellan of Venchieredo, of their opinions about him, and even more frequently about themselves and their own feelings, of the most beautiful sky that enchanted them, and of the lovely sunset that made them halt for a long time to watch in ecstasy.

'That is how I would like to live,' exclaimed Clara ingenuously.

'How? Tell me quickly!' said Lucilio in his gentlest voice. 'Let me see if I am able to understand your desires and take my share in them.'

'In truth I said I would like to live like that,' replied Clara. 'But now I don't know how to explain myself. I would like to live with this splendid light of the sky in my eyes, this gay and harmonious peace that enfolds Nature as she falls asleep in my ears, and in my heart and spirit those sweet thoughts of brotherhood, those great feelings without distraction and without measure, that are born from the spectacle of simple and sublime things!'

'You would like to live that life that Nature has prepared for wise, equal and innocent men!' replied Lucilio sorrowfully. 'The life that in our words is known as dream and poetry. Oh yes! I understand it very well because I too breathe the fragrant air of dreams and put my trust in the poetry of hope, so as not to reply to injustice with hatred and to sorrow with desperation. Consider how ill-adjusted we are. Who has arms has no brains, who has brains has no heart, and who has both heart and brains has not authority. God is above us and we call Him just and all-seeing. We, the children of God, blind, unjust and oppressed, deny Him every moment with our words, our writings and our deeds. We deny His providence, His justice, His omnipotence! It is a sorrow vast as the world, continuing through the centuries, that forces us on, that pursues us and confounds us, and one day makes us recollect that we are all equal, but only in death! . . .'

'In death, in death? Say rather in life, the true life that will last for ever,' exclaimed Clara as if inspired. 'Behold where God rises again and is justified despite all the contradictions here below.'

'God must be everywhere,' went on Lucilio in a voice in which one who was devout might have desired a greater warmth of faith. But Clara did not feel that lack and he already knew that it would be so, otherwise he would not have spoken.

'Yes, God is everywhere!' she replied with an angelic smile, looking at the heavens above her. 'Can't you see Him, can't you hear Him, breathe Him everywhere? Pure thoughts, tender feelings, gentle passions, whence come they if not from Him? . . . Oh, I love God as the fountain of every beauty and every good!'

If ever any argument could have converted an unbeliever, it was certainly the divine expression that at that moment spread over Clara's face. Immortality was emblazoned on that serene and confident forehead; certainly no one would have dared to say that such intelligence, feeling and beauty had been provided by Nature merely to serve as a pasture for worms. There are, indeed, dead, stony faces, twisted sensual expressions, bowed and fawning men who justify by their foul examples the terrible speculations of the materialists, who must be denied the eternity of the spirit as are animals or plants. But amid this moribund rabble there may arise some brow that seems illuminated by a supernatural radiance, and before such as these the cynic stutters confused words but cannot prevent a tremor at his heart of hope or of terror of a future life. What life, ask the philosophers? Do not ask me, if it is your misfortune not to be satisfied with that ancient, secret wisdom that is faith. Ask yourselves. But it is certain that if organic matter once divorced from its human conception ferments and lives again materially in the womb of earth, so the thinking spirit must live spiritually in the sea of thought. The movement that never ceases in the weary labour of the veins or the nerves, can it go back and find peace in the indefatigable and subtle element of ideas?

Lucilio gazed at the countenance of his companion with enraptured eyes. Then a gleam of light lit up his face and for the first time a sentiment not purely selfish but inspired by the feelings of another penetrated the dark recesses of his heart. But he recovered swiftly from this brief defeat to become once more master of himself.

'Divine poetry!' he said, turning his eyes from the lovely sunset that was just losing its colours in a vague twilight, ' . . . he who first soared with you in infinite hope was the true consoler of humanity. To teach men happiness, one must educate poets, not scientists or anatomists.'

Clara smiled compassionately and asked him:

'Then you, Signor Lucilio, are not very happy?'

'Yes, yes, I am now, as perhaps I could never be!' exclaimed the young man pressing one of her hands involuntarily. At this clasp there vanished from the girl's face that immortal splendour of faith and a tender and tremulous light of feeling spread over it, like a lovely moonlight after the evening darkening of the sun. 'Yes, I am happy, as perhaps I never shall be again!' went on Lucilio. 'Happy in my desires, for my desires are full of hope and hope beckons to me from afar off like a lovely garden in full bloom. Ah me, do not pluck its flowers! I do not break them from their delicate stalks! For all the care we give them now, they will wither after three days, and after five they will no longer keep their lovely colours and their sweet perfume. In the end they will fall inevitably into the sepulchre of memory!'

'No, do not call memory a sepulchre!' rejoined Clara fervently. 'Memory is a temple, an altar! The bones of the saints that we venerate are underground, but their virtues shine in heaven. The flower loses its freshness and its perfume, but the memory of the flower remains in our soul, incorruptible and fragrant for ever!'

'My God, for ever, for ever!' exclaimed Lucilio, carried onward by the strength of his feelings towards the opportunity of those fateful moments. 'Yes, for ever! Be it an instant, a year, an eternity, this must always fill it, satisfy it, beautify it with love, so that it is no longer one with death. Ah yes, Clara, love returns to the infinite in every way; if there is a part of us that is sublime and immortal, it is certainly this. Let us trust in Him that we may not become callous before our time, that we may not lose at least this instinctive poetry of the soul that alone makes our life beautiful! . . . Yes, I swear it now, I swear it and I will always remember this rapture that raises me above myself. Desire may thus be transformed into faith; our love will last for ever because these things that are really great can never come to an end! . . .'

These words pronounced by the young man in a subdued, yet deep and vibrant voice, awakened to delight the confused desires of Clara. It was no wonder, since for a long time past the things that she heard then had been stirring in her heart. The looks, the words, the patient and subtle arts of Lucilio had prepared a sure place in her soul for this ardent declaration. To hear repeated by his lips what her heart had unconsciously been long awaiting was like the sudden awakening of a timid and latent joy. There took place in her soul what takes place on a photographic plate when it is placed in the acid; the hidden image is developed in all its forms, and if one cannot wonder at that moment, it is perhaps because one is incapable of wonder. A secret and hitherto unfelt agitation prevented her from replying to the ardent words of the young man and as she tried to withdraw her hand from his she was forced to seek a support as she felt overcome by a delicious swoon of pleasure.

'Clara, Clara, please answer me!' Lucilio begged, supporting her in anguish and looking around to see if anyone were coming. 'Answer me only one word! . . . Don't kill me with your silence, don't punish me with the sight of your grief! Pardon me! If nothing else, pardon me!'

He seemed almost as if he would fall on his knees, so overcome he appeared, but it was a studied attitude, perhaps to hasten the moment. Clara recovered herself and gave him for sole response a smile. Who could have seen such a smile and not have remembered it for all his life? That smile that asks compassion, that promises felicity, that says all, that pardons all; that smile that portrays a soul that gives itself to another soul, that has not in itself any reflexion of the images of this world, that shines only with love and for love; that smile that understands, or better forgets, the whole world, to live and let you live by it alone and that in a single flash reveals its love and confounds the mysterious depths of two spirits in a single desire of love and eternity, in a single feeling of beatitude and of faith! The heaven that opens full of visions and ineffable splendour to the eyes of a saint would not surely be more enchanting than this flash of felicity that sparkles radiant and, alas, too fleeting in the face of a woman. It is a meteor, it is a flash, but in this flash, sooner than in ten years of meditation and study, the soul sees instinctively the confused horizons of a future life. Oh, how often in the clouding of these faces is quenched within us the lovely serenity of hope, and thought throws us down blaspheming into the great emptiness of the void, like the doomed Icarus, whose wings of wax melted! What sudden, sorrowful beating of the useless ether, where myriads of spirits swim in the oceans of light, to the dread and chill abyss wherein no ray of sun is ever seen, that will never more give life through the turning of the centuries to the shadow of a dream! Science, the heir of a hundred generations, and pride, the fruit of four thousand years of history, flee like slaves caught in ill-doing before the menacing onslaught of such a feeling. What are we, where are we going, poor straying pilgrims? Where is the guide that assures us of a not unhappy voyage? A thousand voices sound about us; a hundred mysterious hands beckon us to paths still more mysterious; a secret and fatal force presses us onwards to right or to left; love, the winged boy, invites us to Paradise; love, the mocking demon, destroys us in the void. And only the belief that our sacrifices will lessen the sufferings of others, sustains us.

But Lucilio? . . . Lucilio was not thinking of that then. Thought follows after joy, as the night the twilight, or the chill winter the golden and harmonious autumn. He had loved for years; for years he had directed his every counsel, his every art, his every word, to create, in a distant future, the beatitude of that moment; for years he had walked patiently and warily, by tortuous and solitary ways, lit now and again by some flash of hope; he had moved onward slowly and tirelessly towards that flowered height, whence he then surveyed and held for his own all the joys, all the delights, all the riches of this world, as master of the universe. He had been able to create the philosophers' stone; by a laborious mixture of looks, of actions, of words, he had extracted the purest gold of felicity and love. Victorious alchemist, he savoured with all his senses the delights of triumph; enthusiastic and passionate artist, he never ceased admiring and enjoying his own creation in that divine smile that broke out on Clara's face like the dawn of a still more beautiful day. Others would have felt their hearts tremble with gratitude; in him, pride tempered once more the fibres of an unbridled and tyrannical joy. I perhaps, and a thousand others like me, would have given thanks with tears in our eyes; he rewarded the submission of Clara with a fiery kiss.

'You are mine! You are mine!' he said, raising her hand to the sky. And he wished to imply: 'I deserve you, because I have conquered you.'

Clara said nothing in reply. She had loved him till then without realizing it and without revealing it, and the moment in which love is conscious of itself is not the moment for speech. She only felt herself to be for the first time utterly in the power of another, and that feeling did no more than change her smile from the colour of joy to that of hope. At the first moment she had rejoiced for herself; now she rejoiced for Lucilio, and this joy was easier and dearer to her, since it was more modest and more compassionate.

'Clara,' went on Lucilio, 'it is getting late and they will be expecting us at the castle.'

The young girl started as if from a dream, wiped her eyes with her hand and felt them bathed with tears.

'Shall we go?' she replied in a sweet subdued voice that scarcely seemed her own. Lucilio without a word set out again along the road and the girl walked by his side, quiet and gentle as a lamb by the side of its mother. For that day, the young man asked no more. The treasure once revealed, he wanted to enjoy it for long, like a miser; not to squander it madly in prodigies, only to find himself afterwards in greater misery than before, with the added burden of vanished memories.

'Will you love me always?' he asked her, after a few steps in silence.

'Always,' she replied. An angel's harp never made sweeter sound than that word, pronounced by such lips. Love has the genius of Paganini; it confounds in harmony the virtues of the spirit.

'And when your family finds a husband for you?' added Lucilio in a harsh and mournful voice.

'A husband?' echoed the girl, drooping her head.

'Yes,' replied the youth. 'They will sacrifice you to ambition, they will ask of you in the name of religion a love that religion will forbid you in the name of nature.'

'Oh, I will never look at anyone but you!' replied Clara, almost as if talking to herself.

'Swear it by all you hold most sacred! Swear it by your God and the life of your grandmother!' exclaimed Lucilio.

'Yes, I swear it!' Clara replied calmly. To swear what she felt herself impelled to do by an irresistible force seemed to her quite simple and natural. Then they began to see through the evening shadows the first houses of Fratta and Lucilio released the girl's hand to walk respectfully by her side. But the die had been cast; their two souls were joined for ever. Perseverance and reserve on the one hand, gentleness and compassion on the other, had merged them in a flame of love. The resolution of Lucilio and the self-denial of Clara corresponded, like twin stars eternally drawing nearer to one another in the spaces of the sky.

Two armed men came to meet them at the entrance of the village. Lucilio passed them by, thinking they were two rural guards who were on the look-out for someone; but one of them ordered him to halt, saying that on that evening entry into the district was forbidden. The young man was offended and surprised at such unusual temerity and adopted a method that he knew from much experience to be infallible in such encounters. He began to raise his voice and abuse them. But in vain. The two buli held him respectfully by the arms, replying that the service of the Most Serene Signoria so demanded, and that no one could enter Fratta until the search for certain smugglers they were looking for had been completed.

'I presume you will not prevent the Contessina Clara from entering the castle?' replied Lucilio, fuming with rage and pointing to the young girl whom he was accompanying, holding her arm tightly. Clara made a movement as if to restrain him from getting too angry, but he paid no attention and went on threatening and trying to go onwards. The two buli still held him by the arms and warned him that their orders were precise and that they had the right to use force against anyone disobeying them.

'That right to use force I have too, and I make great use of it against impudent fellows!' went on Lucilio still more heatedly, loosing himself with a blow from the two rascals. But a movement from Clara warned him of his danger and the unseasonableness of such acts of violence. He calmed once more and asked the two who they were and on what authority they forbade entry to the castle to the daughter of the Magistrate. The men replied that they were Cernide from Venchieredo, but that their pursuit of the smugglers authorized them to act outside their own jurisdiction if necessary, that the ban of the Signor Syndics spoke clearly and that, furthermore, those were the orders of the Captain of a Hundred, and they were only there to see that they were carried out. Lucilio would have protested further but Clara begged him gently to stop, so he contented himself with turning back with her and threatening the two rascals and their masters with all the thunders of the Viceroy and the Most Serene Signoria, of whose small value he was very well aware.

'Be quiet! It is useless,' Clara whispered in his ear, dragging him away from the two guards. 'I'm sorry that it is night already and they will be anxious about me at home, but with a little detour we shall easily be able to get in by the stables.'

They started to walk across the fields, looking for the path that led to the postern, but they had not gone a hundred paces before they encountered two more guards.

'It's a real ambush!' exclaimed Lucilio angrily. 'Must a young noblewoman spend all night out at the caprice of a few scoundrels?'

'Watch your words, illustrissimo,' shouted one of them, giving a tremendous thump on the ground with the butt of his musket.

The young man trembled with rage and felt with one hand in his pocket for his faithful pistol, but with the other one he felt Clara's arm trembling with fright and had the forbearance to restrain himself.

'Let us try to come to an understanding . . .' he replied, still fuming with rage. 'How much do you want to let the Contessina pass? I assume you do not suspect her of bringing any contraband!'

'Illustrissimo, we suspect nothing,' replied the guard, 'but even if we could shut an eye and let her pass, those in the castle are of different opinion. They have destroyed both the bridges and the Contessina could only enter by walking on the water like St. Peter!'

'Then the danger really must be serious,' said Clara faintly.

'It's nothing. They have got into a panic, or so I suppose,' replied Lucilio. Turning once more to the guard, he asked: 'Where is your Captain of a Hundred?'

''Lustrissimo, he is drinking of the best at the inn, while we are here keeping watch on the bats,' replied the man.

'Very well. I hope at least you will not refuse to accompany us to the inn to talk to him,' suggested Lucilio.

'Well, we have no orders about that . . .' responded the other. 'However, it seems all right to me, especially if Your Honour will pay for a glass or two.'

'Come along then, come with us,' said Lucilio.

The guard turned to his companion, telling him to remain at his post and not to go to sleep; warnings that were heard with very little satisfaction by the one who had to remain eating fog, while the other had in view a good flask of Cividino. However, he resigned himself, grumbling, and Lucilio and Clara, preceded by the guard, set out again across the fields.

This time the two guards let them pass and they were soon at the inn, where reigned such a commotion that it seemed more like a carnival than a chase for smugglers. Indeed Gaetano, after quenching the thirst of his own people, had begun to offer glasses to the onlookers. These, already a little unruly from the start, had by now come to the closest understanding with him in that mute and expressive language. Those who were drinking called for company, and as this grew they revived and drank still more. Thus, mingling and intermingling, at the end of half an hour the posse of Venchieredo had become a single family with the peasants of the neighbourhood and the host never ceased praising to the skies the splendour and unusual correctness of the Captain of a Hundred of the Cernide of Venchieredo. As may well be believed, such munificence was neither arbitrary nor without its reason. The master had suggested to him that he should keep the local people quiet and prevent them from taking sides against them in favour of the castellans. Gaetano had worked cunningly and the aims of his chief had been well served. Had he wished, three hundred topers would have shouted 'Long live the castellan of Venchieredo!' And God knows what effect the menacing sound of such a shout would have had in the Castle of Fratta.

When Lucilio and Clara set foot in the inn the uproar was at its height. The young noblewoman was heart-broken at seeing their most loyal tenants joining in revelry with the enemies of her family; but they paid no heed to her and surprise and dismay at all this tumult prevented her from seeing clearly. She feared some serious peril for her family and was sorry she was not with them to share it, never thinking that their peril, protected as they were by a wide moat, was far less than her own, defended by a single man against this turbulent rabble.

Lucilio, however, was not of a spirit to be easily imposed upon by anyone. He went directly to Gaetano and ordered him, in a rather arrogant tone, to arrange for the Contessina's return to the castle. The truculence of the new arrival and the wine that he had drunk made the Captain of a Hundred even more above himself than ever. He replied that those in the castle were a perverse race of smugglers and that he had the task of keeping them shut up until they had handed over the guilty and returned the smuggled goods, and that as far as the Contessina was concerned, he had better look after her himself seeing that he had her on his arm. Lucilio lifted his fist to strike him for his impudence, but thought better of it and twirled his moustache furiously in the favourite gesture of Captain

Sandracca. The only thing left to do was to get out of this turmoil and take his companion to some secure refuge where she could pass the night.

Clara at first protested against this decision and wanted at all costs to go as far as the bridge to see if it really had been destroyed. Lucilio accompanied her, even though it seemed dangerous to him to adventure abroad with the girl amongst the wine-sodden rascals who were rioting in the piazza. But he did not want to give her any occasion to think that he lacked courage or that he had omitted any chance of helping her to get home. However, after they had looked at the ruin of the bridge and had called vainly to Germano once or twice, they had to hasten to leave because the commotion continued to grow and the posse had begun to crowd around them and provoke them with jests and insults. Lucilio sweated at the necessity for showing moderation; but his principal duty was to keep the girl safe and with this in mind he went down a small byway in the village and turning towards the Venchieredo road soon arrived, hurrying Clara along with him, at the meadow of the mills.

There he stopped to let her get her breath. She sat down, weary and tearful, by a hedge and the young man bent over to look at her pale face, on which the light of the newly-risen moon seemed to be tenderly reflected. The dark buildings of the castle rose before them and an occasional light appeared between the chinks of the balconies only to be once more quickly concealed like stars in a stormy sky. The dark foliage of the poplars waved gently and the uproar of the village, deadened by distance, in no way interrupted the amorous outpourings of the nightingales. Fireflies shone in the grasses, the stars twinkled in the sky and the new moon striped the vague and shadowy forms around them with slanting, veiled rays. Modest Nature surrounded with darkness and silence her summer bride-bed, but her throbbing heart was thrilled now and again by some breeze redolent of fruitfulness.

It was one of those hours in which man does not think, but feels; that is, he receives the thoughts and facts of the universe that absorbs him. Lucilio, a nature pensive and, above all, disdainful, felt small despite himself in a calm so solemn and profound. The joy of love diffused itself through his heart in vain imaginings, melancholy and sweet. It seemed to him that his feelings grew like a cloud of dust dispersed by the wind; but their forms faded, their colour was dissipated; he felt greater and yet less strong, more master of all and less of himself. There seemed a moment when Clara, seated before him, was bathed in a flash of light and he himself, as if thunderstruck, had to close his eyes . . . whence this marvel? . . . He could not understand it himself. Perhaps the solemnity of the night, that binds weak souls with superstitious fears, yet reinforces the spirit of the strong, showed them in the darkness of its shadows the image of destiny, the subduer of all. Perhaps also he was affected by the girl's grief, even as a short time before he had triumphed over her by the force of his resolution. No, her eyes were not flashing then, unless it were with the shining of tears. Her heart, overflowing half an hour before with felicity and love, had flown now to the bedside of her grandmother, to that little neat and silent room where Lucilio had passed long hours with her and where, when he had gone away, there remained hovering in the air a dear memory, an invisible and enchanting memory. How could the poor old woman have managed to get to sleep without the customary kiss from her granddaughter? Who would have remembered her in the perils that menaced the castle that night?

Pity, divine pity, filled the girl's breast with fresh sobs and the hand that Lucilio took to help her rise was bathed in tears. But once more upon their way, Lucilio's usual alacrity returned. His dreams vanished, his thoughts sprang up once more, resolute and virile, and his mind, subdued for a moment, rose up with greater force to resume its command. The story of his and Clara's love, the extraordinary events of that night, the feelings of the young girl and his own, depicted themselves before him in a single picture clearly and in due order. He looked on them with an eagle's eye, seeing the whole scheme before him, and decided that at all costs, either alone or with the girl, he had to enter the castle before the night had passed. Love imposed on him this duty and let us add that the interest of his love also counselled him strongly. Clara prayed to God and the Madonna. Lucilio summoned to his aid all the resources of his nature and his courage; and so, arm in arm, they walked silently towards the mill. What moderation, some would say, thinking of Lucilio. But if so, it is either that I have explained badly or that they have not understood me properly when I was speaking of his temperament. Lucilio was neither a villain nor reckless; he only claimed to see to the depths of human affairs, to desire the best in them and to know how to obtain that best. These pretensions, when tempered by a sane judgement, he could have proved by deeds, since he never allowed himself to be carried away by his passions, but firmly kept the reins and knew how to hold them at need even on the brink of a precipice or on the flattering and treacherous bank of some flowering mead.

The two entered the mill but found nobody there, though fire was still flickering among the embers in the hearth. The polenta left on a trencher made it clear that all had not yet supped and that some of the men had probably stayed late in the village to watch the rioting. But this was the family with whom the Contessina was perhaps most intimate, so that it would not displease them to help in her rescue.

'Listen, dear one,' Lucilio said to Clara in a low voice, poking up the fire to dry her clothes after the dew of the meadows, 'I will call someone and confide you to the care of one of the women, and then, by hook or by crook, I will get into the castle and give them news of you and see how they are there inside.'

Clara blushed under the gaze of the young man. It was the first time she had received, in a room and by the full light of the fire, their mute language of love. She blushed without shame, for it did not seem to her that she had violated any of the Lord's commandments; and she could not see what difference there might be between loving in secret and confessing that love to one another.

'Lie down and try to rest,' went on Lucilio. 'I will think in the meantime of how to get news of what has happened to the Vice-Captain of Portogruaro, so that he may hasten to put an end to the plots of these rogues. . . . They have not come here for nothing and I think I can see clearly enough what this sudden zeal of theirs against smugglers means. . . . It is a vendetta or a reprisal, perhaps even a quarrel, cooked up to finish this business of the trial . . . but I will put things in their true light and the Vice-Captain will be able to see for himself on which side are the true interests of the Signoria. Meanwhile, Clara mine, stay here in peace and sleep well; tomorrow, if they have not come from the castle to take you home, I will come myself; and who knows what might happen during the night if matters are so pressing. . . .'

'But you . . . don't take any risks for God's sake,' murmured the girl.

'You know me,' replied Lucilio. 'I must be active and try to do something or other even if it were a question of strangers. You can judge for yourself how much more it means when it is a question of your family and our beloved old friend!'

'Poor grandmother,' exclaimed Clara, 'Yes, yes, go and comfort her and then return at once to fetch me, since I shall be waiting here with such an anxious heart.'

'You must go and lie down and I will call one of the women,' said Lucilio.

'No, let them sleep, since I cannot,' replied the girl. 'I wonder at myself and am almost ashamed of myself to stay here and not to go with you.'

'Do what?' exclaimed Lucilio. 'No, for Heaven's sake, don't move from here. Also you must shut yourself in well, since they have been so foolish to leave the doors wide open until midnight! Marianna, Marianna!' he began to shout, going to the door at the foot of the stairs.

A moment later a voice replied from above and the scraping of a pair of pattens; and in another minute Marianna, bare-necked and bare-armed, descended to the kitchen.

'God forgive me!' she exclaimed, drawing her shift together over her breasts, 'I thought it was my husband! . . . Is it you, Signor Doctor? . . . And the Contessina too! . . . The devil! What has happened? How did you get in?'

'By the open door,' replied Lucilio. 'But this is not the time for chatter, Marianna; the Contessina cannot get into the castle because there is rioting all around. . . .'

'How . . . what sort of riot? . . . Are our men there? . . . Wretches! . . . They have not even eaten their supper! . . . Going out to see what was going on and leaving all the doors wide open too. . . .'

'Listen to me, Marianna,' went on Lucilio. 'Your men will come back. They are in no danger.'

'In no danger, indeed! If you only knew mine, how rash and headstrong he is! . . . He is quite capable of trying conclusions with a whole army, that he is. . . .'

'Very well, but you can be quite sure he will not try anything to-night. . . . I am going in search of them and will send them home. . . . But you, see that nothing is lacking for the Contessina.'

'Oh, poor Signora! What a thing to happen to you! . . . Excuse me for coming down like this, but I really thought it was my husband . . . Wretch! Rushing off like that without his supper and leaving the door wide open. . . . I'll make him pay for it! . . . Only command me, Signora . . . I'm sorry that you will find nothing here that you are accustomed to . . .'

'So, I rely on you, Marianna,' said Lucilio again.

'Naturally! There is no need for orders! I am sorry I am not dressed. But you, Signor Doctor, are accustomed to such things and the Contessina is so good! . . .'

Marianna, busying herself with the fire, displayed two very beautiful shoulders, their whiteness set off by the brown of her arms and face. It may be that she was not too unwilling to show them and for that reason made so many excuses.

'Good-bye . . . love me, love me!' whispered Lucilio in Clara's ear; then, intercepting a glance from her, full of love and hope, he made his way out of the door into the mist that shrouded the countryside. Clara could do no less than follow him to the threshold, and when he was lost to sight, turned back to sit in the kitchen, but not too close to the fire for the heat was great and would have scorched her clothes. Indeed, her head, her pulses burned like embers and her lips and throat were parched as in a fever. Marianna wanted her at all costs to eat a mouthful, but she would not and contented herself with a glass of water. Then she stretched her arm along the back of a chair and rested her head on it as if preparing for sleep. Marianna tried to persuade her to lie down in her own bed, where she had put a newly washed sheet, but seeing that she was wasting her words, the handsome peasant was silent and, having bolted the door, sat down on a stool.

'I wish you would go and lie down,' said Clara, since, however many thoughts and fears she had for herself, she could never have been guilty of forgetfulness for another.

'No, Signora. I must be here ready to open to our men,' replied Marianna, 'otherwise instead of giving a good scolding, it might be that I should get one.'

Clara again rested her forehead on her arm and remained, as they say, dreaming with open eyes, while Marianna, after having nodded for some time, leant over the table and soon began to breathe with the quiet and regular breathing of a robust country girl who sleeps soundly.

Meanwhile, as Signor Lucilio with every precaution against being seen was approaching the moat at the back of the castle, I, sent out as a scout, was proceeding with equal care, intending to wander in such a way as to arrive at the village from quite another direction and thus remove any possible suspicion of the truth. After I had walked about a musket-shot towards the meadow, I seemed to see in the darkness a man's form advancing among the leaves of the vines with the greatest circumspection. I squatted down behind the wheat and watched, protected from the most curious eye by my smallness and the wheat which was all round me with its heavy ears already blond and pendulent. I looked between the stems and the ears and in a clearing flooded by the moonlight, who was it I seemed to see? . . . Signor Lucilio! . . . I had another look to make sure and then decided to make myself known. I rose and advanced towards him carefully, keeping behind the wheat and ready to drop back like a hare into its forme should need arise. Nothing in the world, in my view, could have been more fortunate than this meeting. Signor Lucilio was the confidant of the old Countess and of Clara; he had shown himself well enough disposed towards me on the occasion of my escapade in the marshes; no one could help me in my search better than he could. And as he had the reputation of being a man of sense, I drew the best possible auguries from this meeting. When I was about ten paces from him, 'Signor Lucilio, Signor Lucilio!' I whispered in a quiet and subdued voice that nevertheless strove to make itself heard.

He stood still and listened.

'I am Carlino of Fratta! I am Carlino of the spit!' I went on in the same tone.

He took out of his pocket an object that I later knew was his pistol and came forward looking straight at me. Since I was still in the shadow of the wheat, it seemed he had some trouble in recognizing me.

'Yes, yes, devil take it! It is really me!' I said with some impatience.

'Hush! Silence!' he murmured with a mere thread of voice. 'There is a guard near here and I don't want him to overhear us.'

He meant the guard who had remained alone after his companion had left to act as guide to Lucilio and the Contessina. But solitude is sometimes a bad counsellor and the guard, after a valorous watch of more than half an hour, had finally been vanquished by sleep. Lucilio and I were able to talk in complete security, sure that no one would disturb us.

'Come close and tell me how you got out of the castle and what the news is inside there,' he whispered.

'The news is that they have the fear of the devil for holy oil,' I replied, 'that they have thrown down all the bridges for fear of being killed by the buli of Venchieredo, that the Signora Clara is lost and that since the Ave Maria they have already said two Rosaries. But now they have sent me out to have a look round and try to get news of the Contessina and then to return and report to them.'

'And what were you thinking of doing, little one?'

'*Capperi!* What was I thinking of doing? . . . of going to the inn, pretending to have lost my way, as happened that other time, do you remember? That time of the fever; then listening to what the posse were saying and asking for news of the Contessina from some peasant, and then going back faithfully the way I came out, crossing the moat on a table.'

'You really are a little devil, you know. I never thought it of you. However, you can thank your good fortune that has spared you a good deal of trouble. I have been at the inn, I have taken the Contessina Clara safely to the mill and if you will show me the way to get into the castle, we can give them all the answers together.'

'If I show you the way? All I need to do is to whistle and Marchetto will push the table across. Afterwards leave it to me. You will see how I cross without getting wet and you have only to watch me and do as I do and stay well in the centre of the table.'

'Let's go then.'

Lucilio took me by the hand and keeping close behind some thick hedges, through which it would have been impossible to see us even by daylight, I led him in a flash to the moat. There I whistled as had been arranged and Marchetto ran out quickly and pushed the table across to me.

'So soon?' he said from the other side of the moat, since for the moment surprise made him forget all precautions.

'Quiet!' I replied, showing Lucilio how to make himself comfortable on the table.

'Who is it?' asked the Serjeant, still more surprised since he could now distinguish two figures instead of one in the darkness.

'Friends. Be quiet!' replied Lucilio and then he too, as if brought up to the trade, gave a push that brought us touching the other bank gently.

'It is I!' he said, jumping to the ground, 'And I bring good news of the Contessina Clara.'

'May Heaven be praised!' exclaimed Marchetto, helping me to get the table out of the water.

When we entered the kitchen they had only just finished repeating the Rosary. The fire had gone out, and in any case they were in such a state that nobody could have looked after it. Nobody even thought of supper and only Monsignor Orlando every now and then threw an uneasy glance at the cook. Martino, too, had become taciturn and was busy grating his cheese; all the others had faces worthy of a funeral. The appearance of Lucilio was like a ray of sunshine in a storm. An 'Oh!' of wonder, of anxiety and of pleasure echoed round the room and everyone stared at him without asking a single question, as if uncertain whether he were a man or a ghost. It was therefore up to him to open his mouth first, and the words of Moses when he descended from the Mount were not listened to with greater attention than his. Even Martino stopped his grating, but not being able to hear anything of the talk around him, ended by taking hold of me and making me tell him by signs a part of the story.

'First of all, I have good news of the Contessina Clara,' Lucilio said. 'She had gone out into the fields towards Fossalta to meet the Signora Contessa as usual and was prevented from coming back by the bravos who are on guard everywhere. I myself had the honour of taking her to safety in the mill.'

The bravos surrounding the castle on every side rather spoilt the good impression made by the news of Clara. All smiled with their lips at this dove of good tidings, but their eyes were more dismayed than ever, and did not smile at all.

'But we are really besieged then, as if they were Turks!' exclaimed the Countess, wringing her hands in despair.

'We can console ourselves that the siege is not really so rigorous, since I have been able to get in here,' suggested Lucilio. 'Though it is true that the merit is all Carlino's and if I had not met him I would have had some difficulty in finding my way so quickly and in getting Marchetto to push the table across to me.'

The eyes of the company all turned on me then with a certain respect. At last they understood that I was good for something more than turning the roast, and I enjoyed this little triumph in a dignified manner.

'Were you at the inn, too?' asked the bailiff.

'Signor Lucilio will tell you everything,' I replied modestly. 'He knows more about it than I do, and has had some encounters with these gentry, I believe.'

'And what do they say? Are they thinking of leaving?' the Count asked anxiously.

'They are thinking of staying!' replied Lucilio. 'For the moment at least there is no hope that they will clear out and we must apply to the Vice-Captain of Portogruaro to make them put their tails between their legs.'

Monsignor Orlando darted another and more expressive glance towards the cook; the Canon of Sant'Andrea settled his collar with a slight yawn; in both these reverend gentlemen the needs of the body began to cry out more strongly than the afflictions of the spirit. If this were a sign of courage, they were at this time the most valiant hearts in the castle.

'But what do you say? What is your opinion in this crisis?' asked the Count with no less anxiety than before.

'There can be only one opinion,' declared Lucilio. 'Are the walls well manned? Are the doors and windows barred? Are the muskets and the field-pieces at the loop-holes? Are there sufficient men in the castle to look to the defences for a night?'

'To you, to you, Captain!' screamed the Countess, envenomed by the highly unreliable appearance of the Slav. 'Answer the Signor Lucilio! Have you ordered things in such a way that we may consider ourselves safe?'

'That is to say . . .' stuttered the Captain. 'I have only four men including Marchetto and Germano; but the muskets and field-pieces are in order; and I have also distributed the powder . . . for lack of bullets I have used my hunting shot. . . .'

'Excellent! Do you think these rogues are sparrows?' shouted the Count. 'We should do well defending ourselves with bird-shot!'

'For five or six hours even bird-shot will be good enough,' answered Lucilio. 'And if you, Signori, will be able to hold these assassins at bay until daylight, I believe that the militia of the Vice-Captain will then be in time to intervene.'

'Till daylight! How can we defend ourselves until daylight if these desperados take it into their heads to make an assault?' howled the Count, tearing pieces out of his wig. 'If we kill one the blood will go to the heads of the others and we shall all be fried before the Vice-Captain has even thought of putting on his boots!'

'I don't see things in quite so dark a way,' replied Lucilio. 'Once one of them has got his deserts, believe me, the others will come to their senses. It is never a bad thing to show one's teeth; and since Captain Sandracca does not seem in his usual spirits, I will take over the defence myself, and I declare and guarantee that I alone will be enough to defend the castle and to put to rout all those braggarts outside.'

'Bravo, Signor Lucilio! You will save us! We are in your hands!' exclaimed the Countess.

Indeed the young man spoke with such assurance that it put a little spirit back into everyone there; life returned to those faces petrified with fear, and the cook made her way towards the dresser to the great comfort of Monsignor. Lucilio had himself briefly informed of the whole course of the affair; he considered with better judgement that it was some trick of the castellan of Venchieredo to disrupt the investigation by a *coup de main* on the Chancellery, and as the first act of his assumption of authority had all the pertinent papers and documents removed to an inner room of the castle. He then carefully examined the moats, the doors and the windows, and posted Marchetto and Germano at the portcullis; the bailiff he put on guard duty by the stables. Two other Cernide who were the strength of the garrison he placed at the loop-holes that overlooked the bridge, apportioned their duties and gave orders that the first person daring to try and cross the moat should be killed without mercy. Captain Sandracca kept close to the young man's heels while he attended to these provisions, but he had not the heart to put on his usual ugly appearance and it was only due to the signs, grunts and encouragements of his wife that he did not invent a stomach-ache and retire into one of the barns.

'How does that seem to you, Captain?' Lucilio said to him with a rather mocking smile. 'Would you have acted in the same way?'

'Yes, Signor . . . I would have already done all this . . .' stammered the Captain, 'but my stomach . . .'

'Poor thing!' interrupted Signora Veronica, 'he has been working right up till now and it is due to him that these rogues have not already found their way into the castle. But he is no longer as young as he used to be. Work is work, and his strength is no longer equal to his good will.'

'I need rest . . .' murmured the Captain.

'Yes, yes, let him rest as much as he likes,' put in Lucilio. 'He has already shown his zeal nobly and now he can retire under the bedclothes with a clear conscience.'

The veteran of Candia did not need to be told twice; he flew up the stairs like a homing angel and despite the shouts of his wife, who was at his heels, to take care not to fall, in four paces he was in his room, well locked and barred. Having to pass close by the loop-holes gave him a fit of giddiness and he felt much better off between the coverlet and the mattress. For future perils God would provide; those he feared above all were the present ones. Signora Veronica gave full vent to her anger, reproving him for his helplessness, but he replied that it was not his task to deal with thieves and had it been a question of real fighting he would have been at his post.

'These young men, these young men!' exclaimed the valiant fellow, stretching his legs. 'They think they are cut out to be heroes because they have not the prudence to look out for bullets when they show their heads at the battlements. Oh my God! It needs more than that. . . . Veronica, don't leave me, don't go away. . . . I want to defend you as my greatest treasure!'

'Thanks,' replied the woman, 'but why don't you get undressed?'

'Undress! Do you want me to undress while we have this tempest at our backs? . . . Veronica, keep close to me . . . whoever wants to harm you must first pass over my dead body!'

She too, still dressed, threw herself on the bed and being a brave woman would have gone to sleep had not her husband jumped up at every fly that buzzed, asking her if she heard anything and exhorting her to rely on him and not to go far from her legitimate defender.

Meanwhile, downstairs, a modest repast of eggs and cutlets had calmed the convulsions of the two Monsignors and with their minds once more preoccupied with their former fears they began to ask one another about the number and quality of the assailants, if they were a hundred, three hundred, a thousand, all gallows birds, the best of whom had escaped the noose by the indulgence of the hang-man. If they talked about contraband, it was only as a pretext for plunder; to hear them shouting and singing on the piazza, they must all be fighting drunk and therefore reason and mercy were not to be expected from them. The rest of the company exchanged terror-stricken glances at these discussions, and it was worse still when one of the picked men came to report on some sound or move-ment in the vicinity of the castle.

Lucilio, after having paid a visit to the old Countess and calmed her with some tale about Clara's absence, had returned to comfort these poor devils. He then wrote, and got the Count to sign, a long and very urgent letter to the Vice-Captain at Portogruaro and asked permission of the company to go himself and deliver it. Mercy! How could he even suggest it! The Countess almost went on her knees to him, the Count gripped him so violently that he almost tore the seams of his coat, the canons, the cook, the scullions and the servants surrounded him on every side as if to prevent his leaving. And all with looks, with gestures, with ejaculations and with words besought him to understand that to let him leave would be to deprive them of their last ray of hope. Lucilio thought of Clara, but none the less decided to remain.

But someone was needed to deliver the letter and once again all eyes were turned on me. Taking advantage of the general confusion, I had been all the time in the Pisana's room, enduring her reproofs for the expedition *extra muros* of which I had defrauded her. But as soon as they began calling me, I had the cunning and good fortune to be found on the staircase. They filled my head with instructions and advice, they sewed the letter into my jacket, they embarked me on the same table and there was I, employed for the second time on a diplomatic mission.

It was then exactly ten o'clock at night and the moon shone in my eyes with little modesty, two things that caused me some uneasiness, the first because of the witches of whom I had heard Marchetto talk and the second because of the ease with which I could be observed. But for all that I had the good luck to arrive safe and sound at the meadow.

I trembled a little at first, but reassured myself as I went on, and on entering the mill, as I had been instructed, I assumed a certain air of importance which did me credit. I reassured the Contessina Clara and replied politely to all her questions; then, having told Marianna to wake her eldest son, I took advantage of her absence to remove the letter from my jacket, and having taken it out placed it as if it were of no importance in a satchel. Sandro was a youth some two years older than I, who had displayed a spirit and courage out of the common, for the bailiff had advised me to try and get him to take the letter to Portogruaro.

He accepted the commission without a murmur, threw his jacket over his shoulders, put the letter in his breast and went out whistling as if he were going to water his oxen. The road he had to take towards Portogruaro took him ever further away from Fratta and there was little danger that he would be surprised and intercepted. I had therefore no misgivings and was more than satisfied at seeing all the commissions entrusted to me thus carried out without a hitch; moreover, my ears were still ringing with the praises that they had heard in the kitchen of the castle. Though I had been recommended by Signor Lucilio to keep the Signorina Clara company until the return of the messenger, the ground was burning underneath my feet, all the coming and going, the mystery, the perils had given scope to my childish imagination and I could not stay inactive. I was bent on re-entering the castle, reporting on that part of my task I had already accomplished, coming out once more and finding out what the Vice-Captain of Justice had replied.

Clara, when she heard of my intention, asked if I had enough courage to help her too to cross the moat. My little heart beat even more quickly with pride than with uncertainty and I replied with flaming face and tense muscles that I would sooner drown myself than allow even a fold of her dress to get wet. Marianna tried to dissuade her young mistress from this idea with many prudent warnings, but the nail was now well in and I had but to drive it home. I could hardly wait until I should find myself once again in the open.

It was all arranged in a moment; leaving the miller's wife with her prudence, we went out into the fields and thence in a short time reached the moat without mishap. The accustomed whistle, the dispatch of the table and the crossing succeeded as perfectly as the others had done. The Contessina was so overjoyed at this surprise that she seemed almost to enjoy crossing the water and she laughed like a child as she knelt down on our contraption. The joy, the wonder, the relief of the family would take too long to tell; but Clara's first thought was to ask about her grandmother; or if not her first thought, it was at least her first word. Lucilio told her that the good old woman, having accepted the story they had told about her, had gone quietly to sleep and it would be better not to wake her again. Then the girl sat down with the rest in the dining-hall; but while the others were listening at the cracks in the shutters at the noises coming from the village, she was speaking to Lucilio with her eyes, thanking him mutely for all that he had done for them. Indeed, all with one voice ascribed to Signor Lucilio the little hope and security that had relieved their spirits after their first dejection. It was he who was ready to reassure them with some good argument, it was he who must provide the castle against a sudden assault, it was he who had conceived that sublime idea of having recourse to the Vice-captain.

Then it was my turn to take the limelight. They asked me about the letter and who had been entrusted with it, and all rejoiced to know that within a couple of hours I would return to the mill to hear the reply from Portogruaro. I received a thousand caresses, I was the hero of the hour. Monsignor pardoned me my ignorance of the Confiteor and the bailiff repented having made a roasting-jack of me. The Count turned honeyed glances on me and the Countess never seemed to tire of caressing my neck. Tardy, but merited, justice!

While the whole company was doing all it could to make much of me, the noise outside suddenly increased and Marchetto, the serjeant, with gun in hand and staring eyes, rushed into the dining-hall. What is it? What is the matter? There was a general flurry, an outcry, an asking of questions, an overturning of chairs and candlesticks. The news was that four men had found their way in behind the tower by a disused water-channel; that they had leapt upon him and Germano and that the latter, with two knife wounds in his side, must be in a bad way. Marchetto himself had only just had time to escape, locking the doors behind him. At this news, the screaming and commotion increased threefold; no one knew what to do; they were like quails confined in a dark basket, darting their heads hither and thither without knowledge and without aim. Lucilio exhausted himself in advising calm and courage, but it was like talking to the deaf. Clara alone listened to him and tried to help by persuading the Countess to take heart and trust in God.

'God! God! It is indeed time to rely on God!' exclaimed the Signora. 'Call my confessor! Monsignor, do you think we should commend our souls?'

The Canon of Sant'Andrea, to whom these words were addressed, had no longer soul enough for himself; you can imagine whether he had any intention or possibility of commending those of others!

At that moment the sound of several gunshots was heard and with them cries, noises and threats of men who seemed to be coming to blows in the tower. The confusion knew no limit. The women in the kitchen came in from one direction, the maids, the Pisana and the servants from another; the Captain, more dead than alive, came in supported by his wife and crying that all was lost. The shrieks and prayers of Fulgenzio's family could be heard from without and also those of the bailiff, all asking for refuge in the master's house as the safest place. In the dining-hall the confusion reached its climax: dismayed and frightened voices, prayers, exclamations, weeping women, blaspheming men and exorcizing Monsignors. The Count had lost his shadow, who had deemed the moment opportune to retire even farther into obscurity under the table-cloth. The Countess, almost fainting, wriggled like an eel. Clara set herself to comfort her as best she could. I for my part had taken the Pisana in my arms, well content to let myself be cut to pieces before I would relinquish her to anyone.

Lucilio alone kept a cool head in all this turmoil. He asked Marchetto and the servants if all the doors were bolted, and then asked the Serjeant if he had seen the two Cernide before escaping from the tower. The Serjeant had not seen them, but in any case, two men alone were not enough to create the uproar that could be heard outside and Lucilio judged quickly that some fresh incident had occurred. Had his appeal to the Vice-Captain already had effect? It seemed too soon the more so since excess of zeal was not the defect of the militia of that time.

It was, however, clear that some sort of aid had arrived, unless indeed the assailants were so drunk as to discharge their arquebuses at each other. To the complaints of Fulgenzio's family and the bailiff, there was now added the noise of men rapping at the windows and demands that they should open without fear because everything was over. The Count and the Countess were in no way reassured, believing this to be a ruse planned to enter the house by treachery. Everyone crowded anxiously round Lucilio, awaiting counsel and salvation from him alone; the Contessina Clara had taken up a position at the foot of the stairs, intending to run to her grandmother as soon as the danger was imminent. Her eyes replied valorously to the glances of the young man, saying that he should pay attention to the others, since for her part she felt strong and steadfast against whatever might happen. I held the Pisana tighter than ever in my arms, but the little girl, moved to emulation by my courage, shouted to me to let her go and she would defend herself. Pride so acted on her imagination that she believed she alone was enough against an army. Meanwhile Lucilio, leaning against the window shutters, asked who was knocking.

'Friends, friends! From San Mauro and Lugugnana!' replied many voices.

'Open! I am the Partistagno! The rascals have been driven off!' broke in another well-known voice, which loosed, if I may so put it, the breath of all those persons wavering between hope and fear.

A cry of relief made the walls and windows of the dining-hall shake and if the whole company had gone mad at the same time they could not have given way to stranger or more grotesque manifestations of joy. I remember, and I shall always remember, the Signor Count who, at the welcome sound of that voice, put his hands to his temples, lifted his wig, and stood with it thus raised to the skies, as if offering it *ex voto* for the grace received. I laughed at this, laughed so much, that it was well for me that the greatness of the relief turned the general attention away from my person! . . . Finally the doors were opened, the windows unbarred; lanterns were lit and lamps and candles, and to the festive splendour of a full illumination, and amid the sound of triumphal songs, of Te Deums and the most pious ejaculations, the Partistagno, with his liberating army, invaded all the ground floor of the castle. The embraces, the tears, the thanks, the astonishment, were unending; the Countess, forgetting all decorum, had fallen on the neck of the young victor; the Count, Monsignor Orlando and the Canon of Sant'Andrea would have liked to imitate her; Clara thanked him with real emotion for having spared her family who knows how many hours of dread and uncertainty and perhaps also some less imaginary evils.

Only Lucilio did not join in the jubilation and chorus of praise. Perhaps this liberation did not altogether please him and he would have wished it to come from anywhere save from the quarter whence it had come. However, he was too just and prudent not to mask this untimely feeling of envy and he was the first to ask the Partistagno of the manner and fortune that had led him to this good work. The Partistagno told him how he had come that evening for his usual visit to the castle, though a little later than usual because of the repairing of some of the dykes which had delayed him at San Mauro. The men of Venchieredo had forbidden him to enter and though he had protested loudly against this high-handedness, it had availed nothing; finally, seeing that his words did not count a fig and realizing that all this shouting about contraband was only a cover for God knew what schemes, he had decided to turn back and return again armed with quite other arguments than words.

'Though I am not a tyrant by profession,' added the Partistagno, 'even I can, when needs must, do something to make myself felt.'

So saying, he stretched his muscles and displayed some sharp teeth that would not have disgraced a lion.

In fact, he had returned at a gallop to San Mauro and there having collected a few of his retainers as well as some Cernide of Lugugnana, who were still there working on the dyke, had returned towards Fratta. They had arrived just at the moment when the tower had been taken by the four bravos. Having first easily routed the drunkards who were rioting on the piazza and at the inn, he had set himself to ford the moat with some of his men. After some difficulty they had reached the farther side, without those who had occupied the tower troubling themselves to drive them back, since they had been too busy smashing hinges and locks in order to get into the archives. Then, after a few shots exchanged in the darkness, more for show than for need, the four rascals had fallen into their hands and he now held them under guard in the same tower into which they had crept with such barefaced villainy. Among them was the leader of the band, Gaetano. As for the gate-keeper of the castle, he was already dead when the Lugugnana Cernide had found him.

'Poor Germano!' exclaimed the Serjeant.

'Is there really no more danger? Have they all gone? Won't they be back again for their revenge?' asked the Signor Count, who could not realize that such a storm could have dissolved into thin air without some great crashing of thunderbolts.

'The leaders are well handcuffed and will be as quiet as babes till the time comes for the hangman to look after them better,' replied the Partistagno. 'As for the others I bet they will remember the biting smell of the air of Fratta and it will take a lot to get them to smell it again.'

'God be praised!' exclaimed the Countess. 'Signor Baron Partistagno, we will do all in our power to recompense you for the immense service you have rendered us.'

'You are the greatest warrior of modern times!' shouted the Captain, wiping from his forehead the sweat of fear.

'It seems that you thought out a good defence,' replied the Partistagno, 'the windows and doors were so barricaded that not even an ant could have found its way in.'

The Captain was silent and leant against the table to hide the fact that he was without his sword. He made a sign towards Lucilio as if to refer the merit of all the precautions to him.

'Ah, so it was the Signor Lucilio?' exclaimed the Partistagno with a tinge of irony. 'It must be admitted that greater prudence could not have been used.'

This panegyric of prudence in the mouth of one who had conquered by audacity seemed rather too much like raillery for Lucilio not to notice it. His spirit must have risen to great heights to enable him to reply with a modest bow to these ambiguous words. The Partistagno, believing that he had pretty well destroyed him thereby, turned to seek on Clara's face the effect of this fresh triumph over his small, unhappy rival. To his surprise he could not see her, for the girl had already run upstairs to listen at her grandmother's door. But the old woman slept soundly, protected by deafness against the sound of the arquebus shots, and Clara returned to the dining-hall very satisfied with her expedition. The Partistagno looked at her with relish and had in return a glance of real good will that confirmed him still more in his pity for the poor doctor of Fratta.

In the meantime questions about this and that were showered upon him; on the number of the rascals, on the method used by him to cross the moat and, as always happens after a danger is over, everyone enjoyed magnifying it and remembering their emotions at the time. The state of mind of one who has, or thinks he has, escaped a mortal danger resembles that of one who has received a favourable reply to a declaration of love. The same joy, the same loquacity, the same prodigality of everything that is asked, the same lightness of body and of mind; to put it better, all great joys are similar in their effect, in contrast to great sorrows which have a far more varied scale of manifestations. Souls have a thousand senses to feel evil and only one for good and Nature has something of the temperament of Guerazzi that has greater imagination for the miseries than for the rewards of life.

The first to consider that the new arrivals might need some refreshment was Monsignor Orlando; I always think that his stomach rather than his gratitude made him aware of such a need. They say that joy is the most potent of the gastric juices, but Monsignor had digested his supper during his fear and his joy had done no more than stimulate his appetite even more. Two eggs and a small cutlet! More than that was needed to stay the appetite of a Monsignor! . . .

So they set to immediately and made short work of Fulgenzio's piglets. The fear of a long siege had vanished, the cook worked for three, the scullions and the servants had four arms each, the fire seemed disposed to cook everything in a minute. Martino, weeping for the death of Germano, of which he had only just been told by the Serjeant, grated half a pound of cheese in three strokes. The Pisana and I made carnival, happy and content to find ourselves forgotten in the universal rejoicing; as far as we were concerned we would have liked an assault on the castle every month if only to enjoy such excitement. But the memory of poor Germano often intervened to cloud my satisfaction. It was the first time that death had passed close by me since I had reached the age of reason. The Pisana diverted me with her chatter and rebuked me for my uncertain humour.

I replied: 'And Germano?' The little girl sulked, but soon began to chatter again, to ask me for details of my nocturnal expeditions, to try and persuade me that she would have done even better and to join in congratulating me that the cook had deigned to put the roasting-jack into service without fastening upon me to do my usual duties. I forgot my sorrows in this chatter and the petty pride at being regarded as of some importance kept me too occupied with myself and my own prowess to think too much of the dead man.

Midnight had already passed by a good half-hour before supper was ready. No distinctions were made of place or of person. In the kitchen, in the dining-hall, in the pantry, everyone ate and drank as he chose. The families of the bailiff and Fulgenzio were invited to the triumphal banquet and between a mouthful and a toast the death of Germano and the disappearance of the sacristan and the Chaplain required only an occasional sigh. But the dead do not move and the living can be found. Indeed, the little priest and Fulgenzio appeared not long after, so pale and miserable that they looked as if they had been shut up in a flour bin. A great burst of applause greeted their entry and they were invited to tell their stories.

These were in fact very simple. . . . Both of them, so they said, without knowing of the other's intentions, had run at the first arrival of the enemy to Portogruaro to ask for aid and they had in fact only just arrived from there with the aid of Pisa.

'What! Are the noble soldiers outside?' exclaimed the Signor Count, who was still not aware that he had lost his wig. 'Tell them to come in! Come along now, let them in!'

The soldiers were six in number, including a corporal, but in appetite they were the equal of a regiment. They arrived at just the right moment to clean from the platters the last remnants of the roast piglets and to revive the gaiety which had already begun to deteriorate into somnolence. But after they had been satisfied and the Canon of Sant'Andrea had recited an Oremus to render thanks to God for the escape from peril, all thoughts turned seriously to bed. Then, higgledy-piggledy, one here and one there, everyone found his niche, the newcomers in the guest rooms, the others, some in the friars' room, some in the coach-house, some in the hayloft. The following day, soldiers, Cernide and constables received at the order of the Signor Count a large gratuity and everyone returned home after having heard three Masses, in none of which was I called upon to recite the Confiteor.

Thus, after the hurricane had passed, we returned to our usual way of life; the Signor Count, however, had recommended that we celebrate our triumph modestly for it in no way suited him to provoke another reprisal.

With such dispositions of soul, it is no wonder that the inquiry instituted into the revelations of Germano did not advance with much celerity; nor did it appear that there was any real desire to punish the four rascals who were held as the Partistagno's prisoners of war. The castellan of Venchieredo, having been tactfully approached about them, admitted that he had really sent them to track down some smugglers who were said to have taken refuge in the neighbourhood of Fratta, but that his instructions had been exceeded in a manner that was criminally culpable, adding that this did not concern him but the Chancellery of Fratta. The Chancellor for his part did not show any great desire to see the matter through and refrained from forcing the prisoners into dangerous confessions. The example of Germano spoke too clearly and the astute lawyer was a man to take things as they came. He therefore allowed the principal inquiry to slide and in the minor matter concerning the assault on the tower was only too happy to have proved the thorough drunkenness of all the four accused. In this way he hoped to wash his hands of the affair and that the dust of oblivion would providentially accumulate on those ill-omened protocols.

Matters tottered on in this way for about a month, when one evening two Capuchin friars asked hospitality in the Castle of Fratta. Fulgenzio, who was acquainted with all the Capuchin beards of the province, could in no way place these two; but since they declared that they came from Illyria, a circumstance proved by their accents, they were courteously welcomed. Had they come from the moon, nobody would have risked refusing hospitality to two Capuchins on the slender excuse that they did not know them by sight. They excused themselves with pious humility from entering the dining-hall, where that night there was a full assembly, and instead edified the servants with some of their holy hypocrisies and tales of Dalmatia and Turkey, which were the usual stock-in-trade of the friars of those parts.

Then they asked permission to go and lie down, and Martino took them to the room reserved for visiting friars that was separated from my mousehole by a simple board partition. Through a crack I watched them enter. A little later the castle was wrapped in the peace of sleep, but I went on watching at the crack because there were certain things about the two Capuchins that piqued my curiosity. As soon as they had entered their room, they shut themselves in with two good turns of the padlock; I then saw them take from under their tunics some implements that it seemed to me, were labourers' tools, also two strong chisels, two heavy knives and two good pairs of pistols, such as friars are not in the habit of carrying. I hardly dared to breathe for fright, but my curiosity to know what all this apparatus was meant for made me stay at my peep-hole. Then one of them began to break away the stones of the wall opposite with a chisel. This wall backed on to the tower, and one blow after another, the man had soon made a large hole.

'The wall is thick,' observed the other one quietly.

'Three and a quarter feet,' said the one who was working. 'We shall need two and a half hours before we can get through.'

'And if someone discovers us in the meantime?'

'Eh? . . . Well, so much the worse for him! Six thousand ducats will soon pay for a couple of knife thrusts.'

'What if we cannot get out because the gatekeeper wakes?'

'What else will you think of? . . . He is a boy, the son of Fulgenzio. . . . We can soon scare him and get the keys to go out at our ease, otherwise . . .'

'Poor Noni,' I thought, seeing the menacing gesture with which the cut-throat interrupted his work. That hypocrite of a Noni had never been in my good books, especially because of the malicious espionage he carried on to the detriment of myself and the Pisana; but at that moment I forgot his unpleasant habits, as I would even have forgotten the jealous and hypocritical manners of his brother Manichetto. Pity silenced every other feeling; furthermore, the threat touched me also if they once realized that I was watching them through the crack in the partition, but having acquired the taste for adventurous exploits, I hoped that night also to show myself a person to be reckoned with.

I opened the door of my mousehole very carefully and crept on tiptoe into Martino's room. Not wanting or daring to speak, I opened the shutters to let in a little light, for the night was very clear, and then approached the bed and tried to waken him. He leapt up immediately, shouting to ask who it was and what was the matter, but I put my hand over his mouth and signed to him to keep quiet. Luckily he recognized me at once and then, by signs, I got him to follow me and leading him down to the landing on the stairs I gave him an account of the matter. Poor Martino's eyes were as big as lanterns.

'We must wake Marchetto, the Signor Count and the Chancellor,' he said, filled with dismay.

'No, Marchetto will be enough,' said I, with much good sense, 'the others would only make a fuss!'

So we waked the Serjeant, who agreed with me that things should be done quietly and by as few people as possible. The wall on which the Capuchins were working backed on to the Chancery archives, which were in a large dark room on the third floor of the tower, full of documents, rats and dust. The best thing would be to get two strong and reliable men who would seize the two friars as they passed through the hole, blindfold them and bind them securely. And so it was done.

The two men were Marchetto himself and one of his kinsmen, who worked in the castle as a gardener. They made their way very quietly into the archives, using the Count's keys which were always in the pocket of his breeches, hanging in the antechamber. They stood one on the right and one on the left of the spot where the muffled sound of the blows of the chisels could be heard. After half an hour a ray of light penetrated into the archives and the two watchers braced themselves at their posts. They were well armed with hatchets and pistols, but hoped to be able to do without them as the friars imagined themselves to be quite secure and in no danger of being disturbed.

'I can get my arm through,' murmured one.

'Two more blows and the worst is over,' replied the other.

With a little more work they enlarged the hole sufficiently to allow a man to pass with difficulty. Then one of the two friars, he who seemed to be the leader, stuck first his head through, then one and then the other arm and, scrabbling with his hands on the floor, managed to pull his legs through also. But when he least expected it, he felt a friendly force aiding him in this and at the same time received a heavy blow on the chin, his jaws were forced open and a gag jammed between them that almost prevented him from breathing, let alone shouting. A cord tied tightly round his wrists and a pistol held to his head completed the job, and persuaded him not to try and move from the wall against which he was propped. His companion friar seemed a little uneasy at the silence which followed the passage of his chief; but he reassured himself by thinking that he would not breathe a word for fear of being heard and plucked up courage to put his head also through the hole. The second man was treated with even less ceremony than the first. As soon as he had got his head through, Marchetto seized it and pulled so vigorously that he might have torn it off had not his shoulders dislodged some stones from the wall. Gagged and bound in his turn, he was well searched, together with his companion; their arms were taken from them and they were led to a damp cellar, remote and well sheltered from the outside air, where each of them was put in a little cell, like real friars. There they were left to meditate, while we went to wake the family and tell the great news.

You can imagine what amazement, what palpitations and what relief! It was certain that this was some fresh trick on the part of Venchieredo. It was decided to keep the whole affair as secret as possible until an account of it could be sent to the Vice-Captain at Portogruaro. Fulgenzio was entrusted with this mission. It caused so great an impression that the castellan of Venchieredo was still waiting for the return of the friars when a company of Slavs surrounded his castle, arrested the Signor Magistrate, and took him duly bound to Portogruaro. Certainly Fulgenzio must have found very decisive arguments to induce the wary Vice-Captain to so violent and immediate a resolve. The prisoner, pale with anger and fear, bit his lip at having fallen into such a trap and thought, with tardy prudence, of the fair fiefs that he possessed beyond the Isonzo. The prisons of Portogruaro were very solid, and the speed of his arrest was too significant for him to be able to delude himself with any hopes of escape.

The inhabitants of Fratta for their part railed against the temerity of this tyrant, and great and small rejoiced at the stroke as if it had been their own. An order arrived a few days later to send the four men accused of breaking in by force of arms, and also the two Capuchins and the documents on the Germano inquiry, to a representative of the Most Serene Council of Ten, which marked the climax of the joy of the Count and the Chancellor of Fratta. They breathed again at having cleansed their hands of this pitch and ordered a 'Te Deum' to be sung 'for motives affecting their souls' when, after two months, it came to their knowledge that the six rascals had been condemned to the galleys and the castellan of Venchieredo to ten years' seclusion in the fortress of Rocca D'Anfo, near Brescia, as a criminal convicted of high treason and of conspiracy with foreign rulers against the Republic.

The letters deposited by Germano were in fact part of a secret correspondence carried on between Venchieredo and some Gorizian nobles, in which there was talk of inducing Maria Theresa to take over the Venetian Friuli and assuring her of the support and co-operation of the local nobles. These letters had remained in Germano's possession owing to the difficulties of transport and delivery, and he had omitted to return them, saying that he had destroyed them for fear of the consequences or for some other vital reason. He had thought thus to provide himself with a good defence against his master in case the latter, as was his custom, should try to get rid of him; but destiny had willed that, in spite of his efforts to defend himself, he had instead managed to offend an even more tyrannical and unjust master.

After the criminal trial of Venchieredo, the civil case came up in the courts. But whether it was the prudent policy of the government not to encroach too sharply on the rights of the Friuli nobles, or the skill of the lawyers, or the good will of the judges, it was decided that the jurisdiction of the Castle of Venchieredo should continue to be exercised in the name of the young son of the condemned man, who was then a student at the college of the Scolopi Fathers in Venice. In a word, the civil sentence pronounced against the father was judged not to have effect to the prejudice of the son. Thus it was that, Gaetano and all other obstacles having been removed, Leopardo Provedoni finally received Doretta in marriage. Signor Antonio had to resign himself to this, as also to seeing the Spaccafumo, despite the bans and sentences against him, take part as a greatly honoured guest in the wedding breakfast. The young couple were regarded as the most beautiful seen in the district for the past fifty years and no one took the trouble to count all the fireworks loosed in their honour. Doretta entered triumphantly into the Provedoni household and the beaux of Cordovado had one beauty the more to ogle during the Sunday Mass. If the Herculean strength and the severity of the husband somewhat restrained their homage, the flirtatiousness of the bride continually encouraged them. And everyone knows that in such matters allurements are more potent than fears.

The Chancellor of Venchieredo, left almost absolute master during the minority of the young Magistrate, reflected part of his glory upon his daughter, and certainly on festival days she preferred the arm of her father to that of her husband, especially when she went to preen herself at the festive gatherings around the spring.

My destiny also in the meantime had greatly changed. I was not yet in a position to take a wife, but I was fully twelve years old, and the discovery of the false Capuchins had greatly advanced me in the general opinion. The Countess no longer provoked me, and sometimes even seemed ready to remember our kinship, though she reacted very quickly from these outbursts of tenderness. However, she did not oppose her husband when he took it into his head to apprentice me to the legal profession and to add me as a scribe to the staff of the Chancellery.

At last I had my place at the common table, quite close to the Pisana, for the financial straits of the family, which continued owing to extremely bad administration, had made them give up the idea of a convent for the younger daughter also. I continued to rage, to play and to martyr myself; but already my growing importance in some way compensated me for the rebuffs which it was still my lot to suffer. When I could pass in front of the Pisana reciting the Latin lesson that I had to repeat next day to the Rector, it seemed to me that I was in some way superior to her. Poor Latinist, how little did I know!

CHAPTER VI

THE years that came and went one after the other at the Castle of Fratta, tranquil and unremarkable, like simple country-folk, brought instead to Venice and the rest of the world events terrible and famous. They were 1786, 1787 and 1788, three dates that seem like any others, but which in the chronology of humanity remain as the symbols of one of its principal revolutions. No one today believes that the French Revolution was the madness of a single people. The impartial muse of history has revealed to us the wide and hidden roots of this delirium of liberty that, long matured in the spirits of men, broke out in the social order blindly, sublimely, inexorably. Where a fact has thundered, be sure of it that the lightning flash was an idea. Only the French nation, reckless and impetuous, plunged before all others from doctrine into experiment. It was regarded as the head of humanity, but was only its hand, a daring and destructive hand that often destroyed its own work, while in the universal mind of the peoples the great design was being more slowly matured.

In Venice, as in every other state of Europe, opinions began to emerge from their accustomed corners to play their part in the vaster circle of human affairs; men felt themselves citizens and as such to have rights in the good government of their country; subjects and rulers: the first prided themselves as capable of having rights, the second became aware of the ties of duty. There was a looking askance, a preparation for battle, of two forces till then in accord; a new boldness on the one side, a suspicious fear on the other. But at Venice, less than elsewhere, were spirits disposed to go beyond the measure of the laws; the Signoria relied astutely on the contented somnolence of the people, and a Northern Prince was not wrong when, arriving at that moment, he said that he had found there not a State but a family. None the less, what may be a providential and natural necessity in a family may become a tyranny in a republic; the differences of age and of experience that induce the obedience of children and the authority of parents are not always to be met with in the varied conditions of rulers and authorities. Good judgement was maturing among the people while the justice of other times remained an obstacle in its way. To continue the metaphor, the moment had come when the sons, having grown in strength, in reason and in age, had the right to escape from parental authority; that family in which the right to think, conceded to an octogenarian, was denied to a man of mature virility, would certainly not be ordered according to the desires of nature and would even stifle the most holy of human rights, the right of liberty.

Venice was such a family. The ruling aristocracy was degenerating; the people enervated by ease, but could still be rejuvenated to a consciousness of itself at the creative breath of philosophy; a corpse that did not want to be revived, a race of living beings forced by long servility to live with it in the common grave. But who does not know those fortunate islands, smiled on by the heavens, caressed by the seas, where even death doffs his black mourning garments and the phantasms dance upon the waters singing the amorous octaves of Tasso? Venice was the grave where Juliet slept dreaming of the embraces of Romeo; to die with the happiness of hope and the roseate illusions of joy will always seem the most delicious climax of life. Thus nobody was aware that the long and noisy carnivals were nothing else but the funeral pomps of the Queen of the Seas. On the 18 February 1788 the Doge Paolo Renier died, but the news of his death was not published until 2 March, lest the public mourning should interrupt the revels of the *semaine gras*. Shameful frivolity, denoting that no love, no faith united these subjects to their Prince, these sons to their father. Live or die at your pleasure, only do not disturb the gaiety of the masks and the amusements of the Ridotto;

such were the sentiments of the people and the nobility who united with the people only to enjoy themselves at lesser cost and with greater security. With equal indifference, Lodovico Manin was elected Doge on 9 March; perhaps the election was hastened in order that its festivals should break the melancholy of the fast. The last Doge mounted the throne of Dandolo and Foscari during the days of fasting; but Venice was then still ignorant of the penance that had been prepared for her.

Amid such recklessness, in the midst of this rotting ineptitude there did not lack some who, seeing confusedly the necessities of the times, should recall the mind of the Signoria to opportune remedy. It may well have been, however, that the remedies proposed were neither opportune nor suited to the need; but it should have sufficed to have touched upon the wound for others to think of better medicines. Instead, the Signoria turned their eyes away from the evil; they denied the necessity of a cure where quiet and content indicated not malady but health; they did not realize that the most perilous maladies are those where even the feeling of pain has ceased to exist.

Not many years before, the Avogadore of the Commune, Angelo Querini, had twice suffered imprisonment by order of the Council of Ten, for having dared to divulge abuses and illegal actions with which the majority of the Great Council had already struck their bargain and dissembled. The second time, after having been promised that these matters should be discussed, he was committed to prison before even the promise could take effect. Such was the independence of a semi-tribunal authority and such the measure of the powers confided thereto. No one agreed with, or all pretended not to agree with, the imprisonment of Angelo Querini, even as no one felt himself desirous of imitating him. But these were times in which reforms advanced despite themselves. In 1779 the administration of justice and the public good had fallen to so low a level that even the most patient and thoughtless of the people resented it.

First Carlo Contarini proposed the correction of abuses and opportune changes in the forms of the constitution in the Great Council and his harangue was so striking and at the same time so moderate that it was agreed with marvellous unanimity that the Signoria should be commanded to proceed at once to the necessary changes. It was notable in these disputes that those who would then have been called the Liberal Party tended to restore all the patriciate to the most ample exercise of its authority, dissolving that oligarchical power that was concentrated in the Signoria and the Council of Ten by long and illegal custom. They were aiming apparently at reforms of little import; in substance they were trying to broaden the rights of sovereignty, restoring it at least to its original proportions and always insisting on the maxim, for long forgotten, that it was for the Great Council to command and for the Signoria to execute those commands; in any case it was recalled that the latter had only a delegated authority.

The partisans of oligarchy fumed at having to endure such words; but the confusion and multiplicity of laws offered them a thousand subterfuges to drag matters on at length. The Signoria pretended to bow to the ruling of the Great Council and then proposed insufficient and ridiculous remedies. After a year of continual debates, in which the Great Council always relied in vain on the votes of the reformers, the Most Serene Doge was dragged into the question. His suggestion was to delegate the examination of the abuses supposed to exist in the constitution of the Republic to a Magistrature of five 'correctors', and the convenience of such an expedient, which amounted to nothing, was justified by him with similar reasons to those which a prudent politician would have used to justify the necessity of total and immediate reform. Renier spoke at length of the monarchies of Europe, that had become powerful at the expense of the few republics, from which he deduced the need for concord and stability. 'I myself,' he added in his patriarchal Venetian, 'I myself being in Vienna during the disturbances in Poland, heard many times repeated: "These Polish gentlemen do not want rights; we shall soon settle them." If there is a state that has need of concord, it is ours. We have no forces; neither by land, by sea, nor by alliance. We are living by luck, "by accident", and we continue to live solely by the prudence of the government.'

By speaking in this way, the Doge, in my opinion, showed more cynicism than courage, especially since as sole remedy for this ruin he could only propose inertia and silence. It was as if he said: 'If we move a stone, the house will collapse! Don't breathe, don't cough, for fear it will fall on top of us.' But for him, the first Magistrate of the Republic, to admit this in full council was so shameful that he should have been made to discard in ignominy the horned cap of the Doge. At last the Procurator, Giorgio Pisani, had shouted that if they had been informed of the necessary changes in the forms of the Republic and it had been judged impossible to effect them, that the memory thereof should not be preserved in an official document, so that though their descendants might bewail the impotent wisdom of their ancestors, they should not curse their lack of foresight and scatter their ashes to the winds. The Great Council, however, accepted the opinion of the Doge, and the five 'correctors' were elected, amongst them Giorgio Pisani himself.

Later, when this momentary ferment had settled down, and when the Inquisitors of State took their vengeance and with no respect for sovereign decrees confined Pisani for ten years in the Castle of Verona, sent Contarini to die in exile at the Bocche di Cattaro and proscribed and condemned many others, no voice was heard of blame or of pity. Thus there was seen, unique example in history, a magistrate condemning as a crime what the Supreme Council of the Republic had judged suitable, opportune and decorous. To endure this barefaced insult without resentment and to leave languishing in prison and in exile those to whom it had entrusted the execution of its own decrees was, as one might say, a sign of the times. Such was the political order, such the endurance, of the Venetian people. Indeed, rather than live in such a way, or 'by accident' as the Most Serene Doge had said, it would have been a more civilized, as well as a more prudent and generous deed to seek death in some other manner. From this pass, it finally came to the day in which the menace of new things sounded with thunders far removed from the weak voices of a few domestic orators. The same day as the convocation of the States General was decreed in Paris, 14 July 1788, the Ambassador Antonio Cappello announced the news to the Doge, adding thereto grave considerations on the straits in which the Republic might find itself and the most suitable means of dealing with them. But the Most Excellent Savi threw the despatch into the file of unread correspondence; nor did the Senate have any knowledge of it. But the Inquisitors of State redoubled their vigilance and there began a continual terror of imprisonings, spyings, threats, bans and oppressions that, without diminishing the peril, made its imminence easily perceived, and maintained in the minds of the people a feeling of mingled fear and hatred. The Count Rocco Sanfermo meanwhile reported from Turin on the disorders in France and the secret plots of the Courts of Europe; Antonio Cappello, returned from Paris, insisted on an immediate debate.

The peril increased to such an extent that it was not feasible to overcome it without sharing it with some of the other contestants. But the Signoria was not accustomed to look beyond the Adda and the Isonzo and did not understand how, in its own tranquillity, the tumults and madnesses of others could be of importance; they thought that neutrality alone was useful and salutary, not foreseeing that it would be impossible. The tumult from without increased, the murmurs and the oppression increased within. The attitude of the government seemed to be to rely with firm confidence on itself and one by one all the governors felt in their hearts the indifference of despair. In such conditions, there were many who, more prudent than the others, got out of the difficulty by going away from Venice. And thus there remained at the helm of public affairs the many vainglorious, the very few studious of the public good and the multitude of the incapable, the thoughtless and the great mass of poor devils.

The most Excellent Almoro Frumier, kinsman of the Count of Fratta, possessed very extensive properties and a magnificent house at Portogruaro. He was among those who, without seeing clearly in the confusion, had none the less scented from afar the bad odour of pitch and had very little desire to soil his hands with it. Therefore, in full accord with his wife who was not unwilling to see once more those lands where her family enjoyed almost sovereign rights, he had moved to Portogruaro in the autumn of 1788. The health of the noble lady, who had need of the air of her native country for her convalescence, served as a pretext for their going; once arrived, they were firmly resolved not to set foot again in Venice until the last, smallest cloud had vanished. The two sons of the nobleman were deemed quite sufficient to guard the interests and the dignity of his house in Venice; as for him, the obsequiousness of the most illustrious provincials and of a whole city, compensated him abundantly for the perilous honour of holding forth in the Senate.

With a great complement of trunks, coffers, armchairs and other movables, the mature pair had embarked on a postal packet and had suffered painfully in the fifty hours of transit by marshes and canals until they had disembarked on the Lemene at their *villegiatura*. Thus the Venetians were wont to call their houses on the *terraferma*, whether at Milan or Paris or even at Portogruaro. The river bathed the foot of their garden and, scarcely arrived, they had the satisfaction of finding assembled all the best that the city had of every order of society. The Bishop, Monsignor de Sant'Andrea, many other of the clergy and the learned professors of the seminary, the Vice-Captain with his wife and other government dignitaries, the Podestà and all the Magistrates of the Commune, the Superintendent of Taxes and the Guardian of the Customs House with their respective consorts, sisters and kinswomen and finally the nobility in mass, and among the five thousand inhabitants of the district there were enough of them to furnish all the cities of Switzerland which, by misfortune, lacked any at all. From Fratta had come the Count with the Signora Contessa and her daughters, his brother the Monsignor, and the inseparable Chancellor. I, who in the meantime had aroused great hopes of my advancement by my very rapid progress in Latin, had obtained the signal grace of being allowed to climb up on the tail of the carriage and so from a corner was permitted to enjoy the spectacle of this solemn reception.

The noble patrician comported himself with the proverbial affability of the Venetians. From the Bishop to the gardener, no one was defrauded of the favour of his smile; with the first, he kissed his ring; with the second, he slapped him on the back, all with equal modesty. Then he turned to tell the boatmen to use especial care in unloading the furniture and that they should pay particular heed to his armchair, and then entered the house, giving his arm to his kinswoman, while his wife followed, accompanied by her brother. Refreshments were served in the great hall, where the old patrician apologized for the chill of the terraces, and then followed the usual greetings, the usual conversations. How beautiful the daughters were and how they had grown, how his kinswoman was looking younger than ever, his kinsman fresh as a rose, and how long, hot and tiring the voyage had been. The city was more flourishing than ever, the society very pleasant and worthy and their welcome very civil. For these ceremonies a good hour was needed, after which the visitors took their leave and only the family remained behind, to speak much good of themselves and some little evil of those who had left. Here also was used that Venetian simplicity and discretion which contented itself with cutting the clothes without scraping the flesh to the bone.

Towards the Ave Maria, those from Fratta took their leave, it being well understood that the visits would be frequently renewed. The noble Frumier had great need of company and also the Most Illustrious Count of Fratta was not a little proud of being related to, and showing his familiarity with, a genuine senator. The two kinswomen bestowed a peck on one another, the kinsmen wrung each other's hands, the girls made two deep curtsies and Monsignor and the Chancellor went on taking off their hats as far as the step into the carriage. They were comfortably installed within; I scrambled to my former place, and then the four strong horses had a hard job to drag this weighty convoy over the cobbles of the road. The Most Excellent Senator retired to his salon, very satisfied with his first appearance at his *villegiatura*.

Portogruaro was not the least among those little cities of the *terraferma* where the example of the Most Serene Dominant was copied and recopied with all possible fidelity. The houses, large, spacious and with triple windows in the centre of the façade, were aligned on both sides of the main street in such a manner that only water was lacking to complete the resemblance to Venice. A café every two sidestreets, before which was the usual awning below which, around a number of small tables, a bunch of idlers sat; a quantity of winged lions on all the public buildings; light women and boatmen in continual chatter in the streets and around the fruit-stalls; pretty girls at the balconies behind cages of canaries and vases of gilliflowers and basil; up and down by the townhall and in the piazza the black togas of advocates, the long tailcoats of notaries and the most worshipful cloaks of patricians; four Slavs in attendance before the prison; from the Lemene canal a stink of salt water, a blaspheming of boat masters and a constant confusion of wherries, anchors and cables; a continual ringing of church bells and great pomp of ceremonies and masses; little stucco Madonnas with flowers, wreaths and festoons at every corner, devout mammas kneeling with their rosaries, blonde daughters occupied with their lovers behind the doors; abbots with their eyes on their shoe-buckles and their cloaks wrapped modestly over their paunches; nothing, nothing was lacking in this miniature.

Even the three standards of San Marco had their facsimile in the piazza; a red mast whereon waved on solemn occasions the banner of the Republic . . . What more was needed? . . . The Venetians of Portogruaro had succeeded after a study of many centuries in unlearning the bastard and barbarous Fruili dialect which was spoken all around them, and now spoke Venetian with even greater caricature than the Venetians themselves. Nothing indeed annoyed them more than their dependence on Udine, which still existed to testify to their ancient ties with the Friuli. They were like the ennobled commoner who abhors the packtwine and awl because they remind him of his father, the shoemaker. But unfortunately its history had already been written and could not be altered. The citizens of Portogruaro retaliated by preparing for themselves a quite different one for the future and in their new phraseology coined the epithet Friulian to represent coarse, rustic, sordid and verminous. Once outside the city gates (they had been built very narrow as if they were expecting gondolas and not carriages and haywains) they seemed like fish out of water, or Venetians out of Venice. They pretended not to know wheat from maize though their market was full of sacks and samples every day, and they stopped to look at the trees like unaccustomed dogs and marvelled at the dust of the roads though their shoes betrayed a daily familiarity with it. When talking to the countrypeople they very nearly said: you of the *terraferma*. In fact, Portogruaro was, in their eyes, a sort of hypothetical island constructed on the model of the Most Serene Dominant, not indeed on the bosom of the seas, but set between large ditches of greenish muddy water. That they were not of the *terraferma* they showed in their own manner by the many walls, campaniles and house-facades that leant perilously. I believe that precisely for this reason they took care to place them on insecure foundations.

But the real, double-dyed Venetians were the ladies. The fashions of the capital were imitated and exaggerated with the greatest affectation. If at San Marco headdresses rose by two fingers, at

Portogruaro they rose by a couple of palms; hoop-petticoats were so inflated that a bunch of women became a real explosion of silks, laces and trimmings. Necklaces, bracelets, brooches and chains inundated their persons. I would not like to guarantee that the gems all came from Golconda or Peru but they dazzled the eye and that was enough. For the rest, the ladies rose at midday, spent four hours over their toilettes and passed the afternoon in paying visits. Since at Venice the main topics of the assemblies were the theatres, the comic opera, the tenors, they considered it obligatory to talk on the same subjects; thus the theatre of Portogruaro which was open for a month every second year, enjoyed the rare privilege of being discussed by a hundred polite voices for all the intervening twenty-three months. This material once exhausted, they gossiped about one another with really heroic fortitude. Everyone, be it understood, had her own *cicisbeo* and sought to steal those of others. Some carried this fashion to such an extent that they had two or even three with variously distributed privileges. One would offer the lady her fan, another her lorgnette, another her handkerchief or snuffbox; one had the pleasure of escorting the lady to Mass, another of taking her for a walk. But of this latter amusement they were in general, very sparing; not being able to enjoy the divine smoothness of a gondola, and being horror-struck at the very idea of the barbarous bumping of a carriage, they found themselves compelled to go out on foot, an insupportable labour for dainty Venetian feet. Some rough country-man or clownish castellan of the Friuli dared to say that this was the latest edition of the fable of the fox and the sour grapes and that, even had they desired it, they would not have been able to get even a peck at a carriage. I do not know which was right, but the great argument of sex decides me in favour of the ladies. Indeed there are now at Portogruaro many carriages; even though our coffers do not enjoy a great reputation in comparison with those of our grand-fathers. It is true that a carriage in those times was a really regal affair; when that of the Counts of Fratta appeared it was a real carnival for all the urchins of the city.

In the evening 'when one did not go to the theatre', cards pro-longed the night into the small hours; in this also they followed the Venetian fashion, and if this passion did not ruin many families, as in the capital, the merit must go to the prudent liberality of their husbands. On the green cloth instead of *zecchini* rolled soldi; but that was a municipal secret and no one would have betrayed it for all the gold in the world; strangers, however, listening to the events, the heartbeats and the triumphs of the evening recounted, could well have believed that the fortunes of a family had been at stake on every game, rather than a twenty soldi piece. Only at the house of the wife of the Correggitore were these limits surpassed, to go as far as half a ducat but envy avenged itself by accusing this lady of avarice and even of cheating. The few Venetian ladies married in Portogruaro or in residence with their husbands there for reasons of the civil administration, made common cause with the ladies of the place against this primacy of the Signora Correggitrice. But she had the good fortune to be beautiful and to know how to use her tongue like a real Venetian and give the most flattering glances that could be imagined. The young men flocked around her in church, in the café, in assemblies; and I could not say whether their homage or the envy of her rivals was the more pleasant to her. The wife of the Podestà, who always gesticulated with her white and delicate hands, used to say that the hands of the lady in question were like those of a scullery maid; the sister of the Superintendent asserted that she had a squint and so saying opened big blue eyes that aspired to be the most beautiful in the city and only succeeded in being the largest. Everyone, in common emulation, found something ugly or defective in those features in which she believed herself to be perfect; but the beautiful object of these calumnies, when her maid reported these jealous rumours, only smiled at her looking-glass. She had two lips so rosy, thirty-two little teeth so white and even, two round cheeks dimpled so amorously, that with her smile alone she could have her revenge on those who accused her.

You can imagine that the noble lady Frumier, as soon as she arrived, had immediately around her a swarm of these affected creatures. As a woman, she was in the spring of an age already more than mature; as a Venetian, she had forgotten the date of her birth and in her manners, her glances, her headdresses, she displayed the perpetual youth that is the singular privilege of her fellow citizens. As I have said, a fair number of Venetian ladies lived in Portogruaro, but all of these belonged either to the burgess class or to the lesser nobility. A great lady, a noblewoman of high lineage, experienced in all the usages, all the refinements of the assemblies, had till then been lacking. They were therefore overjoyed to possess so fine an example, to be able to look at her, idolize her and copy her at their leisure; to be able to say at last: 'Look at me! I speak, I laugh, I dress, I walk like the Senator Frumier's wife.' She, as shrewd as the devil himself, found great amusement in such follies. One evening she would chatter worse than a jackdaw, and on the following day had the amusement of hearing these ladies compete among themselves as to who could say the most words in a minute. Every gathering became a real twittering of sparrows. Another time she would play the languid beauty, spoke only in a subdued voice and with a sob; immediately the chatterboxes became mute and took on the manners of so many ladies in childbed. One day she made a wager with a gentleman recently arrived from Venice that she would put chicken feathers on the heads of all the principal ladies of the city. In fact she showed herself in public with this bizarre adornment on her headdress and the same day the wife of the Podestà deplumed her whole hen-roost to adorn her head in the same manner. However, the lady Frumier was merciful to the city's chickens by not insisting on this fashion, otherwise at the end of three days there would not have remained a single one with the adornments which nature had decreed for them. The assemblies of the noble lady Frumier eclipsed at a stroke all the others and attracted everyone to them. Smart remarks, glances and gestures were carefully prepared for these great events, and what had been said or done the evening before at the Frumier mansion was continually repeated. Let us add that the coffee tasted much better at these entertainments and that from time to time a bottle of maraschino or some cake from the convent of St. Vitus varied the enjoyment of the company.

The nobleman too, on his side, found bread for his teeth. Without showing himself in practice different from his grandfathers, he had been tinged academically with the modern philosophy and could quote at need in his broad Venetian accent some phrases from Voltaire or Diderot. Amongst the lawyers and clergy of the city there were not lacking educated and inquiring spirits like his own, who scrupulously divided precept from practice and when meeting together did not fear to question or even to deny what, had it occurred in the daily course of their professions, they would have declared as certain and indubitable. It is known how tolerant were the customs of the last century on this matter; at Venice they were more tolerant than elsewhere and at Portogruaro, tolerant out of all measure, because the men, like the women, were not content merely to follow the example of the capital but courageously went far beyond it. To mention only one, Monsignor de Sant'Andrea, the most syllogistic theologian of the capital once out of his curia and sitting down to argue in confidence with his equals, was not ashamed to twist the point of many of his own syllogisms. And among the younger inhabitants there was an occasional one who in the daring of his opinions left behind him all but the physicians of the city. The physicians, be it said in parenthesis, were in no way in great repute as devout persons.

However, among the labourers in the Lord's vineyard, there was a coarse, incorruptible, traditional party which opposed itself with the weighty force of inertia to the invasion of this elegant scepticism, garrulous and a trifle dissolute. Indeed, if some old priest, indulgent to the faults of others, maintained in his own life the simplicity and integrity of sacerdotal custom, it was indeed a rare case; in general, old or young, those who slid into anarchic philosophy did not afford a striking example of piety, of chastity or of any other virtue specially commended to the clergy. Such a relaxation of canonical discipline and the dogmatic indifference that accompanied it, could not appeal to the real priests; that is to those who had studied with blind confidence the Summa Theologia of St Thomas and had come out of the seminary with the persuasion of the immutable truth of their faith and of the sanctity of their own ministry. These, less fit because of their rigidity of conscience and the austerity of their manners, to consort with gentlemen and to adapt themselves to the moral artifices of the day, adapted themselves wonderfully to the patriarchal government of the country parishes.

The mountains are the usual nursery of the village clergy and that party which I have termed traditional was reinforced and renewed mainly in the frequent vocation of the youths of Clausedo, a large alpine district of the diocese. The secularists (as their adversaries termed those who in opinions and customs resembled the laymen) however, came from the well-to-do families of the city and the plain. In the first case, gravity, reserve, belief, if not enthusiasm and priestly self-denial, were perpetuated from uncle to nephew, from rector to chaplain; in the second, classical culture, philosophic liberty, the elegance of fashion and religious tolerance were instilled into them by the free discussions of their family circles; they became priests either thoughtlessly by obedience or by desire for a tranquil and comfortable life. Both these classes had their representatives and defenders in the seminary, in the curia and in the chapter; sometimes one and sometimes the other held the lead and every Bishop who succeeded to the diocese was accused either of favouring the secularists or the Clausedans. Clausedans and secularists were at one anothers' throats; the one accused the other of ignorance, tyranny, nepotism and avarice; they were answered by charges of dissoluteness, atheism, bad example and worldliness. The city for the most part supported the latter, the country the former; but the Clausedans by their natural temperament and the maxims that they defended were more in agreement among themselves and better ordered, while amongst their rivals, pettiness and individual levity precluded any sort of discipline or any method of conduct. This, however, did not prevent the dissensions of the clergy providing more fuel than was needful to the gossip of the assemblies, and the vivacious clerics of the easy life, if they did not compensate themselves at least revenged themselves with ridicule and mordant wit for the greater influence that their adversaries had obtained through centuries upon centuries of austerity and perseverance. The younger women were disposed to favour their party and only some old paralytics held for the rigorists, an effect more of envy than of conviction.

In short, I have tried to say that the noble Senator found also among the clergy a select circle that, cut on his own lines and accustomed to similar view points, his equals in learning and in culture, could help him to pass some very pleasant hours. It pleased him to converse, to argue, to discuss freely, to tell and hear stories and somewhat highly flavoured anecdotes and to enliven the discourse with jokes and proverbs without some prude turning up his nose. He found men to his taste. Not even pellets of mercury run together with such pertinacity as men of similar tastes to form a society. Therefore, in the assemblies of the senator was formed little by little a circle separate from the others, which took its place around the master of the house. Everyone, it is true would like to have entered this circle, but not all have the courage to take part in a discussion without understanding it, to laugh when others laugh without knowing why, to receive a stamp on the foot after showing a merry face, and to remain in the midst of a number of good fellows without being questioned and without risking a single word. The ignorant, therefore, the foolish, the hypocrites and the superficial retired very soon, and there remained the purest gold of the refined, the learned, the witty. There remained the Canon of Sant'Andrea, the advocate Santellini, two or three other men of the law, the young Giulio del Ponte, Professor Dessalli and one or two other professors of the fine arts, a certain Don Marco Chierini, renowned as the most perfect example of an elegant abbe, and three or four Counts or Marquises who had known how to combine the love of books with the love of women and the study of antiquity with modern usages. Then, since we are on the subject, it is worth noting that there could be no educated or cultured persons who had not at their fingers' ends the constitutions of Athens and of Sparta. The stories of Lycurgus, of Socrates, of Solon and of Leonidas were the usual theme of school discourses; a most curious contradiction between so much servility and blind obedience and so much heedlessness of virtue and of licence.

The fact was that while the ladies and the rest of the company shuffled packs of cards at the tables, this little Academy of the Senator met in a corner of the Salon to chat about politics and exchange banter on the most scandalous news of the city. It was a very varied orchestra, a real serio-comic opera, full of themes both ridiculous and sublime, comic and serious, gay and spiteful; an interweaving of disputes, gibes, reticences and anecdotes that made up a real mosaic of words, a masterpiece of Venetian temperament that, like the art of a Benvenuto Cellini, was to be admired down to its minutest detail.

There was talk of the affairs of Germany and of France in the most outspoken manner; there was comment on the voyages of Pius VI, the aims of Joseph II, the intentions of Russia and the movements of the Turks. The most varied authorities were quoted in the discussions, Machiavelli, Sallust, Cicero and Aretino; the affairs of those times were compared with the chapters of Titus Livy and in such grave discussions there was never a lack of jokes and laughter and every opportunity for a jest was welcomed.

But I assure you that for these whimsical fellows it was a matter of little moment to leap from the scandals of Catherine II to the amorous adventures of this lady or that cavalier. The name of one person mentioned reminded them of two more, and these two of another four and so always onward. They respected neither the absent nor the present, and the latter had the good taste to put up with the raillery and not try to revenge themselves at once, but to await a favourable moment to turn the tables, which always came, sooner or later. Much culture, rather superficial if you will, but vast and in no way pedantic, much wit, great subtlety of conversation and above all an infinite dose of tolerance comprised the talk of this little areopagitica.

The gentlemen of Fratta, freed from that scarecrow of Venchieredo, had returned to their usual way of life. The chaplain had preserved his cure of souls and did not cease to welcome at his house at least once a week his old friend and penitent, Spaccafumo. The Count and the Chancellor closed an eye; the Rector of Teglio made an occasional reproof. But this skinny little priest who could scarcely stammer a reply to the rebukes of a superior, knew very well how to look after himself as soon as that superior had turned his back. Meanwhile, for official reasons and because he was a neighbour, Dr Natalino of Venchieredo had become friendly with the Chancellor and the Count of Fratta. Signor Lucilio, a close friend of Leopardo Provedoni, had made acquaintance with his wife also and thus, one step after another, the lively Doretta had made an occasional appearance at the evening parties at the castle. But now, twice a week, there were quite different entertainments from evening parties. They had to go to pass the evening at Portogruaro at the assemblies of His Excellency Frumier; a most perilous enterprise with the roads as they were then, but even the Countess was so insistent on appearing at her kinswoman's that she found courage to attempt it. One of her daughters was already ripe for marriage and the other growing like a weed; the first scarcely launched as yet, the second a young girl who, though of some education, needed to be introduced to the world so as to acquire a certain self-reliance. Then, too, it was necessary for them to be seen, for suitors reason above all with their eyes and these two certainly lost nothing for being looked at.

Such were the arguments put forward by the Signora to persuade her husband to adventure with the carriage twice a week on the Portogruaro road. But first of all the most prudent Count sent out a dozen labourers to repair the most scabrous passages and fill the deepest holes on the way, and gave orders to the coachman to drive at a walking pace and that two lackeys with lanterns should precede the equipage. The two lackeys were Manichetto, son of Fulgenzio, and Sandro of the mill, who were dressed for the sake of show in scarlet coats cut out of two old horse-cloths. I mounted on the hind box and through the whole journey, which was three good miles, amused myself by watching the Pisana through the little window at the back. Why I too was allowed to accompany the family on these visits, during which I spent my time drowsing in the Frumier kitchen, I will now explain.

As the Count dragged behind him the Chancellor, so the Chancellor dragged me. I was, in short, the shadow of the shadow; but in this case, my becoming a shadow did not greatly displease me, since it afforded me a pretext to follow the Pisana, between whom and myself love continued at full blast, interrupted and varied by the usual jealousies, only to be resumed by habit and necessity. Between a boy of thirteen and a little girl of eleven such little intrigues were no longer matters for mockery. I at least took them seriously, she no less so; her parents did not concern themselves at all while the maids and the servants, after my memorable exploits and my transformation into a pupil of the Chancellery, had come to respect me as a little gentleman and leave me to my own devices in everything. Our little game therefore continued, becoming ever more serious and I began to conceive certain romances, which if I were to relate them now, my confessions would go on indefinitely.

But however that may be, some changes had taken place in my feelings also; while at one time the caresses of the Pisana had seemed to me due only to her kindness, now, feeling myself grown in importance, I attributed some part of them to my own merits. Capperi! From the little Carlino of the spit, clothed in the servants' cast-offs and Monsignor's rags, to the well-combed Latin scholar, with a fine black cloak on his back, well shod and with two little brass buckles on his shoes and a little jacket of blue velvet and maroon breeches, there was a great difference! . . . My skin, too, no longer exposed to the sun and the vagaries of the weather, had become much more civilized. I discovered that it was even white and that my large brown eyes were at least as good as anyone else's; my figure daily grew taller and slimmer, I had a not unpleasing mouth and a fine set of teeth, not set so close as to cause inconvenience, but which, none the less, shone like ivory. Only those accursed ears, due to the Rector's pullings, took up too much space on my head; but I tried to correct this defect by sleeping one night on one side and the next night on the other, in order to give them a more aesthetic form. Enough! I touch them even now, and perceive that I succeeded moderately well. Martino never tired of admiring me, saying: 'It is really true that to bring out beauty one must be well scolded. You are the handsomest Carlino of the whole neighbourhood, even though you were born out of the ashes of the hearth and most of the milk you got I gave you!' The poor man had become hunchbacked little by little as I grew up, and now his strength was failing; he grated his cheese sitting and could no longer hear even a cannon shot close to his ears. But it made no difference; he and I continued to understand one another by signs and I believe that to remain alone in the world or to live in it without me would have been for him an equal misfortune. As for the old Countess, he still went upstairs to keep her company during Clara's absences, but the difference in their ways and the social gulf between them prevented them from having in common those signs of intelligence by which it is possible to make oneself understood by the deaf.

The appearance of the noble family of Fratta and especially of the Contessina Clara at the assemblies in the Frumier mansion had introduced there a new element of castellans and petty county nobility. One of the first to run there was the Partistagno, who, after the aid he had brought to the castle during the assault by Venchieredo, had become a sort of guardian angel of the family. He, it must be said, wore the aureole of his glory proudly enough, but the facts justified him and even if one laughed at him, it was impossible to deny his right to it. Lucilio suffered greatly from this haughty attitude of the young cavalier, but his sufferings were more from envy than jealousy. It pained him more than anything else that the service rendered by the Partistagno to the Count of Fratta had not been due to him. Otherwise he was sure of Clara; every glance of hers comforted him with fresh hopes; even the calm with which she accepted the gallantries of the Partistagno was to him an earnest that no danger would ever threaten him from that quarter. How could he not confide himself utterly to a heart so pure, to a conscience so upright and fervent? He had spoken many times alone with her, either in the dining-hall or in the corridors, since the first declaration of their love; almost every day he had passed an hour with her in her grandmother's room and was ever more enamoured of this innocent and angelic beauty, this heart fervent and virginal in its mute tranquillity. His fiery and tyrannical nature had need of a soul with which it could rest with the quiet certainty of affection. He had found such a one and loved it as the dying Capuchin loves his part in heaven; and with his heart and with his nature and with all the thousand arts of an imaginative spirit and an omnipotent will, he had striven to bind to her with ever fresh bonds that other part of himself that felt itself existent only in Clara. She let herself yield deliciously to so much force of love; she, the young girl, loved with all the strength of her soul, and thought no more of it, since God protected her innocence, her happiness, and she was sufficiently happy not to fear anything or to blush for anything. That gloomy and false maxim that forbids maidens love as a perversity had never entered the articles of her religion. To love was her law; and she had obeyed it and still obeyed it devoutly.

Thus she did not trouble to hide that sweet sentiment which Lucilio had inspired in her; and if the Count and Countess had not noticed it, it was only because, in their view, such a thing was so outside possibility that they could not even entertain the suspicion. Furthermore, it was not absolutely forbidden to the maidens of that time to fall in love with whomsoever they wished; it was enough if the passion went no further. The people of the castle whispered that when the Contessina married, Dr Lucilio would become her *cavaliere servente*. But one day when Rosa made some joke or other on the subject to the young man, I remember seeing him turn pale and bite his moustaches with a scowl. Even the old Countess, in my opinion, had discovered Clara's secret; but she was so taken with the young man that she twisted the discovery to the advantage of her grand-daughter. Perhaps also her imagination, unconscious servant of her interests, made her find a thousand arguments to forget these fears. Lucilio would, she thought, show so much restraint that Clara would be calmed. She knew, or believed that she knew, the good old woman, those lovely golden clouds that float through the imaginations of young girls. But they are only clouds, she argued, clouds that pass away at the first puff of wind. The puff of wind would be the offer of a good match and the command of her parents.

But how far she really knew Clara's temperament and its resemblance to her own, we shall see later. Certainly, however, the reserved bearing of Lucilio served to lull her in her comfortable assurance, but had it been permitted her to see into the substance of the affair, she would perhaps not have believed so easily in the mild transience of those clouds and would have resolved to deprive herself of the last pleasures that remained to her and to take from the two young people the foundations of those castles in the air that were so impossible of realization. But as things were, she was happy to be able to rely on the discretion and even temperament of Clara and say to herself, when Clara had left the room to light Lucilio down the stairs: 'Oh, what an honest youth! Would one not say that he is afraid to lift his eyes so high since he could never think that my grand-daughter could mean anything to him? If he lifts them it is only to look at me; and at his age! It is really miraculous!' But Lucilio had other moments to let his spirit take flight at its will, and in these moments, it must be confessed, those eyes of his, so honest and so discreet, committed no small sins of infidelity against the old grandmother.

In the dining-hall, when everyone was playing cards and he seemed intent on looking over Monsignor's 'three-seven' or patting Marocco, the Captain's dog, there was a continual exchange of glances between him and Clara which gave him the sense of an angelic voice singing in his heart while his ears were assailed with a tumult of cracked bells. How dear those divine harmonies that beautify the soul without hindering the rough tumult of the drums! The religion of things imperceptible and eternal are married in the mind as are light and colour in the rays of the sun. Sentiment in thought is the finest triumph over the sensations of the body; it proves that the soul lives outside its envelope, even without the added ministry of material things. Love that begins in the spirit cannot end in the flesh; it conquers the experiences of human fragility, to return pure and eternal to the immense love of God the universal. Lucilio felt the divine magic of those thoughts, without justifying them in his judgement as a doctor. They seemed to him phenomena outside of nature and he returned to and studied them without gaining other than a fresh fervour and an even more resolute tenacity of passion.

When Clara was taken by her family to her aunt's assemblies, the little Fossalta doctor easily found a way to enter that circle. The Venetian code of conduct was never so unjust as to deny the entrance of good education, wit and real merit into the halls of the patricians, even if a quartered coat-of-arms was lacking to give support to those good qualities. Lucilio was much esteemed at Portogruaro and enjoyed the favour and close friendship of many young professors of the seminary. He was therefore presented to the illustrious Senator by them, and they shortly had occasion to be thanked for this act as for a signal favour. Further, the Senator had known Dr Sperandio for many years since he had had recourse to him on every matter of need when he was in Venice. He therefore gently reproved the son of his old friend for having thought the intervention of some third person necessary before presenting himself in his house. When he took leave of him the first evening, he had congratulated him, saying that, in his view, the good things that had been said of him were a mere nothing to what he would himself have to say later on. The young man bowed modestly, feigning not to be able to find words to reply to such great condescension. Indeed Lucilio's conversation was so witty, so lively and so varied that few gave so much pleasure as he. Professor Desalli alone surpassed him in erudition, while the palm for wit and subtlety remained in suspense between him and Giulio del Ponte. If del Ponte sometimes excelled him in quickness and fluency, Lucilio soon had his revenge with his depth and irony. He pleased the men as a mature mind. Giulio had the youth of the spirit and an instinctive gift of attracting sympathy; but to make people think, leaves in the spirit deeper traces than to make people laugh. This, as well as being, like the first, a gracious gift from equal to equal, is a real tribute imposed by the great upon the little, by the strong upon the weak. Lucilio knew how to impose it worthily and exact it with discretion; wherefore they were compelled to value it and in addition to be grateful for it.

The presence of Lucilio revived the intimate circle of the Senator with an immediate flame of enthusiasm. He enlivened, kindled, exhorted these spirits, subtle and well-informed, but tepid and unadventurous. In his presence, whatever remained to them of youth and life was stirred to an unaccustomed fervour. They forgot what they had been and what they were, to borrow from him a last dream of youth. They laughed, chattered, jested and disputed no longer like men only intent on killing time, but as persons lively and inquisitive who sought to make the most of it. It seemed that each one of them had found a fresh aim in life. One voice alone, whose words breathed a lofty and mysterious hope, one brow alone on which shone that faith in an intelligence that never dies, had been enough to do so much.

The Senator when he was left alone and had sunk back once more into his usual indifference, was astonished at the warm outbursts of enthusiasm, that vigorous impetuosity of discussions and arguments in which he had felt himself carried away like a schoolboy. He reasoned that it was because of the example and proximity of younger men; it was, in fact, the flame of life which, stirred from its embers by a powerful magician, though still not enough to warm the already frozen fibres of his heart, had filled his head with fire and given fervour to his tongue. 'One would almost believe that I took seriously all those sophistries in which they involve themselves to pass the time,' he mused, sitting in his armchair waiting for his supper, 'and for forty years I have not even smelt the venerable dust of a college!' 'Perhaps it is true that men are eternally boys!' murmured the old man, stroking his flabby and wrinkled cheeks, 'if Heaven so wills!'

After Lucilio had intervened to kindle the enthusiasm of the Senator's courtiers, those who sat at the gaming tables, the ladies in particular, suffered from frequent distractions. This continual uproar of questions and answers, of accusations and rejoinders, of jokes, laughter, exclamations and applause, moved the curiosity and, let us say it, even the envy of the players. The diversions of 'quintilio' and the excitements of 'three-seven' were much less vibrant, and when a 'capot' had drawn the usual ironical congratulations and the usual threats of revenge, that finished that, and everyone turned once again to the monotonous ups and downs of the game, like tired carriage horses.

Meanwhile in the other corner of the salon, the conversation was always varied, gay, general and animated. Ears began to listen to what was going on there and eyes to grow wearied of the cards. 'But, Signora, it's your turn. Didn't you understand the challenge?' 'I'm sorry, I have a slight headache,' or 'I didn't notice; my thoughts were far away.' They bickered at one another across the tables and at last the culprits settled down again to play. Lucilio entered not a little into all this by-play, and he knew it. He knew the effect he had produced on the assembles of the Senator and he flattered himself indirectly on a generous gratitude from Clara. Love has a pride all its own. On the one side it tries to reach greater heights to please the more and on the other it has a pride in seeing others pleased by what is intended to please one alone. Giulio del Ponte, who perhaps like Lucilio had some motive for wanting to make himself pleasant to the ladies, whetted his own talents to play bourdon to his companion. And the rest of the company, towed along by these two youths, competed in quickness and wit in the most serious discussions that could be held on some phrases from the *Gazetta di Venezia*, the mother of all newspapers.

Indeed the Venetians of that time must have invented and in fact did invent the *Gazetta*; it was a genuine and legitimate child of their imagination and it was due to them only that the library of chit-chat was opened. The Senator received his *Gazetta* every week and many comments were made on its contents; but even in this work of refinement and ingenuity, Lucilio left all others far behind. No one knew so well how to search out at one end of the world the reasons for what was happening at the other. 'What an eye you have, my dear doctor!' they said to him in wonder, 'for you England and China are within range of a telescope and you can find as many links between them as between Venice and Fusina!' Lucilio replied that the earth is but a ball, which turns and moves as a whole, and that after Columbus and Vasco di Gama had remade it as it was created, it was no matter for surprise that its blood had resumed its vast circulation through the whole great body from the equator to the poles.

When he embarked on such discourses, the Senator would close one eye and with the other half closed, would observe Lucilio, while he ruminated over past days, when this youth had left a good many black marks on the books of the Inquisitors of State. Perhaps some vague fear still passed through the head of the scrupulous Venetian; but it was now some years since Lucilio had stirred from Fossalta; his life was now that of a tranquil well-to-do youth of the countryside; the Inquisitors must have forgotten him, and he them, and his youthful misdoings. Doctor Sperandio, on a diplomatic visit to his most excellent patron, had reassured him, confessing that he had never flattered himself in the old days, that he would find in his son the docility and calm that he now showed in his modest and laborious life. 'Oh, if he would only consent to take his laureate,' exclaimed the old doctor, 'without stopping at Venice, naturally!' he added with hasty repentance, 'but, I say, if he gets his laureate, what a splendid clientele he would find ready for him!'

'There is still time, there is still time!' replied the Senator. 'Meanwhile you will see that your son grows more mature, that he gets rid of all these follies, that he preserves his good-humour and wit, and does not take seriously the literary fantasies of the writers. The laureate will come along one day or another and there is never a shortage of sick people for a doctor who knows how to heal them.'

'*Morbus omnis arte hippocratica sanatur aut laevatur*,' added the doctor.

Since this conversation took place after lunch, there were certainly another half dozen of such texts; but that I do not know for sure and in any case want to spare my readers their interpretation.

Lucilio had thus become, as the common people say, the 'ladies' pet'. Those feather-brains, according to the capricious laws of love, let themselves be captured easily by whoever becomes in any way a leading figure. No pleasure perhaps exceeds that of being envied by all. But Lucilio did not accord this pleasure to any of them. He was gay, whimsical, brilliant on his rare excursions among the tables; whence he would always return to play the leading part in the Senator's circle without having let even the tip of his handkerchief make a sign to any of those odalisques. Only, while passing to and fro, he found a way of enveloping Clara with one of those glances that seemed to enfold her, like the salamander, in an atmosphere of fire. The young girl trembled in every fibre at this sudden and unexpected conflagration, but the serene and innocent soul replied to his speaking eyes with a calm smile. It seemed that a magnetic current flashed with a thousand strings through the veins of the girl without being able to disturb the deep recesses of her spirit. More impassible than an abyss, more solid than a rock, her conscience interposed. Her modesty, rather than the inconspicuous place in which she usually sat, protected Clara from the inquisitive interest of the other ladies. She knew how to make herself forgotten without difficulty, and no one could suspect that Lucilio's heart beat especially for her, who less than any of the others took pains to gain it for herself. The Signora Correggiatrice did not use such discretion. From the very first evening her eagerness, her coquetries, her affectations, aimed at the desirable youth from Fossalta, had struck the eye of the Podestà's wife and the sister of the Superintendent. But these two in their turn made themselves conspicuous for the over-indifference that they displayed; in fact, Paris among the goddesses could not have been more involved than Lucilio among all these ladies; he extricated himself by not noticing anything at all.

There was, however, one Signorina who perhaps more than any other, even more than the Signora Correggiatrice herself, followed the triumphs of Lucilio, who never took her eyes off him, who blushed whenever he approached her and had no shame in coming up to him to touch his arm or to stroke his clothes, and look him close in the eyes. This impudent one was the Pisana! Imagine to yourself a little flirt of not yet twelve years old, a little lover scarcely four feet high! But it was just as I have said; and I was forced to realize it through the all-seeing eye of jealousy. The third and fourth times I went to the Frumier mansion, I had observed the little one paying greater attention to adorning herself, to curling her hair, to arranging her ribbons. No clothes seemed smart enough for her, no attention enough for the preparation of her hair or nails. Since she had not shown this folly on the first or second visits, I assumed that this was not due to the usual feminine vanity or the desire to be admired by the other ladies. Till then the martyrdom of certainty had seemed to me less formidable than the torments of doubt; but when I later acquired that cruel certainty, I seemed to bewail the unworthy felicity of still being able to doubt.

The fact was that when the servants went upstairs to serve the coffee, I slipped up with them into the salon and, half hidden behind the portiere, watched all that went on. I saw the Pisana with her eyes fixed on Lucilio as if she wanted to eat him. Her little head turned towards him like a sunflower towards the sun; when he spoke with greater warmth, or turned away from his company, I saw her little breast swell proudly like that of a woman grown. She did not speak, did not breathe, did not look save for him. All the signs of the most intense and violent love were expressed in her attitude; only her very tender years saved her from the comments and suspicions of the ladies, even as modesty had saved her sister. I trembled all over, ground my teeth and clutched the portiere in my hands as if I were on the brink of death. Then it flashed into my mind why the Pisana had been so sulky with me those last few days and why she had not talked and laughed as much as usual, but had been pensive and disposed to solitary places and the moon.

'Ah, traitress!' cried with a groan my poor heart. For even more than the anguish of unhappy love, I felt hate swell in my heart. I would have liked to have been clutching a bunch of thunderbolts only to hurl them at that lofty and abhorred brow of Lucilio; I would have liked my spirit to be a poison to dissolve his every fibre and to torment his nerves until death. To me nothing mattered any more since then for the first time I tasted the bitterness of life and hated it almost as much as I hated Lucilio as the occasion, if not the cause, of all my pain.

Then I saw the little flirt, taking advantage of the privilege of her years, take the coffee cup from the hands of a servant and give it herself to the young man. The girl was as red as a burning coal; her eyes shone brighter than jewels as I had never seen them shine before; she seemed at that moment no longer a child, but a pleasing young girl, perfect and, what was worse, in love. When Lucilio took the cup from her hand, her knees trembled and she spilled several drops of coffee on his coat; the young man smiled at her amiably and leant down to rub them with his handkerchief. Oh, if you could have seen her then, that little girl scarcely higher than the ground! . . . Her face had a more voluptuous expression than ever Greek sculptor could have given to his Venus or his Leda; a moist and beatific mist swam in her eyes and her little person seemed to melt with such weakness that Lucilio had to put out an arm to hold her up. I bit my hands and lips and tore my breast and my cheeks; I felt within me an impetus which almost compelled me to break in upon this odious spectacle, but a mysterious force held me rooted to the floor. At last, thank God, Lucilio returned to his discussion and the Pisana to sit close to her mamma. But the sweet confusion that remained on her features continued to torment me until the servants went out with the silver salvers.

'Oh Carlino, what are you doing here?' one of them cried to me. 'Get out of my way and go back to the kitchen. This is no place for you.'

These words seemed to put the climax to my pain, but instead worked on me like a poison, icy and insidious, that calmed it.

'Yes,' I said to myself with gloomy desperation, 'this is not my place.'

I went back to the kitchen tottering like a drunken man and remained there with my eyes fixed on the embers of the hearth until I was told that the horses were harnessed and that it was time to leave. Then I had once more to see, on the staircase, the Pisana obstinately following Lucilio like a pet dog its master. Indifferent to all others, she got into the carriage, still watching him only, and I saw her lean out of the window to look at the spot where he had stood long after he had left it. I meanwhile took up my usual place like the poor disinherited being that I was; and what my thoughts were for all that long hour necessary to get back to the castle, God alone knew! . . .

Thoughts they were not, but rather delirium, blasphemies, laments and curses. That thin wall of leather that divided my place from hers, I knew very well what it presaged for the future. A thousand times I had thought the day would come when the cursed power of human affairs would take her from me and give her to another; but to another not desired, not loved, scarcely even suffered. It was a comfort to me to imagine her inundated with tears and pale with sorrow under the white bridal veil, going to the altar as a victim; and then in the shadows of the marriage-bed giving herself without love and without desire to the master to whom she would have been sold. Her heart would have remained mine and our souls would have continued to love one another; I would have been very happy to see her pass, now and again, among her children; it would have been a blessing for me to take hold of one of them when she was not looking and to crush it to my heart, to kiss it, to adore it, to search in its features for traces of hers and to delude myself into thinking that the mysterious part of her spirit that had been transposed into that child had belonged also to me when she had loved me alone with all the power of her soul.

A boy of not yet fourteen, I had long known the ways of the world; the unbridled chatter of the servants and maids had taught me more than needful; and yet I had tried to beat down the confused tumult of the senses and to put a brake on the enthusiasms of an enamoured imagination to desire an existence rich only in sweet sorrow and melancholy joy. As a reward for my efforts, for my devotion, I had instead reaped forgetfulness and ingratitude. She had not even set me aside for another love; in that there would have been the comfort of struggle, of revenge. No, I had been discarded like a useless tool in order that she might run after a vain idea of pride, to pursue a ridiculous and impossible dream. The hatred that I had first conceived for Lucilio turned little by little into a fierce disdain for the Pisana. Lucilio was for her an old man, who had never before seemed to her either handsome or amiable; it had needed the homage of others before she could value in him qualities too high and virile for her still childish judgement. I saw myself sacrificed without remorse to vanity.

'She hasn't a scrap of heart, not a spark of memory, not a shred of shame! Yes, I despise her as she deserves and I will always despise her!' I cried to myself.

Poor child! I began from then both to love and to despise; the most terrible torment amongst all those that cruel nature has prepared for her sons; a perversion of every moral principle; a servitude without reward and without hope, in which the soul, which yet sees the good and loves it, is compelled to stoop, to pray, to supplicate before the image of evil. I had too much heart and too good a memory. The recollection of those first childish affections pursued me without mercy. I fled from them in vain, in vain I tried to combat them with reason; more ancient than reason, they sought out all the crannies and hiding places of my soul. At their mortal breath a tempest awoke within me, a tempest of desire, of rage, of fury and of tears. Oh, think well on them, these two words, wherein are embodied the whole story of my sorrows and my tears, meditate on them well, and then say if all the eloquence of passion, all the sentiments of pains endured, all the sincerity of repentance would explain to me their horrible significance. I despised and I loved!

Perhaps you will laugh at these two children in my story who are pretending to be grown up; but I swear to you once and for all that I am not embroidering a romance; I am simply repeating the story of my life. I record aloud and write down what I have recorded. I wager too that if any of you try to go back to your first childhood memories, many of you would find in them the germs and almost the mirror of the passions that afterwards ennoble. Believe me; if little girls are born women in miniature, little boys are equally miniatures of men. The lash of the tutor and the necessary round of daily occupations keep them subdued as a rule up to a certain age. But allow them to go, to do and to think as they will and you will soon see reflected in them, as in the restricted circle of a microscope, all the various germs of passions more mature. The Pisana and I had been left to grow as God willed and as was the custom at that time, making allowance for the intervals of college. From such an education, surrounded by such bad examples, was formed that sheep-like flock of men who without faith, without force, without illusions, reach half-alive the threshold of life and thence till death are dragged in the mud of dissipation and oblivion. The worms that await them in the sepulchre could well serve them as companions in this life also.

I for my part, either by luck or by temperament, or by merit of the adversities that had strengthened my spirit from the earliest days, could remain upright and not foul myself in that morass to be smeared by it for ever. But the Pisana, so much better endowed than I with great gifts and very good inclinations, grew up deprived by misfortune of all the expedients that could save her. Moreover her nature, so vivacious, flexible and lively, was clouded and made sterile in that frenzy of dissipation that had completely invaded her, in that flame of the senses in which she was left to burn and to find consumed therein the finest part of her soul. Her courage, her pity, her generosity, her imagination, the soundest fruits of her nature, so far degenerated that they only remained, in moments of respite, as passing flashes, strange and sudden impulses, of instinct, not conscious and meritorious actions of real virtue.

This deplorable ruin had begun in early infancy; at the time of which I am now telling it had already gone so far that although it might still perhaps have been possible to check it, its effects could not be destroyed; when, later, I was in a position to know it well and to recognize in it the cause whereby the defects of her childhood grew ever worse with the years, then no power in the world could have rescued her. Oh, with what tears of desperation and love did I not bewail that the centuries of marvels and miracles had passed! With what ardours of hope did I not devour those books which teach us that souls are regenerated by affection, by patience and by sacrifice! . . . With what humility, with what courage did I not offer myself piece by piece for that holocaust, so that that fallen angel whom I had seen in the dawn of life in all her gay splendour, should once again recover the glory of her light! . . . But the books lie, or else the Pisana was so made that it was beyond the power of man to change her. The heavens opened before her once and I saw what my reason could hardly believe, but which my heart has treasured as the purest of my joys. How near today seems to me that final day of recompense and of infinite sorrow! . . . But when I lived in the Castle of Fratta it was still far away and my mind would have been terrified to know that my love would receive its most certain reward from the hands of death!

In the days following that evening when I had suffered so much, I began to grow so thin and wan that everyone feared I had some illness. They wanted me, at any price, to have my pulse felt by Dr Lucilio, but that I refused obstinately, and, since the evil did not get any worse, they let me be, persuaded that it was some childish ailment. The maids noticed very quickly that the affection between me and the Pisana had greatly cooled, but they were very far from believing that to be the cause of my condition. They were accustomed to these interludes of coldness between us and did not give the whole matter any more importance than to a childish fancy. After a couple of days, the Pisana also noticed my pallor and my withdrawal and then, as if divining my secret, did her best to approach me and be kind to me. But I had already passed from the fury of desperation to the weariness of sorrow and welcomed her with a melancholy and almost piteous expression. This last mood in no way pleased her and she pretended to believe that I had shown that I did not want her and left me alone like a dog. Oh, if she had only thrown her arms around my neck! I would have been sufficiently credulous or cowardly to press her to my heart and forget the cruel moments I had lived through because of her. Perhaps it was better so; since on the next day my sorrow would have shown itself anew and would have left me weaker than before.

Despite my poor health, every time that the family went to Portogruaro I never failed to accompany them, and there every evening I relished with bitter melancholy the certainty of my ill fortune. It strengthened my spirit but my body suffered mortally and I would certainly not have been able to continue such a life for long. Martino often used to ask me why I sighed so much, the Rector marvelled at not finding my Latin exercises as correct as they had been before, but lacked the courage to reprove me, so much did my exhaustion move him to pity. The Contessina Clara was continually near me with tender and kindly attentions. I grew thinner daily and the Pisana pretended not to notice anything and if by chance she vouchsafed me a glancy of pity, it was immediately withdrawn. She wanted in this way to punish me for my pride. But was it indeed pride?

I was dying from heartbreak and yet felt sorrow for the one who was the cause of my death. I pitied her and I loved her, when I ought to have hated her, despised her, punished her. Who can say that the pride was mine? But at that moment, it happened that the Signora Contessa by good fortune fell ill. I say by good fortune because this interrupted the visits to Portogruaro and was the reason why I did not die. Lucilio continued his ministrations in the Castle even more than before since the Countess too called for him as a doctor; but the Pisana was not by a long way as enchanted with him at Fratta as she had been at Portogruaro. Once or twice she paid him some attention, then ceased to do so without effort and little by little returned to her former indifference towards him. Step by step as Lucilio went out of her heart, I re-entered it and I did not hide that my joy at this repentance was so vehement, so full, that it seemed as if I had been restored to the full confidence of our first affections. I was a boy and believed blindly. Despite her passing flirtatiousness I trusted her, sure that in the depths of her heart nobody existed save I, and I soon persuaded myself that the fruits of her repentance must be eternal. I managed to find in her apparent infidelities and rapid repentances one proof the more that she could love no one but me and could not live without me. I told her no word of my sufferings and avoided replying to her questions, guessing that a confession of jealousy is the warmest incentive to a fresh infidelity. I blamed my ill-temper and closed the way to further inquiries in order to give rein to my joy and to the relief of feelings so long repressed.

The Pisana played with me like a little madcap and it seemed that her momentary fancy had left no traces either on her memory or on her conscience; I consoled myself with that, while if I had been well advised, I should have taken fright at it. I therefore gave myself up with complete assurance to that current of happiness that transported me, so much surer and happier in that the Pisana seemed to me in those days more docile and loving and even more humble and patient than she had ever been before. Was it a tacit reward, unconsciously offered me, for the wrongs done me? I could not say. Perhaps even her timid adoration of Lucilio had weaned her little soul from its violent and tyrannical habits; it was therefore my part to reap where another had sown. But this doubt which now so humiliates me did not then even pass through my mind. One must have lived and philosophized for long in order to learn how to torment oneself so exquisitely.

The Contessa, though only slightly indisposed, improved slowly enough. She was so filled with caprices and affectations that all the Italian and Latin eloquence of Dr Sperandio, the patience of Lucilio, the sympathy of Monsignor di Sant'Andrea, the attentions of her husband and Clara, plus four potions a day, were insufficient to calm her even a little. But one day when a visit from her Frumier kinswoman was announced, she rallied immediately and forgot her countless afflictions to comb her hair, tidy herself, put on her head the prettiest and rosiest cap in her wardrobe and bedeck her bed with pillows and coverlets trimmed with lace. From that moment her convalescence was assured and it was possible to sing a Te Deum in the chapel for the recovery of the health of the most excellent patroness. Monsignor Orlando sang that Te Deum out of the fulness of his heart since they had never eaten so badly at Fratta as during the illness of his kinswoman. Everyone had been occupied in distilling concoctions, preparing bread-soups and carrying broths and bowls, and the cauldrons meanwhile remained empty and at lunch-time they had to content themselves with improvised snacks. But to restore the household to its usual daily round and to transform the convalescence of the Countess into rude health, not less than four or five visits from her kinswoman were necessary; by which time we had reached the depths of winter. But the blooming of those precious cheeks was now assured for another thirty years. Monsignor Orlando saw again with pleasure the space before the hearth little by little refurnished by stewpans and bubbling cauldrons. If this régime of semi-abstinence had continued, he would have paid with his own life for the recovery of his kinswoman.

I and the Pisana had meanwhile gained some months of good accord and of peace. Good accord I say in a manner of speaking, since in fact we had returned to our lives as before; that is to say to the petty amours, the affronts, the jealousies and reconciliations of the past. Donato, the apothecary's little son, and Sandro of the mill sometimes made me boil with anger. But these were quite another matter. To these childish spites I had long been accustomed and besides, the Pisana, even if she were hard and stubborn in her relations with me, was three times more so to the other boys. I did not mark anything to their advantage in the change that had made her so humble, so trembling, so preoccupied as she had been with Lucilio in her aunt's salon. The anguish I had suffered then had in truth left no trace in my heart, but I remembered the cause, and many times it had been on the tip of my tongue to allude to it to the Pisana and see how much she remembered of it and in what way. But I always hesitated and perhaps the day would never have come for me to fulfil my wish, had she not herself offered me the occasion.

Lucilio was descending the staircase after having visited the old lady and the countess, who was already almost restored to health, and was making his way towards the bridge by the stables, which had now been rebuilt with all the prudent additions of a good defence, under the direction of Captain Sandracca. Clara was with him, going to the vegetable garden to collect a few herbs and a geranium or two which still struggled against the onset of the frost. Several days had passed without their having been able to see one another alone and their souls were in tumult, filled with those sentiments that need from time to time to be expressed with ardour, with freedom, so as not to turn back within themselves as a poison. They longed for the fresh air, for solitude and already, having crossed the bridge and sure of being alone, they had a foretaste of the joy of being able to repeat those sweet questions and those eternal replies of love which can suffice for the conversation of lovers. Words a thousand times repeated and always heard with different interpretations and different pleasure, which should be enough to prove that the spirit alone possesses the magical virtue of thought and that the movement of the lips is naught else save a vain stammering of monotonous sounds without any inner conception.

Lucilio was just about to lead the way to the expression of all that love that for so many days had stifled him, when he heard hurrying steps behind him and the shrill little voice of the Pisana shouting; 'Clara, Clara, wait for me; I want to come and pick myself a bouquet too!' Lucilio bit his lip and could not, or did not think it necessary to conceal his irritation. Clara, however, who had turned with her usual kindness to look at her sister, must have noticed the pained expression of the young man and became sad also. As far as she was concerned, the pleasure given to the little girl by a bouquet of flowers would perhaps have paid for the lost delights of the so much desired conversation with her lover. She was kind, kind above all things, and in souls so made, the violence of the passions is quenched in the sight of another's pleasure.

But the young man was not pleased by this easy resignation and his irritation greatly increased. He turned with an angry face to the Pisana and asked if she had left her grandmother alone.

'Yes, but she herself gave me permission to come and pick flowers with Clara,' replied the Pisana crossly, since she did not consider Lucilio had the right to criticize her in this way.

'When one has a heart and gentleness of spirit, one should know how not to make use of certain permissions,' remarked Lucilio. 'A sick old woman in need of company should not be left alone without good reason, however much she seems to allow us to do so.'

The Pisana felt tears of anger rise to her eyes; she turned away angrily and did not even reply to Clara, who told her to stay and not be so cross. The little girl ran at once to the antechamber of the Chancellery, where I had my desk, and red with anger and shame, threw her arms about my neck.

'What has happened?' I exclaimed, dropping my pen and getting up from my seat.

'Oh, he shall pay me for that, Mr Blackbird! . . . he shall pay me for that!' raged the Pisana.

I had long been unaccustomed to hear her use this nickname and at first did not understand whom she was talking about.

'But who is this Mr Blackbird and what has he done?' I asked her.

'Eh . . . the Mr Blackbird of Fossalta, who wants to meddle in my affairs and question me and correct me as if I were a servant girl! . . . I, who am a Countess and he only a blood-letter, only good for the poor and for peasants . . .'

I smiled at the many thoughts that ran through my head at these words, though I only knew later the precise reason for her anger. Meanwhile I profited by the opportunity to get a few more explanations from the little girl.

'At first,' I said to her, 'I did not know who you were talking about with that Mr Blackbird of yours! It's a good while now since we stopped calling Dr Lucilio that!'

'You are right,' answered the Pisana, 'it seems a century. And what a fool I was! . . . There was a time when he pleased me, especially at Portogruaro in my aunt's house when I was enchanted to listen to him. Caspita! How all those other Signori used to keep quiet and listen when he was speaking! I would have given I don't know what to have been in his shoes to cut so fine a figure!'

'You really loved him?' I observed with a secret tremor.

'That is . . . loved him? . . .' murmured the Pisana, thinking it over sincerely. 'I scarcely know . . .'

At this point I saw the lie rise to her lips and understood that now, if not before, she certainly knew of what nature was her admiration for Lucilio. It was both shame and fury that made her make such a confession to herself and she began to abuse him in order to justify herself. 'He is ugly, he is proud, he is bad and dresses like Fulgenzio!' She found in him all the faults, all the sins; and for a long time past I had not heard the Pisana talk so long and with such emphasis as in this philippic against Lucilio. But this very virulence, had I but known, should have given me more reason for fear than for confidence in a temperament as complex and impetuous as hers. Indeed, as soon as the custom of the twice weekly trip to Portogruaro was resumed, the Pisana began to grow colder towards me and to play the goose watching and listening to Lucilio. These diatribes, these protests, of hatred for him were as if never made; she went on adoring what, a few days before, she had trampled on, without being ashamed of herself or wondering at herself. This time my pain was less impetuous but deeper, since I understood to what a roundabout of hopes and disillusions I had confided my future.

I tried to show my sorrow to the Pisana and make her realize the extent of the ill she had done; but she would not hear of it. It seemed to me however that in her devotion to Lucilio there was also a good dose of jealousy. She had become aware that she was neglected because of Clara and suffered from it bitterly; but for all that she did not seem to be exasperated either at her sister or at Lucilio; it seemed that she was content to love, or sure that she loved so much that one day or another she would gain the preference.

All these sentiments that I read in her eyes were very far from giving me comfort. Not knowing with whom to take issue, not with Lucilio, who was not aware of it, nor with the Pisana who paid no more attention to me than if I were a wall, I ended as on the other occasion, by taking issue with myself. But the pain, though deeper, as I have told you, was also more reasonable; I came to terms with it and persuaded myself that, rather than excite it by idleness and boredom, the wisest thing was to seek distraction in work and in study. I put my whole heart into Cicero, Virgil and Horace: I translated great chunks of them, commented on them in my own way and wrote original compositions on similar themes. In fact I may say that this second sin of the Pisana was of great benefit to my classical studies. The Rector declared himself more than satisfied with me and indeed everybody, everybody that is except myself, was pleased with this rapid progress.

Do not think that this was merely a matter of days and hours! There were the usual truces, the usual respites. Now the bad weather, now the condition of the roads, now the extreme heat, or the shortness of the evenings, now the trips of the Frumiers to Udine, suspended the frequency of the visits between Fratta and Portogruaro. Then the Pisana's love for me would revive, with the usual supplement of flatteries for Sandro and Donato; she would at last seem to notice my ill-humour even during her phases of infatuation for Lucilio and would pity me and give me as an alms a glance or even an occasional kiss. I took what I was given like a beggar; sorrow had brought me to the ground, as it says in the psalm, and would have let me be trampled on, oppressed or spat upon without feeling resentment. But this did not prevent my becoming a latinist of greater worth every day and I sweated and grew so pale over my books that Martino sometimes said that it would almost have pleased him more to see me turning the spit as in years past. No matter! I had discovered for myself the great aid to life that there is in study and whatever Martino may have thought, I believe I would have been a great deal more miserable if I had to distract myself with diversions or increased my sorrow by idleness. At least I advanced sufficiently to be able, just after my fifteenth birthday, to take an examination at the seminary of Portogruaro in grammar, Latin, composition, prosody, rhetoric and ancient history, from which I emerged with immortal glory. Just imagine that in a bare three years I had learnt what the others had in six! . . .

After so great a triumph, it was decided by the family that I should be sent to Padua to take my doctor's degree, and meanwhile I was given a post in the Chancellery as a junior official with an annual salary of sixty ducats, which amounted to fourteen soldi a day. Little enough, very little, certainly, but I was very happy to pocket the few coins, saying: 'These are really mine, since I have earned them.' The new dignity to which I had risen also ensured that I had my place at the high table and that I was allowed to enter the salon of the Frumier mansion, sitting near to the Chancellor to watch them play 'three-seven'. This occupation did not please me in the least, but on the other hand I was glad to have the Pisana always under my eye and to fret continually at the childish efforts she made to show her love for Lucilio. Thinking it over now, I can only laugh heartily, but at that time matters were different. My heart wept tears of blood!

The Pisana, in the meantime, had grown into a real young woman. Though not yet fourteen, she already seemed mature. Not very tall, no: but of the most perfect figure, above all about the shoulders and neck, a real torso of Giulia, grand-daughter of Augustus; her head was a little on the large side, but with regular features in a most perfect oval. Her hair was exceedingly long and her eyes always a little moist and filled with a hidden fire; her brows delicate and her little mouth ideal to paint or to kiss. Her voice was full and deep, not one of those that seem to tinkle in the head, but which seemed to come from the breast where the heart beats; her movements were sometimes quiet and orderly like those of a person who is wrapped up in herself; sometimes nimble and resolute like those of a schoolgirl on holiday; she was at one time reserved, silent and pensive, but this could change in a moment to an open, laughing and even talkative manner. But this tendency to chatter she very quickly lost and one could already see that, though only fourteen, her thoughts preoccupied her and stilled her tongue. She seemed a real little woman at the assemblies, already mature and indifferent to the regards of others, but the impulses of her tender age sometimes took charge of her well-made little body and made it play the wildest pranks and most bizarre antics that could be imagined. She had then too much of the tomboy in her, though in the salon itself she would behave as an idle and languid young woman. Thus I remember her in those years of transition, now a child and now a woman, but as regards her spirit, her temperament, the defects of the child were already evident in the woman so exactly that I was not always aware where the one took the place of the other. Perhaps the one was no more than the natural continuation and development of the other.

But now I have reached a point where a new torment was about to begin for me, or perhaps better to say that one already commenced was to increase. About this time the Signor Raimondo di Venchieredo left college and came to live at his near-by castle of Cordovado; but since he had not yet reached the years of his majority, a maternal uncle of his at Venice, who was his guardian, had confided him to the care of a tutor, a certain Father Pendola, who, having come to Venice no one knew whence, had acquired a great reputation as a man of erudition. This mysterious cleric certainly had his own very good reasons for accepting this post; and in confidence I believe that he was secretly a favourite of the

Inquisitors of State. It was said that he was a Roman by birth, but he travelled with a Russian passport; it is well known that the Reverend Jesuit Fathers, after the suppression of their Order, had sought refuge at St Petersburg and that the Republic of Venice had never declared itself their protector. In any case, the political maxims of the Signoria were no longer those of Fra Paolo Sarpi when Father Pendola established himself with his pupil at Venchieredo; and both he and the young castellan made a very great impression in Portogruaro society, which hastened to make much of them and invite them. The Pisana, after the first appearance of this young man in the Frumier salon, often forgot Lucilio to pay attention to him, while I, sitting near the Chancellor, would fret my soul and throw my glances to the winds.

CHAPTER VII

It seemed at first that the hopes of the Signora Contessa for marrying off Clara would be fulfilled. All the young men of Portogruaro and the neighbourhood were, as they say, dying of love for her; she had only to choose to be immediately honoured by whoever amongst them had pleased her most. First of all, the Partistagno regarded her as his property; when he observed that others looked on her with too much devotion, he permitted an expression of disapproval to appear on his face, that spoke openly of his intentions. On his entry into the Frumier mansion he had imprudently taken his place in the inner circle of the master of the house, but he later had to extricate himself since he was not so foolish as to fail to see the poor figure that he cut there. He had then taken up his post between two old women and a Monsignor at a card-table and thence followed his established custom of continually regarding Clara with the eye of a conqueror. This habit of his did not rank him very high in the opinion of his companions in the game, so that from that table there came a continual murmur of requests and reproofs. But the handsome cavalier remained imperturbable; he paid for the games that he lost, paid also for his partner, and was in no way embarrassed. Luckily he was young and handsome, therefore the old ladies pardoned his inattention, and the Monsignor, being the father confessor of one of them, had of necessity to do likewise. The Marchesino Fessi, the Count dell'Elsa and one or two other aristocratic dandies of the city were also paying court to Clara. But the gallant siegework of these Signori was less discreet; their glances were the least thing about it, they made every effort to be pleasant, with arms rounded and legs stiff and straight; and when they put on their laced Sunday coats, their vivacity had no limits. They circled around the chairs of the ladies, bending over this one and that one, but took the greatest care not to become involved in any of the games. The young clergy, and the Professor Desalli in particular, sat very willingly for a quarter of an hour or so beside Clara; their cloth protected them from malicious gossip and the behaviour of the young girl much accorded with their sacerdotal gravity.

Indeed the blonde *castellana* of Fratta had set the heads of the whole assembly in a whirl and her unusual modesty kept her unaware of it. Giulio del Ponte, who was far from being the least assiduous, marvelled and was much irritated at so much reserve; he even went further and, though he paid no special heed to it, conceived certain suspicions about Lucilio. Only a heart already touched by love could coldly resist all this tournament of courtship that displayed itself around her. And who could have made that successful assault if not the little doctor from Fossalta? So thought Signor Giulio, and from thinking to whispering something of his suspicions was a step less than an ant's pace.

Such murmurs had already begun to circulate when Father Pendola presented the young Venchieredo to the Frumier mansion. The Count of Fratta was a little embarrassed, since he had not forgotten that if not by his act, then certainly with his acquiescence, the father of the young cavalier was then eating dry bread in the Rocca della Chiusa. But the Countess, who was a woman of talent, leapt a good step forward in imagination, and built up in a trice a design to end the enmity between the two houses. The Partistagno, in whom great hopes had at first been placed, gave no sign of wanting to make a move; therefore what harm would there be in inducing the Venchieredo to a matrimonial alliance with Clara? . . . The interests of the two families being thus reunited, they would have the right to take measures for the release of the condemned man; then gratitude and happiness would draw a veil over the ugly memories of the past; and to attain this happy conclusion, the powerful protection of the Senator Frumier would serve as a pledge. Father Pendola was a priest of conscience and a man of much ability; having once won his pupil over to the advantages of such a marriage, he would certainly be able to persuade him to it, therefore one must begin there, and the prudent lady set herself to work without delay. The Reverend Father was not one of those who see a span before their noses and wish to give the impression that they can see a mile; quite otherwise. He saw very well at a distance and wore his spectacles with a most resigned expression of mockery. But I believe that he had not to look twice to read the mind of the Countess; and content to be thus wooed, he responded to her attentions with a truly edifying modesty.

'Poor thing,' thought the Signora, 'he believes that I am paying court to him for his own merits! Let him go on believing that and he will serve us with the better will.'

The young Venchieredo, however, assented most eagerly to the chaste designs of the Countess. One might say that he fell in love with Clara on the spot. He fell in love with her like a young ass or a young man just out of college. He tried every possible way to please her, took care to sit as near as he could to her, to touch, even if only with his knee, the folds of her dress, watched her continually and dedicated his few and timorous words to her alone. The far-seeing mama was at the height of bliss; both tutor and scholar had fallen innocently into the net which she had spread before them with so much skill.

But Father Pendola was in no way surprised by these amorous weaknesses of the young man; he knew his pupil better than the Countess and let the water fall over the millrace until he found a suitable moment. To speak openly, the Signor Raimondo (such was the name of the son of the castellan of Venchieredo) loved the fair sex in general even more than he loved Clara. Hardly had he set foot in his jurisdiction than he had given indications of this leading trait of his temperament by a furious pursuit of all the beauties of the neighbourhood. The fathers, the brothers, the husbands had trembled at these warlike preliminaries and the dotard old grandmothers recalled in their inglenooks the times of his noble father. The fiery colt respected neither ditches nor hedges, leapt the one at a bound and breached the other mercilessly, and paying no attention either to restraining rein nor menacing voice, kicked out right and left in order to penetrate into those pastures that pleased him most.

His authority, however, was not yet so formidable as to prevent him from getting a flea in the ear for such imprudences. Some father, brother or husband would begin to raise a storm, to threaten reprisals, vendettas. But then would come the Reverend Father Pendola with his wry neck and contrite face. 'What will you? . . . These are the punishments of providence; they are unpleasant but they must be borne like any other evil, for the greater glory of God! . . . As you know, my heart also bleeds to see these antics! . . . But I put my trust in the Lord, do not complain, but seek his consolation. If He so wishes, I hope these will turn out to be no more than boyish follies; but one must earn by patience the good things He will send you! . . . Join with me, my sons. Let us weep and suffer together that we may have our reward in a better world than this!'

And the simple-hearted fellows wept with this pearl among men and suffered with him; he was the guardian angel of their families and the saviour of their souls! Suppose he had not been there! Who knows what scandals, what trials would have disturbed the countryside! Perhaps there would even have been bloodshed, since indignation had reached its utmost limit.

But the good father consoled them, calmed them and they became once again as lambs waiting to be shorn and, worse still, with resignation. Then, after having shown them where their duty lay, Father Pendola had a private conversation with the young scapegrace and imparted to him a bellyful of excellent advice. No, that was not the way to gain the affection of his people and preserve the decorum and standing of his house! Among his ancestors, too, there had been those who had been sinners when young, but at least they had behaved themselves prudently, had not displayed their faults openly, had not exposed themselves stupidly to the anger of others, avoided giving a bad example and did not excite their neighbours to that Turkish and excommunicate sin of vendetta! How blessed was the prudence of your ancestors!

The young man, as was very natural, extracted from these counsels those parts that best suited him; he began to think things out before doing them and to conceal them well after they had been done. The people no longer complained so much; some wives and girls in the countryside acquired a brooch or a new silk apron; Father Pendola was blessed by all, and the new castellan owed perhaps to him if not the salvation of his soul, at least that of his body. Indeed the rumour that had at first depicted him as a real scourge of chastity was unexpectedly silent; Raimondo gained the reputation of being a discreet and noble youth; he was pleased to joke, yes, but not beyond limits and was courteous to all. For example, he adored all the husbands who had young and pretty wives; were they well-to-do or shepherds, there was never a case when he was discourteous to them. He listened patiently to their chatter, recommended them to the Chancellor or bailiff, and even went to their very houses to take the reply to some petition granted or some account paid. If it so happened that the good man of the house was absent, he would patiently await him, and the wife afterwards would praise exceedingly to her husband the modesty and courtesy of the young patron. In truth, Father Pendola alone knew what to make of such a conversion and among all the people and the neighbouring clergy there was a general inclination to regard him as a sort of wonder-worker.

Doretta Provedoni was among the first to attract the ready attentions of Raimondo; but to Leopardo the affectations of the young nobleman had no appeal whatever and despite the great outcry from his wife he found means of ridding himself of them. To listen to the woman, the young Signor was only making use of his privileges; they were foster brother and sister, had played together as children and it was not strange that he should still preserve some affectionate memory of her. Old Antonio, his brothers, all his relations, afraid of incurring the hostility of the magistrate, took her part and censured Leopardo as a jealous and intolerant lover.

As long as Raimondo continued his dissolute ways, Leopardo had arguments enough to oppose to theirs and Doretta remained with a grudge without being able to do anything about it. But then came the moment of conversion; they began to talk about the miracle wrought by Father Pendola and the marvellous moral amendment of the young castellan. Then Leopardo was overwhelmed with reproaches; Doretta took no part in them, made no fuss, but pretended to be offended at the unjust suspicions of her husband. He, sincere, credulous and accustomed to give way to her in every other matter because of his blind affection for her, confessed that he had been unjust and in order not to see her suffer, consented that she should continue to go and see her father at Venchieredo, as had been her custom before Raimondo came out of college.

The young castellan received his foster-sister with much feeling, wondered that he had never found her at home on the many occasions he had been to Cordovado to salute her and was even angry with her because she had not yet introduced him to her husband. Leopardo was finally persuaded that appearances might have deceived him about Raimondo's intentions; in love with his wife as he was, he let her have her say, and finally ended by begging her pardon and hastening to join her on a visit to the castellan whence he returned home much edified by so much affability and so much reserve, even blessing Father Pendola, and at last allowing his wife to go and stay at Venchieredo as much as she pleased.

So Raimondo went on perfecting his technique as a feudatory, while at the same time his adoration for Clara taught him more discreet and cultivated manners. The Countess, fearing lest he might cool off, thought the moment ripe to sound Father Pendola. She invited him several times to lunch, kept him by her side at the evening game and forgot Monsignor di Sant'Andrea to go to him for confession. At last, when she considered the ground well prepared for action, she put her hand to the sowing.

'Father,' she said to him one evening in the Frumier mansion, after having abandoned the game on some pretext or other to retire with him to a corner of the hall, 'Father, you are fortunate in having a pupil who does you honour!'

The Countess turned an almost maternal eye on Raimondo, who was standing behind Clara and waiting until she had finished her coffee to take her cup. The Reverend Father turned on the youth a glance, glowing equally with affection and humility.

'You are right, Signora Contessa,' he replied, 'I am indeed lucky; for the tutor has really very little share in the merits of his pupil. Good land gives good corn and only waits to be harvested, while poor land gives nothing, however much one is willing to water it with buckets of sweat.'

'Never say that, Father,' retorted the Countess. 'I envy you because you have been found worthy of such luck. In my view the good education of a young man, brought up in the right way, is the greatest boon that can be given to society.'

'That of a noblewoman who educates and guides worthy mothers of a family is certainly no less,' replied the Reverend Father.

'Oh, but Father! We put little study into that. If the Lord gives us daughters who are both good and beautiful, the merit is His. For the rest, a wise economy, good housekeeping, a good dose of the fear of God and the gift of modesty are all the qualities needed for our girls!'

'And you say that that is nothing! . . . Economy, good order, fear of God, modesty! . . . But that contains everything, everything! . . . One could even say more: since good order teaches thrift and the fear of God leads to humility. Believe me, Signora Contessa, were such women on the greatest thrones of the world they would cut a worthy figure.'

The heart of the Countess swelled like a rose after a shower. She looked from the good Father Pendola to Clara, from Clara to Raimondo and from him once again to the excellent Father. This tour of glances was like the theme of a symphony about to be played.

'Listen, Reverend Father,' she went on, drawing very close to his side, since Monsignor di Sant'Andrea was darting two basilisk eyes at her from his table of picquet. 'Is it not true that at the first appearance of Signor Raimondo there were many rumours about him . . . about . . . certain matters . . . certain matters . . . ?'

The Countess stammered, almost hoping that the excellent Father would suggest to her the words she lacked; but he remained on guard and replied to her stammering with an expression of wonder.

'You understand me,' went on the Countess. 'I accuse no one but merely repeat what people were saying. It seems that the Signor Raimondo did not set a very good example in his tastes . . . But you know that in this world judgements are often precipitate and that appearances often . . . '

'Only too often, only too often, dear Countess,' the Reverend Father interrupted her with a sigh. 'Would you believe that not even you or myself are entirely safe from that cursed blight of calumny?'

The Signora bit her lips and felt whether the ribbons of her cap were in place. She would have liked to blush, but unable to obtain this effect, she decided to cough.

'What are you saying, your Reverence,' she went on humbly, 'you may believe that out of a hundred thousand mouths here, all combine in one voice to praise your sanctity . . . As for me, I am too small and insignificant a thing to . . .'

'Eh, Contessa, Contessa, you are mocking me. A great lady, in these times, is worth a whole seminary of priests in the eyes of the world and such alone have the privilege of making entire cities speak well or ill. As for us, it is enough if they deign to return our greetings.'

The Countess, too vain to let pass a compliment without picking it up and little skilled at cutting such fripperies out of the conversation, followed wherever the Reverend Father chose to lead her, always getting farther away from the aim she had set herself at the beginning. But the good Father was no owl; before getting involved in any sort of scheme he wanted to understand what advantage he would get out of it and who were the persons with whom he would have to associate. That day he did not judge it opportune to touch on the argument and navigated so cleverly that when the guests rose from the tables to take their leave, the Countess was telling him, I believe, about the follies of her youth and the good times she had had in Venice and God knows what other old tales. Realizing that the moment to leave had come, she bit her nails, but that hour had passed so circumspectly, the good Father had so held her with his interesting talk that the main topic had remained only half uttered. As to suspecting that the most excellent Father had led her, as they say, to pick violets, the Countess was a hundred miles from believing it. On the other hand, she was irritated at her own loquacity and resolved to be more serious on another occasion and to forget the past in order to pay more attention to the present. But the second time was no better than the first and the third like the second; it was not that the good Father seemed to avoid her or that he talked to her with any ill will. No, on the contrary, he sought her out, often visited her and was never the first to leave if the lunch was served or the lateness of the hour forced them to retire. But either the occasion never presented itself or it so happened that the Countess forgot when she might have been able to open her attack.

However, Father Pendola did not remain inactive in the meantime; he studied the country, the people, the magistrates, the clergy; he wormed his way into the graces of this signor or of that lady; he adapted himself to the various tastes of different persons in order to be welcome everywhere; above all he tried in every way to enter into the favour of His Excellency Frumier. But there were many others tarred with the same brush and the Father knew it and preferred to go surely by the longer way rather than to fall down at the first step.

After a couple of weeks he had become a necessary adjunct to the senator's circle. Up till then, a real anarchy of opinions had reigned there; he intervened to accord, to regulate, to reach conclusions. It is true that his conclusions sometimes limped and that often one of Lucilio's epigrams made him tumble off his perch to the loud laughter of the company. But the patient Father came back to rise again, to unite them with fresh proposals; taken all in all, he wearied them so much, both his friends and his adversaries, that they all ended by agreeing that he was right.

The senator soon acquired a taste for these dialectic exercises; he was methodical by nature and accustomed by long practice to academic jousts, he was pleased by these arguments which, after having amused him for half an hour or so, created, if not more, a sort of semblance of truth. Father Pendola succeeded in giving him something he had never been able to obtain from those witty but featherbrained spirits that surrounded him. He enjoyed a great reputation for perfect logic, which in his opinion was the greatest honour that could be conceded to anyone. He did not rack his brains to find out whether Father Pendola was logical with himself or whether his logic chopped and changed every three paces in order to advance. It was enough for him to see it arrive; it was of no consequence if it were with the crutches of Lucilio or with those of Professor Dessalli. Let it be said once and for all that the most excellent Father had a special eye to discern the souls of others; and therefore after a couple of evenings not only had he understood that the nobleman Frumier liked to be overcome by the sound of chatter, but had even divined the quality of the chatter necessary to that end. Lucilio, who in the matter of discernment was as far-seeing as the Reverend Father, was soon aware what cat there was in the bag; but he had much to do to find a chink in that armour. The black tunic was of so dense a texture that mere looks blunted themselves upon it; and the young man saw himself constrained to work with his imagination.

Finally came the day when Father Pendola allowed himself to acquaint the Countess of his long cherished design. He had learnt as much as he needed to learn; he had prepared all that he had to prepare: he no longer feared, he even desired, that the Countess should have recourse to him, so that he could reply with a good grace: 'My dear Signora, I promise you this, if on your side you will promise me this other!' Now, you will ask, what did the most excellent Father desire? A trifle, my friends, only a trifle! Since, after the marriage of the Signor Raimondo to the Contessina Clara, a tutor would become a useless mouth in the Castle of Venchieredo, he aspired to the post of house chaplain with the Senator. The Lady Frumier had the reputation of being devout. He had touched lightly upon this matter and the touch had brought a ready response; it remained for her kinswoman to finish the good work, if indeed she wanted to see her daughter settled in so honourable a manner. The poor Father was tired, was old, was a lover of study; that was an unexacting post which seemed to him the real antechamber of Paradise; the priest who then occupied it wanted a cure of souls; they could satisfy him and at the same time content the good Father, who no longer felt that he possessed either the energy or the wisdom to work actively in the vineyard of the Lord. It must be understood that the excellent Father approached these matters in a way to make it seem that the Countess had dragged them from his lips and not that he had asked them of her.

'Oh, saints of Paradise!' exclaimed the Signora, 'what a comfort for my kinswoman! What a spiritual aid for my kinswoman! Reverend Father, would you really be willing to adapt yourself to the humble life of a house chaplain?'

'Yes, if my pupil should marry,' replied Father Pendola.

'Oh, but they will marry! Can't you see? They seem really made for one another.'

'Indeed, if I should say a word . . . Raimondo . . . But enough! Let me have time to study their temperaments and observe them a little . . .'

'What good is it to study these hearts of twenty years old? Can't you see? One look at their eyes is enough . . . their thoughts, their affections are there! Leave it to me! . . . It is three months since I have been watching them every evening. Can you believe it, Reverend Father, I have been thinking about opening this conversation with you for the last six weeks but I have always lacked the courage!'

'Really, Signora Contessa? . . . What are you telling me? . . . To lack the courage to ask me to play my part in such a good work and of such value and lustre for two families?'

'Is it not true, though, Father, that the idea is a good one? . . . And wouldn't it be a fine wedding present if one could obtain from the Inquisitors a remission of the rest of his sentence for that other poor fellow? . . . So would end a series of dissensions, miseries and adversities which have afflicted the good people of our districts!'

'Yes, indeed! And I would retire contentedly if I could confide the happiness of my spiritual son to so accomplished a little wife; but these are things, my dear Countess, which must be well thought over. Just because I can do so much with Raimondo . . .'

'Yes, just for that I want you to make clear to him all the advantages that could result to both our houses from such a marriage.'

'I wanted to say, Signora Contessa, that just because of this responsibility that weighs upon me, I must move with lead in my shoes . . .'

'Come, Father. All you need is a glance to see everything. . . . How I long to see this most excellent alliance concluded! . . . And my kinsman, how pleased he will be to have in his house a man of your calibre! . . . Tomorrow, immediately, we shall look to provide a parish for his present chaplain. Since he so desires, nothing could be better!'

'Indeed, Signora Contessa . . .'

'No, Father, don't make difficulties . . . promise me to do this favour to my kinsman! Once you have let a word slip, don't try to withdraw it . . .'

'I did not say that I withdrew it, but . . .'

'But . . . but . . . but . . . let us have no more buts! . . . Look, just look for a moment at Signor Raimondo and my Clara! How they look at one another! . . . Don't they seem like two doves?'

'If the Good Lord so wishes, there will never be a more perfect couple.'

'But the Lord's designs must be aided, Father, and that is first of all a matter for you who are his most worthy Minister . . .'

'Unworthy, most unworthy, Signora Contessa!'

'In any case, I shall expect you tomorrow to lunch . . . you will tell me something then of your Raimondo.'

'I accept your kindness, Signora Contessa; but I really don't know . . . so hasty . . . I can't promise anything. . . . It will be a great blow to me to separate from so good a son.'

'I assure you that my kinsfolk will recompense you with interest for all that you will lose.'

'Ah yes, I believe it, I hope it, but . . .'

'Well, Father, till tomorrow. We shall speak together, we shall arrange something; I will drop a hint this evening to the Senator, since it so happens that we are staying here to supper.'

'Please, Signora Contessa, don't commit me, don't compromise me too much. It is really a sacrifice that . . .'

'But really, your Reverence! Would you deprive that dear son of yours of a wife for mere selfishness? What a bad tutor! Till tomorrow, till tomorrow, Father, and come in time for us to have a little chat while the rice is boiling.'

'Your most humble servant, Contessa. I will certainly not fail and may God bring our intentions to a good end.'

The good Father, indeed, as soon as he had left the Frumier mansion with Raimondo and had settled into the deep and comfortable seats of his bombay, immediately began to praise him for the life that he was then leading and for the good use that he had made of his counsels. But the resolutions of men are frail and their passions imperious and one can never sufficiently commend the prudence of checking and controlling them within sacred and legitimate bonds. He was now just reaching his twenty-first year, the moment could not be better, and he, the most excellent Father, offered to assist him in his choice by his long and wary experience.

'Oh, Father, are you speaking seriously?' exclaimed Raimondo. 'Are you exhorting me to get married? . . . But only a year ago you were instilling into me the maxim that one must be mature in years and in mind before deciding to found a family, and that the aid of a tutor of sound heart and mind was more than worth the assistance, often trivial and imperfect, of some mere woman!'

'Yes, my son,' the tutor replied candidly, 'such were the counsels that I gave you in the last year when I was your master in college and I believed them to be excellent; but then I had not observed you in the liberty of the world. Now that I know you better in the practice of everyday life, I am not ashamed to have changed my mind and to confess that I was mistaken. You see, I speak to my own disadvantage. When your wife enters this castle by one door, I of necessity must go out by the other . . .'

'No, no, Father, don't say that! Don't deprive me of the support of your work and your advice . . . I can never forget how much I owe you! . . . Only two months ago those travellers at Morsano would have killed me if you had not reduced them to more discreet sentiments by making them accept some reparation in money! And I had not so much as touched a finger of their sister . . . I swear it, Father!'

'Yes, my son. I believe you implicitly; but you must not offend my modesty by recalling those very humble merits; I pray you to forget them, or at least not to speak of them further. What has been, has been! As I told you, I have changed my opinion of what I thought best for you a year ago; now it would please me to see you firmly and honourably settled. Leaving you with a wife at your side, good, patient and devout, I would retire more contentedly into the niche of my old age . . .'

'But Father, have you not always told me that even when I married you would remain the peacemaker, the comforter, the spiritual link between me and my wife, and that for all the gold in in the world you would never consent to leave me?'

Father Pendola had indeed spoken many times on this theme, since he had not hoped to get a better post. But then, when he had been able to glimpse something better, after fishing in the ecclesiastical rapids of Portogruaro, he gave his words a broader interpretation.

'I did speak so, and I do not deny now that I said so many times.' he went on. 'My spirit will always remain with you, since the better part of me had become transfused in your soul by the sacred channel of education; and as for your wife, since I shall have the task of choosing her according to the maxims of good morality, she will correspond perfectly to the aims that I have in trusting her. That, Raimondo, is the spiritual link which will come from the most intimate recesses of my heart and which will always remain with you and your wife!'

Raimondo, at these explanations of his tutor, did not perhaps show himself so ill-content as he would have been three months earlier. But at that moment they reached the castle and the conversation was interrupted until after supper. Then they came back to it of common accord, since the young man was eager to know the name of the wife who, in Father Pendola's mind, was destined for him.

'Raimondo, you know that name!' the suave Father replied in his most honeyed tone. 'I can read it in your eyes and you have sinned through little confidence in your friend that you have not shared with him the desires of your heart.'

'What! Can it be true? You, Father, have guessed so quickly?'

'Yes, my son, one guesses when one loves. And I confess to you that if your reticence has afflicted me, I am sufficiently consoled by the good choice that you have made and that will not fail to make your life flower with imperishable joys . . .'

'Oh, Father, isn't it true that she is lovely as an angel? . . . Have you noticed, Father, what eyes, what shoulders! . . . Oh, my God, I have never seen such lovely shoulders!'

'Those are fugitive virtues, my son, merely the external ornaments of the vessel, that are of small account if it does not contain within a rich and uncorrupted aroma. I can, however, assure you that the soul of the Contessina entirely corresponds to all that her appearance promises. She will really be an angel, as you have just said . . .'

'And will they give her to me, most beloved Father? Will they consent to give her to me in marriage? I am all eagerness! . . . I would like to have her with me tomorrow, even today were it possible; and she is still so tender, still almost a child . . .'

'You are mistaken, my son; her modesty and complexion make her seem younger than she really is; as regards age, she is quite suitable for you; indeed she must be only a little younger than you.'

'But how? What do you say? The Contessina Pisana about my age?'

'Raimondo, you are confusing their names; the Contessina is called Clara and not Pisana; the Pisana is her little sister, that little girl who was sitting this evening between you and Monsignor di Sant'Andrea.'

'But it is just of her that I am speaking, Father! . . . Haven't you seen with what eyes she looks at me? . . . From yesterday evening I have been madly in love with her . . . Oh, I cannot go on living if I cannot get her to love me!'

'Raimondo, my son, have you gone mad? From what you tell me, you have no eyes and no perception. She is a little girl of ten at most! . . . It can't be that you are attracted by her; surely your heart is deceiving you and what makes her so dear to you is that she is sister of the Contessina Clara?'

'But no, Father, I assure you . . .'

'But yes, my son; be guided by those who know more than you. Let me put a little clarity into a heart I know better than you do yourself. I have the right, after so many years that I have studied it, to direct it for the best. You love the Contessina Clara; I have noticed it from the courteous attentions that you have shown her.'

'Yes, Father, up till last week, but now . . .

'Now, now since the Contessina is too modest and too well brought up to respond openly and without the consent of her parents, you have got the idea that she has not been moved by your attentions and have tried to come closer to her by becoming friendly with her sister. And now since that little one has received you joyfully and shown her gratitude for your good manners, you have taken this for love. Just consider my son, that would be ridiculous and shameful.'

'No matter, Father! I can see that you have never watched her as I have done this last two evenings.'

'I have watched her very carefully, too, and if you have any intentions towards her, my dear Raimondo, you will have to resign yourself to waiting seven or eight years, and there is always the possibility of her changing her mind in the meantime. And then everyone would laugh at you, seeing you so in love with a mere baby! You know that it is really childishness to love a green fruit when you might pluck one already ripe and full of savour.'

'I don't know what to do, Father, I don't know what to do!'

'Think, my son, reflect well. I will make use of your own arguments. You would like to believe that the Pisana can surpass the Contessina Clara in beauty of appearance, in the whiteness of her skin and the perfection of her figure? Remember well, Raimondo . . . Do you still feel able to resist them?'

'I don't know, Father, I don't know, but certainly she would have nothing to do with me.'

'Foolish words! Believe me, appearances and nothing more. Purely the effect of modesty and bashfulness.'

'It might be so, but in any case these chilly temperaments do not attract me.'

'Chilly, my son? One can see that you are without experience! It is just beneath such a composed and reserved manner that is hidden the most intense ardour and the most refined voluptuousness! . . . Believe me, who have studied the human heart.'

'Yes, Father. Indeed it seems to me that it must be so, yet . . .'

'Yet, yet! . . . What are you trying to say? . . . Yet, I will tell you! . . . It is not a deed of charity or of prudence to wound the heart of a beautiful girl who under the appearance of calm and modesty only lives for you and is ready to make a gift to you of the most holy pleasures that a kindly God has allowed for our enjoyment!'

'Oh Father, could it be true? . . . that the Contessina Clara is in love with me?'

'But certainly, I assure you, I swear to you; do you really want to know? Someone in her family has told me! . . . She is in love, poor thing, and is dying with the desire to please you!'

'If it is as you say, I understand, Father, that I have been mistaken. Seven years is a long time. Indeed, I was in love with the Contessina Clara and even now, thinking it over, I . . .'

'Ah, you have confessed, my son, you have confessed! My Lord, I thank You! Now that my ministry is ended, I shall be able to rest in peace on the happiness prepared by my hands for these two beloved creatures. Raimondo, I have revealed the secrets of your heart; let me act now in a way that everything may turn out as you desire.'

'But slowly, Father, I would not that for too great haste . . .'

'The remedy is urgent, my son. Think of the joy you will experience in pressing to your heart in this castle, in this very room, a wife so lovely, so docile, so filled with love for you . . .'

'You are right, Father. Do as you think best . . . Really my intentions. . . . But now after mature reflection and since you assure me that the girl loves me . . .'

'Yes, Raimondo. I would put my hand in the fire for that.'

'Very well, Father. Could we have the wedding on Sunday?'

'Power of God! On Sunday! And you told me not to be too hasty! It will take a week or so, perhaps even a month or so, dear boy. The things of this world move with a certain order and cannot be hurried. However, in the meantime you will be able to see your fiancée, and talk with her, and stay as long as you like with her in the castle of Fratta when her parents are present.'

'What joy, Father! And so I shall also be able to go on seeing the Pisana.'

'Naturally, and to love her and treat her with the honest openness of a future kinsman. Be at peace, my son, trust in me and sleep calmly with your dreams, so that the hopes of your old uncle may not be deceived and when I attend your wedding I shall be able to feel sure that I have left you virtuous and happy.'

The young nobleman wept with emotion, kissed the hand of his wise tutor and went up to his bedroom with the Pisana and Clara dancing confusedly in his imagination. He was not sure which, but he felt that either one of them would have been welcome that evening. Father Pendola had counted on this fickleness of temper to distract his ward from this passing whim for the Pisana and to rekindle his flame for Clara, nor did the result disappoint him. But as he too went up to bed, he marvelled and congratulated himself that this fresh complication had been luckily avoided.

'Ah, the little rogue! . . .' he thought. 'I was aware that in those fourteen years of hers there are at least thirty years of guile concealed . . . but such breakneck speed I never imagined. Really, whoever said that the world is always rushing forward will end by being right.'

Father Pendola, after having once again assured the young nobleman of the proposals of the evening before, told the Countess of Fratta the satisfactory result of his words, keeping silence, however, since it in no way affected the issue, about the part that concerned the Pisana. The Signora was almost ready to throw her arms about his neck, and rewarded him by assuring him that a simple hint let fall about his establishment in the Frumier mansion had been welcomed by the Senator and his wife with such joyful interest as to augur a ready accomplishment of his desires.

'And now,' said the Signora confidentially to the Reverend Father, who was seated at table near her despite the usual ceremony of the house, 'and now leave it to me. Before Clara suspects anything, for girls must be handled with care in these matters, I want my noble kinsfolk to have the blessing of your company.'

'Poor Raimondo,' sighed the Father between one mouthful and another.

'Don't be too sorry for him,' went on the Countess in a low voice and with one eye on her daughter. 'A wife like that is more to the taste of a young man of twenty-one than any priest.'

Indeed next week all Portogruaro was buzzing with the great news. The celebrated, the illustrious, the learned, the holy Father Pendola was to retire to the Frumier mansion, wearied with the labours of a long apostolate. There he had decided to remain in peace, not that he was yet so advanced in years, but still afflicted with the troubles he had experienced and by many infirmities of old age. The former chaplain had been transferred, as he had wished, to a cure of souls near Pordenone, and the Senator and his noble lady could not contain themselves for joy at having in his stead such a shining example of ecclesiastical perfection. Raimondo had gone through the motions of falling into a passion because the Father wished to leave his house before his wife should enter it; but the good Father had no need to waste his breath for long to persuade him that the guardianship of a tutor was not suitable for a young man about to be betrothed, and that for many reasons it was better that his departure from Venchieredo should precede by some little time the wedding ceremony.

Raimondo had in fact seen him leave without many tears and continued to frequent the Castle of Fratta where the confident affability of the Pisana compensated him for the frigid reserve of Clara. To Clara no indication had yet been given of the good fortune awaiting her; and he attributed to this the effort made by her to conceal from him the ardour of her love. For the rest, he did not greatly concern himself and, if Clara failed him, he could at least requite himself with her younger sister. Such were the philosophic sentiments of the Lord of Venchieredo, but the Countess did not see matters in this way at all. After having let the two young people enter, in her opinion, into a decent intimacy, she took it on herself to prepare Clara for the young man's demand, and talking continually of this, she ended by becoming a little uneasy at seeing the girl remain so cold and unmoved, as if she had not herself been in question.

One day she spoke openly of the probable intentions of Raimondo, but even this last stroke in no way dispelled the cloud that had gathered for many days on the young girl's brow. She lowered her eyes, sighed and said neither yes nor no. Her mother began to believe her stupid, a thing she had always suspected, seeing her so grave, so modest and different in every way from what she herself had been in her childhood. But even the stupid are shaken out of themselves when the question of a husband is touched upon and the stupidity of Clara must be something unnatural if she was not moved even by that. She took up the question then with her old mother-in-law, who had always been the girl's confidante, and implored her to try and make Clara understand the intentions of her family in her regard. The old lady spoke, listened, and told her daughter-in-law that Clara had no intention of getting married, but wanted to stay always with her grandmother, to care for her in her illnesses and to comfort her in her loneliness.

'Bah! Those are foolish whims!' exclaimed the Countess. 'I suppose she will go on making sour faces at that poor young man until he finds some pretext to wriggle out of the whole thing. In this family at least it has always been the duty of girls to obey their parents' wishes, and I will have no newfangled ideas here, indeed I won't! As for you, Signora, I hope you will not encourage this folly and will support me and the Signor Count in trying to make the girl see what is best for her.'

The old woman nodded assent and was very glad that after this outburst her daughter-in-law left the room. But she was no less ready for all that to try and touch Clara's heart and to persuade her to accept the husband offered her, who was both noble and worthy in every respect. The young woman took refuge in silence, or replied that God had not called her to matrimony and that she would be quite happy to end her life in the castle beside her grandmother. Everyone had to have his say, but to her father, to Monsignor her uncle, to her grandmother, to her mother, Clara always repeated the same refrain. Whereon the Countess, no matter how furiously she felt anger rising within her, decided to avoid saying anything to the Venchieredo and to make an appeal in the meantime to Father Pendola, since with his great wisdom he might be able to find a way of making Clara obey without having recourse to violent or scandalous measures.

In the meantime rumours of this obstinate resistance of the young woman had leaked out; Lucilio pretended not to be aware of them and maintained his usual manner towards her, and the Partistagno appeared at the evening parties in the castle and at the assemblies in the Frumier mansion more smiling and glorious than ever. Father Pendola, having heard the seriousness of the case, himself offered to act as peacemaker between the Countess and the young *castellana*; all had great hopes of this and when he was left alone with Clara some of them stopped out of curiosity to listen at the door.

'Contessina,' the Reverend Father began, 'what do you think of this lovely weather?'

Clara bowed, a little confused and not knowing what to reply; but the Father himself relieved her of her embarrassment by continuing:

'It is quite a long time since we have enjoyed a season like this, the more so as one might say that we have only just emerged from winter. The Most Excellent Senator has given me permission, indeed I might say has begged me, to go and visit my dear pupil, that excellent young man, that perfect cavalier, whom you must know well. But in passing I wanted to see your family and ask for news of their affairs.'

'I thank you, Father,' stammered the girl, not seeing him disposed to go on.

The Father saw this timidity as a good omen and argued that as he had extracted that 'thank-you' from her, he would later be able to make her say and promise anything he liked.

'Contessina,' he went on in his most honeyed voice, 'your lady mother has placed some confidence in me and today I had hoped to hear from you what my heart has for so long desired. Instead you have only given me half words; it seems that you have not understood the just and honourable intentions of your parents; but I hope that when I have explained them better, you will have no shadow of doubt in accepting them as the commands of the Lord.'

'Go on, Father,' said Clara modestly, but this time with calm and assurance.

'Contessina, you have in your hands the means of restoring joy and concord not only to two illustrious families, but one might even say to an entire countryside; but I have been led to believe that for various pious scruples you do not wish to make use of them. Will you permit me to believe that your reply has not been well interpreted and that what appears to be unreasonable refusal and stubborn rebellion is no more than shyness or the impulse of too great modesty?'

'Father, perhaps I do not know how to explain myself clearly, but merely by repeating the same thing many times I hope that I shall finally be understood. No, I do not feel myself called to matrimony. God calls me by another road; I should make an extremely bad wife and I can continue to be a worthy daughter; my conscience therefore commands me to follow the latter part.'

'Very good, Contessina. I certainly will not be one of those who want to condemn you for this respect of the laws of conscience. Indeed it redoubles the esteem that I already had for you and makes me hope that later we shall find that our opinions are closer than they now seem. Will you permit that, with my most humble but devout judgement, I aid you to make clear that conscience that is perhaps a little disturbed, a little uncertain, owing to the conflicts of the last few days. No one, Contessina, is so great a saint as to believe blindly in his own conscience, disdaining the advice and suggestions of others.'

'Go on, Father, go on; I am here to listen to you and to confess that I am wrong as soon as I am so persuaded.'

'And they say that she is stupid!' thought the good Father, 'Far from it! I can see that I have a wily cat to skin and I shall be lucky if I succeed!' 'Well then,' he went on aloud, 'you will know better than I that obedience is the first law for conscientious and God-fearing daughters. Honour thy father and mother that thy days may be long . . . God himself says so and up till now you have always put His precepts into practice. But obedience, dear daughter, allows no exceptions and looks for no evasions; obedience obeys, that is all. That is conscience as we poor ministers of the Gospel understand it.'

'So also do I understand it,' replied Clara humbly.

'Have I persuaded her already?' the Reverend Father thought. 'I wouldn't wager a cabbage on it.' None the less, he made pretence of believing that he had done so and raised his hands. 'Thank you, beloved daughter in Christ!' he exclaimed, 'thank you for your good words; it is thus by the road of self-denial and sacrifice that one reaches the final goal of perfection, so one allows oneself to be persuaded to one's own advantage, so one can become a most excellent wife and mother of a family, who up till now has always been a good and well-behaved daughter . . . Oh, it will not long remain a great burden, be assured! . . . A husband, destined for you by Heaven, is not so easy to find in these days. I have brought him up myself, Contessina; and I have moulded him with the purest essence of my spirit and according to the most sacred maxims of Christianity. God will reward you for your outstanding piety, for your filial respect! . . . May He continue to bless you and may He be thanked that He has permitted me to bring into your soul the light of persuasion! . . .'

The good Father, still raising his hands and his eyes towards heaven, was preparing to go out of the room to report the good news to the Countess; but Clara was too sincere to leave him in so great an error. In that crisis sincerity served her as well as guile, for the good Father was relying precisely upon her lack of courage and innocent simplicity and believed that she would let herself be persuaded in order to avoid the necessity of having to contradict him. He was therefore much surprised when he found himself halted by a gesture from the girl, and he understood what that gesture meant. None the less, he did not want to own himself defeated and turned to her with truly paternal unction.

'What is it, my daughter?' he said, sugaring every word with a seraphic smile. 'Ah, I understand! You wish to be the first to tell your parents of so great a consolation! After having grieved them so much, even though with good intentions, it seems to you just to throw yourself at their feet, to ask their pardon, and to assure them of your filial submission! Let us go then, come with me!'

'Father,' replied Clara, in no way confused by the feigned assurance of the preacher. 'Perhaps I understand obedience in a manner different from you. It seems to me that to obey should mean a yielding to the commands of one's superiors not merely in the letter but also in the spirit. But when one feels unable to observe fully one of those commands, it would be hypocrisy to yield to it in appearance only.'

'Ah, my daughter, what are you saying? Those are subtleties of the schoolmen. St Thomas . . .'

'St Thomas was a great saint, and I respect and venerate him. As for me, I repeat to you what you must tell my lady mother, to papa and to my uncle. I cannot promise to love a husband whom I can never love. To obey by giving myself to this husband would be an obedience of the body, with the lips only, but not with the heart. With the heart I could never do so. Therefore allow me, Father, to remain unmarried.'

'Oh Contessina! Consider and reconsider it. Your reasoning is faulty in form and in substance. Obedience has not so long a tongue.'

'Obedience when it is questioned replies, and I, if you had not questioned me, would never have replied, I assure you, Reverend Father.'

'Stop, Contessina, one word more! Must I tell you all? . . . Must I explain to you all the virtues to which an exemplary daughter should aspire? You profess yourself ready to obey all those commands of your parents which you feel yourself capable of carrying out. Most excellent, my daughter! . . . But what is it that your parents command? They command you to marry a young man who had been proposed to you, one noble, worthy, rich, cultivated, in an alliance which should result in great benefits to both families and to the whole district! As to your heart, they do not command it. Your heart will think for itself later; but religion desires us to yield ourselves in what we can, and you may be sure that, as a reward for so much submission, God will extend to you also the grace to fulfil all the duties of your new condition.'

Clara remained for a time perplexed at the casuistry of the moralist; so much so indeed that he again felt that he might have succeeded in making her bend to his will, but his victory was very short, since the perplexity of the young woman was shorter still.

'Father,' she said, with the resolute air of one who ends a dispute and wishes to hear no more of it. 'What would you say of one who, riddled with debts and bare of all else, should give security for eighty thousand ducats for the day after tomorrow? . . . I will tell you what I should think: that he was either a madman or a rogue. You will understand me, father. Conscious of my poverty, I will not give security for a single soldo.'

So saying, Clara bowed and made a movement in her turn to withdraw, and it was the Reverend Father's turn to try and detain her with further words, with further objections; but understanding that he would be merely pouring water into a sieve, he contented himself with following her out with the disconsolate appearance of a retriever who returns to its master without the game it has been sent to find. Those who were listening at the door had scarcely time to make their way back to the sitting-room; but they were not sufficiently skilful to conceal that they knew all. Father Pendola had not yet approached the Countess before she leapt at Clara with every sort of threat and abuse; so much so that many rushed in from the kitchen at the uproar. But her husband and Monsignor set themselves to restrain her, and Father Pendola found the moment opportune to take French leave, washing his hands of the whole affair, like Pilate.

Once he had gone, the reproaches touched on him; and the Signora gave vent to her rage by shouting that he was a great hypocrite, a useless fellow, a barefaced cheat who had worked to get what he wanted and then brazenly abandoned her in her embarrassment. Monsignor implored his kinswoman to stop abusing a clergyman who in a few days of residence at Portogruaro had already taken the lead among the clergy and even with the Curia. But women pay little heed to such things when their tongues itch. She wanted to pour out all her excess of gall before heeding the advice of her kinsman. Finally, having exhausted this subject, she returned to rebuking Clara; and the curious onlookers from the kitchen having returned to their own affairs, even the Count and Monsignor approached the young girl and tormented her unceasingly. She bore it all, not with that cold resignation that is rooted in contempt, but with the real sorrow of one who wished to, but could not, gratify the wishes of others.

This martyrdom lasted for many days and the Countess gave her word that she should either marry the Venchieredo or be sent without mercy to a convent. Already the rumours regarding Lucilio were louder than ever and that young man had to behave himself more discreetly than ever before on his visits. But mingled with these rumours were others about the obstinate refusal of Clara to ally herself with the Venchieredo, and there were some who gave as a reason for this a secret love for the Partistagno. Amongst these, the leader was the Partistagno himself who, having had an account of the whole matter, arrived at the castle more radiant and haughty than ever; he looked the whole company over from head to foot and in the tender glances that he kept in reserve for Clara, one could not have guessed whether love surpassed compassion or *vice versa*. Indeed this hypothesis had also occurred to the Countess; and since she did not deign to have any suspicions of Lucilio, it seemed to her well enough founded.

But that blessed Partistagno would never make up his mind to make a step forward. For years now he had been working with his glances and his smiles without in any way revealing his intentions. Raimondo on the other hand, had come, so to speak, ring in hand and it was only a matter of saying yes for him to be happy and grateful to put it on Clara's finger. These considerations in no way diminished the Countess's bad blood towards her daughter; the more so since even these recent events did not seem to have made the noble castellan of Lugugnana hasten his pace in any way.

One day, however, when the Frumiers had invited their Fratta relations to lunch in order to relieve their minds from these family unpleasantnesses, the most illustrious Signor Count was exceedingly uneasy to hear himself called by his kinsman into a little room apart. Every time he chanced to be separated from the faithful Chancellor, we know that he remained like a candle without a wick. However, he made a virtue of necessity and with many sighs followed his kinsman wherever he wished. The Senator closed the door with a double lock, drew the green curtains over the windows, opened with many precautions the most secret recess of his writing-desk, took out a folded paper and handed it to him, saying:

'Read, but for God's sake don't say a word! I trust you because I know you.'

The poor Count saw a mist before his eyes and rubbed and re-rubbed his spectacles with the lining of his coat, more to gain time than for anything else, but in the end with some difficulty succeeded in deciphering the writing. The message was anonymous, from a man who seemed to have great authority in the counsels of the Signoria, who was replying confidentially to the noble Senator concerning the reprieve asked for in favour of the old Venchieredo. He was first of all astounded at the very idea; this was not a time when the Republic could unleash its most inveterate enemies, occupied as it was in rooting them out and rendering them impotent as far as might be. The castellans of 'up there' were all badly disposed to the Signoria; the example of Venchieredo should serve to admonish them and was perhaps even insufficient since exceeding indulgence had been shown to his family and his property saved from confiscation. Nothing is more pernicious than power conceded to the supporters of our enemies; one must always cut the evil at its roots so that it cannot sprout again. The Signoria only repented that it had not done so. There was, of course, no question of the Senator, who was above all suspicion and had acted in this matter on the suggestion and requests of others, but the friends of Venchieredo should take good care not to let themselves be involved in too great benevolence towards those whose wavering fidelity and uncertain views, perhaps tinctured by those subversive ideas that originated on the other side of the mountains, menaced with ruin the ancient and venerable administration of St Mark. In hard times greater prudence was needed; this should be their guide, since the Inquisition of State was always watchful and no respector of persons.

The Senator, in his role of Venetian patrician, followed with pride the varied expressions of astonishment, sorrow and consternation that showed on his kinsman's face as he made out little by little each phrase of the letter. When he had finished, the sheets fell from his hand and he stammered I know not what excuses and protests.

'Be at ease,' said the Senator, picking up the letter and putting a hand on his shoulder, 'it is a warning and nothing more, but you can see that it was almost a grace from Heaven that your daughter refused that alliance. If she had consented, by this time the wedding would have been celebrated . . .'

'No, for all the saints in Heaven!' exclaimed the Count with a shudder. 'If she wished it now, or if my wife with all her rages tried to have it celebrated, I would with two words only . . .'

'Pst! Pst!' interrupted the Senator, 'remember that this is a delicate affair.'

The castellan remained with mouth wide open like a little boy caught doing wrong; then, forcing down a lump in his throat, he added: 'God be thanked that He has wished us well; we have been saved from a great danger. My wife must be informed that for secret, hidden but extremely stringent reasons there must be no more talk of this marriage. It must not even be dreamed of. But she is discreet and will act correctly! . . . *Cospettanaccio!* I fear she let herself be led by the nose by that blessed Father Pendola!'

Here he suddenly fell silent and once again stood open-mouthed, since from the Senator's wry face he realized that he was about to make, or perhaps already had made, a great indiscretion.

'In confidence,' Frumier replied, with that air of superiority of a master over his pupil, 'from certain phrases that the worthy Father has let drop I believe that it was not for nothing that they placed him with the young Venchieredo! . . . It could also be that, seeing your wife so bent on giving your daughter to that young man, he only pretended to help her. But then you understand, he wished you well, he wished me well . . . and without violating the conventions . . . Indeed, that conversation that he had with Clara . . .'

'But no, I was behind the door and can assure you,' broke in the Count.

'But what can you know about it?' the Senator interrupted him, 'there are a thousand ways of saying one thing with the lips and making another understood by the expression of the face, or by certain reticences . . . The Father perhaps suspected that you and your wife were listening; but really I can assure you that if this marriage did not go forward, then much of the merit for it is due to him.'

'Oh, that dear Father! I will thank him . . .'

'For pity's sake! That would be a fine thing! After all the pains that he has taken to keep it hidden and to make you believe that he approved your idea! Sometimes you are really too smart!'

On this occasion which of those concerned had shown himself to be smarter would be hard to say. Father Pendola, having overheard at table the sudden disapproval of the Senator for the marriage of his niece to Venchieredo, though he had up till then always approved it, had smelt out if not the letter from Venice then certainly something very similar. So with veiled words, headshakes and other ways at his disposal, he had given the Senator to understand exactly the reverse of what had actually occurred. Furthermore, the Senator on rising from table had clasped his hand in a mysterious way, and said:

'I have understood you, Father, and thank you in the name of all our kinsfolk.'

If the Senator was shrewd and had given many proofs of that quality in his long public and private life, here was certainly a case to prove the truth of the proverb that we all have in a single day our quarter hour of trickery. Nor is there any thief so cunning that he cannot be robbed by another even more cunning than he.

When the conversation between the two kinsmen was over and the fatal letter carefully burnt, they returned to the dining-room, chatting about Clara and the good fortune it would be if she could be settled in the Partistagno house. The Count had still some scruples, since all the relations of the young man were not in the good books of the Most Serene Republic; but the Senator replied that he should not be over-cautious, since they were only distant relations and that the young man had shown himself so respectful in his manner to the magistrates of the Republic that he would certainly be honoured from that side also.

'There is another difficulty,' added the Count, 'since however much we think Clara to be in love with him and he with her, yet there has been no sign on his part that he is disposed to declare himself.'

'Leave that to me,' replied the Senator. 'The young man pleases me. We have need of men like him, devout and respectful yes, but none the less strong and courageous. Leave it to me; I will see that he declares himself very soon.'

For the rest of the day they put such discussions aside and only that evening, in the silence of the nuptial bed, did the Count risk a hint to his wife of a grave and mysterious danger from which they had been saved by Clara's refusal of young Venchieredo. The Signora wanted to hear more and grumbled that she did not believe a word of it; but as soon as her husband had whispered the name of the Most Excellent Frumier, she became credulous and submissive and no longer insisted on trying to guess what her illustrious kinsman had kept wrapped in impenetrable mystery. Her husband also told her that the Senator had shown himself well disposed towards the marriage of Clara and the Partistagno and was even ready to take measures to see that the young man came to the point of a formal demand. The couple agreed together in marital content, which I do not imagine had any further consequences. The best result was however for Clara who, without knowing the reason why, ceased to be tormented and had a few days of respite in which to respond to the grateful and impassioned glances directed at her stealthily by Lucilio.

Meanwhile the Senator had kept his promise to intervene with the Partistagno that he should finally make up his mind to demand the hand of Clara. The correggiatrice, who was the chief counsellor of the young man, was happy to assist the noble Frumier in this matter, and knew so well the simplicity and conceit that were his principal qualities that she was able to succeed in her intentions even earlier than she had hoped. The Partistagno expressed his sorrow that the girl was dying for love of him, felt proud that he was considered worthy of becoming the nephew of a Venetian senator and confessed that he had long been fascinated by the girl and that only a natural indolence had hitherto prevented him from changing this love from the purely platonic sphere. After pronouncing this last phrase, the young man almost gasped at the difficulty of having constructed it.

'Take heart, then, and let us move quickly!' said the lady. He took his leave of her with the most sincere assurances that the condition of the maiden moved him to pity and that he would make every haste.

But the Partistagnos were born with ceremonial in their blood and several days passed before the young man had prepared all the ingredients for a solemn demand in marriage. In the meantime he came to Fratta as usual and looked at Clara as a housewife would look at a turkey held in reserve for the Easter banquet. At last, one day, two cavaliers presented themselves at the castle drawbridge, on two palfreys caparisoned with gold and purple. Manichetto ran at full speed to the kitchen to announce this solemn embassy while the two cavaliers, grave and solemn, advanced towards the stables. One was the Partistagno with a plumed three-cornered hat and lace enough on his shirt to stick out a full span from his chest and so many rings, pins and brooches that he looked exactly like a pincushion. He was accompanied by a maternal uncle, one of the thousand Barons of Cormons, dressed all in black with silver embroideries as befitting the solemnity of his office. The Partistagno remained upright on his horse like the statue of Gattamelata, while the other dismounted, and having handed the reins to a groom, entered by the door of the great staircase whose two wings were opened wide to receive him.

He was shown into the great hall, where he had to wait for a little, for the Counts of Fratta also knew the ceremonial code and did not want to show themselves less familiar with it than their noble guests. At last the Count, wearing a waistcoat literally covered with lace and the Countess with twenty feet of ribbon dangling from her cap, presented themselves with a thousand excuses for their involuntary delay. Clara, clothed in white and as pale as wax, was beside her mother; the Chancellor and Monsignor Orlando, who had his napkin in hand and was trying to conceal it in the pocket of his coat, stood on either side. There followed a deep silence, while both parties made low bows; it looked as if they were getting ready to dance a minuet. I, the Pisana and the maids, who were standing by the door to watch, were amazed by the imposing nature of the scene. The Signor Baron put one hand on his breast and extending the other, recited his part magnificently:

'In the name of my nephew, the Most Illustrious and Most Excellent Signor Alberto of Partistagno, Baron of Dorsa, Magistrate of Fratta, Elder of San Mauro, etc., etc., I, Baron Duringo of Caporetto, have the honour to ask the hand in marriage of the Most Illustrious and Excellent Lady, the Countess Clara of Fratta, daughter of the Most Illustrious and Excellent Signor Count Giovanni of Fratta and of the noble lady Cleonice Navagero.'

A murmur of approval welcomed these words and the maids were on the verge of breaking into applause. It seemed to them just like a marionette show. The Countess turned to Clara who had clenched her hands and seemed nearer to dying than to getting betrothed.

'My daughter,' she took it upon herself to say, 'welcomes with gratitude the honoured offer, and . . .'

'No, mother,' interrupted Clara in a voice choked with sobs but in which force of will mastered the tremors of emotion and respect, 'no, mother. I will never marry . . . I thank the Signor Baron, but . . .'

At this point her voice died away, every trace of living colour vanished from her face and her knees seemed at the point of failing her. The maids, not thinking that they thus betrayed the fact that they had been listening, rushed into the hall shouting: 'The young mistress is dying! The young mistress is dying!' and picked her up in their arms. I, with the Pisana and a few others behind us, who had crowded in to enjoy the spectacle, followed them with curiosity. The Countess raged and clenched her fists, the Count swayed to and fro like a flagstaff that has lost its balance, the Chancellor stood behind him as if to support him if he fell, Monsignor pulled his napkin out of his pocket and wiped his forehead with it and the Baron alone remained boldly with outstretched arm as if it had been he who with his magic gesture had produced all this confusion. The Countess busied herself about her daughter to try and bring her to, but seeing that, as soon as she came to her senses, she went on shaking her head in a sign of negation and almost fainted again, she turned to the Baron and said in a voice stifled with anger:

'Signor, you can see for yourself; an unforeseen accident has spoilt the ceremony for today; but I can assure you in the name of my daughter, that never was girl so honoured by any proposal as she by the demand made for her in the name of the Most Excellent Partistagno. He may count upon having an obedient and faithful wife. Only I implore him to delay till a more opportune moment his first visit as the betrothed.'

The maids then carried their young mistress out of the hall. She, though almost unconscious, continued to make signs of denial with her head and hands. But the Baron no longer looked at her any more than at an article of furniture in the house, but braced himself to recite the second and final part of his oration.

'I thank, in the name of my nephew,' he said, 'the noble bride and all her most excellent family for the honour done him in accepting him as the betrothed. Once the banns have been duly published, the ceremony will be celebrated in the chapel of this Jurisdiction of Fratta. I, Baron of Caporetto, offer myself now as guardian of the ring and may the blessings of heaven fall benignly on this most happy jointure of the illustrious and ancient houses of Fratta and of Partistagno.'

At this point he made a threefold bow, turned on his heel and went down the staircase with all the majesty with which he had ascended.

'Well?' asked his nephew, preparing to dismount.

'Stay where you are, my nephew,' replied the Baron, preventing him from dismounting and himself mounting once more. 'For today they excuse you from the first visit of the betrothed. The bride has collapsed from delight; I am still quite overcome.'

'Really?' said the Partistagno, blushing with pleasure.

'Look!' replied the Baron, showing two moist and bloodshot eyes which one might have thought accustomed only to look into the bottoms of many glasses. 'I believe that I wept.'

'Do you think a diamond necklace will be enough for a wedding gift?' his nephew asked, riding up alongside him as soon as they were outside the castle.

'In view of this fresh incident, let us add an emerald clasp,' replied the Baron. 'The Partistagnos must honour the feelings that they inspire.'

So they proceeded as far as Lugugnana, devising the splendours of the feasts and ceremonies that would be held on the occasion of the wedding. But what was the astonishment of both of them when, on the following day, they received a letter from the Count of Fratta that proclaimed his displeasure at the decision expressed by his daughter to consecrate her virginity to the Lord in a convent! The young man doubted if any girl in the world could possibly prefer a convent to him; but he had to realize this fact and remained therefore a little humiliated. But it was still worse when, through local gossip, he came to hear that the young girl did not want to retire to a convent, but that her parents intended to place her in one as a punishment for having refused such a match as his, and that Lucilio Vianello was his rival for Clara's heart. The Baron fled to Caporetto to hide his shame; the Partistagno remained to shout to all the corners of the province that he would be revenged on Lucilio, on Clara and on all her relations and woe to them if, nun or no nun, they did not send his bride to his house. He went on to say that he was quite sure of her love for him, and that it was only the bad faith of her parents and the evil arts of the little doctor that had prevented her from declaring it.

At Portogruaro meanwhile there was a great family counsel in the Frumier mansion on what should be done, and the case was indeed quite an unusual one, since there were not at that time so many young girls who would have opposed the wishes of their parents with such stubbornness. They wanted to have recourse to the Bishop, but Father Pendola at once rejected this idea. All were tacitly in agreement that the gossip of the countryside was only too true and that Lucilio Vianello was the stumbling block. To send him away was not possible; it was therefore a question of sending Clara away. The Frumier palace in Venice was then unoccupied, and the Countess did not seem averse to going to live there. After much discussion it was decided that they should move to Venice. But to avoid all ceremony and any occasion for great expenditure, only she and her daughter would take up residence there and the family would continue to live at Fratta. She flattered herself that the whims would soon leave Clara's head and, if not, then there were plenty of convents in Venice where she could be corrected. The Count complained rather at being relegated to Fratta, for he had a considerable fear of the Partistagno; but his kinsman assured him that he would be quite safe and that he himself would be surety for it.

And indeed, a month after these discussions, the Countess and Clara were already settled in Venice in the Frumier Palace, but she had to confess that she had made very little progress towards changing her daughter's views. At Fratta we were happier than ever before, since now that the cat was away, the mice could play.

Furthermore, as if to nip in the bud all the hopes of the Countess, an event took place which no one would ever have believed possible. Lucilio, who had dragged out for so long the question of his laureate, suddenly decided to follow the Countess and her daughter and despite the opposition of Doctor Sperandio, left for Padua, was made doctor there, and then instead of returning to Fratta, settled down in Venice, where he intended to practice medicine. This great news was received at Portogruaro only after he had already mustered a clientele which relieved him of any dependence on his family. Imagine the perplexity! One proposed to have him arrested, another wanted the Countess and Clara to return at once, another proposed that the whole family should leave for Venice in order to counter his audacities. But nothing came of all this. The Countess wrote that she was not afraid, that Clara appeared to be devoting herself seriously to her vocation and that, even if they were to change their residence, Lucilio, with his profession as a doctor, would be able to follow them to the ends of the world if he wanted.

They therefore confined themselves to asking the Senator to write to one of his colleagues in the Council of Ten asking him to keep the little doctor under observation; to which he replied that they already had him under observation day and night but that no noise should be made about it, since it was rumoured that he was under the protection of a Secretary of the French Legation, a certain Jacob, who was in these days the real Ambassador since the leaders of the revolution in Paris had confidence mainly in him. The Count, hearing of such high matters, seemed as if possessed, but the Senator comforted him and told him to have courage and try instead to satisfy his wife who was always lamenting his parsimony in sending her money. The poor man sighed, thinking that it was for the sake of economy that he had been relegated to Fratta, but that, notwithstanding, they spent more money than seemed necessary for the most splendid maintenance of the whole family. He sighed, I say, but none the less scrabbled in his half-empty coffer for those wretched ducats and made little rolls of them, which fell like all the others into the Venetian abyss. The bailiff warned him that if he went on in this way the Fratta incomes would shortly be mortgaged for fifty years to come. But his master replied that there was no help for it and with this philosophy went on as before. The happiest member of the family was undoubtedly Monsignor who was quite oblivious to all this and continued to gobble the capons and ducks of his honoured relatives.

As for me, I had finished my studies in the humanities and philosophy, a little in the gypsy manner it is true, but still finished. And in my final examination they found me no more and no less of an ass than the others who had attended the course regularly. Then came the moment when they should have sent me to Padua, but the Count's finances did not allow of this munificence and justice demands that I give praise to whom it belongs for a good deed. Father Pendola was not the sort of man to relapse into sloth in a post as house chaplain at the age of fifty, just when his ambition was growing greater and more resolute. As Chaplain and favourite counsellor of the Frumier mansion, he had been able to strike a bargain and gain the esteem of many priests and Monsignors who frequented it; he was never lacking in holy maxims or the expedients of conscience to become beloved of both parties, and he succeeded so well in this and knew so well how to profit by his success that the matter came to the ears of the Bishop. It was said that at every perplexity that distracted the diocese, the Bishop used to exclaim: 'Oh, if only I were Father Pendola! If only I had Father Pendola in the Curia!'

The humility of the good Father gave greater prominence to these episcopal expressions and the secretary having died suddenly, there were priests of both parties, Clausedans and plainsmen, who implored the Frumiers to persuade the Father to accept this post. By this means, each of them hoped to establish his own party more firmly than ever in the episcopate. The Senator spoke of the matter to the Father, who pretended to refuse, rejected the crown like Caesar but let himself be crowned like Augustus; and soon he became secretary to the Bishop and by his skill and manoeuvring became master, to say the least, of the whole diocese. Great things were expected but for the moment all were deceived; but all on the other hand were very pleased since they had hopes for the future and relied on the expansive promises of the good Father.

He had only recently been installed in his new dignity when the

Rector of Teglio introduced me to him in his parsonage, where the Bishop was making a visit. I pleased him, it must be admitted, and he promised me to intercede in my favour with the Senator Frumier. The Senator, in fact, enjoyed the right of nominating a candidate to a place in a free college for poor students at the University of Padua; and this place being vacant, he allotted it to me in the coming November. He even complained to his kinsman that he had not previously mentioned my case, for he would have made provision for me with all his heart. But the benefit came in time and I thanked most fervently both my Maecenas and my valued intercessor. For then I could see no further and had not yet learnt how to ring my coins on the table to hear if they were genuine.

I was not displeased to change my surroundings. The Pisana, after Lucilio had left for Venice and Venchieredo had abandoned the house, was making eyes at Giulio del Ponte, and this time seriously, since she was now fifteen and looked and doubtless felt eighteen. It was just at this point that, to divert myself from so much heartbreak, I began to carouse and flirt in company with all the buli of the countryside and in brief soon became the gallant of all the peasant and artisan girls. When I returned from some festa or wedding feast on the old grey nag lent me by Marchetto and playing my pipes like a mountaineer, I had a dozen of them around me dancing the furlana all down the road. It seems to me now that I must have looked like a caricature of the Birth of the Sun, painted by Guido Reni, with his retinue of the dancing hours. However, I must say that this life wearied me; and it was further interrupted by a mournful incident: the death of Martino, who expired in my arms after a very short attack of apoplexy. I believe I was the only one to weep over his grave, for it had been judged wise to conceal this loss from the old Countess, who was already almost a hundred years old and lapsing into her second childhood after the departure of Clara. The Pisana, confided to the far from sure guidance of that tailless fox, the Signora Veronica, flew more and more into passions and the evil strain in her character became even worse than before in utter idleness. The day before I was to leave for Padua, I saw her returning from a walk, red and fuming.

'What is the matter, Pisana?' I asked her, my heart swelling with pity and even more, I confess, with that great love that was stronger and more powerful than myself.

'That dog of a Giulio did not come!' she replied furiously.

Then, breaking into sobs, she threw her arms around my neck, crying: 'You really love me, it is you who have always loved me!' and she kissed me and I returned her kisses frantically.

Four days later I attended my first lecture on jurisprudence, but understood not a word of it, for the memory of those kisses whirled diabolically through my head. The students were in great tumult, in violent discussion, because the news from France was more and more warlike and against the old governments. For my part I sadly gnawed the meagre crusts of the college and the abundant glosses thereon of my digestion, thinking always of the Pisana and of the joys, now sweet, now bitter, but always dear to memory, of our childhood years. And so closed for me the Year of Grace 1792. Only, I recall that when the news of the beheading of King Louis XVI came towards the end of the coming January, I recited a Requiem for the repose of his soul, a proof of the moderate nature of my opinions at that time.

CHAPTER VIII

FRANCE had decapitated a king and abolished the monarchy; the inner rumblings of the volcano announced a coming eruption; all the old governments looked horrified at one another and hastily advanced their armies to quell the conflagration at its birth. They no longer fought to avenge royal blood but to work out their own salvation. Driven back by the invincible fury of the republican legions, Nice and Savoy, the two western gates of Italy had unfolded the tricolor; already one could recognize the power of the invaders in the greatness of the promises, and the greater urgency of the peril in the internal seething of the states. Alliances and treaties were being concluded on every side. Naples and the Pope shook with craven fears; the old Europe, aroused from its sleep by a blood-stained fantasm, struggled to exorcise it. What then of the Most Serene Republic of Venice? The stupid College of the Savi decreed that the French Revolution was no more to them than an academic question of history, rejected every proposal of alliance with Austria, with St Petersburg, with Naples and persuaded the Senate unanimously to rely upon the null and ruinous policy of unarmed neutrality.

Despite the frenzied forensic eloquence of Francesco Pesaro, on 26 January 1793, Gerolamo Zuliani, Savio of the Week, won his point that Giovanni Jacob should be recognized as Ambassador of the French Republic. Free and reasoned, such a decision would have had nothing imprudent or humiliating about it; moreover, neither family ties nor community of interest nor sworn pacts required the Republic to revenge the imprisonment of Louis XVI, but the venality of the proposer and the precipitate assent of the Senate impressed on this act the stigma of real and craven treason.

The news, quickly widespread, of the murder of the king, changed in the opinion of the governments, this infatuated docility of the Venetians to a venal complicity; disdained on one side, hated on the other, the menaces accumulated. The French Legation in Venice concentrated about itself all the underhand dealings and all the hopes of the Italian innovators; it gave opportunity to other emissaries to instigate the Ottoman Porte against the Empire and the most Serene Republic, and so to divert the Russian and German forces. The College of Savi, always renewed and always imbecile, concealed these perils from the Senate; those retiring transferred to the newly appointed their stolid assurances and their flaccid indolence. Existing for fourteen centuries amongst so many ruins of orders and of empires, a sudden collapse seemed to them impossible; like a decrepit old man who, since he had lived to be ninety, considers that he will never die.

Finally, towards the close of spring 1794, after the unwarlike neutrality of Genoa had been violated by France to the future damage of Piedmont and Lombardy, Pesaro loftily admitted the nearness of the danger and the possible consequence that, between the Imperials descending from the Tyrol into the Duchy of Mantua and the French opposed to them, a conflict might arise on the states of the *terraferma*. That shook even the somnolent Senate and, contrary to the opinion of Zuliani, of Battaia and of other rabbits, even greater rabbits than these, it decreed that the *terraferma* should be reinforced with fresh militia from Istria and Dalmatia, the fortresses repaired and the artillery reconditioned. Thus was saved, not the state, but its decorum. The Savi of the time, first among them Zuliani, took it upon themselves to render even this ineffective. To revenge themselves for the defeat they had experienced in the Senate, they consulted how best to thwart the execution of this decree and finally decided to make use of the method of the celebrated Boerhaave, who sugared the pills for his patients so that they should swallow them without tasting the bitterness within. It was shown that little could be done, and that slowly, because of the poverty of the treasury; in fact, they did nothing at all. The whole reinforcement was reduced to seven thousand men, recruited with great difficulty and little by little from Lombard Venetia. Pesaro, Pietro his brother, and one among the Savi themselves whose name is free, at least in this, from the common ignominy, Filippe Calbo, pointed out to the Senate the bad faith of such prevarications, but the Senate had fallen back once more into its blind torpor, swallowed the pill sugared for it by the Savi, and never tasted, or at least not then, its bitterness, though it later felt its poisonous effect.

So my life began to develop amidst these ruins, my mind grew stronger every day in long and furious study; there grew in me, together with my defences against sorrow, the force and the will to work; love tortured me, I had no family, my country was dying. But how could I have loved, or better how could that torpid, marshy, impotent country have been able to awake in me a worthy, useful and active affection? One does not love corpses, one weeps for them. The freedom of rights, the sanctity of the laws, the religion of glory, which give to a country a majesty almost divine, had not existed for long years under the wings of the Lion. Of the fatherland, there remained the old, uprooted, contaminated limbs; the spirit had departed and whoever felt in his heart devotion to things sublime and eternal, sought for other images to which to dedicate the hope and faith of his soul. If Venice was, of all the Italian governments, the most null and senile, all of them from the greatest to the least were in their death throes because of this lack of thought and of moral vitality. Therefore the number of spirits who dedicated themselves to the cult of liberty and the other rights of man, proclaimed in France, was far greater in Italy than elsewhere.

This, rather than the servitude we suffered or the similarity of race, served the French leaders and aided them to subvert the musty dictates of Venice, of Genoa, of Naples and of Rome, in fact of all the national governments. So true is it that, as in individuals so in society and all human institutions, without the germ, without the kernel, without the spiritual fire, not even the material organism can prolong by much its life. And if external force does not violently destroy its designs, then life little by little weakens and ceases of itself.

My life in Padua was really that of a poor student. I looked like the servant of some priest and bore modestly the symbols of the Italian nation as was still the custom of students, as it had been in the times of Galileo, when Greeks, Spaniards, English, Germans, Poles and Norwegians competed at this university. It was said that Gustavus Adolphus was there a disciple of the great astronomer; which was of very little importance in the destiny either of the one or of the other. My companions at college were for the most part mountain boors, coarse, dirty, ignorant, the seedbed of future chancellors for those proud magistrates or of venal notaries for the criminal courts. They caroused and squabbled among themselves and picked continual quarrels with the police, the butchers or the innkeepers; above all with these last, since they had the strange idea of not allowing anyone to leave the taverns before they had paid their bills. These disputes ended before the privileged tribunal of the students, where the judges showed the easy good sense of always giving judgement in favour of the students, in order not to incur their wrath, as implacable as it was lacking in justice and moderation. The patrician students kept as aloof as possible from this rabble, more from fear than from pride, I imagine. And there was not lacking a middle class, also, that of the majority, of the waverers, of the moderates, who during the fat days of the month took part in the expensive pleasures of the nobles, and in the last lean days had recourse to the villainous and impudent junketings of the others. They spoke ill of these with the others and of the others with these; afterwards among themselves, they mocked at both of them. They were the real precursors of that middle class, brainless and heartless, who considered themselves democrats since they were equally unable to obey nobly as to command usefully.

Meanwhile, the French disorders soon began in one way or another to stir up even the empty and frivolous talents of this student mob. Blood boils and must boil at all costs in young veins; the young are like flies who without reason must go on flying and buzzing. Among the patricians there would be scholastic innovators who applauded, and timid hypocrites who were terrified; among the plebeians, some who shouted for Marat, but the inquisitors taught them wisdom and the greater number, sheeplike in their adoration of St Mark, stormed against the distant French, showing the usual courage of those who revere and then serve the present holders of power. Those of the middle class waited, hoped, chattered; it seemed to them that the reins of government must pass from the nobles to them in the natural course of events, and that they would seize them and then argue among themselves how to prevent their falling still lower. But they did not shout at the tops of their voices; they whispered, they murmured like one who reserves his voice and his skin for better times.

The Inquisitors, one can well believe, watched with a thousand eyes this swarm of opinions, of hopes, of passions; every so often some hornet that had buzzed too loud fell into the web woven by these spiders. The hornet was taken in a wherry to Venice, and once past the Bridge of Sighs nobody ever heard him named again. With such tricks and sleights of hand, ideally suited to frighten a people in its infancy, they thought to save the Republic from the impending storm.

For myself, I had too many memories to think over, too many sorrows to contend with, to let me worry my brains about fishing in such troubled waters. I had heard France spoken of once or twice as a region so far removed that I could in no way understand how the madness raging there could affect us. Indeed, the French had seemed to me figures of delirium and nothing more. The autumn following my first year of jurisprudence finally put a seal on my political incuriosity. The journey on foot to Fratta, seeing once again the Pisana, loves reborn and once again broken off for some fresh extravagance or some new jealousy, the duties laid on me by way of experiment by the Chancellor, the eulogies of the Count and of the Frumiers, the escapades of the Venchieredo, the disorders in the Provedoni family, the dissensions between Doretta and Leopardo, the fresh exploits of the Spaccafumo, the advice of the old rector and the singular counsels of Father Pendola; all these gave me too much to think about, to meditate on, to enjoy or to suffer, that I should repent having left to my companions the care of the affairs of France and the pastime of reading the newspapers.

Despite all that the Pisana made me suffer in those two months, all these things seemed to me like a comedy to be enjoyed. That the Pisana's character should have improved in the interval, nobody would want to believe, even were I enough of a barefaced liar to affirm it. However, she had grown in beauty both in face and form. She had really become a woman; not one of those who resemble delicate flowers from whom the first November breeze takes the colour and the fragrance, but an upright, proud firm countenance, softened by a rosy freshness and a mobility of feature that was strange and swiftly changing, but always gracious and fascinating. When her proud and sculptured brow bent for an instant to the bold glances of some young man and the veiled and troubled eyes looked downward, such a flame of desire, of voluptuousness and of love shone through her whole being that the air around her seemed as if on fire. I was jealous of whoever looked at her. How could I not be, I who loved her so much, who knew her to the innermost parts of her being? Poor Pisana! Was it her fault if nature, having abandoned her to her own devices, had spoilt with its hand all that that same hand had prepared, and that the loving prudence of art had extracted from it a miracle of intelligence, of beauty, and of virtue? And I, was it my fault that I loved her always, however ungrateful, perfidious and unworthy, when I knew that I was the sole person in the world who would feel pity for her? Has the terrible misfortune of sin not to have some recompense of comfort here below?

Oh memory, memory, how can I describe you? Our torment, our reward, our tyrant, you devour our days, hour by hour, minute by minute and then restore them to us in a moment as in a symbol of eternity! You take all from us, you give all back to us; you destroy everything, you preserve everything; you speak of death to the living and of life to those already buried! The memory of man is the sun of knowledge, the faith of justice, the spectre of immortality, the terrestrial and finite image of God who is limitless and who is everywhere! But my memory, meanwhile, serves me ill enough; it binds me, youth to man, with the caprices of a boyhood passion. But yet I pardon it; since in my judgement it is better to recall too much and sorrow over it, than to forget all for the sake of tranquillity. To tell you how much I suffered in the course of those few weeks would need a long volume. But I must confess, in my own praise, that compassion even more than jealousy tormented me; no cross is so hard to bear as that of having to censure and bewail the object of our love. The extravagances of the Pisana, often amounting to injustice, would frequently have seemed shameless, had I not remembered how reckless she was by nature.

Her infatuations no longer had either reason or excuse, duration or method. One week she would be seized with a respectful and vehement affection for the old Rector of Teglio; she would go out with a black veil on her head and her eyes lowered and would chat with him at the door of the parsonage, turning her back on the passers-by; she would listen patiently to his advice and even to his semi-sermons. She got it into her head to become a holy Magdalen and dressed her hair as she had seen it on that saint in a little picture at the head of her bed. The next day she would change as if by enchantment; her delight was no longer the Rector but Marchetto the Serjeant; she wanted him at all costs to teach her to ride; she would scour the countryside bareback on some old nag, like an amazon, scratching her forehead and her knees on the branches in the wood. At such times she only wanted poor people and the peasants around her; she thought herself, probably, a *castellana* of the Middle Ages; she would walk by the brook arm in arm with Sandro the miller and even little Donato, the apothecary's son, seemed to her then too dressed up and artificial. A little later she would completely change register; she wanted to be taken morning and evening to Portogruaro and foundered all her father's horses in the muddy ruts of those abominable roads, for she must needs always drive at a gallop. She enjoyed outshining the Podestà's wife, the Correggiatrice and all the ladies of the city. Giulio del Ponte, the liveliest and most sought-after beau, served her as an echo; she would talk with him and gesticulate not because she had anything to say to him, but merely to get the reputation of being witty and sharp-tongued. Giulio was madly in love with her and would have sworn that she was wittier than all the sharpest tongues in Venice. She, however, was always discontented, always tormented by ill-defined desires, and filled with an unbridled wish to please all, to do good to all; she thought only of that, only studied to that end, and seldom took the trouble even to listen to what others were saying.

One most singular trait of her character was that when she could be certain of satisfying someone there was nothing, however difficult or unpleasant, that she would refuse to do. If a cripple, a beggar, a monster, had shown a desire to get a flattering glance from her, she would have given him one, as amiable, as long and as fiery as to the smartest and most resplendent dandy. Was it generosity, recklessness or pride? Perhaps all three of these motives united to make her as she was; for however odious and despicable the person, he would never fail by an attitude of entreaty to obtain from her confidence and pity, if not affection and esteem. Even with Fulgenzio she was sometimes so familiar that she would sit at his hearth while they were stirring the polenta. Then, having gone away, the very memory of that greasy and hypocritical sacristan would make her shudder. The Signora Veronica was well aware of all this and however antipathetic she had been at first, had known how to make herself supportable and even dear by force of blandishments. You can imagine what perfection of education the Pisana would get from the interested indulgence of this street-corner maidservant. Faustina had finally entered into her favour by acting as a go-between and helping Giulio del Ponte to escape by way of the stables if the Count or Monsignor woke earlier than usual. These town-bred tarts, when reduced to living in the country, become mistresses of vice and corruption; and Faustina was perhaps worse than any of the others since she brought to it a temperament far from prudish. The complicity of her mistress seemed to her the best pledge of impunity and you can realize that she assisted her with zeal and excited her with suggestions and example!

I still marvel that no really serious scandal broke out under the eyes of the Count and Monsignor; but perhaps appearances were worse than reality, and the bodily fatigues of her wild and vagabond life quenched for a time the fiery and sensual instincts of the Pisana. In such matters I was wholly disposed to see more black than white; since having been a witness and a companion of her childish escapades, I had great difficulty in believing that a more mature age would have stifled in her what she was accustomed to excite in others. The Pisana was a creature so made that only one who was, so to speak, born with her and brought up with her, could have divined her completely.

The Pisana behaved with her grandmother as she did with others; one week yes and another week no; only her father, the Chancellor, and Monsignor her uncle did not enjoy her insulting tendernesses; but these were mere figures of cardboard who had no soul, no colour or temperament of their own and the Pisana ignored them. I have no doubt she would also have forgotten all about her mother and sister, since distance always prodigiously moderated her feelings. But a letter from the Countess with a postscript from Clara made her remember every two months that part of her family that lived in Venice; the more so since in these letters there was also news of the young Count who was completing the last years of his education, so that every two months she remembered that she had a brother. Her uncle and aunt, the Frumiers, were the only persons, near or distant whose names were always in her mind or on her lips. The ability to name a senator, a relation of the Doge Manin, and to say 'he is my uncle', was a considerable satisfaction for her and she often availed herself of it without any real necessity. Giulio del Ponte and Veronica often mentioned her uncle the Senator when they saw her dull or out of sorts. At these magic words she would revive at once and begin to chatter about the power and authority of the Senator, his palaces, his villas, his gondolas, his silk robes, his jewels and her aunt's diamonds. The greater splendours she narrated, the more she let her tongue slide over them carelessly, as if to show that such things were so familiar to her that they were no longer of importance. Poor girl, she had never seen either jewels, villas or palaces save the Frumier mansion at Portogruaro and her mamma's little diamond cross. But imagination supplied the lack and she behaved like actresses who talk in comedies of all their treasures but who have never ridden even a donkey or seen the colour of a *zecchino*.

But I was always astonished that, despite all the exaggerations with which she spoke of the mansion of the Most Excellent Frumiers, she remained quiet, restrained and almost dull when she appeared at the assemblies there. I can understand now that the necessity of ceding the leading place to her aunt was alone sufficient to clip the wings of her pride; and then, grown wild in the solitude of Fratta and the company of rough countryfolk and impudent gossips, she would not risk herself in the discussions and became angry at having to show herself inferior in point of wit and elegance. Wanting to revenge herself with the splendours and attractions of her beauty, she fell into the other extreme of always making a thousand childish actions and remaining for ever preoccupied with herself in a way that seemed almost stupid. Monsignor di Sant'Andrea who, despite his barbarous abandonment by the Countess, had still preserved a warm liking for the girl, often protected her from the raillery of the malicious. He affirmed that she was full of wit, talent and knowledge, but what she needed to enhance all these natural gifts was a sharp attack of smallpox.

'But may God preserve her,' added the learned cleric, 'since there is enough genius and doctrine on the shelves of the libraries, while beauty like that is not to be found in Heaven or earth and one would have to be made of stone not to be stirred to the bottom of one's heart even by looking at her.'

Giulio del Ponte supported with drawn sword the words of Monsignor; but the Most Excellent Frumier threw at the young man an occasional bitter-sweet glance when he grew too warm in support of this argument. It is true that the Pisana in no way resembled Clara, but Giulio rather too obviously resembled Lucilio, and the Senator had made several hints to his kinsman on the subject. But it needed more than that to spur on the imagination of the Signor Count! He had unloaded all the duties of his paternity on the shoulders of the Signora Veronica, and since her unending chatter always made him feel dizzy, he contented himself with asking the Captain:

'Eh, Captain! What does your wife say of the Pisana? Is she satisfied with her behaviour, her manners, her work? Is she becoming expert in looking after a house?'

The Captain, well primed by Veronica, replied yes to everything and then twisted and retwisted his poor moustaches, which by dint of being fingered, twirled and generally ill-treated, had been reduced from black to grey, from grey to white and from white to a yellowish hue. They now had the lovely colour of spun sugar; and only the tail of Marocco, by merit of age and being continually scorched by the fire, had acquired a similar colour. Marchetto had offered the Captain for that tail alone the reversion of all his winnings at games, and Andreini and the Chaplain had asserted that only the valorous Sandracca and his noble pointer could compete with the dawn in the colour of their hair. These perpetual guests of the Castle of Fratta had become more domestic and even jovial after the departure of the Countess; and not even the Chaplain suffered any longer from subjection. Even the kitchen cats had lost their former savagery and crouched among the ashes or on the feet of the company. A large old tabby, grave as a counsellor, had joined in the closest friendship with Marocco; they slept together in a community of straw and fleas, and walked together, ate from the same dish and took exercise in the same hunting, that of mice. But with what moderation and lordliness! One saw in them only dilettante hunters who indulged themselves only to kill time and ceded their prey to the menials, the other toms and tabbies of the kitchen.

To tell the truth, after the first days had passed, in which the Pisana had become once more my confidante as of old, I no longer felt at my ease among these people. When I had been a little boy, I had contented myself in not understanding and in admiring them; now, instead, I understood them very well and could not imagine how they could enjoy such dull foolishness. Therefore I withdrew into the Chancery in desperation, and there scribbled reports and copied judgements, repairing little by little the countless blunders that flowed so freely from the most fecund pen of my principal. But my head was always in the clouds, at every footfall I heard in the courtyard I would run to the window to see if it were the Pisana going out or returning from her solitary jaunts. I was so besotted that not even the clatter of a pair of pattens left me unmoved; I heard only the Pisana, saw her everywhere and however much she avoided me, or however much she sulked when she met me by chance, I never ceased to desire her as the sole good that I had.

The Signora Veronica used to deride me for this mania of mine and often entertained me with tales of the great impression the Pisana made at Portogruaro, of Giulio del Ponte who was dying of love for her and of Raimondo Venchieredo who, excluded from seeing her at Fratta or in the Frumier mansion, used to wait for her in the road or in the places where she was accustomed to walk. I swallowed my anger and fled from that babbler. Then I would go over again, step by step, the rambles of earlier times and even went as far as the Bastion of Attila to watch the sunset there and to soak myself in that feeling of the infinite with which nature enchants us in open and solitary places. I looked at the sky, the lagoon, the sea, recalling again the memories of my childhood and thinking how different things were now and what still greater differences were promised, or menaced, me in the future.

From time to time I would go to Cordovado to the Provedoni household where at least I could refresh my soul with a little peace, a little family contentment, at least when Doretta had not spoilt it with her escapades or her whims of being a great lady. The younger Provedoni brothers, Bruto, Grifone and Mastino, were three fine hard-working boys, obedient as sheep and strong as bulls. Bradamante and Acquilina pleased me with their simple ingenuousness and the continual and cheerful occupations of their little hands for the good of the family. Acquilina was a little girl, scarcely ten years old, but careful, grave and farseeing as a housewife. To see her at the trough at the bottom of the vegetable garden with her sleeveless jacket and her shirt rolled up to her elbows, she looked like a real little woman, and I would stay there near her for long hours, feeling myself a little boy again and enjoying, at least in fancy, a little peace of mind. Brown as a gypsy, of that golden brown that recalls the splendours of the Arabs, compact and robust in body, with two thick yet delicate eyebrows that met as if disdainfully across her forehead, two large deep grey eyes and a mass of curling raven-black hair that half hid her neck and ears, Acquilina had an air of calm and competence that contrasted with the hesitations of her elder sister. She, despite her twenty years, seemed more of a baby than the other; but none the less she was a nice girl and the Signor Antonio said jokingly that whoever wanted to marry her would have to pay him dear. But both of them showed themselves admirably patient in their behaviour towards Leopardo and their sister-in-law.

She, arrogant and cross-grained, was discontented with everything; her husband always hoodwinked and irritated with her, was unjust and cruel in turn; it is difficult to describe how greatly his temperament had changed under the domination of his wife. He could hardly be recognized and everybody tried to guess what potion Doretta had brewed to bewitch him in such a way. But it was only love: love which is an angel's fan in the hands of goodness but which becomes a firebrand in hell when snatched up by pride and malice. Doretta repented agreeing to marriage with Leopardo and never failed to say so to everyone, himself included, making him realize her condescension in marrying him. Raimondo's courtship had made her believe that if she had had the patience to remain single she might have been able to aspire to a much higher position than that of the wife of a small country landowner, with hard, bigoted and frugal peasants for mother- and sisters-in-law. Living in that house seemed intolerable to her; she often spent whole days at Venchieredo and when they asked her where she had been she did not even deign to answer, but shrugged her shoulders and went her own way. In order to appear with great ceremony at Portogruaro, she had found the excuse of choosing Father Pendola as confessor. But her frequent confessions contributed little enough, it seemed, to improve her habits.

She had ceased to be on good terms even with her father, as is always the way with morose temperaments, she began by being irritated with one person and ended by being a burden to all. She nursed a grudge against him for having consented to her marriage with Leopardo and when Doctor Natalino said that it had been she who wanted it, would turn on him like a viper and shout that it was the duty of fathers to aid by their common sense the immature judgement of their daughters and certainly if she had shown any desire to go and throw herself into a well, she would have had the consolation of knowing that her father would have given her the first push. It was the task of the young castellan to calm her after such rages, and how he succeeded and to what honour of the credulous Leopardo, I leave it to my readers to guess. In the end the whole countryside was whispering about her and the family bore it all resignedly, while the poor husband never saw anything she desired without spouting fire from his nostrils to get it for her. I drew from the spectacle of these domestic scenes my own conclusions and my own comforts; I realized that happiness is relative and transient and, even more, rare and fallacious. On returning to Fratta, if very little remained to me of these comforts, I had at least passed an hour or so without tearing open my own wounds; sometimes, indeed, they slowly healed over, but the scars remained down to the bone and I became like those travelling barometers whose every rib and joint indicate by aches and pains and creakings every change in the weather.

Thus I continued, vagabond and melancholy all that autumn vacation, till one day when I thought I had glimpsed in the Pisana a more amiable mien than usual, I followed her out by the vegetable garden on to the Fossalta road and, drawing near, took her arm in mine and asked if she would accept me as a companion. I should not have dared so much! The eyes of the girl turned upon me seemed to want to tear me apart, she then tried to give vent to her anger in some great insult, but her voice was suffocated in her throat and she bit her lip till the blood dripped down on her chin.

'Pisana!' I cried, 'for pity's sake, Pisana, don't look at me like that!'

She dragged her arm away from mine violently and stopped biting her lip, since her rage had now found words.

'What are you doing? What are you asking?' she replied scornfully. 'We are not children any more, or so it seems to me! It is time now for each of us to know his place and I wonder that you, instead of helping me to forget it, should recall it to my mind when my too great goodness makes me forget. You know very well that I am wayward and impetuous; it is up to you, who are cold and reasonable by nature, to remember who you are and who I am . . .'

When she had finished, she turned her back on me and made her way towards the shade of some willows where Giulio del Ponte was waiting for her, musket on shoulder. I knew then that she had made a tryst with him there and the idea that I had followed her to spy upon her had inspired those hard words. I suffered then to the depths of my being and returned to the castle more dead than alive. I wandered here and there, up and down the stairs, like a damned soul and thoughtlessly entered the old Countess room.

'See if that is Clara!' she said to her nurse, for her eyes no longer served her save to weep the comfortless tears of old age.

I fled, sorrowful and convulsed; and ran upstairs to my old den where everything remained just as I had left it a year before. Thence, after a long hour, I went into Martino's room. My devotion and the incuriosity of the others had not laid a finger on the things left by the old man. On the floor still lay some nails left by the sextons when they had enclosed him in his coffin; a bottle of I know not what cordial, dried up and gone bad, stood on the table. On the wall still hung, leafless and dusty, some olive branches put there by him on the last Palm Sunday of his life. I threw myself down on the bed, still moulded to the shape of the corpse; there I wept bitterly, evoking the memory of my first and perhaps my only friend. I called his name countless times and prayed him to remember me and to send some spirit or phantom to console me with its company. But my faith wavered in these invocations; I no longer hoped, I no longer believed. Only later, by force of torments and efforts, I managed to strengthen my soul with some vague and confused belief, but none the less sure and intrepid, in things spiritual and eternal. Then I stammered out, indeed, the prayers of the Church, but my soul was arid as a skeleton, my mind withered from the sharp air of the world and my discouraged heart clung to the hope of nothingness as the only refuge of peace. This inner discouragement brought back to me terribly and bitterly the memory of that good old man whom, despite my desperate invocations, I had not been able to see, and who slept in the grave while I tramped onward through life.

* * * * *

I feared that I had shown up till then little zeal in my novitiate in the Chancellery; but I resolved to show it in future and from the next day commenced to write twice as much as I had done on previous days.

One day, after having written for many hours and without having found in that occupation any great enjoyment, I thought of going to Portogruaro to take my leave of the Most Excellent Frumier. It was already nearing the close of October and in a little while I would be embarking for Padua. But by a strange chance the Pisana, on that very day, was going to lunch with her uncle and even if I swore that I had known nothing of this, you certainly would not believe me. They were celebrating the name day of the noble lady and at the table were Giulio del Ponte, Father Pendola, Monsignor di Sant' Andrea and all the others from the usual gatherings. The Senator welcomed me as if I had indeed been invited and I played the Indian, but as I sat down I was not without suspicion that the Pisana, to get me out of the way, had kept silence about the invitation. Indeed, her nearness to Giulio, the glances that they exchanged and their confusion when asked a question, made it clear to me that I must be, if not an embarrassment to her, certainly a most unwanted witness. Embarrassment, no indeed, for they would not have bothered to conceal anything for my sake. Even in the better parts of her soul, the Pisana completely lacked the tact which is often mere habit and sometimes even hypocrisy, but which preserves the respect of virtue in an exquisite sense of shame. But whence could she have learnt this refinement of feminine manners? Her sister Clara, who alone would have been able to teach her, had always lived far from her in their grandmother's room; she, left with the power of showing and imposing all her caprices, had learnt little by little not only to give them loose rein but even not to take the trouble to examine them or hide them if they were ugly or shameful. The mastery of instinct kills the modesty of the soul, which is born of reason and of conscience.

I sat near Father Pendola, eating little, talking less, but observing a good deal and more than anything else eating my heart out with fury and jealousy. Giulio del Ponte exerted himself from time to time in pouring out, like an inroad into the general conversation, a volley of gibes, anecdotes and epigrams; then he would resume his silent colloquy with his neighbour with a movement that seemed to say: 'We can talk more sweetly so!' It could be seen that his gaiety was not spontaneous and that it was not the abundance of his wit that made it overflow. Rather it might be said that, had he remained silent, he would have lost his reputation as a gay and sparkling youth that had conquered for him the heart of the Pisana. She indeed, who smiled only at his glances, blushed to the ears, sighed and was confused when he spoke so quickly, wittily and brightly and made all around him break into the irresistible applause of laughter. Giulio del Ponte had guessed the quality of his own fascination; he pleased her because of his capacity of enlivening, of making others gay, of keeping control of the conversation.

Father Pendola kept both Giulio del Ponte and the Pisana under his eye and stole an occasional glance at me; two eyes like his were not busy for nothing and every time I encountered them I felt his cold glances sliding down to the bottom of my soul. The others at the table paid no heed; they chattered among themselves, laughed uproariously at the sallies improvised by Giulio and above all, ate. But when they rose from the table and the company began to go down into the garden to take their coffee on the terrace, Father Pendola took me affectionately by the arm and invited me to stay behind. The pity that I could read on his face bewildered me a little; but I thought also that it gave me a better idea of his nature than perhaps I had had up till then. What would you? The magnet on the one side attracts, on the other repels the steel, and no one knows why. Also between man and man can be observed the phenomenon of magnetism. I remained out of curiosity, for politeness and a little also because my eyes had already seen too much.

'Carlino,' said the Father, walking with me up and down the hall while the servants finished clearing away, 'you are about to go back to Padua?'

'Yes, Father,' I replied with two great sighs, unreasonable perhaps but certainly sincere.

'It is best for you, Carlino. Come, admit it, you are not satisfied with your position; uncertainty and idleness are ruining you and you are wasting the best years of your youth.'

'It is true, Father. For some time I have begun to taste the weariness of life.'

'Good, good! You will return to find life at Padua ten or twenty times more pleasant. Everything shows that you will sacrifice yourself to the fulfilment of your duties.'

This exhortation from the mouth of the Reverend Father surprised me considerably.

'I may tell you,' I said, 'that for some time past I have been seeking precisely in that fulfilment of my duties a refuge against . . . against tedium . . .'

'And have you found it?'

'I don't know. Writing in the Chancellery is too material a task and the Signor Chancellor is not the best person to make the task pleasant. I occupy my hands, it is true, but my thoughts fly where they will, and only too often the displeasures and the hours are measured more with the brain than with the fingers.'

'You speak very well, Carlino. But you must know better than I that the most important thing in getting cured is to have a firm desire to be cured. Here, here, Carlino, your soul is sick; if you want to heal it, go away from here. You will doubtless tell me that the malady goes with the sufferer. No, no, Carlino, that is not a good enough reason. Come, don't blush; I am saying nothing to you. I counsel you as a good friend, as a father, and nothing more. You are without family, you have no one who loves you, who looks after you; I would like to adopt you as a son and assist you with that light of experience that the Lord has granted me. Have faith in me and try; I ask no more. You must go away from here; and you must go away not only with your legs but also with your thoughts. You will doubtless have already guessed the way to incline them to the right knowledge and to the laborious observance of your duties. You have said very well: sorrows are counted with the brain and, I will add, also with the heart and not with the fingers. You must therefore occupy not only your hands, but your brain and your heart also.'

'Father,' I stammered, really moved, 'speak. I am listening to you with real faith and I will prove to you that I understand and obey.'

'Listen to me,' he went on, 'you have no family ties and the debt of gratitude towards those who have befriended you is quickly paid by one who cannot pay otherwise than with the gratitude of affection. From that side, your duty should not give you a moment's preoccupation, were it not to spur you on to study according to the intention of your benefactors. But that is not enough. So, you can occupy the brain but the heart remains idle. The more so since the family in which you were brought up has not known how to educate you to its profit. No, do not be ashamed, Carlino. It is certain that you cannot be bound with the love of a son to the Signor Count and the Signora Contessa who have scarcely known how to make themselves loved as parents by their own children. Benefits do not so much create obligations as the manner of conferring them, especially to children. Do not be ashamed then. It is so because it must be so. And to compel such feelings now would indeed be a sign of an excellent character, of a docile and grateful spirit, but you would not succeed. Love is a spontaneous growth and not a hothouse plant. Carlino, your heart is as empty of family affection as that of a foundling. It is a great misfortune that excuses many faults . . . let us understand one another, my son! It excuses you, yes, but it does not deliver you from the duty of purging those faults, nor should it in any way serve to make you hard. In early years one instinctively seeks for remedies for such misfortune, and a good angel may see that such a desire hits the mark! But often adverse destiny or childish ignorance finds poisons in place of remedies. Then, Carlino, as soon as the grown reason is aware, it needs must change and abandon those false and noxious remedies to cling to the true one. You are now eighteen, my son; you are young, but you are a man. You have not, you cannot have, any sure affection, holy and legitimate, that worthily occupies your heart, since no one has till now taught you its origin or announced its necessity! I am perhaps the first to speak to you of the voice of duty and I know how welcome . . .'

'Go on, Father, go on. Your words are those for which my thoughts have been searching in vain these many days past. I begin to see daylight growing in my mind and you may rest assured that I shall have the courage not to turn my eyes away from it.'

'Good, Carlino! Have you ever thought that you are not merely a man, but also a citizen and a Christian?'

This question, put to me by the Father with a grave and solemn air, completely bewildered me; what did he mean to say and what did it mean to be a citizen? I in no way knew; as to being a Christian I was never in doubt that I was, since in my catechism they had always taught me to answer yes. I remained therefore a little perplexed and confused, before replying in an unsteady voice:

'Yes, Father, I know that I am by the grace of God a Christian.'

'So the Rector has taught you to reply,' he rejoined, 'and I have every reason to believe that you are not accustomed to tell lies.

Until now, Carlino, all men were Christians and therefore such a question was almost needless. Religion was above discussion, and good and evil, if not the rule of habit, as in the first centuries of the church, at least the chain of faith bound all together in the great family of the Church. But now, my son, times have changed; to be a Christian one must not imitate others, but even consider doing exactly the opposite of what many others are doing. Behind the indifference of all lies hidden the enmity of many, and against these many the few real believers must struggle and fight with every sort of weapon in order not to be overwhelmed. That is, let us understand, not for personal pride but also so that religion, outside of which there is no salvation, shall not be trampled down . . . Carlino, I repeat to you, you are young, you are a Christian, you live in difficult times and the times you have before you will be more difficult still; but their very difficulty, if it is a common misfortune, if it is a miserable thing for you also, is yet, as far as you are concerned, for your immediate interest and for the tenor of your life, a real good fortune. Think, my son. Do you want to rot in indifference, without thought and without dignity? Or would you rather mingle in the battle of eternity against time, of the spirit against the flesh? These present skirmishes lead in the end to such conflicts, do not doubt. You are of an open and generous nature and you must incline towards the good cause. With religion, idealism and faith in immortal justice and the triumph of right is the rational life and the victory of the spirit; with atheism, materialism, epicurean scepticism, the negation of conscience and the anarchy of the passions, is the carnal life with all its vile consequences. Choose, Carlino, choose!'

'Oh, I am a Christian,' I exclaimed fervently.

'It is not enough to want to be,' said the Father in a dry voice tinged with melancholy. 'One must seek the good and one must do it, so that it may really triumph. One must give oneself body and soul to those who sweat, who work, who fight for that; one must use the same artifices as the enemy; one must strengthen one's heart with all the constancy of which one is capable, to arm one's hands with force, one's mind with prudence and be afraid of nothing and endure, always vigilant at one's post and if driven away, return and suffer disdain; one must dissimulate in order to conquer later, even, should it be necessary, yield, only to rise again, compromise only to gain time. In sum, one must believe in the eternity of the spirit and sacrifice this earthly and transient life to a future and better immortality.'

'Yes, Father. The vista opening before my eyes is so vast that I no longer have the courage to bewail my own little misfortunes. I will widen my views and the trifles that now seem to me obstacles will disappear. I want to go forward.'

'Really, Carlino! Now I am indeed pleased with you; but remember that enthusiasm is not enough without the equipment of a good dose of constancy and judgement. Now that I have shown you what high and noble duties demand your labour, you will be filled with fervour for their splendid promise. Along the way, you may perhaps fall back into human levity and pettiness. Do not be afraid, Carlino! It is like a traveller who in order to get to Rome must pass the night many times in filthy taverns in the company of porters and coachmen. Suffer all, do not be daunted by passing events, but lift your thoughts towards your goal and keep them there always.'

I understood and yet did not understand; I was dazzled by the splendid and resounding words which first shone upon my mind with those great phantasms of humanity, religion, sacrifice, faith, that so readily populate the dreams of youth. I understood also that, for good or evil, I had entered into a new sphere where I was only an intelligent atom involved in some sublime and mysterious work. By what means, to what end? I did not know for sure; but end and means alike by far surpassed my amorous preoccupations and childish regrets. Invited to show myself a Christian, I felt myself a man in the great stream of humanity and seemed to grow in stature.

'So much as regards religion,' went on the Reverend Father with emphasis. 'As regards your quality as citizen, the conditions are similar. Only think it over and every individual act falls into its place in the great social mechanism, wherein all are agreed in traditional respect for the fatherland and its institutions. The fatherland, my son, is the religion of the citizen; its laws are his creed. Woe to whoever touches them! We must defend by words, by the pen, by example, by blood, the inviolability of its decrees, the wise inheritance of twenty, of thirty generations! Today, unhappily, a hidden and untiring phalanx of ravagers try to set in doubt all that the tribunal of the centuries has decreed to be true, just and immutable. You must fight against many barbarities that are breaking out. You must return to our enemies that harm they are seeking to inflict on us, sowing amongst them corruption and discord. Evil must be adapted courageously against evil in the manner of a surgeon. If not, we shall certainly fail and shall all fall, friends and enemies alike, into the power of those spiteful and malignant beings that preach an insensate liberty in order to impose upon us a real slavery, a slavery to immoral, unconsidered and tyrannical codes; a slavery of the soul to the profit of some greater enjoyment that is merely earthly and transient. We must be strong against pride, my son. For that we must be humble; we must obey, obey, obey. The law of God commands it, the law that was, the law that is, not the opinion of a few innovators who say that they are making things anew but do nothing save devour! Do you understand, my son, what I am trying to say? . . . Religion and fatherland show you the way, and prepare for you a magnificent battlefield to sacrifice yourself more worthily than in the culpable idolatry of affections or private interests.'

With one hand the Reverend Father cast me prostrate in the mire and with the other lifted me towards the stars. I shook off with an effort my yoke of sorrow, and lifting my head, free but dismayed, replied:

'Here I am. I hope to cancel the first part of my life by placing over it a second, more exalted and more generous. I will forget myself where I cannot change myself; I will seek out duties more sacred, greater loves . . .'

'Slowly with those loves!' the Father interrupted me. 'Do not use the same words in matters so diverse. Love is a flash that glitters, a shooting-star that passes. And in the new life to which I encourage you faith and zeal are wanted. The cross of sacrifice and the sword of persuasion; those are our symbols, superior by far to the crown of myrtles or the paired doves. Persuasion, my son, persuasion issued out of sacrifice is received in the souls of others as the heat produced by the sun is adapted to the seed that it ferments and germinates. You must not allow yourself to be overcome by the contradictions, by the rancours, of others; persuasion will come; make a way for it by perseverance and by force. When the triumph of the good matures, it is suitable to persecute the evil; but do so wisely, usefully, since, my son, the army of martyrs is by no means so numerous and from their sacrifice it is meet that they obtain the prize they merit, so that it be not wasted.'

'Father,' I said with some reserve, for his long discourse had increased the mystery, 'I hope that I shall understand better when my spirit is purified from the clouds that dim it. I will think and I will conquer.'

'You would have conquered already if you had tried to fight,' replied the Reverend Father 'but you, Carlino, are shut up within your shell and have not sought the aid of those who could do much for you. Ideas are not born, but are developed, my son; and you have done very ill to coil yourself up in your own little passions without trusting those honest and sagacious persons who could have led you forward along that road which I have now shown you. Last year, for example, I recommended you to go and see the advocate Ormenta at Padua, a most incorruptible, just and generous man who would have turned your temperament to its true ministry and would have pointed out to you the true scope and full usefulness of life. Men of such a stamp should be venerated by youth and taken as an example.'

'Father, I have seen the advocate Ormenta several times, precisely upon your recommendation; but I was wrapped up in other thoughts. It also seems to me that I was a little frightened at his coldness and a certain air of disdain that little reassured me. I do not know if it was because he seemed too great or too different from me; but certainly I did not feel at ease in his presence and the room in which he received me was so cold and dark as to make me afraid.'

'Those are signs of a sublime and austere life, my son. What at one time frightened you will tomorrow please and fascinate you. Things exalted seem cold, as the snows cover the tops of the highest mountains; but those are the first to be kissed by the sun and the last that it abandons. You will go back this year to the advocate, you will become friendly with him and, unless my judgement deceives me, I shall have rendered a great service in finding you a good and sure guide for the life to which you are destined. Now, I have planted in your heart a tiny seed. Let us hope that it will bear fruit. The good advocate, finding you better disposed, will welcome you with greater confidence. I too, you see, only ten months ago, hoped for little from you; I confess it to you freely, seeing that today I hope for much.'

* * * * *

So I arrived at Padua with the enthusiasm of one who wished to make himself a friar out of amorous desperation. Almost as soon as I arrived, I ran to the advocate Ormenta, to whom Father Pendola had already written, and who received me as a guardian, or as a Provincial would have received a novice. The worthy advocate, who had seemed to me the previous year a little suspicious, a little mocking, a little chilly, seemed to me instead the most open, smooth and mellifluous person on earth. His looks seemed as if he were in an ecstasy, his every gesture was a caress; every word struck right to the heart. I was content with everything, even enraptured: with myself, with Father Pendola and above all with the precious gift that he had made me by confiding me to such tutelage.

Ormenta spoke to me of trust, of meditation, of patience; he invited me to lunch any day I liked, except Wednesdays, on which he used to fast, which would not perhaps suit my youthful appetite. He congratulated me on the freshness of my youth, which gave me a double opportunity to do good; I must seek out the ideas, the intentions of my comrades and consult with him how to correct them and direct them to better ends if they appeared erroneous or strayed from the true path; I should serve as a channel since a mature mind could use to advantage by its experience the fiery activity of youth. There were not enough of such mediators! But they already had some, and the fruit of their work had already begun to increase and to manifest itself among the more docile and reflective students. I would be among the most worthy of them, with my temperament, my handsome and pleasant face and my ready and inspiring eloquence. I would have my recompense either in the satisfaction of my conscience (and that was without doubt the greatest) or in temporal honours and eternal rewards. The State had need of zealous, circumspect and laborious magistrates and would find them amongst us. I should not refuse, since love for my neighbour and the welfare of the fatherland and of religion must impose silence upon my modesty. All men were brothers, but the more skilful brother must not allow the less skilful to hurl himself into the abyss. Love must always be wary and sometimes severe. The hand could strike and in certain cases must even do so; but the heart must, of course, continue to be loving, indulgent and pitiful and weep for the sad necessity of having to punish in order to improve, to cut down in order to correct. Oh the heart, the heart! To listen to the advocate Ormenta, he had one so large, so tender, so ardent that it could err only by excess and never by lack of love.

However, certain things that I had noticed about the Signor Advocate did not fail to cause me some little astonishment. First of all that damp barrack of a house, dark and almost bare, continued to provoke in my nerves a sense of repulsion as at the lair of a snake. How could a man so open and loyal live in such gloom, in such dark and mortuary surroundings? And then, during my visit, I addressed some question, I know not what, to his wife, a slim little woman, pallid and full of lamentations. The advocate turned on her with a sour and discordant voice and with the air more of a master than of a husband and the little woman slipped out of the room biting her lips and not daring to refuse.

Then, too, the Signor Advocate seemed to have a double register in his voice; the one that he had adopted with me the previous year and now with his wife, and the other which he had been using with me a few moments since and which he continued to use until he had accompanied me to his door. A yellowish, dirty, dishevelled brat, clothed like St Anthony, who was playing with some odds and ends from the sacristy in a corner of the vestibule, made me want to laugh. The advocate introduced him to me as his only son, a little prodigy of wisdom and sanctity, who had voluntarily consecrated himself to St Anthony, as was then the custom, and still is sometimes, at Padua. That hair of his, his shaven crown with edges ruffed up like the hedges of an abandoned garden, his squinting and rheumy eyes, his hands spotted with every sort of filth and his clothes all torn and grey in their sanctity, made a strange contrast with the panegyric woven for me in a low voice by the advocate. I thought to myself that his fatherly love had deluded him; the boy might be about fourteen (he was sixteen, I discovered later) but nothing in his young person confirmed the praises that had been made to me, if one did not confound dirt with holiness, as is the extraordinary view of some bigots. As soon as the door had closed, I heard him intoning a devout canticle at the top of his voice; I believe I would have preferred the baying of a dog, even though sacred psalmody with its sad and solemn tones had always thrilled every fibre of my being. But devotions cease to be sacred when they are degraded to a senseless game and a useless noise and I believe that permitting them and teaching them to boys only serves to spoil them, even according to the views of those who only want to make good Christians of them. Spiritual things, according to me, should be taken seriously, otherwise they should be left alone. It may be a misfortune not to be aware of them, but it is a sacrilege to make a mockery of them.

In accordance with the injunctions of Father Pendola and the advocate Ormenta, I made every effort to abandon my usual reserve; I devoted a small part of my time to study and with distractions and intentions towards greater and more exalted things, I lulled the bitter sorrow of my soul over the forgetfulness of the Pisana. It was not hard for me to find among my comrades that profound and general indifference in regard to religion of which the Father had warned me. They went even further than that, indulging in derision, parodies and ridicule. This would have served to rekindle faith in my heart if my masters had taken the trouble to light it, but no one thought of that. On this point one might say that I had been born dead and a miracle was needed to revive me, a miracle that so far had not occurred. However, the disgust that I felt at these buffooneries made me think for some time that I possessed those beliefs since I suffered so much at seeing them made a matter for mockery. The generosity of youth deceived me about the state of my opinions and made me tend to defend the attacked rather than the attackers. I told the advocate what I had seen and he encouraged me to observe more closely, to note what connection this religious anarchy had with political and moral license, to find out the ringleaders of the movement, to get into touch with them and converse with them so that they should open their hearts to me, so that he might know where to begin to correct and to repair. He incited me above all not to be too obvious in my attitude, to become one with the crowd and for the moment to reply little but limit myself to questioning and listening.

'Sheep that have strayed are recalled to the fold by kindness,' said the advocate, 'they must be flattered that they may come to believe in us; we must first follow them so that later they may willingly follow us.'

He never failed to invite me to visit him frequently and to favour him with my company for a meal, but if I agreed to the first I was not much disposed to profit by the second part of his invitation. One Sunday, when he had pressed me at all costs to stay and dine with him, I found myself in such a company that all my appetite disappeared at once. A wheezing and hairy old woman whom they called the Signora Marchesa, an old solicitor, half policeman and half priest, who drank continuously and watched me above his glass, two youths, coarse, dirty and lumpy, who ate with fingers and teeth, in addition to the little St Anthony and the whimpering phantom of the lady of the house, aroused in me the deepest melancholy I had ever felt. The advocate, however, seemed in the seventh heaven to have around him such a company; but I observed that he never once invited the solicitor to drink nor the youths to eat. All his exhortations he turned on the Marchesa, who could no longer either eat or drink because of the cough that distressed her. The Signor Advocate carved with a perfection truly mathematical and managed to cut eight portions from a miserable roast chicken, an operation which in my opinion solved all the difficulties of squaring the circle. I had no desire even to touch the food and ceded my portion to the two youths who did not leave on their plates even the vestige of a bone.

The advocate introduced me little by little to everyone at the table and did not fail to draw me aside to tell me all about them. The Marchesa was a worthy patron of all the pious institutions of the city; it was said that she was rich to the tune of eighty thousand *zecchini* and he, the advocate, was her favourite adviser. The solicitor was a Venetian, a very close friend of the Podestà of the time, for whom he did everything he wanted and flattered him on every possible occasion. The youths were two students from Verona who had, like me, devoted themselves to the good cause and had resolved to aid it with all their zeal. A pity that they had neither my talent nor my good manners, but God knew how to turn stones into bread and with good will everything was possible! I thought that if they put the same zeal into all their occupations as they did into their eating, they would have been in greater need of restraint than encouragement. I also remembered having met them from time to time under the portico of the University and they seemed to me neither the most exemplary nor the most modest of those who attended it between one lecture and another.

'Enough! They do so perhaps to follow the strayed sheep and to rouse in them the desire to follow us!' I thought. But I had not the least desire to try and make friends with them as the advocate advised me. I also accepted with a bow the invitation made me by the Marchesa to go sometimes to her parties, where I could pass a couple of hours among earnest and God-fearing persons. The bow was meant to say 'Thank-you! I can do without your parties!' but the advocate hastened to reply in my name that I was very grateful for the courtesy of the Signora Marchesa and that I would respond by being seen at her house as often as my studies would allow me. I was on the point of adding some out-of-place remark, so furious was I at the use he had made of my will without so much as a by your leave; but the advocate calmed me with a glance and said in a low voice: 'The Marchesa is a good friend of young men; you should be obliged to her for her good intentions and put up with her shortcomings for the great benefits she can confer on you.'

However, despite these beautiful words, I left the advocate's house quite decided not to involve myself any more in his luncheons or in the Marchesa's parties. The next two days I had the benefit of finding the college soup much more to my taste and with a pound of bread crumbled up in it, it seemed veritably a royal banquet. My room at least enjoyed plenty of sunlight and I could look up without meeting the cat-like glances of the solicitor. The two students from Verona met me a few days later in the corridors of the University, but seemed as little desirous of exchanging a few words with me as I was of going near them. I asked some of my fellows about them and learnt that they were among the most drunken and dissolute of the students. They had been studying medicine for seven years and had not yet obtained their degrees, and being without any means of their own lived by fraud and lawlessness at the expense of their companions. I pitied the advocate Ormenta at having become the gull of such libertines; but when I tried to open his eyes about them, he received me badly. He replied that these were calumnies and that he was surprised that I should pay any attention to them and that I should confine myself to revealing and destroying the vices of the wicked and not exaggerate the peccadilloes of the good. I began to think that the faith of the good advocate was a great deal purer than his morals; since, if these were peccadilloes, I no longer understood what could be the vices I was called upon to fight against.

CHAPTER IX

Among those who should have been recommended to the advocate Ormenta and Father Pendola as in need of conversion, I knew several who were a great deal more to my taste than those two young men of Verona, my allies. I even began to make sundry incursions into the enemy camp for the benefit of the advocate; thence I drew my own conclusions and in the end discovered such a difference between the evil told of these young men and that which in fact existed, that I began to doubt the good faith of the advocate and the propriety of the office assigned to me. That I should seek to lessen the sorrows that tormented me in the fulfilment of more exalted duties was undoubtedly a very good thing; that I should seek to forget an unworthy and unfortunate, although most fervent, love by lifting my soul in adoration of those great ideas that are the poetry of humanity, I indeed considered nothing but good. But that my homage to these great ideals should descend to a continual deceit and indecorous espionage; that those ideas of mine, so exalted and sublime, should fail so markedly in practice, I began to doubt. Furthermore, I had made the test that Father Pendola had recommended, but remained very dissatisfied with the result. My mind had been distracted but my soul was very far from that ideal content that should reward it for all other troubles. In brief, my brain was occupied but not my heart and that, thwarted of its one-time love and not filled with any other affection, gave me the greatest trouble with its useless beating. At first I was filled with fervour by the ardour of others, but later, whether it was that this ardour was false, or whether it did not find in me the material on which to feed, I grew so cold that I no longer recognized myself as being what I had once been. This continual manoeuvring with measured steps, foresight, circumspection and calculation kept a youthful and ebullient spirit very ill employed. I aspired to something greater, more active; I understood very well that I was not made for ascetic ecstasies and I have already stated how weak I was in matters of faith.

You may imagine what efforts I made to strengthen myself! But the advocate Ormenta, rather than trying to aid me, always ran counter to my ideas with his too mundane attitude. It was good that my aim should have been so high, so spiritual and God knows what else; but I had lost that aim from view and could no longer recall it when I asked myself about it. A student from Treviso, a certain

Amilcare Dossi, had attached himself to me with the bonds of the closest friendship; he had a strong and very daring nature and a heart for which there was not gold enough to pay. We often walked together arguing about metaphysics and philosophy, since I had my head in the clouds and no longer knew how to free myself from them. Also he had been studying for some little time and was able to help me in my work. After a day or two, I realized that he was just of the type of those whom Father Pendola had defined as spiritual adversaries, ruthless to all idealism and every noble enthusiasm. He doubted everything, discussed everything, argued over everything. Therefore I wondered to find in him a love of science and a fire of pity which seemed to me incompatible with the arid coldness of his doctrines. I ended by showing him my astonishment and he laughed at it.

'Poor Carlino,' he said, 'you are behind the times! You wonder that I have been seized by so violent a love for those sciences that dissect in the manner of the anatomists? It is, my friend, that the love of truth conquers all other loves in truth and in nobility. Truth, however poor and naked, is more adorable and more holy than hooded and splendid lies. Therefore every time that I am able to reveal some tinselled fraud, my heart leaps in my breast and my mind weaves for itself a triumphal crown! Blessed is that philosophy that still teaches us, mortal, weak and unhappy, that we can be great in equality, in liberty, and in love! . . . That is my fire, Carlino, that is my faith, my thought, every day, every moment! Truth at all costs and love among men, liberty of opinions and conscience! . . . What being seems to you greater or happier than he who tries with all his strength to make of humanity one single person in concord, all knowing and content, in so far as the laws of nature permit? . . . To-day then, today when such ideas are increasing and balance quivering upon the reluctant sphere of action, today when I see weaken every day that mist that hides it from the eyes of men, who more happy than I? . . . Oh that, that my friend, is the real peace of the spirit! . . . Once having raised yourself to that liberal and rational faith, neither adverse fortune, nor betrayals nor sorrows can ever disturb the serenity of the spirit. I am strong and unshaken in myself because I believe and hope for myself and for others.'

You can imagine! During this profession of faith that responded so closely to my own needs, I blushed with shame. I remember that I had not the heart to say a single word and Amilcare thought that I had understood nothing of what I had heard. I was ashamed that I had been vacillating for so long; I was sorry for Father Pendola and the advocate Ormenta (who, be it said in passing, had no need of it whatsoever) and decided to study like Amilcare and to ask my heart once and for all what it really aspired to love. I caught a glimpse for a second time of a world filled with exalted ideas, noble sentiments, and hoped that, even without the Pisana, my soul would be able to find the head of the skein of existence.

This revolution in my opinions had already taken place when I next saw the advocate Ormenta; and that day, being little disposed to tell him that everything was all right as usual, I began what was almost a quarrel with him. He was greatly dissatisfied with me because I had never been to one of the Marchesa's parties, for she had shown herself, it seemed, very interested in me. Therefore we separated on bad terms, he saying that the good cause only knew how to make use of qualified and reasoning servants. I did not reply, though I was boiling inside, but ran quickly to Amilcare and for the first time told him of my relations with the advocate and the whole course of events from the sermon of Father Pendola up to the dispute of the same day.

At my account, he pursed his lips like someone who smells something unpleasant and darted a glance at my face that I shall never forget. He said to me: 'Are you a wolf or a sheep?' I was so flabbergasted that I nearly regretted having slipped into this long confession. But the suspicion was gone in a flash; Amilcare was not one of those who, expert in evil, see it everywhere. He was good and recovered at once from his brief uncertainty; his goodness did not make him vindictive as is so often the case. He told me then of the reputation that the advocate had gained in the city and how he was considered a most vigilant minister of the State Inquisition.

'The dog!' I exclaimed.

'What is it?' Amilcare asked me.

I did not have the courage to confess to him that the knave had perhaps made use of me as an instrument of his rascality; and my courage completely failed me when Amilcare told me that the arrest of certain students had taken place the night before; and the expulsion intimated to some others and the perquisitions on many were commonly attributed to the work of the Signor Advocate.

'That Father Pendola of yours must be some Inquisitor disguised, who is playing a double game in order to keep us in the dark,' went on Amilcare. 'At Venice they are still living in the fourteen hundreds and are afraid of the eighteen hundreds that are upon them, but we, no, by God, we shall not change the faith in which we are born. Good sense is no longer the heritage of a hundred noble families. All want to think and whoever thinks has the right to work for his own and the common good. They have led us too long in blinkers; Father Pendola can be pensioned off; we want to walk unaided.'

Amilcare, in pronouncing these words, seemed altogether transformed; his high prominent forehead, his deep eyes, his delicate flared nostrils, seemed to send out flames. He seemed to grow in stature and a passion of pride and virtue seemed to rush through his veins.

'Who were the Greeks? Who were the Romans?' he went on. 'People who lived before us and from whose experience we can profit, who were powerful because they were virtuous and virtuous because they were free. Whether virtue comes from liberty or the other way round we must take the risk. The effort towards liberty will be the strong and efficacious instruction in virtue. How did Lycurgus restore power to Sparta? He restored it by laws and salutory customs. Let us imitate him! New laws, valid laws, universal laws, clear, severe, without loopholes and without privileges! Let us remember that our ancestors were named Brutus, Cornelius and Scipio! History repeats itself on a larger scale; the new order is being born in the old disorder. The time has come for equality, for truth, for virtue! Humanity unified means to reign alone; we shall be its heralds!'

I clasped my friend's hand without saying a word; but my whole soul was with him. I had no other thought than to fly and embrace these great hopes ardently. Justice, truth, virtue; the three stars that govern the spiritual world; away from them everything was dark, every heart trembled or was corrupted! I saw them rise on my horizon like a divine constellation and all the love of which I was capable flowed out to them with irresistible impetus. One more mist to grow clear, one more flutter in that deep heaven and my religion was found, my heart calm for ever. But that fine mist was like those infinitesimal fractions that always grow smaller without ever disappearing altogether. That light was still so far away that just when I believed I touched its fiery breath, a new layer of air intervened between me and it.

I talked with Amilcare many times later of my doubts, and he assured me that they came from lack of thought. I believe however that my having first looked without overtaxing my eyes to try and see what was not there helped me to discover what really was. Justice, truth, virtue; three excellent things, three words, three ideas to entrap a soul to madness and to death; but who would fetch them down from heaven to earth, to use the expression of Socrates? . . . That was the thorn in my heart and though I did not understand so clearly then, it drew blood. New institutions, new laws, said Amilcare, create new men. But to wish for them, even to believe in them, was one thing; but who would give these perfect institutions, these excellent laws? Certainly not the inept and thoughtless governments of that time. Who then? . . . A new people, just, virtuous and all-knowing; but whence would they come and how could they be found, and how brought to the leadership of public affairs? . . . In truth I could then have scarcely understood that the hotch-potch of that time would prove me right; but in that era of intellectual fuddle, of scarcely stirred lethargy and political infancy, was there any great man of government who would have understood more than I?

Then I remained with my vague and entirely sentimental ideal like one who has fallen in love with a woman in a dream. I admired Amilcare who was able to give to these dreams the confident firmness of reality, but I could not imitate him. Meanwhile the affairs of France advanced at breakneck speed and the great news from there, purified by distance and the youthful imagination of my comrades, inspired my confidence. This allowed me to hope and wait with the others and in the meantime I read the philosophers of the Encyclopaedia and Rousseau, above all the Social Contract, and the profession of faith of Vicario Savoiardo. Little by little, my mind began to give a bodily form to these phantasms and when at last I saw them alive and breathing, I threw my arms around Amilcare's neck shouting: 'Yes, my brother, today at last I believe! One day we shall be men!'

The advocate Ormenta, who saw me rarely and then ever more taciturn and cautious, had me spied upon by one or other of his familiars; he knew of my new habits and of my friendship with the Trevisan, and was able to guess the rest. The world at that time was not going according to his desires and the poor fellow had much to do about it; he understood very well that they were ants trying vainly and sadly to arrest an avalanche and even had he not understood, the fact was that he was completely bewildered. Warned by Amilcare, I was on my guard and for my part watched the advocate's face like a barometer. When I saw him quiet, humble, overcast, I ran to join the revels of my companions and we drank gay toasts to liberty, equality and the triumph of France, the Republic and universal peace. Wine at that time cost very little and with the three ducats a month allowed me by the Count I was well able to take my part in the agapes of these featherbrains. This political and philanthropic enthusiasm could satisfy the spirit of a youth such as I was then, in a way that the intrigues, the mundane and underhand religion of the Signor Advocate was quite unable to do. Perhaps the pure gospel of charity and holiness could have found a place within; but by now the step had been taken. I became an active and fanatic Voltairean. I stood up ever more willingly to harangue, or to discuss among my fellows, and being now more similar to them myself, I was the less able to judge them weak and despicable. At bottom, perhaps, fear, vice, sloth, inertia still lurked; but above them rushed a tide of faith, capable of great things, though in such natures merely momentary.

But enough! I was contented, and, having got to know Amilcare through and through, I had got it into my head that they were all like him, which was far from the truth. Like all judges with beardless chins, I then sinned in one extreme as, the previous year, I had sinned in the other. Amilcare dragged me onwards with his impetuosity of faith, enthusiasm, liberty, with his reckless, gay and daring ways; for him the sentiment that could not be consecrated to the good of humanity seemed a sentiment of little worth.

Meanwhile the sound of the French arms grew louder at the gates of Italy, resounding with great promises of liberty and of equality; the spectres of the Roman republic were invoked, the young men cut their hair in imitation of Brutus; everywhere there was a fury of hope that responded to these flattering visions ever nearer and more victorious. Amilcare seemed to me to grow mad; he gesticulated, he shouted, he harangued among the most turbulent groups, in the cafes and on the squares. The advocate Ormenta became still more lugubrious and livid: I believe he was even infuriated against the Marchesa who could not make up her mind to die. I, on my rare visits, used to mock him. One day he spoke to me with a certain bitter flavour about my friendship with the young man from Treviso and warned me, almost as if in jest, that if I loved him I should warn him to be less gullible and to whisper rather than shout. That same evening Amilcare, with certain other students, was taken prisoner and conveyed to Venice by order of the Most Excellent Inquisitors; and I believe that I was spared that same pleasure only because they hoped to frighten me and get me in their grasp again. But cowardice, thank Heaven, has never taken root in my nature. After this misfortune to my friend, I felt such sorrow that it made me hate his enemies three times as much and I became more fervent than ever in our common hopes. Since my own salvation depended on their confirmation, my impatience no longer knew bounds.

Time alone did something to calm me. After the first enthusiasms there succeeded a long and dubious truce. The continental alliances were reinforced; France retreated upon herself like a tiger preparing for a prouder leap but, outside, people began to believe in a fatal discouragement. The Most Serene Republic made pacts with all and sundry, endured and steered cautiously; the Inquisitors smiled to themselves to see dissipated a storm that had caused so much uproar; they smiled, holding in their claws those unfortunates who had hoped so much from the hail and the thunderbolts, while all seemed ripe for a fresh calm. Of Amilcare, and of many others who had preceded or followed him into the prisons, there was no word; but it was whispered that the French Legation was looking after them and would not allow them to be sacrificed. But if the next campaign turned out unfavourable for France? I trembled only to think of the consequences.

Meanwhile, one morning there arrived for me a letter sealed in black. The Signor Count advised me of the death of his Chancellor and added that in nearly two years of study I should have managed to learn enough to be able to pass the examination whenever I wished and that I should hasten to him to direct his Chancellery. What I felt on reading this letter I could not tell you; but I believe that in the depths of my heart I was well content that necessity should call me back once more to the Pisana. Without Amilcare and without the hope of seeing him again soon, Padua seemed to me a tomb.

My hopes grew vaguer and vaguer every day; youthful impatience, once deluded, turns easily to discouragement and the joyful and triumphant mien of the advocate Ormenta began to irritate me. Thanks to a letter of recommendation from the Senator Frumier, I passed my second year examination with credit and then left Padua, so confused and bewildered that I could no longer put two and two together in my mind.

However, I found it hard to drag myself away without getting some more information about the Amilcare affair and, relying on the patronage of the Countess and her noble relatives, I hoped that at Venice I might be able to get to the bottom of it. I therefore asked counsel of my few ducats, which permitted me this brief diversion if I used the greatest parsimony. I made a bundle of my belongings and took passage on a wherry; and then, for politeness' sake, went to take my leave of the advocate Ormenta.

'Oh, bon voyage, my dear fellow,' he said. 'A pity that you are not staying with us for the rest of the year; you are a prudent youth and should have come to visit me more often and perhaps, too, the Signora Marchesa would have accepted you into her circle. Give my regards to Father Pendola, my dear fellow, and trust once again in those who are older than you. The young believe too easily and often make bad bargains.'

I understand now what the dear advocate meant; he thought me an old fox, sly and avaricious like himself, but at the time I understood nothing at all. I had, moreover, as a result of his invitation, to kiss his filthy son who was functioning as usual in the vestibule in his black and smelly robe. This ceremony made my departure from Padua twice as agreeable as before; for the rest, I left my burdens to fate and hoped to make a young man of not yet twenty appear a worthy Chancellor.

Once in Venice, I lost no time either in admiring St Mark's or in strolling along the riva, but left my bundle at an inn and ran to the Frumier Palace. My God! How changed I found the Signora Contessa in those few years! She had become darker and more evil in expression; her nose had become as crooked as a hawk's and her eyes flashed with a sort of greenish fire that augured nothing good, while she showed a carelessness in her dress that was almost disgusting. She no longer had any rosy ribbons or lace on her bonnet and her grey hair tumbled uncombed over her forehead and temples. I confess that not even pity for Amilcare could induce me to try anything from that quarter. I pretended that I had come to Venice to pay my respects to her and had thought this was a most excellent excuse to make myself agreeable; but she replied with a 'thank-you' so abrupt that I scarcely awaited the moment when I would find myself once more in the street, and felt all my strength drain out of my knees as I dragged myself out of the room.

However once in the antechamber, I took heart again and decided to try and see the Contessina Clara and confide in her. While I was looking for a servant who would take me to her, I stumbled upon her by chance. She had heard of my arrival and had not wanted to let me go without a greeting. So much courtesy moved me and gave me heart. The poor Contessina was just as I had last seen her, but a little paler, a little graver and with red circles round her eyes which told of much weeping and long vigils. But these signs of sorrow, rather than lessening my trust, added to it the incentive of pity. I opened my heart to her, telling her of my friend and my wish to know at least why they were keeping him in prison and when there might be a hope of his being released. The Contessina seemed rather disturbed at hearing about Amilcare and even more at the cause of his imprisonment, and two or three times seemed about to make some suggestion, but held back, sighing.

Finally the sight of my grief overcame her and she said that there was one person in Venice who would know about that better than any other, and whom I knew, and that I should find Dr Lucilio Vianello, who would certainly be able to tell me everything I desired to know about the young man from Treviso. She told me that blushing, poor thing, and asked me not to divulge this advice of hers to others; and then when I asked her where I could find Dr Lucilio, she replied that she did not know, but that he would surely not fail to appear some time or other on the piazza which was then, as now, the great gathering place of all the Venetians.

At last I took my leave of her, thanking her for her kindness;

and going to the piazza, walked up and down waiting until the Signor Lucilio should show his nose there. Jealousy no longer whispered in my head and, full of zeal for the greater good of Amilcare, I accosted Lucilio resolutely. He either had difficulty in recognizing me, or pretended to have; but after that he showed me a thousand civilities, asking me about my studies, about my life and finally if I had seen the Contessa and her daughter. I told him everything and how I had found them. He told me then that the Contessa had given herself up completely to the passion of gambling, as Venetian ladies of the time often did; that she lost large sums of money every day; that the moneylenders were treading on her skirts and that she thought of nothing else but of winning back what she had lost at even greater and more perilous risk. Her character had grown steadily worse; she tyrannized over her daughter worse than ever and it was now seven months since the poor girl had set foot outside the house save to go to Mass at San Zaccaria, where he saw her once a week. Then she disappeared like a shadow and she was not even allowed to show herself at an outside window since the rooms allotted to her were in an inner court of the palace.

As for being allowed to enter there, he had never been able to succeed, even though his reputation in his profession was very high and the most select mansions of the nobility had opened their doors to him. The Countess was inexorable and he knew from a sure source that she was in negotiation with the nuns of Santa Theresa for Clara to be accepted by them as a novice; the only remaining obstacle was the dowry as, according to their rule, they could not accept her until it had been paid in full, and the Countess was not at the moment in a position to pay more than half. The young woman had bowed to her mother's wishes and if the sacrifice was not already consummated, it was due to this difference of interests. Only he hoped that she would not obey when it came to making her profession and that she would not be cut off from the world by the insuperable barrier of vows.

Lucilio told me all this with the fury, long suppressed, of one who cannot overcome an obstacle that he considered frivolous and ridiculous; but finally he took heart once more and I was aware that he had lost none of his former courage, that he still hoped and that his hopes were not mere dreams. That vigorous and prudent spirit of his was not one to reassure itself with vain illusions and therefore the assurance that I could sense dimly in his last words gave me confidence. Seeing him calmer, I told him the reason I had been waiting for him so long and did not conceal, perhaps with a touch of cunning, that Clara herself had directed me to him. It seemed that many confused memories passed through his mind, and he turned to look at me as if for the first time.

'How long is it since you had news of Father Pendola?' he asked me without replying to my question.

'Oh, a long time,' I replied with some wonder at being questioned in this way. 'I believe I am no longer in the good books of the Reverend Father and that he is not overpleased with me.'

'Didn't he give you some letters of introduction at Padua?' Lucilio asked me with an amused expression.

'Yes, indeed,' I said, 'to a certain advocate Ormenta, with whom I have completely lost touch since a few months ago I learnt that he had the reputation of being a spy of the Most Excellent Inquisitors.'

'Very good, it might well be so; but don't talk of such things out loud here in Venice; your friend must have fallen into evil waters just because of that.'

'Oh yes, very easily! He used to talk so loudly that one could hear him from one end of the city to the other and he made no secret of his opinions.'

'Well, he was rewarded, as you can see, for his sincerity; however you can comfort yourself that he and his companions are, I believe, under the protection of the French Legation and nothing bad will happen to them.'

'Are you quite sure? But if France is invaded by the allies . . .'

Lucilio cut me short with a burst of laughter and I looked at him in some wonder. 'Do you too believe, like the newspaper writers in Germany, that France is exhausted? That she is in discord and will let the first comer set foot on her soil? . . . Look me in the face again! . . . I am only a doctor, but I guarantee that I can see further ahead than all the political numbskulls in wig and toga. France is not only in France, she is in Switzerland, in Holland, in Germany, in Piedmont, in Naples, in Rome and even here; here where we are speaking, you and I. She knows this and is gathering herself together to draw around her all the active forces of her enemies and to rid herself of them in a couple of blows and then let loose the zest of her brothers here! . . . Do you see? It was by force of habit that a few minutes ago I told you to talk with restraint, and now I am shouting and care nothing for it. It is they now, as you see, who are afraid and there is no longer any danger. You can repeat all that I have told you to the advocate Ormenta and even to Father Pendola and it will not matter very much to me.'

As he said that, Lucilio looked at me with flashing and stern eyes so that I was forced, against my custom, to lower my own. But perhaps he had pity on my embarrassment, for he offered me a chance to recover myself.

'How old are you?' he asked.

'I shall soon be twenty.'

'Only twenty? Take courage then; you have been a baby and they have thought to put nappies on you, but I hope you will not let yourself be bamboozled and will repent while there is still time. Take courage; confess to me that your friendship for Amilcare and your interest in him is a result of the advice of others and not your own spontaneous feeling.'

'But who would have made me do that?'

'Who? Father Pendola, for example, or the advocate Ormenta.'

'They? On the contrary! I even believe that they were very displeased at my close friendship with that young man and indeed it was due to him that I became sick of them and their frivolous and dishonest scheming.'

'Their scheming frivolous? Not so fast, my friend. Dishonest it may well be, but do not let us make hasty judgements on those who are defending their bread. Do you think that the reverend Father and the worthy advocate would be persons of authority and importance if there should come a wind of justice that would throw to the ground, yes, throw to the ground all the privileges of the nobility and the clergy? . . . They are working for their own advantage, as others for theirs; what more can I say?'

I was greatly astonished at that viewpoint of Lucilio; open hatred would have been more to my taste than this cold, calculating hostility, and my friend from Treviso thought, in my opinion, more rightly than the Fossalta doctor. But I forgot that in him youth had boiled away and sentiment had become petrified in a profound conviction.

'But let us talk about you,' Lucilio continued meanwhile. 'I would like to believe that the Contessina Clara sent you to me and not the advocate Ormenta. If that is so, be at peace; your friend Amilcare is safer in his prison than you or I in this piazza. I would even say that to the College of Savi, who if they were as wise as their name, would know how to extract profit from that judgement. I repeat that there are people watching his interests and there is no danger that they will allow young men as valuable as he to come to harm. Meanwhile, take care not to let yourself be deceived by Father Pendola. For pity's sake, Carlino! You used to be a boy of intelligence and, what is more, of good heart. Don't spoil yourself utterly. I must leave you now, since I have to make some visits in the hovels of these poor devils. What will you? The love of his patients is the best reward of the physician. But if you are staying in Venice, look me up at the hospital where I am every day until ten in the morning.'

'Thank you,' I said, 'if you can really assure me that Amilcare . . .'

'Yes, I assure you that no harm will come to him. What more can you ask?'

'Then I thank you and pay you my respects. For my part, I am leaving Venice today.'

'Give my regards to the Count, the Contessina, the Frumiers and my father, should you see him,' said Lucilio. 'Ah me! Give my regards to Fratta and Fossalta as well! Who knows if those remote little places will ever see me again!'

He embraced me and left me, I think with a better opinion of me than when we had met. Certainly, on thinking it over afterwards it seemed to me that some none too honourable things had been told him about me, and later I came to know that he had thought me sold, body and soul, to Father Pendola. But the ingenuousness of my confession had modified that hasty judgement and my youth encouraged him to hope that I was not so calloused in imposture as they had assumed.

In any case, once I had embarked with my little bundle for Portogruaro, I had plenty to think over. In going over in my mind the conversation I had had with Lucilio, and above all the authority there seemed to be in his words, his attitude appeared more strange than admirable. A simple doctor, a countryman only recently moved to Venice, to speak and make decisions in this way! To put himself almost as the arbiter of the destinies of a republic, or if not the arbiter, at least a judge or a prophet . . . there seemed a trace of comedy in it! Had I been made a fool of? I almost regretted having abandoned Amilcare to so imperfect a surety; though it was true that I could have tried nothing more for him, I still doubted to myself whether this too easily given trust was the effect of a lack of will power or of laziness. But I consoled myself with the thought that Lucilio had never been a braggart and that he so surpassed other men in knowledge and in talent that it gave me the right to believe him their superior in foresight and in authority. The previous autumn, in Portogruaro, I had already heard rumours that he was secretly attached to the French Legation and certain of his words had later supported the truth of these rumours. Such relations perhaps put him in a position of being able to know and to see into matters more deeply than others; and finally I could see no reason why he should want to mock at me or amuse himself at my expense.

These considerations, united to the instinctive respect that I had always had for Lucilio and the fact that I had no hope of being able to help Amilcare by any other means, combined to reassure me about what I had done, and I ceased little by little to concern myself about the fate of my friend in order to pay attention to my own. Mile by mile, as I went further away from the lagoons into that labyrinth of creeks, drainage channels and canals that link the lower Friuli with Venice, the events of the past year grew more obscure in my mind and those lived before reappeared with the dazzling shimmer of dreams. It seemed to me that the boat in which I was, was carrying me towards the past and that every dip of the oars cancelled a day of my life, or, to put it better, reconquered a day from the past.

Nothing is more conducive to meditation, to moodiness, to poetry than a long voyage across the marshes in the full majesty of summer. Those immense horizons of lakes, ponds, marshes and rivers, inundated by the shifting colours of the light, those green brakes, those reeds and waterlilies, where the splendour of their colours vies with the richness of their perfume to dominate the senses, already languid in the heavy and sultry air, that torrid and shining sky that curves so immensely above; that continuous and monotonous tremor of all things animate and inanimate, in that splendid wilderness changed by the magic of nature into an ephemeral paradise, all this fills the soul with an inexhaustible thirst of passion and a feeling of the infinite. The life of the universe in solitude is the most sublime, the most indescribable, spectacle that ever strikes the eye of man! Therefore it is that we admire the sea in its eternal battle, the sky in its tempestuous overclouding, the night in its fecund silences and its summer phosphorescence. It is life that is felt, and seems to communicate to us the feeling of a vaster, more complete existence. Then we are no longer the critics and the legislators, but the eyes, the ears and the thoughts of the world: intelligence is no more a whole, but a part; man no longer pretends to understand and to dominate the universe, but feels, quivers, breathes with it. So I thought then in that scurry of dreams and of thoughts that thrust me back caressingly into the blessed memories of childhood. The white-haired exile who returns to his domestic hearth after having dragged out his days in ungrateful and foreign lands was certainly not more moved and joyful than I was then. But it was none the less a feeling of melancholy since the appearance in the twilight of memory of a joy long passed resembles the nocturnal visit of a loved one long dead and invites us to the luxury of tears.

I remembered and at the same time forgot and dreamed; I remembered the happiness of the boy, I forgot the torments of the adolescent, the repentance of the young man and dreamed of a gay and fortunate return to those enchanted shores of Halcyon whence, once driven out, one tries in vain to land once more. Who, after such an absence, has not dared to imagine his loved one changed by a miracle into the ideal love of his dreams, the creature of his heart and of his poesy? . . . Childish fancies, without truth and without expectation, in which the mind is in love, and hope and love and every other treasure of the soul imagines some vain figure draped in beauty. I saw then my Pisana in her cradle; I saw nothing but her long hair, her lovely eyes, her angelic smiles; I saw the little girl and remembered the grace, the talent, the pity and the sweet and caressing voice; I saw her then grown in pride and in beauty, I remembered her generous impulses, her proud movements, her fiery kisses; I felt her arm tremble in mine, I saw her breast swell at my glance and her look . . . Oh! who could describe how she once used to look at me and I remembered then, as I remember still, the magic message of those two enchanting eyes. How could I remember one only of those flashes of love and recall with it the clouds that darkened it? No, her soul, that most beautiful and spiritual part of her that lived in those eyes had not been soiled in the mire of sin.

No, man is not a mechanical contrivance that produces moods and thoughts, but is truly a mingling of the eternal and the temporal, of the sublime and the degraded, in whom life, diffused sometimes equably, is condensed now in this part and now in that to transform him into a hero or a beast. Some part divine shone in the eyes of the Pisana and remained always pure because incapable of sin. There lay the reason for that violent, immortal and complete passion that she had known how to inspire in me and that no prestige of beauty, no blandishment of the senses, would have been able to prolong beyond the tomb in the heart of an old man of eighty. I adored, I pitied the soul, enslaved and helpless, but always sorrowing and ready to rise from its long torpor.

At Portogruaro these fantasies of mine experienced a violent somersault. Everyone was talking about the caprices of the Pisana; even her aunt spoke to me of them, praying me to use my common sense to find some remedy since the Count, despite all that they said to him, would not interfere. She had even gone so far as to advise him to send the Pisana to her house; but he had been told that the girl did not want this at any price and he had allowed his daughter to lead him by the nose, thus seriously damaging his reputation.

'Listen, Carlino,' she said to me, 'Could there be anything worse? Raimondo Venchieredo hangs about her continually; she keeps him there by a hundred thousand whims so that it is a real scandal to see them; but later, when he comes to ask her seriously in marriage, for she is now turned eighteen and could very well consider it, she declares solemnly that she would never accept him as a husband

and that they should leave her in peace. It has been said that an earlier love for Giulio del Ponte is concealed behind this answer somewhere, but that can hardly be the case, for she ill-treats that young man, while continuing to flatter the other one whose proposal she has refused. In any case Giulio is almost penniless and so low in health that the doctors only give him till next spring!'

'What do you say? Is Giulio really as bad as that?' I exclaimed.

'Yes, poor fellow,' said the noble lady, 'and to tell you the truth it would be almost better that he should go, so as not to have to live through another episode with the Pisana, as Lucilio had with Clara. She at least was calm, reasonable and Christian and they were able to prevent any follies. But with this one? Uhm! One could expect anything and I fear she might become a dishonour to the family.'

I forgot the Pisana for a moment to remember Giulio and, I say it to my own credit, the sad news about his health distressed me. Indeed, the last time I had seen him, I had noticed his pallor as more intense than usual and a difficulty in breathing that often cut him short in the middle of a sentence. But I had attributed this solely to the trials and tribulations inseparable from a love for the Pisana and, seeing his sorrows, I almost felt that they were my revenge and rejoiced barbarously at them. After the evil prognostications of the lady Frumier I began to see more clearly and to fear lest he might become the first victim of the ebullient and unrestrained nature of the girl. I felt sorrow for his misfortune and perhaps even more at the crime which would have soiled the conscience of the one who killed him in this way, pitilessly and thoughtlessly. The faults of those whom I love have always had the quality of afflicting me even more than my own sorrows; I believe that at that time I could have pardoned the Pisana for loving Giulio if by doing so she could have restored him his health and his life. Indeed, I had every opportunity of assuring myself that the fears of the lady Frumier were not ill-founded. That same evening I saw the Pisana at Portogruaro; affectionate, timid and quiet with me, as one who had need of love and pity, flattering and provocative with the Venchieredo, indifferent and mocking with Giulio. Raimondo had forgotten Clara's refusal and the Pisana's flatteries had brought him back to the Frumier mansion, where he had hoped perhaps to make up for this refusal by the acquisition of an even more delicate and desirable mouthful. And her evasions had only served to stir up the embers of his desires even more violently, since the Pisana, while refusing him as a husband, accepted him and flattered him as a gallant. The dissolute young man, if he could obtain by contraband what he had tried to obtain legally, would have been considered the most cunning and fortunate of men, and the attitude of the Pisana gave him pretext enough for this hope. If you could have seen to what extremities she had reduced the unfortunate Giulio, you would have understood how pity silenced in me even the interests of my own love. A thing almost incredible. I loathed the Venchieredo not only on my own account, but on Giulio's; I was jealous of the Pisana more for his sake than for my own and the spectacle of that young man, full of spirit, of heart, of wit, who had been so miserably undone by the secret and inexorable cancer of an unhappy passion, filled my heart with a remorse for the hatred I had felt for him in former times. Do I seem too righteous for your taste? . . . It was not so; I was made that way. That long school of renunciation and patience in regard to the Pisana had produced a feeling of pity. I gave a proof of this later by my conduct for which many could brand me as a fool, but none could fail to grant me some praise for courage and generosity.

The Venchieredo had around him the aura of happiness. In his face, his gestures, his clothes, his speech, one recognized a young man well satisfied with himself, who has nothing to desire and nothing to consider save his own enjoyment, so great and powerful is he. Content embellished his cheeks with a rosy and bright colour, made his person slender and graceful, his words fluent and colourful. He saw everything good, everything beautiful, everything enchanting. He was welcome everywhere, since the spectacle of a great happiness comforts men with the confidence that one day or another they will be able to attain it themselves. The Pisana was all for him; she trembled and dropped her eyes at his glances, smiled at the sound of his voice, followed his every movement. As I had seen her, when a little girl, for Lucilio, so I saw her then, already a young woman, for Raimondo, the same confusions, the same ardour unrestrained either by modesty or fear, and an enchantment of desire grown a thousand times more great in the full splendour of her eighteen years old beauty. I loved her then desperately for myself; I hated her for the pitiless martyrdom to which she had condemned poor Giulio and I despised her for her shallow flirtation with a worthless and ill-bred young fellow such as Venchieredo. I know not what fury I felt in my heart to trample her underfoot, to insult and abuse her; I felt proud that I could love her still and yet be able to say that I would have ceded her to another in order to save his life! She, however, went her way as blind as an executioner. Blind! That alone excused her. I believe that she saw nothing, was aware of nothing. Her passions were always so exaggerated that they prevented her from seeing anything beyond them. To see the lacerated soul of Giulio struggling in a body so wasted and exhausted to fight on and defend himself against the easy and serene predominance of Raimondo, made tears come to my eyes.

The fire of the eyes, the splendour of the spirit that had at one time shone in his face, had disappeared; with that, all his beauty had gone, since he had nothing else; even the distinction of his pallor seemed soiled by brown and greenish patches with which his poisoned blood had corrupted him. He looked like a man sick with pellagra and his shame at his own appearance had taken all assurance from his glances and confidence from his words. His gaiety, already crushed by the oppression of his love, tried in vain to lift the lid from this coffin of desperation. He shone in flashes like an ignis fatuus in a cemetery and the force of his will, which momentarily rekindled him, relapsed a little later into a still deeper depression. It was for that that he had pleased others, for that he had himself been loved and without that he must perish; he knew this and was furious with himself not to be able to enliven at least some funerary flash from the ashes of his soul. To die, confounding his enemies, was now his only hope of love or of revenge; but the more he obstinately persisted, the less his will, enfeebled by illness and by passion, obeyed him.

I was horrified by these final efforts of a moribund soul, that amid the ruins of a body already resembling a tomb, still longed for that part of good that had been his and had been snatched from him by a young, arrogant and careless force. I seemed to see Lazarus agonizing with hunger, begging the gourmands for the crumbs from their table and obtaining nothing but rebuffs and scorn. But had it only been like that! Giulio could have found a final joy in venting his just and righteous anger; he could have died in the belief that his words, in revenge for his misfortune, would have resounded eternally in the soul of the foresworn one. But there was nothing of that; the Pisana had neither eyes nor ears for him; he was dying drop by drop, without being able to flatter himself that the death rattle of his curses would have disturbed even for an instant the happiness of her smile!

Next day I set out for Fratta before dawn, since I had done nothing all night save turn over in my mind the strangest plans and the most unlikely hopes, and spent many hours in the Chancellery, putting the affairs of the office in order.

I had the vanity to believe that from the times of the Romans onwards, justice had not been administered in the jurisdiction of Fratta with the honesty and care that were shown by me. A trifle of good will, a little study and consideration added to a reasonable amount of common sense dictated to me sentences which did honour to the Count's signature. Everyone praised to the skies the patience, the goodness and the justice of the Signor Vice-Chancellor; the patience above all, which is as rare as it is necessary for a country justice. I have sometimes seen one of these fly into a passion and get infuriated because of the slow understanding of the parties involved; to thrust his fist in the face of the supposed criminal and threaten him with a beating and then expect from him that moderation, that clearsightedness and reserve that are the fruits only of a long education. Quite contrary to these arguments, it must always be borne in mind that ignorant people are like children; one must use with them the slow and detailed logic of an elementary schoolmaster and not the brief rhetoric of a University professor.

Justice should be widespread but not imposed; it is right to maintain its reputation and decorum with persuasion, not give it the colour of arbitrariness with rebukes and arrogance. Since the formal code of the legal tribunals cannot be altered, these codes seem to country people in no way different from the predictions of the Sibyls. They give sentence because it is so, and he who is in the right often understands it no better than he who is in the wrong. Accustomed from the cradle to live amongst rough and ignorant people, I found it no trouble to clothe myself with such tolerance, which came to me of its own free will; and indeed little was to be done without it.

My example was also of influence on the men of the Commune who were entrusted with the settlement of minor cases, since there were no longer so many complaints to be heard of the negligence of such a one in favour of another, or of the reprisals of one man against another. The old man, Andreini, had died a little before the Chancellor, and his son, who had succeeded him, was only too eager to back up my zeal for the good management of judicial affairs. The Chaplain was beside himself for joy; he was no longer worried about his friendship with the Spaccafumo and the latter, who had begun to give way to drink, no longer disturbed the peace of the festas with his quarrels and was able to visit whomsoever he pleased. The term of his banishment had expired and though his life, it is true, was not like that of his fellows, yet no one spoke ill of him and that was enough for me not to harry him without reason. A few winters before, he had lost the Martinella who used to supply him with salt, polenta and other necessaries of life, so he had to come out of the lagoons more often to fend for himself; but for the rest nothing was known of him and he lived like an oyster amongst oysters. The Chaplain told me that he still remembered that evening when he had brought me back to the castle on his crupper and that he always praised himself for my success and for the great claim that I had on the gratitude of the Commune.

The praises of the Spaccafumo flattered me not a little; but those of the Rector of Teglio sent me into ecstasies. He would declaim them with an authoritative and moderate air, like one qualified to bestow or to withold them, and it must not be forgotten that the glories of the disciple were reflected upon the master. For him I always remained the little scholar with the prominent ears and the Latinist who made four grammatical errors in every sentence. Even Marchetto was satisfied with my administration, since his paunch had begun to give trouble and to grumble at too lengthy rides, so I spared him these with very frequent arrangements. The busybodies and my assistant Fulgenzio used to grumble because the quarrels of others were often to their benefit but I paid no attention to the ill humours of the perverse and I used to scorch the hide of the latter often enough until he amended his former habit of extorting double pay for his labours, once from the magistrate and once from the litigants. Giulio del Ponte had warned me not to antagonize him too much since for all his humility and his hump he had the reputation of standing very well with those in power. And I, thinking over the trial of the old Venchieredo, was well persuaded of the truth of these suspicions; but I put my duty above all and would have washed the faces of the Most Serene Inquisitors themselves, to say nothing of some base little spy of theirs, had I caught them in the act of dishonouring my office.

There was, however, another person who, without seeming to do so, sent all the devils to my heart, and that was the bailiff. My presence, my authority, had curtailed certain old privileges of his in extortion and petty theft. I had discovered the thread of his misdoings and had pardoned him, but I did not pardon subsequent offences; he knew this and bore my surveillance with considerable ill-humour.

The Count, for his part, was only too glad to save the salary of a Chancellor and neither talked of letting me take my final examinations or of settling me regularly in the position. These expedients of his suited me well enough. I went my own way, content with the blessings that were showered upon me from all sides for my impartiality, my wisdom and above all for my moderation in collecting taxes. Donato, the apothecary's son, and Sandro the miller, old rivals though they had once been, had now become my friends and companions, and increased my favour among the people by continually singing my praises. In fact, I proved then the truth of that maxim that in the zealous fulfilment of one's duties is hidden the secret of forgetting one's sorrows and in doing as little evil as one could.

But Fratta did not constitute the world and outside it the rumours, the mischances, the threats of war and of revolution continually increased. The news from Venice was asked for anxiously, commented on, distorted, exaggerated and later formed the theme of many stormy sessions around the castle hearth.

The Captain proved that, as two and two make four, the fears were exaggerated and that the Signoria had acted wisely in refraining from extraordinary measures, since the French, even with a fair wind in their sails, would have to spend three years in crossing the Alps and another four for their advance from Bormida to the Mincio. He enumerated the lines of defence, the enemy forces, the captains, the fortresses; indeed, according to him the war would either be finished on the other side of the Alps or, if on this side, would become the inheritance of the next generation. Giulio del Ponte and one or two others who came from Portogruaro were not of this opinion; according to them, the advantages of the allies were very far from assuring the Republic against the enormities of the French and that in either two or three months it could very well be that they would already have invaded the states of the *terraferma* and even the Friuli itself. The Count and Monsignor shuddered at these prognostications and it fell to me to destroy the evil effects of such overpowering and premature fears.

Drifting along in this way, the spring of 1797 arrived. The Republic of Venice had already formally recognized the new democratic government of France; its representative, Alvise Querini, had said his piece to the Directory and to cement the alliance had already agreed to the expulsion of the Count of Provence from Verona. The Captain said: 'They are doing very well. It needs patience not to put one's hand at once to the purse or to the sword. Do you see? Things are already beginning to cool down over there. Those who have killed the priests, the friars and the nobles have ended on the scaffold themselves; the crisis can be said to be decreasing and the Republic has got out of it without endangering the life of a single one of its subjects.' Giulio replied: 'They have done very ill; they are putting their feet on our necks. They are quiet now, but they will shout all the louder later on. Now we have become accustomed to the danger when the danger is non-existent, but then the real danger will come and will find us asleep or unprepared. God send that all will be well, but at the best we shall cut a very poor figure!'

I inclined to Giulio's opinion, the more so since Lucilio had written to me from Venice that I should hope for the best and that the fate of my friend was never nearer to a change for the better. But his own fate, the fate of the poor little doctor, underwent in those same days a serious setback. Clara had been finally relegated to the Convent of St. Theresa, and we knew of this at Fratta when the

Contessa wrote that they should send her the money for the dowry; she said that she had in the meantime taken up the matter with a money-lender but that he would not hear of long terms with conditions as disturbed as they were then. The Count sighed very deeply, but once more gathered together the money and sent it to his wife.

I was only too well aware that the family was rushing to ruin, but had to limit myself to stanching a few drops while the spigot was pouring out at full flood, since for my part I could do nothing more to remedy it. To the Count I could not risk saying anything, to Monsignor it was worse than useless, while to the bailiff it would be definitely harmful. The Pisana, in whom I confided now and again, replied with a shrug of her shoulders that matters had always gone on in this way, that it was impossible to give orders to her mamma and that for her part she did not worry greatly about it, since they would go on living in one way or another.

She seemed to be much chastened in her caprices. Without showing either irritation or pleasure at my reserve, she honoured me with her confidence and was always pleasant to Giulio, though it could easily be seen that she was not displaying the ardour that she usually showed in her affairs of the heart. The greater part of the day she spent in her grandmother's room and it seemed that she had taken up the task of trying to make the old woman forget the absence of the elder sister; but the poor old creature, now completely senile, was no longer in a state to appreciate her services. These, however, were not for that reason any the less worthy of merit.

When the news of Clara's noviciate became known in the countryside, the Partistagno, who had not shown himself since the tragicomic outcome of his formal demand, appeared at the castle. He shouted, he stormed, he argued and frightened the Count and Monsignor. He then left, declaring that he was going to Venice to demand justice and to liberate a noble damsel from the unconscionable tyranny of her family. The time that had passed had only served to convince him even more deeply of the irresistible value of his own merits and against all reasons that he had to the contrary, he insisted on believing that Clara was in love with him and that her relations would not give her to him for some mysterious reason which he was determined to bring to light. Indeed it was rumoured a little later that he had left Lugugnana and moved to Venice and they hastened to send a report of this from Fratta, but since there came no further news from there, they ended by assuring themselves that the uproar created by the Partistagno had evaporated in idle words.

Meanwhile what I had forseen for some time came eventually to pass. The health of the Signor Count began to grow worse from day to day and in the end he fell seriously ill. Before the Contessa could be warned of the danger, he expired without regaining consciousness, surrounded by the Chaplain, Monsignor and the Pisana. Doctor Sperandio had already extracted about eighty pounds of blood from him and had recited an extraordinary number of Latin texts to prove that this death had taken place according to the laws of nature. But the deceased, had he been able to take a look around him from his coffin, would have been almost content to be dead, so great was the pomp of the funeral. Monsignor Orlando wept with moderation and himself sang the Office of the Dead in a voice more nasal than usual. The Pisana gave way to despair those first few days more than I would have thought possible; and then suddenly seemed completely forgetful. When the Frumiers came to take her and to tell her that it was her mother's wish that she should go to Venice, it seemed that she forgot everything in the great joy of exchanging the boredom of Fratta for the diversions of the capital.

She left a fortnight later and only when taking leave of me did it seem that sorrow at having to part from me overcame her pleasure at rushing off to a new life full of splendid hopes. I was grateful for her grief and let her see this without any pride. I knew once more that her heart was not bad, and I resigned myself and remained.

My presence at Fratta was now really necessary. To tell of the confusion that followed the death of the Count would be too long a tale. Money-lenders, creditors, claimants descended upon us from all sides. The goods put up for auction, the sequestrations and the mortgages were like a city put to sack. The bailiff made off after burning the registers; I remained alone, poor little chicken, to try and unravel that skein. To top it all, I was without any instructions and from Venice came only continual and voracious demands for money. The Frumiers were of very little assistance to me; I believe that Father Pendola had whispered against me and they looked askance at me. I, however, resolved to reply to them with facts; I sweated, I worked, I kept myself occupied all the time, always with the thought in my mind that I was aiding the Pisana and being of use to those who, for good or evil, had brought me up, and when the young Count Rinaldo came to take over the reins of government the eighty thousand ducats for the Contessina's dowry had been assured, the creditors paid or staved off, the income was coming in freely and the properties, though diminished here and there, still made up a good patrimony. There was still great damage certainly, but of such a nature that only time was needed to heal it. Nor was I the last to believe that for such an affair a young gentleman of twenty-four only just out of college (the Countess would have left him there till the age of thirty had it not been for the death of her husband) was not the most suitable person. But enough! I did not know what to do about it and proposed merely to keep an eye on him and be ready to help him with some advice. For the rest, I retired into the Chancellery where, having passed my final examinations, I became a little later Chancellor *in formis*.

Giulio del Ponte, no longer able to bear the torment of separation, had followed the Pisana to Venice. I remained quite alone with only the good that I had done to console me, and determined to go on doing what I could, to live on memories, and to hope for better things in the future. This life, if not happy, was tranquil, busy and useful. I had the virtue to content myself with it.

CHAPTER X

THE Count Rinaldo was a studious and reserved young man, who paid very little attention to his affairs and still less to amusing himself as one might have expected him to do at his age. He would remain for long periods shut up in his room and with me especially practically never exchanged a word. Certainly, I shared in the honours of his table, but he ate little and spoke less. On entering and leaving, he saluted Monsignor his uncle, and left it at that. Well-mannered, affable and even just on occasion, I had no reason to complain of him, and attributed his shyness to illness or to the fear of some organic complaint; indeed, his complexion was rather unfortunate, as of those who suffer with their liver. I for my part carried on my duties day after day, always tranquil, always the same, like the beads of a rosary.

I seldom went to Portogruaro to visit the Frumiers, for fear of Father Pendola, the more so since the diocese had begun to complain of his masked arrogance and the Curia and the Chapter and even the Bishop himself to resent being led, however gently, by the nose. The worthy Father suffered from epilepsy, too, and I had no wish to be present at such a painful spectacle. However, I often used to go to Cordovado to the Provedoni household, where I had made great friends with the young people, and Bradamante and Acquilina enlivened the conversation with their feminine magic that makes us men twice as vivacious, twice as nimble and gay, when we find ourselves in the company of women. For me, at least, it was always so; save for conversations tied to a specific argument, what may be called true, spontaneous, witty small talk I have never been able to bring to my lips in the company of men, even when they are old friends. Mostly I am silent if I have nothing new or of interest to say, so that I have looked like a fool a thousand times. But when a woman joins in the conversation! At once the roseate gates of fantasy are opened and there flow out all the secrets of our feelings, images and thoughts and humorous confidences.

You will note, however, that I have never had any excessive facility for falling in love; and indeed I will not say that all women have had this flattering effect on me, but I have proved it many times with many who were neither young nor beautiful. It was enough that a ray of kindness or a flash of the ideal shone in their faces, and the rest was done by that necessity that inferiors feel to make a good show before their superiors in order to be favourably judged. Women superior to us? Yes, my brothers, accept this unusual opinion from the mouth of an old man who has known many of them. They are superior to us in the constancy of their sacrifices, in faith, in resignation; they die better than we; and they are indeed our superiors in that most important thing of all, in that practical science of life which is, as you know, but a race towards death. On this side of the Alps, women are also our superiors because men can do nothing without inspiration from them; a glance at our history, at our literature, will persuade you that I speak the truth. And this contributes to the praise and the justification of women, as also to their disfavour in all those countries in which nothing great ever takes place. The fault is theirs alone. If they amend in time, the Appenines in labour will bring forth not mice, but heroes.

Sometimes I would make a trip as far as Venchieredo to visit Leopardo, always more and more besotted owing to the tyranny and frivolity of his wife. I remember having been with him on Sundays also at the evening gatherings around the spring. Only to think that it was here that had first flashed upon him the smile of happiness and love! Now he would walk with drooping head, arm in arm with Doretta, and everyone sniggering behind their backs, the usual fate of the deceived husband. But at least he had the felicity of being aware of nothing, so much did that viper of a woman keep in servitude even his understanding. Oh, she was certainly no example of those women superior to us of whom I spoke a short while back! Woe to the woman who has become degenerate! The proverb is an old one; she becomes a devil! Raimondo also came to the spring sometimes. If he talked or joked with Doretta, he did so without any reserve and in a way to make one's stomach turn; if, however, he paid no heed to her in order to run after the other country girls and flirts of the neighbourhood, she did not ignore him, but shamelessly followed him around, always with her husband in tow. And she indulged in such acts of vulgarity, scorn and jealousy that the good people of the company would laugh mockingly behind Leopardo's back.

The other Provedonis, who also went there from time to time, withdrew for shame, and I myself had to move away since the sight of a trust so complete and so basely betrayed nauseated me. However it is often only too true that the sight of the misfortunes of others is a comfort to our own. As we advance in life, we seem to grow hardened to the blows of sorrow, but this is not from habit but because the eyes, looking far afield, descry at every moment some other unfortunate even more oppressed and harassed than we ourselves. Pity for the misfortunes that I beheld armed me with patience for those I suffered myself. The Pisana had promised to write to me from time to time; I had let her promise, and knew now how much reliance I should have placed in her word. In fact several months passed before I had news from her and only towards the end of the summer I received a strange, absurd, scrawled letter in which the vehemence of her affection and the humility of her expressions consoled me a little for her past neglect. That is, they would have been a consolation for any other save myself. For I knew that volcanic little head and knew that, having once given rein to her rush of repentance, she would return for God knows how long to her earlier indifference. Some verses of Dante's came into my mind like so many poisoned knives:

'. . . indi s'apprende
Quanto in femmina il foco d'amor dura
Si l'occhio o il tatto spesso nol raccende.'
(' . . . and so is learnt
How long in women the fire of love endures
If eye or touch do not oft rekindle it.')

I had fished that little Dante out of the *mare magnum* of old books, odds and ends and registers whence Clara, years before, had collected her little library. To her this little red worm-eaten book full of mysterious verses, contractions still more mysterious and pictures of the damned and their devilries, had made no sort of appeal. To me, on the other hand, who had heard it praised at Portogruaro and Padua, usually out of context, it seemed that I had found a little treasure; I began to sharpen my teeth on it and at the first attempt had got as far as the canto of Francesca when I felt that the pleasure received was a good deal less than the labour involved. But at that point I began to fall in love with it. I put my nose to the grindstone and read it through to the end, then I read it again, enjoying what I then understood and what at first had seemed to me unintelligible.

I finally ended by venerating Dante as a sort of domestic godhead and swore so much by him that even the verses quoted a short while back seemed to me articles of my creed. You must remember that at that time there was no mad enthusiasm for the *trecento*, that Monti had not yet written the Basvilliana and the Visioni of Varano were not popular save among the erudite. You will certainly laugh at me; but you will be aware that this passion for Dante, created by myself alone, a young man who was no philologian and certainly not erudite, was a thing that I might claim as no small triumph. And you would be right. I pride myself on it since, even more than the verses, even more than the poetry, I loved the heart and the soul of Dante. As to his passions, they were great, powerful and intellectual and they pleased me the more because of these qualities, at that time only too rare.

All this has little to do with the proverb: 'out of sight, out of mind'; but it had pleased Dante to apply that proverb to the fidelity of women and I have drawn him and my hare-brained studies of sixty years ago into the pictures as the memory returns to me. Only too often he who recounts his own life has to suffer from such digressions. However, in going onwards, I shall have real need of your generosity, my dear readers; and on this question of my literary glories you will have to grant me double indulgence just because I understand their paucity. Our great authors I have guessed at rather than understood, loved rather than studied, and I must admit that the greater number of them set my teeth on edge. I am sure that the fault must have been mine alone, but none the less I flatter myself that in the future he who writes will remember how he used to speak and that the aim of speaking is precisely to make oneself understood. Is it not far better to make oneself understood by the many than to be understood only by the few? In France they print, they sell and they read more books that we do for no other reason than because of the universality of the language and the clarity of the discourse. With us, there are three or four vocabularies and the learned have the habit of employing the least used of these. As for logic, they use it as a springboard to make continuous leaps of an octave or a tenth. Those who are accustomed to ascend step by step remain a good half mile behind and having lost their guide from view, sit down contentedly to wait for another one who perhaps may never come. Take courage, then, I speak ill of no one, but in writing think that many will have to read. In this way we shall see if our literature may perhaps afford an assistance greater than it has so far given to our national renaissance.

And the Pisana's letter, where have I left it? Reassure yourself; I am an idle fellow, but one way or another, will come back to it in the end. The Pisana's letter I have still, together with others, in the deepest recess of my writing table; and, if you would care to, you could find there some little flower of language of a nature passing strange. But it will suffice you to know that it gave me news of Clara, still a novice in a convent, and a little also of Lucilio, who was getting himself much talked about in Venice for his fanatical devotion to the French. If they failed, this prognosticated a bad end for him.

But these demoniac French did not even dream of failing! The war against them had slackened; only Austria and Piedmont remained in the field and even though reduced, they sustained it with better spirit and greater hopes than at first. However, there was no great news until the winter and then let each hold what he had got; he who would create a war every month had not yet poked his head from behind the Alps, and the snows marked the usual armistice. That winter was the longest and most tranquil I ever passed in my life. The cares of my office kept me busy and assiduous. Beyond these, thoughts of the Pisana always hammered in my brain, but my distance from her added a gentle melancholy and took away all bitterness from my grief. I found some recompense in the thought of having done my duty. Giulio del Ponte wrote to me once or twice, scatterbrained and sibylline letters, true letters of a man in love to a friend. From them I could understand that he was not entirely happy and that even his semi-happiness of the past year when he had been in Venice was being whittled away, either because of the caprices of the Pisana or because of the increase in his desire. These letters distressed me for him, but for myself cheered me up considerably. I understood that had I also been in Venice I would perhaps not have enjoyed any greater happiness than I had at Fratta.

Nothing in our solitude was changed. The young Count always in his room, the Countess asking for money by every post, and the old grandmother confined to her bed under the care of the Signora Veronica and Faustina. Around the hearth there remained the Captain and Monsignor Orlando, who quarrelled every evening about making up the fire. Each wanted to wield the poker, and each wanted it arranged in his own way and they usually ended by burning the tail of old Marocco, who would take refuge disconsolately under the coalscuttle. In every old newspaper that arrived, the Captain triumphed to see those cursed French beleagured in the Appenines and the Alps. It was no longer four, but six or even eight years, they would need to cross them. 'Moreover,' he said, 'we could bring all armed Slavonia to the Mincio and then tell me how the game would go!'

Marchetto, Fulgenzio and the cook, who alone formed their audience, would certainly not have sought for a pretext to demolish the Captain's lovely castles in the air; and the Chaplain, when he was present, aided him in building them with his credulous ignorance. I for my part just shook my head and do not remember well what I thought. Certainly the opinions of the Captain would not have had any great weight with me, precisely because they were his. Then one day came the news that a French general, young and quite unknown, was to lead the French Army of the Alps, a certain Napoleon Bonaparte.

'Napoleon! What sort of a name is that!' asked the Chaplain, 'some schismatic, perhaps.'

'It will be one of those names which have recently become the fashion in Paris,' replied the Captain. 'One of those names that resemble those Signor Antonio Provedoni likes so much, like Brutus, Alcibiades, Miltiades or Cimon; all names of the damned, which will send to perdition, I hope, those who bear them.'

'Bonaparte! Bonaparte!' murmured Monsignor Orlando, 'It would almost seem to be one of our names.'

'Eh! We are agreed on that. Masks, masks, all masks!' said the Captain. 'They must have put forward a name like that in order to get into our good books, or perhaps those great generals are afraid at having to cut a sorry figure and have taken a false name, a name that no one knows, so that all the evil repute would go to it. That's it! That is certainly it! It is an escape from shame! Napoleon Bonaparte! . . . One can feel its falsity even in pronouncing it, because nothing is more difficult than to make up a name that sounds really natural. For instance they should have said Giorgio Sandracca, or Giacomo Andreini, or Carlo Altoviti, all easy names and in the customary form; no, sirs, they have slipped up with that Napoleon Bonaparte where one can easily detect the fraud!'

It was therefore decided in the Castle of Fratta that General Bonaparte was an imaginary being, a cover for some old Captain who did not want to dishonour himself in a war in which he had no hope of victory, an empty name invented by the Directory to flatter Italian ears. But two months later, this imaginary being, after winning four battles and forcing the King of Sardinia to sue for peace, entered Milan amid the plaudits and celebrations of those whom Botta called the Italian Utopians. In June, having closely besieged Mantua, he already had in his hands the fate of all Italy; from all sides came a pleading for alliances, a demand for truces. Venice, still deliberating, when the time for doing so had already passed, relied for the last time on unarmed neutrality. The French General took advantage of this at his ease. He made incursions, pillaged, invaded; levied contributions on provinces, cities and castles. He broke the two armies of Wurmser and d'Alvinzi on the Garda, on the Brenta, on the Adige, and a third at Provera, near Mantua, and in February '97 the fortress surrendered. At Fratta they still doubted, but in Venice they really trembled; one could almost hear the thunder of the cannon at St Mark's and there was no time left for idle chatter. They merely went on believing that, as they had lived till then, so they would continue to be preserved 'by luck, by accident', to use the celebrated expression of Doge Renier.

The Contessa, however, in the midst of these disorders, did not look so calmly on them; nor did it seem to her to be a good risk to take refuge in the *terraferma*, seeing that everyone from there was leaving to take refuge in Venice. The Frumiers had already returned there, to the great regret of the select society of Portogruaro. So the Countess wrote to her son that he would do very well to come to her too, since a man in the family was a great assurance, and at the same time told him to bring with him, for every emergency, as much money as he could. Count Rinaldo arrived in Venice just at the moment when the war was rumbling at the gates of the Friuli and even Captain Sandracca realized that the young Corsican General was neither a hypothetical being nor a romantic name invented by the Directory. The Captain now feared the French General real and present, as much as he had laughed at him when distant and imaginary. The report suddenly spread that the Archduke Charles was going down to the Tagliamento with a fresh army and that the French were moving against him, that there would be a massacre, a general pillage and universal ruin. Houses were abandoned, castles were barricaded against the marauding bands of stragglers and deserters, the church treasures were buried, the priests dressed themselves as peasants and fled to the lagoons. Already from Brescia from Bergamo and from Verona came reports of atrocities, rapes and acts of violence which were both bewailed and greatly exaggerated; hatred and fear alternated in equal degree, but the second made the first cowardly also. All fled without a thought, without shame and without providing either for themselves or their families. The Captain and the Signora Veronica escaped, I believe, to Lugugnana, where they remained hidden at a fisherman's hut in a little island in the lagoon. Monsignor went no further than Portogruaro since the prospect of fasting scared him even more than did Bonaparte. Fulgenzio and his sons had disappeared. Marchetto, being ill, got himself taken to hospital. There was a great to-do to keep Faustina so that I should not be left alone with the old Countess. There stayed with me, however, the gardener and the steward who, perhaps because they had nothing to lose, were not in such a hurry to place themselves in safety. But I could not remain so, the more so since the oafs of the neighbourhood, made bold by the universal consternation, were becoming even bolder and had begun to rob some of the more solitary and less defended places.

Furthermore, I was by no means sure of the gardener or of the steward, and least of all of Faustina; so I resolved, before the peril should close in on us even more, to make a trip to Portogruaro to ask for help. I hoped that the Vice-Captain would allot me a dozen of those Slavs who arrived every day on their way from Venice, and that Monsieur Orlando would find me a woman, a nurse, to remain at the bedside of his mother. Therefore I saddled Marchetto's horse, which had been eating its head off in the stables for the past week, and set off at a gallop for Portogruaro.

News at that time had neither steamships nor the telegraph to take it round the world at the fall of an eyelid. At Fratta it arrived either by the miller's donkey or in the courier's saddlebags; therefore it was no wonder if, three miles from the castle, great events were taking place. At Portogruaro, to say the least, the devil's own shindy was going on, unemployed artisans shouting, groups of peasants uttering threats, priests trying to deter them, policemen slinking into corners out of the way and, in the midst of all this, in the place of the usual standard, a famous Tree of Liberty, the first that I had ever seen, and which at that time and in that place, did not make a great impression on me.

However, I was young, I had been at Padua, I had escaped from the wiles of Father Pendola, I in no way adored the Inquisitors of State and this full-throated bawling rather pleased me and it seemed to me that some progress had been made. I was almost convinced that these commonplace ne'er-do-wells could have become men of Athens or of Sparta and I sought among the crowd some person who, in the Senator's circle, used to praise to the skies the legislation of Lycurgus and of Draco. However, I could not see one of them. All these brawlers were unknown to me, had come from no one knew where, and were men to whom the day before I would have questioned the right of reasoning and who were now imposing laws with four tosses of their caps in the air and a few leaps around a wooden pole. There had sprung up out of the earth, if not armed men, then certainly a new power, arrogant and presumptuous; its strength lay in the fright and incapacity of the dispossessed; it was the triumph of the Unknown God, the bacchanal of the freedmen who, without knowing it, felt themselves to have become men. That they would have had the virtue to become such I do not know; but the feeling of being able to, to have to be so, was already a step forward. I too, from the height of my old nag, began to shout with all the breath in my body; and it is certain that I was considered a ring-leader of the tumult, since there soon gathered around me a shirtless and frantic mob which applauded my shouts and accompanied me as if in a procession. So much can a horse do for one at certain moments. I confess that this aura of popularity went to my head and I took a wild pleasure in seeing myself thus followed and applauded by so many persons, none of whom knew me and none of whom I knew.

I repeat, my horse was a great advantage to me, as perhaps also was the fine blue coat that I was wearing; people, whatever you may say, go mad at the sight of a splendid livery and to all these men in rags and tatters it seemed as if they had won a treble chance in the lottery in finding a leader so well equipped and, in addition, on horseback. Amongst the dissentient countryfolk who looked askance at the Tree of Liberty were some from the jurisdiction of Fratta who knew me for my impartiality and my love of justice. They certainly believed that I had joined in the affair to arrange everything for the best and began to shout:

'It is our Chancellor! It is the Signor Carlino! Long live our Chancellor! Long live Signor Carlino!'

The mob of real rioters, to whom it did not seem right to join in an equal enthusiasm with that suspicious and almost hostile throng, found to its taste if not the Chancellor at least the Signor Carlino, and all of a sudden began to shout:

'Long live Signor Carlino! Make way for Signor Carlino! Let the Signor Carlino speak!'

As far as thanking them for these honours and going forward, I got out of the difficulty excellently; but as for speaking, I had, on my faith, not the slightest idea what to say; it was lucky that the uproar around me dispensed with the necessity. But there was some wretch who began to call for silence and to beg them to stop and listen to me, since it seemed that from the eminence of my nag and the inspiration of my fine clothes, I ought to be able to tell them some most agreeable things. Indeed, as the front ranks halted, those behind could not advance and those in the rear began to ask what was the matter. 'It is the Signor Carlino who wants to speak! . . . Silence! . . . Halt! . . . Pay attention! . . . The Signor Carlino speaks!'

Now my horse was surrounded by a throng, restless and eager for my words. I felt the spirit of Demosthenes upon my tongue and opened my lips . . . 'Ps, ps! . . . Quiet. He is speaking!' But the first attempt was not a very happy one; my lips closed again without having uttered a word.

'Did you hear? . . . What did he say? . . . He said to keep quiet . . . Silence then! . . . Long live Signor Carlino!'

Reassured by such a favourable reception, I opened my mouth once more and this time really spoke.

'Citizens!' (It was Amilcare's favourite word), 'Citizens, what do you want?'

The question was more grandiloquent than was warranted; in a breath I destroyed Doge, Senate, Major Council, Podesteria and Inquisition; I put myself at a bound in the place of Providence, a step above every human authority. I could no longer discern the Castle of Fratta and its Chancellery from so sublime a height; I became a sort of dictator, a Washington on horseback amid a noisy crowd of men on foot.

'What do we want? . . . What does he say? . . . He has asked what we want . . . We want liberty! . . . Long live Liberty! . . . Bread, bread! Polenta, polenta!' shouted the peasants.

This shout for bread and polenta ended by creating complete agreement between the peasants of the countryside and the artisans from the city. The Lion and St Mark lost their last hope.

'Bread! Bread! Liberty! . . . Polenta! . . . Hang the merchants! . . . Open the granaries! . . . Quiet! Quiet! . . . Signor Carlino speaks! . . . Silence!'

It was true that a whirlwind of eloquence rose in my brain and I was myself all on fire to speak since there were so many well disposed to listen to me.

'Citizens,' I went on in a loud voice, 'citizens, the bread of liberty is the most healthy of all; everyone has a right to have it, since what is a man without bread and without liberty? . . . I say, without bread and liberty, what is a man?'

I repeated this demand to myself, since really I was somewhat perplexed to reply to it; but necessity forced me on and a deeper silence and a more profound attention urged me to make haste; in my haste I did not seek for anything subtle, but for a metaphor that would be immediately striking.

'Man,' I continued, 'is then like a mad dog, a stray dog!'

'Hurrah! Hurrah! . . . Very good! . . . Very good! . . . Polenta polenta! . . . We are as mad dogs! Long live Signor Carlino . . . The Signor Carlino speaks well! The Signor Carlino knows everything, sees everything!'

The Signor Carlino would have been hard put to it to explain how a man without liberty, that is to say a man with at least one master, had anything in common with a masterless dog who has, for that very reason, the most complete liberty; but I felt this was not the moment to enter into sophistries.

'Citizens,' I went on. 'You want liberty; consequently, you have it. As for bread and polenta, I cannot give them to you; if I had them I would willingly invite you all to supper. But Providence thinks of everything; let us commend ourselves to it!'

A long and varied murmur that denoted a certain disparity of opinion, welcomed my proposal. Then followed a tumult of voices, of shouts, of threats and of proposals that differed considerably from mine.

'To the granaries, to the granaries! . . . Let us elect a podestà. . . . Run to the belfry! . . . Call out the Bishop! . . . No, no, let us go to the Vice-Captain! . . . Let us put the Vice-Captain in the stocks!'

The impulse of those who wanted to go to the Bishop prevailed and I, on my nag, was pushed and dragged before the Bishop's Palace.

'Let the Signor Carlino speak! We want Monsignor! Let Monsignor the Bishop come out!'

It could be seen that my speech, without obtaining any definite result, but calling on them to submit to the decrees of Providence had at least persuaded them to confide in its legitimate representative. But in the Bishop's Palace, meanwhile, all was far from tranquil. Priests, canons and members of the Curia, each gave his own opinion and not one could be found that was really of use. Father Pendola, who had for some time now been tottering on his throne, thought the moment opportune to establish himself more securely. Having decided on a grand coup, he put out a hand from within as a sign of trust, then courageously opened the casement and came out on the balcony, his body half leaning over the rail. A salvo of whistles and catcalls saluted his appearance; I saw his lips stammer a word or two, then he grew pale and retired hastily within as the hands of the crowd sought the ground to pick up stones. Monsignor de Sant' Andrea rejoiced sincerely at that repulse to the most excellent Father and, with him, all within, from the greatest to the least, echoed in the depths of their hearts the cries and whistles of the mob. The Bishop, who was a saintly man, looked pityingly at his secretary, but it was already some time that he had had it in mind to dismiss him, just because he was a saintly man, and if he did not thank him then and there for the work that he had done, that too was the result of his sanctity. He turned with a calm face to Monsignor di Sant' Andrea, asking him if he would make himself the interpreter of the desires of the people who were rioting outside. I was watching the balcony continually and finally saw the synodal figure of the Canon appear there; there were no whistles and no howls at his appearance, but a whisper of 'Hush! Hush!', a murmur of approval and nothing more.

'Brothers,' he began, 'Monsignor the Bishop asks you through me what desire has led you to make an uproar beneath his windows.'

There followed an astounded silence since none of us, I no more than any of the others, knew why we had come. But at last a voice broke out: 'We want to see Monsignor the Bishop,' and was followed by a fresh outburst of cries: 'We want Monsignor! We want Monsignor!'

The Canon retired and already there were milling around Monsignor two parties of different views concerning the expediency or otherwise of his exposing himself to the turbulence of the mob. But he, the Bishop, supported the more courageous party; making his way with gentle violence through the ranks of his opponents, he showed himself on the balcony. His face was calm and serene, the dignity with which he was invested and the sanctity that was evident in his whole aspect moved the crowd and changed its feelings of hate and licence almost into shame. When the commotion caused by his appearance had subsided, he looked tranquilly down and then, in a voice of almost paternal reproof, asked:

'My sons, what do you want from your spiritual father?'

A silence like that which had welcomed the words of the Canon followed this demand; but the repentance overcame the wonder of the mob and already one began to bend his knee and others raised their hands in the attitude of prayer, when a unanimous voice broke from a thousand throats that seemed but one:

'Your blessing, your blessing!'

All knelt, I bowed my head over the ruffled mane of my nag, and the asked for benediction descended upon us. Then, before the Bishop could add, as he wished, some words of peace, the crowd moved onward, howling that we must go to the Vice-Captain and I and my horse were pushed along to the Town Hall. Four Slavs who were sitting at the doors, rushed into the courtyard, closing and barring the entrances; then, after many demands and many consultations, the Signor Vice-Captain decided to show himself in the loggia. The mob had neither muskets nor pistols and the worthy magistrate decided to trust himself before them.

'What is this, my sons?' . . . he began in a quavering tone. 'Today is a working day and every one of you has a family, as I have also; each of us must attend to his own affairs, and instead . . .'

A cheer for liberty by the frenzied fools in the square drowned the voice of the orator.

'Liberty you have taken yourselves, or so it seems to me,' he continued with an air of real humility. 'Enjoy it, my sons, for in these matters I cannot go with you.'

'Away with the Slavs! . . . Hang the Slavs!' rose several shouts.

'The French! Long live the French! We want liberty!' replied others.

These gentlemen, the French, then came into my mind for the first time in all this tumult and put a certain clarity into my ideas. At the same time I remembered Fratta and the reason why I had come to Portogruaro; but the Signor Vice-Captain did not seem to be in such good waters himself as to be able to help others. He showed a most evident desire to withdraw from the loggia and it needed the continual shouts of the crowd to ensure that he remained there.

'But my good sirs,' he stammered, 'I do not know what use it is either to me or to you to keep me standing here on show. I am only an official, a blind instrument of the Most Excellent Viceroy and I take my orders only from him . . .'

'No, no! . . . You must take orders from us! We have no masters any more! Long live liberty! Down with the Viceroy! . . .'

'Take care, Signori! You have no constituted authority, you have no legitimate magistrates . . .'

'Good! Then we will make some! Let us nominate an Avogadore. To the vote, to the vote, for an Avogadore! You will obey our Avogadore!'

'But, for pity's sake,' the Vice-Captain protested desperately, 'this is open rebellion. To elect an Avogadore is all very well, but give us time to write to the Most Excellent Viceroy, so that he may inform the Most Serene College . . .'

'Death to the College! We want our Avogadore! Stop there! Stop there! Death to the Vice-Captain if he moves! To the vote for our Avogadore! To the vote!'

The confusion continued to increase and with it the noise, and here and there about ten names were being whispered for the part of Avogadore; but those who were absent had no merit to conquer those present. A peasant began to shout: 'Let us nominate the Signor Carlino!' Those behind him began crying: 'He is the Avogadore of the people! Long live the Signor Carlino! Down with the Vice-Captain!'

I had not in truth ventured into this turmoil with any such ambitious aims; but once I saw myself exalted so high, I had not the courage to descend; it still remained in doubt, however, if I should be able. They began to press about me, to lift almost on to their shoulders the belly of my horse and to flap grimy kerchiefs, hats and caps in my face and to clap their hands as for an actor who has played a part well. The Vice-Captain watched me from the loggia like a chained watchdog would look at an unleashed cur; but every time he made a movement a thousand gaolbird faces at once turned towards him with threats to set fire to the house if he did not obey the new Avogadore.

'Yes, Signori! Only disperse, and send the Signor Avogadore up here . . . we shall come to an arrangement between us.'

The throng had been rioting without knowing why and already many of the merely curious had gone away and some of the peasants, tired of this comedy, had begun to walk back to their homes. As for me, I did not know whether I was in this world or the next since they had nominated me Avogadore, nor what would be the result of the interview to which the Vice-Captain had invited me. But I was pleased at having become a man of importance and sacrificed everything in the hope of glory.

'Open, open the gates! . . . Let the Avogadore enter!' shouted the crowd.

'My good sirs,' replied the Vice-Captain, 'I have a wife and children and have no wish to see them die of fright. . . . I will open the gates when you have dispersed. . . . You see I am not entirely in the wrong. . . . Clear agreements make long friendships.'

The people did not want to disperse but I, either because I was tired of sitting on horseback or because I was only too eager to treat with a Vice-Captain as an equal, set myself to persuade them.

'Citizens,' I began to say, 'I thank you and will be eternally grateful to you! I am moved and honoured by so many signs of affection and esteem. Moreover, the Vice-Captain is not wrong. We must show our trust in him as he has shown his in us. . . . Disperse then, and remain quiet. . . . Wait for me in the square. . . . Meanwhile I will defend your rights.'

'Long live the Avogadore! . . . Good! . . . Very good! . . . To the square, to the square! . . . We want the town granaries opened up! . . . We want the proceeds of the grinding tax restored! . . . It is the blood of the poor!'

'Yes, but remain quiet . . . trust in me! . . . Justice will be done, but in the meantime wait quietly in the square for me.'

'To the square, to the square! . . . Long live the Signor Carlino! Long live the Avogadore! . . . Down with San Marco! . . . Long live liberty!'

With such cries the crowd rushed pell-mell to the square to pillage some bakers' and greengrocers' stalls, but the noise they made was greater than their hunger, and little damage was done. Some of the more suspicious remained to see if the Vice-Captain kept his promise; I dismounted with the greatest of pleasure, handed the reins of my nag to one of the men who were waiting, and went to the gate to wait till it should be opened. At last, with every care and precaution, a Corporal of the Slavs opened it a crack and I sidled in. Then they put back the bars and the padlocks as if they intended to keep me there a prisoner. This grinding of bars and keys made me somewhat suspicious, but then I remembered that I was an important person, an Avogadore, and mounted the stairs with my head erect and arm arched at my side just as if I had all my people in my pocket ready to defend me. The Vice-Captain, who had prudently retired from the loggia was waiting for me in a salon among a gang of clerks and policemen who did not suit my book at all. He no longer had that humble and compliant air that he had shown to the crowd five minutes before. The flushed face, the curled lip and the sharp glance around in no way recalled the greenish pallor, the wavering looks and the tremulous gestures of the former victim. He came boldly forward to greet me, asking:

'Excuse me, but what is your name?'

I thanked him silently for having relieved me of the task of asking the first question, since I really did not know what peg to hang myself on. So, my *amour propre* offended, I lifted my head like a fighting cock.

'My name is Carlo Altoviti, gentleman of Torcello, Chancellor of Fratta and a short time ago created Avogadore of the men of Portogruaro!'

'Avogadore, Avogadore!' spluttered the Vice-Captain, 'so you tell me; but I hope you don't take seriously this jest of a drunken mob; it would be too risky for you.'

The band of bullies approved their leader's words with nods of the head. I felt my fury rise and nearly uttered some reckless phrase to make them realize how little I cared for their threats. But an exalted sense of my dignity held me back and I replied to the Vice-Captain that though certainly I was not worthy of the great honour conferred on me, I did not mean to disgrace myself by appearing more unfit than I in fact was. Therefore I wanted to know what concessions he would be disposed to make, since the people, my clients, wished to take advantage of their newly acquired liberty.

'What concessions, what liberty? I know nothing of them,' replied the Vice-Captain. 'No orders have come from Venice and liberty has been so long established in the Most Serene Republic that there is no need for the people of Portogruaro to invent it for themselves!'

'Softly, softly, with this liberty of the Serenissima!' I replied, being already well accustomed to similar arguments by my Paduan novitiate. 'If by liberty you mean the arbitrary will of three State Inquisitors, I agree that you are right; they can execute high and low justice as they will. But as regards the other subjects of the Most Excellent Signoria, I humbly demand in what almanac you have discovered that they could be called free.'

'The Inquisition of State is a magistrature proved excellent for many centuries past,' said the Vice-Captain in an uncertain voice, in which long established veneration struggled with his present uncertainty.

'It was found excellent in the centuries that are passed,' I returned. 'As for the present, we are of a different opinion. The people find it very bad indeed and, making use of their right of sovereignty, liberate you for ever from the inconvenience of having to serve it.'

'Signor . . . Signor Carlino, it seems to me,' replied the Vice-Captain, 'that you had better realize that this sovereignty no one has so far seen fit to grant to the people of Portogruaro and they have done nothing to win it. I am still an official of the Most Serene Signoria and I certainly cannot permit. . . .'

'Come, enough of that!' I interrupted. 'Have the officials of the Serenissima given any such permission at Verona, at Brescia, at Padua and everywhere else the French have entered?'

'Mere fire in straw, my dear sir!' The Vice-Captain exclaimed imprudently. 'Sometimes one pretends to make concessions in order to recover better later on. I know from a sure source that the noble Ottolin is holding thirty thousand armed men ready in the valleys around Bergamo and they assure me that the return of the French will not be at all like their arrival.'

'Nevertheless, Signor,' I retorted, 'here it is not a question of what will happen to morrow; it is a question of carrying out or not the wishes of a free people. It is a question of restoring to them what was extorted from them by that tyrannical grinding tax and of opening for their benefit those granaries of the public treasury which have now in any case become useless, since the Slavs can return to their homes whenever they have a mind.'

A murmur of disapproval came from the mouths of all, but the Captain was sharper of hearing and was listening to the sounds of a fresh commotion outside and was therefore more moderate than the others.

'I am the Vice-Captain of the militia and the prisons,' he replied. 'This man,'—he pointed out to me a large, knobbly lout—'is the treasurer of the Customs and Excise; this one here,'—he indicated a figure as long and thin as hunger—'is the custodian of the public granaries. Invested by the Signoria with our duties, we certainly cannot recognize you as a legitimate magistrate nor obey your pleasure without a rescript from the Signoria itself.'

'Body and blood!' I shouted, 'Am I then Avogadore for nothing!'

They looked at each other as if thunderstruck by such boldness; and I, more pledged than ever to maintain my position, went on as if I had taken leave of my senses:

'I, gentlemen, have promised to safeguard the interests of the people and safeguard them I shall. More, I must return to Fratta before evening, and before evening I want to settle all these affairs. Have you understood me, gentlemen? Otherwise I will have recourse to the people and leave it in their hands.'

'I have understood,' said the Vice-Captain with more tenacity than I had expected of him, 'but without orders from the Signoria I can recognize no other authority than that of the Most Excellent Viceroy. As for the people, they will not want to go on behaving like madmen, for we shall be holding you here as a hostage.'

'I, to be held as a hostage! . . . An Avogadore!'

'You are not an Avogadore for nothing! I am the Vice-Captain!'

'I thank you. That, too, we shall see.'

'We shall certainly see; but I do not advise you to be in a hurry. We already know something about you, and how you treat the closest confidants of the Inquisition with little respect.'

'Ah, so they know something about me! . . . That I can well believe! Their closest confidant I shall have hanged as soon as I get back to Fratta! Let them know that too!'

'By order of the Most Excellent Signoria, this person is arrested as guilty of *lese majeste.*'

At this really dramatic outburst by the Vice-Captain, his gang gathered around me as if to prevent me from escaping; but I now wonder what point there was in this precaution, since all the gates were barred. If I had been Pompey, I would have thrown the hem of my toga over my head, but instead, I crossed my arms on my breast and showed the cowardly rabble the sublime spectacle of an Avogadore without supporters and without fear. This dramatic tableau lasted no more than a minute when a clatter of horses hooves and the howling of the crowd in the street beneath attracted the attention of my would-be gaolers. They all rushed towards the window when the noise of this fresh disorder below became more distinct.

'The French! The French! Long live liberty! . . . Make way for the French!'

They remained rooted like so many statues at a banquet of Medusa, scattered round the room, one here and one there. I was at the window with a bound and saw arrive at the gates of the building a troop of light horse with their lances, and around them a tumult of confusion of hot-heads, of curious onlookers and of fanatics, who seemed ready to break one another's heads for the varied passions that convulsed them.

'Long live the French! . . . Make way for the French!'

There was no doubt; these horsemen were French and they began to beat with their lances at the gate of the building, shouting and blaspheming with all the '*pestes*' and '*sacrebleus*' of their vocabulary. I shouted down that the gates would be opened immediately and my words were welcomed by a redoubling of the shouts and enthusiasm of the crowd.

'Bravo, Signor Avogadore! . . . Forward the Signor Avogadore!'

Moved by such a reception, I bowed and then ran inside to make sure that they opened the gates. But inside no one listened to me; everyone was running madly here and there around the room; some cowered in the empty cupboards of the archives, others searched for the keys of the prison in order to mingle with the prisoners, the picked Slavs took to their heels through a side door leading to an alley, and I had to descend myself to remove the bars from the gates. Everyone did their best to save themselves; and as soon as the entrances were unbarred, some cursed Sergeant, with levelled lance, rushed on horseback into the courtyard and nearly ran me through; behind him came all the other lunatics. Before the actual threshold there was a seven-step staircase and in the forecourt they wheeled at full trot, pell-mell, as if they wanted to ride up the staircase or God knows where. The Vice-Captain and his gang, hearing this uproar beneath their feet, which made the walls shake, commended themselves to the Holy Virgin of Earthquakes.

I meanwhile tried to make myself understood by the Sergeant and induce him to dismount if he wanted to go up the stairs, as seemed to be his intention. The Sergeant, to my great surprise, replied in good Italian that he was looking for the custodian of the granaries and the Vice-Captain and that if they did not appear immediately he would have them hanged on the Tree of Liberty. A frantic cheer for liberty on the people's part greeted this decision; the forecourt had already been invaded by the rabble and what with the horses of the Frenchmen and the howls of the crowd, there was a real inferno. Finally the Sergeant, seeing that he could not go up the staircase on horseback and that the Vice-Captain did not seem to have any intention of coming down, leapt from his horse and told me to take him to these gentlemen magistrates. At seeing me going up as the equal of a French officer, another shout shook the building to its foundations.

'Long live the Signor Avogadore!'

Once I and the Sergeant had gone up, we managed after much searching to unearth the treasurer of the public dues, the custodian of the granaries and the Vice-Captain who were squeezed together in a heap, like three snakes, in a corner of the attic. We had a great to-do to save them from the clutches of the people who had followed us; and only by my authority backed up by an occasional blasphemy from the Sergeant, did we succeed in imposing a little order. The Sergeant then demanded with a most menacing air that a contribution of five thousand ducats should be at once made for travelling expenses and that the granaries should be left open in the service of liberty and of the French Army. The people found this also a pretext for another cheer for liberty. The three magistrates trembled in unison like three saplings quivering in the wind; but the treasurer found breath enough to reply that he had no orders and that if force were used. . . .

'What's all this about force!' shouted the Sergeant threateningly. 'General Bonaparte yesterday morning won a battle on the Tagliamento; we have shed our blood in the defence of liberty, and does a free people now grudge us a little reward? The five thousand ducats must be paid out within an hour and as for the rest of the monies, the General commands that it be placed at the disposal of the people. As to the granaries, as soon as the camp at Dignano has been supplied, they are to be left open for the most needy families. Such are the beneficent intentions of the French republicans!'

'Long live the French! Down with San Marco! Long live liberty!' shouted the crowd, roaring about the official offices, smashing furniture and throwing files and bookshelves out of the windows. Those outside set up even louder howls in their rage at not being able to do anything else. I marvelled to myself to see that fear, so pressing and so close, still had not freed the magistrates from the old and dutiful terror of the Inquisition of State. All three had the same idea, but the Vice-Captain was the first to risk expressing it.

'Signor,' he stuttered, 'Signor, most worthy officer, the people, as you say, is free; and we . . . we do not come into the matter any more. . . . They know where the treasury and the granaries are. Here (he pointed to me), here before you is the Most Illustrious Signor Avogadore, created this very day for the service of the Commune; be good enough to refer to him. As for us . . . We hand over our authority into the hands . . . into the hands . . .'

He did not know into whose hands to hand over his authority, but a fresh outbreak from the crowd relieved him of the weight of this decision.

'Long live liberty! Long live the French! . . . Long live the Signor Avogadore!'

The Sergeant turned his back on the three unfortunates, took me by the arm and led me down the stairs. And while a part of the crowd remained to amuse themselves with their former magistrates, making them wear the cockade and shout long live this and long live that, another group followed the French troop who, surrounding my most important person, made their way to the office of the treasury. On the way I remarked to the Sergeant that I had not got the keys, but he replied with a little smile of pity and only spurred his horse onwards. The doors were broken down by two sappers, the Sergeant went into the treasury, placed the monies that he found there in his bag, declared that there were not even four thousand ducats there, and continued his way towards the granaries, again leaving the populace to vent its rage on the furniture and on the files. Under the granaries we found ready a long file of carts, partly military and partly requisitioned from nearby farms, guarded by Provençal chasseurs. Thanks to their labours, the barley, the wheat and the flour was put into sacks and loaded within a very short space of time; the people were left with the dust which floated out of the windows, but none the less they went on shouting: 'Long live the French! Down with San Marco! . . . Long live liberty!'

The convoy once made ready, the Captain who was in charge of it, having received the Sergeant's report, called me solemnly to him, honouring me at every two words with the titles of Citizen and Avogadore. He proclaimed me well deserving of liberty, saviour of my country and adopted son of the French people. Then the carts made their way in good order towards San Vito, the cavalrymen disappeared with the money bag and I remained, flabbergasted and ridiculous amid a discontented and unsatisfied mob.

None the less, they went on shouting: 'Long live the French!' 'Long live liberty!', but by now they had forgotten their Avogadore, and this at least procured me the advantage of being able to slip away as soon as darkness began to fall. The old nag had had no time to find its way back to me and I had no longer the heart to entrust myself on it to some fresh triumph; also I realized that it would be more prudent to remain on foot. On foot, therefore, and regretting having lost in vain fooleries the whole of that day, I once more took the byways and bridlepaths towards Fratta. Many political and philosophical considerations on the instability of human glory and popular favour and on the unusual customs of the paladins of liberty filled my mind and prevented it from dwelling on the fear that some misfortune might have taken place in the meantime at the Castle. However, the deserted farms and the traces of disorder that I observed in them gave me something to think about and made me hasten my pace involuntarily so that, step by step, as I got nearer home, I repented more and more of having forgotten for so many hours the real purpose for which I had set out.

My fears were only too well founded! At Fratta I found literally what is called the devil's kitchen, the houses of the village were abandoned; splintered heaps of barrels, carts and furniture were piled up here and there and the remains of fires were still smoking;

on the square were still traces of the worst bacchanal the imagination could picture. Meat, half raw and half roasted, wine spilt in pools, sacks of flour torn and overturned, fragments of pots and pans, plates and glasses; and in the midst of this the beasts loosed from their stalls were pasturing. The shades of the coming night gave the whole scene the look of a fantastic vision. I rushed into the castle shouting at the top of my voice: 'Giacomo! Lorenzo! Faustina!' but my shouts were lost in the deserted courts and only from beside the porch the neighing of a horse replied to me. It was Marchetto's old nag who, having broken loose in the confusion at Portogruaro, had returned home, more faithful and more courageous, poor animal, than all those other animals who prided themselves on having brains and hearts.

A cruel doubt rent my soul concerning the old Countess and I rushed at full speed through the courts and corridors at the risk of breaking my neck against some column. There within, since the moonlight could not enter, I could not see the traces of the devilish band, but I smelt in passing a most stomach-rending stench. Scrambling over broken doors and smashed furniture, I got upstairs almost on all fours. In the salon I almost lost my way, so great was the confusion of objects that littered it, but fear cleared my mind and I reached the old woman's room and plunged into a terrible darkness, shouting wildly. From the obscurity there came a terrifying sound, like the strangled and menacing panting of a wild beast, mingled with the moaning of a child in a low continuous croaking.

'Signora, Signora!' I cried out, my hair standing on end, 'It is I! It is Carlino! Answer me!'

I heard the sound of a body raising itself with difficulty and my eyes seemed to start out of their sockets in my efforts to see something in that terrifying darkness. It did not even occur to me to feel my way forward or to go back and look for a light, so much did the terror of that uncertainty horrify and unnerve me.

'Listen,' began a voice, which with difficulty I recognized as that of the old Countess, 'listen, Carlino, since I have no priest, I want to confess to you. Know . . . therefore . . . know that I have never intentionally harmed anyone . . . that I have done all, all the good of which I have been capable . . . that I have loved my children, my grandchildren and all my kin . . . that I have loved my neighbour . . . that I have put my trust in God. . . . And now I have lived a hundred years, a hundred years, Carlino! What use has it been to me to have lived a century? I am a hundred years old, Carlino, and I am dying in solitude, in sorrow and in despair! . . .'

I trembled from head to foot and saw with the eye of pity all the secrets of that soul, returned to life only to know the terrors of death.

'Signora,' I cried, 'Signora, do you not believe in God?'

'I have believed in Him up till now,' she replied, in a voice which was growing weaker, and I divined behind those words a smile without hope. Then, no longer hearing either movement or breathing, I advanced to the bedside and touched, shivering, an arm already stiffening in death. There was a moment in which I seemed to see her; I seemed to see her although the darkness in that room of death grew ever thicker, and I felt the poisoned darts of her last glances transfix me mercilessly and it seemed to me that her soul, in abandoning its life-long companion, breathed a curse into my face. Cursed be this life, seductive and transient, which leads us to pleasure by smooth and enchanted gulfs only to fling us, poor shipwrecked mariners, upon some rock! Cursed be the air that caresses us all, young, old or decrepit, only to suffocate us when we lie dying! Cursed be the family that pampers us and surrounds us when we are happy and gay, but scatters far and wide and abandons us in our hour of need and in the solitude of despair! Cursed be the peace that ends in anguish, the faith that turns to blasphemy, the charity that reaps ingratitude! . . .

In these dismal ravings my mind swung between fury and stupefaction; the thought of that holy and venerable life cut off in such a way, amid convulsions of terror, clouded my reason and I remained for long with that icy hand in mine, hardly knowing if I were alive or dead. At last I started up, seeing a light appear in the room, and then I saw it was the chaplain, who marvelled not a little at seeing me there. The Spaccafumo was behind him, carrying a candle. At any other moment the disorder of their appearance, their pallor, their deep sunk eyes and the traces of blood upon them would have horrified me; but at that time I paid no need. The priest seated himself without a word by the old woman's bedside and, after raising her other arm, let it fall again.

'Those dogs of French!' he murmured, 'now she has died without the comforts of religion! . . . And it was my fault, O God, my fault!'

As he said this, he looked at that face, all bruised and torn by the brutality of the soldiers, whose anger he had defied by insisting on remaining by the old woman's bedside. They had dragged him away, mocking and striking him, but he had gone on wandering round the castle and had returned there as soon as the marauders had left. As for the Spaccafumo, he could divine the misfortunes of the chaplain a hundred miles off and never failed to rush to his aid; it was really a sort of second sight, sharpened by gratitude and friendship. I could not then, nor did I wish later, to embitter the good priest's sorrow by describing to him the death of the Signora. I was therefore silent and knelt with them to recite the litany for the dead, though I felt in my mind it was more for the comfort of the living than for the repose of the dead.

We then composed the dead body in a more Christian attitude; but the expression fixed by death on those features contrasted terribly with the hands crossed in the act of prayer. I who alone was aware of the secret of that contrast, went away a little later leaving the priest and his companion to recite with devout fervour the orisons for the dead. I wandered for long, like a ghost, through the country-side; and then, on returning towards the castle, I heard from some fugitive the terrible story of the incursion of the soldiers, who having despoiled the whole territory, had rushed in drunken fury on the castle of Fratta. The shameful acts committed by that gang of cut-throats against the poor helpless old woman who had remained alone to confront them were beyond my imagination. But the little that the chaplain had seen, the pitiable condition of the corpse, the disorder of the room, were all witness to the merciless brutality that she had suffered.

I confess that my enthusiasm for the French was somewhat dampened, but then, on thinking it over, it seemed impossible that they could have committed such atrocities with premeditation and, deciding that they must be imputed to the bestial impulse of a few soldiers, I resolved to ask for justice on them. Rumour had depicted General Bonaparte as a real republican, a defender of liberty, so it came into my head to refer to him and, two days later, when the body of the Countess had been deposited with the usual honours in the family tomb, I set out for Udine, which was then the seat of the French General Staff. From the details that I had learnt, I was able to guess that the guilty ones belonged to the same battalion of sharpshooters who had escorted the grain convoy which had left Portogruaro the same day; so I did not despair of being able to trace them and getting for them an exemplary punishment. The antique virtue of the young liberator of Italy seemed, in my opinion, a pledge of prompt justice.

At Udine, I found the usual confusion. Here it was the guests who commanded and the hosts who obeyed. The Venetian authorities, were without power, without dignity and without council, the people and the local signori divided into many and varied factions, each stranger and more false than the last. Very many who but a few days before had cheered the Hungarian hussars and the Bohemian dragoons, now applauded the Parisian *sansculottes*. Such was the fruit of the political nullity of so many centuries; they no longer believed themselves to be in this world as anything but on-lookers, spectators and not actors. Actors are paid and whoever is in the stalls must justly compensate those who appear before them.

The General in command, Napoleon Bonaparte (as he was then called) lived in the Florio mansion. I asked for an interview with him, stating that I had some very serious allegations to make about some matters that had taken place in the province, and since he had up till then, had only too much to do with discontented Venetians, I was granted an audience. This was probably because he did not know what it was all about.

The General was in the hands of his servant, who was busy shaving him; at that time he did not disdain to appear a man, but rather displayed a certain Catonian simplicity, so that at first sight I felt somewhat reassured. He was thin, wan and restless; with long straggling hair that fell around his forehead, his temples and his neck and even down to below his coat-collar. He looked exactly like that fine portrait that Appiani has left us and which is to be seen in the Villa Melzi at Bellagio, a gift of the first Consul-President to the Vice-President, a superb flattery of the wolf to the lamb. Only at that time he seemed even more emaciated, so that one would have given him only a few more years to live, and had a look of slenderness that seemed to add the halo of the martyr to the glory of the liberator. He sacrificed his life for the good of the peoples; who would not be sacrificed for him?

'What do you want, citizen?' he said curtly, brushing his lips with the fringe of the towel.

'Citizen General,' I replied, with only a slight bow so as not to offend his Republican modesty, 'the matters of which I have to speak are of the greatest importance and of still greater delicacy.'

'Speak on,' he said, pointing to the servant who was going on with his work. 'Mercier here knows no more Italian than my horse.'

'Then,' I went on, 'I will explain with all the frankness of a man who trusts in the justice of one who is fighting for such justice and liberty. A horrible crime was committed three days ago at the Castle of Fratta by certain French sharpshooters. While the main body were sacking the public granaries and the treasury of Portogruaro, some other stragglers invaded an honourable seigneurial dwelling and so abused an old and infirm lady, more than a hundred years old, who had remained alone in the house, that she has died of grief and horror.'

'You see how the Most Supreme Signoria exasperates my soldiers,' said the General, springing to his feet, since the servant had finished wiping his chin. 'They tell my people that they are assassins, that they are heretics; everyone runs away when they appear and everyone abandons their homes. How can you wonder that such a welcome does not predispose them to humanity and moderation? . . . I tell you, I shall have to retrace my steps and clear my way of these miserable insects.'

'Citizen General, I too understand that lying rumours may have hampered the cordiality of their first welcome; but there is a way to give the lie to such rumours and that is by a shining example of justice . . .'

'Yes, you talk to me of justice, today when we are on the eve of a pitched battle on the Isonzo! . . . Justice should have been given to us two or three years back! . . . Now they are reaping what they have sown. But I have the comfort of knowing that the worst damage does not come to them from my soldiers. . . . Bergamo, Brescia and Crema have already divorced themselves from San Marco and that stupid and fraudulent oligarchy will at last recognize that their worst enemies are not the French. The hour of liberty has struck! One must rise and fight for it or let oneself be crushed. The French Republic offers its hand to all peoples so that they may refashion their liberty in the full exercise of their innate and imprescribable rights! One must enrol oneself!'

'But, Citizen General, I am not speaking of refusing any useful sacrifice for the cause of liberty. Only it seems to me that the martyrdom of an old Countess . . .'

'I repeat, citizen, who is it that has so exasperated the spirit of my soldiers? Who has turned them against the priests and peasants of the countryside? . . . It has been the Senate and the Inquisition of Venice. Do not doubt that justice will be done on those who are really guilty . . .'

'Yes indeed, but it seems to me that an example should be made to avoid similar disorders in the future . . .'

'That example, citizen, my soldiers will give on the field of battle. Justice will be meted out to them also; you will not demand that they should all be killed! . . . Very well; they will be in the front rank; they will wash away with their blood and for the cause of liberty the disgrace of the crime that they have committed. So the evil will be turned into good and the cause of the people will be advanced by the very crimes that have disfigured it . . .'

'But, Citizen General, I beg you to note . . .'

'Enough, citizen, I have noted everything. The good of the Republic comes before all else. Do you want to be a hero? . . . Forget every private point of honour and join us, united with those upright and loyal men who are carrying on in your country also a long, obstinate, underground struggle against the privileges of imbecility and gout. Within a fortnight you will see. Then peace, glory, universal liberty will have wiped out the memory of these momentary excesses.'

With these words the great Napoleon finished dressing and moved towards an adjoining room where a number of senior officers were waiting for him. Seeing that he was neither very pleased at my visit, nor disposed to pay any more attention to me, I made my way quietly down the stairs, going over once more in my mind the whole gist of our conversation. I did not, in fact, understand very much of it; but those fine words of his about liberty and about the people and his curt and austere manner had confused me and when I left, after all was said and done, my hatred of the Venetian patricians outweighed even my resentment against the French soldiers. The terrible fate of the Countess seemed but a drop of water in comparison with the sea of blessedness which would come to us from the protection of the Republican army. This Citizen Bonaparte seemed to me a little harsh, a little unfeeling, even a little heartless, but I made excuses for him, thinking that his profession at this moment required him to be so. In this way, I little by little left the dead to rest in peace and turned to thoughts of the living; so that in the letter which I wrote to Venice to inform the family of the melancholy incident, I perhaps gave greater blame to the want of forethought of the Venetian magistrates than to the barbarous licentiousness of the invaders. The Chaplain marvelled much to see me when I returned to Fratta empty-handed, but yet calmer and more content than when I had set out. Monsignor and the Captain, who had crept back to their holes in the castle, heard with terror my account of my conversation with General Bonaparte.

'Did you really see him?' the Captain asked.

'Certainly I saw him! He was being shaved!'

'Ah! So he shaves? I always thought he wore a long beard.'

'By the way,' interrupted Monsignor, 'after Mamma's death (a long sigh) I have never shaved or been tonsured. Faustina (she had also returned) come here and put on a saucepan of water!'

In such a way Monsignor Orlando of Fratta felt his own and the public griefs. I must say that the beasts of the castle showed themselves the most feeling of all its inhabitants in the circumstances, not even excepting myself, whose thoughtlessness on that terrible day was only to be purged by a tardy and vain repentance. In addition to Marchetto's old nag, who had left the turmoil of Portogruaro to return home, as I ought to have done, there was the Captain's dog, old Marocco, who had disdained to follow his master on his flight to Lugugnana. He had remained wandering in the deserted castle, sniffing here and there as if in search of a soul better than his own; but it was not given to him to find one, and some dissolute Frenchman had amused himself by hacking the poor creature up with his bayonet right in the middle of the courtyard. On their return home, the covey of cowards had been so flabbergasted and bewildered that they did not even notice the stench of that carrion that had already been poisoning the air for three days.

It therefore fell to me, on my return from Udine, to do something about it and I gave orders to a peasant for it to be thrown into some ditch. But the peasant, having gone out to do the job, called me a moment later to look at a most remarkable thing. On the already worm-infested corpse of Marocco, the old tabby-cat had taken up his place and there was no way of dislodging him. Caresses, threats and force were of no avail, and in the end I was filled with pity and even felt respect for that poor dead beast that had known how to arouse so deep a devotion in a cat. I had him removed by force and ordered that Marocco should be buried there where he had received the fatal reward of his fidelity. The peasant dug the hole full three feet deep and then covered it with earth and considered that his task was done. But for months afterwards I had every morning to put the earth back in place because the faithful cat spent his nights scratching it up in order to find once more the remains of his friend.

I respected the sorrow of that beast and did not have the heart to remove those relics so beloved by him, yet so long a trial to the noses of the castellans. I had them covered by a stone. Then the cat settled down there day and night, wailing and wandering about the grave with melancholy miaouings. He lived thus some months longer and then died. I know this fact because I did not fail to inform myself later of the end of that tragic friendship. And they say that cats have not also their little portion of soul! As for dogs, their fame in this regard is sufficiently assured. Their affection has its place among the family affections; the lowest place, certainly, but the most constant one. I wager that the first to rejoice at the return of the prodigal son was the house dog! And when I hear someone croaking about the uselessness and danger of this numerous canine family that competes with humans for their food and sometimes infects them with a terrible and incurable illness, I have to exclaim: Respect dogs! They may be now on a level with us, and perhaps, God knows, there will come a time when they will be judged even better than we are! There have been such occasions in the history of humanity! We bipeds waver between the hero and the hangman, between the angel and the fiend. The dog is always the same; he never changes, like the Pole Star. Always loving, patient, and devoted unto death. What more can you ask?

However, I must confess that, as far as I was concerned, life at Fratta no longer seemed either as tranquil nor as worth while as it had seemed a month before. Thoughts of the French kept whirring in my head, I dreamed of becoming someone of importance as this seemed to me the best way to win back the love of the Pisana, I thought always of Venice and the fall of San Marco, of the new order which should emerge, of liberty and equality of the peoples. That General Bonaparte was only a little older than I was. Why could I not too change myself at a bound into a victor of battles and a saviour of peoples? Ambition beckoned, arm in arm with love, and I no longer felt that compassionate respect for the sorrowful passion of Giulio del Ponte. I neglected the affairs of the Chancellery, and spent most of my time competing with Bruto Provedoni in fencing or marksmanship. Bruto was the most fervent of the young brothers for the cause of liberty and often enough Bradamante and Acquilina used to laugh at us. They had seen the French without forming the favourable opinion of them that we had and we, for our part, used to grow angry when they tried to break the spell in which we were bound by calling to mind some of the evil deeds of these propagators of civilization. Above all, I did not like to hear mentioned the injury done to the old Countess of Fratta. I felt they were right in condemning them, but did not want to admit it and for that reason grew three times more exasperated. I do not know how matters would have ended had things continued in this way; but fortune intervened to grant me the fulfilment of my dreams of ambition and of pride.

One fine day (we were towards the end of March) a letter arrived from Venice for me from the Signora Contessa. I read and re-read the signature. But there was no illusion about it; it was really from her. I was thunderstruck at her writing to me and even more since the letter began with the words 'Dear Nephew'. I was almost out of my mind with amazement, but had the good sense to control myself sufficiently to read and understand the rest. Imagine who had arrived in Venice! . . . My father! None other than my father! It was incredible! . . . A man who had been thought dead and who had not given a sign of life for twenty-five years!

My reason almost refused to believe, but my heart, eager for love, said yes, and was already flying on its way to Venice before I had reached the end of the letter. It is true that I spent a good half day in reading it and later, during the journey, skimmed through it every so often for fear of having misunderstood it and of having had my hopes raised in vain. After handing the Chancellery over to Fulgenzio, I left the same day. My heart would not remain calm and my brain was teeming with so many hopes, memories, passions, and desires for the impossible that it gave me no peace. The Countess had warned me to be prepared to take up in society the place due to me as a representative of the patrician house of Altoviti; she added that my father did not write himself because he had become unfamiliar with the Italian alphabet, and that at first I should stay with her, no longer in the Frumier palace but at the Parabini mansion in Canareggio. She ended by sending her well-beloved nephew her kisses and those of his cousin the Pisana. My father and these latter were a good deal closer to my heart than the embraces of my Aunt.

CHAPTER XI

THE first person whom I saw and whom I kissed in Venice was the Pisana, but the first who spoke to me was the Countess, who ran towards me from the far end of the apartment and at once began to cry out: 'Bravo, my Carlino, bravo! . . . How glad I am to see you! . . . Come now, a real kiss from a real nephew! . . .' I passed with the utmost ill-will from the kisses of the Pisana to those of the Countess, even yellower and more made up than usual. But even in this tumult of affection which raged about me, I retained enough sense to wonder in a corner of my mind at the marvel of such an unusual welcome. I resigned myself to receiving some explanation in due course and meanwhile the Countess sent Rosa out in search of my father. This mission of the faithful maid also surprised me a little, the more so since she, no longer young but as cross-grained as before, set off on her errand with many grumbles. Such duties belonged to the footmen and I began to wonder whether the Countess' suite was not so very numerous.

Indeed, waiting there, I observed in the rooms what I hardly thought possible; there was an intense disorder in their very bareness; dust and cobwebs covered the furniture, consisting of an occasional mirror fixed to the walls and a few spindly and threadbare chairs here and there; the very picture of misery in a palace. But what distracted my mind from this melancholy sight was the appearance of the Pisana. She was lovelier, fresher and more gay than I had ever seen her, as she well knew how to be, though a thousand fresh tricks that she had learned at Venice served somewhat to obscure the freshness of her charm. But whether it was a gift of nature, or perhaps my own blindness, even these artifices became in her an added grace. However, she was quieter and more subdued than usual, and looked at me from time to time with her soul in her eyes, lowering her gaze with a blush as if my words delighted her hearing voluptuously, without penetrating to her mind. I noted all this while my aunt the Countess smothered me in a deluge of chatter of which I understood not an iota, save that she frequently mentioned the name of my father and I began to see that she also was overjoyed at his unexpected and miraculous return.

'That fool of a Rosa is never coming back!' muttered the Countess. 'I didn't want you to go, because I wanted to give you back to your dear papa myself, and to be present at the joy of your reunion. Oh, what a good papa you have, my Carlino!'

It seemed to me that the Pisana blushed more than ever at these words and was embarrassed at the look that I kept firmly fixed on her. At last Rosa returned to say that my father would be with us as soon as he had finished some business in the piazza. I again wanted to go out in search of him, to anticipate the joy of that sweet moment, but the Countess pressed me so hard that I was forced to remain.

An hour later the bell rang and a vigorous little old man with a game leg, half-Turkish and half-Christian in his dress, hopped into the antechamber. I ran to meet him, and the Countess, running after me, began crying out: 'Carlino, it's your father! Kiss your father!' I rushed into the arms of the newcomer, shedding in the folds of his Armenian cloak the first tears of joy that I had ever shed.

My father was neither very affectionate nor very talkative with me; he marvelled enough that, with the name I bore, I should have been tucked away in the obscure mousehole of a country chancellery, and promised that I should be inscribed as his legitimate son in the Golden Book and that I should become a leading figure in the Great Council.

The cunning old man spoke of such things in such a way that one could not tell if he were mocking or serious, and at every stop and comma, as if to corroborate his argument, he would beat with his hand on the pocket of his overcoat, which responded with an alluring tinkle of *zecchini* and doubloons. At each of these metallic harmonies, the yellowish face of the Countess was irradiated by a rosy glow, as the sky darkened by storm lights up at a beam of the sun. I listened and watched as if in a dream. This father of mine, arrived from Turkey with riches in one hand and power in the other, and with a large dose of humbug in all his ways, made a singular impression on me. I was never tired of watching the little grey eyes, slightly bloodshot and with a trace of a squint, that had for so many years seen the sun of the orient, and those deep and wayward wrinkles formed under the turban by the corrosive action of God knows what thoughts, and those gestures, a little authoritative, a little sailorly, that always seemed to comment on the halting obscurity of a jargon more Arabic than Venetian. I saw a man experienced in life, that is one who no longer took much account of anything, believed little, hoped still less, and who had for long sacrificed himself in the hope of future ease, finding everything simple, everything convenient, since all things led to the same end.

In this way at least I judged my father; and I confess sincerely that I looked on him with more curiosity than love. It seemed to me that such must have been those old Venetian merchants of Tana or Smyrna who, by many ruses, by their words and by their deeds, made the Tartars pardon or forget their difference of faith. Turks at Constantinople, Christians at St Mark, and merchants everywhere, they had made Venice the mediatrix of the two worlds of their time. Yet the short sparse beard, grey and jutting, made my father's face rather like the masque of Pantaloon. But he had come late on the World's stage. He seemed like one of those comic characters who, disguised as Persians or Mamelukes, come out after the curtain has fallen to announce the comedy of the morrow. Yet all this without prejudice to his paternal authority.

After staying with us for a short time, interrupted by many ejaculations of cordiality and wonder from the Countess and an occasional stifled sigh from the Pisana, my father invited me to go out with him and took me to San Zaccaria, where he was lodged in a fine house furnished almost in the Turkish style, with rugs, divans and narghilehs. There was a lack of tables and coffers to put things away in, but to make up for this there was a large number of cupboards whence was extracted, as if by magic, everything that one could desire. A very black mulatto woman, over forty years old, prepared coffee from morning till night, and she and her master understood each other by signs and monosyllables that were a real entertainment to watch. I do not believe that they spoke any known language and it might well have been that the demons talked like them on their visits to this earth.

My father set down his three-cornered hat, lit his pipe, ordered coffee to be poured and asked me to sit like him, crossing my legs on a rug. Here was a future patrician of the Great Council busy learning the etiquette of Bagdad. He told me he was grateful to his wife for having left so fine an heir as I was, perhaps as a compensation for the few joys afforded him by his marriage; he let me guess that he had closed his eyes to some of the musty suspicions that had clouded their concord and had brought my mother back to Venice, and finished by admitting that I looked like him, especially about the eyes and the turn of the nostrils; so much sufficed to reunite him with his only son in an immortal affection.

I thanked him on my side for his kind feelings towards me and begged him to put down any faults that he might find in my education to the condition of orphan in which I had been left; I did not want to open his eyes to the scarcely honourable nature of the protection afforded me by my uncle and aunt until his arrival, and won, I believe, his esteem by my modest bearing at that first conversation. He observed me out of the tail of his eye and though apparently inattentive to my words he paid the more heed to all those other signs by which, in his long experience, he had learnt to know men.

I made in his judgement a moderately favourable impression. At least so I was led to infer from the greater affection shown me as a result. He asked me to tell him about the Contessina Clara, and how she had become a nun, and often mentioned Dr Lucilio with the greatest signs of respect, marvelling how the family of Fratta had not considered itself honoured by an alliance with him. The Moslem equality tempered in him his natural aristocracy, or at least so I believed, and I was further confirmed in my opinion when he started to make fun of the most illustrious Partistagno who wished to hold back the centuries with his grandfather's sword. I was astonished to find my father as well informed in these matters as I was, and wondered that he should ask account from others when he himself knew so much. However, the testimony of two mouths is better than one, and he behaved exactly as the wise man in that proverb. In the course of our talk, he spoke to me of the Pisana and the many suitors that she had in Venice and said she was much at fault not to rely upon the richest of them to restore the dignity of her house and the fortunes of her mother.

'Ahi, ahi!' I thought to myself, 'here is aristocracy peeping out again.'

Giulio del Ponte, above all, seemed to him, to use his own phrase, a Jack-in-the-box. The Pisana was playing her cards badly not to get rid of him, since he was only a balladmonger full of coughs, misery and melancholy. Pretty girls must look to handsome youths, and manikins like that would be sent in the Levant to peddle monkey-nuts in the streets. I got so worked up by these aphorisms of my father that I was almost ready to make a general confession to him. It was not compassion for Giulio that held me back, but a certain shame at showing myself as an enamoured boy to so experienced and reasonable a man of the world. He continued to observe me out of the tail of his eye, while narrating the downfall of the Countess and the ruinous indifference of the Count Rinaldo, who forgot himself in making astronomical observations in the libraries, while bassetta and faro snatched from his mother the last scrapings of her coffers. He confessed to me with malicious complacency that the Countess had tried to feel the weight of his doubloons, but had not even been able to see the colour of them; and beat his hand again on his pocket to the tinkling accompaniment of coins.

Such cautious stinginess did not altogether please me and I am almost certain that he saw it. But he did not do me the courtesy of changing the subject, but returned to it again like a man confirmed in his own opinion that money was the one thing appreciated and appreciable. I, on the other hand, would have given the half of the few ducats I had in my pocket to the first imposter who asked them of me; and perhaps I thought in this way because I had so few of them. Poverty was my tutor in generosity; her precepts guided me even when she was no longer by me as mentor or companion. None the less, I had reason to find out that my father was no miser. He took me the same day to all the best shops, so that they should equip me as the most complete dandy of St Mark. Then he took me to my room, which had a separate door on to the staircase, and left me with the promise that he would make of me the second founder of the family of Altoviti.

'Our ancestors were among the founders of Venice,' he said to me before leaving, 'we came from Aquileia and were Romans of the gens Metellus. Now that Venice is about to found herself anew, an Altoviti must have a hand in it. Leave that to me!'

In such words my father displayed all the proverbial pride of the petty nobility of Torcello; but the Levantine doubloons worked so well that my right to be inscribed in the Golden Book was at once recognized and I appeared for the first time as a patrician voting in the Great Council in the session of April 2, 1797. As for him, he did not want to be mixed up in all this; it seemed that he did not deem himself worthy of taking a place at the top, but was content to furnish me with the means to do so. Those few days that I had lived as a patrician in Venice, and the entry afforded me through the Countess of Fratta and the Most Excellent Frumiers to the best society, had won for me a most extraordinary reputation. I was not unpleasing to look at, my manners lifted me a little above the usual effeminacy, my culture was not entirely lacking, and the modest degree of wit granted me by nature had not been suffocated by pedantry, and above all I believe that my reputation for wealth had recommended me as an excellent *parti* to all the young ladies and all the mothers of Venice. Carlino here, Carlino there, everyone invited me, everyone loved me. Even one or two young matrons were not too disdainful, and in fact I had but to choose amongst many ways to happiness. For the moment, I chose none of them and the novelty of my position occupied me to such an extent that I did not even think of the Pisana herself when she was not within eyesight.

Meanwhile the affairs of Italy became more and more involved. For more than six months already Modena, Bologna and Ferrara had given the example, with French instigation, of a servile imitation of France; they had improvised, like a soap bubble, the Cispadana Republic. Carlo Emanuele had succeeded Vittorio Amedeo in the Sardinian Kingdom, already reduced to a French military province. All Italy dirtied its knees behind the triumphal footsteps of Bonaparte, who deceived one and mocked another with alliances, flatteries and half measures. The Venetian states of the *terraferma*, cleverly stirred up by his agents, began to murmur against the Standard of the Lion; everywhere trees of liberty arose, he alone knew with what roots. There was even a moment when he doubted his own fortune among the great cloud of enemies and the great distances of none too loyal provinces, fully aware that they separated him from France; but, refusing the proferred negotiations, he put aside his fears and went on as far as Loeben to impose upon Austria the preliminaries of peace.

The Signoria of the Most Serene Republic had seen pass before it this whirlwind of war, like a man on his death-bed who glimpses in a clouded fantasy the spectre of death. It had done nothing save humiliate itself, remain patient, pray, and implore before an overbearing enemy who broke its power bit by bit and dishonoured it with deception and humiliation. Francesco Battaia, Provveditore Extraordinary in the *terraferma*, was the most worthy interpreter of these vilest feelings of servitude and made his cowardly obedience still more infamous by disobedience and treachery still more cowardly.

To the humiliating protests against the invasion of cities, the occupation of castles and fortresses, the stirring up of peoples to revolt, the plunder of public funds and the universal devastation, Bonaparte replied with mocking proposals of alliance, with ironic laments and demands for tribute. The Procurator, Francesco Pesaro, and the Savio of the *terraferma*, Giambattista Corner, were cloistered with him at Gorizia to protest against the part taken by French officers in the revolts of Brescia and Bergamo, and the acts of piracy carried out by French privateers in the inmost recesses of the Gulf. They received such a reply that, at the end of their report, the two envoys did not hesitate to say that only from divine aid could they hope for any result, since nothing could otherwise be expected in the difficult circumstances. Francesco Pesaro had an upright soul and clear foresight; but he lacked constancy and enthusiasm, as I shall show later. For that reason, he was not able to save the Republic or even to imprint upon its fall the seal of greatness.

The turbulent spirits, however, continued their clamour and the timid gave lipservice to the party, so that in the Great Council was seen the strange spectacle of philosophy and fear voting against stability and courage. But true philosophy in those days should have been able to give counsel to uphold one's own dignity and not to have to implore it on bended knees from the political wisdom of a freebooter. I, for my part, was among the deluded and I repent and sorrow for it; but I worked for a good end, and my friendships with Amilcare, still in prison, with Lucilio, close associate of the French Ambassador, and with my father, pushed me further on this way. A hard lesson! To repudiate, to deride the virtue of old times without first having strengthened one's heart with the virtue of the new, and to implore liberty with the leaven of slavery still working in the soul! There are rights which only those who deserve them can claim; liberty is not asked for, it is commanded, and to those who beg it cravenly, the right reply is to spit in their faces; Bonaparte was right and Venice wrong. Only a hero who is in the right can behave as a coward to attain that right.

The democratic party, which could then call itself, and indeed was, French, did not dominate Venice by its numbers, but by its force of spirit, its vigour in action and above all by the power of the aid granted it. Those opposed to it did not form a party but an inert mass of cowardice and impotence, which gained no increase of power from its mere size. Nerves obey the spirit and arms the idea, but where there are neither spirit nor ideas, is either the dullness of lethargy or the liveliness of frivolity. For the Venetian bigwigs it was the former. The French Legation, not the Senate or the College of Savi, were the governors. Under the very eye and in open defiance of the Inquisitors, it prepared the threads of the conspiracy that was to cast down from their thrones the nerveless aristocracy; and a great number of the men of letters or of talent aided them in their machinations. The Leads and the Dungeons were vain scarecrows and a warning from Ambassador Vallement opened wide to the criminals of that state those doors that as a rule never reopened save to corpses or to those condemned to death.

Dr Lucilio had made himself notorious for his fervent devotion to the French cause and perhaps the key to this zeal could have been found in the mysterious turbulence of his youth. It was known that he was, as it was then termed, a philosopher; and it was from the philosophers that usually emerged the ring-leaders of the secret societies who worked, deep and corrosive, under the cracking veneer of the old society. In any case, he had put into his gospel of liberality all the warmth and all the sagacity of which he was capable; and the patricians who came across him in the piazza trembled, like sinners at the nocturnal appearance of a demon. It is true that if one of them fell ill, he was not averse to running to Doctor Lucilio for help. Then the celebrated doctor would feel those pulses and look at those faces, with a sort of sneer that vindicated the hate he had suffered. He seemed to say: 'I despise you so much that I even want to cure you. I know that you are my enemies, but that does not affect me.'

The ladies showed for Lucilio that timid and shamefaced respect that seems fascination, and at a single glance, at a single gesture would look at him with veneration and servitude rather than love. They said he was a master in the art of Mesmer and could do miracles with it; it is certain, however, that he used this art rarely enough, and there was no woman who could claim she had received from his eyes a single glint of desire. He preserved his independence, his chastity and the mystery of a magician; and I perhaps alone knew the secret of his self-possession, since the customs of the time and even more his reputation as a great doctor and a great philosopher would not allow even the suspicion of a love that completely preoccupied him. Yet so it was, as I was able to confirm, and that love extending throughout a soul such as his, still maintained the force and grandeur of an irresistible passion. You will say that he had left Clara tranquil with her mother, that he had not tried to put a ladder under her balcony or to sing her serenades from a gondola, that he had allowed her to enter a convent, and so on. But his love was not of the everyday type; he did not want to conquer but to obtain; sure of Clara, he would have waited a century without changing and without despairing, and he longed for and nourished with all the fervour of his deeds and of his sacrifices that moment when they would implore him to take her to him and hold themselves honoured by his kinship. Love and political faith were so mingled in a single sentiment, so vivid, powerful and enduring, as could only be in a nature so robust, so reserved and yet so involved. When he chanced on the proud acquiline features of the Countess, or the vague, wan, aristocratic face of the Count Rinaldo, or those mawkish, gracious faces of the Frumiers, he would smile secretly. He felt he was drawing near to the time when he would be the master and would be able to lay down the law to these dandies. Their flexible, pliant natures and the ease with which they could be frightened, assured him against any fear of opposition.

But the Countess, on her side, did not rest with folded arms; she knew Lucilio perhaps better than he thought, and the walls of a convent seemed to her a weak shelter against his temerity. She had therefore recommended her daughter to a certain Mother Redenta Navagero, the greatest saint and the most astute nun of the convent, to strengthen with her arguments the soul of Clara against the temptations of the devil. Mother Redenta had undertaken this task willingly but I will not say that up till then she had made any great progress. However she had already made Clara forget, if not Lucilio, at least all the other things of this world. It was no small achievement. Many threads had been cut, but there still remained the main one, the master cable, but, sawing continually at it, she did not despair of cutting this one also and reducing this beloved little soul to the blessed isolation of cloistral ecstasy. Clara sometimes received news of Lucilio through a lay sister of the convent, but this happened seldom and, in the intervals, she sought comfort in devotion and in memories.

But devotion little by little replaced memory, especially after her confessor and Mother Redenta had persuaded her not to give way too much to mundane thoughts and to be constant in prayer now that there was so much need of it for the urgent perils of the Republic and of religion. For these nuns, almost all of them patricians, the Republic of St Mark and the Christian religion were closely mingled, and to hear them speak of the affairs of France and of the French would have seemed the maddest thing in the world. To name Paris or Hell was for them the same thing, and the older amongst them trembled with fear thinking of the terrible deeds that those incarnate devils would be able to commit, once entered into Venice. The younger ones would say: 'There is no need to be frightened; God will help us!' and one or two, perhaps, who had taken their vows for obedience or for distraction, hoped for other things from this divine assistance. It is not the place here to say that that would have been like the aid of Pisa, fruitless because too late: but in any case, those who have not a definite vocation are not obliged to search out and adore the necessity of pretending to have one. Clara, more sincere and less bigoted, was scandalized at these semi-heresies. As regards the French, she agreed with the older women, especially after the terrible tragedy of her grandmother, which had made her weep long days and longer nights. She believed them in good faith to be heretics, brutes and demons; and in the litanies of the saints, after having prayed the Lord to keep them from every evil, she would pray secretly that Venice should be liberated from the French, who seemed the greatest of all evils.

For Venice, indeed, if not the greatest, they were certainly the most recent and most imminent of evils. Her other misfortunes, already gangrenous, no longer caused her any pain. This was the wound, open and bleeding, that was mortal to the State, making flow back to the heart all its sour and stagnant humours. Every day brought the story of some new defection, some fresh treason, another revolt. The Doge felt his horned cap unsteady on his head even in the greatest ceremonies, the Savi completely lost their heads and commissioned the Ambassador in Paris to buy from some lackey the secrets of the Directory. They even tried to reach the heart of

Bonaparte through a long list of friends, whose head was a French banker established in Venice and paid for this purpose, I believe, some thousands of ducats.

You can imagine what sort of props these were to sustain a failing government! The story of the Republic of Venice was like the entertainments of the winter season; a tragedy was not enough to fill the too long hours; a farce was needed afterwards. And the farce there was, though not all for laughing. Many young men, not for liberality of opinion, but for mere bravado, devoted themselves to satirizing these great brainless periwigs; and as always happens to the great become small and to the powerful reduced to impotence, they were overwhelmed with curses, prejudices and jests. The broadsheets, ballads and doggerel circulated at that time served for long afterwards to pack sardines, but the merit then attributed to the authors of these unseemly and vile parodies seems almost impossible.

Even I had fallen into disgrace with my lady aunt for my democratic whims; but the doubloons of my father stood me in good stead and she used often to nudge her daughter to make her show greater courtesy towards me. These nudges and my continual distractions annoyed the Pisana and kept her thoughts away from me, but there still remained an occasional fugitive glance or sudden blush which, had I observed them as they should have been observed, would have flattered me.

One day came the news of the French entry into Verona, believed up till then the city most averse to novelty. The town militia was dispersed and the troops collected to reduce Bergamo and Brescia retired to Padua and Vicenza. It was a great festa for the supporters of the French. A few days later came the shock of the tremendous Verona Easter with all the atrocities against the French that disgraced it. Then came the furious protests of Bonaparte and the formal declaration of war. Senators, Savi, Counsellors and all had begun to believe that what has endured for a long time can none the less come to an end; they began providing supplies for the Most Serene Dominant; as to defence, they thought little enough about it because, to speak plainly, nobody believed in the possibility. Finally General Baraguay d'Hilliers surrounded the estuary with his camp, the communications were cut off and Dona and Giustinian, sent to General Bonaparte, revealed his intention that a new form of government, more liberal and broader should be introduced into the Republic. He also demanded that the Admiral of the Port and the Inquisitors of State should be handed over to him, as guilty of hostile acts against a French ship that had tried to force an entry into the port of the Lido.

The Signori Savi understood the warning and disposed themselves humbly to serve the General's beard and wig, as they say in Venice. It seemed to them that the deliberations of the Great Council were too slow for the urgency of the need, so they improvised a sort of funerary magistrature, a college of sextons, for the moribund Republic, which was composed of the officers of the Signoria, the Savi of the Council, the three Chiefs of the Council of Ten and the three Avogadori of the Commune, in all forty-one persons, with the Most Serene Doge at the head and with the extremely convenient title of the Conference. Moreover they whispered in Venice that sixteen thousand conspirators armed with daggers, were already posted in the city to renew upon the nobles the massacre of the innocents. I remember that, with the air of a conspirator, I asked Lucilio how much truth there was in this rumour and that the doctor replied, shrugging his shoulders:

'My dear Carlino! Do you think the French are mad enough to pay sixteen thousand real conspirators while the rumour of quite imaginary ones will produce the same effect? . . . Believe me, there is not a pinpoint of truth in all this, though it might well be true, for there is no necessity to kill all these patricians. They are as good as dead already!'

The Conference met for the first time on the evening of 30 April in the private chambers of the Doge. He repeated an exordium that began: 'The gravity and distress of the present circumstances . . .' But the nonsense that was said there, though it showed clearly enough the distress, did not at all correspond to the gravity of the circumstances. It proposed to touch the heart of General Bonaparte through a certain Haller, a very close friend of his. The Cavaliere Dolfin was the initiator of this definite piece of advice. The Procurator Antonio Cappello, known to me from the Frumier palace, rose to deride its puerility and Pesaro associated himself with him in a demand for a discussion on defence and nothing more.

In fact, there was no longer any need to explain the intentions of the French, and it was fruitless to deceive ourselves with vain chimeras. But the Savi intervened in such a way that the whole thread of the discussion was lost, when at the height of it the Savio of the week produced a sheaf of letters from the Admiral Tommaso Condulmer who reported the advance of the French across the lagoons with the aid of rafts made of floating barrels. The consternation was immediate and almost universal; some tried to escape, others proposed negotiations, or, better still, surrender.

It was in these circumstances that the most Serene Doge, Lodovico Manin, pacing up and down the room and tugging at his belt, pronounced these memorable words: 'To-night we are not safe even in our beds.' The Procurator Cappello assured me that most of the

Counsellors were equal to His Serenity in greatness of spirit and in courage. It was decided at breakneck speed that it should be proposed to the Great Council that two envoys should be chosen to treat with Bonaparte about changes in the form of Government.

Pesaro, indignant at such cowardly counsel, broke in with tears in his eyes, with words of pity for the ruin of the Fatherland, now assured; and declared that he would leave that night to find refuge among the Swiss. However, he did not do so; I believe, indeed, that he left by the postal packet for Vienna. In truth I have hardly spirit enough to try and palliate with a miserable national pride the vile buffoonery of these scenes. They got their lesson, a great one and a severe one. Be men, if you want to be citizens; believe in your virtues, if you have any, not in those of others which may fail you, not in indulgence or justice from a victor no longer restrained by fears or by laws.

On 1 May, in wig and toga, I entered the Great Council arm in arm with the nobleman Agostino Frumier, second son of the Senator. The elder son belonged to Pesaro's party and would not deign to be seen with us. That day the attendance was sparse, and scarcely reached the number of six hundred voters without which, by law, the deliberations were not valid. The older members were pale, not with grief, but fear; the younger ones vaunted a haughty and satisfied mien, though many knew within themselves that they were forced to act against their own interests, and their gaiety was not sincere. The decree was read which gave authority to the negotiators to change the form of the Republic at their discretion, and which promised Bonaparte the liberation of all political prisoners arrested from the date of the first entry of the French armies into Italy. In this last clause I discerned the influence of Dr Lucilio and I thought of Amilcare and was perhaps the sole person there to rejoice not indecorously.

I must have had the brain of a goose not to understand the cowardice of this promise and to find it just for an entirely personal reason. The decree was approved with only seven dissenting votes; there were another fourteen who abstained, neither welcoming nor rejecting the proposal, but refusing to take advantage of the present opportunity. As soon as it was known in the piazza, the supporters of the French, who were rioting there, suddenly rushed at all speed to the prisons. With the innocent came out the gaolbirds, with the fanatics the depraved, and the story of sixteen thousand conspirators obtained greater credence than ever before. The patricians believed that they had given proof of the utmost courage in that they had not debated the delivery demanded by Bonaparte of the Admiral of the Lido and the three Inquisitors. But General Bonaparte once more declared to Dona and Giustinian that he would not receive them as envoys of the Great Council if these four magistrates were not first imprisoned and punished. The most humble Great Council bowed its head once more, no longer with five hundred but with seven hundred votes, and the Captain of the Port and the three Inquisitors were imprisoned that very day for the strange crime of having obeyed, with less ill faith than others, the laws of their own country. Francesco Bottaia, the traitor, was among the three Avogadori of the Commune entrusted with the execution of this sacrilegious decree.

But that was not sufficient for the impatience of the innovators or the terror-stricken condescension of the nobles. The Conference unanimously passed another decree ordering Condulmer not to resist with force the military operations of the French, but only to persuade them not to enter the Most Serene Dominant until there had been time to send away the Slav regiments in order to avoid possible unpleasant consequences. They wanted to pare even their own nails, so as not to give by mistake a scratch to him who was hastening to suffocate them.

If this were not the most marvellous weakness, unique in the world, I defy even sheep to invent a better. My father had returned from Turkey just in time to make poor me a participant, unknowingly, in these cowardly stupidities. But, on the other hand, what use was knowledge? Dr Lucilio was smeared even more than I by this filthy pitch. Woe to the wise who are not in tune with the spirit of their times; who upheld by their conscience in their own doctrines, rise easily to dwell in the clouds, who, if at first they do not despair for the discretion of their judgements, must at last despair by the necessity of experience. Amilcare, meanwhile, had come out of prison and we had picked up anew our old friendship; another fanatic, he too regarded the French as the liberators of the world and as far as that went perhaps his judgement kept its feet, but it stumbled badly when he looked on them as the liberators of Venice.

That did not prevent Amilcare from helping to rouse my zeal and persuading me too, since his ardour was not restrained like that of Lucilio, but filled with all the boundless enthusiasm of youth. With Amilcare I leave you to guess who was liberated from the talons of the Inquisition: the Signor of Venchieredo! This was hardly to be expected, since his crime was certainly not that of favouring the French. But I believe either that he had contact with them in the prison, or that his pardon was granted by some mistake, or perhaps that his sentence was in any case shortly due to end. The fact remains that Lucilio gave me the news, adding mysteriously that he had fled from the Rocca d'Anfo to Milan where was then the residence of

General Bonaparte and where the destinies of the Venetian Republic were being discussed diplomatically.

One evening (we were already rushing headlong towards the abyss of 12 May) my father called me to his room, saying that he had great things to tell me and that I should pay close attention and think over everything carefully since on my sagacity would depend my own fortune and the splendour of the family.

'Tomorrow,' he said to me, 'there will be a revolution in Venice.'

I gave a start of surprise, because with the supple acquiescence of the Great Council and the negotiations still pending in Milan, I saw no need of a revolution.

'Yes,' he continued, 'you needn't be surprised because everything will be clear to-morrow. In the meantime, I want to put you on the right path, so that you do not miss the decisive moment. Do you know, my son, what a democratic Republic means?'

'Certainly,' I exclaimed with the ingenuous ardour of a young man of twenty-four. 'It is the union of ideal justice with practical life, it is the kingdom not of this or that man, but of the free and collective thought of all society. Who thinks rightly has the right to rule and will rule well. That is its motto.'

'Very good, very good, Carlino,' mumbled my father. 'That is a very good scientific conception that you can put aside or give to Signor Giulio to rave about in some canzonetta. But a government of all, sought by few, imposed by fewer still and created by a Corsican general; a free government of people who do not want to be free, and cannot be free; do you know what part you would be disposed to take?'

I looked around in embarrassment, because in all such matters I was apt to make my account without taking heed of men, and added and multiplied and divided as if all were gold, but finally instead of finding myself with a good sum down in *zecchini*, it might well be that I remained with a ragbag of wretched soldi and farthings. As I have said, I had not thought of this and therefore was completely confounded by my father's question.

'Listen!' he went on, like a master patiently beginning his lesson all over again, 'these things that you so beautify with dreams and illusions, I have foreseen for years exactly as they are. If you had ever been at loggerheads with a pasha or with the Grand Vezir, I think you would spew out less philosophy but would see further and clearer. The clumsy knavery of the Mamelukes teaches us to appreciate the more subtle cunning of the Christians. Believe me, who have proved it. And I have not proved it for nothing, since I have always worked for my own good ends and I would now be playing my part had I not, on returning to Venice, recollected you.

Consider that I thought to myself: "By Allah! Providence has set the ball at your feet at just the right moment! You are old, and fate has rejuvenated you by forty years at a turn of the hand. Courage, Bey. Leave the race to the younger horse and you will win." In a few words, Carlino, I have accepted you as my true and legitimate son and I have wanted to leave you before I die the inheritance of all my hopes. Will you be the one to justify them? . . . That is it, in short . . .'

'Go on, Father!' I broke out, feeling that the pause after this long and semi-Mohammedan harangue was becoming too prolonged.

'Go on, go on! . . . It is not so easy as you think. These are things to be caught on the wing. But all the same, seeing your ignorance, I will try to explain myself more clearly. You must know that I have certain influence with these frenchified gentry and even with the French themselves, who today control the destinies of Italy. Secret, even very distant, influence if you will, but still influence. Some millions of piastres serve me as a crown and their rays do not count too badly towards the central fire of my glory. Carlino, I leave everything to you, to you I give everything, so long as you can provide me with a divan, a pipe and ten cups of coffee a day. I leave it all to you for the greater glory of the house of Altoviti. What will you? It is my fixed idea! To have a Doge in the family! I assure you we will succeed if you are willing to trust in me.'

'Who? I . . . I, the Doge?' I stammered, scarcely able to breathe, 'do you mean that I, I in person, should become the Doge?'

'Certainly, Carlino, you can catch ideas on the wing quicker than I had hoped. The profession of Doge will become more profitable as it becomes less troublesome and dangerous. You will gain many ducats and I will make them bear fruit. After six years we will buy all Torcello and the Altoviti family will become a dynasty.'

'But father, father, what are you saying? . . .' I assure you that I believed him to be in the last stages of madness.

'Yes,' he replied, 'there is nothing to be surprised at. With the new regulations which we shall set up, he who has merits should be able to surpass those who have none. But that is an abstraction. Concretely, with your habits and your customs here, don't you think that the richest and the most cunning cannot easily be judged also the most meritorious? . . . Every age has its children of fortune, my son, and we should be fools not to make our profit of it . . . !'

'But in all charity, Father, you seem to see everything ugly and corrupted. What sort of part are you giving me to play, who was prepared to fight for liberty and for justice!'

'Very good, Carlino! To prepare for that there is only my way open to you; otherwise you will remain among the mob and there I defy you to fight; you would only be beaten. Therefore, to ensure the triumph of the true and the good, you must be among the first even if you have to push your way there, it does not matter how. Think of the harm if some depraved good-for-nothing should be in such a position. Onward then, my son, to help others on; the end justifies the means. I do not say that you must make yourself Doge tomorrow or even the day after; have patience a little and the medlars will ripen quicker than you think! . . . In the meantime I want to warn you that because you support the aims of your friends you do not have to keep yourself back for false modesty. Do you believe that you have an upright soul and good and sound intentions? Do you believe that it would be better to place at the head of public affairs a man who loves his country and does not degrade himself to parley with its enemies?'

'Yes, Father, I believe it!'

'Take courage then, Carlino. This evening Signor Lucilio will talk to you more openly. Then you will understand, you will see for yourself, you will decide. Keep in close touch with him. Don't waver, don't draw back. Whoever has heart and conscience must press on courageously, generously, not for the sake of his pride, but for the benefit of all.'

'Don't be afraid, Father. I shall press on.'

'It is enough for the moment if you are pressed on. Meanwhile, we are agreed. You will be backed by the nobles and you have the favour of the democrats; fortune cannot fail you. I am going to Signor Villetard to put a few final clauses in order. We shall see one another again this evening.'

After such a conversation I was so astonished and perplexed that I did not know what wall to beat my head on. I had to rise to the first posts, perhaps to the very highest place in the Republic? What did these dreams mean? Certainly, my father must have brought back with him from the Orient some additional volumes of the Thousand and One Nights. And what was the meaning of his vague words about revolutions, clauses and God knows what else? Signor Villetard was a young secretary of the French Legation, but what authority had my father to meddle with him in the affairs of the State? The more I thought, the more my thoughts were in the clouds. And I would never have descended thence, had not Lucilio come to orientate me. He asked me to follow him to a place where they were to discuss matters of great importance to the public good; in the streets we were joined by other and unknown persons who were awaiting us, and all together we made our way towards one of the most deserted by-ways of the city, behind the Ponte Dell'Arsenale.

After a long walk, anxious and silent, we entered a large hall, dark and empty; we ascended the staircase by the dubious light of a small oil lamp; nobody spoke to us, nobody let us in, we seemed like a cohort of phantoms going to haunt the dreams of some evil-doer. At last, after we had entered a bare, damp room, we were permitted a less miserable illumination and by the light of four candles on a table I saw one by one all the persons in our assembly and could more or less distinguish their features. We were about thirty in all, most of us young; I recognized amongst them Amilcare and Giulio del Ponte, the former with his face kindled with enthusiasm and with impatient eyes, the second very pale and with a sluggish air that dispirited me. There was Agostino Frumier and there was also Barzoni, a young man, robust, impetuous and enamoured of Plutarch and his heroes, who later wrote a pamphlet against the French entitled 'The Romans in Greece'.

Among the older men I knew the Avogadore Francesco Battaia, the grocer Zorzi, the old General Salimbeni, a certain Giuliani da Desenzano, Vidiman, the most honest and liberal patrician of Venice, and a certain Dandolo, who had acquired a great reputation as a heckler in the most tempestuous gatherings; the others were almost all unknown to me, although in one or two cases the faces did not seem unfamiliar. . . . They were grouped with close attention around an insignificant little man, scurfy and reddish, who spoke little and in a low voice, but who waved his arms like a primo ballerino. Dr Lucilio paced the room silent and thoughtful; all made way for him respectfully and seemed to await orders from him alone.

Once Battaia tried to push himself forward noisily and draw everyone's attention to himself; but no one paid any heed to him; one broke away and then another, one cleared his throat and another coughed into his handkerchief; nobody trusted him, and in the end he remained like the crow that tried to sing. So matters stood for a considerable time, without my being able to understand anything at all, either of my premonitions or from the curt words of Amilcare or the sighs of Giulio; finally a man in a wig, yellow, exhausted and livid with fear, rushed into the room. Lucilio went to greet him at the door and at his arrival the whole company stood tense as if to hear some great and expected piece of news.

'It is the deputy Savio of the week!' whispered Amilcare in my ear. 'Now we shall see if they are disposed to give way with a good grace.'

I pretended to understand, and considered the man with the wig with greater attention. He did not seem in any way eager to display his eloquence to the numerous band surrounding him. Battaia came up and took hold of him to question him, but Lucilio cut him short and everyone stood silent to hear what he was going to say.

'Signor Procurator,' he began, 'you know the deplorable state of the Most Serene Dominant, now that all the provinces of the *terraferma* have hoisted the standard of true liberty. You know the helplessness of the government after the embarkation of the first Slav regiments and the work that it has been to restrain the fury of the populace . . .'

'Yes . . . yes, Signor, I know it all,' stuttered the Savio of the week.

'I have considered it my duty to explain to the Most Excellent Procurator the sad condition of the Republic,' put in Battaia.

Lucilio, without even deigning to look at him, went on speaking: 'You know also, Signor Procurator, the summary demands of the treaty that will shortly be signed at Milan between the moribund Great Council and the French Directory!'

This cruel reminder drew from the eyes of the Procurator two great tears which, if they did not show his courage, were not at least without a certain dignity of grief and resignation. They made tortuous runnels in the powder with which he had sprinkled his cheeks, and made him yellower and even less prepossessing than before.

'Signor Procurator,' continued Lucilio, 'I am a simple citizen, but I look for the good, the real good, of all citizens. I say that we are doing an act of patriotic charity and showing a proof of our independence in thus anticipating the best intentions of others; in this way we shall be spared many internal disorders, which will not fail to complicate matters if the conclusion of the treaty is still delayed. I for my part am not moved by ambition; you will see that in the position which it has been agreed to give me in the frame of the future municipality. Signor Villetard, (he motioned towards the little, restless, reddish man) 'has been good enough to draw up the conditions according to which, having changed the form of the government, a French presidium will enter to protect the first establishment of real liberty in Venice. . . . They are the usual articles (as he said this he took from the table a document and scanned it rapidly); 'hoisting of the standard of liberty, proclamation of a democracy with representatives chosen by the people, a provisional Municipality of twenty-four Venetians, at the head of which will be the ex-Doge Manin and Giovanni Spada, the entry of four thousand French into Venice as allies, an invitation to the cities of the *terraferma*, of Dalmatia and of the islands to associate themselves with the mother country, the final disbandment of the Slavs, and the arrest of Signor d'Entragnes, accomplice of the Bourbons and the cession of his documents to the Directory through the channel of the French Legation. All these things have been noted and approved by the unanimous agreement of the people. Indeed, yesterday evening the Doge declared himself ready, in full assembly, to resign the ducal insignia and to restore the reins of government to the hands of the democrats, as a pledge of stability and independence of the future Republic; is that not so, Signor Villetard?'

The little man agreed with many gestures and grimaces. Lucilio then turned once more to the Savio of the week and handed him the document that he had been reading a little before.

'Behold, Signor Procurator,' he went on, 'here are the destinies of the Fatherland; see that you enable the spirit of the Most Serene Doge and of his other noble colleagues to . . . otherwise . . . may God preserve Venice! I have done all that I humanly can to save her.'

The Procurator replied with tears in his eyes:

'I am truly grateful at the great deference of the most illustrious signori (the incorruptible citizens shuddered at these excommunicated titles); 'the Most Serene Doge and his colleagues the Procurators, as perpetual officers of the Republic, are ready to sacrifice themselves' (to sacrifice themselves meant simply to get out), 'the more so as the fidelity of the remaining Slavs is beginning to waver and it would not be strange to see them unite with our enemies . . .' (the Procurator realized that he had made a blunder and began to cough until he was as scarlet as his tunic), 'I mean to say unite with our friends who . . . who . . . who . . . wish to save us . . . at all costs. Therefore I reaffirm that these conditions (he showed the document that he held between his hands as if it had been a viper) 'will be accepted by the Most Serene Signoria, that the Great Council will ratify our salutary judgement and that we shall henceforth become a single family of equal and happy citizens . . .'

The voice died away in the Procurator's throat in a sob, but his last words were drowned in a round of applause. He flushed, poor man, conscious of shame, and then hastened to ask if some member of this distinguished company should accompany him to hand the document to His Serenity. Zorzi was chosen unanimously; a grocer to pair with a Procurator to intimate his abdication to a Doge! . . . Two centuries before, the entire Council of Ten had presented themselves to Foscari to demand from him the horn and the ring: all Venice, silent and trembling, waited at the threshold of the palace for the great news of obedience or refusal . . . the great and glorious Doge preferred obedience, and died of grief, the last solemn and terrible scene of a mysterious drama. How times had changed! . . . the abdication of the Doge Manin could have taken its place as an incident in a comedy by Goldoni without danger of lessening its dignity.

After the Procurator and Zorzi had left, Villetard left also with Barraia and a few other patricians, traitors to their class; there remained we few, the elect, the flower of Venetian democracy. Dandolo was he who talked the most, I most certainly he who understood the least. Lucilio had again started to pace up and down, silently thinking. Suddenly he turned on us with a far from contented expression and said, almost as if thinking aloud:

'I fear we shall make a fine hole in the water!'

'What do you mean?' Dandolo broke in, 'a hole in the water, now that everything smiles upon our desires . . . now that the gaolers of liberty are disputing among themselves who shall take the chisel to break off our fetters? Now that a world redeemed by justice is preparing for us a worthy place, honoured and independent, at the great banquet of the peoples, and that the liberator of Italy, the subduer of tyranny, himself offers us his hand to lift us from the abjection into which we had fallen?'

'I am a doctor,' went on Lucilio peaceably. 'To diagnose illness is my profession. I fear that our good intentions have not sufficient root in the people.'

'Citizen, do not despair of virtue, like Brutus!' almost roared a young, practically beardless, man of violent appearance.

This young man was a Levantine from Zante, son of a ship's surgeon in the service of the Republic, who after the death of his father had taken a room in Venice. His opinions had not always been of the soundest since it was whispered that only a few months before he had taken it into his head to enter the priesthood; but however that may have been, instead of the priest he had wanted to be, he had become a tragic poet; and one of his tragedies, the *Tieste*, had been given the previous January at the Theatre of Sant'Angelo and had created a furore for seven consecutive evenings. This young man, noisy and revolutionary, was called Ugo Foscolo. Giulio del Ponte, who had not breathed a word all evening, shuddered at this outburst and sent him a side glance that was like a dagger thrust. Between him and Foscolo was the envy of genius, the coldest and most fervent of all jealousies; but poor Giulio realized that he had been surpassed and had tried to make up for it by adding venom to his rancour. The little lion of Zante did not even deign to glance at this flea nipping his ear and if he gave him a slap or two it was more from annoyance than anything else. He had more than a good dose of self-importance, and I do not know if the glory of the singer of the *Sepolcri* could ever have equalled the hopes and the desires of the author of *Tieste*. More than a mere man of letters, he was the most curious and comic specimen of a citizen that could have been found, a real Republican bear-cub, snarling and intractable, a model of civic virtue that would willingly be exhibited to universal admiration; but he admired himself as sincerely as he disdained others and had taken the great principle of equality so seriously that he would have written a letter of advice, as man to man, to the Emperor of all the Russias and would have been greatly offended if the Imperial ears had not listened to him. For the rest, he hoped much, despite his lugubrious tirades and his despairing periods, since temperaments like his, so bursting with life and passion, do not easily resign themselves to apathy or to death. For them, struggle is a necessity; and without hope there can be no struggle . . . Giulio del Ponte was not the only one who started at the Roman apostrophe of Foscolo; even Lucilio honoured him with a smile, half friendly, half compassionate, but did not think it opportune to reply directly.

'Which of you,' he added, 'watched Villetard this evening while I was expounding his conditions to the ex-Procurator?'

'I was watching him,' broke in a tall and sturdily built man whom I knew to be Spada, he whom they wanted to associate with Manin in the new Government. 'In my opinion, he looks like a traitor.'

'Bravo, citizen Spada!' went on Lucilio, 'only he believes himself to be no more than a good servant of his country, a prudent and fortunate minister. It is some time already since glory has taken the place of liberty on the banners of France.'

'And what do you want us to do?' said Spada brutally.

'Nothing,' went on Lucilio, 'since we can do nothing. Only for those who wish to know, I want to make clear our opinions on the conduct of this revolution before the formal command comes from Milan. Distrust is an excellent virtue, especially for the weak, but I fear that it will not be enough. We want the French to be our allies but not our executors; that is the idea. We want to change of our own accord, not to be forced to change like people who have lost the ability to move for themselves. The French are bound to come, because they can do so and want to do so; but they will at least find everything done and will not hang round our necks like masters.'

'Let the French come, to spare us civil war and the proscriptions of Sulla,' exclaimed Foscolo.

Barzoni, who had not spoken at all, looked up to dart a shattering glance at the imprudent orator.

'Well said,' continued Lucilio imperturbably, 'but you should have said let them come to spare us another century of torpor like those past, though in a different form. Let them come, to startle us, to frighten us, to shame us, to solicit in fear of their tyranny the active and sublime awakening of our liberty. . . that is what you should have added! . . . Whether we are to take them for examples or for masters we shall know a few months from now. Villetard does not doubt and does not fear, and that makes me suppose that those above him have other desires!'

'What does that matter?' Amilcare interrupted him. 'We respect your words, citizen Vianello, but we feel our pulses intolerant of slavery and we laugh at Villetard and he who stands above him, even as we laugh at St Mark and at Procurator Pesaro.'

Lucilio turned his thoughts away from such considerations, as perhaps too sad or perhaps too late to do anything about, and looked at me with an almost paternal air.

'Citizen Altoviti,' he said, 'your father has done very much in the cause of liberty; he is owed a reward that he prefers shall be given to you. Not that that would have been enough, had not your nature and your actions already given hopes to see continued in you the great examples of your family. You are one of the youngest members of the Great Council and one of the few, even the very few, who have voted for liberty not out of cowardice, but from the greatness of your soul. I notify you, therefore, that you have been chosen as the first secretary of the new government.'

A murmur of surprise from the young men present welcomed these words.

'Yes,' continued Lucilio, 'his father has spent some millions at Constantinople to turn Turkey against the Holy Alliance, and has sacrificed many years of his life in weaving in the distant Orient the web of this work of redemption which will perhaps make us free, and certainly will make us men. He who has done this may well lay claim to as much again for his only son! . . . I am able to tell you this, because on the day after our triumph I myself will return to the hospital to bleed my patients! . . .'

A burst of applause broke unanimously from the whole company and ten pairs of arms competed for the honour of clasping Doctor Vianello in their embrace. In this frenzy of enthusiasm I withdrew thoughtfully into a corner, with the millstone of my secretaryship round my neck. The discussion then became general; they spoke of the fleet, of Dalmatia, of the surest means to obtain the agreement of General Bonaparte to the new form of government. Much breath was wasted until midnight, when Zorzi re-entered the hall with the self-important manner of a shopkeeper who has just overturned a government thirteen centuries old.

'Is it done?' all asked.

'It is done,' replied Zorzi, 'the Doge asked me to go to Villetard to obtain his conditions in writing; His Serenity did not know that we already had them in our pocket. Tomorrow, therefore, there will be a resolution moved in the Great Council that the Venetian Republic immediately adopt the democratic system of the new provisional government as drawn up by us.'

'Long live liberty!' they all shouted.

There was such a clamour of joy and enthusiasm that I felt it run like fire through my veins. In that moment, had I been commanded to believe in the resurrection of Rome with the Comilii and the Manlii, I would have found nothing strange in obeying. A little later we separated and, although it was very late, the Venetian fashion still permitted myself and Giulio to stop at the Countess' house. I was quite out of my senses without knowing why; so must feel a noble horse at the sound of the trumpet. Giulio on the other hand seemed discontented at the too modest part he had played at the evening's meeting, the more so as he should have been accustomed to such gatherings, for both he and Foscolo had the reputation of mixing themselves up in these affairs, and the latter's mother was said to have counselled him to perish rather than reveal any of his companions. Spartan mothers had come back then into fashion. The fact was that the Pisana that evening had eyes only for me, but I was too wrapped up in thoughts of the new government to worry about this amorous play. I looked at her, yes, but only as an attentive listener to my declamations, and this attitude of mine did not please her at all. As for Giulio, seeing him so depressed, she scarcely paid him any attention, and his weary gallantries did not obtain the reward of a fourth part of the trouble that they cost him. It was certainly true that the Countess rewarded him with a deluge of questions on the news of the day, but the little poetaster did not appreciate it, and risked being considered ungrateful rather than become a martyr to boredom. The wary old woman, little by little, as the times grew worse, had begun to trim her sails and now, as far as words went, had become almost a sans culotte. Inside, however, God knows how much hate and bile was hidden.

'What do you say, Signor Giulio? Will these French come? . . . Will they cancel the mortgages on the feudal domains? . . . And will the patricians be sure of a pension or a position? and will St Mark be kept on the standards?'

Giulio sighed, yawned, ground his teeth, grimaced, but the inexorable Countess wanted to get an answer and I believe that he would have allowed one of his teeth to be pulled out with a better grace. I meanwhile could not resist the pleasure of boasting before the Pisana of my future splendours and let it be inferred that in the new government there would be a good place for me.

'But, Carlino,' she asked me quietly, 'were we not agreed that we must place equality upon the throne?'

I shrugged my shoulders angrily. What use was it to philosophize with women? But I do not know if I was silent for disdain or because I did not know what to reply. The fact was that on that evening ambition had dishorsed love and that when I parted from the Pisana I would not even have been able to tell you the colour of her eyes. I said farewell to Giulio abstractedly in the Frezzeria and made my way alone and skipping with impatience to the Riva degli Schiavoni.

I will always remember that memorable evening of the 11th of May! . . . It was an evening so beautiful and serene that it seemed made for the colloquies of love, for lonely meditations, for gay serenades, and nothing more. But, instead, in so great a calm of heaven and earth, in this poetical enchantment of life and of spring, a great Republic was falling to pieces like a body rotting with scurvy; a great queen for fourteen centuries was dying, without tears, without pomp, without obsequies. Her sons either slept indifferently, or trembled with fear; she herself, a dishonoured phantom, floated down the Grand Canal in a fantastic Bucentaur and disappeared into this liquid grave. Could it only have been so. . . . Instead, this dead mask remained exposed for several months, maimed and disfigured, to the contumely of the world; the sea, her ancient spouse, refused her ashes, and a French corporal scattered them to the four winds, a fatal gift to whoever dared to collect them. There was a moment when I lifted my eyes involuntarily to the Palace of the Doges and looked at the moon that beautified with a veneer of poetry its long loggias and great bizarre windows. It seemed to me that thousands of heads, covered with the sailor's caps of ancient times, peered out for the last time from those thousand niches with the pale gaze of phantoms; and then a whisper of air came from the sea that seemed a lament.

I assure you that I trembled even though I hated aristocracy and hoped from its extermination for the triumph of liberty and justice. There is no doubt; to see great things shadowed by the past, disappear for ever, is a grave and inexpressible grief. But the greater these creations of man, so much the more they resist even the breath of time, until there comes that little shock that turns the corpse to powder and takes away the memory and even the appearance of life. Who perceived the fall of the Western Empire of Romulus Augustulus? It had already fallen at the abdication of Diocletian. Who noted in 1806 the end of the Holy Roman Empire of Germany? It had disappeared from the sight of the peoples with the abdication of Charles V . . . Who wept the entry of the French into Venice, the ruin of a great Republic, heir to all the Roman wisdom and civilization, and the mediatrix of Christianity throughout the Middle Ages? She had withdrawn herself voluntarily from the attention of the world after the abdication of Foscari. Abdications mark the downfall of states because the pilot neither abandons nor is obliged to abandon the helm of a ship whose cordage is well furnished and whose crew is expert and disciplined. Desperation, weakness, indifference, distrust, precede but shortly dissolution and shipwreck.

Therefore I turned my eyes to the Palace of the Doges and trembled. Why not destroy this superb and mysterious structure now that the last spirit that animated it was lost? . . . In that unmoving, eternal marble I had a foreboding that was more than memory, it was remorse. Meanwhile I saw, further down the Riva, the faithful Slavs sadly and silently embarking; perhaps their tears alone consoled the dying Venice. Then there arose in me a more definite fear. This new liberty, this happy equality, this impartial justice, with the French in our house, began to seem to me a little untoward. Lucilio had given good advice, to carry out the revolution before Bonaparte sent his orders and instructions from Milan; but that did not prevent the fact that the French would be coming from Mestre, and, once come, who knew? . . . I was ready to evoke the superb magnanimity of Amilcare to free myself from these forebodings. . . . We are men like others, I thought, and the new fire of liberty that animates us will be fecund of prodigies. Europe, too, could not be ungrateful to us; her own interests would not consent. With constancy, with good will, we shall return to be ourselves again; and assistance cannot be lacking whether we look to starboard or to port.

Comforting myself thus, I turned towards home, where my father told me that he was very satisfied at the place reserved for me in the future Municipality, and that I should take care to conduct myself according to his counsels if I wished to go on still further. I do not remember what I replied to him; I know only that I went to bed and did not close an eye till morning. It must have been about a quarter to nine when the bell of the Great Council rang out and I made my way towards the Staircase of the Giants.

Whatever haste the nobles may have had to commit the great matricide, the delights of bed did not allow them to anticipate by more than a quarter of an hour their usual timetable. Those present numbered five hundred and thirty-seven, an illegal number, since by inviolable statute every resolution which was not discussed in a meeting of at least six hundred was considered illegal and null. The greater number were trembling with fear and impatience; they were in haste to get the affair over, to return home and to take off that toga, now a too dangerous symbol of a decadent rule. Some pretended assurance and joy; they were the traitors; others sparkled with a real content, with a fine and generous pride that the sacrifice that they made cancelling their names from the Golden Book would make them free citizens. Amongst these were myself and Agostino Frumier, who were sitting hand in hand. In a corner of the hall, twenty patricians at the most stood wrapped in their togas, rigid and silent, a few old and venerable men who had not appeared at the Council for many years, but who came that morning to honour the fatherland with their last and dignified vote; an occasional youth amongst them, some honest man inspired by the magnanimous sentiments of his grandfather, his father-in-law or his father.

I was a little surprised to see amongst them the Senator Frumier and his eldest son, Alfonso, since I knew them devoted to St Mark, but not so courageously as they appeared to me then. They stood united in a close little bunch by themselves, and they looked at their companions not with the haughtiness of disdain or with the envy of hatred, but with the firm gentleness of martyrs. Blessed be the religion of the fatherland and of the given oath. There it shone with a last ray, without hope, and yet filled with faith and majesty. They were no longer aristocrats, they were not tyrants and inquisitors; they were the grandsons of the Zenos and the Dandolos, recollecting in that hall for the last time the glories, the sacrifices, the virtues of their ancestors. I looked at them then, amazed and hostile; I recall them now, moved and wondering, and at least I can laugh outright at the false fables of later times and not evoke from the last Great Council of Venice a malediction on human nature.

Throughout the hall there was a murmur, a sort of indistinct roar; only in this obscure and hidden corner reigned silence and grief. Outside, the populace was rioting; the ships returning disarmed to the estuary, some last banners of the Slavs, still embarking, and guards who, against every precedent, were guarding the entrances to the Doge's palace; all funereal presages. Oh, the slumber of death is deep indeed, if then did not awake out of their graves, the heroes, the doges, the captains of the ancient Republic! . . .

The Doge rose to his feet, pallid and trembling, before the sovereignty of the Great Council of which he was the representative, and to which he now dared to propose a baseness without example. He read the conditions proposed by Villetard to meet the desires of the French Directory and the letter to placate the fury of General Bonaparte. He approved them in ignorance, supported them in incapacity, and did not know that Villetard, traitor throughout, had promised what no one had ever had in mind to perform, Bonaparte least of all. Ludovico Manin stuttered a few words on the necessity of accepting these conditions, on the uselessness, even the impossibility of resistance, on the magnanimity of General Bonaparte, on the hopes we had of better fortune in the future through the reforms recommended. At last he proposed barefacedly the abolition of the old forms of government and the establishment of a democracy. For the half of such a crime, Marin Faliero had perished on the scaffold; Ludovico Manin went on, dishonouring with his stammering words himself, the Great Council, and his country, and there was not a man's hand to dare snatch from his shoulders the Doge's mantle and pound his craven head on that pavement where once had bent the heads of the Ministers of Kings and the Legates of Pontiffs! Even I pitied him; I who in the fear and degradation of a Doge saw nothing then save the triumph of liberty and equality.

Suddenly a few musket volleys resounded outside; the Doge stopped in consternation and was about to descend the steps of the throne; a frightened crowd of patricians clustered about him, shouting: 'To the vote!' . . . The people howled outside; inside the confusion and dismay increased. 'They are the rebel Slavs!' (the last of them were then leaving and had saluted with these shots the ingratitude of Venice). 'They are the sixteen thousand conspirators!' (the dreams of Lucilio). 'It is the people who want to wash their hands in the blood of the nobles!' (the people, who not only preferred obedience to these nobles to the harder slavery that menaced them, but even loved that obedience and did not want to forget it). All in all, between the shouts, the howls, the haste, and the fear, the vote was finally taken.

Five hundred and twelve voters approved the part not yet read, which contained the abdication of the nobility and the establishment of a Provisional Democratic Government, always insofar as it was in accord with the desires of General Bonaparte. The reason given for not awaiting from Milan his supreme wishes and the terms of the treaty now being negotiated was the urgency of the internal danger. Only twenty votes opposed this vile precipitancy; five abstained. The spectacle of these deliberations will always remain in my memory; many faces that I saw then among this troop of miserable sheep I can still see today, after sixty years, with profound humiliation. I still remember the distorted corpse-like faces of some, the bewilderment of others, almost as if they were drunk, and the sorrowful haste of many who would, I believe, have willingly thrown themselves out of the windows in order to leave as soon as possible the scene of their humiliation. The Doge hurried to his rooms, divesting himself as he went of his insignia and ordering the doganal emblems to be removed from the walls; many gathered around him, as if to forget their own infamy in the spectacle of one still greater. Those who went out into the piazza were careful first to throw away their wigs and patrician togas. We alone, the few and deluded worshippers of liberty among that flock of slaves (we were five or six in all), ran to the windows and the staircase, shouting: 'Long live liberty!' . . . General Salimbeni, watching with one or two of the conspirators, had already begun to agitate among the crowd, exciting them to dance and riot. But the crowd turned furiously on him and forced him to shout: 'Long live St Mark!' The new cries drowned the first ones, and many amongst those farthest away believed that the old Republic had emerged safely from the terrible hazard of the voting. 'Long live the Republic! Long live St Mark!' rose like a single voice from the whole piazza packed with people; the image of the Evangelist was carried in triumph; and a menacing wave of people ran to the houses of those patricians who were believed to have conspired to call in the French.

In the midst of the crowd, uncertain, confused and divided from my companions, I came upon my father and Lucilio, perhaps less confused, but more humiliated than I. They took me with them and dragged me towards the Frezzeria. Those few patricians who had voted for the independence and continuance of their country passed us with their wigs awry and their togas trailing on the ground. The people made way for them, without insults, but without applause. Lucilio gripped my arm: 'Do you see?' he whispered in my ear, 'the people cry "Long live St Mark" and yet has not the courage to bear in triumph one of the last and worthy masters left to them and to make him Doge . . . slaves, slaves, eternally slaves . . .' My father did not waste time in sophistries; he hurried us on as well as he could; he wanted to be once more safely in his room to think over the pros and cons of the situation.

A proclamation of the new Municipality that painted the base acquiescence of the patricians as a free and spontaneous sacrifice to the spirit of the times, to justice and universal good, restored tranquillity to this good Venetian people. Even as a rat's tooth is enough to sink a worm-eaten ship, so the intrigue of a petty Parisian secretary, of five or six traitors and a handful of Republicans, had sufficed to overthrow that political edifice that had resisted Suleiman II and the League of Cambrai. These were revolutions without grandeur because without aim, and the ringleaders of the party should have asked for the light of experience when fortune had consigned into their hands the destinies of the Fatherland.

Four days later, Venetian ships brought the French troops to Venice; and a city defended only a few days before by eleven thousand Slavs, eight hundred pieces of artillery and two hundred warships, now gave itself up, voluntarily enchained, as the spoil of the soldiers, four thousand adventurers, captained by Baraguay d'Hilliers. The Municipality walked in their retinue, amid the silence and the scorn of the crowd. I too, as secretary, had my share in these silent insults; but the enthusiasm of the Pisana and the exhortations of my father gave me courage to endure everything for the love of liberty.

But my courage was somewhat affected by the replies received from the provinces of the *terraferma* to the invitation to associate themselves with our government. The podestàs wavered and the French generals openly laughed at us. Venice remained alone with her counterfeit liberty. Istria and Dalmatia had meanwhile been occupied by Austria, according to the permission granted her at the negotiations of Loeben. But even this was not the end. France, with the Venetian fleet, made herself master of our possessions in Albania and the Ionian Sea; and worse misfortunes threatened. Poor secretary! I had not sense enough to reconcile all these contradictions and to form a judgement for myself. I sighed, I worked, I waited for better things. Meanwhile I took rueful pleasure in noting the sins for which Venice had fallen, unhonoured and unwept, after fourteen centuries of noble and glorious life. No one, I believe, had till then thought of them or tried to formulate the reasons for her ruin. The peoples alone in modern history live and fight and, if they fall, they fall strong and honoured, because certain of their resurrection.

CHAPTER XII

FAREWELL fresh and carefree youth, everlasting bliss of the ancient Gods of Olympus and celestial but transient gift to us mortals! Farewell dewy dawns sparkling with smiles and promises, clouded only by the lovely colours of illusion! Farewell serene sunsets watched lazily from the shady brink of some stream or from the flowered balcony of the loved one! Farewell virgin moon, inspirer of vague melancholies and poetic loves, you who play round the curly heads of babes and lovingly caress the thoughtful eyes of youth! The dawn of life passes like the dawn of a day and the night tears of heaven are turned in the immensity of nature into restless and vital humours. No more ease, but work; no more beauty but activity; no more peace and fancy, but truth and struggle. The sun awakes us to grave thoughts, to weary tasks, to long and vain hopes; it conceals itself in the evenings, granting us a short but longed for reward of oblivion. The moon then mounts the starry circle of the heavens and diffuses over the sleepless nights an azure and cloudy veil, woven of light, of sadness, of remembrance and of sorrow. The years follow one another, always more stern and sullen, like masters discontented with their servants; they seem old and failing to the sight and the whiter the brow, the more rapid and swift their flight. It is like the pace of the shadow that becomes gigantic at the approach of sunset. Farewell shining porticos, enchanted gardens, harmonious preludes to life! . . . Farewell green countrysides filled with wandering paths, of pensive meditation, of infinite beauty, of light, of freedom and the song of birds! Farewell, first nest of childhood, houses vast and busy, huge to us children, like the world to men, where the work of others was a delight, where the guardian angel watched over our slumbers, consoling us with a thousand enchanted visions! We were content without effort, happy without knowing it; and the frown of the master or the reproofs of the governess were the only furrows that destiny engraved on our foreheads! The universe ended at the walls of the courtyard; if there was not within all the plenitude of bliss, at least our desires were modest and injustice seemed to us so trivial that the next day we laughed at it as at a joke. The old servants, the grave and austere priest, the harsh and mysterious parents, the voluble and chattering maids, the quarrelsome companions, the lively little girls, saucy and coaxing, pass before us like the figures on a magic lantern screen. We were afraid of the cats who played under the dressers; near the fireside we caressed the old hunting dog and admired the coachman when he groomed the horses without fear of their hooves.

For me, it is true, there was also the spit to turn, but I pardon even the spit and would undertake to turn it again to have once more the innocent happiness of one of those blissful evenings between Martino's knees or beside the cradle of the Pisana. Beloved and melancholy shadows of the persons whom I loved, you still live within me; faithful into old age, you do not fly either from its chilly breast or its frigid appearance; I see you always hovering around me as a cloud of thoughts and affections, and then disappearing far far away in the glowing rainbow of youth. Time is not time save for him who has money out at interest; for me it was never other than memory, longing, love and hope. Youth remains alive in the mind of man and the old man recalls without a curse the memory of his manhood. How could this treasure of thoughts and of affections that is for ever growing and accumulating end in nothing? . . . Intelligence is a sea and we the brooks and rivers. Ocean bottomless and boundless, I confide fearlessly to your billows my memories, this life of mine, long and wearied of rushing onward. Time is not time for him who feels himself immortal.

And so I have written a worthy epitaph on those delicious years in that world of ancient times, the world of powdered wigs, of buli and of feudal magistrates. I emerged from them the secretary of a democratic government that had nothing to govern; with hair shorn in the manner of Brutus, with a round cap with wings rising at the sides, the shoulders of my jacket stuffed out like two Bologna mortadellas and high boots with heels so arrogant that one could hear me coming from one end to the other of the Procuratorial offices. What a jump from the soft and sliding slippers of the old noblemen! It was the greatest revolution that had so far taken place in Venice!

Save for this, the water went down the mill-stream as usual, save that the French gentry racked their brains every day in devising some fresh way to pluck us the better. Pictures, medallions, codices, statues, the four horses of San Marco, all went their way to Paris; let us console ourselves that science had not yet invented any way to move buildings or transport towers and cupolas, or Venice would have remained what she was in the times of the first successors of Attila.

Bergamo and Crema had already been finally occupied to round off the Cisalpine Republic; from the other provinces deputies rushed to a meeting at Brescia to decide whose side to take. Berthier, the clever old fox, presided in order to thwart any useful decisions. I wrote the desires of the Municipality to Bassano and received the replies. Doctor Lucilio who, without seeming to be so, continued to be the moving spirit of the new government, did not want this last sheet-anchor to be abandoned and he too intrigued and stubbornly pressed his point. It seemed that we were close to an agreement to the satisfaction of all when the cunning Berthier unexpectedly declared that any agreement was impossible and so—Good night! Venice remained with her oysters, and the provinces with their Presidents and their French generals. Victor at Padua croaked impudently that no one should pay any attention to the Venetians, a putrid and incorrigible race of aristocrats. Bernadette, more sincere, simply forbade deputies to go from Udine to the comedy at Bassano. The times were so depraved that cruelty was little less than mercy and certainly more meritorious than hypocrisy.

None the less, I pressed onward with bandages on my eyes and pen in my hand, thinking I was rushing onwards to the times of Camillus or of Cincinnatus. My father shook his head; I paid no heed to him and perhaps thought that the wishes or the presumption of a few hotheads would be enough to wean this liberty of babes already worse than decrepit.

One evening I went in search of the Countess of Fratta at the usual house, but was told that she had moved and had gone to lodge on the Zattere at the other end of the city. I trotted there, climbed a battered and worm-eaten wooden staircase and finally reached her apartment, damp, dark and almost without furniture. I could not contain myself for wonder. In the antechamber the Pisana came to greet me with a lamp; my astonishment increased and I followed her as if sleep-walking to the guest room. My God, what shame!

I found the Countess huddled in an old armchair of peeling black morocco leather; an oil lamp was flickering on a side table propped against the wall so as not to fall down. All in all, a typical room to let, without furniture, without curtains, with a floor of uneven boards and badly whitewashed ceiling of crude beams. The walls were bare and leprous, the doors and windows in such bad repair that the miserable flame of the lamp seemed always on the point of going out.

Beside the Contessa a little old man, washed-out, white and puffy, sat on a rough straw chair; he wore the elegant trappings of the patricians, but a chronic and rasping cough contrasted greatly with that youthful get-up. The Countess saw on my face my wonder and my grief; she put on her liveliest expression to give me the lie.

'You see, Carlino?' she said with a somewhat forced gaiety. 'You see, Carlino, whether I am a provident mother? The revolution has ruined us and I am compelled to tighten my belt and save for these dear children of mine! . . .'

As she said this, she looked at the Pisana who was seated by the nobleman with downcast eyes and hands folded in her lap.

'May I present my cousin, the noble Mauro Navagero,' she went on. 'A generous cousin and furthermore one disposed to ally himself with us in the bonds of kinship. In short, since this morning he is the betrothed of our Pisana.'

I believe that in that moment I saw all the stars of the firmament, as if a heavy rock had fallen on me and crushed me; then, to that flashing of stars succeeded a blackness lasting for several seconds before I could go on listening, without being able to discern anything of the faces about me or to comprehend the buzzing in my ears. I imagine that the Countess had been expounding at great length the magnificence and suitability of that alliance; certainly the noble Navagero, because of his cough, and the Pisana, because of her embarrassment, had no time to waste in idle chatter. I confess that the love of liberty and all the other fancies so instilled in me by my own open nature and the intrigues of my father fled like dogs scalded by a saucepan of boiling water. The Pisana remained alone queen of my mind; I repented, I reproved myself, I despaired that I had neglected her for all that time and I realized that I was too weak or too vicious to find any happiness in great abstractions. Blessed is that state where private affections are the stair to civil virtue and where moral and domestic education prepares in a man the citizen and the hero! But I was born on another mushroom-bed; my affections contrasted with one another too greatly, like the customs of the past century with the aspirations of the present. This is a misfortune that is perpetuated in the youth of our own times and of which one laments the ills without being able to provide the remedy.

When I dared to turn my eyes towards the girl, I felt as if some obstacle made me look away again; it was the chilly and peevish glance of the tender bridegroom that wandered from the face of the Pisana to mine with all the anxiety of a miser. There are certain looks that one feels before seeing them; those of the Most Excellent Navagero directly wounded the spirit without troubling the optic nerve. Moreover they embarrassed me so much that I had to turn as a last and desperate resort to the mask-like face of the Contessa. She appeared radiant with satisfaction, so that I became three times more furious, and ended by completely losing my bearings. A man who, unprovided with arguments, joins in a discussion where all are against him would have been in a better position than I was then. The Pisana with her almost mocking reserve irritated me more than all the others.

I wanted to rise, to escape in desperation and to give vent to my sorrow anywhere I could, when my father skipped in. He was even more nimble and strange than usual and seemed to be well aware of all that had so greatly surprised and dismayed me, since he congratulated the Navagero on his good fortune and turned on the young betrothed one of his glances that spoke more eloquently than any tongue. What would you? To see my father too taking his place among my enemies, and gorging himself on my misfortune as on so much manna, made me so furious that I no longer thought of going away and felt within myself something of the heroism of Horatius alone against all Tuscany.

I sat down again, proudly defying the Countess' cunning smirk, the Pisana's indifference, the Navagero's jealousy and my father's cruelty. Later, when I had to rise to take my leave, I noticed too late that my knees scarcely obeyed me and whoever might have observed us three, myself, my father and the Navagero walking, might well have taken us for three of the happiest drunkards. I could not stomach the lectures my father read me and for the first time got into bed without thinking of the gilded cap of the future democratic Doge of Venice.

A thousand ideas, varied, strange and terrifying, whirled in my brain in such arabesques that I could not succeed in controlling them. To confront the Navagero with sword and dagger, to stick him like a frog, then to give the Pisana my solemn curse and throw myself into the canal by the convenient road of the window; or else, after killing him, to take her in my arms, to fly on a Smyrna Xebec and carry her off with me to a life in the desert, among the ruins of Palmyra or on the sands of Arabia Petraea, were among the least extravagant of my pindaric flights. For the rest, I poetized without numbers, without metre and without rhyme; I did not think anything was difficult or impossible and had I had by me a hippogryph and the treasures of Croesus in my pockets, I could not have built castles in the air with greater freedom and magnificence.

Thus dreaming, I fell asleep and dreamed again while sleeping. Waking the next morning I picked up once more the thread of my dreams of the day before. Amilcare asked me the reason for my continual fantasies and I allowed myself to tell him perhaps more than I had intended. . . . Shame! That a Secretary of the Municipality should lose himself in such follies! Did I not blush to be jealous of a slobbering and slipshod old aristocrat and to behave like a weakling over some little flirt who would have wedded a satyr just in order to be married? That could now be seen clearly; and a fine bargain I would have made to maintain such a role! Better to wait and show oneself a man, to give all for one's country, to the cult of liberty, especially now, when there seemed so great a need!

Amilcare spoke from the heart and persuaded me; it was really not worth while to make an ass of myself for the Pisana; moreover the cares of government took up all my time and occupied all my attention. I made an effort with myself, granted the Navagero his life and the scene that I had imagined when I should present myself to the Pisana before either drowning myself or leaving for Arabia, I changed into a silent apostrophe: 'Do as you will, faithless one! You are unworthy of me!'

I have my doubts now whether I had any right to pronounce such a sentence. The girl had never promised me anything. However, I knew very well that I had never been so infatuated as then; but the strangeness and unreasonableness of my temperament made me hide all these things even from myself. The fact was, however, that I decided to break with her in the firm conviction that I was the victim; and this allowed me to play the martyr, even more than my own heroic intentions and the jealousy of the Navagero allowed. The Count Rinaldo, who rarely came to his mother's room, had had some moments of irritation at seeing me turtle-doving with his sister. He too, poor fellow, joined in with all the others, but I was not in the least concerned, being completely persuaded that I should be wrapped up in my secretary's office and not think at all either of the Pisana or of her marriage.

The domestic affairs of the house of Fratta had become more involved than ever. The Signora Contessa went on gambling feverishly and when there was no money left, looked for it in the pawn shops. The philosophy of the young Count and the thoughtlessness of the Pisana were no deterrent, and I believe that, in their view, His Excellency Navagero would be called on to settle all these difficulties. But what gave me most cause for wonder was the intimacy that continued between my father and the Contessa, even though the former had not slackened his pursestrings in the slightest and had countered by a thousand different wiles the designs of the Countess for a marriage between myself and the Pisana. I had vaguely understood that these projects were not to my father's taste and that he, without actually mentioning it, had guessed my wishes and had done his best to turn them in another direction.

But how had he been able to oppose the aims of the Countess and at the same time remain in her good graces? That was what I strove to make clear to myself and I finally discovered that he had been the go-between in the marriage arrangement with the Navagero and that I owed my misfortune mainly to him. As for me, the old schemer had very exalted ideas; a very rich maiden of the Contarini family would have suited him as a daughter-in-law and he did not fail to give me a hint from time to time that I should single her out from among the many girls who, their pride forgotten, would not have disdained at that time to link their name with mine. All actors upon the world stage have their benefit nights, and this was mine. The citizen Carlo Altoviti, ex-gentleman of Torcello, Secretary of the Municipality, favourite of Doctor Lucilio and celebrated in the Piazza San Marco for his fine clothes, his self-reliance and above all for his father's millions, was not a man to be put to one side.

I, however, humbled in my self-esteem by the treachery of the Pisana, no longer puffed myself up for such qualities, though, despite the exhortations of Amilcare, I no longer knew how to maintain my flight in the sublime heavens of liberty and of glory. That heaven had begun to cloud over and great storms were menacing from all round. But had the earth opened under my feet, it could not have been worse for me! None the less, as I was a man of heart and of honour, I did not neglect my duties at the Municipal Palace. Only it pleased me better to chafe and fret with rage at the side of the Pisana than to sense in that Palace the future aura of the Doges foretold me by my father.

About this time, when Venice was already settled into servitude to the French and uncertainly awaiting a future that seemed ever more melancholy, Doctor Lucilio presented himself at the house of the Countess of Fratta. She had been dreading this visit for more than a month but no longer had the courage to refuse to see him. The doctor sat down in front of the Countess with his usual air, neither humble nor arrogant, and asked her with all due form for Clara's hand. The Countess feigned great surprise and pretended to be scandalized at such a request. She replied that her daughter was about to take her vows and in no way intended to expose herself to the perils of the world that she had so far avoided with such prudence; finally she referred to the prior rights of the Signor Partistagno, who had been continually braying to all Venice of the sacrifice imposed on Clara and certainly would never have consented that she should leave her convent to become the bride of someone else. Lucilio retorted fairly and squarely that Clara had promised herself to him long before anyone else, that her vows had not yet been taken and that the democratic laws in no way hindered their union and that, as far as the Partistagno was concerned, he laughed at him and his grumbling which had been the joke of every circle in the city for a whole year past. The Contessa replied with tight lips and a malicious little smile that, since he had brought up the question of Clara now being of age, he should refer directly to her and that she congratulated him on being so fixed in his purpose, though perhaps a little tardy in declaring himself and said that, for her part, she wished him every luck in his venture.

'Signora Contessa,' concluded Lucilio, 'I am fixed, as you have said, in my intentions and have been so for many years, though I would have preferred to turn the world upside down rather than violate the codes of decency or implore a favour on bended knees. Now that circumstances have placed me on an equality, I do not hesitate to ask what others are ready to concede me. I count myself fortunate that you do not wish to oppose your maternal authority to my dearest hope.'

'As you will, just as you will!' the Countess added hastily. It seemed that she spoke out of fear of Lucilio, but perhaps she was thinking of Mother Redenta to whom she had confidently delegated the difficult task of defending the soul of Clara against the wiles of the devil. The Reverend Mother had already been on the alert for some time, and Doctor Lucilio, as he took his leave of the Countess, perhaps did not think that his enterprise was beginning any too well. I would not like to affirm that he was so very sure of himself. He had kept on delaying from day to day to see the triumph of his party and of democratic opinions first assured in Venice. Then, perhaps before anyone else, he had sensed a change in the wind and, proud in face but desperate in soul, had hastened to take advantage of these last gifts of fortune in order to satisfy the supreme desire of his heart. He saw falling to pieces around him those proud castles in the air of political liberty, glory and public prosperity, and hoped to save for himself, as if with an anchor, the last refuge of domestic happiness. With such thoughts in his head, he made his way to the Convent of Santa Teresa, gave his name to the gatekeeper and asked that the Contessina Clara of Fratta be brought to the parlatorium.

The gatekeeper disappeared into the convent and returned to say that the noble lady wanted to know the reason of his visit and that she would try to satisfy his desires without disturbing her claustral meditations. Lucilio started up with surprise and rage, but seeing behind this request some clerical jugglery, repeated to the gatekeeper that his interview with the Signora Clara was necessary and indispensable and that the Signora herself must know very well what it was about and that nothing in the world could deny him the right to demand it. The lay-sister went in once more and returned after a few minutes to say with a scowling face that the lady would come down shortly, accompanied by the Mother Superior.

This Mother Superior was in no way to Lucilio's taste, but he was not the man to be daunted by a nun and waited, a little uneasily, measuring out with great strides the red and white marble pavement of the parlatorium. He had been walking thus for a considerable time when Mother Redenta and Clara entered; the one with a cantankerous air, lowered eyes, hands crossed on her stomach and the hairs on her upper lip more prominent than usual, the other calm and serene as ever, her beauty a little tarnished by the enclosed life of the convent, but her soul shining through, more pure and ardent than ever, like a star that breaks through a mist of cloud.

It was many years since the two lovers had seen one another so close to, but they gave no sign of great emotion; their strength, their love, lay so deeply embedded in their hearts that one saw on their features only a faint and distant reflection of it. Mother Redenta sought a spyhole in the dense hedgerows of her lashes whence she might look on without being observed and her ears kept so sharp a vigil that they could have heard a fly at the other end of the room.

'Clara,' Lucilio began in a voice perhaps more moved than he would have wished, 'Clara, I have come here after a very long time to remind you of your promise to me. I believe that for you, as for me, these long years have been no more than a single day of waiting. Now no obstacle opposes the desire of our hearts; no longer with the impatience and the carelessness of youth, but with the strengthened judgement and the unchangeable intention of maturity, I ask you to renew, with but a single word, the promise of happiness that you made me in the sight of Heaven. Neither the wish of your parents nor the tyranny of the laws nor the conventions of society any longer hinder your liberty or my discretion. I offer you a heart filled with one love only, kindled by a flame that shall never die, and proved time and again by labour, by patience and by misfortune. Clara, look me in the face. When will you be mine?'

The girl trembled from head to foot, but it was only for an instant. She placed on her breast a hand whose whiteness contrasted with her black novice's tunic and lifted her eyes to Lucilio's face with a long and baffling look which seemed as if searching through everything for the hope of Heaven.

'Lucilio,' she replied, pressing that hand gently on her heart. 'I have sworn to God to love you, I have sworn in my heart to make you happy so far as in me lies. It is true; I remember it always and I will always ensure that my promises shall have that greater effect which God allows them.'

'Which means to say?' exclaimed Lucilio anxiously.

Mother Redenta risked raising her eyelids to reveal two eyes so horrorstruck that they might have been looking at the horns of Beelzebub. But the calm appearance of Clara reassured her and she once more hid her glances behind their former loopholes.

'I will tell you all,' the girl meanwhile went on. 'I will tell you everything, Lucilio, and you shall judge. I entered this place of peace to confide my soul to God and his providence; I have found here affection, thoughts and comfort which made me look with repulsion at the rest of the world. . . . Oh no, no, Lucilio, do not disdain me. . . . Our souls were not made to find happiness in this century of vice and perdition. Let us resign ourselves and we shall find happiness above!'

'What are you saying? What words are you saying now that tear my heart asunder and yet come from your lips with the sweetness of a melody? Clara, for pity's sake, come to yourself! . . . Think of me! . . . Look me in the eyes! I repeat with my two hands on the cross—think of me!'

'Oh, I do think of you! I think even too much, Lucilio, since I am too involved in the affairs of this world to raise myself, simple and pure, to God! . . . But what do you want, Lucilio, what do you want of me? . . . Our Republic has fallen into the power of strangers without religion and without faith. There is no more good, there is no more hope save in Heaven for God-fearing souls. Why do you trust yourself, Lucilio, to the vain hopes of this world? . . . Why found a family in this society that no longer respects God and His Church? . . . Why? . . .'

'Enough, enough, Clara! . . . Do not scorn my sorrow or my rage! Think of what you are saying; think that you must give an account of my soul to that God whom you adore and whom you intend to serve better by committing so atrocious a crime. The Republic has fallen, you say? . . . Religion is in danger? . . . But what has all that to do with the promises that I had from you? . . . Clara, reflect that the first and most sublime precept of the Gospel commands you to love your neighbour. Now, as your neighbour, as no more than your neighbour, I ask you to remember your oaths and not to make a merit before God of being faithless to them! God abhors and condemns the faithless; God refuses sacrifices offered at the price of the tears and blood of another! . . . If you must sacrifice yourself, at least sacrifice yourself to me! . . . If not as happiness, then accept me as a martyrdom!'

Mother Redenta coughed noisily to spoil the effect of these words declaimed by Lucilio in such a frenzy of desperation and entreaty as to split the soul. But Clara turned, reassuring her with a gesture, and did not fear to go nearer to Lucilio and place a hand gently on his shoulder. The poor fellow was intelligent enough to guess everything from that look and from that gesture and felt with a breaking heart his inability to follow into Heaven that soul that, blessed in its own sorrows, was escaping from him.

'But why, why, Clara?' he went on without even waiting for her to declare the terrible meaning of that gesture. 'Why do you want to kill me when you could bring me back to life again? . . . Why do you forget that holy, that indissoluble love that you swore to me?'

'Oh, that love, more holy, more eternal, more indissoluble than ever I swear to you now too!' replied the girl, 'Only our wedding will be in Heaven, since upon earth God forbids it to his faithful! . . . I swear to you Lucilio! I shall always love you, I love no one else save you! This love I have been able to purify, to sanctify, and I cannot expel it from my being save in death! Just for that reason, you can see if my vocation is true and lasting. I will love you always, I will live with you always in communion of prayer and of spirit. But more, Lucilio, more you have not the right to ask me! . . . More I cannot give you, since God forbids it!'

'God then commands you to kill me!' exclaimed Lucilio with a cry.

Mother Redenta broke in to ask for moderation since the sisters were at that time in meditation and might have been disturbed by such cries. Clara lowered her eyes and, poor thing, began to weep; but she neither wavered nor was in the least shaken in her firm intention. The suffering that she endured was intense; but the Mother Superior had reckoned well on the wiles used to bewitch her in this way. For long now the soul of Clara had dwelt in Heaven and saw the things of this world as if from an immeasurable height. She would have made amends by her own death for a venial sin of

Lucilio, but she would also have killed him herself in order to assure his eternal salvation. In fact she swooned and trembled all over, but recovering herself and coming still closer to him she suddenly went on:

'Lucilio, do you love me? Well, fly from me! . . . We shall meet you may be sure, in a better place than this. . . . I will pray for you, I will pray for you in sackcloth and in fasting.'

'Blasphemy!' shouted the other. 'You will pray for me? . . . The executioner is to intercede for his victim? . . . God will abhor such prayers!'

'Lucilio,' said Clara humbly, 'we are all sinners, but when . . .'

Mother Redenta interrupted these words with an opportune nudge: 'Humility, humility, my daughter,' she muttered, 'there is no need to speak to or to teach others when it is not strictly necessary . . .'

Lucilio darted a glance at the old woman such as a lion might give from between the bars of its cage.

'No, no!' he cried bitterly, 'Teach me also, since I am really a novice in this art and will certainly die of heartbreak before having learnt it! . . .'

'And I, do you think I am striving to live much longer?' said Clara sadly. 'You know that I ask no grace of the Madonna with such insistence and with so much fervour as to die very soon and go up to Heaven to intercede for you! . . .'

'But I, I despise your intercession!' Lucilio burst out, 'I want you, I want my happiness, my good . . .'

'Be calm! Have pity on me too! . . . In this world there is no more good, I know that only too well! . . . You know there are already rumours that the religious orders will be abolished and the convents destroyed!'

'Yes, yes, and that rumour will come true! . . . I swear to you it will come true. I myself will see to it that of these tombs of the living not one stone shall stand upon another! . . .'

'Be silent, Lucilio, be silent for pity's sake!' replied Clara, looking uneasily at the Mother Superior who was shifting on her seat with what was perhaps a secret complacency. 'Be converted to the fear of God and to the true faith outside which there is no salvation! . . . Do not commit these sins of heresy which make you mortally guilty before God! Do not outrage the sanctity of those souls who down here on this earth are wedded to their Creator to make life more clement for their brothers in exile.'

'Hypocritical souls, false and corrupt,' exclaimed Lucilio grinding his teeth, 'who try to break down other souls that are simple and weak! . . .'

'No, my dear Signor Doctor,' broke in the Mother Superior in a dry and nasal voice, 'do not try to calumniate blindly those souls as hypocritical who sacrifice their whole life to try and strengthen the weak and who alone defend the faith and good observances against the perversities of the world. It is their merit if many weak souls become so strong and sublime as to place all their hopes in God and who regard the words of a simple oath as an insuperable barrier which divides them for ever from the company of the perverse and the unbelieving. It is true,' she went on, bowing her head, 'that we remain united to them by the spiritual bond of prayer, which, we would like to hope, will serve to save one or two of them from the infernal wiles.'

'Oh quickly, very quickly will those perverse and unbelieving rescind your vows!' thundered Lucilio. 'Society is the work of God and whoever withdraws himself from it has the remorse of crime, or the cowardice of fear or the unfitness of inertia of the soul! . . . As for you,' and he turned to Clara, 'as for you who have perverted your conscience by robbing it of all humanity, as for you who rise to Heaven by treading beneath your feet the corpse of one who loves you, who does not see, does not live, does not think save in you and for you, may wrath and malediction rest upon your head . . . !'

'Enough, Lucilio,' exclaimed the girl with a solemn air, 'do you want to know all? Very well, I will tell you! The vows that I shall solemnly pronounce on Sunday before the altar of God, I had already made in my heart on that fatal night when the enemies of religion and of Venice entered this city. There were eight of us who offered our liberty and our lives for the removal of this scourge, and if these base criminals are compelled to abandon their prey so vilely gained, then God may perhaps have looked kindly upon our sacrifice!'

Mother Redenta sneered under her cap and Lucilio, his fury a little modified, began to make a step or two towards the way out, when he turned once more to Clara is if he felt it impossible to leave her in this way.

'Clara,' he repeated, 'I will implore you no longer; I see that it would be useless. But I will leave with you the spectacle of so much unhappiness that remorse will pursue you even in the silence and the peace of the cloister. Oh you do not know, you have never known how much I love you! . . . You have never measured the deep and flaming abysses of my soul, all filled with you; you have never forgotten yourself as I have forgotten myself in order to live only in you. The sacrifices that you impose upon yourself with a thousand mental subtleties you do not accept with the holy spontaneity of affection and of feeling! . . . Clara, I leave you to God, but will

God come to you? Is adultery permitted to Him by those holy commandments which are the sublime compendium of our duties?'

I do not know whether, by speaking in this way, Lucilio intended to surrender or to make a last attempt. But between him and Clara it was a contest like that of two fencers out of range of each other or two litigants each of whom was speaking a language unknown to the other. Mother Redenta triumphed secretly over this powerful and indefatigable intriguer who had, one might say, given the *coup de grace* to a government fourteen centuries old and changed the face of a good part of the world. Why did she so enjoy doing this? First of all, there is no pride that can surpass the pride of the humble; then too she wished to avenge upon others her own unhappiness, and finally she wanted to keep all her promises to the Countess. After so many years of patient labour, she could admire in the constancy of Clara the fruits of her own work and she would not have bartered those moments for the most important abbacy of her order.

As for Lucilio, after so many years of toil, of perseverance and of certainty, after having overcome every barrier and removed every obstacle, to see himself gently repulsed by the devout scruples of a young girl and not to be able to master a soul wherein he knew that he still reigned, was a madness that surpassed imagination itself! With every force of his mind and his heart he had reached a point where it was impossible for him either to advance or to retreat; he had begun to lose faith in himself after so long a train of continuous triumphs. The confidence that he had had before now added a real desperation to this defeat. None the less, I do not believe that he gave himself up for beaten since his nature was such that gives way only before the final breach of death. But love turned within him to rage, to hate, to fury; and in these last words hurled at Clara pride alone perhaps still struggled. Love had entered so deeply into his soul that it had stirred up there a conflagration of all those passions that had at first served him so obediently and almost reasonably.

The girl replied nothing to the insults that he heaped upon her, but her silence expressed more than any long speeches and Lucilio began to assail her with a fury of reproofs and imprecations, like a maddened bull which, prevented from getting out of the arena, smashes its skull against the stockades. He became infuriated to the great scandal of Mother Redenta and the great compassion of Clara; then his will recovered its control of these disordered passions and was strong and proud enough to dispel them and persuade him to go away, leaving as his last salute to the girl a look of pity mingled with defiance. I repeat once more; the wound to his pride was perhaps deeper than that to his love; in fact, even in those terrible moments he was able to think how to retire with the honours of war. I should have died of heartbreak; but he forced himself to live in order to persuade himself that he was still master of his own passions, of his own life. I cannot assure you that this was true, but I recall having seen him during those days and though I was very much concerned with my own affairs, the desolation that he tried in vain to conceal under his usual austere imperturbability did not escape me. Little by little, however, his former self prevailed; he arose once more with titanic pride from this brief defeat; the misfortunes of his country found him stronger, and more invincible, the more despairing he was within himself. Clara solemnly pronounced her vows and Lucilio kept to himself his anguish and his rage at this irremediable loss.

The Pisana was married a short time afterwards to the noble Navagero, and Giulio del Ponte followed them to the altar with a smile of hope on his lips. I alone remained to display my grief and my fury; I could not find peace and could not think of the future without an effort but yet, even in the delirium of sorrow, I did not dare to curse the Pisana and reserved all my maledictions for the Countess who had debased her own daughter by a monstrous marriage in order to enjoy the opulence and the advantages of the Navagero house. I even discovered that the arts employed to turn Clara into a bigot stemmed from the question of cash. The old woman had paid only half the dowry to the convent and had promised the rest on the security of her jewels; but the coffers were empty, the jewels were glittering in the pawnshops, and she greatly feared lest Clara, on getting married, should ask for an account of her properties. How many misfortunes were due to the frenzied mania of this woman for bassetta and faro! The Count Rinaldo had extricated himself from the ruin and from the dishonourable heritage of his family by accepting a very obscure post in the State Audit Department. A silver ducat a day and the use of the Marciana Library assured him all his needs. But none the less I saw him walking in the streets with bowed head and hollow eyes and I wager he was not the last to feel sorrow at the baseness of those customs and those times.

I confess it with shame; it was really baseness. All knew whither we were rushing and all pretended not to know so as to be freed from the bitterness of bewailing it. Barzoni alone among the writers dared to raise his voice against the French with his book *The Romans in Greece*. But his false erudition in this booklet and his strained analogies were already the indication of a weak temperament and an emasculated literature. There was a great to-do about the book and its anonymous author. People read it behind closed doors and with a candle as their only witness, ready to throw it on the fire at the first whisper and to declaim the next day that the depredations of Lucullus and the astute nobility of Flaminius in no way resembled the generous and liberal government of Bonaparte. In reality, he deprived us of our very shirts in order to make a present of them to the liberty of France; the future slaves must remain as naked as the helots of Sparta.

He had already reconstituted around Milan the Cisalpine Republic, rather a menace than a promise to the still provincial Municipality of Venice. The liberation of M. d'Entragnes, the Bourbon Minister, basely handed over to him by the degraded Signoria, had given him the reputation of a gentleman among the emigrés; they hoped for another Monk. What an idea! But the incorrigible Republicans, the destroyers of the Bastille, the adorers of the Tree of Liberty, the Bruti, the Curtii, the Timoleons looked on him askance, accusing him of pride, falseness and tyranny. The Municipality, which after the checkmate of Bassano, had felt the earth giving way beneath its feet, had the ingenuous whim to ask for the incorporation of the Venetian States in the new Lombard Republic. But the rulers of that Republic replied with proud and haughty words; it would have been fratricide if the undeclared will of Bonaparte had not explained their servility. In any case there remained branded for ever the names of those who signed the document that denied aid to a sister city in her misfortune and her peril. Better to drown together than to save oneself without extending a hand to a neighbour or a friend piteously imploring help.

I for my part hoped like all the others in the arrival of the General. I hoped that the vestiges, the monuments of our past greatness would have dissuaded him from the cruel and premeditated indifference which he had commenced to display in our regard. But instead of the General, restrained by shame or by remorse, there came to us only his wife, the beautiful Josephine. She disembarked at the Piazzetta with all the pomp of a Doge's wife and had, if not the majesty, then certainly the splendour in her true creole features. All Venice was at her feet; those who had flattered the banker Haller, the friend of Bonaparte, in order to obtain a prolongation of its agony for the old republic, flattered and fawned upon the wife of the people's representative, to try and prevent her killing before birth this new abortion of liberty! I too peacocked about in the cortège of the Parisian Aspasia in my splendid travesty as a Secretary. I saw her lovely mouth smile at the Venetian courtesies, heard her caressing voice whisper French almost like an Italian dialect; I, who had studied it a little in those days of universal gallicization, stammered in my turn my '*oui*' and my '*n'est-ce pas*' with some of the *aides-de-camp* who accompanied her. All in all, whether it were the prestige of beauty or the appearance of good will or the tenacity of false illusions, the spirits of the deluded were somewhat cheered by the visit of this woman. Even my father no longer shook his head, but pressed me onward to be seen in the front rank of her admirers.

'Women, my son, women are everything,' he said to me. 'Who knows? Perhaps Heaven has sent her; from small seeds great trees grow. Nothing would surprise me.'

Meanwhile Doctor Lucilio who, as a familiar of the French Minister was admitted more freely than anyone into the confidence of the beautiful visitor, took no part, as far as I could see, in this general enchantment. He studied in Josephine not the woman but the wife, whence he could divine the husband, and the diagnosis he drew thence for our destiny, which was in her hands, was not very favourable. It confirmed him more than ever in his deep desperation and I saw him in those days more gloomy and melancholy than usual.

The others were all dancing around as if we were on the eve of the millenium. Members of the Municipality, leaders of the people, ex-senators, ex-nobles, ladies, young beauties, abbés and gondoliers, all crowded around the wife of the great Captain. Beauty could do much in Venice, could even do anything when it was enlivened within by some exalted sentiment, as we were shortly to have proof. Women make men, but enthusiasm creates women even when their education has prepared them only to be dolls.

Many times, when in the retinue of the Beauharnais or in her antechambers, the Pisana and her doting husband passed by me almost grazing my elbow, I felt as if a bucket of cold water had been poured down my back. But then I remembered my position and my father's advice and made myself dignified and graceful to draw the attention of the illustrious guest.

She did indeed notice me and I saw her ask account of me from His Excellency Cappello, who had given her his arm; they spoke together in low voices and then she smiled at me and gave me her hand which I kissed with much respect. It was thus that one treated the wives of liberators, with respectful lips and bended knee. It is true that this hand was so shapely, so soft and so perfect that one could not think of it for a moment as the hand of a *citoyenne*; many empresses would have liked a pair of hands like that and Catherine II never had such, despite the many soaps and toilet-waters that her distillers concocted for her. I became, after that kiss, a person of great importance and the Pisana honoured me with a glance that was certainly not indifferent. His Excellency Navagero looked at me also with even less indifference than his wife and clearly wanted to get me well out of the way.

At just the right moment Giulio del Ponte came to my aid. He was, it seemed, following the fortunate couple and I turned in embarrassment to talk to him. I do not know of what we spoke, but I remember that the conversation touched on the Pisana and her marriage. Giulio no longer had even the one per cent of that happiness he had hoped for on the day of her wedding; indeed when I looked at him then, he seemed almost corpse-like, as a lover who has been deceived.

'Look!' he whispered in my ear, fiercely grinding his teeth. 'Just look! Do you see that sly little officer who is always following the Pisana and is always skipping about by her side or by her husband's and who is now approaching the lovely Beauharnais, bowing to her and pressing her fingers with such charm? . . . Well, that is the Citizen Ascanio Minato from Ajaccio, half-Italian, half-French, a compatriot of Bonaparte and *aide-de-camp* to General Baraguay d'Hilliers, and billeted by order of the Municipality in the Navagero house. As you can see, he is a handsome youth, slim and dark and well-built, full of wit, of pride and of health; he is brave, they say, to desperation and a better swordsman than Don Quixote. . . . Furthermore he has the uniform of a soldier, which often pleases women more than virtue. The old Navagero, who will not allow in his house the dandies and gallants of Venice, has had to put up without protest with this intruder from overseas. The poor old fool is afraid and rather than incur the suspicion of being thought aristocratic and francophobe, he would even be capable of letting . . . But enough! . . . There is a heroism of fear and it goes well enough with that senile and decrepit face, mottled with red and yellow like a parrot-tulip. The little Signora becomes more French every day; already she twitters half a dictionary like a Parisienne and I fear that the most interesting words have already found their way into her conversation. Of course, it is understood that the Corsican official does not deign to speak Italian! . . . Just think . . . But we have taken the measure of these liberators of ours! They have cancelled the *Pax Tibi Marce* from the book of the Lion to incorporate therein instead the Rights of Man. So much the worse for us who wanted it so! . . . But a thousand times worse for those who merely resign themselves to it! . . . Oh, one needs long sight for that . . .'

Till then I had let this spate of eloquence flow without hindrance, but when he set himself to mock so melancholy a hope and to desire from so great a public misfortune some revenge for his own essentially personal troubles, I felt a tempest of disdain swell within me and broke into an apostrophe that kept him rooted to the ground like a statue.

'And you would resign yourself to that?' I said to him with scornful wonder. I repeat, he stood there like a statue, save that he breathed with a difficulty that statues at least are spared. Indeed I too had experienced a fresh pang for this new exploit of the Pisana of which he had told me, but none the less, I swear there was no place in my heart for such a grief, so great had been my horror at Giulio's cynical outburst. I went on to rebuke him for his sacrilegious hopes and showed him that the most cowardly are not those who resign themselves so much as those who find their satisfaction in the vileness of others and the ruin of their country.

I became so eloquent that we were left there alone without my having noticed it; the rest of the company had followed the Beauharnais into the treasure chamber of San Marco whence they had to extract a magnificent collar of cameos and make her a present of it. When we went to join them, they had already come out on to the Piazza and were moving towards the Government Palace. You can hardly imagine my surprise when I saw among the people paying their court to the Frenchwoman, Raimondo Venchieredo, and, among the crowd, Leopardo Provedoni and his wife, who had also let themselves be drawn into the procession out of curiosity. But for that day the ceremony was over and I, leaving Del Ponte to his anger, greeted those two with the hearty welcome and the many 'ohs' of wonder and pleasure as are usual between old friends from the same country met in a foreign land.

Doretta's eyes were following Raimondo, who was disappearing into the atrium of the Palace with the most assiduous of the courtiers; Leopardo gripped me by the hand but had not the heart to smile. However, after he had seen his wife home, which was two rooms near the Ponte Storto, and was alone with me, he recovered a little of his self-confidence and told me the why and the how of their coming to Venice. The old Lord of Venchieredo seemed to have become very intimate with General Bonaparte in Milan and had accompanied him to Montebello at a secret interview with the Austrian Ministers and had then made a journey hot-foot from Milan to Gorizia, from Gorizia to Vienna and from Vienna once more to Milan, only to return once more to Vienna a little later. In the course of this last journey to and fro, through Lombardy, he had stopped at Venchieredo to see his son, and had ordered him to go at once to Venice where the forthcoming development of affairs would assure a great future for him. Leopardo had not liked this at all and had it not been for the entreaties of his wife, would have remained willingly enough in the Friuli. During this recital, the poor young man turned all colours and restrained his feelings only by a great effort. I noticed this and changed the subject by asking for news of our country and of our friends and acquaintances.

Talking thus and strolling through the streets and along the quays, he forgot his usual gloominess and almost forgot his own troubles; but I suffered for him, thinking of the moment when he would remember only too well. Meanwhile, he confirmed the reports of the very sad state into which the affairs of the Fratta family had fallen. The Captain and Monsignor no longer thought of anything but eating and poking the fire; the old servants, who had either died or been dismissed, had been succeeded by a gang of petty thieves who set themselves to pilfer the little that remained. There were no longer even enough casseroles or frying-pans for Monsignor's lunch. Faustina had married Gaetano, the serjeant at Venchieredo, who had been released from prison a short while before and, on leaving, had carried away or sold a good part of the household linen. The Captain and Monsignor squabbled almost as much about the shirts as about the poker; Signora Veronica used to mend them, tearing them away from the two of them. And the most ridiculous thing of all was that the old Sandracca used sometimes to get bitten by the bug of jealousy which created a third source of argument and altercation between him and the Canon. Otherwise, Fulgenzio was doing just as he pleased. Immediately after my departure he had bought a property belonging to the Frumier family near Portovecchio, and then had begun rounding it off by converting into mortgages the sums that he anticipated from the family of his patrons. For example, there was corn in the granary and from Venice they were shouting for money; if corn became cheap, he pretended to buy it with the sum that he should have sent to Venice and then, when commodities rose in price, he gained from its sale a good percentage for himself. If the price continued to fall, he would forget this fictional contract and the amount of the purchase became a loan out at interest from which he deducted seven, eight, or ten per cent. Thus he preserved the peace of his conscience, increasing immoderately the profits of his own position.

His sons were no longer sacristans or doorkeepers. Domenico was acting as a notary at Portogruaro while Girolamo was studying theology at the seminary. In the district it was foreseen that at one time or another Fulgenzio would become the castellan of Fratta or something very like it. The young Andreini, to whom Count Rinaldo had entrusted before leaving the general supervision of the affairs of the castle, had undertaken his task with such complaisance that it seemed as if he too had joined in the general chicanery. The Chaplain, poor devil, was even afraid of the sacristan and did not poke his nose into details; the Rector of Teglio, looked at askance in the parish for his harsh manner, had too many troubles in his own home to wish to meddle with other people's affairs. Already the diocese, after the coming of the French and the departure of Father Pendola (according to Leopardo he, too, must be in Venice) had been divided and subdivided into parties and gangs, for the accord patched together by the craft of the Reverend Father had not been very durable.

'Father Pendola in Venice!' I exclaimed. 'What has he come to do here? . . . It seems to me that this is neither the time nor the place for him.'

Leopardo sighed at my words and added in a low voice that if the signs did not lie it was only carrion that attracted crows. As he was saying this, we arrived at the Piazzetta where he, lifting his eyes, looked at that marvellous building, the Palace of the Doges, and tears began to flow down his cheeks.

'No, do not let us think of that!' he cried, crushing my arm with great force, 'we will have to think of that in its own good time.'

Then he went on to give me an account of things at his home; how his sister Bradamante had married Donato of Fossalta, and Bruto his brother and Sandro the miller, seized by a heroic frenzy, had enrolled in a French regiment. This news surprised me not a little, but as far as Sandro was concerned, I thought it would turn out well and that he would cut a good figure, and indeed events proved me to have been right. Bruto in my opinion got too overheated to make a perfect soldier and though handling arms would be to his taste, infantry drill would not suit him at all. Leopardo's words about the great sorrow of his father at this decision touched me deeply. The poor old man had lost his memory and the use of his legs and the affairs of the Commune went on in their own good way, as God willed. In other matters there was the usual hotch-potch; and this interregnum of all government, this confusion, this conflict of three or four jurisdictions, some impotent from age, others tyrannical from their arbitrary or military nature, all oppressed in their own way the people who implored in unison that one master should come to drive off these three or four who maltreated them without being either capable of, or interested in, defending them. Between City Municipalities, communal and legal assemblies, feudal tyranny and French military government, no one knew where to start to obtain a crumb of justice.

In this continual coming and going of rulers, private justice had considered it necessary to intervene; crimes of violence, fights and murders were of daily occurrence; the gallows worked overtime and knives did their best to do the same. Only where there was a General Staff billet was there perpetual feasting and good humour; there the officers luxuriated with the goods seized throughout the countryside and in the smaller places the rabble junketed in plenty with every gift of God, and the ladies kept the fashion by flirting with the gay and elegant Frenchmen.

What better way of being patriotic and liberal than making love? . . . It happened everywhere as at Venice; at first they looked at one another askance and ended by embracing one another as the best of friends.

The usual vices are go-betweens for every vileness and there were many who without having the incalculable temperament of the Pisana made the same sort of adjustments as she did with some Lieutenant of the line in order to escape from the troubles of that provisional period. I know that these were defects and cowardice inherited from their fathers and grandfathers but there is no need to pass over them as blameless just because they were inherited; one inherits scrofula also, which is certainly nothing to hold dear. As for democracy and the cult of reason, they were more than anything else protests put forward by fear and vanity; indeed those who danced around the Tree of Liberty were those who danced at the next carnival in the halls of the Ridotto, despite the Treaty of Campoformio and later dirtied their knees before the divinities of Austerlitz.

I believe that a popular festival more funereal and grotesque than the planting of the Tree of Liberty in the Piazza San Marco could not have been seen in the whole world. Behind the four drunkards and twenty maenads leaping about, could be heard the dragging of the French sabres on the pavements and the officials of the Municipality (I amongst them) stood silent and rigid on their loggias like those old corpses just disinterred who only wait a single puff of air to dissolve into dust. Leopardo accompanied me to this ceremony and bit his lips like a man in a fury. In a loggia opposite ours his wife was sitting near Raimondo and displaying all the Venetian affectations that she had learnt after a week's novitiate to add to those she already possessed.

The days passed, sad, monotonous, oppressive. My father had become drowsy like a Turk; he talked only with his servant and that only by blows and monosyllables, rarely smacked his pouch of doubloons and ceased to worry me with panegyrics about the Contarini. The Frumiers remained immured in their palace as if in fear of some plague-stricken air; only Agostino appeared now and again at the café on the Riva to recite aloud his Jacobin creed. He was among those who believed in the duration of the French rule and hoped to reacquire by force or favour at least some part of his vanished importance. Lucilio went from house to house like a shadow; one could see in him the doctor who no longer pays any heed either to his own life or that of others and continues to heal more by habit than by conviction that he is of some use to humanity. Leopardo became even more sullen and taciturn; his idleness ended by eating up his spirit. He made no show of his sorrows but contented himself by dying of them inch by inch. Raimondo and Doretta no longer paid any attention to him and became so brazen that they would indulge in scenes of jealousy under his very nose. He would hide his hand in his breast and draw it out again with nails deeply blood-stained and deep lines soon began to show on his handsome face. His only relief was to pour out to me not his own sorrows but the bitter recollections of lost felicity. Then he would break for a while his Carthusian silence; the words seemed like a song on those pure and fervent lips as he recalled those times with infinite sorrow and bitter pleasure, without a trace of hatred or rancour.

Summer was drawing to its close. Already the fiery Bocchesi of Perast had burnt, weeping, the last standard of St Mark. The Republic of Venice was dead, but its last embers still glowed on the remote horizons of life on the seacoasts of the Levant. Vidiman, Governor of Corfu, brother of the wisest and most generous of the men of the Municipality, delivered up his soul in pain at the continual oppressions of the French who had landed there as masters. The population, revolted by Venetian weakness, disdained to serve slaves; better directly the French, or whoever else might be, than the flaccid ineptitude of a hundred patricians. That which many centuries back was respected for its power, then venerated for its wisdom and then tolerated by custom, ultimately merited that disdain which is always the consequence of homage too long falsely enjoyed.

In the Municipality the same councils of despair created discord; Dandolo and Giuliani preached the universal republic, the latter without any regard to the suspicions of our allies. Vidiman counselled moderation, since history taught him that if there was ever salvation for new governments it lay in prudence and slow change. They shouted at each other in that hall of the Great Council where on other occasions the simple word of a patrician had decided the destinies of Italy. The greatest perplexity was mine, who had to give form to reports and mutual recriminations without scope and without end.

Finally the great news which had been whispered fearfully here and there, broke from the lips in words of true and certain despair. France had agreed by the Treaty of Campoformio that the Imperial troops should occupy Venice and the States of the Levant and the *terraferma* as far as the Adige, while she herself retained the Austrian lowlands and kept the provinces of Venetian Lombardy for the

Cisalpine Republic. The pact and the words were worthy of those who wrote them. Venice awoke once more shivering in her lethargy like those dying men who recover the clarity of their mind in the fatal moments of the death agony.

The Municipality sent envoys to the Directory, to Bonaparte, to be allowed to defend themselves. The phrase was quite in accordance with that other in the above-mentioned treaty in which the occupation of Venice was 'allowed'. To ask the executioner for arms to defend oneself against him was ingenuous beyond all belief. But the men of the Municipality knew their own impotence and in no way tried to delude themselves at the last. Bonaparte put their envoys in prison; those sent to Paris did not even arrive in time to recite their little comedy.

One morning, Villetard, with crocodile tears, came to announce in full session that Venice must sacrifice herself for the good of all Europe, that his heart wept at such a necessity but that she must submit with a brave heart; that the Cisalpine Republic offered fatherland, citizenship and even a site for a new Venice for however many sought refuge from this fresh slavery and that the monies of the public purse and the sale of public lands would serve to comfort their exile with a little ease.

The proud Italian temperament immediately reacted against this proposal. Weak, discordant, credulous, garrulous, incapable, yes: but venal, never! The whole assembly gave a shout of indignation, repulsed the ignoble offer and refused to approve what the French Republic had so cynically and barbarously permitted. It decided to place the whole question before the people, demanding of them the choice between slavery and liberty. The people voted in crowds and in silence; their vote was for liberty.

Then the Municipality dissolved and many left for exile whence some, Vidiman among them, never returned. Villetard wrote to Milan and Bonaparte replied, scoffing but furious. To allow oneself to be crushed and then not to obey is still a crime to tyrants.

In those days Serrurier, the real gravedigger of the Republic, entered the city. He dismantled the shipyards and sent guns, cordage, frigates and ships to Toulon, gave the finishing touch to the pillaging of the Public Treasury, the churches and the art galleries, scraped the gilding off the Bucentoro, made merry with what little remained and assured himself for ever from remorse at having left to the new masters the living value of a quattrino. Such was the respect shown to sworn alliances, to promised protection, to sacrifices imposed and basely perhaps rather than nobly accepted. So did they behave towards Venice who for so many centuries had defended all Christendom against the barbarities of the Moslems. But these pigs had not read history; they only prepared some horrible chapters for the historians of the future.

That same evening the Municipality laid down its authority, and those of us who had remained friends of liberty and courageous enemies of betrayal met at the usual house behind the Arsenal Bridge. The number was less than usual; some had not come because they were afraid and many had already left the city with various intentions. The session was more for mutual comfort and to shake one another by the hand than for deliberations. Agostino Frumier did not appear, though an hour earlier; he had given me his promise, speaking softly, to do so Barzoni was missing too, since after a public altercation with Villetard, he had embarked for Malta, intending to publish there an anti-French newspaper; I did not see Giulio del Ponte, and guessed the reason. Lucilio walked up and down as usual with unmoved face but with a storm in his heart. Amilcare shouted and gesticulated against the Directory, against Bonaparte, against everyone; he asserted that we must live for revenge. Ugo Foscolo sat in a corner with the first words of his Jacopo Ortis marked upon his brow. I for my part do not know what I felt in my heart or showed on my features. I felt absolutely nothing, like one who suffers without understanding why. I heard the majority decide in favour of seeking refuge on the territory of the Cisalpine Republic where there would always remain some hope for Venice; and I too found such a decision fitting, as it made exile honourable and active by accepting it in a fraternal and already almost Italian country. The peevish pride of some who would not deign to accept a hospitality offered in the name of France and guaranteed by France herself seemed out of place in those moments of supreme necessity.

We were offered the route to Milan where, either in the government or in the army, either by our words, our pens or our hands, we could hope to be of some use for our common salvation. The shocks and changes of fortune came in those days so close upon one another that hope budded anew in desperation itself, more confident and more unreasonable than ever. In any case we had to give an example of Venetian fortitude and dignity in face of the terrible accusations that had been hurled at us. Now one, now another departed to put his affairs in order or to collect some personal belongings before going into exile. One ran to embrace his mother, another his sister or his mistress, one crushed to his heart his innocent children, while another sorrowfully passed this last night contemplating from the edge of the Piazzetta the Palace of the Doges, the cupolas of San Marco, the Procuratie, those venerated and dishonoured relics of the ancient Queen of the Seas.

Tears flowed from these devoted eyes, the last tears to be freely given and gloriously commemorated.

I had remained alone with Doctor Lucilio since I had no longer the force to move, when we heard coming up the staircase the sound of hasty steps and Giulio del Ponte with the hue of death upon his face rushed into the room. The doctor, who had said very little up till then, turned to him with great vehemence to ask what was the matter with him and why he had come so late. Giulio did not reply; his eyes were wild, his tongue seemed to stick to the roof of his mouth and he seemed incapable of understanding what was said to him. Lucilio threw back with one hand his black hair, through which already glistened an occasional thread of silver, gripped the young man's arm and drew him by force into the circle of the lamp-light.

'Giulio, I will tell you what is the matter with you!' he said in a low but firm voice. 'You are dying for a personal sorrow of your own when it is no longer permissible to die save for the sorrow of us all! . . . You have basely surrendered yourself to the evil that consumes you, when you should be ascending with a strong spirit the path of martyrdom! . . . I am a doctor, Giulio, I do not want to deceive you. A passion composed of rage, of pride, of ambition is eating you up; its bite is poisonous and incurable. You will succumb without any doubt. But do you believe that the soul cannot exalt itself above the maladies of the body and prescribe for itself a great and glorious end?'

Giulio wildly mopped his eyes, his cheeks, his brow. He trembled from head to foot, coughed from time to time, but still could not utter a word.

'Do you think,' went on Lucilio, 'that beneath my hard and icy shell there are not hidden such torments that I would prefer hell, to say nothing of the grave, to the weariness of life? Very well, but I do not want to die bewailing my own lot, being sorry for myself and thinking only of myself like a sheep with its throat about to be cut! When the body has been consumed, the soul will fly thence freer, stronger, more blessed than ever! . . . Giulio, let your body die, but defend your immortal spirit against baseness and abjection!'

I looked with wonder at this tableau of two figures, one of which seemed to pour into the other life and courage. At the words, at the touch of the doctor, Giulio seemed to pull himself together and come alive again before our eyes; shame darkened his brow, but his spirit, newly awakened to a great sentiment, coloured the signs of his approaching death with a sublime splendour. He no longer coughed, he no longer trembled; the sweat of enthusiasm took the place of that of fever and though he still stuttered unfinished and confused words, this was only due to the impatience of repentance and generosity of feeling. It was a real miracle.

'You are right,' he replied at last in a deep and calm voice. 'I have been a coward until now; I will be so no longer. I must most certainly die, but I shall die bravely and my soul shall be saved from the ruin of my body! . . . I thank you, Lucilio! I came here by chance, by habit, in despair; I came desolate, humiliated, sick; I will leave with you, healed and in a becoming manner. Tell me where we have to go now; I am ready!'

'We shall leave tomorrow for Milan,' replied Lucilio, 'there will be a rifle for each of us; one does not ask of a soldier in these days whether he is sick or healthy but only if he has greatness of soul and of will! . . . Giulio, I assure you, you will not die trembling with fear and longing for life. Let us abandon together this century of fraud and poltroonery and take refuge contentedly in the bosom of eternity!'

'I too,' I exclaimed, 'I will come with you!'

I gripped the doctor's hand and threw my arms round Giulio's neck as round a brother's. I was so moved that I could see no fate better than dying at the side of such companions.

'No, for the moment you must not go,' said Lucilio gently. 'Your father has other plans for you; you must take counsel with him, since that is your duty. As for mine, just today I received the news of his death. You can see for yourselves that I am quite alone now, completely denuded of all those affections that enclose so great a part of our lives within family walls. For me the horizons grow ever wider before me; from the Alps to Sicily is all one house. I will inhabit it with one sentiment alone that will not die even with my own death.'

A memory of the convent of St Teresa passed, like a flash, across Lucilio's eyes as he pronounced these words, but it did not disturb the quiet tone of his voice or leave on his features any trace of melancholy or sorrow. Every anguish had vanished in that proud assurance of a spirit that felt in itself some part of the eternal. We separated then; the leavetakings were austere, without regrets and without tears. In our last words there was no mention of the names of Clara or the Pisana, even though for all three of us, even for Lucilio I am certain, an unhappy love tore at our vitals. They went towards the hospital, agreeing to set out the next morning at dawn; I hastened on my way, in search of my father. I did not know what his plans could be, for Lucilio had been unwilling to tell me more of them, but I was eager to learn them so as to unburden myself of my private sorrows by some great and not altogether useless sacrifice, as poor Giulio had shown me the way.

CHAPTER XIII

I DID not find my father at home, and the old Mohammedan woman expressed herself with so many signs and shakes of the head that I got the impression that she wanted to say that she did not even know when he would return. I thought to myself that I would wait for him, but she handed me a little note, making signs that it was a matter of very great importance. I thought perhaps it was some message from my father, but saw, instead, that it was from Leopardo. 'I did not find you at home,' he wrote, 'so am leaving you these few lines. I have need of you most urgently for a service which three hours from now you will no longer be able to render me.' There was no further explanation.

I tried to make the old woman understand as well as I could that I should come back soon, took my hat and rushed off at top speed to the Ponte Storto. The note had told me nothing at all; that very morning I had left Leopardo grave and taciturn as ever, but sane and reasonable. My heart warned me of some disaster and I wished I had wings on my feet to get there more rapidly. The gateway to the house was open and a rushlight was lying on the ground at the foot of the staircase. I went up to Leopardo's room and found him seated in an armchair with his usual serious expression but looking much paler. His eyes were fixed on the lamp but on my entrance he turned them towards me and without speaking made a sign of welcome. 'Thank you,' they seemed to say, 'that you have come in time!' I was frightened at his attitude and at his silence and asked him anxiously what was the matter and how I could help.

'You cannot help,' he replied, half-opening his lips like one who is trying to speak at the moment of falling asleep. 'I only want you to keep me company; excuse me if I do not talk much, but I am in great pain.'

'For God's sake let me call a doctor, then!' I exclaimed.

I knew that Leopardo was not in the habit of complaining about nothing and his nocturnal summons revived all my fears.

'A doctor,' he replied with a sad little smile. 'I must tell you, Carlino, that an hour ago I swallowed two grains of corrosive sublimate.'

I gave a cry of horror, but he put his fingers to his ears, saying: 'Quiet, quiet, Carlino! My wife is asleep there in the next room! . . . It would be a pity to disturb her, the more so as she is with child and her condition makes her irritable.'

'But for pity's sake, Leopardo, let me go . . .' but he gripped my wrist with all his remaining strength. 'Perhaps we may still be in time; a good emetic, a heroic remedy that I know of . . . let me, let me . . .'

'Carlino, it is all useless! The only favour I will accept from you is as I said, a last hour of your company. Resign yourself, since you see me even more than resigned, even desirous to be going; the emetic and the doctor would in any case come a good half hour too late; for a week past I have been studying the chapter on toxicology that was needful to me. Don't you see? These are the second symptoms! . . . I can feel my eyes protruding from my head. . . . If only the priest whom the portress went to look for arrives soon. . . . I am a Christian and I want to die according to the rites.'

'No, no, Leopardo, I beg you, let me try, if nothing else! It is impossible to let you die in this way! . . .'

'I want it so, Carlino, I want it; if you are my friend, you must grant me this favour. Sit near me and we shall finish it all in conversation, like Socrates.'

I knew then that there was nothing to hope for from so vast a tranquillity. I sat beside him, deploring this sad aberration that was destroying so miserably one of the finest souls I had ever known. The precaution of sending for a priest showed the disordered brain of a suicide, since he could not be unaware that the act he had committed was regarded by religion as a mortal sin. It seemed that he had guessed my thoughts, for he set himself to justify his action before I had even considered putting them into words.

'Isn't it true, Carlino, that this foible of mine for a confessor surprises you? But what will you? . . . By a lucky chance I had forgotten for many months past that God forbids suicide; but now I remember it, for it is really true that the approach of death aids the memory wonderfully. But, luckily, it is now too late! . . . It is too late! The Lord will punish me for this long forgetfulness but I hope He will not be too hard on me and that I shall be allowed a passage to Purgatory. I have suffered too much, Carlino, I have suffered so much in this life!'

'Oh, curses, curses, on the heads of those who forced you to so miserable an end! . . . Leopardo, I will avenge you; I swear to you that I will avenge you!'

'Quietly, quietly, my friend, don't wake my wife. She is sleeping. I exhort you, moreover, to forgive her, as I forgive her. I also name you the executor of my forgiveness so that no one shall have any harm from my death, and I charge you not to make it known that I caused it myself. It would be a great scandal and others would have to bear the discomfort and remorse of it. . . . I will arrange it all with the priest and so I hope to die in peace and to leave all in peace after me.'

'Oh, Leopardo, Leopardo! A soul like yours to die in this way! With all your goodness, all your strength and fortitude!'

'You are right! Two years ago I would not even have imagined such a thing! But now I have done it and there is no more to be said. The sorrows, the humiliations, the disillusionments have piled up here inside me,' he touched his chest, 'until one fine day the vessel overflowed and, farewell good judgement! I must express myself so in order to make my excuses before God.'

I could see then, or better, I could guess, the long torments of that poor heart, so honest and sincere, the anguish of that open and loyal nature so unworthily betrayed, the delicacy of that heroic soul determined to see nothing and to die without leaving to his assassins even the punishment of remorse. I did not breathe a word to him about this, out of respect for the wonderful restraint of the dying man. Leopardo went on talking in a voice deeper and more fatigued; his limbs were stiffening and his flesh took on little by little an ashen colour.

'Do you see, my friend? Up till yesterday I thought as you do and held out bravely. I had a country to love and hoped when the time came to serve it and to forget all the rest. Now that illusion too has vanished . . . that was the blow that decided me!'

'No, no, Leopardo, all hope has not vanished! Get well, return and live with us; we will bear our country in our hearts wherever we go, we will teach, we will propagate that holy faith! We are young, better times will smile for us! Let . . .'

I had risen to my feet, but he held me tightly by the arm with a convulsive force and I had to sit down again. A vague and melancholy smile passed over that face already overshadowed by death; never had the beauty of the soul a greater triumph over that of the body. The latter had quite disappeared, the former still breathed with all its splendour in that already corpse-like face.

'Stay, I tell you,' he said with a pitiful effort, 'in any case, it would be too late. Preserve, my friend, the purity of your faith; I commend you that, since it is, even if no more, a most powerful incentive to fine and honourable deeds. . . . As for me, I am going without regret. . . . I am sure that I would have waited in vain. I am tired . . . tired . . . tired . . .'

As he said this, his body relaxed and his head fell lolling on my shoulder. I was about to move and call for help, but he recovered himself sufficiently to realize my intention and forbid me.

'Can't you understand?' he murmured weakly, 'I want only you and the priest!'

I understood him only too well and turned a look full of hatred and disgust at the door behind which Doretta was sleeping peacefully. Then I put my arm around Leopardo's neck and, seeing that in this position his spasms seemed to grow less, forced myself to support his head in this way. Its weight upon my arm increased and I began trembling, I know not whether from fatigue or sorrow, when the portress returned with a priest. Having knocked in vain at the door of the parish priest, she had brought with her one whom she had chanced to meet by the way. He, at first reluctant, had decided to go with her when he heard that it was a question of a stroke, as Leopardo had himself told her. But what was my astonishment when, on lifting my eyes to look at the priest, I recognized Father Pendola! . . . The good Father too gave a start certainly not less than mine, and so we remained for a moment, since our surprise prevented any other movement. At this silence, Leopardo looked up painfully, but as soon as he realized who the priest was, he leapt to his feet as if bitten by a snake. The Father retreated a couple of steps and the portress in her fright let the lamp fall from her hand.

'I don't want him! Make him go away, make him go away at once!' shouted Leopardo, struggling in my arms like a madman.

The Reverend Father had the greatest desire to comply, but shame before the portress held him back and he wanted, at the worst, to save the honour of his cloth. But this was easier than he had feared, since Leopardo calmed down rapidly from his momentary fury and became once more gentle as a lamb. The good Father approached him tentatively and with an angelic smile, and began to utter words for the comfort of his soul in a thin voice that really seemed sincere.

'Reverend Father, I beg you to go away!' whispered Leopardo in a hollow and menacing voice.

'But, my dearest son, think of your soul, and think that you have but a few moments left and that, however unworthy a minister of the Lord, I can . . .'

'Better no one than you, Father,' Leopardo interrupted brusquely.

The portress, at this unedifying spectacle, had returned to her duties so that the prudent Father did not consider it necessary to insist. He bestowed his holy benediction and began to go out the way he had come. Leopardo stopped him in the doorway with a cry.

'A last reminder to you, Father, from the brink of the grave; a last spiritual reminder to you who are used to minister to the souls of others. You see the way I am dying: tranquil, gay, serene! . . . To die so, one must live as I have lived. You may long in vain for such good fortune and will pass into the other world trembling and panic-stricken as one who already feels in his flesh the claws of the devils! Good night, Father; at dawn I shall sleep more peacefully than you!'

But Father Pendola was already beating his retreat, making a gesture of horror and of pity; and I wager that once down the staircase he added many other gestures to express his intense pleasure at having escaped so cheaply. Leopardo thought no more of him and begged me urgently to go and fetch some other confessor. I placed little confidence in the portress and went out myself, hurrying to the door of the parish priest whom I routed out of bed and brought back with me to the bedside of the dying man. During my absence, he had grown so much worse that, had I seen him somewhere else, I should have had difficulty in recognizing him. However, the arrival of the priest comforted him a little and for a while I left them together. On re-entering I found him in the grip of the final phases of the death agony, but none the less calmer and more serene than ever.

'Then, my son, you have really repented of the very grave sin that you have committed?' the confessor repeated to him. 'You agree with me that you have despaired of Providence, that you have wanted to destroy by force the work of God and that it is not permitted to one of his creatures to make himself judge of His divine dispositions?'

'Yes, yes, Father,' replied Leopardo with a slight tinge of irony that he could not repress and that I alone perhaps discerned, since even the dying man himself could not have realized it.

'And you have done all in your power to prevent the effects of your crime?' the priest asked once again.

'We must resign ourselves,' said the dying man in a weak voice. 'There was no time . . . Father, two grains of sublimate are too powerful an expedient! . . .'

'Very well. The absolution that I have given you, God himself will confirm.'

And he began to repeat the prayers for the dying; he then administered the last sacraments and Leopardo composed himself to await death with the grave piety of a true Christian. Peace had returned to him, the solemn peace that precedes death; I could realize how great was the power of religion in that proud and manly soul and envied for the first time those sublime convictions denied to me for ever. The death of the old Countess of Fratta had put them in discredit with me; that of Leopardo made them once more seem sublime and worthy of veneration. It is true that the nature of that death was such as to be good proof in itself, with or without faith.

A little later he had an attack of very sharp pain, but it was the last; his breathing became more and more feeble and difficult, his eyes half closed as if in contemplation of an enchanting vision and his hand rose now and again as if to caress one of those angels who came to meet his soul. They were the golden fantasies of youth that wandered before him in the confused twilight of delirium; they were his most beautiful hopes, his most splendid dreams that took on visible forms and the features of reality to the eyes of the dying man; it was the reward of a virtuous and stainless life, or a foretaste of Paradise. At intervals he would fix his gaze smilingly on me and show that he recognized me; he took my hand in his to bring it close to his heart, that heart that was by now scarcely beating, but was still overflowing with courage and affection! There was a moment in which he seemed about to rise and I almost seemed to see him start upward in a majestic attitude of inspiration and of prophecy. He uttered proudly the name of Venice and then returned once more, as if exhausted, to his fantasies.

When he was near the final moment, I saw him open his lips in a smile such as had not for long past shone on that strong and noble face; he put his hand to his breast and drew out a locket on which he pressed his lips many times. Each kiss was slower and less intense, and finally he dropped the locket, smiling, to give up his soul to God. His last breath came so full and strong from his breast that it seemed to mean: 'Here I am at last, free and happy!' The relic, to which he had consecrated his last breath, fell into my hand at the slackening of his grip; I received it as a pledge, as a sacred heirloom, and knelt down by the dead man and before God. I had never seen a death like that. The priest sprinkled the corpse with holy water and went away wiping his eyes and assuring me that he would be granted Christian burial however much the canons of the church forbade. The sanctity of that passing commanded him not to pay too close attention to the rules. Then, as I remained alone, I could give vent to my sorrow. The lamp was at its last flicker, the first dim light of the day was seeping through the shutters when it occurred to me that I should have to tell Doretta of the death of her husband. The thought made me shudder. But none the less, I braced myself to knock at the door when I heard from behind it the sound of approaching steps; the door opened very softly and there appeared before me the face, a little pale and mistrustful, of Raimondo Venchieredo. I gave such a cry that it roused all the echoes in the house and rushed to put my arms around Leopardo as if to protect him or console him for this posthumous insult. Raimondo at first understood nothing, stammered I know not what about a gondola and Fusina and hastened to be gone. I learnt later that he had sent Leopardo to Fusina with orders to remain there all day to wait for his father who was due to arrive there, and to give him a most important letter.

Leopardo had left at the Ave Maria but realizing half way through his voyage that he had forgotten the letter, had returned to get it, arriving about three o'clock in the morning. He had then seen Raimondo enter his house stealthily and go to Doretta's room; the rest anyone can imagine. It is true, however, that he had obtained the sublimate from an apothecary that morning after having taken part in the session of the Municipality in which Villetard had pronounced his sentence of death against Venice. It seemed that this last infamy had done no more than hasten a decision already matured and taken for many motives. The letter directed to Venchieredo, in the handwriting of Father Pendola, was found in the drawer of his table.

But all this I did not know then, though I guessed something of the sort. Therefore I did not allow Raimondo to make his escape thus, without knowing anything of the tragedy of which he had been the cause. I ran to the doorway after him, seized him by the shoulders and dragged him trembling and half-kneeling before Leopardo's corpse.

'Look!' I said to him, 'traitor, look!'

He looked horror-stricken and only then became aware of the livid pallor of death covering those inanimate remains. To become aware and to utter a cry even louder than mine was but the work of a moment. The second cry brought the portress into the room, together with Doretta and all the other people in the house. Raimondo had come to his senses but could hardly stand on his feet; Doretta tore her hair and I know not if she screamed or wept, while the others looked with horror at the mournful sight and asked one another in low voices what had happened. It fell to me to lie, but this was not difficult since I thought thus to carry out scrupulously the last wishes of my friend. But though I could only ascribe Leopardo's death to a sudden stroke, the tone of my voice spoke otherwise. Raimondo and Doretta understood me and quailed before my accusing gaze with the shame of criminals. Then I left the house, intending to return later to accompany my friend to his last dwelling. What my feelings were I would not like to confess now. I looked with an inexpressible longing at the deep and turgid waters of the canals, but my father was waiting for me and there were other martyrs ready to invite me along the way to Milan to the hard expiation of exile.

My father had indeed been waiting for me for an hour and was impatient at not seeing me return. But I made my excuses, telling him of the terrible event. He cut the words short in my mouth, exclaiming: 'Mad, mad! Life is a treasure and one must use it well down to the last soldo!' I was rather sickened at such callousness, and had no wish to fall in with his desires as the partial confidences of Lucilio had persuaded me the previous evening. He, however, without letting me interrupt, came straight to the point.

'Carlino,' he asked me, 'tell me the truth; how much money a year do you need to live?'

'I was born with a good pair of arms,' I replied coldly, 'They will aid me!'

'Mad, mad, you too!' he replied. 'I too was born with arms and have made them work for me wonderfully, but I have never refused the good assistance of friendship. Take it as you like, but I am your father and I have the right to give you advice and even at times to command you. Don't look at me so haughtily! . . . There is no need! . . . I am sorry for you; you are young and you have lost control of yourself. I too spent all yesterday not knowing if I were alive or dead; I too have suffered, you see, more than anyone in the world, seeing all my hopes overthrown by those very people upon whom I had counted to see them accomplished. I too have wept, I have wept for rage, finding myself scorned and ridiculed and paid for seven years of services and sacrifices with ingratitude and betrayal. . . . But today, today I laugh at it! . . . I have great ideas in my mind which will keep me busy for months, perhaps for many years; I hope to succeed better than at this first experiment, and we shall see one another again. A man, you see, is a pretty weak animal, a future relative of nothingness! . . . but though he is nothing himself, he may become the first link of a chain upon which the whole depends . . . Pay attention to me, Carlino. . . . I am your father, I esteem you and even love you; you must accept the counsels of my experience and must reserve yourself for that future which I shall strive to prepare for you and for our country. Remember that you are not alone, that you have friends and relations in exile, impotent and in need, and that it will be pleasant for you sometimes to have a crust to share with them. Here in this wallet are certain millions that I am devoting to a great experiment of justice and of revenge; they were intended for you, but are now so no more. You see I speak openly and sincerely! Give me, therefore, equal trust and tell me how much you need to live reasonably for a year.'

I gave way under this urgent paternal logic and said that three hundred ducats would be more than sufficient for me.

'Bravo, my son!' replied my father. 'You are a fine man. Here is a letter of credit for seven thousand ducats on the house of Apostulos in San Zaccaria which you will consign this very day to their representative. You will find there excellent people, noble and loyal; an old man who is a pearl among honest merchants and who will be for you another father, like myself; a young man just returned from Greece who is worth twenty of us Venetians, a young girl whom you will love as a sister and a mother who will love you as a son. Have trust in them; through them you will have news of me, since I intend to embark before noon as I do not wish to see the infamy of this day. This house, which I have bought for two thousand ducats, I hand over to you; I have already registered the deed of gift. In that writing table you will find some documents that belonged to your mother. They are her heritage and will go to you direct. As to your future destiny, I give you no advice since you have no need of it. Others still trust to the French and are departing to the Cisalpine. Look after your own interests and do not let yourself be dazzled either by fortune or by wealth or by glory. There is glory only when one has a country; esteem fortune and wealth only when they are assured by liberty and justice.'

'Don't be afraid, father,' I said, greatly moved by these words which, even though expressed disjointedly in a jargon more Turkish than Venetian, were none the less noble. 'I will think always of Venice! . . . But why may I not go away with you and take part in your designs as a companion of your labours?'

'I will tell you, my son; you are not enough of a Turk to approve all my methods. I am like a surgeon who while he works does not want a crowd of silly women blubbering around him. I do not say this to insult you but, I repeat, you are not enough of a Turk. That is all the more honour to you. But it would lose me that freedom of action which alone gives speed to the things of this world. I am a man of sixty, Carlino, I must make haste! And even more, there are not enough strong and right-thinking young men like you in these lands; it is better that you remain here, if you are to act for us. Already in one corner or another the skein is getting tangled. At Ancona, at Naples, there is a fervour that is wonderful; when the fire spreads whoever touches it will be burnt; then it will be up to you, that is, to us. For that reason, I tell you to remain and let me go where old age can succeed better than youth and money has more power than strength of body or valour of spirit.'

'Father, what can I say? . . . I will remain. . . . But if I could at least know where you are going?'

'I am going to the Orient to come to an understanding with the Turks, since here I could not make myself understood. In a little while, even if you hear nothing of me, you will hear something of the Turks. Then you will know that I have a finger in the pie. More I cannot tell you, since all this is still fantasy and project.'

My father had to go to be in time for the Captain of the tartane that was leaving for the Levant. I accompanied him and could find out no more than that he was going directly to Constantinople where he might remain either a long or a short time according to circumstances.

Certainly his thoughts were neither petty nor base, since they even seemed to make him grow larger and gave him an air of authority unusual in him up till then. He wore his old berretta and breeches in the Armenian style, but a new fire shone under his white eyebrows. About nine o'clock he went on board the ship with his faithful servant woman and a small trunk; he did not give a sigh, left farewells for no one and took of his own free will the road to exile with the valour of a youth who has before him the certainty of a coming triumph. He kissed me as if we were to meet again the following day, advised me to visit the Apostulos and then went below, while I returned in the gondola that had taken me to the ship.

How alone, how miserable, how forsaken I felt when my foot once again touched the pavement of the Piazzetta! . . . My thoughts rushed with a sigh to the Pisana, but I stopped them half way with the thought of Giulio and the Corsican officer. It then remained to me to mourn the death of Leopardo and to honour his memory with the posthumous lamentations that make up the funeral elegy of a friend.

I wept and raved for a while until, to distract myself, I thought of the letter of credit and turned towards San Zaccaria for my interview with the Greek merchant. I found him a large-moustached, grey-haired man of very few words, who honoured my father's signature and asked me without more ado how I wished to be paid. I replied that I only wanted the interest from year to year and that I would willingly leave the capital in such safe hands. The old man gave a sort of grunt and a young man appeared to whom he gave the document, adding some words in Greek that I could not understand. He told me that the young man was his son and that I should go with him to the safe where the sum would be given me as I chose. But though the old merchant was rough and uncultivated, the son Spiridione, on the other hand, pleased me at once for his pleasant and polite manner. Tall and slender in figure, with a most striking modern Greek profile, a deep olive skin and two shining eyes, I liked him from the very first moment. I could discern a great soul behind those features and in my usual manner I loved him at once. He paid me out three hundred and fifty newly minted ducats and asked my pardon smilingly for the crabbed welcome his father had given me, adding that I should not be alarmed since he had spoken of me that same morning with every favour and that I would always be welcome at their house where I would find once again the peace and trust of a family. I thanked him for his kind words and said that it would be my greatest pleasure to visit them whenever by some strange chance I should find myself again in Venice. Thus we separated friends from then onwards, so it seemed to me, to the depths of our souls.

I dined that day, with what appetite you can imagine, in a little tavern where porters and gondoliers were discussing the withdrawal of the French and the coming of the Austrians. I had every opportunity deeply to lament the destiny of a people who, after fourteen centuries of liberty had not been able to preserve either a flash of judgement or a consciousness of their own existence. Perhaps that was due to the fact that they had not had real liberty and, accustomed to the rule of an oligarchy, they saw no reason to loathe the military dictatorship of foreign rule. For them it was all one. They had to serve, and discussed the humour of their masters and their wages and nothing else. Any less disinterested voice would have seemed out of place in that harmony and they might well have been afraid of listening to it, so well had the Inquisition of State trained them. I marvel that a single generation should have been able to change them so much and I bless either the unhoped-for consolations of Providence or the mysterious and sudden reactions of human nature.

After I had gone home, gloom and fear of solitude overcame me. I remember that I wept unrestrainedly at finding my father's pipe still full of ashes. I thought to myself that everything ended so, and an involuntary suspicion filled my heart that this might be an omen. In such a state of mind, poor Leopardo drew me to him with an irresistible force; indeed I passed the rest of the day by the bier where the pitying neighbours had laid him out. The portress told me that the gentleman's widow had gone away with her belongings, leaving eight ducats for the expenses of the funeral; and had told her before leaving that she had not the heart to remain an hour longer under the same roof with the inanimate remains of him she had loved so much.

'However,' said the portress, 'the Signora seemed extremely enraged that the handsome cavalier who was here that morning had not come to fetch her and she was also no little irritated with my little girl because she let one of her bonnets fall on the ground. I can hardly think that those are the signs of a great sorrow.'

I did not reply. I asked the woman not to put herself out on my account and since she persisted in her gossip I turned without ceremony to the dead man's bier. Then she left me alone and I could plunge at will into the gloomy abyss of my meditations. I said to myself the *mementòmo* of the first day of Lent; all things turn to ashes. Small and large, good and evil, ignorant and wise, all seem the same, in the end as in the beginning. That is the judgement of the eyes; but the mind? The mind is too venturesome, too proud to content itself with tangible reasons. The stupendous and sublime actions inspired by the Gospels, are they not the legitimate outcome of the thoughts, of the doctrine, of the soul of Christ? There is a divinity, an eternity in us that does not end in ashes. Did not the mute and cold Leopardo live in me, did he not still warm my heart with the fiery memory of his noble and vigorous nature? There is a spiritual life that passes from being to being and sees no limit to its future. The philosophers may find sounder and fuller comforts; I am satisfied with these and it is enough for me to believe that good is not evil nor life a momentary hole in the water.

Then, with these sad thoughts in my mind, I drew out of my pocket that locket that had fallen the day before from the hand of the dying man into my own and opening a slit fastened with a tiny button I drew out an image of the Madonna and a few withered flowers. It was like a wide horizon that opened before me, far, far away, filled with poetry, love and youth; between that horizon and me stretched the abyss of death but the mind passed over it without repulsion. Ghosts have no terrors to one who loves for ever. I remembered the simple and beautiful words of Leopardo, I saw once again the spring of Venchieredo and the graceful nymph who dipped one foot into it while with the other she stirred the surface of the water; I heard the nightingale intone his prelude and felt the harmony of love arise from two souls as from two instruments one of which echoes the melody of the other. I saw a splendour of happiness and of hope spread under the thick foliage of the alders and the willows. . . . Then my gaze turned from those remote imaginings to the real things around me; I trembled as I looked at the corpse that was sleeping before me. There was another happiness, but alas, how different!

Weariness overcame me and I slept for some hours on the same bed where Leopardo had gone to sleep for ever and my sleep was deep and tranquil as on the breast of a mother. Death seen from so near and in such guise has nothing horrible or disgusting about it; it seems a friend, cold and severe indeed but eternally faithful.

I rose to perform the last offices for my friend, to place him in his last bed and to accompany him on the silent waters to the island of San Michele. I envy the Venetian dead this posthumous voyage; if a far-away sense of life remains in them, as the American Poe believes, the gentle swaying of the gondola must come very sweetly to their deadened senses. On that narrow and desert shore, peopled only with crosses and sea-birds, a few shovelfuls of earth divided me for ever from those loved remains. I did not weep, so much was I turned to stone within myself like Dante's Ugolino; I returned in the same gondola that had carried the bier and the live man who returned seemed not then more alive than the dead man who remained.

Once more in Venice, I noticed a coming and going of curious crowds and greater movement than usual in the French garrison. I overheard someone say that the imperial commissioners had arrived to make arrangements for the handing over; they had been seen entering the Government Palace and the people crowded to see them come out again. I don't know for what reason I stopped, but at the worst I believe that I was seeking a fresh sorrow to distract me from my mood. A little later the Commissioners did indeed come out, with a great clatter of sabres and pomp of plumes. They were talking and laughing loudly with the French officers who accompanied them and thus, joking and laughing, they embarked on a barge sumptuously furnished by Serrurier to take them back to their camp. One alone separated from his companions in order to remain in Venice, and he was no other than the Signor of Venchieredo. Half an hour later I saw him again walking in the Piazza arm in arm with Father Pendola, but he no longer had sabre or plumes but was wearing a black coat cut in the French style. Raimondo and the Partistagno, whom I then saw in Venice for the first time, followed him with an air of triumph. The association of that last with such people displeased me not a little; not so much for him as because it was an indication of the great harvest that the cunning would know how to reap from the pliable natures of the ignorant. The blade does not think but is none the less a deadly instrument in an experienced hand.

I ended by running home, since I felt I could no longer contro myself and I confess that at that moment I was quite incapable of any deep thought. However much I had heard rumours of arrests, of condemnations and of proscriptions, I could not make up my mind to leave. I had fallen into that unthinking depression in which the nerves and the will fail to respond, when a thunderbolt striking one or a beam falling on one's head would seem as a gift from Heaven. Then only I remembered those papers belonging to my mother which I was to find in the writing desk, the pitiful heritage of an unfortunate to an orphan still more unfortunate. I tremblingly opened the drawer and taking out an old pasteboard envelope, set myself to skim through the many dusty and yellowish pages that it contained.

I scanned through one or two love-letters written in the Venetian manner and sprinkled with spelling mistakes. They were from a nobleman, perhaps long dead and buried with the ghosts of his loves; the name did not appear, but the nobility of his household was vouched for in many passages scattered here and there in that long correspondence. I might give you one or two extracts to show the manner in which one courted young ladies about the middle of last century.

It seemed that more serious matters were not committed to writing; instead the lover paid great attention to placing on show his own good qualities and describing the impression made on him by the good graces of the loved one in various circumstances; but however much he lacked delicacy he more than made up for it in ardour; above all, the letters diffused a charm of good faith, of calm, of goodness, which nowadays has been relegated to the letters which schoolboys write to their relations for Christmas. None the less, as you may well believe, their reading was not much in keeping with my mood on that day. I passed on. Other letters were from teachers and school-friends, more insipid than the first. I went on further. There followed the complete set of my father's love letters. They were foolish enough, and he seemed as deeply in love as any man could have been in this world; and his last note fixed the day and hour of that flight which my parents made to conceive me in the Levant.

With these letters I found a diary in the handwriting of my mother dated from many cities in the Levant and Asia Minor. There began her story. Her happiness had lasted until about half way through the voyage. Storms and seasickness for the rest of the voyage, the miseries and squabbles of their first pilgrimages and later, illness, overwork, and even hunger had considerably quenched the flames of love. None the less, she did not weary of following her husband, supporting his caprices patiently, together with his moods of indifference and above all of jealousy, which seemed unaccountable to her. He would remain absent for whole weeks from the places where he had confided his wife to the care of some poor Turkish family for whom she had to act as servant and cook in order to earn her keep. My father meanwhile wandered in the harems and the kiosks of the rich Moslems, doing business in brooches, little mirrors and other knick-knacks that he knew well how to sell at most incredible prices or so at least my mother, reduced to the limit of her resources, affirmed. One day it seemed that his fits of jealousy began again even more violently on account of her being with child. The accused was a witty *fellah* of the neighbourhood; my mother wrote words of fire about the injustice of her husband; it seemed that she suspected him of a premeditated system to weary her of life, to finish her completely or at least to force her to run away. Then her pride began to reassert itself; from laments and despair she became once more the noblewoman whose honour has been offended; more and more exasperation was displayed in these little notes set down on paper, day after day, with a furious hand; till finally they ended on an almost blank page whereon nothing was written save the three words: 'I have decided'.

So ended these records; but they were completed by a letter written by my mother to my father after she had made her decision. I cannot do less than report these few lines, which may serve to give a better indication of my mother's character. Ah me, why can I not speak of it at greater length? . . . Why has a son's love never had anything through all his life on which to base itself save this confused gleam of distant memories? Such is the destiny of orphans. Even now, at eighty years old, regret at never having been able to see in my memory the image of my mother still remains. The lips that do not recall the savour of your kisses grow dry more quickly in the noxious breezes of the air of the world.

'My husband' (so began the letter wherein she took farewell of my father for ever), 'I have wanted to love you, I have wanted to trust myself to you, I have wanted to follow you to the ends of the earth against the advice of my parents, who described you as a rogue without heart and without brain. Was I right or wrong? Your conscience will tell you. I, for my part, know that I can no longer support suspicions that dishonour me and that the child in my womb must not be imposed by force upon a father who disowns it. I have been a vain and frivolous woman; love of you has made me pay deeply for these faults of mine. I resign myself with fortitude to make a fuller repentance. In all, I have but twenty ducats; I will do everything possible to return to Venice, where I shall find awaiting me only shame and disdain. But once my little one has been consigned to its relatives, who will not have the heart to disown it, God may make of me what he wills! You will be away another week; on returning, you will no longer find me. Of that I am sure. Everything else is in the hands of God!'

The letter was dated from Bagdad. From Bagdad to Venice, over four thousand miles of desert and sea, in a suffocating time of year, with little knowledge of the language, with a body broken by fasting and passion, I can see once more in thought my poor mother.

She set out with twenty ducats in her pocket from the home of a suspicious and brutal husband; she made her way, through a voyage of perils and hardships, to the rebuffs and shame that awaited her in her own country. A devoted and loving wife, she would be counted with the women of easy virtue and it would be lucky for her if someone amongst her relatives would be generous enough to take her little son from the streets! . . . Ah me! It was because of me that she had suffered so much infamy, so many hardships. I felt almost resentful at having been born; I felt that a very long life, all consecrated to consoling her, to make blessed that holy soul, could scarcely have sufficed to appease my heart; and I have neither seen her face, nor smiled at her glances nor sucked a single drop of her milk! . . . By my birth I had set her upon the road to perdition; I had abandoned her there without help and without comfort. I almost detested my father and thanked God that he had gone away and that a long space of time must elapse between the reading of these pages and the first moment when I should see him again. Otherwise I could not foresee what would be the result of this battle of my affections. Some reproach, some curse would surely have escaped my lips!

Oh how I wept that day! . . . Oh how I plucked eagerly at the relief, not merely permitted, but sacred and noble, of filial love, in order to lessen by my tears the infinite burden of my sorrows! . . . There united strangely in the anguish that overflowed my soul in cries and sobs, my country sold to slavery, my friend dead by his own hand, my loved one faithless and forsworn and the face of my mother with the sufferings of her life still imprinted on her features! . . . Oh how furiously and terribly I raged against all those who had sought to defame her memory and take from me by sacrilegious calumnies that respect that I owed to her! . . . Yes, I wanted them to be calumnies at all costs; for they are always calumnies, those accusations against the poor dead, the accusations without proof and without shame hurled against a tomb. Did those who so eagerly believed and exaggerated my mother's faults know of her sacrifices, her torments, her tears and the long martyrdom that had perhaps exhausted her strength and overset her reason? . . . I tore at my breast, raging at my impotence to rise in vengeance against those cowardly slanderers; the silence maintained throughout my childhood by this furtive malice gnawed at me like the memory of a crime. Why had I not risen to wipe out her shame with all the courage of innocence and the vehemence of a son who feels himself insulted in the memory of his mother? Why had not my little eyes flashed with disdain and my heart refused to accept the charity of those who had made me pay the price of infamy for a crust of bread and a grudging hospitality? The blush of shame flooded my cheeks; I would have given my blood, my very life to have once more one of those days to revenge myself for so dishonourable a servitude.

But it was now too late. They had instilled into me as one might say with my milk, patience, fear and I would almost say hypocrisy, the three cardinal sins of beggars. I had grown up meek; my temperament, softened by submission, looked only for pretexts to yield and masters to obey. Then I realized all the dangers of letting oneself be moulded by the opinions and affections of others. I resolved for the first time to be myself, none other than myself. Could I have succeeded in such a resolution? Sometimes yes, but more often no. Reason is not always prepared to pull in an opposite direction to instinct; sometimes it is an ignorant accomplice, at other times it even maliciously allies itself with the stronger party; then we believe ourselves strong and commit base actions that are the more despicable the more they are unknown to or safe from the censure of the world. There is no remedy or hope. In the nature of the young there remains enclosed the compendium, the theme of an entire life; thus I never tire of repeating: 'Oh you who are governors of the people, you minds confident of the future, souls kindled with love, faith and hope, return to innocence and take heed of the young! There lies faith, humanity and love of country.'

The inventory of my mother's heritage ended here; but between my mother's last letter and the pasteboard of the envelope I found some pages with a number of lines evidently written recently. They bore, indeed, the date of only two days before and were in the handwriting of my father. I cannot conceal that I looked at them almost with repulsion and it seemed to me that they would burn my fingers. However, after I had calmed down, I read as follows:—

'My son, all that you have read of your mother I could have concealed from you for ever; you may thank me for having re-established her in your esteem though perhaps at the loss of that esteem which I have been able to inspire in you. I have seen that you have need of consolation and I have wanted to leave you such, even at the cost of paying dearly for it. I married your mother for love, that I cannot deny; but I believe that I was not made for that sort of passion and so love was extinguished only too quickly in my mind. My departure for the Levant, my trials and my voyages there, were intended for quite a different aim; in a few words, I wanted to make millions and that aim I subsequently achieved. But my temper was soured and the cruelty with which I tyrannized over myself, reducing my needs to the barest necessities, she believed to be a method expressly thought out to make a martyr of her. My continual absences and my preoccupation with that great design which was always whirling in my head, provided excuses for altercations and continual quarrels. She ended by finding herself very satisfied with any company, Turkish or renegade, so long as it was not mine. Often, on returning home, I would hear her high-pitched Venetian laughter echoing from behind the shutters; but my presence brought back anger, blows and tears. With one *fellah* above all, my wife forgot easily enough her morose and absent husband.

'Then transpired what often happens in temperaments none too generous nor sufficiently sincere. I became jealous; but perhaps in the depths of my being I perceived that my jealousy was only a pretext to give so much pain to my wife that she would be forced to leave me. I swear to you that I awaited with impatience some scene of despair on her part and a direct demand to return to Venice. But I was very far from suspecting her flight. She was timid, delicate and more prone to talk than to act. Her unexpected departure took me by surprise and grieved me not a little; but I had been then in Persia and did not return until a month later when it was no longer possible even to try and catch her up.

'Having got the idea of enriching myself even more fixed in my mind, all the thoughts that turned me from this project I regarded as enemies; you will know already, or at least it will be easy for you to understand, that state of our minds in which we pretend to believe true and excellent those ideas that please us; and by force of habit we indeed believe them so in the end. To repress the remorse that worried me, I persuaded myself that my jealousy was not without good cause and that I was not responsible for my wife being with child. I so accustomed myself to this convenient opinion that I gave no further thought either to her or to the child that would be born of her.

'I learnt that, for good or ill, she had reached Venice and, glad that I was finally rid of a bond that irked me, I gave myself up entirely and with even greater pertinacity to my trading. Only while returning to my own country with the dreamed-of millions already converted into beautiful *zecchini* and great doubloons as the result of my self-denial, did I have time to look, for diversion, at the papers left me by your mother. A sea trip of forty-two days gave me time to think things over at length. Therefore, on disembarking at Venice, I saw you with a certain pleasure and the suspicions that I had had concerning your birth were dispelled. But what will you? I convinced myself with difficulty. I felt I was caught in my own trap and acted like those silly fellows who, after having concealed a crime for twenty years, rush to confess it to a judge and get themselves hanged. I marvelled, and will always marvel that my Levantine morals should have allowed me this damaging confession. It is true that I was accustomed to deal with Turks and Armenians like beasts and to swindle and ruin them unscrupulously; but I had never dug my claws into Christian flesh and your mother, whatever her sister the Contessa may say, was a better Christian than any amongst us.

'Perhaps also my own interests helped me to reconsider my unjust suspicions. The resurrection of the house of Altoviti had become allied little by little in my mind with the resurrection of Venice and I hoped, as they say, to kill two birds with one stone. I had busied myself at Constantinople with inducing the Turks to break away from the Holy Alliance and to divert its forces from Germany and Italy. Having succeeded, if no more, in holding them in the balance, I had some credit with the French who were then believed, at a distance, to be the regenerators of the world. With the favour of the French and with the assistance of some internal conspirators who were even in advance of me in their Oriental intrigues, with my own perspicacity and with my millions, I had hoped to influence affairs in such a way that one day or another the destinies of the Republic would be in my hands. Do I frighten you? . . . None the less, it nearly came off; only the Republic was lacking. Also I discovered that I was rather too old for this, and therein I can claim a certain merit! . . . I could tell you that, having realized that I was an old man as soon as I met you, it was a good motive that induced me to right the wrongs I had committed. But however that may be, I willingly leave obscure those deeper motives for my actions and will not make a show of virtues that are more dubious than sure. I saw you, I embraced you, I took you for my true and legitimate son and loved you with all the heart that I have and gave you your place in my ambitions. Intimacy with you added strength and sweetness to such feelings and by that which I now write it seems to me that I am giving you a proof that I am really your father.

'At the point of returning to my old adventurous life, full of perils, to go on following that dream that has escaped me just at the moment when I thought to have held it in my hands, I do not wish to pass over as a trifle the ties of blood that unite us. I have a great revenge to accomplish and I will try to carry it out with every means that fortune has placed at my disposal, but once this great act of justice has been accomplished it will be your task to reap its honours and its fruit. For this reason, I have wanted you to remain, over and above the other reasons of which I have already told you. You must remain under the eyes of your fellow citizens to bespeak their affections and their esteem. Remain, remain, my son! The fire of youth is germinating among all men from Venice to Naples; whoever thinks to profit by it for his own advantage might well experience a great shock. So at least I trust will be the case. Were it for me to point out a suitable spot for you I would choose Ancona or Milan, but you will be a better judge than I, according to circumstances. Moreover you have taken the measure of those chattering Frenchmen; turn their own arts against them, use them to your advantage as they use us merely for their own convenience. Think always of Venice, of that Venice when Venetians ruled her.

'Now nothing is hidden from you; you can pass judgement on me as you please, since if I did not make this confession to you by word of mouth it was simply because I was the father and you the son. I have not wanted to defend myself, I have wanted only to tell how things were; I see that I have been philosophizing more than was necessary to explain both my good and my evil feelings. Judge me then, but give credit for my sincerity and do not forget that if your mother were in this world she would be pleased to see you a kind and loving son.'

Having read through this long letter, so different from the usual taciturnity of my father and in which his nature was so entirely revealed with all its great gifts and all its many faults and with the remarkable acumen of his talent, I remained for some time plunged in thought. Finally I had the inspiration to raise my thoughts to the plane of things holy and eternal; I found there inscribed in indelible characters that most worthy of God's commandments: 'Honour thy father and thy mother'. This double affection cannot be divided and to honour my mother implied in itself to pardon him whom she would certainly have pardoned, seeing him contrite and penitent for his perverse and devious ways. That hard and savage, yet tenacious and straightforward character of my father had a certain influence over me; the small are always disposed to admire the great and when impelled by duty their admiration transcends all measure.

I thought, I thought and spontaneously yielded all my heart to him who alone called me by the sacred right of blood. What were those new designs that had called him back to the Levant I could not even imagine. In all, I put my trust in him; waiting to see him whenever some great event should happen, and though he had been deceived by the same delusion as we had been, I esteemed him so superior by his broadness of view and force of will, that I could not think of him so deluded and discomfited for a second time. Then I was still young; not even sorrow had blunted hope, which still held its ground in the midst of my discomforts, trepidation and anguish of soul.

Having somewhat returned to myself after this inner searching of my emotions, I dined on a crust of bread that I found in a cupboard and went out after nightfall to look for Agostino Frumier if he were still in Venice in order to make arrangements with him about our departure. The truth is that a deeper and more shameful reason of which I cannot speak provided a pretext for this delay; but it is true that, having set out to go to the Frumier mansion, I wandered without noticing as far as the Campo of Santa Maria Zobenigo where the Navagero palace was. Once there I repented of my action, but could not prevent myself stopping and looking at all the windows and even descended to the ferry to see the palace from the Grand Canal side. The shutters were closed throughout and I could not even glimpse if there were light or darkness in the rooms. Very slowly and with dragging feet I turned with an ill will towards the Frumier house, where I was told that His Excellency Agostino was in the country. A week before the servant would not have dared to pronounce this title aloud; but the nobility were once more in the ascendant. I did not worry unduly about this, but the sudden 'weather-cocking' displeased me though later I had ample time to grow accustomed to it.

'In the country!' I exclaimed with considerable incredulity.

'Yes, in the country near Treviso,' replied the servant, 'and he has left word that he will return next week.'

'And the nobleman Alfonso?' I asked.

'He has gone to bed these two hours.'

'And the Signor Senator?'

'Asleep . . . they are all asleep.'

'Good night,' I concluded.

And with these words I set at rest all the thoughts, all the fears that had been stirring in my mind. The better part, the more civilized and sensible part of the Venetian patriciate would pretend to be asleep; the others . . . God preserve me from them! . . . I did not feel it my place to apportion the blame.

What was sure was that, the following week, on the establishment of the Imperial Government in Venice, Francesco Pesaro, the unshakeable citizen, the admirer of the Swiss, the Attilius Regulus of the fallen Republic, took the oath of allegiance; I note it here, so that names at least shall not veil actions. I went on, meanwhile, with my moonlight walk. Patrols of the arsenal workers, of the Municipal Guards and of French soldiers met shoulder to shoulder in the narrow *calles* and avoided one another as if plague-stricken and each went about his business. The business of the French was to embark all that they could of the riches of the Venetians on the boats due to sail for Toulon. To console us their leaders said: 'Be quiet! This is a strategic move! We shall soon return!' But for all that they so debased themselves that few still desired their return. The people, betrayed, abused, despoiled with impunity, took refuge in their houses to weep and in their churches to pray; and whereas at one time they had prayed God to keep the devil far from them, now they implored Him to send the French to the devil.

The common people yielded in surrender to the lesser evil nor need one expect more from those who feel rather than think. Of the good they had lost they expected to be able to save at least something; liberty is precious, but for working people the security of work, and peace in abundance, are also not things to be thrown away lightly. It is a grave mistake to expect similar views from men at a different stage of culture; as, too, it is a gross and ruinous error of politicians to rely upon this fallible pretension for their plots and their ordinances.

From the Frumiers I went to look for the Apostulos, for solitude made me think and I had no great wish to think. There I found enough to help me waste a couple of hours; I wager, too, that I never expected to waste them so pleasantly. The old Greek banker was still in his workroom; around a brazier in the Spanish style were his old wife, a truly matriarchal figure, with a fine pair of spectacles on her nose and the Lives of the Saints on her knees, a lovely girl clothed in dark colours, all charm and grace, and all Greek from the roots of her hair to her saucy little Morean sandals, who was embroidering an altar cloth, and finally the sympathetic Spiro, who was examining his nails. The two last leapt to their feet at my arrival and the old woman looked at me in a dignified manner over her spectacles. The young man introduced me formally to his mother and his sister, Aglaura, and I became a fourth in the conversation.

A discussion between Greeks could not be carried on without four pipe-stems; they offered one to me that seemed to stretch right out of the room, but since settling in Venice I had also mastered this most important art of modern life and so was able to play my part without disgracing myself. I had quite other wishes than to smoke and in my distraction several mouthfuls got into my lungs.

'What do you think of Venice? What have you been doing today?' Spiro asked me to get the conversation moving.

'Venice seems to me a tomb where the gravediggers are rifling the corpse,' I replied.

And as for what I had been doing, I told him of my friend who was dead and of the last sad offices I had had to carry out for him.

'I heard talk of it in the Piazza,' said Spiro. 'They said he poisoned himself out of patriotic despair.'

'He certainly had the spirit to despair thus nobly,' I replied without directly assenting.

'But do you think that such are acts of real courage?' he asked me.

'I don't know,' I said. 'Those who do not kill themselves say that it is not courage, but it is in their interest to say so and furthermore they have never tried it. For my part I believe that, even as to live well, so also to die by one's own will, needs a good dose of courage.'

'Yes, that too is courage,' replied Spiro, 'but it is a blind courage and badly conceived. For me, true courage is that which reasons on the value of its own sacrifices. For example I do not call courage the fall of a rock from the top of a mountain which shatters into fragments at the bottom of the valley. That is obedience to physical laws, it is necessity.

'I do not know if I believe that, but I hold, none the less, that a man would not really be strong and courageous who kills himself today uselessly, when tomorrow his sacrifice might be of value. When all the human race will be free and happy, then it would be incontestible heroism to take one's own life. You can cite me the unique case of Sardanapalus but again I would reply that Camillus was the greater man and more courageous than Sardanapalus.'

The old woman closed her Lives of the Saints and the dark Aglaura listened to her brother's words, looking sullenly at him with her hand resting on her embroidery. I glanced stealthily at the young girl, since this hard and disdainful attitude piqued my curiosity; but her mother intervened to change the conversation from this tragic subject and Aglaura went back to passing her needle through the beautiful purple cloth.

We talked then of the news in everyone's mouth, of the coming withdrawal of the French and the entry of the Imperialists into Venice, of the peace so gloriously hoped for and so despotically imposed; in short, we talked of everything and the two women took part in the conversation without vanity and without affectation and with a well considered discretion that Venetian women seldom know how to employ, even less so then than now. Aglaura seemed very worked up against the French and let no occasion slip to call them assassins, faithless and merchants of human flesh. But I learnt later that the flight of her lover after the new order of the State, following the Treaty of Campoformio, had made her youthful Greek blood boil in her veins and made her extravagant in her accusations. The day before she had been on the point of killing herself, but her brother had stopped her, hurling into the canal a little phial of arsenic already prepared; therefore she looked at him so sullenly; but in her heart of hearts and perhaps also out of regard for her mother, she was not dissatisfied that he had prevented her action. And so, even if she was still maturing some extravagant decision in her heart, at least that one of killing herself no longer plagued her.

When it was midnight, I took my leave of the Apostulos and returned home, turning over in my mind Spiro, Aglaura and the Lives of the Saints, everything in fact save the steps I should have to take concerning my own future destiny.

CHAPTER XIV

THE next day, I am not ashamed to say, I spent all morning wandering about Santa Maria Zobenigo, and I wondered not a little to see all the windows of the Navagero Palace tightly closed. It is true that a couple of times I ran across the Lieutenant from Ajaccio, who seemed in a great state of mind; but this gave me no comfort, however much the restlessness and ill-humour of Signor Minato seemed a good omen for me. None the less I went back to my lair with the greatest discomfiture to think that even if the French were leaving, he was not leaving and that, furthermore, in addition to the obstacle of a husband, I would have against me this other enormity of the Pisana. At that moment neither the reading of the Encyclopaedists nor the passion for liberty was a sufficient excuse for her sudden infatuation for some youth in uniform. I shut myself in the house and then in my own room, to gnaw, as if fasting, a crust of mouldy bread; those days I had become as thin as a rail, but not even hunger induced me to capitulate. Thus, on the surface of my mind, was a flood of patriotic indignation, of funeral elegies and vague designs; had one looked beneath, one would have found my thoughts of sixteen years ago as vigilant and tenacious as sentries. As to going far away from the Pisana, for God knew how long, without being able to see her, to speak to her, to help her with my advice against the dangers that surrounded her, this dismayed me so much that I preferred to risk my neck in order to remain.

Indeed the risks that I ran, by remaining after the withdrawal of the French, served to bolster up my conscience which from time to time reminded me of those who were awaiting me in Milan. However, already there were skirmishes in my spirit preceding a coming conflict. My father's words resounded in my ears and I could see from afar Lucilio's severe and penetrating glance. . . . Ah me! I think that fear of that alone made me run to look at my trunks, but just as I was dusting them off and had lit a light to see in the darkness of the rooms, there was a violent peal at the bell.

'Who can that be?' I thought.

The buli of the Inquisitors, the French security guards and the Austrian scouts all mingled confusedly in my imagination. I preferred to go down the stairs myself rather than pull the entry cord, and through the cracks of the door I shouted loudly: 'Who's there?'

A woman's tremulous voice replied:

'It is I. Open the door, Carlino!'

Despite the tremor in her voice I knew her at once and hastened to open the door with so deep an anguish in my breast that I could scarcely control myself. The Pisana, dressed in black, with her lovely eyes reddened by indignation and tears, her hair in disorder and only a taffeta shawl on her head, threw herself into my arms, crying out to me to save her. Believing that she had been insulted in the street, I was just about to leap out of the door to avenge her against whomsoever it might be, when she stopped me, holding my arm and then, leaning on it, led me to the staircase and up to the reception room as if she knew intimately all the nooks and crannies of the house even though, or so I believed, she had never set foot in it before. When we had sat down facing one another on my father's Turkish divan and her heavy breathing had calmed down, I could not refrain from asking her point blank what this disorder, this trembling and this sudden appearance meant.

'What does it mean?' replied the Pisana in an angry voice that seemed to rattle against her teeth before it left her lips. 'I will tell you what it means! I have left my husband, I am tired of my mother, I have been renounced by my relatives. I have come to stay with you! . . .'

'Mercy!'

That really was my exclamation; I remember it exactly. I also remember that the Pisana was in no way offended and did not abate a jot of her resolution. As for me, I do not wonder that such a violent change of outlook threw me into a painful confusion, greater at that moment than any joy or any fear. However that may be, I felt myself so overwhelmed and astounded that I felt a sort of constriction in my throat and only after some moments did I come to myself sufficiently to ask the Pisana how I could be in any way useful to her.

'Well!' she said. 'You already know that now and again I am too sincere, even as at others I am rather too much of a liar and secretive and reserved by habit. Today I can hide nothing from you; my whole soul is at the tip of my tongue and it is a good thing for you that you know me so well. I got married to spite you and to please my mother, but that was a revenge and a sacrifice that quickly became wearisome and with my temperament I cannot love a decrepit, dissipated and jealous husband for twenty-four hours a day. . . . Furthermore, my soul was overflowing with love for my country and the passion for liberty, while all my husband could do was to come to me coughing and preaching calm and moderation since one never knew how things would turn out! . . . I was pleased enough at first to see my mother relishing with gusto the ragouts of the Navagero Palace and squandering the *zecchini* of her son-in-law at *bassetta*;

but a little later I was ashamed of what had at first pleased me and between my mother and all those other old freaks, charlatans and wiseacres who were always around me, I felt like a sheep among wolves. I was tired, Carlino, I was so tired that a hundred times I was on the point of writing to you and forgetting all my pride, but I held back . . . I held back for fear of a rebuff . . .'

'How could you ever think it?' I exclaimed. 'A rebuff from me? How could you even imagine it!'

As you can see, while the Pisana had been talking, I had sought and at last found the thread to enable me to find my way out of the labyrinth; that I must love her, love her above all, without trying to probe too deeply and without passing through the alembic of reason the eternal desire of the heart.

'Yes, I was afraid of a rebuff, since I had never led you to expect any pledge of my exemplary conduct,' she said, 'but now I want to give you one and lay bare all my little wounds until you are thoroughly disgusted with them, if I can.'

I shook my head, smiling at this fresh fear. She began arranging the hair on her forehead and readjusting some brooch or other on her blouse that had become insecure. Then she went on:

'Just then there was billeted on my husband a French officer a certain Ascanio Minato . . .'

'I know him . . .' I said.

'Ah! So you know him? . . . Well, you cannot say he is not a handsome youth, of manly and noble appearance, though I later found him, at the critical moment, to be treacherous, faithless and disloyal, a real goose-head and rabbit-heart . . .'

I listened with some uneasiness to this string of insults which, in my opinion, explained only too well the truth of what Giulio del Ponte had told me the day of the ceremonies for the Beauharnais. The Pisana was not afraid to confess brazenly her own feelings and did not seem to notice the pain that her importunate sincerity was giving me. I bit my lips, gnawed my fingernails and reproached Providence that it had not made me as deaf as Martino.

'Yes,' she went on, 'I repent and am ashamed of that little trust that I reposed in him; I had always thought that the Corsicans were spirited and valiant, but I see that Rousseau was wrong to expect from their breed some great example of strength and civic wisdom! . . .'

'Rousseau, Rousseau . . .' I thought to myself.

These philippics and these quotations irritated me and I should have liked to get to the end of the story and to know everything without dotting so many i's and crossing so many t's; therefore I settled myself on the cushions and shuffled my feet, rather in the manner of a boy who has got bored with a sermon.

'What did I ask of him? What did I want from him?' the Pisana went on with even greater energy, 'Were those wishes so abnormal or impossible or base? . . . I asked him nothing else than to make himself the benefactor of humanity, the Timoleon of my country! . . . I wanted to make him the idol, the father, the saviour of a whole people; and in addition to this gift I promised him all my heart, all that he might want from me! . . . Coward, rogue! . . . And he knelt before me and swore and forswore that he loved me more than his own life, more than God Himself! What did he think? That I would give myself to the first man who came, for his fine eyes and his broad shoulders? . . . Let him be satisfied now, when he bears on his face the marks of a woman's blows! Since there are no men to do it, it is up to us women!'

'Calm yourself, Pisana, calm yourself!' I began to say, still uncertain whether I had properly understood her. 'Tell me all as it happened; tell me why you are so angry with Signor Minato, what he asked of you and what you, on your side, expected of him.'

'What did he ask me? . . . That we should make love together under the eyes of a jealous old man who would have pretended to be asleep out of too much respect for the French fury. . . . What did I expect of him? I expected that he should persuade, should stir up his fellows in arms to an act of solemn justice, to offer alliance in place of the faithless concessions of the Directory and Bonaparte, to join with us to defend Venice against those who tomorrow will become her masters without striking a blow! . . . Any one of them, even the most beardless, even the most chicken-hearted, would have done it without other persuasion than the right of conscience and the hatred of unjust and disloyal commands. . . . Should not one who loves a woman and hears her urging him on to noble deeds, do even more? . . . Should he not adopt the country of that woman and repudiate his own that was shamefully guilty of such misdeeds? . . . Should not every Frenchman who heard such exhortations from the lips of her whom he had sworn to love, lift his visor like Coriolanus and declare eternal hatred and rush furiously against that Medea who devours her own children? . . . Manlius condemned his own son to death, Brutus killed his own father. Those are examples for those who have heart and strength to imitate them! . . .'

I confess I would not have had heart and strength enough to withstand a tirade as violent as that of the Pisana; but I had heart and intellect enough to understand her, while admiring above all those proud motives of an ardent and noble nature, but I repented that at first I had so misjudged her. The epithets that she had hurled at the tepid and sluggish republican I had thought addressed to a weak and unfaithful lover. Thus at times one gets hold of the wrong end of the stick and neglects the general characteristics of a temperament in order to seize on one point only.

'Tell me, tell me,' I said, 'how you came to this outburst against him and everyone?'

'It happened because time was pressing and because for some little while he had been leading me on from day to day with certain smiles of his and with airs and graces that in no way reassured me, perhaps believing that I would drape myself *alla Romana* in order to make him still more enamoured and that finally I would have granted him everything for his sweet words! . . . Oh, now I can see him! And I am indeed glad that this Italian bastard has come to know a real Italian woman! . . . You know that yesterday already the Imperial Commissioners came to discuss the form of the transfer of authority; therefore I found myself forced to action and I began to press him, the more so as he was becoming more ardent than ever. Just imagine what he had the audacity to propose to me! . . . He asked me to abandon His Excellency Navagero and to leave with him when the French retired from Venice. "Yes," I replied, "I will come with you when you have proclaimed in the Piazza the liberty of my country, when you will lead your fellow soldiers to surprise, to conquer and to overwhelm those who think to make themselves our masters without firing a shot! . . . Then I will be to you wife, mistress, servant, whatever you like!" And I would have done what I said; I felt myself able to do it. I would have given all of myself to whoever would attempt so noble a revenge! . . . I would have given myself to him with the blind enthusiasm of a martyr even if not with the passion of a mistress! . . . Do you want to know what he replied? He twisted his lip angrily, then recovered himself and, putting out his hand to give me a caress that I rejected, he whispered in a low voice: "You really are an enchanting little madcap!" Oh, if you could have seen me then! . . . All my strength was concentrated in these five fingers. I marked his face with a slap so loud that my mother, my husband, the servants and the maids came running from the other rooms . . . the beautiful officer roared like a lion. Liar! . . . with the heart of a rabbit! . . . His hand went to his sword but he thought better of it seeing himself confronted by a woman's breast; then he rushed out of the room, throwing furious glances and gestures of defiance around him. "What have you done? For pity's sake! Look! You will be the ruin of this house! Better to tolerate the bad in order to avoid the worse!" It was with such words that my mother and my husband rewarded me; my husband above all moved me to disgust . . . and they said that he was jealous! . . . "Oh, so I am the bad omen in this house?" I shouted, "very well, I will change my house and leave you in peace!" And on the spot I went running out without anyone preventing me, took a shawl from my room in haste and went to look for my brother. They didn't know where he was, they thought he had gone away. I asked then about my Frumier uncles at their palace. They were all sleeping and had given orders that no one should enter, neither man nor woman, relative nor friend. Who remained to me at last? . . . Carlino, no one remained to me but you!' (Thanks for the compliment.) 'I repented that I had not come to you first of all.' (Somewhat better!) 'I learnt at the Frumier's door that you were still in Venice and where you were living. Now I am here, under your protection, without fear and without regret since, to tell you the truth, I have really loved you only and if you do not want me any more because of my caprices and all the follies I have committed, the fault, the damage and the trouble will be mine alone. A fair share is however due to you too, since in any case, by virtue of our old friendship, convenient or inconvenient, I am putting myself at your side and not going to move again. If your father still wants to give you the Contarini, let him give her to you in holy peace; but it will be up to the bride to support this bitter pill with patience since she will have at least one female relative always under her feet . . .'

As she said this, the Pisana began bouncing up and down on the divan as if to confirm her share of authority and to have heard her before and to see her now, one would certainly not have said that it was the same person. The spirited Republican, the Greek and Roman philosopher was converted into a carefree and vain little woman, so much so that one could have believed the blow given to poor Ascanio was not wholly merited. None the less, those two persons, so diverse and so intermingled in one person only, thought, talked, acted with equal sincerity, each in her turn. The first, I am sure, would have despised the second and the second would never have recognized the first; yet they lived together in excellent harmony like the sun and the moon.

But the strangest case was mine, for I was in love with both of them, not knowing to which to give the preference. The one for abundance of life, for pureness of sentiment and for eloquence, bore away my heart; the other for tenderness, for trust, for beauty; in fact, rightly or wrongly, I was head over heels in love, but any one of my readers, finding himself in my shoes, would have been equally so. Only those two brown eyes which looked at me, piteous and frightened, entreating me, would have won the contest. On the other hand, even if this tragic pose, sustained with so much vehemence by the Pisana, overwhelmed me, there were other arguments to compensate me. It was the effect of too much reading, working avidly in a volatile and impetuous brain; that fire in straw would soon have been quenched; but there would have remained that sparkle of nobility that she had lighted and I could live with her in very good accord knowing her of old as I did. Furthermore, the unbridled eloquence and the classic pomp of these speeches assured me that she must have been a considerable time without opening her mouth. So they used to say when she was a child and often Faustina, to make up for a difficult and uproarious Sunday used to say to herself: 'Today the Signorina has her tongue in her teeth and pepper in her blood. It will be a good thing for us if only she leaves us in peace for the rest of the week!' In fact it usually so happened. Nor was I ever mistaken, even later on, in applying Faustina's reasoning.

I replied with all my heart that she was welcome in my house; and having first drawn her attention to the serious step that she was taking and to the grave damage to her own reputation that might result from it, and seeing her none the less firm in her intention, limited myself to saying that she must do as she thought best and that I and all that was mine were at her disposal. I knew her too well to think that she would have altered her ideas because of my objections; perhaps also I loved her too much to try, but that was only a doubt that crossed my mind.

Once having accepted her plan so wholly and without scruples, it now had to be put into practice and in a moment a number of difficulties appeared to me. First of all, could I assume a sort of guardianship over her, uncertain as I was if I could remain in Venice and sure that because of the promises I had given and the laws of honour I should have to go away? And what would her family say, first and foremost His Excellency Navagero, the old and jealous husband? Would they not find some pretext to have a decree of banishment pronounced against me? Even that was not enough; there was the final scruple, the greatest perplexity, the capital difficulty. How could I justify our conduct in the eyes of the world and in the long run my own conscience too, that life in close intimacy with a beautiful young woman whom I loved and by whom I had every reason to believe myself loved? Should I say that we were awaiting in this way less wearisomely the death of her husband? The darn would be worse than the hole, as the people say.

All these perplexities leapt to my mind and uselessly afflicted me, while the Pisana enjoyed her reacquired liberty, singing and dancing, and not sparing a care in the world for what people might whisper about her. She made me take her all through the house from cellar to attic, found the carpets, the divans and even the pipes to her taste and took no heed either of appearances or of convention.

You know very well that when a woman is not dismayed about certain details, it is not for us to be worried about them; it would be an insult to her delicacy and confessors are not lauded who suggest sins to their penitents. Suddenly, while I was admiring the gaiety and impudent thoughtlessness of the Pisana, not knowing if I should ascribe it to a sincere love of myself, to freedom of habits or to pure levity of mind, she stopped with folded arms in the middle of the room, lifted her eyes to mine with a somewhat troubled expression and said:

'And your father?'

Only then it suddenly occurred to me that she knew nothing of his departure, and I marvelled even more at her openness in coming to establish herself with me, while at the same time I realized that after all she had not been so forgetful of her feminine modesty. When there is a father in question, two young people are safer from temptation and from the gossip of the neighbours. Together with this thought, another flashed into my mind, that she would be frightened at finding me alone and would regret her excessive trust in me. Only a while before I had been complaining at finding her so heedless of her honour and of social conventions, but now I would have wished her to be even more shameless than a street-woman if only she would remain satisfied with my company. See how we are made! However, my exceeding desire to have her with me did not go so far as to put lies in my mouth. I told her openly of my father's departure and how I was living quite alone in the house without even a servant maid to sweep away the cobwebs.

'Better still, better still,' she cried, jumping up and clapping her hands. 'Your father always rather frightened me and who knows if he would have looked on me with a friendly eye!'

But after this outburst of joyfulness, she suddenly became pensive and seemed to have no breath to go on. She pursed her lips as if about to cry and her lovely cheeks lost their colour.

'What is the matter, Pisana?' I asked her. 'Why are you frowning like that?' Are you afraid at finding yourself alone with me?'

'It is nothing,' she replied, a little vexed, but more with herself, it seemed to me, than with anyone in particular.

She walked once or twice about the room with her eyes fixed on the points of her shoes. I awaited my sentence with the tremor of a man who although he is innocent has yet a certain fear that he may be condemned; but the Pisana's hesitation buoyed up my heart sweetly as if assuring me that I was really loved as I wished to be loved. Up to then her assurance in face of every trial and her supreme confidence had for me a flavour somewhat fraternal that did not tickle my palate in the least.

'Where do you want me to sleep?' she asked suddenly with a tremor in her voice and with so lovely a blush on her face that it made her a hundred times more beautiful. I remember that she looked me in the face at the first of these words, but the others she pronounced in a low voice and with her glances straying here and there.

'Here on my heart,' I would have liked to reply, 'on my heart, where you slept so many times as a child and never wanted to complain.'

But the Pisana seemed so charming in that moment of mingled love and shame, of brazenness and reserve, that I felt forced to respect so beautiful an act of virtue and restrained even the breath of desire so as not to tarnish its purity. I had gone so far as to forget my familiarity with her in other times and to believe that if I had dared to touch her then it would really have been for the first time. I seemed like a skilful player of the violin who sets himself the greatest technical difficulties in order to have the pleasure of mastering them; he is sure of his ability but is always satisfied and pleased to prove it.

'Pisana,' I replied with a fairly steady voice and a most exemplary restraint, 'here you are the mistress of the house as I told you at the beginning. You honour me with your trust and it is up to me to show myself worthy of it. Every room has a strong lock and here is the key of the house; you can lock me out in the street if you will and I shall not complain.'

Her only reply was to throw her arms about my neck and I recognized in that sudden transport my Pisana of earlier times. None the less, I had the tact and the prudence not to take advantage of it and to give her time to come to herself and correct with words the excessive sincerity of her heart.

'We are like brother and sister, aren't we?' she said, her tongue stumbling over the words and finally resolving her perplexity by a sudden fit of coughing. 'Isn't it true that we will get on well together as in our happy days at Fratta?'

It was my turn then to quiver all over with a shiver that ran through all my veins. The Pisana looked away and did not know what to add and in the end I saw in time that we had gone too far and ought to separate.

'Look,' I went on, making the effort and taking her into my father's room, 'here you will be safe and free at your pleasure; I will arrange the bed for you in a few moments.'

'Do you think I will let you make the bed? . . . That is a job for women and belongs to them by right; I want even to make yours as well in the morning, and since there is a coffee pot here (there was one in every corner of my father's room) I will bring you coffee.'

Then there was a little battle of politeness, which quenched our earlier temptations and satisfied to have stopped there, I hastened to retire, happy to sleep yet another night in the company of my desires; a most tiresome company when one has not the hope of fulfilling them, but which is full of delicate pleasure and poetic joy for those who believe themselves about to realize them. I thought either rightly or wrongly that I was in the latter case. I had every reason for this as the next night proved to me.

Here would be the place to reply to a delicate question which few of my lady readers but many of the men would be bold enough to ask me. How stood, at that time, the virtue of the Pisana? It is true that I have spoken of her up till now with very little respect, dragging all her defects into the brightest light and saying a hundred times over that she was more inclined to evil than to good. But disposition is not everything. In reality, how many steps of the staircase of evil had she descended? Had she indeed descended, step by step, in reality all that her imagination and perhaps even her desire had suggested? But does it not seem that from smelling a rose to picking it and putting it in one's bosom is a long step? Any gardener, however jealous he be, will not forbid you to smell a flower, but if you make a movement to try and pick it, then he may indeed turn ugly and hasten to chase you out of the hot-house. . . . The question is a delicate one; but even more delicate is the necessity of replying. As you may well believe I do not want to go full bail for anyone; but as regards the Pisana I firmly believe that her husband found her, if not a chaste, at least a virgin wife, and that he so left her by the enforced moderation of his white hairs.

Whether it was by her merit or the early knowledge of vice that enlightened her, whether luck or Providence was in question, the fact was that, for my own excellent reasons, I believe that it was so. With that temperament, with those examples, with that liberty, with that upbringing, in the company of the Signora Veronica and Faustina, this was no small miracle. It is useless to deny it. Religion is for women the most potent check since it dominates sentiment with a stronger and more elevated sentiment. Even honour is not a sufficient check, since it exists only in our own judgement and is imposed upon us by ourselves alone. Religion, moreover, has the momentum of its power in a place inaccessible to human judgements. It commands us not to do something, since He who so wishes can do all, He can see all, He can punish and reward the deeds of men according to their inner value. There is no escape from His justice, no evasion of His decrees, there are no human considerations or duties or circumstances that make permissible what He has forbidden once and for all. The Pisana, deprived of this support and with a most imperfect notion of honour, was lucky enough to stop at premeditation of sin without proceeding to its consummation.

I do not wish to claim for her any great merit since, I repeat, it still seems to me more like a miracle than anything else; but I must state the fact and thereby satisfy the curiosity of my readers. They will excuse me for having treated this matter at such length, since the customs of those times were different enough from ours in this respect. But it is true that the difference could be more in the varnish than the substance.

The next morning it was not yet eight o'clock when the Pisana came into my room with coffee. She wanted, she said, to assume from the very first day the duties of a good and careful housewife. The enamoured dreams of the night in which I had lost all memory of my sorrows, the semi-darkness of the room, protected against the already strong rays of the sun by blue silk curtains in the oriental manner, our reminiscences that gushed forth at every glance, at every word, at every action, the enchanting beauty of her smiling little face, whose roses were only just recovering their colour after the early dews of sleep, all excited me to begin once more to create a link in that chain that had so long been cast aside. I took from her lips only a single kiss. I swear to you; only one kiss and even that mixed its sweetness with the bitterness of the coffee. And they say that in the last century there was no virtue! . . . There was, yes, but it meant twice the effort owing to the lack of moral education. I assure you that Saint Anthony would not have had such merit in withstanding in the desert the temptations of the devil as I had in drawing back my lips from that cup before my thirst was quenched. But I was certain that I would quench it one day or another and this changed my virtue into a refinement of gourmandise. Then, as soon as we had risen, we had to think of how we were going to live; that is, to go in search of a woman who would look after the kitchen and do the heavy work of the house. One could not live on coffee alone, especially with the love that devoured us. For the first time in my life I occupied myself with every pleasure in these household details.

I knew a goodwife in the nearby Campo, who recommended me to this one and that one, and they in turn fixed me up with a servant, who, at least in appearance, would have been sufficient by herself to guard a house against the Turks and Uskoks. Ugly as a guy, tall and lean as a grenadier after four months in the field, with grey eyes and grey hair and a red kerchief wrapped about her head in the manner of Medusa's serpents, she squinted a little and was somewhat bearded, and had a harsh nasal voice that spoke neither Venetian nor Slav but a bastard jargon somewhere between the two. She had received from Mother Nature all the ugliest imprints of fidelity; since I have always observed that fidelity and comeliness often quarrel and rarely come to an agreement in a tranquil and everyday life.

Even more, I was certain that whoever wanted to enter the house and came face to face with this apparition would rather have gone to the house of the devil himself than advance a pace across the threshold, so lovely and pleasant she appeared. Naturally I gave her instructions always to say that the masters of the house were out of Venice, for we had many good reasons for wanting to remain concealed. That should have been sufficient for our happiness, for as soon as other men were aware of that happiness they could do no less than crush and spoil it. Therefore, once my Cerberus was installed in the kitchen and our safety and our victuals suitably provided for, I turned once again to the Pisana and forgot everything else.

That was perhaps not the best thing to have done since, may God forgive me, other duties still called me and this was no time to wander like Rinaldo in the garden of Armida; but note that I did not say that I had made any effort to forget the rest. I forgot it so spontaneously that when ulterior circumstances recalled me to public life, it seemed to me a new world. If there were ever excuses in the delirium of love and the intoxication of pleasure, then I certainly had them all. However, I do not want to conceal my faults and am always willing to confess myself a sinner. This heedless month of bliss and enjoyment that I lived during the humiliation of my country, that I robbed from the decorous misery of exile, has left on my soul an eternal remorse. Oh, what a distance there is between the miserable begging of excuses and the proud independence of innocence! With how many lies was I not constrained to hide from the eyes of others my clandestine and cowardly happiness. No, I will never be indulgent towards myself, not even for a single forgetful moment, when honour commands me to record everything honestly and for always. The Pisana wept often enough when she at last saw that all her efforts to make me happy succeeded in doing no more than interrupt by some carefree flash an unease that continued to grow greater and which covered me with shame. Oh, why did she not turn to me with that inspired and vigorous love that had daunted the little soul of her gallant, Ascanio Minato? I would have died as a hero, whereas I was living like a pig.

* * * * *

None the less, the days passed, short, unheeded, delirious. I did not see any way of escape and felt neither the courage nor the desire to do so. I would have liked to try on the Pisana that miracle that she had tried on the young Corsican, and to lift her spirit to some elevation where love becomes the mainspring of great deeds and noble enterprises. But I had not the heart even to dream of a separation and as to making her a companion of my life, of my exile and of my poverty, I did not feel that I had the right. I disregarded everything, waiting counsel of events and sufficiently compensated for my inner torments by the happiness that shone, beautiful and radiant, on her features. I could not refrain from wondering, to see how her humour had changed and softened in those few blissful days; never a complaint, never a moment of irritation, never an access of vanity. It seemed as if she were determined to give the lie to the poor judgement that I had made of her at other times. A girl just out of a convent and entrusted to the care of a loving mother would not have been more serene, more gay, more open-hearted. All that was outside our love or was not in some way connected with it, seemed in no way to occupy her thoughts.

The tales that she told me of her past life, though strange and varied, did no more than convince me of her lasting and fervent love. She told me of the exhortations of her mother to look favourably upon this one or that one of her suitors in order to achieve a good match.

'What would you?' she said. 'The more splendid, beautiful or charming they were, the more aversion they roused in me; so that if ever I gave any sign of kindness or of pleasure, it was always to the ugliest and most ill-favoured, to my own great surprise and that of all around me, who thought this to be some refined art of flirtation. In truth, I allured those who seemed to me too awkward to allure me in return and if my favours were insults, may God forgive me, for I could do nothing else!'

I discovered then certain family secrets of which I would have preferred to remain ignorant, so much did they disgust me. The Contessa, her mother, gambled desperately, and would not admit poverty, so that she was always asking for money from this one or that one; when she found herself completely in the red, she and Rosa, her old chambermaid, would devise some trick to extract money from the pockets of acquaintances and friends. When they grew tired of these calls upon their resources, Rosa had proposed to put the Pisana into the game and to soften the hearts of those who seemed the most devoted admirers of her beauty by tales of her lack of means. Thus, without knowing it, she had lived on shameful and disgraceful alms. But finally she became aware of this, and despite the silent indifference of the Contessa, had thrown Rosa out of the house. This was one of the reasons that had induced her to accept the hand of the Navagero, since she was ashamed of seeing herself exposed to such infamy by her own mother.

I asked her why she had not preferred to rely on the generosity of the Frumiers; but she replied that even the Frumiers were finding themselves in deep waters and that even had they been able to save her from penury by some sacrifice on their part, they had no intention of ruining themselves completely to satisfy the insatiable passion of the Contessa. I marvelled how far this passion for gambling had gone in her.

'Oh, I do not wonder at it at all!' replied the Pisana. 'She is always so sure of winning that it seems to her a real shame not to play; and furthermore, she pretends that she always wins and that I and my brother eat up her immense winnings! Just imagine it! For my part I had never anything on my back save a simple linen dress and I have always left in her hands the interest from my eight thousand ducats. My brother ate and drank like a friar and I would undertake to maintain him for four soldi a day. But she was so convinced that she was right that it was not worth talking to her; and I am sorry for her, poor thing, for she had always been accustomed to eat without thinking of the morrow and it is impossible to take account when one is not used to noticing what one saves or what one spends. Anyhow, her passion is not unusual. All the Venetian ladies are now possessed by it, so that the very best houses are being ruined at the gaming tables. They understand nothing . . . everyone is being ruined and not one ever recovers herself.'

'Like the old proverb,' I said. 'The devil's flour does not make good bread. One who today risks the fortune of her own children at faro will certainly not tomorrow become so farseeing as to invest the winnings at five per cent. It will all be wasted in vain spending and all that will remain as a result will be the net loss. But your mother was more inexcusable than the others, since she was not ashamed to endanger the reputation of her own daughter to satisfy her craving! . . .'

'What are you saying!' exclaimed the Pisana. 'I am sorry for her even despite that! It was that covetous wretch of a Rosa who put it into her head, and for my part I am certain that she used to keep for herself a good half of the gifts. And since my mother had first asked in her own name, she might as well ask in mine too. She is not my mother for nothing.'

'Pisana, you are being too lenient! I don't want you to get used to thinking in such a way, for thus everything can be excused and everything forgiven and the frontiers between right and wrong disappear entirely. Indulgence is an excellent thing but it must keep eyes in its head both as regards ourselves and others. Let us forgive faults, yes, when they can be forgiven, but let us call them faults. If they are put in a single bundle with virtues, then one completely loses all measure!'

The Pisana smiled, saying that I was too severe, and added jokingly that if she excused everything it was just because others had forgiven her for all her own little faults. For the moment, she said, she had not even one, unless it was to make herself too much loved, which was more my fault than hers, but I put my hand over her mouth, saying:

'Be quiet! Don't revenge yourself on me now for my unjust severity of times past.'

After some weeks of life in the house, devoted to love, I thought it time to go to the Apostulos to get some news of my father. I was remorseful at having forgotten all about him and wanted to make amends with an urgency that, considering the shortness of the time, was bound to be useless. But when we want to persuade ourselves that we have failed in something, we pay no heed to reason. As I was going out the Pisana asked me to escort her to the convent of Santa Theresa to pay a visit to her sister. I agreed, and we set out arm in arm, I with my hat close over my eyes and she with a veil down to her chin, looking around suspiciously to avoid, if it were possible, being stopped by acquaintances. In fact, I saw in the distance Raimondo Venchieredo and the Partistagno, but succeeded in dodging around a corner in time. I left my companion at the convent and made my way thence towards the house of the Greek banker.

As you can well imagine, in so short a time my father had not even been able to reach Constantinople, still less to send any news from there. They all wondered, Spiro most of all, to see me still in Venice, but I replied that I had not left because of certain very important business matters that had detained me and that it was in my interest to defy the many risks I ran in remaining, despite the suspicions I had aroused. I did not dare to add, however, who they were who might have had such suspicions since I was still ignorant who might be the masters of Venice for though I imagined that the French had already gone, I had no certain proof of it.

Aglaura asked me where I intended to go when those business matters of mine had been concluded and I replied in confusion that I should probably leave for Milan. The young girl looked down with a shiver and her brother shot an angry glance at her. I had too many other things on my mind to pay attention to this pantomime and took my leave, assuring them that they would see me again before I left. I then went into the street, even more chary of being seen, since I now felt shame as well as fear.

It was of the greatest importance for me not to be seen since the perfect freedom from every vexation in which I and the Pisana had been living until then convinced me that her relatives were unaware of my presence in Venice. Had it been otherwise, it would not have been easy to imagine that she could have taken refuge with me. I did not then believe that the scene between the Pisana and the Lieutenant Minato had made such a sensation and that the Navagero and the Countess had not pursued the matter for fear of compromising themselves. At the turn of a *calle*, I found myself face to face with Agostino Frumier, fresher and rosier than ever. Both of us by mutual consent pretended not to recognize one another but he must have wondered at me more than I wondered at him and the shame was certainly greater on my side.

At last I reached the convent, the stones of the street seeming to scald my feet, and I repented at every step that I had not waited until nightfall to take this walk. I determined to have it out with the Pisana on the first occasion and to try and show her that the happiness with which she intoxicated me was at the cost of my honour, and that respect for my country, good faith towards my friends and my given word all compelled me to leave. It was with such thoughts that I entered the parlatorium, without thinking that Sister Clara might be surprised at seeing her sister in my company; but this had never occurred to the Pisana and I had paid no heed to it.

It was the first time I had seen Clara since she had taken her vows. I found her pitifully pale and wasted, with the transparency of those alabaster vases in which one puts a light to burn; also a little bowed as if by long habit of obedience and prayer. On her lips the kindly smile of olden times had been succeeded by a cold monastic rigidity; at long last it could be seen that the isolation from earthly things so much sighed after by Mother Redenta had reached her also; she not only despised and forgot, but she no longer understood, the world. Indeed, she wondered not at all at my intimacy with the Pisana, as I had feared, but merely gave us good and wise advice; she did not mention the past save to shudder at it and only once did I see the straight and thin curve of her lips soften when I mentioned her old grandmother.

How many memories there were in that half-smile! . . . But she recovered herself at once and reassumed her usual coldness that was the obligatory vestment of her soul, even as the black gown must invariably clothe her limbs. I believe that at that moment even Lucilio flashed into her thoughts, but they fled horrified from that memory. Where, indeed, was Lucilio at that time? What was he doing? That terrible uncertainty must have entered her soul with the invisible but deep gimlet of remorse. She exerted indeed a certain effort to become as impassive and severe as before; her eyes were no longer expressionless nor her voice so tranquil and monotonous.

'Alas,' she said suddenly, 'I promised to pray for the soul of my good old grandmother with a hundred masses, but have not yet been in a position to carry out my vow. That is the one thorn that I still have in my heart.'

The Pisana hastened to reply with her usual thoughtless generosity that she could take this also from her heart, for she would aid her, and have those masses celebrated according to Clara's intention.

'Oh thank you, thank you, my sister in Christ!' exclaimed Clara. 'Bring me the record of the priest who has celebrated them and you will indeed have acquired every right to my prayers and an even greater merit before God.'

I did not find myself quite at ease during this discussion and was surprised at the Pisana's facility in attuning her own feelings to those of others. But generous as she was, and an exquisite mistress of lies, I would have marvelled even more had she acted otherwise. . . . However, after we had taken our leave of Clara and had returned to the street, the fear again assailed me that we should be seen together and I proposed to the Pisana that she should go home unaccompanied and that we should each choose a different route. In fact we did so and I had occasion to be thankful since, after I had gone perhaps a hundred yards, I again ran into the Venchieredo and the Partistagno, who this time followed on my heels and would not lose track of me. The detours that I forced them to make through the interminable labyrinths of Venice I could not describe, but I tired sooner than they, since I was worried at having to leave the Pisana alone so long. I therefore decided to make for home, but what was my astonishment when at the door I saw the Pisana, who must have arrived some time before, chattering amiably with Rosa, that chambermaid who had been used to beg alms from the Pisana's admirers. She seemed in no way disturbed at my arrival, bade farewell to Rosa with the greatest affability, inviting her to come and visit us, and then entered the house with me, scolding me for being late. Out of the tail of my eye, I could see the Partistagno and Raimondo who were still watching from a nearby corner. I slammed the door and went up the stairs feeling somewhat irritable.

Once upstairs, I did not know how to make the Pisana realize the folly of her behaviour and in the end decided to tax her with it openly, the more so as she had aroused in me a certain turbulent emotion of anger. I told her that I was utterly amazed to see her in close conversation with a shameless woman of that type, who had insulted her unpardonably, and that I did not understand how she could have stopped to chatter at the door of the house in view of all the interest we had in not being seen. She replied that she had stopped without thinking and that as far as Rosa was concerned she had been sorry to see her dressed in rags and with her face wasted by poverty. She had even asked her to come and see us for that reason, since she hoped to be able to help her in some way. Also the woman had repented of her misdeeds, so that she had felt obliged to forgive her, and had indeed forgiven her, since she had protested that she had never intended to do her any harm and all that she had done had been for a good end and at the instigation of the Signora Contessa. The Pisana seemed so persuaded by this last argument that she was almost remorseful at having thrown Rosa out and took upon her own conscience all the hardships that Rosa had suffered through her unmerited severity.

In vain I countered by saying that certain wrongs could never be excused and that honour is perhaps the only thing that one has the right and the duty to defend even at the cost of one's own life and that of others. The Pisana said she did not agree with me, since in some things one must look to one's own feelings and that hers advised her to repair the ill that she had done.

Moreover, she implored me to help her in this deed of mercy, beginning by conceding a room in our house where Rosa could stay. At this request I began to storm and she to shout and to weep. We ended by agreeing that I should pay the rent of Rosa's present lodgings and only after I had promised this did the Pisana agree not to take her into our house. That was the first time when our love was forgotten and our two temperaments once again clashed somewhat violently. I went to bed with many evil forebodings and the mocking and inquisitive glances of Raimondo stuck in my throat all that night.

The next morning there was another skirmish. The Pisana begged me to let her go out to arrange for the celebration of the hundred masses she had promised her sister. You can imagine how this fresh whim pleased me in view of the shortage of money that was beginning to make itself felt! . . . For obvious reasons I had not let the Pisana know that my father had taken all his wealth with him when he went away, leaving me with only a modest sum. What with the house expenses, the servant's wages and some purchases made by the Pisana, who had taken refuge with me with little more than the clothes she stood up in, the greater part of what was supposed to suffice me for a year had already slipped through my fingers. None the less I did my best to conceal these worries of mine and tried with a hundred other reasons to check the Pisana's generosity about the masses. She would not even listen to me. She had promised, she said, and it was a question of her promise to her sister and if I loved her the least little bit I would do as she wanted. Then I told her openly how things stood.

'Is that the only difficulty?' she replied without turning a hair. 'First we will fulfil our obligations and then if there is nothing left, we will starve.'

'You talk very freely about starving,' I said, 'but I would just like to see what you make of it when you are too weak to stand.'

'Well, if I cannot stand, I shall fall. But it shall never be said of me that I grew fat with what should be used for the good of others.'

'Consider that after paying for the hundred masses, very few lire will be left for us.'

'Yes, you are right, Carlino! It is not right that I should sacrifice you to one of my whims. It is better that I should go. . . . I will go and stay with Rosa. . . . I will work at sewing and embroidery . . .'

'What has taken you now?' I shouted indignantly. 'I would rather flay the skin from my back than leave you in such evil straits.'

'Then, Carlino, we are agreed; do what I ask of you and then let Providence look to the rest.'

'You know, Pisana, you simply amaze me! I have never seen you so resigned and confident in Providence as now, when Providence seems to have no thought for you.'

'If only that were true! I should be only too pleased if this virtue should grow in me at need. None the less, I can tell you that now I have begun to have faith in Providence, I can already feel its courage and its force. At the bottom of our hearts some devotion to religion always remains in us women. Very well then! I abandon myself to the arms of God! I assure you that if we strip ourselves of everything, you will never find two hands that would work more valorously than mine to provide a living for the two of us.'

I shook my head, for I had not much faith in that courage which was still far from being proved; but however little I believed, I still had to pay for the hundred masses and for Rosa's rent and when at last the Pisana was satisfied there remained only about twenty ducats with which to face the future.

But not so far away there were those who were taking a great interest in my actions and were working behind the scenes to relieve us of our perplexities; they wanted to throw me from the frying pan into the fire, and they succeeded. My duty for the past month had been to get myself roasted and I could thank them for the great merit they acquired in lightening my burden. The scene between the Pisana and the Corsican officer had caused a great stir in Venice; her disappearance from her husband's house had added mystery to the adventure and strange and remarkable things were said about it, which would have seemed fabulous in the telling. One had seen her clothed in white, wandering under the arches of the Procuratie in the dead of night; another claimed to have met her in some deserted *calle* with a dagger in one hand and a flaming torch in the other, like the statue of discord; the boatmen told how she would wander all night through the lagoons in a gondola that moved without oars and left behind it in the silent waters a phosphorescent trail. Some splashes were heard from time to time around this mysterious apparition; they were the enemies of Venice magically wrenched by her from the quiet of their sleep and hurled into the maw of the canals.

These imaginative fairytales to which every day popular credulity added some fresh flower of fancy, pleased the new provisional government established by the Austrians after the departure of Serrurier, little or not at all. They were signs of little sympathy and it was best, they thought, to cure the people of these poetic fancies. Therefore they did their best to discover the whereabouts of the Pisana. But their inquiries were without result and certainly no one could have imagined that she was living with me, since I was believed at that time to be far from the lagoons. Our gypsy had been incorruptible; she had told whatever disguised policemen who had come to the house to ask about the masters, that they had left Venice for some time past, and so they stopped importuning her. Knowing that my father had embarked for the Levant, they assumed that I had left with him, or else with the other unfortunates who had sought a new country either in the quiet cities of Tuscany or in the turbulent provinces of the Cisalpine.

The discovery made by Raimondo Venchieredo set the police spies on my track. He had spoken of it to his father as a piece of gossip, but the old fox sought to take advantage of it and after consulting the Reverend Father Pendola, he had decided to win himself a good mark in the eyes of the government by describing me as a dangerous conspirator hiding in Venice and ready for God knew what desperate enterprise. My life with that fabled heroine who had made the common people and the unemployed talk so much, merely added force to the accusation.

Indeed, one morning as we were peacefully drinking our coffee and thinking how to stretch as far as possible the most useful service of those seven or eight ducats that still remained to us, I heard a furious ringing at the door and then a confused sound of voices shouting and replying to one another from the window to the *calle* and from the *calle* to the window. As I was listening to the uproar I heard a crash as of a door being broken in by force and then a second blow even louder than the first and a shouting and commotion that seemed endless. The Pisana and I were just about to go out and see what was the matter when our gypsy rushed into the room with her nose bleeding, her clothes in ribbons and an enormous fire shovel in her hand. It was the one on which my father used to burn perfumes in the Constantinople manner.

'Master,' she shouted, out of breath. 'I have taken one of them prisoner. He is shut up in the kitchen with his face spotted like a pudding. . . . Save yourself if you can. . . . They have come to arrest you. . . . They say it is for a crime against the State . . .'

The Pisana did not let her go on but ran to close the door, and peering out of the window that gave on to the canal, began to tell me that I should look to myself, escape, and save myself as urgently as possible. I did not know what to do, but a leap out of the window seemed the most suitable way of getting out of the difficulty. To think and to act were but the work of an instant; I leapt out without looking either where or how I was to land, fully convinced that I should hit something or other. In fact I hit a gondola within which I glimpsed during my leap the face of Raimondo Venchieredo, who was watching our windows. The blow that I gave to the bottom of the boat almost dislocated my back but the somersaults of my childhood and my gymnastics with Marchetto had accustomed my bones to such shocks. I jumped up like a cat, more active than before, and ran towards the prow in order to leap on to the further bank, but Raimondo, who was just about to emerge from under the cover, involuntarily got in my way and stopped astonished at this body which had made the gondola rock under his feet in falling.

'Ah, so it's you, villain,' I cried furiously. 'Take the reward of your spying!'

And I gave him such a blow that it made him roll on to the raised prow, almost putting his eyes out. In the meantime I had reached the further bank and paused to wave to the Pisana who was watching me from the window and urging me to fly as quickly as possible. My saviour, the gypsy, was still standing with her shovel at the smashed door, terrifying the police agents with her belligerent attitude. None of them felt willing to follow his leader into the house and risk encountering the ugly fate that he had perhaps already encountered. Had they paid closer heed, they might have heard him yelling; shut up in the kitchen with his face well battered by that tremendous shovel, he was wailing on the highest notes of his bass register like a piglet being taken to market.

I had seen all this in a flash and before Raimondo could recover himself or the police agents discover me, I had disappeared down a narrow *calle* that cut through near by. In that confusion of deeds and ideas, it was a real providence that put into my mind the idea of taking refuge with the Apostulos. To think was to act, and I arrived at my sanctuary having undergone no greater peril than that most hazardous leap from the window. My friends were very glad to see me safe after so great a danger; but none the less I could not yet sing a paean of victory and until I was well clear of the lagoons and even of the provinces on this side of the Adige my liberty ran great risks.

'Where are you thinking of going?' the old banker asked me.

'But . . . to Milan,' I replied, scarcely knowing what I was saying.

'Are you really determined to go there?' Aglaura asked me in her turn.

'It seems the best thing to do,' I said. 'At least, some of my best friends are there and they have been expecting me for some time.'

Spiro had run downstairs to dismiss the clerks in the office while we were talking and Aglaura seemed about to ask some favour of me, when he returned. Then she changed her mind and began to listen as if she were not really interested; but she watched me intently and every so often glanced at her brother. I heard her sigh as her father told me that, with a Greek dress and a passport as one of their representatives, I would be able to leave the next morning.

'Not before,' he said, 'for the police are always very watchful and alert at first and you could easily fall into their hands. Tomorrow, however, they will not be watching so carefully because they will think that you have already left the city and, as it is a *festa*, the customs guards will be too busy examining the pockets of all the country people coming into the city.'

The old lady who had come to congratulate me on my escape, nodded approval. Spiro said that, once at Padua, I would do well to take off my disguise and take any convenient way to the frontier, as the Greek dress would be too noticeable. I replied yes to everything and turned to another problem, that of money. With the seven ducats that I had in my purse I could not even dream of reaching Milan; I really needed a considerable sum; even an advance on the interest for another year would not be sufficient and moreover I wanted to leave some means of subsistence for the Pisana. I proposed to the Greek that he should pay me a thousand ducats and pay the interest on the remaining capital to the Noble Contessina Pisana of Fratta, the lady Navagero. The Greek was quite agreeable and I signed a receipt and a power of attorney in due order and advised the Pisana by letter of what I had done, including also a document with which I invested her with the profits from my house. It was impossible to know how long I should have to remain absent and the best thing was to make provision for a considerable time; nor did I fear that the Pisana would think herself offended by these provisions since our love was not of the kind that thinks itself humiliated by such trifles. Who has, gives; that is the general rule amongst neighbours and you can imagine that between two lovers even more than between neighbours, there can be only one common interest!

Once these business matters had been attended to, it was time to think of my stomach in order to sustain the hardships of the first day of exile. It was already evening and I had taken nothing for twenty-four hours except coffee; none the less, I was no more hungry than if I had just risen from a wedding banquet. On the table, to left and right of me, were great bottles of Cyprus wine and I devoted myself to these and while the others ate and encouraged me to eat, I set out instead to drink out of sheer despair.

I drank so much that I understood nothing of the lively conversation that took place after supper, but it seemed to me that, having been left for a moment alone with the ladies, Aglaura had whispered something in my ear and followed it up by pressing my knee and kicking me under the table when Spiro and her father returned. Out of courtesy they had placed her in the next seat to mine. I understood nothing of this manoeuvre but somehow dragged myself to the bed that had been prepared for me and slept so much like a pig that I could hear myself snoring. But in the morning, when they awakened me, it was quite another pair of shoes! Calm had followed the storm and sorrow succeeded bewilderment. Up till then I had stubbornly persisted in my hopes like a consumptive; but in the end I had to give way to brutal necessity; to draw back or to hope was equally useless. I could not even say that I had the strength to get out of bed, dress myself in my new attire *alla greca* and take leave of my hosts. My body did my will with the foolish obedience of an automaton and as for my soul, I could well believe that I had left it in the Cyprus wine.

Spiro accompanied me to the Riva del Carbone where the courier left for Padua, promised me that any news of my father would be forwarded immediately to me and left me with a grip of the hand. I stood there on the bridge silently contemplating the dark waters of the Grand Canal, where the palaces of the admirals and of the doges seemed reflected almost as if desirous of that abyss. I felt as if my very vitals were being torn out of me and remained downcast and quite lifeless like one who finds himself face to face with a misfortune that can end only in death.

I did not notice the departure of the boat; we were already far out into the lagoon though I could still see the Foscari Palace and the Rialto Bridge. But when we arrived at the customs house and were given the order to halt in an accent that was certainly not

Venetian, I emerged suddenly from those fantastic griefs to find myself gripped by a real and very deep sorrow! Then all the misfortunes of my country ranged themselves beside my own, and all, one by one, pierced my heart with their knives.

We had already untied from the landing stage of the customs house when we were overtaken by a swift caïque and a voice shouted to us to wait. The pilot indeed stopped and I was most astonished a moment later to see young Apostulos on the deck of the courier. He greeted me with some perturbation, peering left and right, and said a little confusedly that he had hastened in order to tell me the names of certain of his friends who could be of great use to me in Milan. I was astonished at this attention, since it is the custom in such circumstances to furnish the traveller with letters of introduction; none the less I thanked him and he then left me to look for the captain, to whom he said he wanted to recommend me. On this pretext he went down into the cabin and in fact I saw him whispering with the captain, who hastened to reply 'no' and made a sign as if granting him permission to do as he liked and look where he pleased. Spiro then went right to the far end of the cabin where he saw a few boatmen who were sleeping, wrapped in their cloaks, and then returned with an expression that he tried to make indifferent.

'Capperi! What a *courier de luxe* you have!' he exclaimed, examining everything from bow to stern with his falcon eyes; he stuck his nose into every dark corner to the evident irritation of the pilot who was waiting to give his orders to the helmsman.

'May we leave?' he asked the captain in order to get rid of this importunate visitor.

'Wait a moment, I am just going,' said Spiro, leaping from the courier into the caicque and waving me an abstracted farewell.

I realized that he had not overtaken the boat and inspected it with such care for the reasons that he had given me, but I was too bewildered and miserable to occupy myself with speculation and in a short time the incident passed from my mind and I went back to watching Venice receding farther and farther away from me amid the bluish mist of the lagoons. It seemed more and more like a theatre curtain discoloured by the dust and smoke of the footlights.

Oh Venice, oh ancient mother of wisdom and of liberty, though your spirit now seemed paler and more intangible than your appearance! It disappeared at length in that blind obscurity of the past that destroys even the traces of life; there remains memory, but naught else save fantasies; there remains hope, the long dream of torment. Did I love you, dying and decrepit? . . . I do not know, I do not wish to say. But when I saw you wrapped in the cerecloths of the grave, when I admired you, lovely and majestic in the arms of death, when I felt your heart cold and the last breath spent upon your lips, then a storm of sorrow, of despair, of remorse, stirred up in me the deepest passions of my soul! . . . Then I felt the rage of the exile, the desolation of the orphan, the torment of the parricide! . . . Parricide, parricide! still shouted the mournful echoes in the Palace of the Doges. You could have left your mother to die in peace on the standards of Lepanto and the Morea; instead you tear her with abominable cruelty from that noble bed and leave her to die upon the pavements, you dance around her, drunken and cowardly, you offer to her enemies the cord with which to strangle her. . . . There are certain moments in the life of peoples when the incapable are traitors when they pretend to the rights of valour and of wisdom. Were you impotent to save her? Why did you not confess it to the world? Why have you mingled with the executioners? Why did some of you, after being horrified by the odious bargain, then stretch out your hands for alms to the purchasers? Pesaro was alone in virtue; but, first and most vile of all to abase himself, he found many, only too many, imitators. I do not accuse but vindicate; I do not insult but confess. I confess what I should have done and did not do, what I could have seen and did not wish to see, what I did for heedlessness and will always deplore as a vile crime. The Directory and Bonaparte betrayed us, it is true; but in such a way only cowards allow themselves to be betrayed. Bonaparte did with Venice as a man does with a mistress to whom love means slavery and who kisses the hand that strikes her. He neglected her in the beginning, then outraged her, enjoyed her only to deceive her, only at last to put her under his feet and trample on her as a harlot, saying to her scornfully: 'Go! Seek another master!'

Perhaps no one can understand without having experienced it, my deep dejection of soul at such thoughts. When I compared it with the gay and carefree happiness that had delayed me those few days, my discouragement and anxiety grew, if possible, even greater. It was really true; I had touched the summit of my desires, I had held within my arms, beautiful, contented and loving, the first, the only woman whom I had ever loved. What I had imagined from my earliest years to be the consolation of my life and the cure for every sorrow had filled me, intoxicated me with as much enjoyment as could ever be realized in any human breast! And what had I left after all that? Only remorse! Drunk but not satiated, ashamed yet not repentant, I now left the ways of love for those of exile, and if the police agents had not taken the trouble to warn me I would have remained to profane the funeral mourning of Venice with the effrontery of my pleasure. So in the end the food of my soul turned to poison in me and I was forced to despise what I still desired more ardently than ever to possess.

Pale, convulsed, agitated, without touching either food or drink, without looking my companions in the face or replying to their questions, jumping up now and again to avoid the elbows of the rowers, I finally arrived at Padua. I disembarked, no longer remembering where I was and not recognizing that canal bank where I had so often walked with Amilcare. I made inquiries, however, about an inn and was directed to one on the right of the Porta Codalunga. I approached it with my bundle under my arm and followed by one or two urchins who admired my oriental dress; I entered, asked for a room and some refreshment. Then I changed my clothes, ate a little food, refused wine with loathing, and then having paid my modest bill went out to the local tavern saying in a loud voice that dressed in this way I hoped I should not attract the attention of all the rogues in the city.

In fact I pretended to be leaving, but having reached the gateway I turned aside and went down a sidestreet which I remembered would take me out on to the Vicenza road. On leaving the inn, I had noticed a certain person who had the air of keeping a purposeful eye on me and I wanted to find out if this were true. Indeed, looking obliquely, I saw that shadow still following mine, slowing its pace and keeping a little behind me. Having turned down this sidestreet, I could still hear a light and cautious step accompanying me, so that there was no longer any doubt that he was definitely after me. I thought immediately of Venchieredo, of Father Pendola and of the advocate Ormenta, since I did not know then that the worthy advocate was sitting in the government through the wise protection of the Reverend Father. None the less, it seemed that boldness would be the best course and when I had got my hired assassin to stop in the open country I turned suddenly and rushed at him to lay hold of him and make him pay in double coin for his unwanted company. To my great surprise he neither moved nor gave any sign of fear; he had a sailor's cloak wrapped around him and lowered the hood to reveal himself better. I forgot the violence of my anger and contented myself with pointing out to him that it was not permissible to follow in this way on the heels of a gentleman. While I was speaking, he looked at me with a frown that seemed more undecided than troubled and I seemed to recall in his appearance the memory of some person well known to me. I passed rapidly in review all my Paduan friends, but not one in any way resembled him; indeed a certain intuition persisted in revealing this figure to me as one seen only a short time before and vivid, indeed very vivid, in my recollections.

'Then you really don't mean to recognize me?' he said, putting a hand up to his face and in a voice that immediately brought recognition to me.

'Aglaura, Aglaura,' I exclaimed, 'Can I believe my eyes?'

'Yes, I am Aglaura; I have followed you all the way from Venice, was with you on the same boat, refreshed myself at the same inn and would not have had the courage to reveal myself to you if your suspicions had not made you turn on me.'

'Then,' I said, 'it was you for whom Spiro was searching this morning?'

'Yes, he was looking for me. Returning home and not finding me there, since I had left for the courier in the meantime, after having changed my clothes at the laundry-woman's, he suspected what he has feared for some time. It is true that I went out with the maid, but she had returned, as I had begged her to leave me alone in the church to pray, and so his suspicions increased. It was lucky that, because of his haste, he had not the time to find out if that were the truth or an excuse, and so when he asked the captain if he had any women on board and had been told no, he really thought that I had stayed behind to pray and was perhaps seeking in prayer the force to resist the temptations that had for so long assailed me. Poor Spiro! . . . He loves me, but he does not understand or pity me! . . . Rather than take my part, he is ready to make himself the instrument of my father's curses.'

From these words, from her looks and from the tone of her voice, I became persuaded that poor Aglaura had fallen in love with me and that the pain of losing me had led her to the desperate course of following me. I felt full of gratitude and pity for her. If the Pisana had remained with His Excellency Navagero or perhaps run away with Lieutenant Minato, I might have fallen in love with Aglaura on the spot, if only for gratitude.

CHAPTER XV

THE young Greek girl in her sailor's get-up was as lovely as a picture by Giorgione. There was such a mingling of strength and gentleness, of boldness and of modesty about her that a hermit from the Thebaid would have fallen in love with her. But I did not let myself succumb to her charms and by a supreme effort prepared myself to show her the folly of her actions and recall to her the memory of her parents, her brother, her moral and religious obligations, and perhaps also to persuade her that it was not love that she felt but a transient passion which would cool in a couple of days and to declare that my heart was already in bond and every effort to win it would be useless. My heroism even went as far as that! But luckily it was not necessary and the girl's sincerity spared me the ridiculous Quixotry of tilting against windmills.

'Do not condemn me,' she went on, motioning me to be silent, 'listen to me first! Emilio is my betrothed; he would certainly never have thought of mixing in affairs of state or in plots and intrigues when I first knew him. It was I who spurred him on this road that led to his prescription so that now, deprived of everything, without relatives, without friends and in poor health, through me he was sent to suffer, perhaps to die, in a distant and foreign land! . . . Judge for yourself! Was it not my duty to abandon everything, to sacrifice everything to lessen the evil caused by my urgings? . . . You can understand. Spiro was wrong in trying to restrain me. It is not love alone that has made me leave home; it is pity, religion, duty! Let everything perish so long as this atrocious remorse does not remain in my heart! . . .'

I remained, as they say, flabbergasted: but I played the Indian in a dignified manner and although shame coloured my cheeks for the blunder I had been about to make, I managed to find words that did not reveal my embarrassment and at once concealed it. Above all, this Signor Emilio, deprived of everything, this interesting invalid, puzzled me, since Aglaura had declared him to be her betrothed but of whom I had never heard a word mentioned by her parents. Probably she assumed that Spiro would have talked to me of him, and indeed she went on with her story as if I knew as much about him as she did.

'Last week,' she said, 'I was obsessed with the idea of killing myself; but when I saw you and heard that you intended going to Milan, another and less extravagant idea flashed into my mind. Why should I not go with you? Emilio was in Milan also. A long silence had kept me in the dark about everything that concerned him. In killing myself, I would have known no more than at first, and I would not even have been able to give him any comfort; while by rejoining him who knows but I might be able, by taking my place at his side and remaining with him always, to lessen the misfortunes which I had brought upon him by my liberal follies. I decided therefore that I would go with you, since the very thought of setting out alone on such a journey scared me. Just think! I rarely used to set foot outside the house! My courage would not have failed me, but experience would, and who knows in what sort of difficulties I could have fallen! But in company of an honest and trusted friend, I could be sure of going even to the end of the world.

'Having taken this decision, I had to make another. Should I tell you of my intention or follow you without your knowledge, so that the position in which we found ourselves would have compelled you to take me as your companion? Sincerity inclined me to the first course, but fear of a refusal urged me to the second. None the less, the greatest obstacle to be overcome was my brother. He and I are almost like a single soul, as if the thoughts drawn in him were coloured in me. We are like two lutes of which one echoes spontaneously if a little uncertainly the sounds played on the strings of the other. He indeed divined my intentions from the first moment that you entered our house; I do not say that he guessed the plan that I had formed to accompany you, but he read clearly in my eyes my desire to run away to Milan. That was enough to make my flight impossible, or at least extremely difficult, since I know my brother's great affection for me and that he would rather die than be parted from me.

'At certain times it seems to me that, for a brother, this love is exaggerated, but he is made that way and one must agree that it is a good fault. You cannot imagine the ruses I adopted to rid his mind of these suspicions, the lies that I poured out with the most ingenuous manner in the world, the fondness beyond normal custom that I showed him and the attention that I paid to all the affairs of the family! Only one who believes herself called by God and her own conscience to make amends for her own faults could have done so much and be able to confess it without dying of shame.

'My old parents and Spiro himself were deceived. . . . You see, I weep for them even now! But God so wills and may His will be done! They were all deceived, as I tell you, and certainly this morning when I said my devotions with Mamma and wished Papa good morning, none could have suspected that I was hatching a plan to abandon them a half an hour later, change into a sailor's dress and wander the world with you in expiation of my sins! Now I am resolved; the great step has been taken. If God granted me the strength to dissimulate for so long and the cunning to deceive such shrewd and loving guardians, it is a sign that He approves and defends my conduct. He will take care to repair the evils that my flight may give rise to! . . . As for my parents, I have no great regrets! . . . Whether it be my sex, or my lack of merit, or their advanced years that incline them to egotism, I have never felt that their affection for me was in any way remarkable. My mother sometimes seems to me to feel that she has neglected me and heaps caresses on me that seek to be maternal, but always seem a little artificial; my father does not even take this trouble; he forgets about me for whole days on end and it seems to me that he treats me as if I had arrived in his house that same day and would be leaving it the next. In fact, we women are for our fathers only a transient blessing, a plaything for a few years; they consider us, I believe, as someone else's good and certainly my father never shows that he considers me his.

'So I tell you that as far as they are concerned I have no great anxiety; they will be satisfied if they know that I am alive. But as to Spiro I cannot do less than be anxious! . . . I know his proud and impulsive nature and his heart which knows nothing of patience or moderation! Who knows what commotion he may cause! But I hope that love and respect for our parents will restrain him a little. In any case, I will write to him to set his mind at rest and will always pray Heaven to grant me the boon of being reunited with him.'

Speaking thus, she had already begun to walk in the direction in which I had been going before I had turned to confront her and I too, without thinking, walked along beside her. But when she had finished her story I stood still, saying:

'Aglaura, where are we going now?'

'Why to Milan, where you were going,' she replied.

I confess that such assurance confounded me and I put back unused all the arguments I had ready to dissuade her for her hasty decision. I saw there was no help for it and thought involuntarily of my father's words, when he told me that in the daughter of Apostulos I should find a sister and that I should love her as such. Could he have been a prophet? It seemed so; but in any case I felt I could not abandon the girl and determined to assist her with advice, to accompany her and to afford her, in fact, that brotherly aid that was hers of right for the long-standing friendship between her father and mine. If not brother and sister, we were practically cousins; and so I reconciled myself and decided to behave in the future as circumstances dictated and not to neglect any means open to me to restore Aglaura to her family.

However, I in no way changed my plan, which was to go forward on foot as far as a little district near by and thence to the foothills in a farmer's cart and so, from one cart to another, from district to district, slipping between the cities and the mountains until I reached the Lake of Garda and there cross by boat to the Brescian shore.

However, before carrying out the first part of my plan, I asked the girl if this Signor Emilio was indeed her betrothed and if she knew for certain that he was lying sick in Milan.

'You ask me if Emilio is my betrothed? Don't you know Emilio

Tornoni?' Aglaura exclaimed in great surprise. 'Surely Spiro must have spoken of him to you?'

'Not as far as I remember,' I replied.

'Very strange,' she muttered to herself.

To relieve my perplexity, she told me briefly that before Spiro had returned from Greece where he had been staying with an uncle for the past fifteen years, she had been asked in marriage by Emilio, a good-looking youth, by her account, belonging to one of the best families of Istria and employed in Venice as an official of the Arsenal. The return of her brother and some family complications that had occured had first delayed the marriage and then the revolution had left everything in the air, since Emilio had had to fly with all the others because of the shameful Treaty of Campo-formio.

She continued to declare that the sole cause of his misfortunes had been herself, since it had been she who had first turned Emilio's head and caused him to take part in the bacchanal of that ephemeral liberty and diverted him from his naval duties. I denied this, saying that a man must always be responsible for his own actions and it is his own fault if he lets himself be led by the nose by women. But Aglaura would not submit to this reasoning and persisted in considering it her duty to rejoin her betrothed to compensate in some way for all that she had made him suffer. As to his illness and his being in Milan, she could not doubt it because in his last letter he had informed her that he would not move from there, and since she had received no further news from him she believed he must either be dead or seriously ill. Perhaps the poor exile, while writing to her, had already felt the first symptoms of the malady that had confined him to the plague-ridden bed of some hospital. Aglaura's imagination was so lively that she already seemed to see him abandoned to the carelessness rather than the care of some mercenary nurse, in despair at having to die without even her kiss upon his lips.

Talking thus, we arrived at a little village and made the best of a country wagon which took us as far as Cittadella. To tell you how philosophically Aglaura accepted the discomforts and hardships of that journey like an old campaigner would make you laugh. As a rule we put up for the night in some filthy country alehouse where generally there was only one room and only one bed. It is true that this was usually big enough to sleep a regiment, but modesty, be it understood, did not permit certain risks. As soon as we entered the room, we put out the light and she undressed and lay down on the bed, while I curled up as best I could on a table or in some wicker chair. Woe to me if I had been accustomed all my life to the softness of Venetian feather beds! In a couple of nights all my bones would have been broken! But luckily they still remembered my kennel at Fratta and the implacable lumps of those donkey's breakfasts, so that when put to the trial they endured valiantly and the next day could support the violent jolting of yet another rough cart.

Thus enduring, joking and (it must be said) laughing also, we crossed the Vicentino and the Veronese and on the fourth day arrived at Bardolino on the blue waters of the Benaco. Despite all my misfortunes, my fears and the distractions caused by my companion, I remembered Virgil and greeted the great lake which trembled like the sea, with its swelling waves sometimes tossed sky high. Far off in the waters one could make out the lovely Sirmione, the eye of the lake, queen of the islands and peninsulas, as Catullus, the sweet lover of Lesbia, used to call it. I saw the melancholy hues of its olive groves and imagined myself beneath their shade, wandering with sweet verses on my lips like the poet of the Latin graces.

I pondered blissfully in the moonlight on my classical memories, thanking in my heart the old Rector of Teglio who had revealed to me a source of joy so pure and of consolation so powerful in its simplicity. Orphaned one might say of parents and country, tossed here and there by a mysterious destiny, guardian by force of circumstances of a girl not bound to me by ties either of parentage or love, I saw once more a flash of happiness in the poetic imagination of men who had lived eighteen centuries before me. How blessed is poetry! The harmonious and unfleeting echo of all that humanity feels greatest and imagines most beautiful! . . . Shining virgin dawn of human reason! . . . misty and glowing sunset of divinity in the inspired mind of genius. It proceeds on its eternal way, drawing to itself one by one the generations of this earth, and by every step that we advance along that sublime way it opens to us a wider horizon of virtue, of happiness and of beauty. The anatomists lean over to examine and dissect its corpse; but thought and feeling escape their knives and enveloped in the mystic and eternal pyre of intellect rush towards the sky in tongues of flame.

We went for a walk along the crest of the hill while the host prepared our supper of little trout and a few sardines. After a tiring climb, we came to a place where we followed the ridge of a rock rising precipitously from the lake. The descent fell dark and cavernous, sadly outlined by the moonlight at some more precipitous point, while below the waters stretched dark, deep and silent; the sky was reflected in them without illuminating them as always happens when the light does not fall crosswise but direct. I stopped to contemplate that gloomy and solemn spectacle that deserves a more finished description from some pen more masterly than mine. Aglaura stretched herself out on the precipitous slope of the rock and seemed absorbed for the moment in even more gloomy meditations. I thought meanwhile of the calm horizons, the green meadows and the glimmering seacoast of Fratta; I saw once again in thought the Bastion of Attila and its vast and marvellous panorama that had first made me bow my head before the controlling Deity of the universe. How many flowers of a thousand shapes, a thousand colours, does Nature hold in her lap to scatter widefold upon the varied face of the world! . . . I was shaken out of such reflections by a long and deep sigh from my companion; then I saw her move forward and fall headlong into the abyss that yawned beneath her. I shuddered at the thought of looking down into those depths only to see therein perhaps the inanimate and bleeding remains of the unhappy Aglaura. Then I seemed to hear below me and not very far away a faint cry. I leant over the edge of the rock, straining my ears and could just hear a groan; she still lived! I strained my eyes to the utmost and at last made out near a bunch of shrubs a black object like a body which seemed to be caught there. Impatient to help her and to save her from the imminent danger of a bough that might break or a root that might tear out, I lowered myself resolutely down the almost vertical wall of the rock. I slithered down beside her quickly, scratching my face, knees and elbows but that very fact and the few tufts of grass which I managed to catch hold of in passing broke the violence of my descent; I do not know by what miracle I arrived safe and sound, that is at least with whole limbs and sound vertebrae, at the patch of cornel that had stopped her fall. Then I had time to think, as I drew her away from the clump of brier in which the fringes of her cloak had become entangled and laid her, still only semi-conscious, on the ledge. Without water, without aid, in that brier-patch which seemed like a great eagles' nest, I could do no more than wait until she came to herself or watch her die. I had heard tell how human breath helps to restore to their senses those who have fainted because of some violent emotion and I set myself to breathe on her eyes and temples, watching anxiously for the least sign of movement. At last she opened her eyes and I sighed as if a millstone had been lifted from my breast.

'Ah me! I still live,' she murmured, 'so it is indeed a sign that God so wills!'

'Aglaura, Aglaura!' I whispered imploringly and affectionately in her ear, 'have you no faith in me? . . . Has my protection, my company only ended in making life burdensome to you?'

'You, you?' she said weakly, 'you are the dearest and most

faithful friend I could have. For your sake I could condemn myself to go on living, if needs be even twice the span allotted me by destiny. But what value has my life ever had for others? . . .'

'A very great one, Aglaura! First of all for your parents and for your brother who loves you, who adores you, you alone know how much. Then because there is one heart in the world which has the right of love and of authority over yours. Your love, Aglaura; you have lost the right to kill yourself, if it can be allowed that anyone ever has that right.'

'Yes, it is true, I love!' replied the girl in such a tone of voice that I could not tell whether it was due to shortness of breath or to bitter irony. 'I love,' she repeated, and this time with deep sincerity. 'I must live to love; you are right, my friend! . . . Give me your arm and we will walk back.'

Grasping at a branch that jutted out from the rock, knotty and flexible, she let herself down; then she let go of the branch and I saw her descend, slithering down as I had done a few moments before. A minute later and her feet were on the soft wet sand, where the waves of the lake lapped quietly. You may well believe I did not want to show myself less daring than a woman, so I too risked the leap and after a second dose of bumps and scratches, joined her. Then I gave such a deep sigh of thankfulness that the very air seemed to sense its weight. My companion, however, went nimbly on her way as if just coming out of a ball or a theatre. And to think that a quarter of an hour earlier she had thrown herself down from the height of two campaniles! Women, women, women! . . . What are the names of the hundred thousand elements, always new, always different, always discordant that compose you? I had never seen Aglaura so gay, so light-hearted as then, after having played me that desperate trick. But when I wanted to try and make her talk sense, she changed the subject somewhat sulkily, only to bring it up again a moment later with even greater gaiety and redoubled effrontery:

'Do you really want to know? . . . I am mad and that is all there is to it!'

So she finally silenced me and we spoke no more of it. So gay, carefree and talkative was she for the rest of that walk that I even began to share in her good-humour, and though my knees remembered much, my mind in that half hour forgot all.

'What I am sorry about is that our trout will be cold and our sardines will have gone soft!' said Aglaura jestingly as we set foot on the flagstones of the port.

I am telling you the truth when I say that however much I had recovered from the incident, I was still unable to have such concrete ideas about trout and sardines. But I pretended to laugh at Aglaura's regrets and promised her an omelette if the fish had been spoiled.

'An omelette would be welcome, but I would like to make it myself,' exclaimed the girl.

Sappho, who after her leap from thc Leucadian rock sets about preparing an omelette, is quite a fresh character in the great drama of human nature. But I can assure you that such a character is no grotesque poetic fiction but has lived in flesh and blood, just as you and I are living. In fact Aglaura not finding the trout to her taste, set herself to beating the eggs. I believe that the poor trout was most unjustly slandered just for the wilfulness of the girl in trying to get out of this impasse. I wondered open-mouthed. Bent over the fireplace with the handle of the frying-pan in one hand and the cover in the other to protect her face from the heat of the fire, she seemed like the cabin-boy of a Levantine caïque preparing a meal. The omelette proved to be excellent and after it the trout vindicated the insult offered to it by getting itself eaten. The sardines also did their best to go where the trout had gone before. In the end there remained only a few bones on our plates and from then on I have been persuaded that nothing so sharpens the appetite as having tried to commit suicide an hour before. Aglaura thought no more of it and I too began to regard this ugly incident as a dream or a jest and our appetites worked with such good will that seemed impossible to me after the anguished heartbeats of a short time before. I confess that I suspected some magic in this violent appetite and that Aglaura had bewitched me. Every sardine that she swallowed was an ugly thought that flew away while a gay and laughing one took its place. Sucking the tail of the last one, I tried to imagine the happiness I would have felt in a time of calm, of love and of harmony, enjoyed with the Pisana on these enchanted shores.

'Who knows?' I thought, swallowing the mouthful.

So I trusted to my good star after the great storm of that evening! How true it is that extremes meet, as the proverb says.

That evening was in fact the gayest and most agreeable that I passed with Aglaura during the journey, but much of that was perhaps due to my satisfaction at seeing her safe after so great a danger. When I saw her to her room (the tavern at Bardolino had from the end of the previous century pretensions to be an inn) I could not refrain from saying:

'You won't frighten me again like that, will you, Aglaura?'

'Certainly not, I swear to you,' she replied, pressing my hand.

Indeed next morning crossing the lake and for the next few days travelling through the newly born provinces of the Cisalpine Republic, she was so calm and composed that I continually wondered at her. Several times I risked touching upon that perilous leap of hers, but she always silenced me, saying that she had already confessed a hundred times that she had been mad and that I could be at peace since in that madness at least she would not be caught again. So we entered Milan happily enough, where we found the hero Bonaparte with a dozen or so Lombard muddlers busy improvising that botched up replica of the one and indivisible French Republic.

It was 21 November; a huge and festive crowd was surging from one street and another on to the Corso of the Porta Orientale and thence to the Campo del Lazzaretto, newly baptized the Campo della Federazione. Artillery thundered, thousands of tricolor flags waved in the breeze; there was a persistent ringing of festival bells, shouting, hats tossed in the air and a waving of scarves and handkerchiefs throughout that gay and tumultuous throng that was far from being calm and dignified. Neither Aglaura nor I had the heart to stay inside, while in the sunlight, under the free air of heaven, the established Italian government of the Cisalpine Republic was so soon to be inaugurated. Having put down my bundle and Aglaura being unwilling to quit her male disguise, we mingled with the crowd, very glad to have arrived in time for this solemn and memorable spectacle.

When we reached the square where the Archbishop was blessing the flags, between the Altar of God and that of the country, before the popular authority of the new government and the glorious guardianship of Bonaparte who was present on a special throne, I too confess that all my scruples were driven out of my head.

That was really the birth of a people and whether it had been Frenchmen or Turks who had awakened them, I cared not in the least. Those faces, those breasts, those cries filled with enthusiasm and great presage; this sudden concord of so many provinces, freed from various foreign dominations, to compose a single independence, a single liberty, spurred the imagination to greater hopes. When Serbelloni, President of the new Directory, swore by the memory of Curtius, of Cato and of Scaevola, that he would maintain, if necessary with his life, the Directory, the Constitution and the Laws, those great Roman names seemed perfectly attuned to the solemnity of the moment. We laugh now, when we know what the outcome was, but at that time the trust was immense, the republican virtues and hard earned liberties of the Middle Ages seemed things of small account, recalling the great shade of Caesar. In that carnival of liberty, my thoughts turned to Venice and I felt my eyes moisten; but the present ceremony drove out that distant memory. The edicts and the speeches were so pregnant with meaning that the flatteries made to the Venetians by Villetard no longer seemed either lies or deceptions. Those Venetians who attended the ceremony wept more for emotion than for sorrow and thenceforth considered it impossible that France, after having first granted liberty to such servile and indifferent provinces, would deny it to those who had always possessed it and had shown to the last that they held it most dear.

Bonaparte was once again uppermost in the affection and admiration of all; at the worst, they murmured against the French Directory who kept his hands tied, the usual excuse of thieves and swindlers of the public good. Even I began to believe that the Treaty of Campoformio was a momentary necessity, a temporary concession in order to recover afterwards more than had been conceded and seeing, close to, the work of these Frenchmen and the civilization of the Cisalpini it no longer surprised me that Amilcare had written to me quite cured of his Brutus-like ravings and that Giulio del Ponte and Lucilio had enlisted in the Lombard Legion, kernel of future armies.

I glanced along the ranks of the militia drawn up on the Campo del Lazzaretto looking for some of my friends and it seemed to me that I could in fact see some of them, though at that distance I could not be sure. But one I clearly recognized was holding a French flag; it was Sandro, my old friend the miller, with great plumes on his head and gold braid and tassels all over him. It seemed to me impossible that they could have decked him out so finely in so short a time, but it was really he, I could swear to it. I asked Aglaura if she could see the Signor Emilio, but she replied in a very dry tone that she could not. She seemed to be carried away by the festa and her cries and applause so struck those around her that she soon became the centre of a little group.

'Aglaura, Aglaura,' I whispered to her, 'remember you are a woman!'

'Man or woman, what does it matter?' she replied loudly, 'the worshippers of liberty have no difference of sex. They are all heroes!'

'Bravo bravo! Well said! Man or woman. Long live the Republic! Long live Bonaparte! . . . Long live the brave woman!'

I had to draw her away or they would have carried her off shoulder high; and she would have submitted, I believe, most willingly to this honour and I saw in her eyes a certain fire that recalled the fury of the Pythoness. With much trouble I was able to get her into a corner where a great crowd of women, the most troublesome and talkative that ever filled a market, was gathered. It was really a republic, that is to say an anarchy of empty heads. For my part, I know of no being that utters so many stupidities as a political woman. After a lot of talk they ended by tearing out each other's hair and those around joined in the fray, trying to calm them down. Then a

French corporal intervened and restored order with the butt of his musket. One who had asserted a short time before that instead of being no one, there were the Cisalpini and the French, was proved right. Above all, there could be no doubt that there were the French. When one looked well, one could see that they had ordained the government, chosen the Directory and nominated the members of the assemblies, the secretaries and the Ministers and had reserved the right to elect in due course the members of the Great Council and that of the Elders. But the people, new to this fervour of life, had all they could do to carry out their orders. From obeying blindly and like sheep to obeying actively and well had been a great step; the rest would be seen later, with Bonaparte as surety.

I confess that at that moment I too had my full share of the popular illusions, nor would I have called them illusions had it not been for the downfall that was to come later. For the rest, they had great and good reasons for hope. That day indeed was a great day and worthy of being honoured by their Italian descendants. It marked the first renaissance of Italian life; and Napoleon, in whom I then hoped and whom I afterwards defied, will always have some part of my gratitude for having so hastened the course of our annals. Venice had to fall; he accelerated and dishonoured that fall. The great dream of Macchiavelli had some time or other to detach itself from the world of fantasies and be transformed into action. It was Napoleon who caused the metamorphosis. That was a real merit, a real glory; and though he only did it by chance and afterwards betrayed it for later ambitions, it does not remain less true that the favour of chance and the interests of his ambition conspired for a moment with the salvation of the Italian nation and imposed upon him the first step towards its renaissance. Napoleon, with all his pride, with all his mistakes, with all his tyranny, was fatal to the old Republic of Venice, but useful to Italy. I tear now from my heart all the petty angers, the petty hatreds, the petty loves. False, liar and tyrant, he was none the less welcome.

If I was so fervent, you can imagine the effect on Aglaura whose head you will already have noted had been quite turned by all this enthusiasm for the republic and for liberty. To such preoccupations I ascribed her lack of interest that day in her Emilio; but I spoke to her that evening after we had taken lodgings in two tiny rooms in a very modest inn on the Corso di Porta Romana.

'It is you,' she replied, 'who imagine that I showed no interest. All the morning I did nothing but look for him and if I did not succeed in seeing him, that is not my fault. . . . But haven't you many Venetian friends whom you mean to go and look for this evening? . . . Very well then, go and bring them here; through them I will get some news. Meanwhile I will do my best to alter the women's clothes that you bought me. You know how much I thank you, my friend! I swear I will be eternally grateful to you. . . . But, above all, if you meet Spiro, pretend to know nothing of me. It wouldn't surprise me in the least if he had got to Milan before us.'

I promised to do as she asked, but begged her in return to keep her promise to send news of herself to her parents. She said that she would and I went out, first of all to the post to see if there were any letters for her or for me. . . . There were four, of which three were for me and two of those from the Pisana. In one she told me of all that had happened after my flight; the other contained only complaints, tears for my absence and longing for the time when we could once again embrace. I was astonished at the news she gave me. His Excellency Navagero had expelled his cousin, the Contessa, from his house and she had gone to live with her son, who had recovered his post with the State Audit. The elder Venchieredo had made a great uproar about my flight and stormed and shouted that he would place a sequestration order on all my property; but since nothing had been found save one insignificant old house, his zeal had calmed somewhat and he had even forgotten about the house, in which the Pisana was still living. It seemed, moreover, that the intercession of Raimondo had greatly contributed to impose some restraint on his reprisals, since the quick-witted youth had not completely forgotten the coquetries of the Pisana and it seemed that he reconsidered them seriously. At least I suspected something of the kind for the Pisana wrote to me that one day she had thoughtlessly received Doretta. This visit was certainly a move on Raimondo's part, who hoped to worm his way in by means of his mistress; Doretta served him blindly though he would certainly cast aside the instrument once his aim had been achieved. Familiarity between this vile woman and the Pisana was in no way to my taste and I considered writing a solemn paternal remonstrance to her with a caution to keep well away from Doretta—it is true that she merely laughed and made jokes about their meeting, but how could I tell what might happen, given that flighty little head of hers! But enough, I thought! May the French make haste to light the touchmatch, for if they did not I could see little good for me. That little madcap must be loved very much and at very close quarters to remain faithful and this experiment of distance I could not afford to prolong unduly!

Two other remarkable items of news were the uproar that the Partistagno was still creating about Clara and the installation of Father Pendola in a canonry of San Marco. The former, recently made a Cavalry Captain in the Imperial Army, probably through the influence of the famous Baron, his uncle, clinked his spurs day and night before the Convent of St Theresa, so much so indeed that Mother Redenta had asked for a sentry to reinforce the defences of the portress. The sentry was kept busy night and day presenting arms to the terrible Partistagno, who continually passed to and fro. He had really persuaded himself that the Contessa had forced Clara to take her vows because of the hatred and envy she felt for his family. Therefore his desire for revenge had revived once more and amongst other methods he had put into operation that most dangerous one of buying up many mortgages on the Fratta estates and harassing with petitions and executive orders the last remnants of that unfortunate patrimony. Certainly the Partistagno by himself was not capable of devising anything so diabolically cunning, but one could see behind him the devil's hoof of the elder Venchieredo who, after his condemnation, had sworn eternal hatred against the family of the Count of Fratta down to the last generation.

Moreover, between his efforts and those of the Partistagno, the thefts of Fulgenzio that aided their efforts and the carelessness of the Count Rinaldo, the active substance of the estate had become passive and a bankruptcy would have been little less than a good speculation. The castle, abandoned by all, was falling into ruins and only Monsignor's room still had doors and shutters to the windows. In the others, bailiffs, stewards and rogues had wrought unhindered, one sold the window-panes, another the locks, another the flagstones and another the beams of the ceilings. They had even carried off the poor Captain's door, for which reason the Signora Veronica suffered worse than ever from coughs and chills so that the weight of his matrimonial cross had increased some fifty times. Marchetto had left the castle and instead of being serjeant had become the parish sacristan. A strange transformation! . . . But buli were no longer of any use so they were forced to become saints!

What was still worse was that the Contessa, instead of receiving money from her property, now only got dunning letters and executive threats. She no longer knew where to turn and if it had not been for the miserable interest on the Pisana's dowry she would even have lacked for bread. None the less, she continued to gamble and Rinaldo's meagre monthly salary for the most part went into the bottomless pockets of some notorious sharpers.

The news from Fratta, the Pisana said she had got from her relatives at Cisterna, who had moved with their children to Venice in the hope of finding some profitable career for them since their family was in good odour with the Austrians. One way or another, there were only too many hands ready to dip into the public purse.

Who would want to remain uncommitted since by so doing there would be no hope whatever of any pickings? I confess that I have seen few such miracles in my life and not a single one among men of mature age. Disdain for honours and riches belongs to youth. It alone knows how to hold dear its most sacred part which alone makes possible great intentions and magnanimous deeds.

The other letter was from old Apostulos. In it he informed me of the flight of his daughter and the measures taken to trace her everywhere save in Milan. In that city, this duty was confided to me. I was to ask for news of her and search for her and, once found, either send her back to Venice or keep her with me, as she preferred. Certainly he would not want to exercise his paternal rights over a rebellious and fugitive daughter. Let her do as she liked. He did not curse her, since those who are mad do not deserve this, but he took no further interest in her.

However, he added in a postscript, he had made arrangements for the most searching investigations in the other cities of the *terraferma* and his representatives there had orders to bring the erring one back to Venice with them immediately. He relented only in my favour and if I considered that the girl's aberration would be better cured in Milan than in Venice, I was to act as I thought fit. These last words were underlined but I in no way understood their hidden significance. I thought of asking Aglaura for an explanation, whether they perhaps alluded to a marriage with Signor Emilio; but I did not then understand the reason for speaking of it with such mystery. Mine was certainly a strange fate, to be considered by both sides as the confidant of the other and everyone speaking to me with nods and veiled words which I understood no more than Arabic. For the rest, there was still no news from my father, and he did not expect to have any before Christmas, though the general news from the Levant was good.

With this medley of thoughts, news and perplexities in my mind I stopped at a café to ask the whereabouts of the headquarters of the Cisalpine Legion. They directed me to Santa Vincenzina, a couple of yards from the Piazza d'Armi. Once there I asked for news of Doctor Lucilio Vianello, of Amilcare Dossi and Giulio del Ponte from a greasy and sullen soldier who was furiously cleaning the shoes of one of his colleagues for the fee of a half-carafe.

'They belong to the first battalion; turn left,' said that helot of equality.

I turned to the left and repeated my inquiry to another soldier, even dirtier than the first, who was polishing the barrel of a musket with oil and wadding.

'I know all of them, God curse 'em!' he replied. 'Vianello is the doctor of this very battalion; he's the one who will cut all our throats by order of the French, who are tired of us. Do you know, citizen, that they have closed the hall of public instruction? . . .'

'I know nothing about it,' I replied, 'but where can I . . .'

'Wait a bit. As I was telling you, Vianello is our doctor and Dossi the standard-bearer of our battalion. Del Ponte is the corporal, a real drunken deathshead who can hardly stand on his feet and puts all his service duties on my back. Look at this! This is his musket which it is up to me to polish! . . . And that fine festival of this morning . . . making us stand upright like stakes for ten hours and sniff the air that has more winter in it than it should! . . . Devil take it! We enlisted to make war, to destroy the race of kings and aristocrats—not to pay court to the Directory and carry the candles for them in procession! . . . If they want such duties, let them send for the lackeys of the Archduke governor. It is a real insult . . . All today I have drunk nothing save a pint of Canneto. . . . Is it for nothing that one has become a Republican! . . . Citizen, will you honour me with a small loan to buy a pint? Giacomo della Porta, file-leader of the first battalion of the Cisalpine Legion at your service.'

I offered him, naturally as a loan, a Milanese lira on the understanding that he would take me without more ado to any one of the three that I had named. He threw aside the musket, the oil and wadding, made four little jumps like a marionette, with the lira between his thumb and forefinger and then spreading the fingers of his other hand wide open on his nose, rushed down the staircase in search of an innkeeper.

'So much for republican honesty!' I thought to myself, grumbling like an old man.

I had quite forgotten that with a piece of stamped paper and a festa on the Campo della Federazione one could only begin but not complete the reform of habits and furthermore that there will always remain in all the republics on this earth a certain number of persons who will prefer a glass of wine to giving a hand to their neighbours.

Finally I found in a corridor another soldier, well set up and smart, almost elegant, who replied to my salute by an almost courtly bow and called me citizen as four months before he might have called me Count or Excellency, so well-mannered and fine-spoken was he. He must have been some Marchese fired with the love of liberty who had thought to make himself a devotee of this new religion by enlisting with the Cisalpine legionaries. Elegant and thoughtless martyrs, who abound in all revolutions and of whom whosoever speaks ill merits excommunication, since with a little patience they end by becoming heroes! He indeed helped me on my way, leading me very efficiently to the room of Doctor Lucilio, at the door of which we turned to take leave of one another like two ministers after a conference.

I entered. I have no words to tell you of the surprise, the congratulations and the embraces of the doctor and of Giulio, who was with him. I really believe they would not have given warmer greetings to a brother so that I knew they had indeed a small place in their hearts for me. I felt a sort of remorse at clasping Giulio to my breast and kissing him. One might say that I still felt warm on my lips the kisses of the Pisana, whom he too had loved and who perhaps by her thoughtlessness and her coquetries had instilled into his veins the fire of fever that consumed him. But, on the other hand, he had renounced this love for one more worthy and rewarding. I found him pale and wasted indeed, but certainly in no worse state than he had been in Venice despite the hard military life of the barracks. Lucilio reassured me concerning him, saying that his malady had made no progress and that good companionship moderate and regular duties and spare and regular food might perhaps at length induce some improvement. Giulio smiled as one who perhaps believed, but did not consider it worth while to hope; he had become a soldier in order to die and not to be cured and was so accustomed to this idea that it led him forward gaily, and, like Anacreon, he crowned himself with roses at the grave side. I asked them about their hopes, their duties, their life. All was for the better. They had impatient and extravagant hopes of the revolution that was raging in Rome, in Genoa, in Piedmont and in Naples and of the movement towards unity that was beginning from the forthcoming association of Bologna, of Modena and even of Pesaro and Rimini to the Cisalpina.

'At Massa we shall touch the Mediterranean,' said Lucilio, 'what hinders us from touching the Adriatic at Venice?'

'And the French?' I asked.

'The French aid us well, since we are not yet in a position to aid ourselves. Certainly we must keep our eyes open and not swallow the lies of some fool like Villetard and we must above all hold firm tooth and nail to our liberties and not let them be taken from us for all the gold in the world.'

These were more or less my own ideas; but from the warmth of his voice and the vivacity of his gestures, I could see that the great ceremonies of the morning had kindled even the cautious imagination of Lucilio and that he was that evening no longer the passionless doctor of two months ago. In this guise he pleased me more, but was less infallible and however much his prognostics agreed with mine, I still did not wish to entrust myself blindly to them. I therefore expressed some doubts about the inexperience of the people, who seemed unready for the wise civilization of the republican ordinances, and about the insubordination I had myself observed among the recently formed militia.

'Those are two objections to which one gives a single reply,' said Lucilio. 'What is needed to create disciplined soldiers? . . . Discipline. What is needed to make true, virtuous and complete republicans? . . . The republic. Neither soldiers nor republicans are born spontaneously; all are born men, that is beings to educate either well or ill, future slaves or future Catos, according to whether they fall into honest or knavish hands. You will agree with me, too, that if the Republic does not succeed in forming perfect republicans, then in a short time tyranny will be even more willing and able to prepare them!'

'Who knows?' I said, 'The Rome of Brutus arose out of the Rome of Tarquin!'

'Oh, you can set your mind at ease, Carlino, on that point; we have not lacked Tarquins in four or five centuries of madness and slavery! . . . By now we must be sufficiently educated. But rather tell me something about yourself. Why did you delay so long in Venice? How did you manage to live there?'

I gave them as an excuse the death of Leopardo, the business affairs left unfinished by my father and finally plucked up courage to mention the name of the Pisana, sending a secret glance at Giulio. Both of them started to ask me about the row with the French officer, rumours of which had been trumpeted as far as Milan. I described the incident in detail and said that the inconvenience and dangers arising from it for the Pisana would have compelled me in any case to remain there to defend her and give what advice I could. I dwelt especially on the description of my flight, to impress them with the risks I had run by remaining in Venice, to which I would certainly not have exposed myself had there been no need. In a few words, I confessed to myself that I had been guilty of indolent delay but did not want others to be able to acquire information to make an accusation against me. In order not to labour this sore point unduly, I spoke about the provisional arrangements in Venice, of the last pillaging of the city by Serrurier, and of the new government set up there, in which the Venchieredo seemed to me to have some influence.

'Caspita! Didn't you know?' said Lucilio. 'He was the courier between the Imperialists at Gorizia and the Paris Directory! . . .'

'Or rather Bonaparte at Milan,' Giulio corrected him.

'As you like; it's all the same. Bonaparte could not undo what the

Directory had already plotted. The fact remains that Venchieredo was well paid but I fear, or hope, that he will go too far, since he always serves badly and has all the prejudices and mockery of one who serves too much.'

'By the by,' I asked, 'what can you tell me about Sandro of Fratta? I saw him this morning at the festa with so many constellations on him that he looked like the Zodiac!'

'He is now called Captain Alessandro Giorgi of the Chasseurs à Pied,' Lucilio replied. 'He won great honour in the repression of some seditious movements in the district of Genovesato. His advancement continues. They made him lieutenant and then captain in one month; but of his company I believe only four remained alive, what with the musket-shots, the assassinations and the great hardships. One of these had to become Captain; the others were two cobblers and one shepherd, therefore the miller was chosen, as he should have been! . . . You will see how puffed up he is! But he's an honest and good fellow who offers his protection to everyone he meets and will not hesitate to offer it to you too.'

'Many thanks, 'I replied. 'I will accept it if need be.'

'Not now,' replied Lucilio, 'your place is with us and with Amilcare.'

They then told me about Amilcare, that he was prouder and more exaggerated than ever and that he maintained the morale of their company with expedients that only he knew how to find in the worst extremities. Reduced to living on their pay, you can imagine they were often in the red; it was then for Amilcare to find ways of making money and to think up ingenious methods of saving until their next pay was due. The mention of Amilcare recalled to my mind Bruto Provedoni also, who, it was said, had left at the same time as Georgi and of whom I had had no news. It seems he was involved in the petty skirmishes in Liguria and the Piedmont where, despite the fact that the king was a good friend and a better servant of the Directory, they were always trying to keep the resistance alive in order to be able to find some support there whenever the moment came to strike a blow. The botched-up Ligurian Republic had been spurred on to make war on him and he had been forbidden to defend himself. The poor king therefore did not know where to turn, since precipices yawned all around him. It was lucky that warlike and faithful Piedmont in no way resembled somnolent Venice, otherwise some similar ignominy would have been seen. Ignominy there was indeed, but all on the French side. . . . It then struck me that this was a favourable moment to ask about Emilio Tornoni. I pretended to know him and asked for news of him. Lucilio stuck out his lip and did not reply. Giulio told me with a sneer that he had left for Rome with a beautiful Milanese countess, probably to take part in the revolution there. Their contemptuous attitude made me somewhat suspicious, but I could get no more out of them. A little later, that hothead Amilcare returned—more embraces, more astonishment! He had become as dark as an Arab, with a voice that seemed attuned to the sound of musket-shots; but they explained to me that he had spoilt it in this way in continually teaching recruits to march. Indeed, taking a step, which is in itself the easiest thing in the world, has been reduced by the tactics of war to the most laborious art. Nevertheless, before Frederick II, battles were fought either without marching or marching very badly; but it is not incredible that a hundred years from now they will be teaching soldiers *entrechats* or to march in polka step. That evening never seemed to come to an end; there were so many things to talk about; we had gone out on to the city walls and at the drum-beat Lucilio made a sign to the other two that it was time to retire.

'Ah yes!' said Amilcare, shrugging his shoulders, 'in my view an officer should obey the drum.'

'I am sick and supposed to be in hospital,' said Giulio.

I relied on Lucilio to recall them to their duty, for I was impatiently awaiting the moment to rejoin Aglaura and take her the letter from her father and the news of Emilio, but the two conscripts paid no attention to the doctor's words and I was forced to enjoy their company until after nine. Then they accompanied me to my lodgings, but since I did not invite them in and they saw the shadow of a woman outlined on the blinds by the light behind they began to make fun of me, to indulge in a thousand conjectures and rally me on my good fortune. That reckless fool Amilcare indeed made so much commotion that I feared at any moment to see Aglaura appear on the balcony. When God so willed, Lucilio persuaded them to go away and I was able to go upstairs to the girl and console her for having been left so long alone. I gave her the letter and saw her sigh and weep on reading it, but pretended not to notice.

'May I ask who is writing to you?' I said.

She told me it was her brother Spiro. But she hastily evaded all the other questions I asked her and merely told me that he was very well informed and believed her to be in Milan in my company. How was it then that he had not come to join her, seeing all the great affection that he had for her? That was what I could not make out, but it became clear later when I learnt that Spiro had been thrown into prison as an accomplice to my flight. That very letter had been sent from prison and it was for that reason that Aglaura had been so moved. She then asked me if I had received any letters from Venice and when I said yes asked me for the news in them.

Without more ado, I handed her the letter from her father and the one in which the Pisana had told me about the troubles in Venice. She read them through without batting an eyelid; only when she reached the place where Raimondo Venchieredo and Doretta were mentioned she gave a little start of surprise and repeated the name of Doretta over to herself as if to make sure of it.

'What is it?' I asked.

'Nothing; only I know this signora, at least by repute, and I wondered at finding her name in a letter addressed to you. I would have been almost as astonished if I had heard that the Venchieredo was on your side.'

'And how comes it that you know the Venchieredo?'

'I know him . . . just because I know him! . . . Not well, though, I must admit. He had some business or other, I think, with Emilio.'

'By the way, I have some bad news for you.'

'What is it?'

'The Signor Emilio Tornoni has left for Rome.' (I maintained a discreet silence about the Countess.)

'I knew it, but he will return,' replied Aglaura with an almost defiant air. 'However, I beg you to try and find out tomorrow if the Signor Ascanio Minato is here, the aide-de-camp of General Baraguay, or the Signor d'Hauteville, secretary to General Berthier. They are persons who can be of use to me in regard to news of Emilio which I can get from them at need.'

'At your service.'

'And tell me, have you learnt nothing more about him?'

'Nothing else.'

'Nothing—nothing . . . really nothing?'

'Nothing, I tell you.' I was quite impressed by the young girl and all her talk, apparently so indifferent, about aides-de-camp and generals, and did not want to let her know of the silent disdain I had noted in Lucilio and del Ponte when I had mentioned Tornoni to them. I know the sort of pleasure it gives girls to hear ill spoken of their lovers.

'Aglaura,' I went on after a pause, to start the conversation once more, 'you are a little mysterious and you will agree that my kindness and my discretion . . .'

'. . . are unequalled . . .' she finished.

'No, I did not mean to say that; I would rather have added that I deserved a small grain of trust on your part.'

'It is true, my friend. Ask, and I shall reply.'

'If you stand there as rigid and as serious as a queen, the words will die in my mouth. Come, be confused and happy as that evening when I first saw you . . . so, you really please me! . . . Tell me then; why are you so familiar with all these names of the French General Staff? A little while ago you sounded like a commander arranging his forces for a battle.'

'That is all you want to know?'

'That is all. For the moment my curiosity stops there.'

'Very well; these Signori were close friends of Emilio; that is why I know them.'

'The Signor Minato also?'

'Even more than the others; but he is also the most gallant; that is to say, less of a rogue than all these other thieves.'

'Gently, Aglaura! . . . You are no longer the same girl as this morning. . . . How can you abuse now the very same persons you were praising to the skies a few hours ago?'

'I? I praised the Republic to the skies, not those who made it. Even an ass may sometimes be laden with precious stones. . . . In any case, those who are thieves indoors may become heroes outdoors; but butcher heroes, not . . .'

'Tell me, does Spiro write that he will come and fetch you, or that you must go to Venice?'

'Why this question? . . . Are you tired of having me with you?'

'Good night, Aglaura. We will talk again tomorrow. Tonight you are ill-disposed.'

In fact, I withdrew into my little room next to hers and lay down, thinking of the Pisana, of the hardships she must have endured and of the dangers of her solitude. Above all, that reconciliation with Rosa and Doretta's visit worried me; then Raimondo, for I understood that he was the ram who would pass through the gap made for him by the sheep. I thought over a long letter to be written the next day and then from thoughts of the Pisana I turned to thoughts of Aglaura, which pained me less but were even less comprehensible. Who could have discerned a ray of clarity in that little whirlwind? . . . Not I, surely . . . from Padua to Mantua she had led me on from one surprise to another; she did not seem to be a girl intent on living her own life, but a French novelist intent on composing an epic. Her actions, her words, were continually changing, retiring, scrambling over facts, as full of contradictions and surprises as a Pindaric ode badly refashioned by the scholiasts. I dreamed about them all night, and thought over them a good part of the morning, before I went out with the letter to the Pisana in my pocket, but without coming to any conclusion about them. I enclosed a letter for Apostulos, in which I told him all about Aglaura and put myself at his disposal in all matters concerning her; I begged him also to make whatever provision might be necessary for the Pisana, as if it had been for myself. Naturally I did all this without saying a word to the young girl, since it was a question of my conscience and I wanted no ceremony about it. To be a brother to her, yes, but not to make myself a rogue for her sake.

About midday I encountered Lucilio at the Duomo café which at that time was the fashionable meeting-place and there we had made an appointment. He was very sorry that he had not been able to enroll me in the Cisalpine Legion where there was not a single place to be had; but rather than leave someone like myself unoccupied, he said, he would have sought inspiration from the devil himself and I could be sure that one of the very best inspirations had come to him.

'Now I will take you to your General,' he said, 'General, Commander, fellow-soldier, whatever you like! He is one of those men who are too superior to others to take the trouble to show it; one can hardly believe that he has only one spirit for it seems that his great activity should be able to tire out a dozen a day. None the less, he admires quiet people and even sympathizes with the indolent. On the field I wager that he alone would be enough to win a battle, although it is not clear at the first glance where his extraordinary powers lie. He is a Neapolitan and in Naples they say he has the throwing power or, as they call it in our district, the evil eye; not to be confused, however, with that evil, even more evil, eye of the late Chancellor of Fratta.'

'And who is this Phoenix?' I asked him.

'You will see for yourself and if he is not to your taste I will change my very name.'

With these words he hurried me out of the café and went at top speed beyond the Naviglio di Porta Nuova towards the city walls. We entered a huge house with a courtyard crammed with horses, grooms, horsecopers, saddles and trappings of all sorts as in a cavalry barracks. There was a coming and going of soldiers up and down the staircase, of sergeants, of orderlies, as in a General Staff Headquarters. In the antechamber there were arms stacked or piled in heaps in the corners; in one corner there was even heaped up a little store of tunics, shoulder belts and military boots.

'What is this?' I thought. 'Is it the Arsenal?'

Lucilio pressed on without paying attention to anyone. Indeed, without even announcing himself in the last antechamber to a sort of aide-de-camp who stood there counting the ceiling beams, he opened a door and entered, leading me by the hand into the presence of the master of this military academy. This was a tall young man of about thirty, the real image of a military adventurer, the living portrait of one of those Orsini, those Medici, those Colonna, whose lives were a continual series of battles, sacks, duels and prison sentences. He was even called Ettore Carafa, a most noble name made even more illustrious by the independence of the one who bore it and by his love of liberty and country. He had suffered a long imprisonment for his republican intrigues in the famous Castel Sant'Elmo; thence, a fugitive, he had taken refuge in Rome, and came from there to Milan to form at his own expense a legion to liberate Naples. He had one of those spirits that, with others or alone, wish to act at all costs; and his greatness of soul shone gloriously in his features. Only between his eyebrows there was a tiny scar, which seemed like the sign of a sad fatality for the noble hopes of a brave man. He rose from the pallet on which he had been lying, gave his hand to Lucilio and congratulated him on the fine officer who accompanied him.

'A very poor officer,' I replied. 'The real military art I know only by name.'

'Have you the courage to get yourself killed to defend your country and your honour?' replied Carafa.

'Not one, but a hundred lives,' I said, 'I would give for such noble reasons.'

'There you are, my friend; I permit you from now on to consider yourself a perfect soldier.'

'Soldier, yes,' replied Lucilio, 'but officer?'

'Let me be the judge of that! . . . Can you ride, load a musket and handle a sword?'

'I know something of all three.'

That was due to Marchetto and I thanked him for it then as a little while before I had thanked the Rector for his classical education.

'Then you may consider yourself an officer too. In a Legion like mine which wages war piecemeal, a good eye and a good will are worth more than knowledge. Come back to me this evening at last post and I will give you your company and you may be sure that in three months from now we shall have conquered the Kingdom of Naples.'

I seemed to hear Robert Guiscard or some paladin of Ariosto speaking, but he was quite serious as I realized later from experience.

I was a little embarrassed to ask him if I might sleep out of barracks, but at last summoned up courage. He said to me smiling that that was an officer's privilege.

'I understand,' he added, 'that your nights are occupied with another Colonel.'

I was too embarrassed to deny it. Lucilio smiled. The fact remained that I could not leave Aglaura alone but what pleasure it was to me to mount guard over her, God alone knew! I was at the time charmed with the Signor Ettore Carafa and twice as much so later. I shall always remember with pleasure that austere, energetic military life. In the morning, drill with my company, then lunch and a long session of talk with Amilcare, with Giulio or with Lucilio; in the afternoon and evening long talks with Aglaura, who was still waiting for Emilio and would not even hear of returning to Venice. In the meantime, some bitter-sweet letters from the Pisana. So we came to the moment of the revolution in Rome which was to give the first foothold to the military operations of Carafa in the Kingdom of Naples.

CHAPTER XVI

On 15 February 1798, five notaries had drawn up the Act of Liberty of the Roman people in the Campo Vaccino. There took part as liberator that same Berthier who had taken part as betrayer in the Congress of Bassano for the preservation of the Venetian Republic. The Pope remained shut up in the Vatican among his priests and Swiss guards and having refused to divest himself of his temporal authority was taken from Rome by armed force and sent into Tuscany. He was Pius VI, a unique example of Italian inflexibility in those times of continual change and of well-founded fears. However little of a Christian I may be, I remember that I admired the fortitude of that grand old man and, contrasting it with the tremulous weakness of the Doge Manin, I made a painful comparison between these two most ancient governments of Italy.

Rome, already consummated by the Treaty of Tolentino was completely despoiled by the republicans; the assassination of General Duphot, the pretext for war, was celebrated by obsequies, by illuminations and by the sack of all the churches. Heavy cases of precious stones made their way to France, while the army was deprived of everything and rioted against Massena, the successor to Berthier. The countryside was in revolt and there were daily murders; in fact there began one of those social dramas still possible only in southern Italy or in Spain.

In that turn of events, once the organization of Carafa's legion had been completed, there was nothing else to do save to await the consent of the French commander-in-chief to set out. I found myself in a fine muddle. Aglaura wanted to leave with me, since the trip to

Rome accorded with her ideas; I did not want to refuse her nor to expose her to the dangers of a long march at so perilous a moment. I therefore wrote to Venice, but they did not reply. The Pisana, too, had kept me in the dark about her intentions for some time past. The expedition to Rome seemed to begin for me under very sad auspices. None the less, I went on hoping from day to day, and while Carafa raged about that blessed consent always withheld, I consoled myself with the idea that a wider field for some vague hope still remained. My three friends, with a part of the Lombard Legion, had already moved southwards towards Rome and I remained alone and with no other company than that of the splendid Captain Alessandro.

The worst thing was that, whether from Venice or from Milan, the rumour was widespread that I was living with a beautiful Greek and there were continual jests about it among my fellow-soldiers. You may imagine what a comfort that was to me, with the fine construction that could be drawn from it. I assure you that I would have given a hand like Mucius Scaevola for the Signor Emilio to get tired of his Milanese Countess and come back to claim Aglaura. Not that she was much of a burden to me and in any case I was already accustomed and acted as her guardian with an exemplary patience, but it irritated me to have the appearance of a happiness that in fact belonged to another.

But on 1 March the Legion had orders to start at once for Rome and there join up with the Franco-Cisalpine army for future operations.

There was no longer time to put my trust in fortune. Aglaura was still on my hands and I would have to leave without news of the Pisana or of my father. If the sentiment of honour, the love of country and of liberty had not been so strong in me, I would certainly have made some grave blunder. Meanwhile the hail that was to descend upon my head rattled among the clouds and I was aware of nothing at all.

Desperate at the long silence of the Pisana and the Apostulos family, I had written to Agostino Frumier, imploring him by our former friendship to give me news of persons so near to my heart. I had mentioned this letter to no one, since both Lucilio and the other Venetians had much against Frumier and considered him as a deserter. None the less, I sent it, not knowing to whom else to turn, and waiting and waiting, I had already given up hope when an answer arrived.

But can you guess who it was that wrote to me? . . . It was Raimondo Venchieredo! Certainly Frumier had taken fright at maintaining a correspondence with an exile and had passed the burden to another. Raimondo wrote that everyone in Venice wondered to hear that I had been without news of the Pisana for so long, he most of all; that they had very good reason to believe her in Milan with my connivance and consent, sharing with me the pleasures thereof; that he had delayed writing to me for that very reason since he had judged it superfluous for my peace of mind, considering my despair only a trick to put the old Countess, the Count Rinaldo and the Navagero off the scent. They, for their part, had washed their hands of the whole affair and I should tell the Pisana that as far as he was concerned, even if she had been received peaceably by her own family, there would still be plenty of time for him to take his revenge.

The letter ended abruptly at this point so that I continued to rack my brains for answers to suit these allusions. Why was Raimondo so furious with the Pisana? What did her disappearance from Venice mean? . . . Could it really be true? . . . Could she be in Milan without giving me a sign of life? It did not seem possible. And how could she have set out on a journey and on an expensive existence in inns? . . . It is true that she had a diamond or two and could even have had recourse to the Apostulos. But of them Raimondo said never a word. What could have happened? Was Spiro still languishing in prison? But why didn't his father write? In fact, the news from Venice only added another thorn to those I already had in my heart and made me most unwilling to leave. Carafa also no longer seemed to be so impatient, or so I explained it to myself, since he was no longer so irritated at my ill-concealed wish to delay. One day, I remember, he took me aside privately and put me through a very strange interrogation. Who was the beautiful Greek who was staying with me? Why were we living together? (I myself did not know that!) Had I other loves, and where and who were they? In fact he seemed to me like the confessor of some young nobleman just returned from his first year at the university. I replied truthfully, but with some perplexity especially in regard to Aglaura. How could it be otherwise? It was so complicated a matter that it only required the astonishment of my interrogator to make it entirely inexplicable.

'So you love a Signora from Venice yet notwithstanding you are living in Milan with this beautiful Greek?'

'Unfortunately, that is so.'

'I find that hard to believe, it is so unusual. In fact I don't believe it, I don't believe you! Good-bye, Carlino! . . .'

He went away very gaily as if his disbelief in this intrigue had meant some immeasurable good fortune for him. However I was by now accustomed to Signor Ettore's whims and I concluded that he was pleased to have something to laugh about. As for me, since the departure of Amilcare, I no longer felt any desire for amusement and if there was anyone who sometimes cleared my brow a little of its troubles it was Aglaura with her high-spirited wilfulness. She owed me this slight recompense for all the anger and anxiety she had made me suffer since our meeting in Padua.

One evening just before we were due to leave she and I were sitting together in our little lodging at the Porta Romana, where two little trunks and the emptiness of the drawers and cupboards recalled the journey that we were about to undertake, even if we had not remembered it only too well from the fears we both had about it, though we did not confess them to one another. For some days past I had been rather bad tempered with Aglaura; her determination to accompany me to Rome, even without any word from her parents, made me a little suspicious of her good faith. I was almost prepared to throw the bomb and tell her of the perfidy and infidelity of the one for whom she seemed ready to sacrifice everything, even the most sacred duties of a daughter, when, I don't know exactly how, at one of her glances filled with humility and pain, I felt myself soften. From the judge that I had wished to be, I felt myself change little by little to a penitent. The anxieties, the uncertainties that had so long tormented me had grown to such an extent that they demanded outlet. That glance of Aglaura implored me so piteously that I could no longer hold out, and I told her of the suspense in which I had been living concerning the Pisana, her long and cruel silence, and her leaving me in ignorance of her departure from Venice.

'Ah me!' I exclaimed, 'it would be too great a folly to try and delude myself! . . . She has gone back to what she always was. Distance has made her love die through abstinence. She will have taken up with someone else, perhaps some rich man or some scapegrace who will satiate her with pleasure for a year or so, and then. . . . Oh Aglaura! To despise the one person whom he loves more than his own life is a torment greater than any man can bear!'

Aglaura clutched at my hand that I had raised while saying these words. Her eyes flashed, her nostrils dilated and two tears of fury reflected in the lantern light the baleful fire of her glances.

'Yes,' she shouted, almost beside herself. 'Curse, curse in my name too the vile and the unfaithful! With this hand that you have raised to God as if to entrust to him your vengeance, seize a bundle of his thunderbolts and loose them on their heads!'

I realized that I had touched some secret and bleeding wound in her heart and the sympathy of my grief with hers opened my heart more than ever to trust and compassion. I seemed to have found in her a friend, even a real sister, and I let flow freely on her breast the tears that had for so long been pent up within me. Her indignation too was softened by the feeling of pity and we embraced like brother and sister; we wept together and wept unrestrainedly, the wretched comfort of the wretched.

At that moment the door burst open and a man, enveloped in a cloak sprinkled with snowflakes, entered the room. He gave a cry, threw back his hood and we both recognized the pale features of Spiro.

'Have I come too late?' he asked in a tone of voice that I shall never forget.

I was the first to throw myself into his arms.

'Oh, blessings on you!' I stammered, covering his face with kisses. 'How long I have been hoping that you would come! . . . Spiro, Spiro, my brother!'

He pushed me away, tugging at his collar as if he was stifling, and replied to my kisses only with a hoarse roar.

'Spiro, for pity's sake, what is the matter?' Aglaura asked him timidly, throwing her arms about his neck.

At the touch of her hand and the sound of her voice, he trembled all over.

'Listen to me, Aglaura,' he began in a voice that he tried to control but which none the less was still rough and harsh. 'Listen to me, in the name of the love I bear you! . . . I was about to follow you when I was put into prison. In my cell, every day, every minute, I sought for some way to escape and rejoin you, to save you from the abyss into which you have fallen. At last I succeeded. . . . A boat brought me as far as Ravenna; from there I had decided to go on to Milan since my heart told me that you were there. But, after arriving at Bologna, some Venetians who had taken refuge there gave me news of Emilio Tornoni, who had passed through that city, flying from Milan with a lady, and heading for Rome . . . you can well understand that I could not afford to waste time in getting details and dates. My conjectures, on broad lines, were justified; I turned in haste towards Rome and learnt there that the Republic had already been proclaimed! . . . Well, you must know, Aglaura! . . . Your Emilio is a vile traitor, as I always told you, but you wouldn't listen to me. . . . He betrayed you for a noble whore from Milan! He betrayed the Venetians to the French and betrayed the French too for the Imperial *zecchini* that the Signor Venchieredo brought him from Gorizia! . . . He had fled to Rome only to betray again! . . . On the recommendation of a Reverend Father of Venice, he was taken into the good graces of some Cardinals in order to work on the credulity of the Pope, claiming to be a most influential friend of Berthier. Moreover, he deceived Berthier too, appropriating to his own use a great part of the spoils of Rome. The people, disgusted, seized him while he was directing the sacking of a church; French and Romans alike were overjoyed at this and he was publicly hanged on the Campidoglio! . . . His whore had taken flight the day before for Ancona with her very good friend Ascanio Minato!'

Aglaura had turned all colours during Spiro's furious tirade. When he had finished, she had already resumed her usual gravity.

'Very well,' she said, looking directly at Spiro, 'justice has been done. God has taken it for Himself, and did not wish me to stain my hands with it. Blessed be God's kindness!'

'So it is really true?' said Spiro bitterly. 'And you are brazen enough to confess it to me? . . . Don't you love him any longer? . . . You should be afraid, Aglaura, for a single word of mine could avenge me for your effrontery!'

'Be afraid of you?' replied Aglaura, still calmly. 'I am afraid only of two things, my conscience and God! . . . In a short while I shall be afraid of nothing!'

'What are you thinking of doing?' asked Spiro almost menacingly.

'I mean to kill myself!' Aglaura replied, coldly and disdainfully.

'No, by all the Saints!' I intervened. 'I have your word and you will keep it.'

'You are right, Carlino,' she replied 'I will not kill myself! . . . But unhappy you, unhappy me; let us make common cause. Let us marry and leave the rest to God.'

I thought the ceiling would have fallen on my head, so loud was the bellow that escaped from Spiro.

'And if . . .' he began to say as if in answer to an inner suspicion that went no farther. Then suddenly his features became more composed, a pallor spread over his face, his limbs ceased to tremble and he once more seemed to become a man after appearing like a wild beast. These details remained fixed in my mind so that all the next night I did nothing but turn them over in my thoughts and try to guess from them what tremendous and mysterious passions had stirred Spiro's soul. It seemed to me impossible that the indignation of a brother would display itself so brutally and violently.

Having apparently recovered his calm, the young Greek sat down between us; we were well aware of the effort he made in remaining, but did not dare reproach him for it. He watched the two of us with a furtive eye and from time to time pity, despair and a last trace of rage alternated on his anxious features. He told us then that the absence of letters from his father was due to the fact that he had been forced to leave suddenly for Albania and Greece, whence he had not yet returned.

'And so,' he said, 'you do not want to come with me to Venice, Aglaura, where I remain alone, without happiness and without hope?'

'No, Spiro, I cannot go with you,' replied the girl, lowering her eyes before the young man's flaming glances.

Spiro looked at me again and if his glance did not devour me on the spot it was only because it could not; then he turned once again to the girl.

'What hope now leads you on, Aglaura? . . . For pity's sake tell me! . . . At least I have the right to know! I am your brother!'

These last words were hissed between clenched teeth so that they were scarcely comprehensible.

'Tell me if you have any tie of affection or of duty,' he went on, 'I swear to you that I will help you to sactify them.'

This was another cry even more tormented than the first.

'No, I have none,' replied Aglaura in a faint voice.

'Why won't you come with me then?' Spiro asked, rising in front of her like a master before a slave.

'I think you know!' said Aglaura, letting these words fall one by one on Spiro's anger which was already about to flare up again. But instead they had the effect of calming him once more.

He turned on the room a long and searching glance; then he left, saying that he would see us again and that everything, in one way or another, would then be settled. However much I implored Aglaura to explain some parts of the dialogue that had been beyond my understanding, it was impossible to get another word out of her. She wept, she tore her hair, but she would not utter a word. A little indignant, a little pitying, I went to my room and a tormented imagination kept me up until after midnight. Then I heard a knocking at my door and thinking that it would be orders from my captain I told whoever was there with some irritation to come in. My room opened on to the staircase and I had forgotten to bar the door. To my great surprise, instead of a soldier, I saw Spiro again, but so changed in a couple of hours that he no longer seemed himself. He begged me humbly to forgive him his furious outburst of anger and begged me, by all that I held most sacred, to intervene with Aglaura to get her forgiveness also. I felt as if I had completely lost touch with what was going on, and he ended by bewildering me completely when he cried, his eyes wild, that he loved her and could no longer contain himself.

'You love her?' I replied, 'but that seems to me quite natural. Are you not of the same blood, of the same parents? Love her, then, and may God bless you!'

'You do not understand, Carlino,' he said. 'Very well, I will explain! Aglaura is not my sister; she is your mother's daughter; you are her brother!'

A sudden light illuminated the darkness of my thoughts and I was about to ask for an explanation of this extraordinary development when Aglaura, having heard those words spoken by Spiro in a loud voice, rushed into the room and straight into my arms, weeping for joy.

'I felt it,' she said. 'I felt it and dared not believe it.'

Bewildered, confused, still not knowing what to believe, yet moved to the depths of my heart, I pressed Aglaura's tear-stained face to my breast. Later I would ask for explanations and proofs; for the moment I enjoyed the supreme comfort of finding a sister in that world where I had wandered desolate and an orphan. Spiro watched us in silence with an expression that showed that he both shared our joy and repented of his rage. After we had recovered from that sweet and very tender reconciliation, he told us that my mother had sent Aglaura to his father from the hospital where she had given birth to her and had died a few days later. My father, when he was told of this, had written to Apostulos from Constantinople asking him to take charge of the child and bring her up as if she were his own, so that she would not be ashamed of her birth. Who would have suspected so much love, so much delicacy in my father? I blessed him with all my heart and reflected that the diamond is to be found among the roughest and hardest rocks. Spiro then told me of certain words uttered by his mother from which he had guessed the mystery of Aglaura's birth even before he had left for Greece.

On his return, with the dreams of fifteen years' absence in his head, to see her and to fall in love with her had been the work of a single moment; but he had found an invincible opposition in her love for that Emilio, for whom, without ever knowing him, he had vowed eternal hatred. That hate had turned to fury, and love had grown in all the tenderness of pity, when he had learnt of the infamous conduct, the frauds and treachery of that youth, some inkling of which must have reached Aglaura also.

'Yes, indeed,' Aglaura broke in. 'For what other reason, do you suppose I left Venice if not to punish him for his betrayal of our country?'

'Why then did you always forbid me to blame him?' said Spiro.

'Because,' replied Aglaura in a faint thread of a voice, 'I was afraid of you . . . of you . . . my brother!'

'It is true,' cried out the poor young man. 'I was a wretch! . . . But how can one always command one's eyes? How could I believe you to be a sister and treat you as one when I knew that you were not and when I was hiding a love for you fifteen years old and strengthened by all the stimulus of separation? . . . Pardon my eyes, Aglaura! . . . If they sometimes sinned, my will was not guilty! . . .'

'Oh, I forgive you, Spiro, 'Aglaura exclaimed suddenly. 'But if I had really felt myself to be your sister, I would have mistrusted those glances; let me believe that the ill was neither mine nor yours, or at least half and half!'

I then asked Spiro somewhat ingenuously why he had not revealed this sweet secret three hours before and had instead amused himself by enacting that ferocious Orestean scene. He was embarrassed, but finally replied that having learnt of Emilio's new love and that the lady who had fled with him from Milan was not Aglaura, monstrous suspicions had tormented him.

'When I first came here yesterday evening and found you together in one another's arms, those suspicions finally overcame my reason! . . . Oh God, what a misfortune! I say misfortune, since it would not have been your fault, but none the less there are fatalities that like the greatest crimes leave in the soul an eternal remorse. Do you understand me now, Carlino? . . . I was mad!'

I shuddered, thinking what he must then have suffered.

'Yet you told us nothing!' I replied.

'There was a moment when I was about to tell you everything! I believed that so I should have been revenged.'

'Yet you refrained?'

'For pity, Carlino, and for justice, I refrained. If the evil had already been done, why punish you who were innocent? It was better that I should go away, taking with me my despair and my jealousy and leaving your happiness to you.'

'Spiro, how noble of you!' I exclaimed. 'A soul like yours commands admiration even more than love and gratitude.'

Aglaura wept unrestrainedly, pressing my arm with one hand and looking at Spiro through the fingers of the other.

'Tell me, then, where were you all those hours?' I asked, turning to Spiro.

'First of all I went outside, into the fresh air, to breathe and to ask enlightenment of God; then, as my heart counselled me, I came back to the inn and questioned the host and the porters. . . . Oh, it needed little, Carlino, it needed little for me to believe again. That cloud of despair had dissolved; already it seemed to me impossible that God would allow such an evil to occur in all innocence. When I heard of the life you were leading here, just like brother and sister, simple, modest and reserved, when I heard of your delicate behaviour towards Aglaura, the certainty of your innocence filled my heart and

I bewailed and cursed my foolish haste and swore I would not let the night pass without taking from your heart the knife with which I had stabbed you! . . . For pity's sake, Carlino! . . . Aglaura, if by my great affection I have ever deserved anything of you, pity me, forgive me, reserve for me if nothing else, at least a little corner in your memory . . . and if my presence recalls to you some angry thoughts . . . then . . .'

I turned silently to Aglaura since I felt that this was not enough to reward the fine magnanimity of Spiro. She understood me, or perhaps understood her own heart; she took the hand of the young man and putting it in mine, as if we were all three united in one single embrace, she said:

'Enough, Spiro! This is our reply? Let us become a single family!'

The rest of the night we enjoyed in friendly and joyful talk and in examining the records brought by Spiro and left by his father in Venice, from which the birth of Aglaura in the hospital was clearly proven. The name of the father did not appear and you can well imagine that it did not occur to any of us to pay attention to this unpleasant omission.

We behaved as if a father was a matter superfluous in the mystery of generation; I knew enough of the heavy burdens weighing on my mother's soul in the last stage of her life and I understood them, but neither filial piety nor respect for my own and my father's name counselled me to disclose them. I therefore accepted Aglaura as a sister and with all my heart thanked Heaven for an unhoped for and most precious gift and did my best to try and make everything even more pleasant by changing into ties of blood the friendship that already united me to Spiro. The transformation from ideas of death, hatred and revenge to those of peace, love and marriage was a little hard for Aglaura, but with my aid and Spiro's we overcame her doubts. From thenceforward she saw that everything fell into its right place, and women, to see everyone satisfied, are even capable of getting themselves married, especially when by such an expedient they satisfy themselves in the first place. In those times few formalities were necessary for a wedding. Interpreting the tacit wishes of Spiro, I occupied myself so much and with such happy results that before the departure of the Legion I had the satisfaction of seeing him Aglaura's husband. We then left Milan in company, since the Signor Ettore willingly gave me permission to accompany them as far as Mantua. Thence I could rejoin him at Florence on the road to Ferrara.

This brief glimpse of family content was necessary to me to break the darkness of my outlook, which had begun to be too threatening, since Spiro had also brought me some news of my father which, even if not direct, was at least credible. It reported that he had arrived without mishap at Constantinople and had there occupied himself more than ever in that most difficult task that preoccupied him, but that unexpected obstacles had held him up. He was well and would send news of himself, or return when his enterprise was completed. The departure of old Apostulos for Greece could well have been connected with my father's machinations in Turkey but I gathered that Spiro either did not know or would not tell me more, and I changed the subject, only charging him to send me as quickly as possible, and anywhere that I might be found, whatever news of my father he might get.

Aglaura, who had taken the view that we shared a father since in fact we shared a mother, said that she would see that this was done and that she would seek for every means of getting frequent news of him since so good a papa was dear to her also. We separated at Mantua on the very day when that city had finally obtained permission to join the Cisalpina and the gloom of our leavetaking was lost in the universal joy and hope. I had found a sister and seemed to be well on the way to finding a country; it seemed good to be alive even if I had lost my love for ever.

I left Mantua in better humour than I could ever have imagined. My purse was quite depleted (you can imagine that the thousand ducats had suffered somewhat from our long residence in Milan) so that this thin purse and a certain soldierly modesty only permitted me a carriage as far as Bologna; one of those vehicles that gives the sufferer some of the illusion of sitting in a chaise with all the inconveniences of trotting on a miller's horse. The carts of the Vicentino had nothing in common with these; they seemed like gondolas in comparison with these boneshakers. Therefore I arrived in Bologna with frayed and angry nerves; and it was to stretch my legs a little that I made the trip across the Apennines on foot.

At Florence I found Carafa but not the whole Legion which had set out towards Ancona because of the protestations of neutrality made by the Grand Duke. The Signor Ettore seemed very pensive; I thought that he was thinking of his soldiers, but he grew irritated as soon as I recalled them to his mind. He cursed women through clenched teeth, saying that it was real madness that we had stooped to come into the light of day by means of such demons.

'The devil, Captain, and how would you like to have been born?'

'From Vesuvius, from Etna, from the tempestuous waves of the sea,' he replied, 'but not from those little monsters armed with a viperine force who revenge themselves for having produced us by taking our lives away from us inch by inch.'

'Captain, are you really so unhappy and pessimistic in love?'

'Most surely! . . . With a mistress who loves me and who does not love me; that is to say has loved me and let herself be loved as I desired for a week and now wants to love me in her manner which is the strangest and most insupportable on earth.'

'What manner, Captain?'

'Like the date-palms who make love when one of them is in Sicily and the other in Barbary.'

I laughed a little at this comparison but in the depths of my heart whenever we touched on amorous misfortunes in our talk I had very little desire to laugh. But since I did not consider the Signor Ettore to be a finished master in such matters, and furthermore I liked him very much, I took the liberty of offering some advice.

'Offend her pride,' I advised him. 'Create a rival for her.'

'I will see,' he said. 'Meanwhile you go and rejoin our fellows at Ancona. When we get to Rome I will be able to tell you of the worth or otherwise of your advice, which seems to me rather stale and much corrupted by long use.'

'Old wisdom brings fresh fruit,' I replied.

From the Arno to the Adriatic took three days and from Ancona to Rome ten, since we were moving with the entire Legion which, not being accustomed to the march, had to begin cautiously. Then I had the opportunity to convince myself that the first enemies that a new army meets in its operations are the chickens and the priests. Neither threats, nor reproofs, nor punishments availed. A chicken meant a musket-shot and a priest jests and ribaldry. They would kill the chickens in order to eat them at the priest's house and to drink his wine; that was the end of it and if the abbés were men of law with a scrap of self-reliance and a political patina, we ended by parting the best of friends. One of these archpriests was sufficient to incline the souls of the whole legion in favour of Pius VI; it is true that at that time the Cardinal Chiaramonti had reconciled Religion and Republic in his famous Homily and was able to influence almost everybody. For my part, the more I advance in years, the more I see that all religion gains considerably by keeping well away from politics. It is useless. Oil will never mix with vinegar nor sentiment with reason without something spurious and insipid being born of the mixture.

Here we were at last in Rome. I had so great a desire to see it that it could hardly have been greater. I felt that only Rome could make me forget the Pisana, yet while I relied on such forgetfulness I would go about puzzling my brains what could have happened to her. I built up conjectures, I created and exaggerated fears and gave substance and life to the most monstrous fancies imaginable. Her cousins of Cisterna, recently arrived in Venice, that washed-out

Agostino Frumier, that scoffer Raimondo Venchieredo, all appeared at one time or another as so many rivals; but all the suppositions vanished when letters from Aglaura and Spiro confirmed the absence of the Pisana and said that her family knew nothing of her and seemed to care less. The Contessa gorged on the interest on her eight thousand ducats and that was enough for her; the Count Rinaldo passed from his office to the Library and from the Library to his meals and his bed without a thought that others might also be living in the world; both of them wretched, most wretched, but not troubling themselves unduly about others.

You will agree with me that mine, if not heroism, was certainly a fine fortitude, to go on ordering odds and ends and drilling my men on Monte Pincio when I wanted to scour and rummage the world to find my loved one! I really loved her more than myself, and for me, who am not selling the rags of trite phrases but making profession to tell the truth, that is to say all. Notwithstanding, I had the fortitude to put my country first and even then, though I had to make an effort to include Naples also in that idea, Rome aided me to pass the test.

Once there my sorrow suffered the fate of every small thing when faced with one surpassingly more great; it was overcome, stifled, almost forgotten. What indeed could be the unhappiness of a single man in the face of the mourning of an entire people? . . . I found once more a weary peace, a sorrow without bitterness, in watching this stormy prelude to the great downfall; above it all the pomps, the events of the Christian centuries seemed to me mere games and futilities. Only in the catacombs there still lingered a spirit of faith and martyrdom that elevated Christendom above those grandiose pagan sepulchres. I bowed trembling before those holy memories of sacrifice and blood, and the tortures, the scourgings, the infamies and outrages and the deaths joyfully suffered for an ideal, that I admired without understanding, and that made the weight of anxieties that I inflicted upon myself and could not forget, seem small to my eyes. In the emulation of the great lies the redemption of the small.

However, if living in the ancient Rome of consuls and of martyrs brought me some comfort, the Rome of those times filled me with horror and almost with consternation.

The Pope had left without mockery but without applause, since, having had to renounce much of the pomp and magnificence in which he was accustomed to live, the people paid no further heed to him. The excellences of the Prince of Christendom were measured rather by the splendour of his court and ceremonies than by the virtue and sanctity of his life. A medley of things venerable for their religious virtue and their age contemptuously reviled, of nastiness exalted to the skies and splendidly adorned, of stupid superstitions, of vile renegades, of pillaging and famine, of gluttons and men starving, of cardinals persecuted by dragoons and dragoons with their throats cut by brigands; everything was in confusion, was rushing to perdition; the clouded and deluded view of each individual was judge of good or of evil; there was a mingling of priestly resistance, of French control, of popular licence and of private murder. There was a putting forward of great and honourable names to mask the infamy of the petty, continual shifts without faith and without assurance caused by the rapacity of those who liked to fish in troubled waters, of French who cursed the Italian traitors and of Trasteverini who revolted, shouting: 'Long live Maria!' . . . Blood flowed in the woods, in the marshes, in the caves; city and country armed with equal fury, but even in the underground passages of the Colosseum, even in the recesses of the mountains, in the arms of their wives, at the feet of their aged parents, the rebels were persecuted. Murat shot, killed, hanged; the survivors went to the galleys and some called them martyrs and others gallows-birds.

There could be no greater sowing of discord and of future rebellions than this opinion of the people who exalted the scaffold to the altar. Four Commissioners of the French Directory came to resuscitate the ancient names of consul, senate, tribune and quaestor, taking their authority from them and making use of them to cover things quite new, servile rather than republican for the haste with which they were imposed. The five consuls changed with every change of mood of the French General; none the less the Confederation of the Roman Republic (a weighty name to bear) was celebrated with a solemnity equal to that of the Cisalpina. A medal was coined bearing on its two faces the two inscriptions: *Berthier restitutor urbis* and *Gallia salvus generis humani*. Of the first we knew how much to believe; of the second, God alone knew!

After the general insurrection of the countryside, the army, almost all concentrated in Rome, was scattered into patrols, garrisons and reinforcements in the various little cities and walled places of the Romagna. I remained for a few days with Lucilio, Amilcare and Giulio, and in their company visited the beautiful things of Rome and its surroundings, but when the break-up of the military occupation began, Giulio and Amilcare were sent to Spoleto, while Lucilio and I remained in Castel Sant'Angelo. My Legion was still awaiting its Captain who was delaying his arrival from Florence; but perhaps he was in no hurry since the paucity of the French forces and the formidable fortifications of King Ferdinand left few grounds for hope, at that time, for a Neapolitan war. It was as good to sit idle in an armchair, the fate of a soldier in peace-time, in one of the cafés of Florence, as in any of the many cafés of Rome. So at least I explained Carafa's delay. Meanwhile, I continued to enjoy with Lucilio the wonderful antiquities of Rome and to study its history through its monuments. It was the sole distraction that remained to me against the ever-growing uneasiness due to the lack of news from Venice.

My sister and her husband wrote to me, and even my father wrote through them from Constantinople that I should go on hoping and preparing. But these were infrequent solaces and no one could give me news of the Pisana, not even by rumours or conjecture. I heard also that at Venice there was talk of dividing her inheritance, a sign that they believed or hoped her to be dead, and I cannot say how much this fact, behind which I could discern the cruel greed of the Contessa, infuriated me.

In God's good time Carafa arrived from Florence, irritable, surly and severe as never before. He was always rubbing with one hand that scar over his eyebrow, and that was a bad sign. The worst thing was that, wishing, if he could not attack Naples, to be at least closer to the Neapolitan frontier, he took the Legion, and me with it, from the Castel Sant'Angelo and stationed us at Velletri, a little country town like so many that are to be found in the countryside of the Romagna, picturesque from the outside but horrible, dirty and stinking within, filled by day with ploughs, carts and herds of oxen and horses coming and going, and at night rejoicing in the mooing of cows, the crowing of cocks and the bells of convents, truly a place in which to immure some poor devil to cure him of the malady of lovely landscapes and wide horizons.

Carafa lived outside the city in a convent sacked by the French republicans, whither he had forwarded from Rome all that was necessary to make it if not splendid at least comfortable and habitable. A few sentries guarded it with a pair of tiny mule-drawn field-pieces. No one was permitted to enter the private rooms except his servant, who had the reputation in the Legion of being a magician. For the rest, the shepherdesses who wandered round the countryside and the peasant-girls who took milk to the convent reported that they had seen at the window a very beautiful lady who must be the love of Signor Ettore. The other soldiers who had served in the Legion longer than I had and who had always known him continent as one who has no time to waste on such follies, did not believe in such tales; or rather told stories about her being an enchantress or some Neapolitan Princess that he wanted to put in place of Queen Caroline.

Places can have a great effect upon the imagination and the surroundings of Velletri must have inspired in any healthy mind such tales of witchcraft and enchantment, even as the meadows and dairy-farms of the Lodigiano inspire eulogies of cheese and cream. I perhaps alone held aloof from such Gothic imaginings, knowing very well that one can endure continence for a considerable time and then unleash oneself with the gluttony of one who has long fasted. For example I would refer you to Amilcare who used to tell me how he had never tasted wine until he was twenty; but from then onwards nobody drank as much as he. The same thing might have happened to Carafa. But I believed in a genuine and proud passion of love rather than in any witchcraft and on that subject there were many altercations and even bets between me and my companions. After my separation from Lucilio I had become so arrogant and intractible that it required very little to get my back up; I called all those who saw marvels and witchcraft in it fools and simpletons. I was reproached in the Legion as a man better with my tongue than with my actions and I felt it was up to me to show them that this was not true.

On the other hand the continual tumult raging within me and the boredom of that idle and animal existence made its tranquillity irritating to me and I congratulated myself on having found a pretext to do something, even if it were only a practical joke. The Captain had forbidden, on pain of death, any officer or soldier save those on guard to approach the convent where he had set up his headquarters. The place was very close to the frontier; the new Neapolitan army, to form which even the priests and the nuns had been taxed, was massing more and more every day close to the borders of the Abruzzo; some skirmish might occur, indeed had already occurred, but more because of the impatience of the young officers than for any deliberate intention of the leaders; Carafa did not want to station the legionaries on that side of the town lest some incident not at the moment desirable should take place.

But these dictates of prudence were somewhat at variance with his usual recklessness and the truth was that he did not want any inquisitive eyes around the convent. I swore to my companions that I would go and have a look, let happen what might, and one Sunday evening was chosen for the great essay.

My plan was as follows: to give the alarm to the garrison of the convent and then to creep around the walls and enter the garden over its broken-down surrounding wall while everyone was watching the place whence the enemy might be expected. That evening, being a festa, the main body of the troops would be scattered among the Velletri taverns and a large-scale disorder was not likely to take place. The false alarm would be discovered but I would have carried out my plan before the officers would have had time to collect their men. Carafa, who would be outside giving orders, would not be able to see me, while the other persons in the convent, whoever they might be, would certainly not recognize me. The only danger, though a big enough one to be sure, would be if I were discovered escaping from the convent; but I was not without an excuse and would say that I had entered to save myself from an attack by the Neapolitan cavalry. Whether they believed it or not did not greatly concern me and even if I should have to pay for this whim with my blood, I had undertaken to do it and would carry it out.

So indeed, towards sunset, using as a pretext a great cloud of dust which could be seen rising from the mountain side opposite the convent (it was probably some flocks descending) I and a few of my companions who were taking part in the wager pretended to have been surprised in a near-by tavern and ran to the first sentry, shouting that the Neapolitans were advancing and that they must give the alarm while we went up the hill to Velletri to warn the others. In a few minutes the little garrison was on the alert since Carafa, foreseeing some such event, had arranged an ambush on the left side of the road, leaving only one or two sentries around the convent, believing that there would always be time to retire and that the mass of the legion, descending meanwhile from Velletri, would have caught the enemy between two fires. While he disposed his little company in this way in open order on a chain of small hills crowned by cypresses and laurels that flanked the road, he arranged to place his two little cannon with his usual foresight.

I and my companions, laughing at this commotion, made a short detour and reached the back of the convent where the vegetable garden bordered the marshland. The others remained on watch, while I vaulted the wall and ran on through the garden where the cabbages gone to seed and the vegetable beds burnt by the sun bore witness to the unfinished lenten fast of the proscribed Capuchins. When I reached the convent building I examined the windows and door to find a hole by which to enter, but it was a more difficult task than I had imagined. The windows were fitted with very solid grilles, and door and shutters were of hard maple that would have resisted a battering-ram. I found myself, as they say, at Rome without being able to see the Pope. Then I saw, among some near-by trees, a ladder which must have been used by the gardener or the friars to pick peaches and thought to myself that access to the upper floor was perhaps not so jealously guarded as to the ground floor. I made use of it and set myself to the test. Indeed, the shutters of the first window that I tried had merely been closed without further security of bolts and bars. I opened them very quietly and saw a sort of store-room that had been adapted by Signor Ettore for an armoury, and put a leg inside. But just as I was about to put the other one in, a noise, a trampling and shouting which I could hear not far off, caused me to remain suspended, just as I was, straddled across the sill. Over the very wall that I had just climbed appeared a three-cornered hat, then another and yet another. They were men in great haste to enter and seemed to prefer to risk breaking their heads by falling from the wall into the garden rather than remain on the other side. One of them, having reached the top, was hastily descending, when there was a crack like an arquebus shot and he spread out his arms and fell like a dead man. Those who had already got over took to their heels across the cabbages. I recognized them as my companions and had only just done so when other hats began to appear and then arms and legs as though there were no end to them. When one got down, ten others climbed up; it was a real invasion, a plague of locusts darkening the sky.

'The Neapolitans! The Neapolitans!' shouted my companions who had reached the foot of the convent wall and were climbing rapidly up the ladder at the head of which I was sitting.

'Gently, gently!' I cried, 'otherwise you will all be killed without waiting for them to kill you.'

Indeed the ladder, with a man on every rung creaked like an overburdened pear-tree. I had prudently withdrawn both my legs into the room and thought I was doing all that was necessary in giving them good advice.

'One at a time! Don't get in one another's way! . . . And don't shake the ladder so much!'

All of a sudden there was a whistle here, a whistle there and a crash sounded as if a couple of thunderbolts had collided and there followed such a shock that it shattered all the glass in the room. Seven of my colleagues leapt in and one remained dead outside; luckily he was dead and not merely wounded! Adding the other man killed while he was crossing the wall, we should, if I had got my figures right, have been ten.

The devil and all! There was no doubt about it. Those had been musket shots, and aimed at them! . . . I smelt then for the first time the smell of powder. It affected me so that I burst into a roar of laughter, as one might who had just had a narrow escape. However, I would not like to swear that I felt no fear at all. At least allow me to boast of my sincerity. But even if I was afraid, my fear was not so great as to prevent my going over to the window and making a certain very expressive gesture to those Neapolitan rogues who were looking up at us without being able to follow us since with much acumen we had pulled the ladder up. That gesture was the magic touch that filled my companions' breasts with enthusiasm, but our enemies were not joking and commenced a certain music with their muskets that gave me no great desire to show myself again on the balcony to look at the weather. We armed ourselves with guns, cutlasses and pistols from the armoury so happily at our disposal and returned their salutes with every courtesy; while they were combing our hair, we were splitting their skulls and their paunches and I cannot say if they were very satisfied with the exchange.

However, the continuation of the comedy gave us something to think about. Where had these cursed Neapolitans come from? Did the Captain know about this? Had they already been on their way in reality while we had been shouting a false alarm on the side facing the mountain? That was in fact what had happened and a silly trick might have cost me and all the Legion dear, and might even have given to a joke or a mere piece of daring the appearance of treachery. Meanwhile the shooting went on with greater success from above than from below and it seemed to us that the enemy had considerably slackened their fire. One or two of us were already about to sing a paean of victory and perhaps even to set about the few obstinate stragglers who did not want to retire, and make a foray in the kitchen garden, when we heard a dull thud under our feet and a little later the sound of running and stamping in the rooms on the ground floor, followed by cries, shouts, oaths and exclamations in the usual manner of Neapolitans at war. We were all overcome by terror; while the snipers remained on watch, the mass of the assailants had broken down a door with a small mine, and the convent had been invaded. We were one to ten and it would have been foolish to try and resist. But I, who felt on my conscience all the remorse of this unlucky affair, rushed bravely to rally my comrades. A few words, a good and prompt example and I felt that they would back me up at need.

'Friends, let us give our lives, but let us not surrender the upper floor! Think of our honour and that of the Legion!'

As I said this, I rushed from the store-room to the staircase where I began barricading the doorway with cupboards, tables and any other furniture I could lay my hands on. The Neapolitans were advancing up the stairs with confidence, but found several musket barrels facing them through the chinks in the barricade which made them turn back pell mell.

'Courage, friends,' I cried. 'Help can't be long!'

Indeed it seemed to me impossible that Signor Ettore, on hearing the noise of the arquebus shots, had not sent someone to see what was happening. I could never have imagined that just that day would have been chosen for the first advance of the Neapolitan army and that he would be too busy in keeping their scouts at a distance to give time for the legion to come out of Velletri. In any case, we held out so firmly behind the good shelter of the double door of oak that the enemy gave up their idea of advancing up the stairs. But we soon found that they had abandoned this plan only to adopt another still more dangerous for us. It seemed that they had set the convent on fire beneath our feet; through the cracks in the floor the smoke eddied into the passage where we were and caught our breath; a little later and the beams began to crackle and the flames to make their way through the red-hot bricks.

We fled at top speed into the near-by rooms and a minute later the floor where we had been collapsed with a fearful crash. But we were not much safer in the other rooms. The fire spread very rapidly since it had been kindled in the hay barns. We would have to get out or resign ourselves to being roasted.

My companions, pistols in their hands and knives between their teeth, leapt from the windows and surprising the few of the enemy who were amusing themselves in watching the fire, retired to safety to the hill beyond. Only one tripped in jumping and broke a leg, and immediately those assassins were on him like wolves on a lamb and you would call me a liar if I described all the tortures and ignominies they made him suffer, since it would not seem possible that human beings could be so bestial. I drew back, shuddering; but a supernatural force commanded me not to fly and kept me within those walls devoured by the flames. Other creatures were shut up there, I knew not who; but that was enough to ensure that I, the innocent cause of this massacre, should sacrifice myself in the forlorn hope of being able to save them.

I ran like a madman through the long corridors, passing from door to door of the innumerable cells and through the spacious apartments of the cloisters; the air became hotter and hotter like an oven where the fire is continually being stoked. Everywhere was solitude and silence; only the howls from without and a distant cracking of arquebus shots added terror to those desperate moments. Having decided not to try to escape until I was quite certain that no human being remained in that inferno, I ventured on the almost hopeless passage through that corridor whose flooı had almost collapsed under our feet. A few smouldering beams still remained and on one side of the wall a sort of arch covered the entrance to a back staircase. I passed over them at a run and decided to make for the other side of the building. I came upon a closed door that certainly would not have resisted such a desperate attack as mine. None the less, I first shouted loudly: 'Open, open!' I was answered by a cry that sounded like that of a woman, and at the same time a pistol ball, coming from a hole in the doorway, grazed my forehead and embedded itself in the opposite wall.

'Friends, friends!' I shouted.

But fresh cries drowned my voice and another pistol shot came from behind the door. The bullet grazed my arm and made the blood spout.

I threw myself against the door, determined to save whoever was within even against their will, if a friend, or to get myself killed if an enemy. The door shattered into pieces and, smoke-blackened and covered with blood, I must surely have looked like a damned soul as I rushed into the room. In my rush I cannoned into a woman who was running to and fro with her hands raised, tearing at her hair, overcome by fear. Another woman was running from me and it looked as if she intended to save herself by leaping from the window; but I was too quick for her and caught her in my arms just as her body was hanging over the sill. The flames that were coming from the floor below had singed her hair and two or three arquebus shots greeted our appearance at the window. I began to drag her away from this dangerous position, saying that I was a friend who had come to save her and that she must not lose heart or we were lost. Her face, beautiful with a sublime despair, turned suddenly towards me. . . . I staggered as if I had received a musket ball in my breast. . . . It was the Pisana!

The Pisana! . . . Oh God! Who could describe the storm that raged in my heart? Who could tell of the passions that overwhelmed me? . . . But love, love was the first and strongest, the one that redoubled my resolve and gave my spirit an invincible boldness.

I picked her up and rushed with her through the flames, among the cracking beams, the ruined walls and the crash of collapsing arches. . . . I got down to the front portico where the flames still allowed us passage, but to right and left I felt a fiery blast catch me by the throat. One last effort! Who would dare to say that I could fall with such a burden in my arms? . . . Who would dare to suggest that I could abandon to the flames those lovely limbs whose perfection I had so often admired and that enchanting face where her great soul shone through like lightning through the clouds? . . . I would have crossed a volcano without fear of losing my hold of so much as a hair of that precious and almost inanimate body. Were she dead, then I would die also, if only to be able to think at the supreme moment: 'I have perished for her sake and by her side!' Fears, suspicions, jealousy, revenge, all that had swelled my heart for an instant had disappeared; love alone remained, with a faith reborn as a Phoenix from its ashes, full of a strength that conquers death itself, since it despises and ignores it.

With the Pisana in my arms and despair in my heart, a frightful danger confronting me, I swung my sword wildly, throwing into confusion a file of the enemy who were warming themselves heedlessly at the flames from the burning convent. I remember noticing among them a monk who was praying and devoutly haranguing the soldiers. It was the Prior of the convent who had led the soldiers of the Holy Faith in this mighty revenge; he said that the enemies of religion had been left to roast in their own fat. The last of these, however, no enemy of religion but an enemy of the fanatics who place arms in its hand, escaped miraculously from their fury. If God at that moment had been looking down upon Velletri, it is certain that his favours were with me and the Pisana. Still running, I reached the hill where Carafa had placed his ambush and there the fate of the combat had been very different. We met some of the legionaries who, after having forced the Neapolitans back to the mountain gorge, had turned to attack those who had set fire to the convent. Ettore himself, who had only just received news of what had been happening behind his back, rushed thither at the head of his men, not sure if he would be in time but certain that his defence or his revenge would be devastating and invincible.

I hid among the laurels until he had passed, but then I felt sorry for him and stopped a Corporal who was following him with a new flag picked up at Velletri and told him to give the message that she of whom he knew was already safely in the city. I had only gone a few steps farther when I ran into two of my men and got them to take the Pisana from me as I was completely exhausted and had great difficulty in following them to the top of the hill where Velletri stood. Once arrived there, I put her on my bed, sent for a neighbouring barber to open a vein, and when she came to herself, to save her from the shock of surprise, went out on to a balcony that overlooked the countryside. I could see the convent like a great bonfire, the reddish smoky flames outlining it ever more clearly against the sky turned brown by smoke and in their sombre light I could see flashing the bayonets of the legionaries on the heels of the flying Neapolitans. The battle had been won and bad omens attended the first entry of the liberators into the confines of the Roman Republic.

When I re-entered, the Pisana was already sitting up on the bed and she greeted me with less confusion that I would have expected. She was the first to speak, which surprised me still more, remembering her customary reticence in moments of considerably less difficulty.

'Carlo,' she said, 'why didn't you leave me where I was? . . . I would have died like a heroine and they would have put me in the new Pantheon in Rome.'

I looked at her, stupefied, thinking that she must be mad. But she seemed to be talking sanely and I had to reply in the same vein.

'In that case I would have had to stay too,' I said in a voice so moved that I could hardly go on. 'I swear to you, Pisana, that at the first moment I saw you I longed to kill you and then to die myself.'

'Then why didn't you?' she cried and her tone was such that I had to realize her sincerity and despair.

'I didn't . . . I didn't do it because I love you!' I replied with bent head, like one who confesses to a fault.

She was in no way abashed by my frown; she even raised her eyes like an offended virgin.

'Oh, so you love me, you love me!' she exclaimed. 'Inhuman, traitor, perjurer! May Heaven hear your lies and pour them down your throat changed to molten lead! . . . You have trampled on me as if I were a slave, you have deceived me like a credulous fool; at my side, in my very arms, you were contemplating the perfidy you have committed! . . . Oh happy you! Happy that a man has taken his place between you and me! . . . One who has taken my revenge out of my hands and offered me another that is my shame and my torment every day, every minute! Otherwise on the very breast of your whore I would have plunged a dagger into your heart and there is enough strength in this arm of mine to have wiped out both of you at a single stroke! . . . Go now, go! . . . Enjoy my humiliation and your triumph! . . . You have saved my life! . . . How noble of you! . . . At the next decade you will have a civic crown about your brows, but I will be so bold as to refuse the dregs of that cup of dishonour that you want to impose on me! I will have the courage to defy that mad love that I have renounced with such passion! . . . It is six months now since I have scorned it and now I will ridicule it! Revenge for revenge! . . . A dagger thrust from this hand will bring death to me and eternal remorse to your cowardly heart!'

To hear myself abused in this way by one who had so cruelly betrayed me, for whom I had preserved a pure trust and a constant love of which I had but then given proof by risking my own life to save hers, in spite of the manner and the place in which I had found her, should have made my rage even more bitter and changed my affection into fury; to see her raging and angry with me while I waited, trembling and humble, was such a blow that it broke my heart. My anger rose even against God who allowed innocence to be so unworthily maltreated and allowed vice, armed with thunderbolts, to enjoy striking from its throne of shame.

'Pisana,' I shouted, in a voice overcome by sobs, 'Pisana, enough! I will not, I cannot listen to you any more! . . . The words you have just spoken are viler and more degrading than your unfaithfulness! . . . It is not your place, indeed it is not your place to accuse me! . . . While you confess to the most monstrous crime that one lover can commit against another, you have still the cruelty to gloat over my tears and pretend to be offended and insulted, while threatening me with a revenge more bloody but less unworthy than the one you have already inflicted on me! Be silent, Pisana, not another word or I shall deny whatever is left just and holy in this world. I shall tear honour from my breast and throw it to the dogs as an abomination. Yes, I renounce that false honour that suffers the shame owed to the faithless without replying by a burst like a volcano against such barefaced calumnies!'

The Pisana buried her face in her hands and began to weep; then she suddenly leapt from the bed where she had been lying fully clothed and made as if to leave the room. I held her back.

'Where do you mean to go now?'

'I want to go to Signor Ettore Carafa; take me to him at once.'

'The Captain is busy pursuing the Neapolitans and it will not be easy to find him; moreover, he has been told that you are safe and will certainly come to join you as soon as he can.'

I seasoned these last words with a strong dose of irony, and she said with the air of a prophetess:

'Woe to him or woe to you!'

'Woe to nobody,' I replied calmly. 'Woe to nobody! . . . I shall be very glad to be able to kill someone!'

'Why not kill me?' she asked with great simplicity.

'Because . . . because . . . because you are too beautiful . . . because I remember that you were once good too.'

'Silence, Carlo, silence! . . . Do you think Signor Ettore will come soon?'

'I told you. He will come as soon as he can.'

She remained silent for a time and by the uncertain moonlight that entered from the balcony I could see that many and varied thoughts were passing through her mind. Now gloomy, now radiant, now stormy like a sky heavy with cloud, now calm and serene as a summer sea; sometimes she adopted an attitude of prayer, only a little later to clench her fist as if she had a dagger in her hand to strike repeatedly at some abhorred breast. With her clothes in disorder, stained with blood and dust, her features bearing the imprint of the terrible events of that day, she leaned her elbows on the table and rested her forehead on her hand, equally blackened and bloodstained. She seemed like some black Pythoness just come from Erebus and meditating the frightful mysteries of her infernal visions. I did not dare to break that gloomy silence. Then, too, I had need to collect my own thoughts before provoking the revelations of that melancholy Sybil. The story of her heart and of her life after my departure glimmered in flashes of light through my horrified imagination. If someone had said to me: at the price of making you a fool I promise to convince you of the Pisana's innocence, I would have accepted the bargain.

About an hour later, Carafa entered the room, alone and frowning. He had lost his hat in the mêlée and had a swordless scabbard at his side having broken his sword on the skull of some dragoon after having cleft his helmet right through the crest. His scar shone whitely with an almost incandescent pallor. He saluted and stood between me and the Pisana, waiting for one of us to speak.

The Pisana did not keep him waiting long and with a proud and angry air demanded that he repeat the story of my amours with the beautiful Greek and tell everything exactly as he had told it to her. Carafa, having asked my permission, repeated shamefacedly what he had learnt of those amours in the circles of Milan, of the beauty of the young woman and of the jealousy with which I had kept her hidden from every eye.

'There you are, Pisana, that is what I told you,' he concluded, 'when you arrived in Milan and came to ask me if I knew anything of my officer Carlo Altoviti and his love affairs that were creating so much talk because of their mystery. In telling you that, I did no more than repeat what was in everybody's mouth and the honour of the one who was the hero of such amours certainly did not go unscathed. Did I do wrong? . . . It does not seem so to me. . . . I have not to answer for it to anyone!'

The Pisana appeared satisfied with this very temperate speech by Carafa and turned to me like a judge to a criminal after the testimony of an irrefutable witness.

'Pisana, why do you look at me like that?'

'Why?' she cried. 'Because I hate you, because I despise you, because I would like to shame you even more than I have already done by throwing myself into the arms of another. . . .'

I was horrified by her cynicism; she perceived it and writhed like a scorpion touched by a hot coal. She repented having shown herself as she really was, mad and like a devil in that moment of rage.

'Yes,' she said, 'look at me as you will. . . . I can love a different man every day, since when you swore to love me you were already planning the rape of Aglaura.'

'You are mad!' I shouted.

I ran to my trunk, pulled out a couple of letters from my sister and threw them on the table before her.

'Lights!' I ordered and having put them near the Pisana, I said: 'Read!'

Fortune aided me in that she was ignorant of the fact that I knew nothing of my relationship to Aglaura when we had fled from Venice; I thought it better to keep Carafa also ignorant of it, rather than have to enlarge on a thousand details during that sad and difficult moment. She read the letters, then handed them to Ettore, saying: 'You read them too!' and while he skimmed through them, showing every sign of astonishment and displeasure, she went on muttering:

'They betrayed me! . . . It was a plot! . . . Curse them, curse them! . . . I will destroy all of them!'

'No, Pisana, no one has betrayed you!' I said. 'It was you who betrayed me! . . . Yes, you! . . . Don't be angry with me! . . . If you had really loved me, then I could have been unfaithful, infamous, a scoundrel and you would still have loved me! . . . You know, Pisana, you know, so why should I say it? . . . It is because I felt it. It is because, even such as you are now, though I am ashamed to say it, I love you, I adore you still! . . . No, don't worry. I will go and you will never see me again! . . . Let me take this revenge only, to let you know that you have made the eternal unhappiness of the man to whom you could have been the joy, the comfort, the happiness of a whole lifetime.'

Carafa had meanwhile glanced through the letters and handed them back to me, saying:

'I beg your pardon. Gossip deceived me, but I had no intention to deceive.'

Such an apology from such a man moved me greatly; I could see that great effort made by Signor Ettore to wring even so much from his spirit. Pride bowed fuming under the inexorable force of will. The Pisana wept, and a double shame prevented her from turning either to Signor Ettore or to me. But he had mercy, I know not whether for the Pisana or for me, and called me for a few minutes from the room. He told me how his first interview with the Pisana had come about, since she, knowing that I was an officer in his service, had come to him for fuller information. He said that she was already mad with jealousy and he fascinated by her from the first glance. In fact he confessed to me that, believing me to be madly in love with my Greek, he had not considered it unseemly for him to make good use of the chance that had come to his hand, the sweeter and more desired in that love had rarely touched his soldier's heart. He therefore had tried his best to turn to his own advantage the Pisana's fury and had indeed for the first few days succeeded.

'But then,' he said, 'it seemed as if she no longer wanted to remember those first few days of rapture. From Milan, to Florence, to Rome, she accompanied me, but always mute, haughty, and cold, enjoying my transports and replying to all my prayers and threats with the bitter words: 'I am only too well avenged!' Oh, how I suffered, Carlo, how I suffered! I swear to you that you too were well avenged! I implored, I entreated, I wept, I made vows to God and all the saints, I no longer recognized myself! . . . I even had recourse to bribery and tempted her chambermaid, a certain Venetian from whom she would never be separated, with gold!'

'Who was she?' I asked. 'What was she called?'

'She was called Rosa, a wretch who would have sold her own sister for ten shillings. But today she received a terrible punishment for her sins, for I saw her body burnt to a cinder in the ruins of the convent. . . . But even through her infamous intercession I could gain nothing. I was, it seems to me, sufficiently humiliated. I took her from Rome to bring her to this solitude where I had even considered resorting to force to satisfy my desires! . . . A vain thought, Carlo! . . . Force fell on its knees before her look. I understood that some supreme decision, some invincible passion had taken her from me for ever after the almost involuntary concession of a moment of shock! . . . I have told you the whole truth, though I have no reason to boast about it; draw your own conclusions and arrange your affairs accordingly. From tomorrow evening my headquarters will be at Frascati because the Commander-in-Chief, Championnet, has ordered a general retreat along the whole line. Discuss it with the Pisana. My house will always be open to her, because I never forget either the favours of others or my own promises.'

So saying, Carafa gripped my hand without over much effusion and strode away, once again assuming his proud soldierly frown; it seemed to me that in expanding his chest and tossing back his hair, he threw off the gynecaeum and turned once more to wear the lion skin of Alcide.

I went back to the Pisana and waited until she questioned me before saying a word.

'Where has the Signor Carafa gone?' she asked me eagerly.

'To give orders for the retreat to Frascati,' I replied.

'Leaving me here? . . . And not even saying where he was going?'

'He has told me what he has meant to you. You can see he is not lacking in any of his duties as a gentleman and he does not refuse to carry out any of his obligations towards you.'

'Obligations to me? . . . He? I wonder at him! . . . He could have no obligations towards me save to return what he has stolen from me; but those are things that cannot be returned. In the last resort, I shall not be the first woman who has made herself respected without having at her side the naked sword of a paladin! . . . Will you call my maid?'

'Have you forgotten where we left her? . . . She fell victim to the fire.'

'Who? . . . Rosa? . . . Rosa is dead? . . . Poor me, unhappy me! It was I, I who left her to perish so! . . . I forgot all about her at the very moment when I should have looked after her best. A curse on me who have always on my conscience the blood of the innocent!'

I forced myself to make her understand that since she had fainted in the commotion and having need of my aid to escape herself, she could not have given a thought to Rosa or to anyone else. She went on lamenting, sighing, talking with an incredible volubility, without however saying a word about following Carafa or wanting to leave me. For my part, I felt such pity for her, that though my love would not have stooped to become gentle and caressing as before, it would still have pretended to desire to.

'Carlino,' she said suddenly to me, 'when you left Venice you did not know that Aglaura was your sister, otherwise you would have told me.'

'No, I didn't know,' I said, seeing no reason to lie any further.

'And none the less you lived together really like brother and sister?'

'There was nothing else to be done.'

'How long did this innocent life of yours together go on?'

'Some months.'

The Pisana thought this over for a little while, then said:

'Would you mind, Carlo, if I slept on this chair?'

I replied that she could take her ease on the bed since I had a mattress downstairs where I could try and get some rest. She seemed very pleased at this permission, but waited until I had gone downstairs before taking advantage of it. I stopped to listen out of curiosity and I heard her shoot the bolt on the door, taking great care not to make a noise. The year before at Venice she would not have done this, but the precautions that she took not to be heard made me understand that it was because she was ashamed.

On the morrow we spoke no more of what had happened the day before. This was an easy matter for the Pisana who had forgotten everything, but a very difficult one for me, who was accustomed to realize the present through memories of the past. She asked me how we should leave, as if we had been travelling together for many years past, and having settled ourselves together as best we could in a travelling carriage, her natural gaiety made the trip to Frascati seem to me a very short one. Love was no longer in question but a friendship as between brother and sister, full of pity and forgetfulness, took its place. You must remember that I am speaking of our words and our actions; as to what was boiling beneath I would not like to give any assurance, and sometimes I would surprise myself in some gesture of irritation at the simplicity with which I had accepted this cold and silent compromise. The Pisana seemed happy to be, I will not say loved, but tolerated by me; so simple, so obedient, so gently she behaved that a daughter could not have been better. It was, I believe, a sort of way of asking forgiveness, but would she not have obtained it had she asked for it? Only too often I had shown that capacity, that I had so often blamed in her, for pardoning and forgetting wrongs altogether unpardonable. None the less, I in no way relaxed my reserved manner and at Spoleto, at Nepi, at Acquapendente, at Perugia and in all the places where Championnet led the army to reassemble its scattered fragments, we led the life of two companions in arms who had already enjoyed their youth and who, as they say, descended ever more into the complaisance of companionship.

Meanwhile King Ferdinand of Naples and his General Mack had entered Rome in triumph. The French had prudently retired and the General attributed the merit to his very complicated plan of strategy. The Roman Republic fell into disorder like a house of cards; under the protection of the King a Provisional Government was established. But meanwhile Baron Mack did not sit with folded arms, and complicated his plans even more to chase Championnet out of the Roman State and perhaps even from Italy itself. Naselli had disembarked at Livorno, Ruggiero di Damas at Orbetello and he, having divided his army into five corps, advanced along both banks of the Tiber. Championnet, without so many complications, raged, broke, routed them from the rear, from the van, to right and to left. Mack, tangled in his own plan, was obliged to fly. His king preceded him along the road to Caserta and to Naples, and after seventeen days of catalepsy the Roman Republic once again awoke to its miserable life. Championnet pressed victoriously on the frontiers of the kingdom; Rusca with his Cisalpini and Carafa with the Parthenopean Legion skirmished in the van. Already the revolution growled threateningly at the gates of Naples.

CHAPTER XVII

THE people of Naples, armed and in the field had been scattered by a handful of Frenchmen through the complicated ignorance of Baron Mack. The people abandoned by their king, their queen, and Acton the evil genius of the kingdom, sold by the Viceroy Pignatelli to a hasty and humiliating armistice, without arms and without organization, still defended themselves for two days against the growing arrogance of the victors. They retired into their lairs conquered but not crushed, and Championnet, entering in triumph on 22 January 1799, felt the ground trembling beneath his feet. A new Parthenopean Republic arose, notable for the singular honesty, strength and wisdom of its leaders, to be pitied for the anarchy and for the merciless and perverse passions that rent it, and unfortunate and remarkable for its tragic end.

The new government had not yet been properly established when Cardinal Ruffo with his bands disembarked in Calabria from Sicily and placed the republican authority in this extreme heel of Italy in great danger. Some welcomed him as a liberator, others rejected him as an assassin and either defended themselves successfully or were taken, burnt and destroyed. Troops of brigands captained by Mammone, Sciarpa or Fra Diavolo supported the Cardinal's movements. Seven Corsican emigrés, having passed off one of their number as hereditary prince, had sufficed to throw into confusion a good part of the Abruzzi, but the French resisted vigorously and hanged several of them as a solemn example of justice. That was not a war between man and man but a combat to the death between wild beasts. In Naples they were waiting to strengthen the government, to instil republican sentiments into the people and to make them learn a democratic gospel translated into dialect by a Capuchin to make them understand that St Januarius had become a good democrat. But from afar could be heard the Russian armies of Suvaroff and the Austrian armies of Kray knocking at the gates of Italy; the fleet of Nelson, victor of Aboukir, and the Russian and Ottoman fleets, masters of the Ionian Islands, scoured the Adriatic and the Mediterranean. Bonaparte, the Benjamin of victory, amused himself cutting capers with Bedouins and Mamelukes. With him, fortune had deserted the French colours and bravery alone still defended them in the foreign lands where he, the resplendent victor, had placed them. After a few months what had been feared had come to pass. Macdonald inherited and Championnet was recalled into Upper Italy against the Austro-Russians who had invaded it; having left a few small garrisons in the Castel Sant'Elmo, at Capua and at Gaeta he had to open the way before him by force of arms, so much had rebellion everywhere been emboldened, even on the frontiers of the Roman State.

I had placed the Pisana with the Princess of Santacroce, the sister of a Roman prince who had been killed a few months before at Aversa defending the Republic against Mack's invasion. I felt easy in my mind about her, and Carafa treated me with great kindness and reposed a special trust in me. I had no other desire, no other passion than to see triumph that cause of liberty to which I was devoted body and soul. The departure of the French was a terrible blow to the Neapolitan republicans. They had done enough but not sufficient to recompense the loss of so valuable a support.

At that time Ettore Carafa's column had been sent into Puglia to oppose the rebellion that had been gaining ground in that province also. I left after kissing my friends and the Pisana perhaps for the last time. Her presence in Naples had been noted not only by Lucilio; Giulio suspected it but did not dare to think of it, while Amilcare had too many other things to think about! . . . He saw nothing save Ruffo, Sciarpa and Mammone and could not even see them in imagination without wanting to strangle them. As to the Pisana, that was the first kiss she had suffered from me since the meeting at Velletri; she tried to remain cold and reserved but when our lips touched, neither of us could restrain the impulse of our hearts and I straightened up, trembling all over and her face was bathed in tears.

'We shall meet again!' she said to me with a look full of assurance.

I replied with a gesture of resignation and went on my way. The Princess of Santacroce, sending on a few days later some letters that had arrived for me at Naples, wrote that a frenzy of despair had brought the Pisana almost to death's door after my departure. She beat her face and breast in a frenzy, crying that without my forgiveness it was impossible for her to live. The good Princess did not say to what forgiveness the poor girl was alluding and surrounded her with attention and the most tender care; but I did not want to be less generous and wrote direct to the Pisana, asked her pardon for my cold and proud manner towards her in recent months, and said that I knew very well that the affectation of fraternal friendship was equivalent to an insult, and that just for that reason, considering myself guilty, I offered her in reparation all my love, more tender, more vehement, more devoted than ever. In this way I hoped to bring her peace of mind even at the cost of my own dignity; furthermore, feigning ignorance of what the Princess had written to me, I gave to my protestations all the semblance of spontaneity.

I learnt later that my action had given the greatest comfort to the Pisana and that she always praised me to her protectress as the kindest and most generous person in the world. Even if the Princess had told me all these things in order to bring about our full reconciliation, I would still be grateful to her for a great service. Too much severity is wounding to women and in dealing with them it is necessary that our very virtues should take on something of the softness of their natures. One can even be too good without incurring the suspicion of baseness or of fear.

Meanwhile I arrived in Puglia fairly satisfied with myself and my affairs. I had very good news from Venice: Aglaura was pregnant, old Apostulos had returned safely and my father was on his way back. As regards this last item of news, which intrigued me more than all the rest, I puzzled my brains over it for some time, but only through some guarded words said by Lucilio was I able to throw any light on it. It seemed that, having organized a republic from Milan to Naples, some people wished, or had the intention, of bidding a kind farewell to the French and launching out for themselves. Therefore they wanted to induce the Ottoman Porte to league itself with Russia and to fall upon France in the Mediterranean; from powers so distant there was no danger of direct control and it was also understood that they would be opposed to the influence of governments nearer and more likely to exercise permanent lordship. From all this I began to suspect that my father had occupied himself up till then with this Turco-Russian alliance which so astonished the world for its speed and its unnatural aspect. But what they expected to get out of it just at the moment when the French seemed more disposed to withdraw than to play the master, I could not imagine. It seemed to my poor judgement that our independence, in relying on the Turks and the Russians, gave a very poor proof of its own stability. But there were those at that time who pushed these illusions to the limit and one could understand that better after the miserable death of General Lahoz near Ancona. Meanwhile we remained in Puglia to watch the Turkish-Russian vessels that cruised off the beaches of Puglia from the conquered ports of Zante and Corfu.

Ettore Carafa was not a man of half measures. Having gone to his fief of Andria, whose inhabitants had elected for Ruffo, he met them first with fair words of moderation and of peace. But when they would not listen to them, he drew his sword and ordered the assault; and an assault by Carafa was equivalent to a victory. Invulnerable as Achilles, he was always at the head of his legion; a skilful soldier, whether with sword, musket or artillery, he would mix with his men as an equal only to reassume at will the manner of their captain, without showing any signs of excessive arrogance. Also there was a shade of sadness in his warlike roughness; his subalterns loved him for it and I admired and felt sorry for him. But he was one of those men who find in their own political creed a comfort and a shield against any misfortune; natures of fire and steel that confound God with country and country with God and never think of themselves when the public good and the defence of liberty bid them gird on the sword of heroes.

There was in all his greatness some trace of the barbarian and his name and reputation soon made the whole province subject to him. He had dictatorial power and if the Naples government had had five other condottieres his equal, the last remnants of the Parthenopean republicans would never have been routed at Marigliano at the very gates of Naples by Ruffo or Mammone. But the government became stupidly jealous of Carafa. It was a fine time, indeed, for jealousy! . . . As if Rome had feared the dictatorship of Fabius when he alone remained to defend her against the Carthaginian victor! . . . They said that Puglia had already been pacified and that they would make fuller use of his activities and that in the Abruzzo, whither they sent him, he would have ample opportunity to render even more important services.

Ettore had the simplicity and docility of a real republican. He did not ask what cat was in the bag, accepted those honeyed words and set off for the Abruzzi. Only, since it seemed to him that the province without his presence would not remain as sure and faithful as they imagined, on his own responsibility he ordered me and Francesco Martelli, another officer of the legion, to remain in Puglia at the head of a little guerilla force which could be of great value against the petty revolts that would surely spring up once more. He placed great trust in me and that trust reposed in me by so great a man I acknowledged with tears of pride and gratitude. May his noble and blessed soul obtain in some other place that reward that it did not obtain here on earth, though he had so worthily deserved it.

Martelli was a young Neapolitan who had left wife, children and business to draw the sword in defence of liberty. Both of us come to the field from the market-place, both of us of a mild but resolute temper, we had been bound in the closest ties of friendship ever since the Velletri incident. He had been one of my companions who had wagered against me about the visit to the convent; so much so that, since the bet had been for a supper and a dance for all the officers of the legion and no one had thought of paying it, he had taken the whim of settling the account for all of them at Puglia, when one was thinking of things very different from suppers and dances. So, returning with our fifty men after having followed some brigands who had sacked a dairy-farm not far away under the guise of royalists, I found one evening the Castle of Andria illuminated and the great hall arranged for a dance, and inside a considerable number of country lasses and girls from the neighbouring houses who, in order to have an evening's enjoyment, were quite willing to forget that we were excommunicated republicans. Martelli welcomed me to the festivities with a princely gesture, saying 'Here you are; the Velletri debt is paid, and you shall have the supper too! Who knows what is in store for us, we may even be dead tomorrow, so I wanted to put my accounts straight'.

Dead or not dead the next day, that evening I danced my fill, though many times I recalled my dear Friuli and those famous festas of San Paolo, of Cordovado, of Rovignano, where we danced enough to lose our senses and our shoes. But the Neapolitans and the Pugliesi played their part nobly. From head to toe of this poor Italy we are not so different one from another as they would like to have us believe. And the resemblances are so odd that one cannot see their like in any other nation. For example, a peasant of the Friuli has all the avarice, all the stubbornness, of a Genoese shop-keeper or a Venetian gondolier, and the atticism of a Florentine dandy and a Veronese broker and a Neapolitan baron are as like one another in boasting and bragging as a Modenese policeman and a Roman priest in craftiness; Piedmontese officials and Milanese men of letters have an equal gravity of demeanour and air of command; watersellers of Caserta and doctors of Bologna compete in eloquence, Calabrian brigands and bersaglieri of Aosta in valour, and Neapolitan lazzaroni and Chioggia fishermen in patience and in superstition.

The duties entrusted to me and to Martelli were not of the easiest. We had plenty to do, with ignorant and boorish country people, with barons hard and surly, worse than the followers of Robespierre if they were Republicans, or armed with the most accursed hypocrisy if partisans of Ruffo, with ignorant and credulous priests who reminded me, with some even worse additions, of the Chaplain of Fratta, with enemies cunning and by no means over-nice in their choice of means to do us harm. None the less, the authority of Carafa, in whose name we commanded, and the example of Trani sacked and burnt for its obstinacy in rebellion, imposed some restraint upon these gentry, and the government of the Republic was silently tolerated along the whole coast of the Adriatic. In the less backward districts, where a certain culture was disseminated among the middle classes, they were afraid of the bands of the Cardinal and even more than the excesses of the French, the massacres of Gravina and Altamura ordered by Ruffo kept their minds in doubt.

In those days I was able to convince myself of the strange moral phenomenon that, in the Kingdom of Naples, a maximum of civilization and a most refined education was concentrated in a small number of men, for the most part nobles or outstanding local gentry, while the common people were left to rot in the slough of ignorance and superstition. Defect of a government, absolutist, jealous and almost despotic in the oriental manner, which held itself aloof from the most cultivated minds and flung itself unrestrainedly into the most absurd theories, relying for support on the fanatical and fostered zeal of a vicious mob. Liberal clergymen like Monsignor di Sant'Andrea and patrician philosophers like Frumier were to be found by the hundred in the little cities of Puglia and from these the republican party drew its main support. But those were times for action and the brigands were more important than the learned.

One day the news arrived that the allied Turco-Russian fleets were in sight off Puglia. We had no precise instructions for such an occurrence, but Carafa had warned us not to lose courage since disembarkation could only be carried out by small forces. In fact rather than losing heart, we made all haste to Bisceglie where they appeared to be concentrating their scattered ships and there, with the aid of a few cannon found in the castle, we set out to defend the beaches as best we could. We had spread the rumour that the fleets were manned by Albanian and Saracen bands, ready to over-run the kingdom and put all to fire and sword. Since hatred of the Turks is traditional in these regions, the people backed us up with all their might.

So they were all well disposed to repulse vigorously any attack on Bisceglie, when there arrived a messenger in hot haste from Molfetta, seven miles away, who reported that a disembarkation was being attempted there and telling of the great efforts made by the populace to prevent it. Seeing that matters in Bisceglie were in good order, Martelli and I judged it opportune to go to Molfetta, since no preparations had been made there against an enemy landing. We had no hope of defending it for any length of time, but preferred to lose our lives rather than risk not having done all we could for the safety of the Republic.

We left a good part of our men at Bisceglie and having saddled whatever horses we could find, set off at full speed. I don't know what was the matter with me that day, but I felt less courageous and optimistic than usual; perhaps it was the certainty that our cause was lost and that we were now fighting for honour only. We tried to believe in these forebodings as little as possible. Martelli, more despairing, but stronger than I, urged me not to lose heart and not to give up any of that wonderful assurance that up till then had served better than an army to keep Puglia in good heart. I told him to let me alone, that I would fight to the last gasp, but that, despite myself, I felt weakened by some inner fatigue.

About a mile outside Molfetta, we began to see smoke and hear the sound of shots. Out at sea, we could make out some ships trying to approach the port, but the high seas prevented them. Once in the town we found the turmoil at its height. Turks and Albanians, disembarked in a few lighters, had begun to sack and kill with such cruelty that it was as if the times of Bajazet had come once more. I raged madly at the barbarity of those who had handed over so fair a part of Italy as prey to these monsters, and encouraged Martelli and my companions with hopes of a tremendous revenge. Those we encountered were cut to pieces and trodden under our horses' hooves, or left to be torn to pieces by the desperate mob growing always larger behind us. On the piazza, where the greater number had already retired to regain their boats and put to sea, the bloodshed was more protracted and even more terrible. It was the one time that I barbarously enjoyed seeing the blood of my fellow-men spouting from their veins and their bloodstained bodies piled gasping and wounded, one upon another, in the convulsions of their death agonies. The crowd howled madly, lusting for blood; already some of the boldest had made themselves masters of the boats. Every escape was cut off and the last of the scoundrels was spitted on my bayonet while a hundred furious hands disputed with me the disgusting trophy. Molfetta was saved. The grandsons of Suleiman had learnt to their cost that one cannot make history retrace her steps without loss, and that Mahomet II (pardon my chronology) was as far from them as Trajan was from us. Meanwhile the streets and the piazza filled with people hurrying to the churches to thank the Madonna for their victory. The names of Captains Altoviti and Martelli were lauded to the skies by thousands of voices, united with the praises of the Blessed Virgin of the Garrison.

Having left orders at Bisceglie that news of what was happening there should be sent to us urgently and not seeing any messenger, and also wanting to give some rest to our men who needed it only too badly, we retired to an inn to take up our quarters there until dawn. We feared, too, that if the sea should calm, fresh disembarkations of Turks or Russians might try to wreak vengeance for their lost boats, though it is true that a most devilish scirocco was blowing so that precautions on this account were more or less superfluous. Notwithstanding, our men welcomed with joy the proposal for this short respite and dancing with the sailors and the women of the district soon banished from their minds the hardships and perils of the day.

Martelli had gone out to the mole with a few notables of the place to speculate on the weather and set the sentries; I remained, alone and melancholy, in the main room of the inn, gazing at the little lamp of a Madonna of Loreto hanging on the opposite wall or going to watch in the courtyard the tarantellas improvised under the vines by our soldiers. The gay life of the south went on its way and reassumed its usual tenor as if nothing had happened, only twenty paces away from the piazza where blood was still flowing and twenty or thirty corpses were awaiting burial. My thoughts were neither animated nor gay despite this ephemeral victory. I cursed inwardly at that perverse instinct that makes us live more in the fears of tomorrow than in the satisfactions of today and envied the carefree happiness of those who dance and drink without giving a thought in the world to what has been or what is going to be.

I was passing from one grief to another, when an old priest, bent and almost in rags, approached me timidly, asking if I were Captain Altoviti. I replied a little harshly, because considerable experience had not made me very tender towards the Neapolitan clergy and there were times when a clerical collar was no great recommendation to the republicans. The old man was in no way put out by my harsh words and coming closer to me said that he had something very important to tell me, and that a person allied to me by the sacred ties of kinship wanted to see me before dying. I leapt to my feet, since my mind ran immediately to some whim of the Pisana, and since I was disposed to see misfortune everywhere, my mind at once inferred the most disastrous and irreparable of them all. I feared that the Pisana, knowing I was alone in Puglia, had had the idea of coming to join me and had fallen a victim of the Molfetta massacre. I seized the priest's arm and dragged him out of the inn, warning him that if he had any idea of making a fool of me, I was not the man to endure it. When we were in the darkness of a deserted side road he whispered in my ear:

'Signor Captain; it is your father!'

I cut him short: 'My father?' I exclaimed. 'What do you mean, my father?'

'I saved him from a maddened crowd that had attacked him,' said the priest. 'He is a small thin man, and when he heard the name of the Signor Captain mentioned, he began to twist and turn on the bed where I had laid him and asked me about you. He said under oath that he was your father and that he would not die content if you did not come to see him first!'

'My father!' I went on muttering to myself, running so fast that the legs of the old abbé could hardly keep up with me. You can well imagine whether at such a moment I could put in order all the thoughts that whirled bewildered through my mind! After rushing along for some moments we reached a door flanked by columns which seemed to be the door of a monastery, and the old priest opened it, picked up a little lamp that was burning in the hall and led me to a room whence I could hear groans like those of a dying man. I entered, overcome by surprise and grief, and fell with a cry beside the bed where my father, mortally wounded in the throat, was putting up a determined struggle against death.

'Father, father!' I murmured.

I had not the breath nor the sense to say anything more. The blow had been so unexpected, so terrible, that it had deprived me of the last traces of strength remaining to me.

He tried to raise himself on his elbow and indeed managed sufficiently to fumble at something or other about his waist. With the priest's help he drew out of the folds of his wide Turkish breeches a long purse, saying with a great effort that that was all he could give me of his fortune and that, as regards the rest, I would have to ask account of the Grand Vizier. . . . He was just about to say a name when a great rush of blood poured from his throat and he fell back on the pillows, breathing stertorously.

'In God's name, Father!' I said, 'think of living. You must not die . . . and abandon me now when everyone else has abandoned me!'

'Carlo,' said my father, this time in a faint but clear voice, since the last flow of blood seemed to have relieved him. 'Carlo, no one is abandoned here below, when there are people living who cannot be abandoned. You are losing your father, but you have a sister hitherto unknown to you . . .'

'No, Father, I know her, I have loved her, for some time. It is Aglaura . . .'

'Ah, so you know and love her? It is well! I die more content at that than you would believe. . . . Listen, my son, I want to leave you something as a precious heritage . . . never, never, despite any changes of times or of men, allow the hope of a noble, generous and immortal cause to depend upon the avarice of others. I have, you see, wasted my wealth, my talents, my life, and all that I have in that false and trivial idea. . . . Ah, those Turks, those Turks! . . . But do not blame me, my son, for having placed my hopes in the Turks. For us, they are all the same. . . . Believe me! . . . I believed in making use of the Turks to drive out the French, after which we should have been left in peace. . . . Fool that I was! . . . Fool! . . . Now, now I see what the Turks want! . . .

As he said this he was seized by a violent delirium; in vain I made every effort to calm him and to support him so that he felt as little pain as possible from his wound; he went on raging and shouting that everyone was a Turk. The priest told me that it was in opposing the violence that the Ottomans had used against the helpless inhabitants as soon as they had disembarked, that my father had received that terrible scimitar wound in the throat and that, being left on the street, the country people would certainly have torn him to pieces if he had not borne him away in secret, having been a witness of the whole scene from one of the window slits of the bell-tower. I thanked the priest for so much Christian charity and asked him quietly if there were no surgeons or doctors in the district to whose skill we might have recourse. The dying man trembled at these words and shook his head.

'No, no,' he said, speaking with a great effort and in a faint voice. 'Remember the Turks! . . . What good are doctors? . . . Remember Venice . . . and if you can see her once again great, mistress of herself and of the sea . . . encircled by a forest of ships and an aureole of glory . . . then, my son, may Heaven bless you! . . .'

And he died.

Such a death was not one of those that leave one thunderstruck and almost afraid to take up life once more; it was an example, a comfort, an inspiration. I closed with reverence the still eloquent eyes of my father; his spirit, strong and active, left almost an impression of animation on those features, already dead. I kissed his forehead and do not know whether I prayed, but certainly my lips murmured some words that I have never since repeated. I would have remained for long in the company of the dead man, had not his last thoughts, indeed his very image, recalled to me those sublime duties of which he had been the unknown martyr, sometimes indeed mistakenly, but always resolute and unshaken.

'Father,' I thought, 'you would be glad to know that I deprive myself of the consolation of accompanying you to your last resting place only to look to the salvation, already almost beyond hope, of our Republic!'

It almost seemed as if a smile of assent flickered on his lips. I hurried from the room with a heart that seemed broken into fragments. With some difficulty I induced the old priest to accept a few doubloons for the expenses of the funeral and to have prayers said for the soul of the dead man. Then I returned to the inn where Martelli had already drawn up our little force for departure and was most uneasy at my absence. The dawn was breaking on the sea, scattering from its white fingers all the colours of the rainbow, but the scirocco of the previous evening has left the sea somewhat rough and on the horizon not a single sail was to be seen. The churchbells called the fishermen to early mass, the women were chattering at their doors about the terrors they had endured and a few ship's boys were singing as they hoisted the sails. Nothing, nothing in that land, in that sky, in that life, was in sympathy with the mourning of a son who had but lately closed the eyes of his father's corpse! . . .

'Where have you been? . . . What is the matter?' Martelli asked me, leaning over the mane of his horse. I leapt on to my own and, driving my spurs into its belly, went off at a gallop without replying. For a time the cheers of the inhabitants who had come out to see us leave, followed us. We had galloped in this way for a good couple of miles when the near-by roll of guns pulled us up short to listen. In this uncertainty one of our men came at full speed to meet us, without arms and without hat, and resolved our doubts. A ship under a flag of truce had entered Bisceglie. The inhabitants, seeing that they were not Turks, but Russians under the command of the Chevalier Micheroux, General of His Majesty King Ferdinand, who asked to disembark only to drive out the French still remaining at Capua and Gaeta, had begun to shout *evvivas*, to throw away their guns and wave their handkerchiefs. One thousand four hundred Russians had disembarked and set out along the Foggia road to surprise the people at the time of the stock-fair and to strike terror into the whole province from this one central point.

Martelli and I took counsel with a glance. The most obvious plan was to forestall the Russians at Foggia and put the city in a state of defence. We therefore turned right for Ruvo and Andria, but at the entrance to the latter castle we were surrounded by an armed and violent throng. It was one of Ruffo's bands, sent to join up with the Russians of Micheroux. Aware too late of having fallen into this hornet's nest, we had our hands full to get out of it again. Martelli with seventeen others succeeded in escaping, ten remained on the field dead and eight others, I amongst them, all more or less seriously wounded, were saved to ornament the gallows at some festival, according to the paragraph on prisoners in the military code of Ruffo.

The band that had taken us prisoner was led by the celebrated Mammone, the ugliest man I have ever seen, who wore countless medallions on his hat like the familiar spirit of Louis XI. Dragged along in their tail, barefoot and exposed to continual insults, I tramped at length through Puglia, the very place where I had reigned five or six days before with almost sovereign powers. I confess that this sort of existence pleased me very little and, since the irons on my hands and feet prevented me from escaping, I had no other hope than to be hanged as quickly as possible. However, one evening when we arrived at the fief of Andria, seat of my former grandeur, a shepherd came up to insult me in the usual manner and after having shouted at the top of his voice the most barefaced indignities that Neapolitan fancy could imagine, added so softly that I scarcely understood him: 'Courage, little master, they are thinking about you in the castle!'

I thought then that I recognized him as one of Carafa's most trusted tenants and later, looking up at the castle, I was astonished to see the windows lit up, seeing that only a few days before I had left it closed and deserted for its true master was still in the Abruzzi and even, it was reported, beseiged by the rebels in the citadel of Pescara. So, having nothing better to do, for that evening I allowed myself to hope.

When it was nearly midnight, one of the brigands came to take me out of the outhouse where they had confined me and having shown the guards an order from the captain, took the irons off my hands and feet and told me to follow him along the road. When we reached a miserable little farmhouse a stone's throw from Andria, he handed me over to a man of smallish stature, wrapped in a cloak, who said very curtly: 'Good!' The brigand then returned whence he had come, leaving me with my new master. I was considering whether to stay where I was or to take to my heels when another person, whom I at once sensed to be a woman, appeared from behind the man in the cloak and threw herself upon my neck with the warmest embraces possible. I did not know, but felt that it must be the Pisana. However, the man in the cloak was impatient at this scene and reminded us that there was no time to lose. I knew his voice also at once and murmured, more moved than surprised: 'Lucilio!'

'Quiet!' he said and led us to a dark corner behind the house where three fine coursers were champing at the bit. He told us to mount and although for twelve hours I had not touched food or drink, I scarcely noticed covering eight leagues in two hours. The roads were horrible, the night as dark as could be and the Pisana, with her horse sandwiched between ours, swung now to the right and now to the left, prevented from falling only by our shoulders that pushed her back in turn. It was the first time that she had ridden a horse for a long time, but at intervals she had the courage to laugh.

'But tell me by what witchcraft you were able to get round Signor Mammone?' Lucilio asked her. It seemed that he knew no more than I about certain parts of the story.

'Capperi!' exclaimed the Pisana, speaking as well as the continual jolting of her horse permitted her. 'He told me I was very beautiful. I promised him everything he asked and even swore it by all the medallions he wears in his hat. At two after midnight he was to go to Andria to receive the price of his generosity! Ha, ha!' (The impudent one laughed at her noble perjury.)

'So that was why you insisted on leaving before two! Now I understand!'

Then it was my turn to ask for explanations about all the rest of the plan and I learnt that Lucilio and the Pisana, having set out to join me under the powerful protection of Carafa, had met some fugitives from Martelli's band who had told them that I had been taken prisoner. Hearing that Mammone was due at Andria the following day, they had preceded him and there the Pisana had copied in part from the story of Judith the trickery that had saved me from the gallows and I know not which of the two, Mammone or Holofernes, had been the better cheated. By daybreak we had reached the first scouts of the republican camp of Schipani, where Giulio and Amilcare were surprised to hear all that I had undergone and had escaped so fortunately. The rejoicing, the embraces, the joy and congratulations were unending; but in the midst of it all we felt a deep melancholy at the pending and inevitable collapse of the Republic and I concealed another, though a different, mourning in my heart for the tragic death of my father. The first to whom I unburdened my heart on this matter was Lucilio. He listened to me with more sorrow than surprise and said: 'It had to end this way! I too was led away by such errors! . . . I too lament so much time, so much talent, so many lives uselessly wasted! . . .'

We reached Naples with Schipani's column, thrown back to the capital by the ever growing hordes under Ruffo. The confusion, the tumult, the fear was at its height. None the less, garrisons were stationed in towers and in castles and if there was no real war, at least there were many who died like heroes. Francesco Martelli was ordered to defend the Torre di Vigliena. Having decided to die rather than surrender, he wrote me a letter confiding to my care his wife and children. Giulio del Ponte, more weakened than ever by his illness, asked the privilege of sharing this dangerous post and obtained it. When he left Naples for this sad mission, the Pisana kissed him on the lips, the last kiss of farewell. Giulio smiled sadly and turned on me a long and resigned look of envy. Two days later the commanders of the Torre di Vigliena, hard pressed by the royalists, by Ruffo, by the brigands, and no longer able to resist, fired the magazines and blew themselves up together with a good hundred of their enemies. Their shattered corpses fell on the smoking ground and the mountain echo repeated their last cry: 'Long live liberty! Long live Italy!'

In the anarchy of those last days, we had lost sight of Amilcare and it was not until some months later I learnt that he had ended his life as a real brigand in the mountains of Sannio; a fate not unusual for strong and impetuous natures in those contrary times and governments.

A few days later the Russians, the English and Ruffo's rabble entered Naples through the infamous cowardice of Megeant, the French commander of Sant'Elmo. Nelson with a stroke of the pen annulled the terms of the capitulation, saying that a king did not bargain with revolted subjects. Then began the assassinations and the martyrdoms. It was a real heroic cycle, a tragedy that had no comparison in history save the massacre of the Pythagorean school in the same region of Magna Graecia. Mario Pagano, Cirillio, Vincenzo Russo, three lights of Italian science, simple and great as the men of ancient times, died as brave men upon the scaffold. Eleonora Fonseca, a woman, drank coffee before mounting the gallows and recited the verse: *Forsan haec olim meminisse juvabit.* Federici the Marshal, Caracciolo the Admiral, the flower of the Neapolitan nobility, the pride of letters, arts and science in that part of Italy, was condemned to die by the hands of the executioner . . . and the English and Nelson pulled at their feet!

There remained Ettore Carafa. He had defended to the last the fortress of Pescara. Consigned by the Neapolitan government itself to the royalists, under the terms of the capitulation, he was brought to Naples. The day when he mounted the scaffold, I, Lucilio and the Pisana slipped away secretly from the Portuguese ship on which we had taken refuge, and had the fortune to salute him. He looked first at the Pisana, then at me and Lucilio, and then once more at the Pisana; and smiled! . . . Oh, blessed be that weak humanity that can with a single such smile redeem itself from a century of abject misery. The Pisana and I lowered our eyes, weeping. Lucilio watched him die. He asked to be beheaded lying on his back so that he could watch the edge of the axe and perhaps too the sky and the only woman he had ever loved, yet loved as unhappily as he had his country.

Nothing more bound us to Naples. Having confided the widow and children of Martelli to the Princess of Santacroce, supplied with a little pension based on the money left me by my father, we set off for Genoa, sole rock remaining of Italian liberty.

By the glorious fall of Naples, by the capitulation of Ancona, by the victories of Suvaroff and of Kray in Lombardy, all the rest of Italy at the beginning of 1800 was in the power of the confederates.

CHAPTER XVIII

WE arrived at Genoa, the Pisana and I bedevilled by seasickness and relieved, thanks to that, from all other preoccupations. Lucilio was always more reserved and meditative as one who begins to despair, though still unwilling to do so. His strength increased according to his need and he really had the soul of a Roman, made to command even in the lowest positions, a gift common enough and fatal to the Italians, since it causes so many of our misfortunes as well as some of our most tragic glories. Secret societies are a refuge for the disgruntled and for the imperious natures of those who either scorn to, or cannot, act within the very narrow limits imposed on them by government. For some time I had become aware that Lucilio belonged, perhaps from his University years, to the philosophical sect of the illuminati or the Freemasons; but then, little by little, I had perceived that his philosophical tendencies leaned towards politics, as the factions of the former Cisalpine Republic and the last events at Ancona had borne witness. Lucilio followed such reports with the greatest eagerness and some of them he had predicted with remarkable accuracy. Whether he had been previously advised or if he were a true prophet, I do not know; but I incline to the latter opinion, since he neither used to discuss what was told him, nor in our condition at that time was it very easy to receive fresh news by letter. At Genoa, later, neither fresh nor salted news was in question and the most recent reports from Venice we got from an Austrian prisoner who had been billeted the month before on the Pisana's husband, perhaps in the very room previously occupied by Lieutenant Minato.

One of the most unpleasant innovations that I found in Genoa was the famine; for the day after our arrival the English fleet began a strict blockade and in a few weeks reduced us to hunting cats. I had, however, one great comfort and that was the protection offered me in every way by my friend Alessandro the miller who was also in Genoa and was no longer Captain, but Colonel. Whoever managed to live in those times was sure of rapid promotion.

Colonel Giorgi was not yet twenty-six and had advanced to become the leader of all his regiment and gave orders right and left in a real miller's voice. He did not know what fear meant, and would rage in the fury of the battle without ever forgetting the companies whom he had to lead and control; those were his merits.

He wrote passably well, though with some difficulty about spelling, had only known for about a month, and then only by name, who Vauban and Frederick II were; those were his defects. But it seems that they gave greater weight to his merits, since in two and a half years he had become Colonel, though the greatest merit was due to the slaughter of all his battalion that, as we have said, had made him Captain by force of necessity. One day I met him, when the stores had already begun to run low and those who had provisions had begun to hoard them. I had the Pisana to fend for, who was in a low state of health, and I had not yet been able to find a pound of meat for soup.

'Ohe, Carlino,' said the Colonel. 'How goes it?'

'As you see,' I replied, 'I am still alive but I fear for tomorrow or the day after. The Pisana is not feeling well and we are going from bad to worse.'

'What? The Contessina is ill? . . . Body of the devil! . . . Would you like me to get you half a dozen army doctors? . . . The regiments are no more but the doctors have survived; good proof of their great knowledge.'

'Thanks, thanks! I have Doctor Vianello, who is enough for me.'

'I am sure he is, but I made the offer in case you needed more advice or opinions.'

'No, no, the malady is clear enough. It comes from lack of air and of food.'

'Nothing else? Then leave it to me! Tomorrow I am on guard duty at Polcevera and there she can breathe enough air in one hour as she could breathe in Fratta in a whole day.'

'Yes, that is true, but what about those fine beetroots that Melas keeps making us a present of?'

'True. I forgot that she is a Contessina and that bombs might irritate her. Well, there is nothing to be done about it. You might take her for a walk on the roofs.'

'If she would like it, and feels strong enough, I would even try the roofs, but a sick girl fed on lettuce soup cannot certainly have much energy.'

'Poor thing! However, I can get you out of your trouble. . . . You see how fat and well-covered I have managed to keep myself! . . .'

'You have indeed! You look like a canon of Portogruaro Cathedral.'

'Far more than a canon! Tell me, does one get muscles like this by chanting in the choir? . . .' and he showed and flexed an arm that almost seemed ready to burst his coat-sleeve: 'You see, I have kept myself like this by foresight. I slaughtered my two horses, had them salted down and guzzle my four pounds a day. Afterwards, let come what may! But if you would like to join me in my land of milk and honey . . .' But one day the miller-Colonel came to see me somewhat less ruddy and jovial than usual. I blamed the salted horse, which was beginning to run short, but he replied that he had quite other things to think about and that he would take me to a place whence I too perhaps might leave with no wish to make jokes. In truth, I no longer felt any great inclination for such badinage, but however much I pressed Alessandro he would tell me nothing and merely repeated that I would see for myself next day.

In fact, the next day he came to fetch me and took me to the military hospital. There we found poor Bruto Provedoni who had just begun to get up again after a long illness; but he had done so with a wooden leg. You can imagine what a shock! Even Alessandro had been unaware of his friend's misfortune and not having had any news of him for a century, had feared perhaps even worse. But when searching the hospitals for one of his soldiers who could not be found and was reported to be ill, he had come across his friend. However, of the three of us, Bruto himself was the least concerned. He laughed, sang and tried to walk and dance on his wooden leg with the most childish and grotesque antics in the world. He said he only regretted not having delayed the loss of his leg until the beginning of the siege, since then he would have been able to eat it with great pleasure. I was very glad to have found him, since I might in some way or another be of use to him. Indeed he passed all his convalescence at our house with the Pisana and Lucilio and thus avoided the tedium and hardships of the military hospital.

At Genoa I once again saw Ugo Foscolo, an officer of the Lombard Legion, and this was the last time we met on terms of our former familiarity. He was already standing on his dignity as a man of genius; he avoided all friendships, especially with men, in order the better to gain their admiration, and wrote odes to his women acquaintances with all the classicism of Anacreon or Horace. This was enough to show that his time was not entirely taken up with dying of hunger and that chicory roots neither extinguish poetic inspiration nor dull completely the high spirits of youth.

But in the long run poetic inspiration melted away and good spirits began to wither. A bean cost then up to three soldi and bread was four francs an ounce and to eat bread and beans alone was to ruin oneself within a month. I had only about twenty thousand lire in all, in cash and Austrian bonds, but this was not the place to obtain payment of these and so my whole property was reduced to a hundred or so doubloons. Trying to restore the uncertain health of the Pisana and feed her with other things besides rats and candied fruits, we lived well enough for a doubloon a day. But in the end I considered myself lucky to be able to fall back on Alessandro's salt horse. But, one way and another, there were only bones left and then it was up to us to do as all the others did; to live off putrid fish, boiled hay when it could be found, grass and sugared pastries, of which there was a great abundance in Genoa since they formed there a most important branch of commerce. Fevers and rashes were added as a final boon, but in our own house health began to revive once more just when it was getting worse outside. The sugared pastries seemed to suit the Pisana; she recovered the lovely roses of her cheeks and her wayward and cross-grained humour, that during her illness had become so sweet and placid as to make me fear some great disaster.

Then I consoled myself once again, judging that no harm had been done and that her health was as it had always been; indeed my consolation went so far that I even began to get worried. She would sometimes jump up savagely, frown and prolong her sulks for a whole day. In these moods she wanted everything her own way and would pass from sullen silence to an almost fabulous garrulity in less time than it takes to say. In this way she seemed to cancel from my memory all those years we had lived in the meantime and bring me back once more to our tempestuous childhood at Fratta. On closing my eyes, I could almost have believed myself no longer at Genoa, the veteran of a long and bitter war, but on the bank of one of the ditches in our meadows boring holes in snail-shells and polishing pebbles. I felt myself growing childish like a great grandfather, even though I was not yet a father, nor had any great eagerness to become one. That was another great point of controversy between us. She wanted a baby at all costs and I, however much I determined to point out that in our position, in that place and in those times, a son would be the worst of complications, had to hold my peace, otherwise the uproar would have brought the ceiling down about our heads. That was the start of more squabbles, more altercations, more jealousies; all for that blessed baby and yet, I swear to you, that if providence had decided to send us one, I would have felt neither sin nor regret for it.

Complaint was universal. The General alone had his own ideas, in order to postpone by a month, by a day, the surrender. Bonaparte in the meantime would have rallied the last republican ardours of France to consume Europe yet once more. Through hardships, sufferings, fortitude and cruelty, we reached the 1st of June, when Bonaparte fell like a thunderbolt to disturb the quiet little skirmishes of Melas against Suchet, and reawaken in Milan the hopes of the

Italians. The surrender of Genoa was called a convention and not a capitulation, the eight thousand men of Massena passed opportunely to swell the ranks of Varus and one heard no more talk from the new conquerors of Liguria about restoring the former government, even as there was no more talk of it in Piedmont. It was a fine time to talk about restorations! Melas, by forced marches, rallied the scattered fragments of the army on the banks of the Bormida, directly opposite that point where Napoleon, before leaving Paris, had put his finger on the map and said: 'I will break them here!' And so they hastened to leave Milan, to cross the Po, to conquer with the Viceroy Lannes at Montebello and press upon the enemy around Alessandria. It was a very strange position for the two armies, each of which had its own country at the back of the enemy!

The exiles in Genoa, according to the terms of the convention, were taken on English ships to Antibes. I myself, the Pisana, Lucilio and Bruto Provedoni were among them. It was a most unpleasant voyage and cost me my last doubloon. At Marseilles I was very pleased to find a moneylender who discounted my Austrian bonds at thirty per cent and, since the news of the victory at Marengo had already arrived, we all retraced our steps to Italy. There was hope enough, indeed we hoped for even more than had been recovered, though what had already been recovered was almost a miracle. But no one could have imagined that Melas would so lose heart after a first defeat, and the continuation of the war widened the field of our illusions, even so far as to discern dimly in the distance the restitution of liberty to Venice or at least her adherence to the Cisalpina.

Instead, we were met on our way by the news of the capitulation of Alessandria whereby Melas withdrew behind the Po and the Mincio and the French reoccupied Piedmont, Lombardy, Liguria, the Duchies, Tuscany and the Papal States. The new Pope, who, elected at Venice, had recently re-entered Rome amid the enthusiastic applause of his Neapolitan allies, thought he would have enough to do to reconquer power from the too tenacious hands of his friends, instead of which, he had to accept it from the clemency of his enemies by signing a Concordat with the French on 15 July. But the First Consul then set himself up as the protector of order, religion and peace; and Pius VII, the good Chiaromonti, believed him implicitly.

New provisional Consulates sprang up on every side in this new atmosphere of peace, order and religion. Lucilio and all the old democrats frowned on them; but Bonaparte flattered and intoxicated the people, blandished those in power and rewarded the soldiers generously, and against such reasons republican irritation could make no headway. I for my part, true to my former principles, hoped for the new order, for I could not imagine that men could have changed so greatly in so short a space of time. For all that, I felt no surprise when Lucilio refused an important position offered him by the new government, but for my part, I accepted willingly enough a post as auditor in the military courts. Thence, so great a shortage was there of capable administrators, they appointed me Secretary of Finances at Ferrara. It did not displease me to gain my bread honourably, since what with the twelve thousand lire left for Martelli's widow in a bank in Naples, the doubloons spent in Genoa and the bonds negotiated at Marseilles, all the monies left me by my father before his death had gone up in smoke. Colonel Giorgi kept coming to me saying that I should rely on him and that he would have me gazetted major in the Engineers or the Artillery, but living as I was with the Pisana a military career was not to my taste and I felt more inclined to civilian employment. Indeed at Ferrara we set up house very honourably. Bruto Provedoni, who had accompanied us as far as Ferrara, on his way back to Venice and the Friuli, promised that he would write us very fully on all that he could find out there. We felt very satisfied at having saved ourselves so fortunately from that great tempest that had swallowed up so many greater and cleverer than we, and set ourselves to await with patience that unforeseen event which would end by putting our lives perfectly in order.

The death of His Excellency Navagero, which could not be long delayed, was very close to my heart. Not that I wished the poor old fellow ill, but after having lived happily enough for more than seventy years he could well afford to make way and allow a trifle of happiness for us also. Without wanting to do so, I believe that I too had moderated my opinions according to the opinions of that second republican period; that reckless, intoxicating, delirious love that had seemed natural enough amid the ardent and unbridled passions of a revolution was somewhat at odds with the sober, legal and considered ideas that had taken their place. Finally, the Concordat with the Holy See had turned me, despite myself, to thoughts of marriage. The Pisana gave no hint of what she hoped or intended to do. Returned to a regular life, she had also returned to her usual unevenness of temper, the usual taciturnity varied by sudden excesses of chatter and laughter, the usual love seasoned with rages, jealousies and recklessness.

Aglaura and Spiro wrote from Venice with news more varied than good. They had had a second baby, but Spiro's mother was dead and they were inconsolable; their business prospered but public affairs seemed more than ever in the hands of the wicked and the depraved. The Elder Venchieredo played the master shamelessly, displaying the manners, language and haughtiness of a foreigner. Spiro, who had had to seek audience of him to entreat for the liberation of a countryman exiled to Cattaro with the republicans captured in the *terraferma*, had had to agree that the foreign masters were worth more than the local stewards and bailiffs. The advocate Ormenta was Venchieredo's companion in that despicable work, but had got an even worse reputation for his secret embezzlements than for his open extortions. The counsels of Father Pendola were in vogue. Despite his expulsion from Portogruaro and the discredit in which he was held by the Venice curia, he had been able to form a certain party among the less educated clergy and by some was considered a martyr and by others a rogue. The old Frumiers had both died, within a month of one another; of the young ones, Alfonso had renounced marriage to obtain a command in the Order of Malta and it was not even known for certain if he were still alive; but it was rumoured that he was courting a certain Lady Dolfin, older than he by some fifteen years, who had already been the wife of a Correggitore at Portogruaro—I remembered her and recalled her to the Pisana and we both laughed.

Agostino, however, had solicited a post in the new government, since otherwise he did not know how to earn his living, having lost all his patrimony after the death of his parents. They had made him Controller of the Customs and he, the fervid republican, was humiliated by this. However, he had ideas of recovering his position by a good marriage and there was some intrigue afoot concerning that young Contarini damsel whom my father had wanted to palm off on me on the pretext of her great dowry and his dreams of my future position of Doge. The Countess of Fratta, being his aunt, beat the big drum for him, but she was more encouraged by the hope of a generous commission than by any affection for her nephew, for her old passion for gaming still possessed her and the family inheritance continued to decrease, being now reduced to a hundred or so fields around the Castle of Fratta, mortgaged against her daughters' credits. The Reverend Clara, after the death of Mother Redenta, had become the leading figure in the convent and there was talk of making her Abbess. She therefore concerned herself less than ever with what happened in the world outside for good or evil. Count Rinaldo remained hunched over his accounts or in the libraries; Raimondo Venchieredo had offered to get him promotion in the administration but he had obstinately refused and went on his way, grimy and in rags, with his ducat a day and even that skinned from him by his lady mother, and did not want, or so I believe, to bend his back more than was absolutely necessary. Aglaura also sent me news of Doretta who, you may remember, had occasionally been in touch with her and, more particularly, had brought her through Venchieredo some letters from Emilio after his departure for Milan. The wretched Doretta, abandoned by Raimondo, had forgotten all restraint and gone from lover to lover, always lower in the scale, and had fallen into the most degraded and infamous slums of Venice.

'You see in whom you trusted?' I said to the Pisana.

She had confessed to me that it had been Doretta who had told her of my supposed love affair and flight with Aglaura, by which the foolish strumpet had served Raimondo's aims against her own interests.

'What do you want me to say?' replied the Pisana. 'You know very well that when one is angry with someone, bad words come quicker than good ones. What if I confessed to you that Raimondo himself described you to me as an intriguer who had remained in Venice after the others had gone and only left for Milan to fish in troubled waters, and very dirty waters too?'

'The rascal!' I exclaimed, 'so Raimondo told you that? . . . I shall have something to say to him!'

'I didn't really believe him,' replied the Pisana, 'and even if I believed him a little, it did him no good. He was trying to get me away from you, but all he did was to hasten my arrival in Milan.'

'That's enough!' I said, since I was not anxious to have this part of our lives recalled. 'Let us see what Bruto Provedoni writes from Cordovado.'

We read the long-awaited letter from the poor invalid I could, as I have done above, give you a summary of it, but my modesty as a writer does not permit. Here I must leave the field to one greater than I, and you will see for yourselves how a noble soul can support misery and watch from a distance the affairs of the world without renouncing his co-operation in them, or his pity. This letter I still preserve among my dearest treasures, in the reliquary of memory, that begins with that tress of hair that the Pisana made me tear from her head. But read meanwhile what Bruto Provedoni, recently returned to his little corner of the world with one leg the less and many anxieties the more, wrote to us:

'My dearest Carlino! I have long wanted to write to you for there are many things I have to tell you and I have received so many sad impressions on returning that it seems that I shall never come to an end of them. But I am little accustomed to hold a pen and must often put aside my thoughts and limit myself to those material things that I can better express. Moreover I can be open with you and let the spirit speak in its own way. Where it does not express itself as well as it should, you will none the less understand, and in any case you will be merciful to my ignorance that is so full of good will.

'If you could only see these parts, Carlino! . . . You would no longer recognize them! . . . What has become of the festas, the reunions, the meetings that were the pride of the neighbourhood and which preserved uncorrupted the ancient traditions of hospitality, Christianity and religion? . . . What blight has all of a sudden attacked that life of lively contests between one village and another, of rivalries and disputes over the favours of some girl, the election of a parish priest or the affirmation of some right? . . . In four years it seems to me that fifty have passed. Here there has been no famine, yet everywhere they complain of misery, no military levies or pestilence as in Piedmont and in France, yet the countryside is depopulated and the houses deserted by the best workers. One has emigrated to Germany, another to the Cisalpina; yet another has gone to seek his fortune in Venice and another remains only because he secretly fears those hidden and more distant powers. Differences of opinion have broken up families; the sorrowings, sufferings and oppressions of war have killed off the old people and made the grown men old. Marriages are no longer being celebrated and rarely do the bells sound for a baptism. If one hears the bell it is for a death agony or a passing. The vigour that had always remained among our countrymen and which showed itself either well or ill in many little village crafts, has altogether gone. Left without arms, without money, and without faith, no one thinks of anything save his own interests and the needs of the day; each works only to assure himself of a refuge against the deceits of his neighbour or the oppression of his superiors. The uncertainty of the public weal and of the law makes them wriggle out of agreements and rather speculate on the good faith of others than trust in it.

'As you know, the former magistratures have been abolished, and Venchieredo and Fratta are no more than villages, subject, like Teglio and Bagnara, to the Prefecture of Portogruaro. Thus they call a new magistrature established to administer justice, but however useful and in accord with the times such an innovation may be, the peasants do not believe in it. I am too ignorant to tell you their reasons, but it may be that they expect little good from those who up to the present have done them such ill. What is sure is that those who have grown fat in the meantime are the wicked and perverse; the good men have been overwhelmed and impoverished for not having had the courage to hold their own in the general misfortune. The bad know the good, know they can rely on them and skin them to the bone. In the contracts that they sign to their own ruin, there is no provision for future compromise nor means of escape. They come into the net and are strangled there without mercy.

'Some of the stewards of the great families, the usurers, the speculators in grain and the furnishers of the communes for military requisitions; these are the men of genius who have arisen in the general desolation. They, serfs and servants until yesterday, have more arrogance than their masters of former times and without the restraints of education and chivalrous custom do not even trouble to give their wickednesses the illusion of honesty. They have lost all knowledge of good or evil; they want to be respected, obeyed, served, because they are rich. Carlino! The revolution up till now has created more evil than good. I am much afraid that in a few years from now we shall find proudly installed an aristocracy of money that will make us regret the aristocracy of birth. I have said "up till now" and I do not withdraw my words; since men who have recognized the vanity of rights solely dependent on the merits of great-grandfathers or great-great-grandfathers will more quickly realize the enormity of a power that is not dependent on any merit, either present or past, but solely on the right of money, which is on a par with the right of force. That he who has money may keep it, spend it or use it, is very good; but he who buys with it that authority which is due to knowledge and virtue alone is a thing that I can never stomach. It is a barbarous and immoral defect of which humanity must at all costs be purged.

'Oh, if only you could see the Castle of Fratta now! . . . The walls are still upright and the towers still rise among the leaves of the poplars and willows that fringe the moat; but for the rest, what desolation! No longer people coming and going, dogs barking, horses neighing and old Germano polishing muskets on the bridge, or the Signor Chancellor going out with the Count, or the servants lined up with their hats off to the Contessinas! Everywhere is solitude, silence, ruin. The drawbridge has fallen to pieces and the moat is filled with cartloads of rubbish and mortar from the gardener's house, which has fallen down. Grass is growing in the courtyards and the windows are not only without shutters, but the frames and sills are rotting away under the continual dropping of the rain. It is said that some creditors, or thieves or some one else, have even bought the roofbeams of the granary; I know nothing of that. But I see that a great piece of the roof is missing and that the rain pours in, with what damage to the apartments you can guess. . . . Marchetto, who is sacristan at Teglio and has grown as lazy as a capon, still goes to the castle from time to time out of long habit. He has told me that the Signora Veronica is dead, and that Monsignor Orlando and the Captain have only Giustina, the Chaplain's old servant, to look after their clothes and prepare their lunch and supper. Monsignor sighs because he may no longer drink wine; the Captain wails because he promised his Veronica upon her deathbed not to take another wife and there is now at Fossalta the widow of the apothecary who is crazy and wants to marry him. I can't think why. In winter they go to bed at five, and Monsignor seeks refuge in deep sleep. Of all his former acquaintances, only the Chaplain has remained true and seems to draw closer to him at every fresh misfortune. Monsignor de Sant'Andrea and the Rector of Teglio are also dead. In fact, as I told you in the beginning, I went away from a countryside and have returned to a cemetery—but that is not all.

'As to their manner of existence, these gentlemen live on their stipends and almost on the alms of the four tenants who still remain to them, for all the revenue trickles to Venice. The bailiffs, stewards and agents have seen to that, after having recouped themselves thoroughly at the expense of the simpletons. Even before I went away, Fulgenzio had bought the Frumier house at Portogruaro and was lording it there like a seigneur; now his son Domenico is a notary and has a position in Venice, while his second son sang his first mass yesterday and will find a place in the curia as registrar. He is a fine little priest, this Don Girolamo, and taken all in all, pleases me more than his brother and his father, though he too is as cunning as a fox.

'Now, Carlino, I come to the most grave misfortunes; I say most grave because they touch me most closely, and I have kept them till the last since if I had begun to enlarge upon them at the beginning I would scarcely have been able to make up my mind to speak of other things. My father has followed my mother, who had already been dead a month when I went away with Sandro Giorgi to become a soldier. He breathed his last, poor fellow, in the arms of Acquilina, since all his sons save I were on bad terms with him and did not believe that he was going to die. Bradamante was in childbed and could not aid her sister in these last pious offices. I do not want to speak ill of my brothers, but the first of them through ignorance, and the others through bravado, have ended by turning the whole house upside down. Filched here, torn away there, wasted, sold, lent, I found the rooms empty; that is, I must correct myself, not empty; Leone, who had moved with his family to San Vito to become a factor, had seen fit to let the house, with the exception of three rooms left to Acquilina and Mastone, since Grifone had already left for Illyria as a master builder. Three months later, Mastone was offered a post as scrivener at Udine and decamped, leaving Acquilina, a girl of fourteen, alone in these three rooms. It is true that she seems almost grown up, and I was very glad to hear the priest praise her, but to act in such a way shows that Mastone kept all his brotherly charity in his heels.

'Of all these misfortunes, Carlino, some I had already heard about by letter, others I only suspected; but I tell you the truth that, in coming face to face with them, they made a terrible effect on me and one which I should never have expected. Perhaps seeing myself so maimed and incapable of putting things to rights ended by embittering my sorrow, which was already great enough. But there was another blow in store for me, just after my arrival, that nearly overwhelmed me. Amongst other things, Acquilina had told me of the death of Doctor Natalino which had taken place a couple of months before. Then, one evening, can you guess who arrived at my house? . . . My kinswoman, that shameless wretch Doretta! . . . She had with her a little whippersnapper of a pen pusher, who is said to be the son of a certain advocate Ormenta of Venice and who had come with her to claim her dowry and the inheritance of her husband. What do you think of that? . . . What a heart! . . . The dowry that had never been paid! The inheritance of a man whom she had, so to speak, killed! But since she had an acknowledgement of indebtedness, written in Leopardo's hand some eight months after their marriage, and furthermore was in so pitiful a state, for the little clerk told me in an aside that without the help of this money the honour of my kinswoman would be in grave danger, in order to get her out, if that were possible, of the evil way of life into which she had fallen, and out of respect for our name and the memory of my brother, I did all I could to pay her. I sold what remained to me of the property of my father; I gave her the money and she hurried off; but it seemed to me that the young man was very eager to relieve her of the trouble of carrying the satchel.

'I learnt later that the money had served her as a dowry to enter an Institute for the Converted, newly opened in Venice, and under the control of various priests, obscure in name, but Christian at heart and full of the most honourable intentions. She stayed there in retirement for a month and then fled, they say, as if possessed by a devil; now, I am greatly afraid that she may be in even worse circumstances than before, for the gift of the dowry was irrevocable and in any case it was not so great a sum as to enable her to live an independent existence.

'Now you know our circumstances and, practically speaking, those of the whole countryside. I play the father to Acquilina, administer the ten fields that remain to her and for my own part gain my bread by giving an occasional lesson in calligraphy in some good family of the neighbourhood that perhaps wants in this way to disguise the giving of alms. On Sundays, our kinsman Donato comes to pick us up with his little cart and takes us to Fossalta to see Bradamante who already has three children, the first one stumbling about like a crane, and the last still at the breast. Despite my wooden leg, I make great prowess with the first, and teach the second, who is a girl and lazy enough for her age, to walk. I do not know whether this state of affairs is final, or a way leading to better fortune, or a truce before worse calamities. I know that I have done my duty and that I will always do it and that if I have taken a hasty decision it was because my duty called me to do so, and indeed my life has never disclaimed these decisions. Things might have been a great deal better, but I would not give my poverty and not even my wooden leg for all the riches, the comforts and the rude health of some rascal.

'Am I right, Carlino? I know you are of the same opinion and therefore I can speak to you from an open heart. For the rest, my hopes are not all bounded by the rooftree of my house. I have some that go in search of you, and others that retrace the road I have already covered and which are not satisfied after the melancholy experience of wars that have ended. Our First Consul has already won a victory at Marengo, but we too can offer him some fine battlefields and he has already known them not to be unpropitious. Oh, if we could only see *that* time! How joyfully I would dance, wooden leg and all! How I would embrace you, the Pisana and Doctor Lucilio. . . . By the way is it true that the Doctor has settled in Milan? . . . Do you know, moreover, that Sandro Giorgi has been sent with his regiment to the wars in Germany? If the wars continue, he will certainly make his way, and I wish it for him, for despite all his little faults, he has a heart, a heart that he would tear into shreds for others. But I shall never come to an end of chattering to you! . . . Love me then, write to me, remember me to the Pisana and do not forget to do everything in your power to hasten our next meeting.'

A great soul! And it was he who had excused himself for not knowing how to write! Where one can feel the heart, who worries about the choice of words? Who looks for style when the writer's soul so sweetly touches our own? I am not ashamed to say that I wept when I read this letter, not for the phrases in themselves, those perhaps no one would find especially moving, but just for that meticulous and merciful care not to move one too deeply, not to reveal to those at a distance all his wounds, so that the pleasure of hearing from a friend should not be embittered by the sorrow of knowing him to be unhappy! The death of his father, the dispersal of his family, the bad conduct of his brothers; I imagined to myself that so many blows, one after the other, must have hurt Bruto more than he wished to show. I pictured Acquilina to myself, that charming little girl, so grave, so loving, who even in childhood showed the sweetest and most compassionate woman's heart that anyone could wish! She would mitigate with her simplicity and her angelic smiles all Bruto's sorrow and would compensate him with the care she took of him. I was certain that those two dear creatures, reunited after so many tempests, would have found in their reunion happiness and peace.

The Pisana joined with me in those simple hopes. A romantic soul, she looked above all for violent contrasts, the proud emotion of tragedy, but understood the roseate innocence and pastoral peace of an idyll. Dwelling on Bruto and Acquilina, our fancies saw once more the tranquil horizons of the meadows between Cordovado and Fratta, the lovely streams flowing through the countryside enamelled with flowers, the sweet-smelling bushes of honeysuckle and juniper, the beautiful surroundings of the spring of Venchieredo with its shady paths and its fresh borders of moss! We longed for them and enjoyed our longing. A shame that a wooden leg should hamper all those beautiful romances that we imagined for Bruto! In the country such a defect is unpardonable and a limping hero is worth less than an upstanding rogue. The ladies of the city are sometimes more indulgent; although even in this indulgence there enters to some extent perhaps the adoration of heroism.

But supposing that Bruto had not had that wooden leg, would he have returned to Cordovado? Where was Amilcare, where Giulio del Ponte, Lucilio, Alessandro Giorgi and where, finally, was I, though less prone by fury of temperament to perilous enterprises? Emigrés, exiled or dead, wanderers on the face of the earth, like servants forced to labour on fields not our own, without assured roof, without families, without country, yet on the very soil of our own land. But who can be sure that a country conceded by the whim of the victor shall not be taken away again by that same whim? . . . Already in France they were beginning to whisper about a new order of government and it was easily perceived that a Consulate was not a Curile Chair but a step towards a more exalted throne. Bruto was now excluded from the struggle where we were jousting blindly without knowing what the prize would be for so many tournaments. At least he had found once more the paternal hearth, the home of his childhood, a sister to love and to protect! His destiny stood written before his eyes, not glorious perhaps nor great, but calm, rich in affection and secure. His hopes would have chosen to fly after ours or would have fallen with them, without the remorse at having been inactive from choice and without the pain of having laboured in vain to follow a phantom.

Thus I began to envy the fate of a young soldier who had returned to his country deprived of a leg and instead of finding his father's arms into which to throw himself, had found nothing save a grave to water with his tears. However, I was not one of the more unfortunate. Temperate in my wishes, my hopes and my passions, when my own private means had begun to fail me, public assistance had come to my aid. Without influence, without intrigue, in a foreign land, to obtain at the age of twenty-six a post as secretary in so new and important a branch of the public administration as was then the finances, was no small or despicable fortune and I contented myself with it, though I was met everywhere with jeers and reproofs. But I, I confess it without shame, always had the quiet instincts of the snail whenever the whirlwind of events did not carry me away with it. To act, to work, to toil, pleased me, in order to prepare for myself a family, a country, a felicity. Whenever this part of my ambition no longer smiled either near or sure, then I returned naturally and with love to my little garden, to my hedge where at least the wind did not blow too fiercely and where I would have lived preparing my children for times more fruitful and fortunate. I had neither the blind and irresistible fury of Amilcare, which once launched could not retreat, nor the indefatigable pertinacity of Lucilio that, when driven back from one road, opened another for itself, always aiming at a noble and sublime goal though at times, after four years of sweat, it seemed more uncertain and distant than it was at the beginning. For me I saw the great master road of moral betterment, of concord and of education, towards which I had every so often to return from the bypaths that had led me astray. I would very willingly have placed my feet upon it, to depart from it only when called by some urgent need. Instead, destiny had made me beat the countryside to right and left. The year before a useless mouth in Genoa, then secretary at Ferrara; the hieroglyphs of my horoscope revealed themselves in characters so various that, to coin an expression, one had to haggle with one's good sense.

Luckily the Pisana afforded me very frequent diversions from these fantasies of mine. Her continual caprices that made the hitherto deaf-mute society of Ferrara talk for a month, kept me occupied for those few hours that remained after the threshing-floor of the office. To pass from sums, from subtractions and the operational scales of taxes, to the strategic circumspections of a jealous lover was not an undertaking as simple as sucking an egg. So I made myself acquainted with all the gymnastics of the spirit and all the skill acquired in fifteen or more years of experience. For the rest, there were days when the Pisana concerned herself only with me and watched over me as over some little boy who wanted to play truant; then I either pretended not to be aware of the change, or began to sulk, but in truth I was delighted since then I could take a rest from past trials and gain a breathing space to prepare for the future. If there were ever lover or husband who strove to govern his lady well without letting her feel the compulsion of the reins, it was certainly I during the time when we lived at Ferrara. The papal gallants, the elegant little French officers, used to say: 'What a good fellow' but would perhaps have wished me a little more out of the way. I was indeed a very considerable inconvenience to them; and the worst of it was that they could not complain or ridicule me as some financial Othello.

To interrupt these manoeuvres and strategies there fell into our midst a report of the illness of the Countess of Fratta. It was Count Rinaldo who told the Pisana without further comment; he said only that since the Reverend Clara could not leave her convent, her mother had remained alone, confided to the care, certainly not over-eager, of a kitchen maid; so, knowing the Pisana to be at Ferrara, he had thought it his duty to overlook everything and bring to her attention the grave misfortune that was threatening. The Pisana looked me in the face. I at once said 'You must go!' But I assure you that it cost me much to say it, and it was a sacrifice to public opinion which otherwise would have blamed me for causing a daughter to act so unnaturally as to deny her closest duties to a mother. The Pisana, however, took it the wrong way, though I believe that if I had remained silent, she would have spoken as I had. None the less, she began to complain that I was tired of her and looking for nothing better than an excuse to get rid of her. You will realize how great an injustice that was. I replied, shrugging my shoulders, that for her part she was, to my belief, doing her best all day long to find the most remarkable pretexts to be disagreeable to me and that she should be grateful that I had been the first to propose such a journey, which was in every way unpleasant and inconvenient to me. In fact, putting aside the loneliness in which I should remain, I was at that time in some little difficulty regarding ready cash. To live well had always been to my taste, the Pisana had never been able to reckon an account in her life and had never had the smallest regard either for her own purse or for those of others; in fact, she spent freely and even left here and there in the shops some little debts. None the less, she wanted to squabble with me and succeeded in doing so.

I could never understand that passion for tormenting me just at the moment when we were to be separated, despite all her great love for me, since I assure you she would have let herself be cut to pieces for me. I imagine that regret at having to go away spoilt her temper and with her usual thoughtlessness she discharged all her ill-humour at me. Now and again her eyes would grow red and she would follow me about the house like a little girl after her mother, but if I turned a loving glance on her or gave her a word of comfort, her face darkened like night and she turned away, obstinately paying no attention to me. In fact, she played all the usual childish tricks, but I must speak of them to show the continual atmosphere of suspicion in which we lived.

Thus, a few days later, having scraped together the necessary monies for the journey, I took her by carriage as far as Pontelagoscuro, whence one took a boat for Venice. There, that is to say on the Po, was the frontier between the Venetian Provinces occupied by the Austrians and the Cisalpine Republic, and I could accompany her no further. However, at the end of the week I had news from her that her mother was out of danger but that her convalescence might be a long one and that we should therefore resign ourselves to a separation of several months. That worried me not a little but in view of the other good news that she sent me I did my best to resign myself. Aglaura and Spiro were living in perfect accord and had two little ones that were a joy to see; their business prospered and they offered to do anything in their power to assist her or me. The Count her brother, despite the coldness of his letter, had received her with every kindness. Then there was another item of news which might suit both of us. His Excellency Navagero, struck by a general paralysis and now completely imbecile, had been confined to his bed for a month; she told me of her husband's sad condition in the most moving words in the world, but her emphasis in describing it as desperate revealed an easy resignation to the final blow that was expected daily. Therefore I resigned myself to my solitude and devoted myself entirely to the duties of my office in order to mitigate its tedium.

At that time, the Council of Lyons was summoned to reorganize the Cisalpina, which came out of it baptized Italiana, but reorganized for good, that is according to the new ideas of the First Consul Bonaparte, who was elected President for ten years. The Vice-President, who had later to govern in person, was Francesco Melzi, a real liberal, of great and patriotic feelings, but who because of his magnificence and noble origin did not accord with the tastes of the more ardent democrats. Lucilio told me of these changes from Milan, with a cold rage that conveyed to me considerably more than he dared to write; certainly he expected me to resign my post and refuse to serve a government from which every true republican had now turned away. Indeed, I felt some desire to do so, not so much for the Republic in itself, but because the republican fervour was still the sole incentive of my obstinate hopes for Venice, for which reason alone I had forced myself to endure the service of the Cisalpina. But then an event occurred that drove all such ideas from my mind. I received nothing less than an appointment as Intendente, that is to say Prefect of Finances, at Bologna.

Whether it was that the new government considered me in favour of its maxims of order and moderation, or whether they wanted to reward me for my assiduous and most fruitful labours of those last few months, the fact was that I heard of this appointment with the greatest surprise. Perhaps they wanted for the post a hard-working, careful and indefatigable man and a younger man was considered more suitable for it than an experienced magistrate. For my part I was carried away by such a frenzy of enthusiasm that for two or three months I never even thought of Lucilio and only occasionally of the Pisana. It already seemed to me that the Ministry of Finances would fall into my hands on the first occasion; and once so high, who knew what might happen? . . . Changing an arm-chair is such a pleasant occupation! I thought of the former illusions of my father and no longer found them either strange or unreasonable; only that decennial presidency of Bonaparte distressed me a little and, however rash I might have been, I did not go so far, I confess, even in my dreams, as to underestimate him. As to the others, I would have employed Prina as a wise administrator and we could have come to an understanding with Melzi. I knew of his growing dissensions with the Consul because of that independence of deed and action that arose from his thoroughly Italian temperament and that he was inclined to regulate the moves of the Italian government independently of the French. In that I would have assisted him with art and cunning, firm in my ambition, my aim, to try and enlarge the Italian Republic as far as Venice. That was the excuse for my madness.

Having taken up my position at Bologna with these great ideas in my head, I became a most eloquent and munificent Intendente of Finances. I wanted to prepare the way to future greatness; I knew however, later on, that for all my pride they called me, in their spiteful Bolognese jargon, the Intendente Puff. After a month or so of haughty bliss and continual labour in the just disposition of the taxes, so unusual in the States, I began to believe that I was not yet in Paradise and to hope that the return of the Pisana would supply much that I felt to be lacking. Indeed, not two, not three, but six months had passed since her departure from Ferrara and not only had she not returned but latterly, after my transfer from Ferrara, her letters had been growing less frequent. It was great luck that I still had my head in the clouds, else I would have beaten it against the walls. The Pisana in her correspondence had the strange habit of never replying at once to the letters that she received, but putting them on one side and then forgetting them till three, four or even eight days later, so that, no longer remembering anything that she had read, her reply dealt with entirely new matters and one was continually playing a game of blind man's buff. Many and many times I had written that I was tired of remaining alone, that I did not know what to think about her, that she should make up her mind to return or at least reveal the true reason for her unreasonable delay. But to no purpose! It was like beating against a wall! She replied that she loved me more than ever, that I must take care not to forget her, that she was bored in Venice, that her mother had now completely recovered and that she would come as soon as circumstances permitted.

I wrote by return of post asking what those circumstances were and if she had any need of money, or if there was some serious reason why she could not come, that she should at least say so, for in that case I would ask for a passport and come and keep her company for as long as I could get leave. I did not fail to ask her for information regarding the most precious health of His Excellency Navagero who, in my view, should have gone to the devil some time since; nevertheless, the Pisana did not even tell me if he were in this world or the next. This neglect of what she knew must be of such importance for me ended by stinging the self-respect of the most magnificent Intendente of Bologna. To complete my grandeur, to ensure that my triumphal chariot had all its four wheels, I needed a wife; and this I could not expect until after the death of Navagero. I was almost astonished that this useless gentleman should not have hastened to die to give pleasure to an Intendente such as I! If it were the Pisana who for her own purposes had delayed sending me the news, then she would have to deal with me! . . . I meant her to sigh for at least a year for the hand of the future Minister of Finance . . . and then? . . . Oh, my heart knew not how to resist longer, not even in imagination. I would have elevated her to my throne, like Ahasuerus the humble Esther, and would have said to her: 'You loved me when I was little, I will reward you now that I am great!' It would be a master stroke; I congratulated myself on it, walking up and down the room, rubbing my chin and chewing over the words with which I should reply to the fervid thanks of the Pisana. The juniors who entered my room with bundles of papers to sign halted on the threshold and then went out again to say how the Intendente Puff was puffing so hard that he seemed to have gone mad.

However, those days, less than any others, had they reason to complain of me and, in general, since I worked much and was patient and cordial, they began to admire me in spite of my puffing. The Bolognese are the most cultivated and worthy backbiters of all Italy; once they are your friends, they are friends in every trial, but you must allow them to speak evil of you and ridicule you at least twice a month. Without this vent for their feelings they would expire and you would lose in them useful and devoted friends and the world would lose gay and sparkling wits. As for the women, they are the gayest and most companionable that one could desire; which shows that the government of priests does not serve to make them rough and uncultivated.

To finish, then, with Bologna; I can say that one lived there then, and can still live now, gaily, splendidly and with great facilities for friendships and merry gatherings. The city stretches out its hand to the villas and the villas to the city; beautiful houses, lovely gardens, without the cavilling of that provincial luxury that says: 'Respect me because I cost a great deal and must endure for a long time'. It is always in movement, always active, always vital. The Bolognese are talkers and wits in order to match the talk and wit of others. They are quick to please all those charming ladies who are themselves so quick and so companionable; they are ready and willing to run here and there and never fail to satisfy anyone's civilized desires. One eats more in one year in Bologna than in two in Venice, three in Rome, five in Turin or twenty in Genoa; though one eats less in Venice because of the scirocco and more in Milan because of the cooks. As to Florence, Naples and Palermo, the first is too prim to encourage its guests to a good bellyful while in the other two the life of contemplation fills the stomach through the pores without wearying the jawbones. One lives in an air impregnated with the volatile oils of cedars and the fecund pollen of the figs. How is it then with all the rest in this question of eating? It is an axiom that the digestion works well because of hard work and good humour. A ready and varied company which touches on all the sensations of the spirit like a hand on a keyboard, that exercises the mind and makes the tongue run faster, to leap here and there to meet every occasion, that excites and over-excites your mind, prepares you for a good lunch better than all the essences and vermouths in the world. They have done well to invent vermouth at Turin where one speaks little and laughs less except in the Chamber; however, when they invented vermouth, they did not have their Statute. Now there is some activity but of the kind that helps to manufacture, not of the kind that stimulates the appetite. That is lucky for those who hope for well being . . . and for the manufacturers of vermouth.

Despite all this chatter that I am stringing together for you now, the Pisana gave no sign whatever of wanting to return and Bologna lost little by little its merit of stimulating my appetite. A distant love is not, for an Intendente of twenty-eight, a misfortune to jest about. It was all very well for one or two months, but eight, nine, almost a year! I had taken none of the three monastic vows and here I was, forced to observe the most scabrous of them. Capperi! I saw everyone laughing at my naivety! . . . But I do not want to retract my words by one iota. At that time I loved the Pisana so much that all the little women of Bologna seemed to me like little men; lovely, pleasant, elegant little men, in all respect to the Bolognese; but still men, and in this there was no rusticity or hypocrisy but all love. So I am not ashamed to confess to you that I played Joseph the Jew on several occasions; while in the meantime during this long separation from the Pisana I found myself gradually changing. I will not say that I loved her any the less, but it was in a different way and whatever the platonists may say, I endured this second separation with much better spirit than I had the first.

However, being in great haste and a most devilish frenzy to see the Pisana again and not being able to learn anything definite from her, I turned to Aglaura, imploring her, if she had any sense of sisterly charity, to tell me without mysteries and without equivocation, all that concerned my cousin. Up till then, my sister had always avoided replying explicitly to my inquiries on this matter by pleading uncertainty or ignorance and had always slipped through some hole in the net. But this time, knowing from the tone of my letter that I was really distraught and ready to commit some folly, she replied at once that she had always kept silent because the Pisana herself had implored her to do so, but that none the less she wanted to set my mind at rest since she realized the state of agitation in which I was; I should know, then, that for the last six months the Pisana had been in her husband's house, very busy acting as his nurse and that she did not seem willing to abandon him. Aglaura assured me that she still loved me and that her life in Venice was really that of a nurse.

Oh, if I could have got His Excellency Navagero into my clutches! . . . I don't think he would have needed a nurse for long. What had got into that putrid carcase to rob me of my share of life? . . . Was it right that a young woman like his wife. . . . But I paused a little at that word 'wife', since it flashed into my mind that the promises sworn at the altar steps might perhaps count for something. I examined my scruples with the greatest care.

'Yes, yes,' I thought to myself. 'Is it right that his wife remains tied to him like a live body to a corpse? Not for a moment! . . . By

Bacchus, I will think how I can detach her, how end this monstrous torment. After all, even without stressing that charity begins at home, surely it is the law of nature that he should die rather than I? Without taking into account that I will indeed die, whereas he is capable of dragging on in this way for years and years, the old imbecile! . . .'

I grasped my magnificent Intendente's pen and wrote such an epistle as would have done honour to a king in anger with his queen. The gist of it was that if she did not come even more quickly than possible to put a little breath back into my body, I, my glory and my fortune would soon be gone underground. That letter of mine remained unanswered for a fortnight, at the end of which, just when I was seriously thinking of going myself, I won't say underground, but at least to Venice, the Pisana suddenly appeared. She was sulky, as a woman who has had to obey someone else's command and before I got either a kiss or a greeting from her she wanted me to promise that I would let her go again whenever she wanted to, then, seeing that this speech took from me half the pleasure of her arrival, she threw her arms about my neck and then —farewell, Signor Intendente!

I was most impatient to let her see all the privileges attached to my new dignity; a sumptuous apartment, footmen in quantity; oil, wood and tobacco at the expense of the State. I smoked like my poor father in order not to leave untasted any of my privileges and ate oil three times a week like a Carthusian; but I had put aside a respectable sum to allow the Pisana to play a worthy part in Bolognese society. It was for one of my temperament such a proof of love that she should have fallen on her knees before it. However, she scarcely noticed it, for to understand the merits of such efforts one must oneself be capable of them and she had more holes in her hands and in her pockets than a Roman beggar in his jacket. She only made two great round eyes at me when she heard four hundred scudi named; it seemed that for some time she had lost the habit even of hearing such a great sum mentioned. But, in fact, it was not so great as we had believed. Dresses, hats, bracelets, excursions, picnics soon put me back to my salary and the scudi did not grow old in my pocket for more than a fortnight.

Diverting herself here and there and everywhere, the Pisana revealed to me another and quite fresh side to her temperament. She became the gayest and most talkative lady of Bologna, keeping four, six or eight conversations going at once; she never sulked, never tired, never was at a loss for a quip, a thought, never listless or forgetful of others; she knew how to distribute her words and smiles so that there was always something for everyone and never too much for anyone. I could trust her, and the torments and trials of Ferrara were over. Everyone spoke either of the cousin, or the wife, or the lover, of the Signor Intendente; there were many who aspired to marry her, others who wanted to seduce her or to take her from me. She took note of all of them, laughed at them politely and if she scattered her wit right and left, her love she reserved for me alone. Such women please other women, for men get tired of falling dead for nothing and end by paying court from habit, reserving their more serious love affairs for others. So after a month, my Pisana, adored by the men and sought after by the women, passed in triumph through the streets of Bologna, so that even the ragamuffins ran after her shouting: 'It is the beautiful Venetian! It is the wife of the Signor Intendente!' I do not want to say that she grew vain at this good fortune but she certainly knew how to make herself valued in my eyes with the best air in the world. And it was my part, naturally, to love her in proportion to all the desires that pressed about her.

Leading this life of continual pleasure and domestic happiness, she no longer spoke of going away again. When letters arrived from Venice she scarcely cast her eyes on them; if the writing went over the page she certainly never turned it and left off reading in the middle. I would then read it to her from beginning to end, but took care to conceal from her the eagerness that her mother or her husband from time to time displayed for her return. The Navagero no longer seemed so covetous nor so near to death; he spoke of me with a real outburst of friendship as of a near and very dear relative and of the years to come as of a Land of Cockaigne which would never come to an end.

'That moribund monster!' I used to grumble. 'He has come to life again!'

I almost felt myself capable of being jealous of all that time that the Pisana had spent with him. But she burst out laughing at my misgivings and I laughed with her; but I took care that once she had thrown the letters aside they should not fall into her hands again. Her natural forgetfulness aided me perfectly in this. As to her long stay in Venice, this is how matters stood, or better to say, this is what she told me bit by bit, mouthful by mouthful, as the mood seized her. Her mother, once convalescent, had implored her at least for the sake of convention to visit her dying husband who, she said, would be very grateful. The Pisana agreed, and then the condition of the poor man, his financial straits (so much, they told her, had he fallen from his earlier opulence) and the disorder in which he lived had touched her heart and persuaded her to remain with him, as he showed her was his wish. She had been all goodness and I, though lamenting its evil effects for me, could do no less than praise her from the bottom of my heart and love her even more for it.

However, as you may well believe, I proceeded very cautiously in dragging such confidences from her; I did not insist even for a moment, since I feared that if I harped too much on it, I would revive all those former qualms in her mind and reawaken her wish to depart. I was just enough to praise, but egoist enough to hamper, those acts of heroic virtue; and, luckily, the Pisana being very good and compassionate, but also thoughtless in the extreme, I was able to keep her with me by festas, songs, and laughter for almost six months. None the less, I saw with consternation the increasing number and urgency of the letters; but seeing that no harm seemed to come from them, I grew accustomed and believed that this bliss would never end. From Minister of Finance and Vice President of the Republic, I had modestly reduced my ambitions to the present post and if others did all the wonderful things that filled my brain, I judged it more convenient not to make any move myself.

Poor mortals, how frail is our felicity! . . . The institution of a diligence service between Padua and Bologna was my downfall. Count Rinaldo who because of a queasy stomach would never have endured a voyage by water as far as Ferrara or Ravenna, profited with pleasure by this diligence and came to trip me up at Bologna although no one had invited him; he insisted on visiting the Madonna di Monte, Montagnola and San Petronio and ended up by taking the Pisana away with him on the third day. At the sight of her brother all her scruples began to plague her once more and it was not she who accepted his invitation but rather proposed herself as his companion on his return. That assassin had said nothing, did not even hint that he had come expressly for her. He wanted to leave me in the credulous illusion that he had trotted all the way from Venice to Bologna merely for curiosity to see San Petronio. But I had read it in his eyes at the first glance, and was furious to see him succeed in his intention without even having had the inconvenience of putting it into words. How could a dirty, blear-eyed library rat be more skilful and powerful in feminine policy than a lover, young, handsome and an Intendente at that? In certain cases, it seemed that he could; so I remained behind to puff and to bite my nails.

I went back again to my duties, to find diversion, if no more, from the irritation that tormented me. And working much and forgetting as much as I could, I became little by little another man, it is for you to say whether better or worse. As the fumes of poetry began to evaporate from my brain, I began to feel the weight of my thirty years that had already begun to hang leaden upon me, and to remain willingly at table and to divide the love that dwells in the soul from that which stimulates the body. Excuse me if I said that I became another man, my real opinion is that I was becoming an animal. In my view, he who loses the youth of his mind can only fall from the human state to some lower and animal-like condition. That part of our mind which differentiates us from the brutes is not that which calculates its own gain, that strives to procure ease and avoid fatigue, but that which bases its judgements on beautiful dreams and the great hopes of the soul. Even the dog knows how to choose the best mouthful and to dig out his bed in the straw before curling himself up in it; if that be reason, then give to dogs this evidence of man's intention. But I will tell you that this myopic and laborious life had its excuse; there was one great intelligence that thought for us and whose will so dominated us all that great deeds were done with but little expense of ideas on our part. Today indeed those ideas still sparkle but of them one sees neither the white nor the black simply because unfortunately those who have brains have not hands; but at that time the hands of Napoleon were extended over half Europe and all Italy to stimulate and reawaken dormant energies. It was enough to obey, since a miraculous activity was developing in an orderly manner from the old unities of the nation.

I do not want to make prognostications; but if it had continued thus for another twenty or so years we would have come to life again and our intellectual life would have reawakened from the material, like a sick person getting well again. To see the fervour of life that then animated the world would be to make one's head turn. Justice had been created one and equal for all; all competed according to his abilities in the great social movement; one no longer thought as a single unit but as a whole. An army had been wanted and in a few years an army had arisen as if by enchantment. From peoples rotten with idleness and vitiated by disorder had been conscripted legions of soldiers, sober, obedient and valiant. Force demanded the renascence of customs and all was obtained by order and discipline. The first time that I saw drawn up in the Piazza the conscripts of my department, I thought I was not seeing clearly; I did not believe that one could attain so much and that one could have transformed by law those vulgar rustics, that city scum who had up till then only taken up arms to pillage the countryside and strip the wayfarer.

From these beginnings I expected miracles and persuaded myself that we were in good hands. I no longer strove to see where we were going, the better to admire the manner of our advance. To see, whenever it might be, my Venice, armed with her own forces and made wiser by fresh experience, again take her place among the Italian peoples amid the great assembly of the nations; that was my wish, my daily faith. The pacifier of the revolution had put this into the number of his future exploits; I thought to see in them the tokens of that new baptism of the Cisalpine Republic that presaged new and more exalted destinies. When Lucilio wrote me that things were going from bad to worse, and that by abdicating its intelligence a people lost every liberty and every force of its own, that he had hoped for a liberator and found a despot, I ridiculed his fears, which seemed to me half madness and half ingratitude, threw his letter into the fire and returned to the affairs of my intendency. I believe that I even congratulated myself on the absence of the Pisana since solitude and a quiet life gave me greater opportunities for work by which I could advance my own interests. Long live the mad Orlando! . . . So I lived through those many months, busy, working, trusting without thinking for myself or looking beyond the narrow frame that I placed before my eyes. I understand now that it was not a life to invigorate the forces of the soul or to arouse its faculties; one ceased to be a man, to become only a cog. And one knows what happens to cogs if one forgets to oil them on the first of every month!

Was it fortune or misfortune? I do not know; but the proclamation of the French Empire drove the mists a little from my eyes. I looked around me and saw that I was no longer my own master, and that my work merely assisted in the interlocking of all those other activities that were developing above and below me to the sound of the drum. To break away was, alas, to become a cypher. If all were in my case, as I began to suspect, then Lucilio's fears were not too far from the truth. I began a close examination of my conscience, to go back again over my past life and see how the present compared with it. I found a diversity, a contradiction that horrified me. There were no longer the same maxims, the same illusions, that directed my actions; first I was the poor artisan, wearied but intelligent and free, then I was a thing of wood, well varnished, well polished, since I bowed myself methodically, stupidly, like a machine. Yet I wanted to stay firm, not to take any hasty decision, so that I should not descend yet another stair in that ladder of servility.

When the news came of the transformation of the Republic into a Kingdom of Italy, I took the few possessions and the few scudi that I had, went immediately to Milan and handed in my resignation. I found another four or five colleagues come on a similar task, whereas everyone had thought to find a hundred in order to make a great impression. They thanked us effusively, laughed at us and entered our names in a huge book that boded no great recommendation for our future. Napoleon came to Milan and placed the iron crown on his head, saying: 'God has given it to me; woe to him who touches it!' I sat myself down, poor and indigent, in the ancient halls of Porta Romana, saying in my turn: 'God has given me a conscience; no one shall buy it!' Then the enemies of Napoleon found strength and hardihood enough to touch that fatal crown and take it from his head; but neither California nor Australia had up till then dug up enough gold to buy my conscience. In that I was the truer and the stronger.

CHAPTER XIX

LUCILIO had taken refuge in London; he had friends everywhere and besides, for such a doctor, all the world is one country. The Pisana kept putting me off with her promises to come and rejoin me and later, having resigned my post, I did not even have the courage to ask her to share my poverty. I disdained to turn to Spiro and Aglaura for money; they sent me punctually my three hundred ducats every Christmas but I had mortgaged two years' income to pay for debts left at Ferrara. I was then, for the first time in my life, without roof and without bread, and with very little ability to procure them. I turned over in my mind a thousand different projects, but for every one of them a good handful of scudi was required merely to begin; and having no more than a dozen of such scudi I contented myself with leaving them as projects and went on my way.

Every day I endeavoured to live on less. I believe I would have made the last scudo last a century if on the day of Napoleon's departure for Germany it had not been stolen from me by one of those famous cutpurses who work, by pious tradition, the streets of Milan. The Emperor had grown fat and was then making his way to the victory of Austerlitz; I remembered him, thin and still resplendent with the glories of Arcole and Rivoli; by Diana, I would not have given the Little Corporal for His Majesty! Seeing him depart amid a thronging and applauding people, I remember having wept with rage. I thought to myself: 'What could I not do, were I that man!' and this thought and the idea of the great things I would have done, moved me deeply. Indeed he was then at the height of his power. He had returned after having made the caves of Albion echo with his roarings, and menaced with his omnipotent talons the necks of two emperors. The youthful genius of Caesar and the mature judgement of Augustus combined to exalt his fortune above all human imagination. He was indeed the new Charlemagne and knew that he was. But I on my side was proud to pass before him without bending the knee. 'You are a giant, but not a God!' I said to him. 'I have taken your measure and have found my faith far greater and more sublime than yours!' For a man who believed that he had in his pocket one poor scudo and in fact had none, that was no small thing!

The best was when it came to eating. I believe that no one in the world could have been in a worse plight. On leaving Bologna, and taking advantage of the discretion of some friends, I had turned every brooch, every ring and everything else that was not immediately necessary into cash. None the less, on making a fresh inventory I was able to find many items in my wardrobe that were superfluous; I made a bundle of them, took them to the old clothes dealer and pocketed four scudi which seemed to me a million. But the million did not last for more than a week. Then I began to get my teeth into many necessary objects also, shirts, shoes, collars, coats, everything went to the old clothes dealer. We had concluded between us a sort of friendship. His shop was on the corner of the Street of the Three Kings going towards the Post Office; I used to stop there for a talk, going from my house towards the Cathedral Square.

Finally I came to an end of all my belongings. Although in the meantime I had tried to foresee every possible means of getting myself out of so pressing a difficulty, not even an idea had occurred to me. One morning I had met Colonel Giorgi who was coming from the Campo di Bologna and was about to rush off to Germany with the hope of being made a general very shortly.

'Go into the army administration,' he said. 'I promise to get you a good post there and will make you rich in a very short time.'

'What is it like in the army?' I said.

'In the army one conquers all Europe, one courts the most beautiful women in the world, one makes a great show of one's glory and then goes on one's way.'

'Yes, yes, but for whose advantage does one conquer Europe?'

'Don't be foolish! Is it common sense to ask?'

'*Alessandro mio*, I will not go into the army, not even as a sweeper.'

'A pity! I had hoped to make something of you!'

'Perhaps I would not have been suitable, Alessandro! It is better for you to concentrate all your efforts on yourself. You will become a General all the quicker.'

'Two more battles to rid me of a couple of seniors and I am one by right. The Russian and Austrian balls are my allies; that is the right way to live in harmony with everyone. But do you really think so little of us poor soldiers?'

'No, Alessandro, I admire you, but I cannot imitate you.'

'Eh, I understand, one needs a certain force in one's muscles. . . . Tell me, have you any news of Bruto Provedoni?'

'The best that can be told. He is living with his sister, a girl of about eighteen or nineteen, Acquilina; do you remember her? He acts as father to her, tries to get together a little dowry for her and earns his bread by giving lessons. With the heritage of his brother Grifone, who died in Ljubljana when a roof fell in on him, he intends to buy the house from his other brother and have it in his own and his sister's name. He will thus be able to free himself from having to drag out a miserable life like so many ragged and cheeseparing lodgers. I believe that if he could settle Acquilina properly there would be no happier man.'

'You see what we old soldiers are like! . . . We remain happy even without our legs!'

'Bravo, Alessandro, but I don't want to lose my legs for nothing. They are capital that should be invested well and kept for oneself.'

'Do you call it nothing to become a General in eight years at most? Isn't that good interest?'

'Yes, but it pleases me better to remain in these clothes and my misery.'

'Then I can't help you in any way? Perhaps I can be of service to you with thirty or so scudi? Not more, I fear, for I am not the most saving of soldiers and between cards, women and God knows what else, my pay soon goes. . . . But, let me think . . . would it suit you to take service in a civil job?'

The good Colonel could see nothing outside the army; he had already forgotten that a quarter of an hour before I had told him all my career in the service of the finances and my voluntary resignation from the post of intendente. Probably he thought that finance was no more than a supplementary service to the army, to provide it with food, clothes and suitable funds to sustain the assaults of faraone and bassetta. To my reply that I would be satisfied with any employment that was not in the public service, he made a face like one who is forced to withdraw from someone a good part of his esteem, but none the less his outstanding kindness was not affected.

'I have a landlady in Milan,' he said.

'You had one at Genoa, too.'

'Quite different! That one was as stingy as an apothecary, but this one is more splendid than a minister. I had to steal cats from the first, but this one, if she liked, could make me a present of a diamond a day. She is incredibly rich and has seen a good deal of life in her time but now, after receiving a handsome inheritance, she has settled down and has the reputation of being a society lady; it is true that she no longer has the peach-bloom on her cheeks, but she can still be charming and elegant on occasion, more especially when she feels a little lively. Just imagine, she took a ridiculous liking to me and wants me to stay with her every time I am in Milan; she has even told me in confidence that if she were twenty instead of thirty, she would like to go to the wars with me.'

'But where do I come in with this lady?'

'Where indeed? The devil! Why, everywhere! She has a lot of important connexions and will recommend you strongly to any post you wish. If you really feel a private job would suit you better, her own household is big enough for you to find a post in it.'

'Remember, I don't want to steal the bread from anyone's mouth and, if I eat it, I intend to earn it by my own labours.'

'Eh, be quiet, you need have no scruples on that score. Perhaps you think you would like to be one of our Friuli factors, where the usual story is that the factor gets rich at the expense of his master and keeps his own hands in his money-belt. Eh, my friend, in Milan they know a thing or two! They pay well but want to be served better; the book-keeper will get fat all right, but the master will not grow lean because of him. I know how these things go!'

This arrangement in no way displeased me, though I was far from having a blind faith in the omnipotent recommendations and the splendour of the good Colonel's patroness, but being well aware that alone I was good for nothing, I was content enough to try the aid of others. I returned home to brush up my coat for the introduction that was to take place the next day. I had recourse to my own landlady's splendour for a little polish to shine my shoes and spread out on a chair the sole shirt that I possessed other than the one which I was wearing. I delighted my eyes in its whiteness, which consoled me for the meagreness of the rest of my wardrobe.

The next morning the Colonel's orderly came to tell me that the Signora had received the suggestion very well and wanted me to be presented to her that very evening, when as it happened she was giving a great reception. I gave a glance at my shoes and my shirt, almost regretting that I had not remained in bed to preserve their original freshness till the solemn moment; but thinking that in the evening they would not be so closely noticed and that a former Intendente should possess enough resources of vivacity and culture to make up for the modesty of his attire, I told the orderly that I would be at the Colonel's house about eight, and went out a little later. It was time for breakfast, but I let it go by without feeling in my pockets; it was a heroic deference to the coming hour of lunch.

But when that time came I put my hands in my pockets and drew out four fine soldi that made in all, I believe, fifteen centesimi. I had not thought, in truth, that I was as poor as all that, and the squaring of the circle seemed to me a problem far easier than the lunch I should have to extract from that miserable sum. But I had not been an Intendente for nothing and should have known how to balance accounts better than anyone! So, without losing courage, I tried. One soldo of bread, two of salad and one of brandy, to brace the stomach and prepare it for the evening's visit. But what was one soldo of bread for someone who had not touched food for twenty-four hours! I went over my accounts again; two soldi of bread, one of pecorino cheese and the usual 'nip'. Then I found that the soldo of cheese was a prejudice, an aristocratic idea for dividing the meal into bread and something to go with it. It was far better to have three soldi of bread.

I courageously entered a baker's, bought the bread and in four bites had swallowed it. I noticed with some bewilderment that I felt not the slightest trace of thirst and therefore, slighting my 'nip', I provided yet another roll which soon joined the others. After this little diversion, my teeth still remained very restless and I searched among them for any crumbs that might have lost their way. They seemed to say with a grinding of consternation: 'Is the banquet over? Is it really finished?' 'It is really finished,' I replied and felt my stomach even more aghast than my teeth. Then I indulged in a permissible pastime of imagination that had already served me for many days to deceive my appetite; I made a list of my friends from whom I could have asked a lunch had they been in Milan. The Abbé Parini, dead six years ago and in any case very unsubstantial in the matter of lunch; Lucilio, gone abroad; Ugo Foscolo, Professor of Eloquence at Pavia; of my former acquaintances I could not turn to a single one; my landlady, when she had given me the shoe-polish the evening before, had cocked that great nose of hers and seemed to say: 'Enough of these bad jokes!'

There remained Colonel Giorgi, but I confess to you that I felt ashamed, as indeed, I do not doubt that I would have been ashamed before all the others had they been in Milan, and I would have died of hunger rather than let Ugo Foscolo pay for a coffee and roll for me. In any case it was always a consolation to be able to think of them while my hunger gnawed at me; so, having exhausted that pastime, I found myself more unhappy than ever and to crown all, when passing through the Piazza Mercanti, I noticed that it was scarcely five o'clock. 'Three hours still!' I feared I would not survive till the time of the visit or at least that I would cut a pretty famished figure. I set out to divert myself with another stratagem.

I thought of all those from whom I might be able to get a loan, a present, some assistance, had I asked it. My kinsman Spiro, my friends in Bologna, the thirty scudi of Colonel Giorgi, the Grand Vizier. . . . By Bacchus! Whether it was hunger or something else, or some particular favour of Providence, that day I thought more than usual about the Grand Vizier. I actually remembered having in my notebook a bill of exchange for a huge sum signed by a certain hieroglyphic which I could in no way understand; but the house of Apostulos had many correspondents at Constantinople and some authority over the Armenian bankers who were skinning the Sultan of that time; I ran to my lodging without thinking any more about my appetite, wrote a letter to Spiro, put the cheque in it and took it gaily to the Post.

As I passed back through the Piazza Mercanti the clock was striking a quarter to eight. I therefore made my way to the Colonel's lodging, but I had left my hopes of the Grand Vizier at the Post and just at the critical moment I again began to feel hungry. Do you know what I had the courage to think of at that moment? I dared to think of those immense Bolognese lunches of the year before and to find more satisfaction in this than in thinking of my famished stomach. I had the courage to comfort myself with the thought that I was alone and that good fortune had preserved the Pisana from sharing my privations. Fortune? . . . I could not let that word pass. Fortune, if one looks at it well, is no more, most of the time, than a figment of man's imagination and therefore I feared, not without reason, that the forgetfulness, the coldness or perhaps even some petty love affair had turned the Pisana from me.

'But have I any real reason to complain?' I went on to myself. 'If she loves me less, is that not just? . . . What have I done during all the past year?'

What could I do? I found everything reasonable, everything just, but that suspicion of having been forgotten and abandoned for ever by the Pisana hammered at my thoughts at least as much as my hunger. It was no longer the fury, the jealous madness of earlier times, but a discomfort filled with bitterness, a discouragement that made me lose all desire to live. Cast down by these various sorrows. I went up to the Colonel who was reading the weekly reports of his Captains, smoking as I had done when I was an Intendente, and moistening his throat from time to time with good Brescia anisette.

'Bravo, Carletto,' he said, offering me a seat. 'Pour yourself out a glass to chase your cares away.'

I thanked him, sat down and glanced around the room to see if there was a roll or a biscuit or some other substance to marry with the anisette for the better relief of my stomach. But there was absolutely nothing. I poured myself out a brimming glass of that balsamic liquor and sent it down at a gulp. It seemed as if a new soul had come into me. But one knows what happens in that quarrel between a new and an old soul, especially on a famished stomach. I completely lost my head and when I rose to follow the Colonel I was as gay and talkative as I had been dull and silent when I sat down. The good soldier congratulated himself that it was a good omen and while going up the stairs he urged me to appear gay, witty and daring since such manners are pleasing to ladies of a certain age who have no time to lose. Imagine to yourself, I was so gay that I nearly fell on my nose on the top step; furthermore, together with other gifts, yet another developed in me, an appalling frankness and that, as might be expected, made me make my first blunder. When the footman had opened the door and the Colonel had taken me into the antechamber, I was dancing and skipping so much that I scarcely seemed to touch the floor.

'Who could ever have imagined,' I said in a very loud voice, 'who could ever have imagined that I am simply fainting for hunger?'

The footman turned in wonder to look at me, however much the canons of his profession forbade it. Alessandro gave me a nudge in the ribs.

'Eh, you fool,' he said, 'you must have your joke!'

'I swear to you it's no joke . . . Oh, oh, oh!'

The Colonel had given me such a pinch that I could not continue the argument and had to break it off with this three-fold exclamation. The footman turned to look at me again and this time with every justification.

'It's nothing,' said the Colonel, 'I trod on one of his corns.'

It was a good excuse at such short notice and I did not think it opportune to defend the virginity of my feet since just at that moment we entered the Signora's room. The Colonel had by then perceived the danger but the dance had begun and we had to dance it out; a veteran of Marengo should not know the meaning of retreat.

In the dull and reddish light that poured down from lamps hanging from the ceiling and shaded by red silk curtains, I saw, or it seemed that I saw, a goddess. She was sitting on the edge of one of those curile chairs that Parisian taste had disinterred from Republican Rome and which had endured as much under the Empire of Augustus as under that of Napoleon. The short and frilled gown revealed a form, I cannot say how firm, but certainly very opulent; an abundant half of her breast was bare; I did not look at it with overmuch pleasure but felt a sort of tickling of my teeth, a desire to eat it. The fumes of the anisette allowed me to see dimly that this was flesh and left me with only that barbarous flash of good sense that remains to cannibals. The Signora seemed very satisfied with the good impression produced upon me and asked the Colonel if I were the young man who wanted a post in her household. The Colonel hastened to reply that I was and did his best to distract the Signora's attention from me. It seemed, however, that she was greatly attracted by my manner, for she never stopped looking at me and turned the conversation in my direction, completely neglecting the Colonel.

'Carlo Altoviti, I believe,' she said with the most gracious effort of memory.

I bowed, becoming so red that I felt as if I were going to burst. I had cramp in my stomach.

'It seems to me,' she went on, 'that I have noticed that name, if I am not mistaken, last year in the rolls of our high magistrature.'

I gave a last puff in memory of my intendency and held myself rigid and upright, while the Colonel replied that I had indeed been nominated to the Bologna finances.

'Ah, we understand,' said the Signora in a low voice, bending towards me . . . 'the new government . . . its maxims . . . in short, you resigned.'

'Yes,' I replied with a most imposing air, not having understood a word.

Then there began to enter Counts, Marquises, Princes, and Abbés, each announced by the stentorian voice of the footman; there was a superabundance of 'Dons' which drummed on my ears and, let me say frankly, that clipped and nasal Milanese dialect is not distinct enough to be fitted to the ears of a drunken man. At a suitable moment the Colonel approached the lady of the house to take leave, as I was quite unable to do so. She whispered to him that everything was arranged and that I should go at once the next day to the counting house where my duties would be assigned to me and I would be told the conditions of her service. I made my thanks, bowing and shuffling my feet so much that a dozen of the 'Dons', silent and rigid, turned to look at me; then proudly clicking my heels at the Colonel's side I made my way out of the hall. The fresh air did me good, since it cooled my wits in a moment and there mingled with my feelings a little shame at the state in which I now perceived I was and at the poor figure that I feared I had cut at the Contessa's gathering. However, a good dose of my frankness still remained and I began to complain of the hunger that I felt.

'Is that all?' said the Colonel, 'Let us go to Mother Rebecca's and I will soon get rid of that for you.'

I do not remember very clearly if it was Rebecca's that he said but at that time that mother of all trattorias existed in Milan.

I let myself be taken and indulged in a good bellyful without drawing breath or saying a word, so that, as my stomach returned to peace, my head too became more organized. Shame grew in me up to the moment of paying the bill and I was just about to play the usual little comedy of the sponger, to feel in my pockets with much surprise and reprove myself for my cursed carelessness in losing or forgetting my purse, when a more honest shame prevented me from such an imposture. I blushed at having been more sincere when I was drunk than when I was sober and confessed fairly and squarely to Alessandro my extreme poverty. He broke out angrily to ask why I had concealed it until now and forced me to take those thirty scudi that he said he still had and which, after the bill had been paid, were reduced to twenty-eight, and made me promise that in every other case of need I would turn to him, since he would always help me, only with a little, it was true, but with all his heart.

'Meanwhile I must leave tomorrow without fail for the camp in Germany,' he said, 'but I leave with the hope that those few scudi will be enough to help you to wait without inconvenience till the first pay that you will receive, perhaps even tomorrow. Courage, Carlino, and remember me. This evening I must hold a meeting of the captains of my regiment to give them some verbal orders, but tomorrow I will come and see you again before leaving.'

What a good fellow Alessandro was! There was in him a certain mingling of military roughness with a feminine kindness that moved me; he lacked the so-called civil virtues of the time, which I would now scarcely know by that name, but he had a super-abundance of so many others that one could excuse him for that. Next morning at dawn he came to take leave of me while I was still abed and bewailed my pigheadedness at wanting to remain an obscure employee at Milan when I might have followed him and become a General without difficulty. One finds few such comrades; however, he heartily wished death to all his colleagues in order to attain a more resplendent 'brass hat' and three hundred francs a month more pay. Such was the fraternal charity taught, nay imposed, even on good and kindly hearts by the Napoleonic government!

At the suitable time I dressed myself with every possible care and went to the counting-house of the Contessa Migliana. A fat, rotund, cleanshaven gentleman, with patriarchal air and manners, welcomed me, so to speak, with open arms. He was the chief accountant, the lady's secretary. He led me first with all ceremony to the safe, where sixty shining scudi were counted over to me as my first quarter's salary. Then he took me to a desk on which were many greasy and crumpled books and amongst them one much larger book on which one could at least put one's hands without soiling them. He told me that for the present I should be master of the household, the majordomo of the Signora Contessa, at least until a post should be found more suitable to my merits. Indeed, to fall from being the Intendente of Bologna to the administration of a wardrobe was no small descent; but even though I was by origin a Venetian patrician of the most ancient and Roman nobility of Torcello, pride was rarely a defect of mine especially when need spoke so much louder. For my part I hold Plutarch's view who, they say, superintended the street-cleaners of Chaeronea with the same dignity as when he presided over the Olympic Games.

My duties included residence in the palace and a greater familiarity with the Signora Contessa. I was not sure whether these two things were to my taste or not, but I intended to remove the bad impression which the Signora must have had of me on the first day. However, I found her very satisfied with me and with my noble and cultivated manners; in truth such eulogies surprised me and I should never have imagined that drunkards could so have pleased the ladies of Milan. She treated me more as equal to equal than as mistress to majordomo, a delicacy that somewhat reconciled me to my position and made me write to Aglaura, to Lucilio, to Bruto Provedoni, to the Colonel and to the Pisana letters filled with enthusiasm and gratitude to the Signora Contessa. As for the Pisana I also intended to revenge myself a little for her neglect and to make her a little jealous. The strange revenge that she had herself inflicted on me on the other occasion of my supposed infidelity had not taught me. But after five or six days I began to notice that the Pisana would not have been altogether wrong in being jealous of my patroness. She behaved towards me in such a way that either I must have been a great dunce or else she invited me to an intimacy that does not as a rule figure among the duties of a majordomo. What could I do? I do not try to excuse myself or to hide anything. I fell.

The Contessa's house was one of the most frequented in Milan, but despite the gay temperament of the mistress of the house, the gatherings there did not seem to me either carefree or animated. A certain distrust, a Spanish gravity, kept the lips and brows of all these gentlemen tight and compressed; and then, in my opinion, youth was rare there and on the few occasions when it made an appearance, was so dull and insipid as to arouse pity. If such were the hope of the country, one could only make the sign of the cross and put one's trust in God. Even the Signora, who when *tête à tête* or within the family circle was lively, and perhaps even more free than was necessary, at these gatherings assumed a heavy and austere manner and seemed more ready to bite than to speak or to smile. At the time I understood nothing of all this.

After a fortnight, I began to understand a little. A guest from Venice was announced and to my great astonishment I saw once more, after so many years, the advocate Ormenta. He did not seem to recognize me, because the years and changing fashions had made me completely different from the little student of Padua; I pretended not to know him since it did not suit me to stir up his recollections in any way. It seemed that he had come from Venice to recommend himself and his views to the powerful protection of the Contessa; indeed in those days there was a greater coming and going than usual of French Generals and high Italian dignitaries. Several ministers of the new government remained closeted for many hours with the distinguished advocate and I wasted my time in vain trying to discover why a leading counsellor of the Austrian government in Venice had to concern himself in the affairs of the French government in Italy. That too I learnt later on. The prudent advocate had foreseen the battle of Austerlitz and its consequences; he passed from the camp of Darius to that of Alexander to save a little something for himself from the results of defeat. Whoever may marvel that feminine fingers were involved in this intrigue, must remember that history teaches that women have never had so much power in affairs of state as during periods of military rule. Greek mythology was aware of this, when it always mixed Mars and Venus together in its tales.

The first reports of the victory of Austerlitz reached Milan before Christmas and created great confusion. This increased when confirmation was received of the peace signed on St Stephen's day at Pressburg by which the kingdom of Italy was enlarged to its natural frontiers on the Isonzo. I forgot for an instant the question of liberty to give rein to my joy at seeing once again Venice and the Pisana, my sister and Spiro and my nephews and the dear places where I had passed my childhood and which still lived in my soul. The letters that the Pisana wrote to me then I do not want to speak of so as not to draw down upon me too great a weight of envy. I could not explain to myself how so much passion could be reconciled with the indifference of the past; but present content overcame all else. Thinking of nothing else, I went to the Signora Contessa with tears in my eyes and told her that after the Peace of Pressburg. . . .

'What do you mean? . . . What difference does the Peace of Pressburg make?' the Signora shouted at me, narrowing her eyes venomously.

'The difference is that I need no longer be Intendente or Majordomo . . .'

'Ah, you villain! And this is the way you choose to tell me? . . . I have really been too good to put all my . . . my trust in you! . . . Get out of my sight and don't let me set eyes on you again!'

I was so beside myself with joy that such treatment had the effect on me of a caress; it was only later, on thinking it over, that I perceived the callousness of taking leave of her in such a way. Certain favours should never be forgotten when once they have been accepted as favours and he who forgets them deserves to be well kicked. I realize now that if the Countess behaved towards me with some kindness, it was all due to her weakness for me, therefore I have never had the heart to join her detractors when I heard later all the evil that was spoken of her.

The Pisana welcomed me at Venice with the exuberant joy of which she was capable in her moments of enthusiasm. Though I had foreseen that she would at least spare me a room or two in my house, she now wanted at all costs to set up house with me, a whim that you will find strange enough in view of all the tenderness and care she had up till then lavished on her husband. But the strangest thing of all was when old Navagero, driven to desperation by his wife's resolution, sent secretly to me to implore me to come and live in his house instead, saying that he would receive me with great pleasure. This was behaviour even beyond Venetian tolerance and it made me realize that his apoplexy had completely cured him of his jealousy. But I did not deign to accede to the polite invitation of the nobleman and showed my scruples to the Pisana and said that nevertheless she ought to stay by her husband. Our love would have gained in freshness and relish what it would have lost in convenience. Spiro and Aglaura wanted me to stay with them but I had taken over the top-floor of my little house in the San Zaccaria and did not want to move.

So I lived, careless of everything and very happy until the spring, keeping as far away as I could from the Countess of Fratta and her son, but passing the most lovely hours of the day in the company of the Pisana. Her pity for that old and sorry carcass of Navagero so far exceeded all bounds that I sometimes even felt a little jealous of it. It happened not infrequently that after some tedious or irritating visits, when we were alone for a moment, she would rush off to change her husband's linen or to pour out his medicine. This excess of zeal annoyed me and I could not refrain from a prayer, not addressed to Heaven, that the poor invalid should soon attain the glories of Paradise.

But there was nothing to be done. Women are lovers, wives, mothers, sisters, but above all they are nurses. There is no dog of a man so profligate, so despicable or so disgusting that, if he be ill and far from aid, will not find in some woman a worthy and pitiful guardian angel. A woman may lose every feeling of love, of religion, of modesty; she may forget her most sacred duties, her sweetest and most natural affections, but she will never lose the instinct of pity for to the sufferings of her dear ones. If woman had not her necessary place in creation as the mother of men, our ills, our infirmities would have made her equally necessary to us as a consoler. In Italy our defects are so great that our women are, so to say, from birth to death, always busy in ministering either to our souls or our bodies. Blessed be their fingers dripping balm and honey! Blessed their lips whence springs that fire that burns and yet heals. . . .

My other acquaintances in Venice did not seem to concern themselves unduly about me, but exception must be made for the Venchieredos, who tried in every way to win me over, but I kept myself at a distance with all the prudence of an excellent memory. Of the Frumiers, the Chevalier of Malta appeared to have been buried alive; the other one, married to the Contarini and pushed forward in his career in the finances, had ended up by being appointed Secretary. Ambition spurred him on in a career which with his newly won wealth he could easily have renounced, but with that goose's head of his, he was ready to place his signature under any report as long as he could keep his eyes fixed on the horses of San Marco and the figures of the Clock Tower. It surprised me, moreover, that in his case, as in those of Venchieredo, Ormenta and certain others employed by the late government, the new one suffered them to remain in their former positions or in fresh ones equally important and delicate. However, since I had to share my apple neither with the outgoing nor the incoming, I did not cudgel my brain to find the reason. What, however, worried me not a little was that many of my friends, as well as the friends of Lucilio, of Amilcare and even of Spiro Apostulos and my kinsman himself, began to treat me at times with a certain coldness. I did not feel that I had in any way ceased to deserve their friendship, so I did not deign to complain about it, merely mentioning it to Aglaura, who evaded the question by saying that her husband often had his head full of business and could not pay attention to festas and ceremonies.

One day I chanced in the Piazza on an ugly mug that I never encountered without a certain irritation: I mean Captain Minato. I tried to avoid him, but he forestalled me from ten perches away with an 'Oh!' of surprise and pleasure and I had to swallow a long draught of his Corsican stupidities in silence.

'By the way,' he said, 'I have just been in Milan and offer you my congratulations; you were there in time to inherit my lovely one.'

'What lovely one?'

'Capperi! Isn't the Contessa Migliana lovely? . . . Ever since I made that trip with her from Rome to Ancona I have found her a little passée, but none the less she is still a fine woman.'

'What! . . . The Countess Migliana is . . .'

'The lady friend of Emilio Tornoni and my little treasure of '96. How the years have flown!'

'Impossible! . . . You're romancing! . . . That was not the name of your adventuress and she had not either the fortune or the entry into society of the Countess Migliana!'

'Oh, as far as names go, I can assure you that the Countess has never stuck to any single one for more than a month! It is a delicate consideration for each of her lovers. As to her fortune, even you should have known that she only laid hands on her inheritance a few years ago. For the rest, society is too cunning to deny entry to anyone who pays it well. You will have seen the type of person that surrounds her, at least at formal times; they were the sort who, at the cost of a little veneer or a donation to the holy cause, would agree to draw a veil over the past and welcome the strayed lamb into the bosom of the aristocracy . . . or as they call it in Milan . . . the sugar-plum aristocracy.'

'And therefore . . .' I started to say . . .

'Therefore . . . you want to say that, being her majordomo, in her very house . . . I hope I make myself clear . . . but you surely did not find the little lamb so faithful to the fold that she did not lose herself every now and again in some wanton game in a deserted pasture . . .'

'Sir, you have no right either to besmirch the honour of a lady, or to . . .'

'Sir, you have no right to prevent me saying what everyone is saying.'

'You come from Milan, but here in Venice . . .'

'Here in Venice, Signor, they are talking even more perhaps than in Milan! . . .'

'But . . . I hope you are making all this up . . .'

'The news came, so to speak, in the briefcase of the Counsellor Ormenta, who gives you credit for your love affairs as for a timely conversion to the cause of the Holy Faith.'

'Counsellor Ormenta, you say?'

'Yes, yes, the Counsellor Ormenta! Don't you know him?'

'Only too well!'

I began to consider why, after having forgotten me to such an extent as not to recognize me, he should have taken the trouble to spread such gossip about me. It did not enter my head that he in his turn might have thought himself unrecognized and that my name, fallen by chance from the Countess' lips, would have helped him to change into certainty the suspicion of a resemblance. Men of his type look for nothing better than to spread distrust and discord, and the reasons for his malicious gossip were only too clear. As to the rest, it didn't matter a fig to me to hear the details; none the less, I was convinced that Minato had rendered me a signal service by opening my eyes to these trickeries and I separated from him with less pleasure than usual and returned to the Pisana to chew over my anger less bitterly.

I found there that day a person whom I would never have expected to see there: Raimondo Venchieredo. After all that we had said about him and the intentions he was supposed to harbour concerning the Pisana, after all the intrigues woven by him against her by means of Doretta and Rosa, I wondered greatly to find her in such company. Further, it might be added that, knowing as she did the hostility still existing between me and Raimondo, she should have kept him at a distance out of regard for me. The crafty fellow, however, did not judge it opportune to inconvenience me for long and withdrew with so deep a bow that it was equivalent to a slap in the face. Once he had left, we began to squabble.

'Why do you receive that kind of trash?'

'I receive whom I like.'

'No, you don't, my lady!'

'We shall see if you can order me about!'

'I don't order you, I beg you.'

'To beg such favours, one must have the right.'

'I have won that right, I think, by many years of penance.'

'A fine penance!'

'What do you mean by that?'

'I know what I'm saying, and that's enough!'

We continued this terse wrangling for some little time, but I could drag nothing further from her.

I left in a fury, but in spite of all my rage I found her when I returned, even more sullen and colder than before. Not only would she not express herself more openly, but she avoided everything that could lead to an explanation, while as to talk of love between us, she would no more hear of it than of sacrilege. On the third and fourth occasions it became still worse; I kept meeting Raimondo in her room, playing with her lapdog. And the little beast even began to bark at me. The first time I put up with it, but the second I really let myself go; I became aware of my brutality from the haughty and mocking behaviour of Raimondo and rushed off down the stairs, pursued by the yelps of that beastly little dog. Oh, those little beasts are really barbarously frank! They make and retract in the name of their masters, declarations of love that do not err, not even by a hair's breadth. By then I was so furious that I could have made a bundle of dog and mistress together and thrown them into the lagoon. You may say that I am accustomed to boast of my quiet and patient nature! Well, what a hot-blooded and impetuous person would have done in my place, I really don't know!

In all this, the sole point that did not remain obscure was the perfidy of the Pisana towards me and her infatuation for Raimondo Venchieredo. That he was the cause of my misfortune I could not say for sure, but I wanted to believe it in order to unload upon someone the burden of hatred that I felt within myself. To bring a climax to my madness, I received about then a letter from Lucilio so icy, so enigmatic that I very nearly tore it up. Had everyone, friend and enemy alike, conspired to lead me to the extreme of humiliation and desperation? . . . The blow that I had received from Lucilio, from the friend whose judgement I respected more than that of any other, from him who up till then had been the guardian of my conscience and maintained all the strength and fortitude that sometimes failed me, such a blow, I say, took from me even the consciousness of my misfortune. What had I not done and what would I not do to preserve Lucilio's esteem? Now, without telling me the why or the wherefore, without even calling upon me to justify myself, he intimated that he had taken it from me. What was the treachery, the baseness, the guilt that deserved such a sentence? . . . My mind could not grasp it. I tormented myself, I grew thin, I wept with rage, sorrow and humiliation; shame made me bow my head, shame which I knew I had not merited. But over-sensitive temperaments such as mine react almost as much to the injustice of an action as to the action itself. I have never possessed the effrontery of virtue.

In those moments Aglaura's kindness diffused my sorrow with an inexpressible sweetness; for the first time I felt the kindness there is in those calm and devoted affections that are never withdrawn from us either for lack of merit or for change of opinion. My kind sister and her little children smiled at me, however hostile society as a whole showed itself to be. Without speaking, they took up my defence with Spiro, since he could not remain surly and sullen with one who was continually receiving embraces and kisses from his wife and children.

The more the trust of my former companions was withdrawn from me, the more I was confronted with a thousand little attentions from the advocate Ormenta, his son, the old Venchieredo, Father Pendola and all their gang. The good Father had made himself the spiritual director of that home for the converted of which the little doctor Ormenta was the accountant. Every so often, when they encountered me, there was a doffing of caps, greetings and little smiles that turned my stomach because they seemed to say: 'You have come over to our side! Bravo! We thank you!' I did everything I could to avoid these fulsome courtesies; but other people saw them, including some to whom I had become suspect; the calumnies took wings and there was no way in which I could refute them. I was like a man in a bog who, struggle as much as he could, only sank the deeper.

The Ormentas, father and son, redoubled their attentions and courtesies towards me; and it must have seemed that I had gained favour with them, or else that their faction had become so depleted that it no longer spared trouble or expense to gain a convert. They surrounded me with tempters, and made use of every kind of go-between and agent; but I remained adamant.

I was suffering because of the injustice of my friends, but I would never have consented to turn even my little finger against them, for behind those deceived and unjust friends was that eternal justice that never fails, which never deceives or is deceived.

Yes, I wept much and suffered much, but I wept and suffered for others, for in myself I felt neither sin nor fault. This is, in my opinion, one of the greatest injustices of nature towards us; that conscience, however clear and quiet, has not the power of opposing itself vigorously to unmerited afflictions. We suffer from the malice of others as from a punishment. The sorrows, the pain, the humiliation, the continual battles of a meek and sensitive nature with an adverse destiny, deeply affected my health. The doctors said it was inflammation of the veins or congestion of the liver; I knew very well what it was, but could say nothing, for the ill known to me was incurable.

I had never seen death so close before; better I should say that I had never had the ease to contemplate it with such calm. I found it neither disgusting, nor grievous nor terrifying. I see it again after so many years still nearer, still more sure. Once again it is the same face, shadowed by a cloud of melancholy and of hope, a courageous but inexorable mother, who murmurs in our ear the last words of final consolation. There will be expectation, there will be expiation or repose; but there will no longer be the confused and empty battles of life.

The doctors did not talk much in my presence but I soon perceived from their silence and the variance of their opinions that they despaired of my recovery. Those last days, I tried my best to pour into the soul of Spiro and my sister all the experience of my life, to show them how my feelings had been formed and how love, friendship, the love of country and of virtue had broken in, at first confusedly, then becoming purer little by little and purging my soul. Aglaura wept. Spiro bent his head and the children looked at me bewildered and asked their mamma why uncle's voice was so low and why he always wanted to sleep and never left his bed.

Spiro was by no means satisfied with my explanations; he felt my pulse, observed my eyes anxiously as if searching for that hidden cause of my illness that had escaped the others. Finally, one day when we were alone, he took courage and said:

'Carlo, in confidence, tell me! Is it that you can't or that you won't get well?'

'No, I cannot, I cannot,' I exclaimed.

At that moment, Aglaura entered the room to tell me that someone, very dear to me in other times, wanted at all costs to see me.

'Let her come, let her come,' I murmured, overcome by this consolation that had come to me so unexpectedly. I saw through the walls, I read the soul of her who came to visit me; I believe that I was half-afraid of that almost superhuman flash of clairvoyance and I feared that I would not be able to sustain that sudden rush back of life.

The Pisana entered; she had eyes for no one but me. She threw her arms around my neck without a cry or a word; her laboured breathing, her wild eyes told me all. There are moments that the memory still feels and will always feel as if they were eternal, but that cannot be examined or described! If you could imagine the light, aerial flame of a bonfire that is dying and realize how it would feel when it revives once more after having a surge of spirit poured over it to rekindle it, then perhaps you would be able to understand the miracle that took place in my being. . . . I was as if stifled by happiness; life burst forth fiercely from that momentary sinking, and I felt a mixture of warmth and freshness flow, health-giving and delightful, through my nerves and veins.

The Pisana refused to leave my bedside; that was her way of asking pardon and of obtaining it immediately and completely. Why do I say obtaining it? A single glance would have been enough for that. Then I understood the real reason for my illness, which my pride had hitherto perhaps concealed from me. I felt life return to me; I dismissed the doctors and refused to take any more of their stupid potions. The Pisana did not sleep a single night, and never left my room. She allowed no hand but hers to touch my limbs, my clothes, my bed. In three days she became so pale and thin that she looked worse than I did. I believe that I forced myself to get well, in order not to see her suffer, and shortened the course of my illness by several weeks. Spiro and Aglaura looked on in wonder. The Pisana seemed to expect no less, such was the faith and sincerity of her love.

What would I not have pardoned her? . . . It was that time as with all the others. The lips were silent but the heart spoke. She had given me back my life and the possibility of loving her again. I professed myself her debtor and the humility and tenderness of an infinite love compensated me for the thoughtless abandonment of a day.

'Carlo,' the Pisana said to me one day when I was sufficiently convalescent to be able to go out. 'The air of Venice does not suit you. You need the country. Shall we pay a visit to my uncle, Monsignor Orlando of Fratta?'

I do not know how I managed to reply to an invitation that interpreted so well the most ardent longings of my heart. To see once more, in the company of the Pisana, the haunts of our earliest happiness would be a real Paradise for me.

She advanced me a small sum of money due from the accumulated rent of my house over the last four years, and a withdrawal to the country would in itself help our finances. Everything combined to make the idea suitable, useful and expedient. In addition, I knew that Raimondo Venchieredo was still in Venice and had learnt of the base and malicious tricks he had made use of to inform the Pisana of my affair with the Countess Migliana and to take advantage of a moment of scorn to further his own interests. I had pardoned the Pisana but not him; nor was I sure that I could control my rage should I chance to run across him. For the next two days the Pisana said nothing about leaving but I saw that she was very preoccupied and it seemed to me that she was making preparations for a long absence. At last she came to my house with her luggage and told me:

'Cousin, I am ready. My husband is not well yet, but his illness is taking a more regular course and the doctors say that he may last like this for many years more. My sister, who is leaving her convent tomorrow . . .'

'What?' I exclaimed. 'Clara is discarding her habit?'

'Didn't you know? Her convent has been suppressed. They have granted her a small pension and she will come out tomorrow. Of course she has no intention of breaking her vows and will continue to keep the four fasts of the year. But meanwhile she has consented to act as nurse to my husband. I have persuaded her that Monsignor my uncle has great need of me, and my mother too, who will get some benefit from this trip of mine, has backed up the idea with all her might.'

'What advantage will your mother have from this trip?'

'The advantage that I have finally ceded to her not only the interest but also the principal of my dowry!'

'What madness! What remains for you?'

'For me there remain the two lire a day that my husband insists on giving me despite the meagreness of his resources. With these I can live in the country like a great lady.'

'But, Pisana . . . the sacrifice that you have made for your mother seems to me as imprudent as it is useless. What advantage will she get in having the principal as well as the interest on your dowry?'

'What advantage? I don't really know, but probably that of being able to eat. And then keeping accounts was never my strong point. My mother has shown me the wretched way in which she lives and her old age is always demanding fresh comforts and fresh expenditure and she is continually worried by debts; also, I have noticed the demands of her little weaknesses and I did not want her to have to sell her bedclothes in order to play a couple of games of "three-seven". I said to her: "Do you want it? . . . Then take it! . . . But let me go, because I need a breath of fresh air and to see our own country again." "Go, go, then, and may Heaven bless you, my daughter," she said. I believe she was really very pleased at seeing me getting ready to go, because my hints would no longer be able to force Rinaldo to buy himself a new hat or a less shabby jacket from time to time and so there would be a *zecchino* or two more for her. I went to a notary and the deed of cession was drawn up and signed.'

'So,' I said, 'you are left with only two miserable lire a day conceded by the wretched munificence of the noble Navagero, so that if the old fool should change his mind he could send you straight to the poorhouse! . . .'

'What matter?' replied the Pisana. 'I am young and strong. I can work, and in any case I will be staying with you and you can reckon my keep as salary.'

Such an arrangement suited the Pisana's way of thinking very well and I certainly had nothing against it; only it seemed to me that I should need some work myself to eke out my most miserable resources until the longed-for death of Navagero should enable us to put things on a suitable footing. But for the time I put the idea aside. The important thing was to leave at once; the improvement in my health had stopped. I had about a hundred ducats in my purse, the Pisana insisted on giving me another two hundred that she had raised on some of her jewels and with this great sum we gaily made our arrangements to leave.

Before leaving Venice, I had the good luck to see for the last time old Apostulos, who had just returned from Greece; he had become involved in those intrigues for the liberation of his country, through the patronage of the so-called Phanariotes, or Greeks of Constantinople, and was rushing here, there and everywhere on the pretence of business. Spiro, who inclined to the younger party that later surpassed all the rest and fomented the final war of independence, obeyed his father with a heavy heart in these ignoble intrigues, in which some half-Turkish Prince or other was also fishing for his own interest. There was therefore a slight chill between them. Old Apostulos also gave me good news of my Grand Vizier; he had been strangled, according to the very convenient system then in vogue at the Porte, rather than that other European way, a thousand times more expensive, with public rejoicings. But his successor had recognized the validity of my title, only, since the credit amounted to seven million piastres and the treasury of His Highness was not at the time very well supplied, he had asked for a delay of a year or so for payment. Thus, millionaires in hope, and with three hundred ducats in our purse, the Pisana and I took a boat for Portogruaro, where we arrived on the second day after many broken tow ropes and much time lost in changing horses and on the shoals of the Lemene.

The voyage was long but gay. The Pisana was then, if I am not mistaken, twenty-eight. She looked twenty and in heart and mind felt herself not more than fifteen. I, a veteran of the Parthenopean war and ex-Intendente of Bologna, became little by little as we drew near to the Friuli a boy again. I believe that, when we disembarked at Portogruaro I wanted to turn somersaults as I had so often done in the Frumier garden while I still had my milk teeth. Our gaiety was, however, mingled with a certain melancholy. Our old acquaintances were almost all dead; of the young or those of our own age, some were scattered here, some there, but very few had remained in their own country. Fulgenzio, now decrepit and in his second childhood, was afraid of his own sons and had fallen into the hands of an astute and avaricious maidservant who tyrannized over him and knew well how to put her meanness to profit and glean a little capital for herself. Dr Domenico fumed, but for all his doctorate never succeeded in freeing his father from this harpy's claws. Don Girolamo, professor in the Seminary and brilliant champion of the popular faction, accepted the situation with philosophy. In his view, one must wait patiently until the Lord should touch his father's heart; but the doctor, who was very eager to get his hand on the purse-strings, was not reconciled to the comforting of his priestly brother. Fulgenzio passed from this world within a few days of our return to the Friuli; his death throes were accompanied by a terrifying delirium in which he felt the soul being clawed out of his body by demons and he clutched the hand of his housekeeper in his fear to such an extent that she was on the point of kicking the inheritance to glory and leaving him in the sexton's care. But avarice made her hold firm, so much so indeed that, after the master was dead, they had to free her arm by force from his frantic nails. When the will was read, she had a fine sum of money in addition to what she had already stolen. There followed many bequests for masses and donations to churches and convents; finally an imposing sum topped the whole that had been set aside by the testator for the construction of a sumptuous campanile near the Fratta church.

With that he believed himself to have made the final gesture for the cleansing of his conscience and to have settled his accounts with the justice of God. There was no word of restitution to the Fratta family; the miserable heirs of the ancient castellans had to content themselves with a view of the new campanile. Don Girolamo contented himself with his far from small share in the inheritance that remained to him even after so great a distribution of legacies, but the doctor leapt into the lists with legal causes and quibbles. However, the will was incontestable. Everyone had their share and piles of stone and mortar began to accumulate on the Fratta square to bear witness to the posthumous beneficence of the defunct sacristan.

Another very strange item of news told us at Portogruaro was of the marriage that had taken place a short time before between Captain Sandracca and the widow of the Fossalta apothecary who had come to live with him with her dowry of seven or eight hundred lire. The Captain, troubled by the promise of celibacy that he had made to the late Signora Veronica, but still more by the poverty that so weighed on him, had set everything in order by composing a glib discourse that he proposed to deliver to his first wife should he chance to meet her in some street in the other world. He proved to her by it that his promise was not valid and in no way bound a poor devil from whom it had been extorted in a moment of real despair, and that in any case pity for her husband should be more powerful than some whim of posthumous jealousy. He assured her that his heart was always true to her and that in reality, the only thing that he loved about the apothecary's widow was her seven hundred lire. With that he flattered himself with the hope that the Signora Veronica would be deeply moved and would be convinced of his reasonableness and would not hold an almost nominal infidelity against him. In any case, had he married a young girl, the damage would have been irreparable; but with a widow, matters could easily be arranged. She would return to her first husband and he to his first wife and there would be no trouble or annoyance *per omnia saecula saeculorum.* The Signor Captain savoured the flavour of the seven hundred lire with the well assured hope of a gracious forgiveness.

Meanwhile we had already made our entry into this ramshackle capital of the ancient jurisdiction of Fratta. Our hearts filled with pity only to look at it from a distance. It seemed like a castle that had only that moment been sacked by some devilish band of Turks and was now inhabited only by the winds and some ill-omened owl. Captain Sandracca saw us again with much uncertainty; he did not fully understand if we had come to take him or it away. Monsignor Orlando, on the other hand, welcomed us as quietly and calmly as if we had only just returned from an hour's walk. His noble shirtfront had more than doubled and he walked dragging his legs, but he congratulated himself on his good health, were it not for that cursed scirocco that made his knees creak. It was the scirocco of his eighty years that I too now experience and that blows from Christmas to Easter and from Easter to Christmas with a persistence that makes a mock of the weather prophets.

While the Pisana, kind-hearted and carefree, made much of her uncle and amused herself by discussing the duration of his scirocco I went out quietly to renew my acquaintance with the old chambers of the castle. I still remember that it was dusk and that at every doorway, at every bend in the corridors, I thought I saw before me the dim spectres of the Signor Count and his Chancellor, or the open, ruddy face of Martino. Instead, the swallows flew in and out of the windows, bringing the first straws, the first beakfuls of mud, for their nests; the bats flew by me on their dark and uncertain wings and in the marriage chamber of the former masters a screech-owl mocked me. I wandered here and there, letting my legs take me where they would, and my legs, faithful to ancient custom, brought me to my old den near the friars' room.

I don't know how I managed to arrive safe and sound across those battered and ruined floors, through those long corridors where the fallen rafters and scraps of mortar from the attics hindered my steps and set some very efficient traps to pitch me down once more on to the floors beneath. A swallow had made its nest on that very beam on which Martino had been accustomed to hang his olive branch on Palm Sundays. Innocence had taken the place of peace. I remembered that night when the Pisana had come upstairs to find me and for the first time had defied for my sake the scoldings and blows of the Contessa. That lock of hair! I have it always with me. I had foreseen in it almost the symbolic story of my love, nor had my premonitions deceived me. Pleasure mingled with tears, humiliation side by side with bliss, servitude with possession, the contradictions and extremes had not been lacking in its promise; they were bound up confusedly in my destiny. What sorrows, what joys, what hopes, how much of life stemmed from that day! . . . Who could have told then how many other troubles and how much variety of experience awaited me before I returned to set foot once more on that crumbling and dusty floor! . . . Who could have told whether the hands of men or the furies of the elements might not have completed the vandalism of Fulgenzio and the other rapacious pillagers of that ancient dwelling! . . . Who could tell if some future master might not have made those falling walls rise again, have replastered those rooms, have scraped from them those signs of old age that spoke with so much power to my heart? Such is the destiny of men, such is the destiny of things; under an appearance of joviality and health is hidden the avarice of the soul and the death of the heart.

When I went back downstairs, my eyes were smarting and my mind filled with strange fancies; but the laughter of the Pisana and the calm, round face of Monsignor dispelled the clouds from my brow. I expected at every moment to be asked if I had learnt the second part of the Confiteor. Instead the good Canon lamented that his revenues were no longer as abundant as they had once been and that those scamps of tenants, instead of bringing him their best capons, as they should have done, gave him nothing but stringy chickens or hens so emaciated that they escaped through the cracks in the hen roost.

'And they insist that they are capons,' he said sighing. 'But when I wake in the night I can hear them crowing loud enough not to disgrace the betrayer of St Peter! . . .'

A little later Captain Sandracca entered with the chaplain, grown so old, my God, that they seemed but shadows of what they once had been; Signora Veneranda, Donato's mother, newly married to the Captain, also came in and it did not seem that the seven hundred lire of her dowry would have been enough to keep her in flesh. It is true that sometimes fat people eat more sparingly than thin ones. She placed on a trencher a slice of fat bacon and six eggs which were due to be converted into an omelette to make supper for us. Then she began, with mouth a little set, to prepare two beds for us as best she could; but we had already been warned of the comforts likely to be found at the castle and knew that if we stayed there, the couple would have had to go and sleep with the hens. So we had pity on them and their six eggs and returned to our carriage to go and ask hospitality of Bruto Provedoni as had been agreed between us before leaving Portogruaro.

I will not try to describe to you the hearty welcome of Bruto and Acquilina or the sincere cordiality with which those two made us make their house our own. Everything had been arranged to the last detail; we found two little rooms at our disposal, for which and for our keep, which we shared in common with them, a very modest sum had been reckoned. It was in no way a bargain but a sharing out of our slender mutual resources to defend ourselves against the poverty that hemmed us in on all sides. Acquilina jumped for joy like a mad thing and however much the Pisana wanted to help her those first few days about the house, she found everything already done and in order. Bruto, who went out to give his lessons each morning, returned by lunch-time and we amused ourselves together till nightfall, working, laughing and taking walks, so that the hours flew past like butterflies on the breath of a spring breeze. I had forgotten to tell you that at Padua during my close friendship with Amilcare I had learnt to pound on the spinet. My very fine ear enabled me to acquire a certain skill as a tuner and there at Cordovado I recollected at the right moment that I had learnt this art and, as the proverb says, put it away for a rainy day. Bruto praised me throughout the neighbourhood as the most tuneful of all men; an occasional priest asked me to play the organ and aided by the local ironmonger and my own audacity I acquitted myself with a certain honour. Then my fame began to spread to the whole district and there was not an organ, a clavichord or a guitar which did not have to be tormented by my hands to make it play as it should. My term of office as Chancellor had made me popular at the time and my name had not been altogether forgotten. In the country, he who has been a good Chancellor has no difficulty in making himself believed to be a good tuner and in the end, by dint of breaking, stretching and torturing strings, I believe I succeeded in doing some good.

Finally I reached the pinnacle of my glory by appearing as organist at some festival or ceremony. At first I used to have my difficulties with the inexorable chanters of the Kyrie or the Gloria; but I learnt the way of it in the end and had the satisfaction of seeing them singing at the tops of their voices without turning every so often their piteous glances to question or reprove the capricious organist.

So from majordomo I became organist; and bear it well in mind that the geneology of my professions is far from a usual one. But I can assure you that I earned my bread and between Bruto as writing-master, the Pisana as seamstress, Acquilina as cook and your Carlino as organist, I swear that in the evenings some brilliant little comedies used to be played that made us all burst out laughing. We were very happy and happiness and peace soon gave me back double the health I had before.

Sometimes I would go to Fratta and take the Captain and his dog out hunting. The Captain never wanted to go outside the few perches of land on which he seemed to have taken a lease and where the duck and water-fowl took very good care never to set foot. His dog, too, had the defect of sniffing too high in the air and looking at the bushes. It seemed more as if he was looking for fruit than for game, but by dint of much shouting I taught him to keep his nose to the ground and if I did not catch in a single morning the twenty-four snipe of Leonardo's grandfather, I often managed to put a dozen in my bag. Five I would give to the Captain and Monsignor, the others I kept for ourselves, and the spit turned and I was often tempted to put myself once more in place of the turnspit; but then I remembered that I had been an Intendente and put on a dignified expression.

Our hosts became dearer to our hearts as the days went on. Bruto had become, so to speak, my brother and Acquilina, I know not whether a sister or a daughter. The poor little thing had a great affection for me and followed me everywhere and did nothing without finding out first if I approved. She saw, as it were, with my eyes, heard with my ears and thought with my mind. I tried to return her affection by making myself useful to her; I began teaching her a little French and to write correctly in Italian. Little skirmishes often broke out between master and pupil, in which the Pisana and Bruto took part with the greatest amusement. I had become so fond of the girl that I felt the bump of fatherhood developing in me and I had no greater wish than to see her settled comfortably with some fine young man who would make her happy. We discussed this a good deal among ourselves when she was busy with the cares of the house, but she did not seem much inclined to fall in with our ideas. Pretty as she was, her features slightly irregular, something of a tomboy, but kind and gentle as a lamb, she did not lack admirers. But though she did not appear in any way shy, she none the less preferred to stay with us beside the spring or in the market square rather than join the swarm of girls with their gallants.

The Pisana urged her to amuse herself, but then, sorry at seeing the pretty face of Acquilina frowning at her exhortations, she would take her in her arms and cover her with kisses. They were like two sisters. The Pisana loved her so much that I grew jealous; if Acquilina called her, she would leave me at once and run to her and get angry if I tried to detain her. What this fresh caprice meant I did not then understand, though perhaps I did so better later, in so far as anyone could understand clearly so mysterious and complex a nature as the Pisana's.

After a few months of this simple life, laborious and peaceful, the affairs of the Fratta family recalled me to Venice. It was a question of obtaining from the Count Rinaldo the authority for the transfer of some barren valleys towards Caorle, which had been asked for by a rich gentleman of the district who was planning a large-scale irrigation project. But the Count, usually so neglectful and easygoing, became very stubborn at the idea of this sale and would not agree despite the evident advantages he would get from it. His was one of those indolent and fanciful natures which flame out in dreams and projects and base their hopes on castles in the air, while completely disregarding the building of anything on the solid earth. He saw in the future cultivation of those marshy lowlands the means to restore his family fortunes and would not defraud his own imagination of this very broad field of exercise for all the gold in the world.

When I arrived in Venice, I found many things greatly changed.

The extraordinary rejoicings at the unification with the Kingdom of Italy had given way little by little to a calmer judgement of the advantages it would bring to the country. France weighed us down like any other master; perhaps the forms were less absolute but the substance remained the same. Laws, initiative, action, all came from Paris, as today the hats and mantles of the ladies. The restrictions literally emasculated the people, taxes and impositions milked their wealth, and material progress did not compensate the country for the spiritual stagnation that made their minds grow sluggish. The nobles of the former governing class were either humbled by inertia or tucked into obscure corners in the most humble administrative posts; the citizens, a new class, still disorganized, was incapable for lack of education of handling affairs; commerce languished, the naval yards were allowed to go to rack and ruin; all this reduced Venice to a provincial city.

Poverty and humiliation were everywhere clearly to be seen, however much the Viceroy tried to conceal them by the glorious pomp of the imperial mantle. The Ormentas, the Venchieredos, still remained in the government, nor was it possible to expel them since they were the only ones who understood its functioning. Placing French or other foreign dignitaries over them would only have wounded municipal pride without making straight the crooked and obscure movement of public affairs. At Milan, where for good or evil there was still the shadow of the republic, public spirit still stirred. At Venice, conquest followed conquest, lackey followed lackey, with the usual indifference of he who seeks only the interest of the master who pays him.

I was somewhat disheartened by these signs of indolence and neglect; I saw that Lucilio had not been altogether wrong in fleeing to London and that he had common sense on his side. But however much I had tried to re-establish correspondence with him, he no longer condescended to reply to my letters. I got tired of knocking where the door was not opened and contented myself by getting news of him from some mutual acquaintance in Portogruaro or from the rumours current on the Piazza. They reported that he had become a doctor of great reputation in London and much esteemed by the leading families of the aristocracy there. He placed high hopes in England for the expulsion of the tyrant Bonaparte from France and for the renascence of Italy; his just and moderate ideas had not lasted long and his mania for making and remaking had for once led him astray. However that may have been, I remained in Venice only about a month, always hoping to obtain from Count Rinaldo the desired authority; but I was unable to get more out of him than the permission to sell a few detached bits of those swamps; the rest he wanted to keep himself for the future redemption of the family. So they got out of the sale only a few thousand lire which merely served to furnish a rather larger stake for the old Countess at the gaming table. It is indeed true that death takes the best and leaves the others; she who was the ruin of her house showed no signs of wishing to go; so too that inconvenient husband Navagero persisted in not wanting to leave his young wife a widow.

I had hoped to bring Aglaura and her children back with me to the Friuli, but the death of her mother-in-law kept her with her family; a real misfortune since the country air would have been very good for certain small ailments from which she was beginning to suffer. Spiro, as strong as a bull, could not understand his wife's fragility; but the fact was that for lack of amusement or change, her health was becoming more and more uncertain and Spiro only realized this when it was too late to remedy it. He kept saying that if she wanted she could go to Greece with his father on the first opportunity, but the tender mother did not want to risk her children, themselves still rather delicate, on a long and dangerous voyage. She replied smiling that she would stay in Venice and that, if her native air did not restore her to health, no other would be likely to have such virtue. I reproved Spiro for being too much the merchant and of paying no heed to anything save the terms of his bills of exchange and the price of coffee, which was continually rising because of the English privateers. But he shook his head without replying and I did not understand what he meant to convey to me by this mysterious gesture.

The fact remained that I had to return to the Friuli alone; the amusements and excursions, the lovely peaceful days, the activity, the country air that I had dreamed of in company with Aglaura and her children remained one of so many hopes that would come true only in another world.

At Cordovado I found the friendship, the intimacy, and if there were a more expressive word I would use it, between the Pisana and Acquilina had grown greater than ever. Now the Pisana's love only reached me through Acquilina. It was Acquilina's task to say: 'See, the Signor Carlo wants this or that!' Only then would the Pisana take heed of me, otherwise it was as if I did not exist, a complete eclipse. Acquilina stood before me and the soul of the Pisana saw only her. Even in certain moments in which thought does not usually wander far abroad, I surprised the mind of the Pisana filled with Acquilina. If we had been in the days of Sappho, I would have believed in some unnatural enchantment. What can I say? . . . I could not make things out at all; Acquilina became sometimes almost hateful to me and the least that I said of the Pisana in my mind was to call her crazy.

I have now come to a stage in my life that I find it very difficult to explain to others, since it has never been very clear even to myself; I mean my marriage. One day the Pisana called me into her room and began without preamble:

'Carlo, I am beginning to feel that I am a hindrance to you. Your love for me now cannot be more than a fraction of what it once was. You have need of a sure affection which will bring you peace and family contentment. I give you your liberty and only want to make you happy.'

'What folly is this?' I exclaimed.

'It is a folly that comes from the heart and which I have been thinking over for some time past. You are going on loving me either from habit or from a feeling of loyalty. But I can no longer sacrifice you and amends must be made to put you on the true road to happiness.'

'The road to happiness, Pisana? But we have long trod together that road blossoming with thornless roses! It will be enough for us to join hands and the roses will bloom under our feet and happiness will smile upon us once more in whatever part of the world we may be.'

'Either you don't understand me, or perhaps you do not understand yourself! This is my dream, Carlo; you are no longer a foolish and inexperienced youth and you cannot any longer be content with a happiness that may fail you from one day to the next. You must take a wife!'

'May God grant it, my soul! May Heaven pardon me this thoughtless longing; but when your husband will have left this world of his infirmities for one of eternal health, my first wish will be to unite your destiny with mine by the sanctity of the sacrament.'

'Carlo, don't waste your time in such dreams. My husband will not die yet and you must not lose the best years of your manhood. I would make a poor enough wife for you; you can see for yourself that Providence has not created me to bear children! . . . and so, what good is a wife? . . . No, no, Carlo, don't delude yourself; to be happy you must have marriage . . .'

'Enough, Pisana! . . . Are you saying that you no longer love me?'

'I am trying to say that I love you more than myself and for that reason you must listen to me and do as I advise . . .'

'I will do nothing but what my heart commands.'

'Well then, your heart has spoken. You will marry her.'

'I marry her? . . . You are talking nonsense. . . . You don't know what you are saying.'

'Yes, I tell you . . . you will marry . . . you will marry Acquilina!'

'Acquilina? . . . Enough! . . . Come to your senses, I beg you.'

'I speak as I judge best. Acquilina is in love with you; you like her and she is in every way suitable. You will marry her!'

'Pisana, Pisana, don't you see how you are hurting me?'

'I see the good I am doing you and if I want to sacrifice myself for your good, nobody can stop me.'

'I will stop you! . . . I have rights over you that you should not, cannot, forget!'

'Carlo, I shall have the courage to live without you. . . . You can gauge my strength by the shamelessness of that confession. But Acquilina will die. Now, choose for yourself. For my part, I have already chosen.'

'No, no, Pisana, think again! . . . You are exaggerating, you are imagining things that don't exist. Acquilina has a calm and tender sisterly feeling for me; she will always take pleasure in our happiness.'

'Be quiet, Carlo! Trust the intuition of a woman. The sight of our happiness would poison her entire youth.'

'Then let us go away, let us return to Venice.'

'You may, if you have the heart to do it. I love Acquilina, I want to make her happy; and I believe that you too will be happy if she marries you, and I myself will join your hands and bless your union.'

'But I would die of it! . . . I would hate her. I will feel all my vitals rise against her and my worst enemy would not be so abominable as to make me hold her in my arms.'

'Acquilina abominable! . . . If you say that again Carlo, I will run away from you. I will no longer even see you! . . . The angels command us to love; you would not be so perverse as to abhor what has come down to us from Heaven as the most beautiful incarnation of the Divine Thought. Look! Open your eyes, Carlo! . . . look at the murder you are committing. You have been blind up till now and have not noticed either her martyrdoms or my remorse. I have been your accomplice up till now, but I swear I will be so no longer; no, I will not murder with my own hands an innocent creature who loves me like a daughter, although. . . . You know, Carlo, her heroism surpasses imagination itself! . . . Never a sign of anger, never a glance of envy; a weary resignation. Instead, a love that makes one weep. No, no, I repeat, I will not repay with murder the hospitality we have received in this house; and you must assist me in this work of charity! . . . Carlo, Carlo, once you were so generous! . . . Once you loved me, and if I had spurred you on to some supreme and courageous enterprise, you would not have wasted so many words!'

What could I do? At first I was speechless, then I wept, implored, tore my hair. Useless! She remained inexorable. She kept on telling me to look, go look, and if I would not consent to what she proposed, I would be despicable, unworthy of love and incapable of any sort of feeling. From then on she denied me every glance, every smile of love; she forbade me to enter her room, was all for Acquilina and nothing for me.

In fact, however much I wanted to deceive myself, I was forced to recognize that, in so far as the girl's love for me was concerned, her suspicions were not so far from the truth. By what enchantment I had not noticed it, I could not tell you, and I was furious at my folly and ingenuousness. I even tried to turn some part of this rage against Acquilina herself, but found I could not. It seemed to me that she was asking pardon for the ill involuntarily committed and I saw her sometimes ask the Pisana to try and intercede with me. She even tried to avoid me, to pretend to be offended, so that I should not become aware of what was taking place in her heart and so allow harmony to come back amongst us. Bruto, who up till then had been overjoyed at the happy life we had been leading, discovered with chagrin these first traces of dissension and estrangement; he did not understand what it was all about and it pained him. He even tried to speak to me about it, but I wriggled out of it with a jest, shrugging my shoulders, which merely made another cause for suspicion and distrust. Acquilina in the meantime was failing in health; doctors were called in and made many fantastic diagnoses but discovered nothing. The Pisana went on urging me and I weakened. In the end, I know not how, I let a 'yes' fall from my lips.

Bruto was astounded at the proposal put to him by the Pisana, but after reiterated assertions of the fact that everything between her and me had ended in spontaneous agreement and that Acquilina was dying for me, he was persuaded. He spoke of it to the girl who at first refused to believe it and then could not conceal her feelings of delight. But when she first spoke of it to me, she was breathless and almost speechless; the poor thing had some presentiment that I had been persuaded to offer myself to her and did not have the courage to accept such a sacrifice of me. Would you believe that her attitude ended by winning me over completely and that I suddenly understood the Pisana's sacrifice? . . . It seemed to me that I was saving the life of an angelic creature at the price of my own and the consciousness of this good action gave to my behaviour the appearance of virtue. To Acquilina it did not seem true; at first she had tried hard to believe what the Pisana had given her to understand, that we two had only loved one another as brother and sister, but then seeing me beside her, quiet, affectionate and sometimes even happy, she had been persuaded. Then there were no bounds to the joyous outbursts of her spirit and I felt I had to be grateful to her for them, if only for pity.

To see this ingenuous creature blossom like a rose watered by the dew and rise again more and more lovely and smiling at a glance from me was a spectacle that made me fall in love, if perhaps not with her then at least with my own action. The Pisana was overflowing with joy at this happy result and her joy sometimes kindled a virtuous emulation in me and at others drove from my heart the stuff of jealousy. Oh what a tumultuous whirlpool of affections is centred in the human heart! Then, too, I gave proof of that extreme pliancy that had impressed so many actions of my life with a strange and bizarre pattern, however much my tranquil and reflective nature was alien to oddity and caprice. But the extravagance was hers who had led me by the nose, though later I could not have said whether on this occasion I had done well to let myself be led or if it would have been better to follow my own instinct and come to an opposite decision. Certainly my feelings, and I say it without flattering myself, then touched the utmost limits of generosity and I have since wondered at it without repenting of it. To regret a great and noble action, whatever may come of it later, is always an act of great cowardice.

It is better now to tell everything in a few words. The marriage was fixed for Easter 1807. The Pisana had enough discretion to get herself invited by Monsignor her uncle and to stay with him to look after his household.

I remained with Bruto and Acquilina and the wedding was celebrated, despite my protests, and at the Pisana's request, with great ceremony. Acquilina, poor girl, was overcome with joy and I found myself forced to take some part in her joy and believe that I did nothing to spoil it. Sometimes I looked back and wondered at myself for having gone so far, not understanding either the why or the wherefore, but the current bore me onwards; if there was ever a time when I believed in fate, it was certainly then.

So I married Acquilina. Monsignor of Fratta blessed the union. The Pisana was the bride's godmother. I felt within me a great desire to weep, but my melancholy was not without its sweetness. At the wedding breakfast there was not too much gaiety, but nevertheless little was left on the plates. Monsignor ate as if he were twenty again; I who was seated near him, and a little bewildered by the unexpected events that had happened to me, asked him about his health I do not know how many times during the meal. He replied between mouthfuls:

'It would be excellent if it weren't for this cursed scirocco! At one time it was not like this! Do you remember, Carlo?'

But it had not rained for a month and among all the people of Italy, Monsignor was the only one who felt the scirocco. Among the wedding guests were, of course, Donato with his wife and children, the Captain with Signora Veneranda and the Chaplain of Fratta. Another guest at the wedding, about whom you have perhaps forgotten, was the Spaccafumo who, amid all that confusion of governments and events that had taken place still continued to administer justice in his own way, but every year passed a month or two in prison and had become old and a drunkard. His prowess was now more an affair of words than of deeds and the ragamuffins used to tease him and make him repeat the oddest nonsense. He lived, one might say, off alms and however strongly Bruto pressed him to sit at the common table, there was no way of getting him out of the kitchen, where he enjoyed the wedding breakfast with the cats, the dogs and the maids. In the evening there was a great dance and the guests thought more of having a good time than of the bride and bridegroom. The gaiety was unrestrained and spontaneous. Marchetto, the sacristan, who looked like the devil in priest's clothes, scraped the double-bass and, despite his age, played with such energy that his legs could scarcely hold him upright. The Pisana tried to slip away that evening without being noticed; but I was aware of her departure in a moment. Our eyes met and exchanged, I believe, a last kiss. Acquilina was then talking with Bradamante and was for a moment disturbed.

'What is it?' her sister asked.

'Nothing, nothing,' the bride replied, half fainting, 'but don't you think it is stifling in here? . . .'

I heard the words, though they were spoken in a very low tone, and had no thought than to carry out the new duties imposed on me. I was gentle and loving with Acquilina until the end of the feast. And then? . . . Then I realized that in certain sacrifices Providence, perhaps to reward their merit, knows how to instil a certain dose of pleasure. The innocence, the charm, of my wife quite won her cause for her and confirmed my intention always to prove myself a good husband. 'What is done, is done,' I thought to myself: 'let us do what is to be done, well.'

I do not think that Acquilina noticed, not even during the first days, the effort expended to show her that fervour of love that in fact I did not feel. But little by little, I grew used to loving her in that new way in which I must; I no longer had to make such efforts and even if I sometimes sighed in thinking of the past, I found that I did not need too much philosophy to be content with the present. Good deeds are a great distraction. That of making my wife happy fully occupied me and I saw myself, after only a month, a far better husband than I should have supposed.

The Pisana witnessed this great internal change in me. Convinced that her great but too easy sacrifice in favour of Acquilina could only be explained by a noticeable cooling of her love for me, I did not take the trouble to hide from her the comfort that I found, greater than I had hoped, in resigning myself to play my part in that sacrifice. I hoped that, seeing me not ill-contented, she would have less remorse for the tyranny with which she had done violence to my will. At first she did understand it in this way, but the days passed and in the frequent visits that she made she became more and more sullen and her congratulations on my courageous spirit changed little by little into suspicion and anger. I believed that she did not consider me sufficiently considerate towards Acquilina and redoubled my zeal and good intentions, but her ill humour continued and even with my wife she no longer seemed so affectionate as before. One morning she appeared at our house in a great hurry when Bruto and Acquilina were both out for some reason or other. Without even waiting for me to greet her, she silenced me with a gesture.

'Be quiet!' she said. 'I am in a hurry. Now that you are really in love you have no more need of me. I am going back to Venice.'

I wanted to speak, but she did not give me time. She called from the doorway to ask me to give her greetings to my wife and Bruto, then climbed back into the carriage in which she had come, accompanied by the Chaplain of Fratta, and, run as fast as I could, I was unable to catch her up. An hour later when I got to the castle, she had already left and no one seemed to know if she had taken the Portogruaro or the Pordenone road in the gardener's cart. I was greatly perplexed how to explain to Acquilina and Bruto the reason for so hasty a departure but had the happy idea of inventing an unexpected illness of the Signora Contessa and was believed without difficulty. Then, neither happy nor forgetful, but tranquil and resigned, I went back to my life as organist and husband.

The months flashed by, simple, laborious, serene, like those autumn skies whence the sun makes nature more beautiful but does not warm it. Acquilina, devoted to me, showed fresh graces every day and made fresh efforts to please me; gratitude for a love so nobly shown inclined me more and more towards her and made ever rarer my regrets for the past. My heart still flew away sometimes but when my mind demanded comparisons, it was forced to admit that Acquilina was the most lovable and perfect of all the women I had ever known. At long length the judgements of the mind have a certain influence over the affections of a man of thirty-four. When later on I saw that she was pregnant and when I held in my arms the strongest and rosiest baby I had ever seen and felt the emotions of a father rise within me, I had to confess myself her debtor and no longer knew where I was. I almost thanked the Pisana for having driven me to this fantastic and misguided marriage. However, my memory was neither dead nor ungrateful. I wanted to have frequent news from Venice and knowing that the Pisana, living with Clara in her husband's house, was solely occupied in caring for him, certain rash judgements that I had made about her flight from Fratta passed out of my mind. If she had been really angry with me, she would never have sent me any news of herself. I had had experience of the Pisana's revenges. Moreover, though distant, I had not ceased being of use to her. I had put back into proper order the administration of those few farms which still belonged to the Castle of Fratta and arranged the collection of a number of quit-rents. The Fratta incomes increased by thirty per cent and Monsignor was able, now and again, to eat a capon that was not a cock, and Count Rinaldo, despite his shyness, had to thank me for having acted so efficiently on their behalf without even being asked to do so.

You will be astonished and perhaps even annoyed that my life, for long so wayward and disordered, should now take on so quiet and monotonous a course. But I am telling a story and not inventing one; on the other hand, this is a very common phenomenon in the life of Italians, which often resembles the course of a great river, calm, slow, marshy, but interrupted at intervals by noisy and violent rapids. Where the people have no permanent part in the government, but take it by force from time to time, these leaps, these metamorphoses, must necessarily take place, for is not the life of the people only the sum of individual lives? As for myself, I had for some years turned the spit, I had been a student and also to some extent a conspirator, then a peaceful Chancellor, later a Venetian patrician of the Great Council and Secretary of the Municipality; from a lover, reckless of everything, I had changed suddenly into a soldier, from a soldier once again to a man of leisure; then an Intendente and a majordomo, and finally ended by getting married and playing the organ.

In these perpetual ups and downs it is for you to judge whether I ascended or descended; for my part I know that I consumed in this way thirty-four years, years for which I lived for myself alone. Later, family ties and duties, precise and material occupations, controlled my emotions. I was no longer the colt that scoured the marshes, leaping ditches and forcing its way through hedges and brakes, but the harnessed horse, whether steadily drawing a cardinal's carriage or a gravel-cart. But do not fear; upheavals and reverses will not lack to give the horse back his liberty and make him return to his mad coursing across the world. Only now am I sure to rush no longer, but have, like Monsignor, the scirocco of eighty years in my legs.

While I was making myself more and more husband and countryman, and to my little Luciano, who was already trotting about the courtyard had been added a second little boy to whom we gave the name Donato in honour of his uncle who was his godfather, the military glories of Napoleon were deafening the world. He conquered Prussia at Jena, Austria at Wagram, he allied himself with the ancient dynasties and, master of Europe, closed the continent to England and menaced the semi-Asiatic Empire of the Tsars. Italy, in the hollow of his hand, was eaten up bit by bit at his whim, but had none the less set up at Milan the standard of unity. They grew accustomed to look on Napoleon more as an enemy than a protector because of his immeasurable ambitions and his heedlessness of history or peoples. But if the sword given us by him should have fallen to the ground, who would have dared to gird it on? They did not think of that. They believed themselves strong, not knowing that force remained with the colossus and with him would be broken. Of a hundred who took up arms perhaps one was inspired, and the other ninety-nine would have laid them down at the final trial. I was not a participator, but I could guess.

Thus the years passed as rapidly as the months of my youth; but do not believe that they were in reality as swift as they seem in telling of them. The longer a time takes to tell the more fugitive it is in reality. At Cordovado the days were tranquil, serene, sweet, if you will, but surpassing velocity was not their defect. The Pisana's letters, rare enough at first, became bit by bit more frequent as the political tempests grew angrier; it seemed that, imagining how much I would have to suffer, she hastened to afford me the comfort of her words. She told me of the great outcry that Venchieredo, Ormenta, Father Pendola and their proselytes had raised in Venice; of the fine positions given to her Cisterna cousins, especially Augusto who had suddenly become, I believe, Secretary of the Government; and of Agostino Frumier, who, wishing to retire from public life and being now very rich, had not deigned to ask for the pension that was his due. Many, as you can see, were the vilenesses; nor could it be otherwise since abstention had become the virtue of the best of men, nor could they do more. Moreover, the old Venchieredo, looked at askance for his excessive zeal, had lost a good deal of his influence and had fallen from the leading roles to that of Director of the Police. He protested, but it was no use. To serve too well is to serve ill; he had not been cunning enough. The Partistagno, meanwhile, had once again set foot in Venice as a Colonel of Uhlans; he had married a Moravian Baroness because, it was said, she closely resembled one of his favourite mares. He still maintained his rancour against the Fratta family and having learnt that Clara, after leaving her convent, was living in the Navagero palace, frequently paraded in full uniform under her windows, hoping to catch her eye and persuade her to say: 'What a shame that I did not love him despite everything!' But Clara, having grown short-sighted by dint of pouring over the Offices of the Madonna, could no longer see what was in the street and could not distinguish the magnificent and spectacular Colonel Partistagno from one of the beggars on the gondola steps.

There were some who said that Alessandro Giorgi had passed from the Italian to the Austrian army, retaining his rank of General gained at Moscow, but I did not believe them. Indeed, some months later, I received news from Brazil where he had taken refuge and found a good post. He did not forget to offer me his intervention with the Emperor Dom Pedro and told me that he had found at Rio de Janeiro a considerable number of Countess Miglianas who would be able to do far more for me than make me a majordomo. Probably he had forgotten that I was a married organist with a family, even though he had seen us all when he had passed through with Prince Eugene on the 1809 march into Hungary. But despite his forty years he was still a little forgetful and a good deal of a libertine.

The ashen years that followed were only a melancholy cemetery. The first to go was the Chaplain of Fratta. Then it was the turn of Marchetto the Serjeant, sacristan and double-bass player, who was struck by lightning as he was ringing the bells during a storm. The inhabitants of the parish revere him to this day as a martyr. During the famine year and the one following, death laid a heavy hand on the poor people; there was continual tolling of the bell; and there also went, though not owing to the famine, the Signora Veneranda, leaving the Captain a widower for the second time, but with seven hundred lire at his disposal which freed him from the necessity of taking a third wife. Even we in that year had to tighten our belts a little, since there was no family to be found to pay for a tutor for their boys or a priest who wanted his organ repaired. So the expenses incurred in that year were the first of our deficit which continued to grow worse and at last led me to fresh changes of which you shall duly hear.

I do not remember exactly when, but certainly about that time, the Count Rinaldo made a trip to the Friuli; he came for money, and since he did not find any, sold the most tumbledown part of the castle to a building contractor. I was present at the demolition and it seemed to me like the funeral of an old friend; even the Count could not bear the spectacle of this ruin and having pocketed the few coins, returned at once to Venice. His mother's illness, which had begun to cause grave fears, also called him back. Scarcely had the stones broken away by the picks and the rubble piled up in heaps during the demolition been cleared from the courtyards when Monsignor began to feel the scirocco more troublesome than ever. One morning he fainted during the Mass and after that he never left his room again. I went to see him on the last day of his life, asked him how he was, and received the usual sol-fa. Always that persistent scirocco! . . . None the less he continued to eat his fill even in bed and in his last hour had his breviary on one side of his bed and half a roast chicken on the other. Giustina came to him asking: 'Not eating, Monsignor?' . . . 'I'm not hungry any more!' he replied in a voice weaker than usual.

So died Monsignor Orlando of Fratta, smiling and eating as he had lived; but at least he had appeased his hunger. But his kinswoman who followed him a few months later raved to the end about her triumphs at cards; she died dreaming of fabulous winnings, with coffers empty and all her possessions in the pawn-shop. The Cisternas had to lend Count Rinaldo a few ducats to get her buried, since neither Clara nor the Pisana had a single ducat to their name and His Excellency Navagero was continually complaining of his poverty. All were going, but he still held out, an evident sign that my most fervent wishes of some years back had not found favour before God. The Pisana wrote me with sorrow of the death of her mother and also told me confidentially of a most unexpected visit they had received. One evening while she and Clara had been repeating the rosary in the private chapel of the house (this was not at all what I had expected of the Pisana) a foreigner was announced, who had been asking urgently for them. He, they said, was small and thin, with a thick beard and very brilliant eyes, despite his age which seemed about fifty, and with a very high forehead and almost bald. Who could he be? . . . They went into the salon and the Pisana recognized, more by his voice than his appearance, Doctor Lucilio Vianello. He had come on an English ship and having heard that Clara had returned to secular life, had come to ask her for the last time to fulfil her promises. The Pisana said that she had been afraid of the doctor, he had seemed so dark and menacing; but Clara replied curtly that she no longer recognized him, that she was married to God and that she would continue to pray for his soul.

'I assure you,' wrote the Pisana, 'that at that moment indignation and fury made him seem thirty years younger; then he turned very pale and his face became ashen like a man of eighty. He went away, bent, stumbling and muttering strange words. Clara made the sign of the cross and invited me in a perfectly controlled voice to continue with the rosary. But I said I must heat up some soup for my husband and went away, since the whole scene had made me feel ill. I would never have believed that so much passion could have been concealed beneath that icy appearance, remaining unchanged through all the events, the ups and downs of a life little less than fabulous. Do you remember Naples and Genoa? Didn't it seem to you that he had completely forgotten Clara? Did he ever ask for news of her? . . . Never! . . . I am convinced that to make a final judgement on men one must wait until they are dead. You too, Carlo, do not try to judge me until I have joined my poor mother!'

Then followed the usual greetings, more affectionate than usual, for Acquilina, Bruto and my sons, now already almost grown up. She also asked me to put up a small memorial in the cemetery at Fratta for Monsignor Orlando; but I had already thought of this some months before, though Don Girolamo, despite his brother the notary, had forestalled me in this pious work. The stone bore an inscription whose elegant falsehoods could be overlooked since no one in the countryside could understand them. However, a certain worthy who knew how to read had succeeded in translating them up to a certain point where it said that the reverend canon had died *octuagenarius*; which according to him, meant that he had died on the 8th of January. Many protested, saying that he had not died on the 8th but on the 15th of January.

'Well, there you are,' replied the worthy: 'do you expect the stonemasons to worry about such details? A day more or a day less, the important thing is that he should be dead in order to carve an inscription on his tombstone.'

I told the Pisana that her pious wish had already been carried out some time before, greatly praising Don Girolamo who, though he was no Vincent of Paul or Francis of Assisi, had none the less known how to get himself pardoned by the poor of Fratta despite the goods that had been stolen by his father. They are not all like Father Pendola, I said. She replied that in so far as Father Pendola was concerned there had been some fine stories about him. Ever since the Pope had reconstituted the Company of Jesus, he had done his utmost to obtain its establishment in Venice. Since his new Institute for the Converted was not prospering, he had tried to obtain by agreement with the few remaining sisters and with the due approval of his superiors permission to lay out the income for a college of novices. However, the government seemed reluctant to favour this idea and even the advocate Ormenta, who had done so, was said to have been pleased.

From this report I could understand all the manoeuvres in that affair and how those good priests, the original founders of the Institute, had been only obedient puppets in the hands of Father Pendola. But even for him the time of rejoicing was a short one; for he too died without seeing the Reverend Fathers established in Venice. Good or evil, in the end all had to go. Father Pendola lacked neither epitaphs, nor satires, nor panegyrics, nor libellous pamphlets. Some wanted to canonize him, others to throw his corpse into the lagoon. He had begged, on dying, to be forgotten as an unworthy servant of the Lord; but surely did not believe that he would be obeyed so implicitly. After a week no one spoke of him any longer and of so much ambition nothing remained save an old and rotting carcase wrapped in a cloak and nailed between four pine boards. They had not even lacquered his coffin, as was usually done for persons of distinction! What ingratitude! But all in all I believe that the Patriarchal Curia was not displeased to have been freed from the perilous assistance of so crafty a zealot of the Glory of God and of his own interests.

It was towards the end of 1820 that, our situation having grown considerably worse and fresh hopes having reached me from Spiro for the settlement of my famous Constantinople credit, I considered going to Venice to have a talk with him. From July the Carbonari had been organizing the Naples revolution, demanding for their country a very liberal constitution; but King Ferdinand had already gone to the Congress of the Allies at Troppau where they did not support even with words the ideas of liberty sent to them from Naples. Down there, they were arming themselves against the storm that was gathering in the north. A trip to the kingdom was, according to Spiro, a necessity for me, in order to look for the death certificate of my father without which the Turkish government did not intend to honour its note. To find witnesses and recall to their minds circumstances long forgotten was not a negotiation that could be carried out by letter. This was my motive for obtaining a passport, but, further, I was entrusted with other duties, delicate enough not to be mentioned aloud. I entrusted my family to Spiro's care, and he even promised to go and visit them during my absence, and set out without regrets, since my considerable knowledge of Neapolitan affairs obliged me to make myself of assistance where I could; and this fact having drawn the attention of others to me, I did not want to seem unworthy of their trust for my own private interests, though perhaps I looked more doubtfully than others at the roseate illusions of that time.

At Venice, as you may well believe, I saw the Pisana and remained in wonder at her. I had looked at myself from time to time in the mirror and knew that my forty-five years could easily be read in my face; she, on the other hand, seemed to me younger than when I had last seen her; a slightly increased plumpness of her features added sweetness to her expression of kindness, but there were always the same melting and voluptuous eyes, the lovely fresh oval of her face and her springing gait. She had much to do to accommodate herself to the claustral frigidity of Clara and almost as much in explaining to me that they were living together like a pair of saints, but I still saw my old Pisana, and enough! . . . If I had not been married! . . . I marvelled the more at her excellent health since they both had, so to speak, to gain their bread by the work of their hands, since the few quattrini that slipped unwillingly from the clawlike hands of old Navagero were not enough to pay the doctors' bills and buy medicine. He, in the short visit I paid him, praised his wife to the skies but, I believe, did not look on me with much favour because of his great fear that I would carry her off with me.

'Signor Carlo,' he said, 'I believe that if my nurse were taken from me, I should not live another day.'

'Eh, old fellow,' the Pisana answered, 'you know well enough that we women love those who are sick even better than our lovers.'

The sick man clasped first her hand and then mine; and I rose to leave him, promising that very soon, when I passed through Venice again, we would meet. But at our leave taking the Pisana remained cold and reserved, as befitted a saint.

The evening before I left I saw in the Piazza the Colonel Partistagno with his wife and rumour was for once justified; his Baroness really did look like a horse, so long were her arms, her legs and her face. None the less, Raimondo Venchieredo was laying siege to her. He did not see me, since I had withdrawn into the quietest corner of the Café Suttil to read my papers carefully. He had greatly aged and was livid and ugly as a vicious libertine, nor do I believe that he was very active since both his father and Ormenta had had the joy of going on half pay. These two old wrecks were ending their deceitful and thievish lives badly enough; but the advocate was in the slightly better case since his son was then in Rome, they said, on a diplomatic mission and he expected great things of it. Certainly I wasted no tears at leaving scum like this behind me in Venice; but it pained me to see, before leaving, that Aglaura was suffering even more from weakness and melancholy. Poor woman! Who could then have recognized the handsome young sailor who had accompanied me from Padua to Milan in the days of the Cisalpina!

CHAPTER XX

Poor Adriatic! When will you see again the glories of the Roman fleets of Brindisi, the Liburnian longships and the galleys of Venice? Today your surges beat, wild and stormy, upon two almost deserted coasts and the marshy lowlands of Puglia face the depopulated mountains of Albania. Venice, a tavern, and Trieste, a shop, are not enough to console your shores for their desolation and the dawn that every day smoothes down your white-maned billows, searches vainly along your shores for aught save ruins and memories.

When we weighed anchor at Malamocco the weather was quiet and serene. It seemed as if winter did not exist, especially on the high seas where the bareness of the trees and the whiteness of the snows could no longer attest the age of the year. The warm breath of the west wind jested with the wave caps and wafted to arid Dalmatia the sighs and memories of sister Africa. Where are now Salona, refuge of Diocletian, or Hippo, episcopal seat of Augustine? . . . Memories, memories, always memories across those waves ever restless and unchanging, of those gentle breezes always sweet and perfumed, over that land eternally insatiable and fecund. The Orient has produced over long ages a civilization that decays in folly; the North has for three hundred years behaved with the infantile pride of one who thinks himself full grown and is perhaps not yet born. Italy has twice surpassed the Orient and forestalled the North, twice was queen and mistress of the world, a miracle of fruitfulness, of power and of disaster. The fires still rage deep within her, despite the elegies of Lamartine or the lack of faith of the pessimists; one day she will overtake those who stand but a pace before her and believe they have advanced a thousand miles. One pace, one pace; no more, I assure you; yet it is a long pace to take.

In the latitudes of Ancona the scirocco began to annoy us and to bar our path. The Chioggia tub stood up to it well, but the wind was too much for our sails and we had to reef. Casting anchor at one place and another, we needed a month to reach Manfredonia, where I had to disembark. When I reached Molfetta from there it was already February 1st and the provincial militia was hurrying to the confines of the Abruzzi to join with General Pepe against the foreign invasion of their land. But the main body of the enemy was waiting on the Roman road and the regular army opposing them under the command of Carascosa was bivouacking on the western coast between Gaeta and the Appenines. My own affairs I settled in a few days. The old priest was dead, but had inscribed my father's name in the register of deaths for 1799. I obtained the death certificate in due form and hastened to the camp of General Pepe according to my instructions.

I was received courteously by the young General who had the greatest confidence in his swarms of volunteers and proposed to fight bravely with them against any diversion which the enemy might make along this coast. It was no longer to be considered that Nugent would fall upon him with the whole army; so, still trusting greatly in the Papal levies, he planned to reinforce his position by taking up a stand at Rieti in the Roman States. He was occupied with this daring plan when I was announced, and handed him my letters of recommendation. He received me very kindly, spoke of his hopes and said that, at the worst, the return of the king must settle everything without foreign intervention. Then on my side I told him what I had been commissioned, which pleased him greatly. He said he would consider it when the enemy, if they did not parley, would have come to blows with him. He would then, he hoped, throw them back behind the Po. He also said that there was a Milanese gentleman in the camp, charged with similar proposals, and that he would make me acquainted with him.

We met in fact at table, and I was somewhat disconcerted to recognize him as one of the most frequent visitors at the assemblies of the Migliana household; such a choice being in no way to my taste. The gentleman spoke little, looked around and muttered a good deal, as indeed had been the usual custom in the Countess' house. He remained only one day more and then, at the moment of the greatest danger, disappeared and we no longer had sight or sound of him, save that he was seen a few days afterwards in Rome with young Doctor Ormenta, to whom he said he had been recommended solely in order to obtain a free pass back to Lombardy. Many believed him, but not I; indeed, he did not figure any too worthily in the trials of the next few years and although he knew little, he made good use of that little to save his own skin and leave his companions in the lurch.

It was reported suddenly after lunch that a squadron of Uhlans had passed by the evening before and peasants flying from the open fields said that the whole army was behind them. The very clever plan of the Imperial Generals was then clear to our leader, namely, to feint at Naples by the Capua road, thus drawing away the principal forces of the defence, and then to approach instead by the badly defended passes of the Abruzzi. However, there was some reason to suppose that these peasants' tales were, as always, exaggerations and that they had multiplied into thousands the few companies of scouts or foragers who were intent on some reconnaissance. We had hoped to concentrate behind Rieti the guards placed here and there, and at least to give time to Carascosa to intervene from his side between Naples and the enemy with Pepe's militia at their back. Since the General wanted to send immediately to Rieti, I and some young Sicilians offered our services. He thanked us, gave us an escort of horsemen and told us to get as much information as possible in the shortest space of time, Meanwhile, he would detach messengers to go to all the commanders and tell them to draw back with their men on to the road from Rieti to Aquila.

What we had feared turned out to be only too true. Nugent pressed on the confines of the Abruzzi with his whole army and a large body of cavalry threatened the very important position of Rieti. Pepe was informed within a couple of hours but it was already too late for him to take measures in so great a crisis. He had only time to rally his forces for the greater danger. Already the Imperial horse had begun the assault. The volunteers, armed with carbines, resisted the shock of the charge badly; the countryside was ravaged, the roads were running with blood, terror grew rapidly at the vast number of the assailants and the lack of means of defence. There was no artillery, the horsemen did not amount in all, I believe, to more than four hundred, while the rest of the troops were dispersed in various positions. After two hours Rieti was lost and Pepe compelled to retreat. But when he had rallied his men and obtained reinforcements it was clear that Rieti was the key position and that, once it was lost, no other hope remained. A council of war met, which considered it impossible to re-take the central square in face of the guns already assembled there in considerable numbers by the Imperial forces. None the less, the General insisted on the bold but necessary decision. He shouted that whoever was willing should follow him, but that he would not abandon the confines of the Abruzzi without having made a last effort to take Rieti. His honour, his duty, commanded it. To this desperate appeal a number of the bravest volunteers hastened to offer him their support, myself and the young Sicilians among the first.

The thought of my wife, of my children, only flashed for an instant into my mind and that only to persuade me that the duty of a father is to leave behind him a good and brave example. You will agree with me that this was not so bad for a Cordovado organist. Death at that moment seemed to me so beautiful and glorious as to crown a life even longer than mine and even more filled with sorrows and misfortunes. In the long years that I have passed through there have been lacking, it is true, many occasions to live well, but those of dying better have not been so rare; this too is a comfort, to be able to leave this world without regret.

Our assault was sudden and violent, but unavailing because of the small number of the assailants; the cannon thundered and caused terrible havoc in our ranks. Of the brave Sicilians only one remained alive and he was taken prisoner at the howitzer's mouth. We rallied for a second assault, but most of us had lost heart; we were met by a hail of bullets, the ranks broke, the volunteers scattered and a considerable number of dead and wounded were left on the field, trodden under by the enemy cavalry that was ravaging far and wide. The General had time to take refuge, almost alone, at Aquila which was the headquarters of the rest of the army, completely discouraged by the first disaster and the unsuccessful action at Rieti. As for me, seriously wounded in the shoulder, I tried every means to stay concealed and drag myself into the bushes, but some scouts found me and when it was discovered that I was not a Neapolitan I was taken to their headquarters for interrogation. Thus, advancing with the Imperial army, I had first-hand knowledge of the rout of Aquila and the defeat at Antrodoco.

In March I was taken to Naples, conveniently lodged in the Castel Sant'Elmo, and consigned to a military tribunal to decide on the nature of my crime. For the fact that I had been fighting as a volunteer for a constitutional government that was not my own, was considered to be high treason. Since my wound had now healed, one fine morning they read to me my sentence of death. I had written nothing of all this home since, according to my ideas, it is always good to postpone news of irreparable misfortune; I therefore disposed myself to die with the greater resignation, and was only greatly annoyed that I should not be able to witness the end of this last sad chapter of history. They came very courteously to offer me mercy if I agreed to tell them who had sent me and why I had come, but to these most indiscreet demands my father's death certificate dated at Molfetta and found upon my person was sufficient answer. I therefore replied that I had come for no other purpose and that, having broken my journey to greet General Pepe, my evil destiny had drawn this unpleasant incident upon me. But it was as if I had never spoken, though I took advantage of the occasion to ask these polite gentlemen if they would send my family the death certificate together with my own in order, if nothing else, to help them to overcome the somewhat niggardly scruples of the Sublime Porte.

These gentlemen smiled ironically at my speech, perhaps thinking that I had said all this to prove myself mad; but I replied with the sweetest smile imaginable that they should do me the honour of believing in my sanity and again implored them to do me this favour. I gave one of them the addresses of Spiro Apostulos at Venice and of Acquilina Provedoni Altoviti at Cordovado in the Friuli. At that they became convinced that I was serious and promised that my wishes should be carried out. I also asked them when I should be taken from the prison for the ceremony since I had been rotting there for three months and it seemed to me a good bargain to give my life for a mouthful of fresh air. When I learnt that the execution was fixed for two days later and that it would take place in the castle moat I was somewhat annoyed. To have to die in Naples without being able to see it again! You will agree with me that that was a trifle hard.

None the less, once they had gone, I consoled myself as best I could. I said to myself that I must not waste these last days in vain and frivolous hopes and that the best thing for me was to take death seriously and give an example of greatness to the executioners at least. Good examples speak with the mouths of all and are always of value, and the executioner often does greater harm by his words than any good he may have done by his trade.

The next day, after having slept with, I confess, a certain restlessness, I heard footsteps approaching in the corridor that were certainly neither those of the guards nor of the gaolers. Therefore when the door was opened I expected to see either the priest or some servant of the executioner coming to shave my head or measure my neck. Nothing of the sort. Three tall figures entered, dressed in funereal black, one of whom took a paper from under his arm, examined it slowly and began to read in a formal and nasal voice. I seemed to be listening to Fulgenzio reading the lesson for the day and the recollection gave me no pleasure. None the less, I was so convinced that I would have to die the day after tomorrow and was so occupied in observing the three sombre figures that I paid no attention to what they were saying. Only the word 'pardon' caught my attention.

'What?' I cried, all astonishment.

'Therefore the death penalty is commuted to forced labour for life to be served in the Ponza penitentiary,' continued the nasal spokesman of the Signor Chancellor.

I then understood what it was all about and do not know if I was very pleased since between death and the penitentiary I have always seen very little difference. Indeed, during the next few days I had plenty of opportunity of convincing myself that if there were any advantage it was all on the side of the gallows. On the island of Ponza and especially in the dungeon where the free arbiter of my human liberty was confined, I could not say that the comforts of life were very abundant: a long narrow room, furnished with wooden benches on which to sleep, water and bean soup and a very numerous company of Neapolitan thieves and Calabrian bandits, with legions of vermin of every type and quality into the bargain, most of which even Job himself had not to suffer lying on his dunghill. Whether it were the effect of what we ate or of the scarcity of the Pythagorean elements, the fact was that we suffered from hunger; the guards told us that the air of Ponza was fattening, but I found that the beans made me thin and it would have been ill for me if I had stayed there more than a month. I do not know how the daughter or the grandson of Augustus could have endured a ten-year residence, but probably they were nourished by something more succulent than beans. It was fortunate, I say, that I remained there for not more than a month; but they sent me to Gaeta where, although I had better company and was better fed, my sight began to suffer.

I had a little cage all to myself, all white mortar, that looked out over the sea, whence the sun shining in the sky and reflected in the water sent such a glare within that it hurt my eyes. I made request after request, but all in vain. Perhaps they considered it permissible to deprive of his sight a man to whom they had made a present of his life, but I do not understand why such a privilege had not been mentioned in the act of pardon. In three months I became almost blind; I saw things blue, green, red, but never their normal colour and day by day lost more of my sense of proportion so that sometimes my little cell seemed to me a boundless salon and my hand an elephant's foot. The gaolers seemed to me rhinoceroses.

In the fourth month I began to see my little piece of the world as through a mist, in the fifth a great darkness began to fall on me and of the colours that I had seen before nothing remained but a gloomy red, a mingling of dust and blood. Then came an order to transfer me to the Castel Sant'Elmo at Naples and the two usual registrars returned to read the usual rigmarole.

I was pardoned the rest of my sentence! Wonderful! If I could no longer see the world in its true colours, I could at least walk in it and smell it at my ease! . . . I would meet again my wife, my sons and go to my own country! . . . But not so fast with these dreams! . . . I was pardoned, yes, but banished from Italy; and you may believe that, banished from Italy, neither France nor Spain would be disposed to open their arms to me. What sort of pardon was this that sent a poor blind man to beg for alms? God alone could say! However, I had the comfort of knowing that my pardon was due to the intercession of the Princess Santacroce and that I had been granted permission to visit her before leaving the port of Naples.

The Princess must have aged considerably, but she still kept her kindly manner and the perpetual youth of woman. She welcomed me very kindly and though I could not see her, I could have sworn that she still had the thirty years she had had at the time of the Parthenopean Republic. She told me that she had tried to intercede for me, both to have me pardoned my death sentence and to obtain my liberation, but had not been successful earlier. Moreover, she confessed that there was another person to whom I owed even more than to her, and that I knew that person very well, but before agreeing to make herself known to me she wanted to be assured of the state of my health and whether my sight had suffered as much as they had said. I do not know whom I expected that unknown and merciful person to be, but I was impatient to see her as well as I could.

'Princess,' I said, 'the clear light of my eyes I have left at Capua and am now condemned to live for ever in a perpetual dusk! . . . The features of the persons I love are hidden from me for ever and only in imagination can I enjoy your serene and amiable features!'

I sensed that the Princess smiled sadly, as one who believed it an advantage not to be seen.

'Since that is so,' she said, opening a door that gave on to a smaller room, 'you may come in, Signora Pisana. The Signor Carlo has real need of you.'

However much my heart may have told me who it was, I believe that at that moment I was nearly raving. The Pisana was my good angel. I had found her everywhere whenever destiny seemed to have abandoned me in my greatest need, the victor in my favour of destiny itself. She rushed into my arms, but drew back when I was about to clasp her to my heart. She then took my hands and contented herself with giving me one of her gloves to kiss. At that moment, I forgot everything; my soul felt only that kiss.

'Carlo,' she said in a voice broken with emotion. 'I came to

Naples seven months ago, with the permission, indeed at the request, of your wife. The Princess had written in great urgency to Venice to know if a certain Carlo Altoviti who had been accused of high treason in the Castel Sant'Elmo was the same whom she had known twenty years before. She wrote to me, not knowing any of your family. You can imagine what I felt at the news since I had been waiting in vain for three months for word from you and was greatly afraid that you had got involved either voluntarily or by chance in the Neapolitan revolution! . . . I wanted to leave at once, but lack of means held me back.

So I took the matter up with your kinsman, explaining to him that I might be able to do much for you through some persons of influence who I had once known in Naples. He wanted to come with me but his wife, your sister, had been failing in health and he was forced to stay behind. So he gave me money for the journey, as you know that we are always short, but before leaving I asked another favour of him: I wanted him to go to your wife, telling her everything and getting her permission to do what I could for you. Acquilina, poor thing, was desperate with worry, but what could she do? Hemmed in by poverty, with two young boys to look after and an almost helpless brother, she none the less wanted to leave everything and come and suffer and die with you. Your kinsman dissuaded her, pointing out to her that her journey could do you no good while her remaining where she was would be of great benefit to the children. She resigned herself and was very happy to learn that I had offered to try every means to save you, and that I had every confidence in the important patronage that I could employ. I came here then and your pardon you owe entirely to the gracious intercession of the Princess; but since God has wished to afflict you with another misfortune that it is not in her power to lessen, here am I, proud of the trust that your wife has reposed in me. I will be your friend, your guide if you will allow me, and in any case your nurse!'

'Pisana, you are too modest,' the Princess broke in. 'Your intercession has done at least as much as mine here in Naples. If I have been able to influence wills, you have known how to convince hearts.'

'Both of you are my dear protectresses!' I exclaimed. 'My life will not be long enough to prove my gratitude, in words if in nothing else.'

'Don't let us waste time in compliments,' said the Princess. 'Now we must turn to something more useful. Tomorrow you must leave for a long journey and we must take care that you lack nothing for it.'

Next day I left without regret those enchanted shores of Naples which had twice proved fatal for me; I could not salute them with my eyes, but my heart measured with its beats a mournful hymn of departure. I knew that I should never see them again and if I had not died for them, they remained as if dead for me.

The following month I was in London. England was the only country where I was permitted to live at that time; but our conditions were such that more often than not we were forced to endure the most painful privations. The high cost of food, the expensive rents, my eye trouble that grew steadily worse, the poverty that drew closer to us day by day with no hope of escaping it in any way: all combined to torment us in the present and make us fear a future still more disastrous. The Pisana, poor thing, had become neither more nor less than a Sister of Charity. She worked for me day and night, and studied English in the hope later on of being able to give lessons in Italian and so provide for my support. But none the less, we spent more than we earned and, despite the doctors and their remedies, I had become completely blind. Just at the moment when we were expecting some help from Venice, Aglaura wrote that she could send us very little since Spiro with his two sons and all his fortune had set sail for Greece at the first cry of rebellion raised by the men of Maina. She herself believed it her duty to encourage him, but because of her uncertain health she had not been able to accompany him and had remained in Venice content, in her poverty and sorrow, to believe that all these sacrifices were useful and necessary to the holy cause of a great and oppressed people.

Though I agreed with her and my kinsman in their greatness of spirit, the last hope of obtaining any assistance from this source had now disappeared. As to the credit at the Porte, this was not even mentioned now that Spiro had declared war on it with his compatriots. It remained to apply to Cordovado, but here some tact was required and we had to tell more lies than truth in describing our needs. Acquilina and Bruto would have drained the blood from their veins to help us; but just in order to prevent their depriving themselves and my sons, we had taken care not to tell them anything but good news. So they knew nothing of our extreme poverty and my blindness and to give an honest appearance to the departure of the Pisana and to my writing, which was as bad as might be expected from a blind man forcing himself to write, we gave them to understand that I was very busy and she very usefully employed with a great family of quality as governess, and was not eager to return, since she knew that she was more of a burden than a help to her husband now that Clara was looking after him.

Meanwhile the Pisana tried every possible means to earn something by her embroidery and although at first she had not wanted to live in the same house as I did, she consented to do so as my affliction grew worse and I had great need of her. We lived as brother and sister, unmindful of that time when we had been bound by sweeter bonds and if I thoughtlessly recalled it, the Pisana would immediately treat it as a joke or change the subject.

However, all our hopes were disappointed. The Pisana had learnt English at incredible speed and already spoke it fairly correctly; but the expected lessons did not mature and despite all her efforts she only found the sons of some petty merchant to whom to teach Italian and French. She then tried to help us by doing lace work, in which the Venetian girls of that time were past masters, but although she earned a good deal by this, she could not keep it up for long. I spent long hours in thanking her for all that she was doing for me and I do not believe that I ever suffered more cruelly than then in accepting sacrifices that cost so much for the preservation of a life so pointless as mine. The Pisana used to laugh at my fine speeches of devotion and gratitude and tried to persuade me that what seemed to me to cost her so much did, in fact, cost her very little trouble. But from the sound of her voice and the thinness of the hand that I pressed now and again, I was well aware that work and hardship were wasting her away. I, however, grew fat as a horse always kept in its stall and that was not the least of my troubles. I feared to be thought insensitive to all these proofs of heroic friendship granted me.

Friendship! I used to spin much on this word, as we Venetians say, and it seemed to me impossible that the Pisana would be capable of remaining within the limits of this moderate sentiment. I do not know if I feared, or if I flattered myself, that the memory of the past alone had merit for the sacrifices of the present. But she mocked me so gently when I touched on some distant allusion, that I was ashamed of my suspicions as born of too much pride in myself or lack of trust in the disinterested heroism of that amazing woman. Furthermore, the continual and fervent talks which she was always ready to start about Acquilina, my sons and the happiness I should experience in having them in my arms again, were enough to dissuade me from that opinion. It seemed that the Pisana of earlier times must be dead and buried for me.

So the months passed without differentiation for me of day or night. I had completely lost hope of recovering my sight and never moved from my room save on Sundays when I went for a short walk on the Pisana's arm. She wearied herself beyond measure, however much she wanted me to think otherwise, and often remained away for whole mornings to get, if I were to believe her, a breath of air or to run from house to house for the numerous lessons that she said she had. In fact, I imagined that she had found work in some shop, nor could I possibly have imagined what I later discovered.

'Pisana,' I once asked her. 'Today is Sunday. Why haven't you got on your silk dress?' I knew it by its rustle.

She replied that she had sent it to be mended; but I knew that she had deprived herself of it to get some money, for a neighbour had told me she had helped her to sell it.

Another day it was her shawl that was missing and I noticed it, because, being cold, I could hear her teeth chattering. She assured me that she had it on and made me feel a piece of wool that she said was the shawl. But I knew from long habit the soft texture of that cashmere and was not deceived by a merino cloak. The shawl had made the same voyage as the silk dress. Sometimes I was consoled for being blind in that I had not to suffer the sight of so many miseries, forgetting that my misfortune was the main cause of them. I was almost in despair at knowing myself so useless that I had to owe my daily bread to the wonderful pity of a woman.

Acquilina, despite our protestations of comfort, sent as much money as she could, but it was a mere drop of water in our ocean of needs. She often wrote that she was putting a little aside every day in order to come to me and that she had done much in Venice to obtain me permission to return to my country. I shook my head, because hope had long left my heart, but the Pisana reproved me, saying that I was foolish to become discouraged and that we were fortunate to be able to live honestly in face of so many difficulties. Sometimes in scolding me for my weakness of spirit she would fall back into the sharp and malicious humour of earlier times, but it was only a moment before she was kind and patient once more, as if either her temperament had completely changed or she forced herself to be as she was. Indeed, there are sons who cost their mothers much, lovers who owe all to their loved ones and husbands who have had from their wives the greatest proofs of affection, but a man who owed a greater debt of gratitude than I to the Pisana would not, I believe, be easy to find. Neither mother, nor lover, nor wife could have done more for the object of her love.

You can imagine how a poor blind man and a woman brought up to all the comforts of the leisured Venetian nobility could live in that vast and busy whirlpool of London. The political exiles were not too well looked upon, nor had fashion made them a curious sort of menagerie animal. They made us pay even for the water we drank and save for the meagre aid sent us from home, the Pisana had to provide everything. But what were the three or four hundred ducats a year from Venice or Cordovado in London? . . . Poverty! Especially in view of my infirmity that the Pisana was always seeking to cure by consultations with the most famous doctors, although I, having lost hope in any help from medical skill, reproved her for it as for a completely useless luxury.

At the beginning of the second year of our exile, she fell seriously ill. What were then the torments, the desperation of the poor blind man I can scarcely describe to you since I am still astonished that I survived them. What was worse, I had to suppress all my feelings so as not to increase her cares with my frenzies; but she tried to lessen my hidden grief with the most tactful consolations that could be imagined. She felt that she was on the brink of death and yet talked of convalescence; she had the fires of a mortal fever in her veins and yet was sympathetic with my troubles as if her own were not worthy of mention. She was always planning to go out the next week, discussed the little credits she had in this place or that in order to meet the increased expenses and the loss of income, and in the meantime tried everything to make me forget her illness or persuade me that she believed in a rapid recovery. None the less, I would pass nights and days at her bedside, feeling her pulse every few moments and listening to her heavy and laboured breathing.

What would I not have given for a flash of light to be able to see her features for a moment to assure myself of how much I should believe of her mercifully false words! With what dismay did I follow the doctor down to the landing imploring and entreating him to tell me the truth! But more than once I suspected that she followed me to prevent him from disobeying her instructions and telling me the whole truth about the danger of her condition! . . . Later, when I refused to believe her protestations, she had the courage to get angry and demand that I should believe her and not martyr myself with imaginary fears. But I was not deceived by these tricks. My heart warned me of the misfortune that threatened us and the medicines that the doctor ordered were not those suitable to a minor complaint. We were reduced to the final extremities and I had to sell the bed-linen and our clothing; I would even have sold myself to get her a moment's relief.

God finally had mercy on her and on my great anguish. Her illness, if not vanquished, took a turn for the better, the fever slackened in her exhausted body and her strength began little by little to return. She got up and wanted to sack the servant immediately in order to reduce expenses, and look after the household duties herself. I opposed her as much as I could but the Pisana's will was unshakeable; neither illness nor misfortune, nor orders availed to change her mind. The first days when she went out she would not even let me try to accompany her as I wanted, but grew so angry that I had to give way in this also and let her go alone.

'But, Pisana,' I kept on telling her, 'didn't you say that you must collect some little bills due for your lessons here and there? Let us go, then, and I will accompany you wherever you like.'

'A fine guide!' she replied mockingly. 'A blind man is a fine guide! Really, I should be ridiculous if I showed myself in their houses with you! . . . What would they think? . . . No, no, Carlo! The English are conventional; I tell you once and for all, that I will not let myself be seen unless I go alone.'

Then, still protesting, and in no way persuaded of the truth of what she told me, I had to let her have her way. Her long absences began again and I had to remain behind with anxious heart wondering if she would ever come back. Indeed, she often came home so exhausted that she could not conceal her weakness however much she tried. I reproved her gently, but finally had to remain silent since even the slightest reproof made her so ill-tempered that she nearly went into convulsions. I do not believe it would be possible to imagine a misery greater than mine.

London, as you know, is large, but the mountains remain unmoved and men, travelling around them, meet. So it happened that one morning the Pisana ran into Doctor Lucilio, whom I had supposed to be in London, but had not wished to approach after the coolness he had so unjustly showed me earlier. He met the Pisana who told him all about my troubles and her own and the reason why we were now in London, deprived of everything. It seemed that my situation persuaded him of the falseness of those accusations that he had previously believed to my discredit. Indeed, he came to see me and was more friendly than perhaps he had ever been to me before. It was a delicate way of asking pardon for his long injustice, nor could I expect more from the proud nature of Lucilio. All in all, I was greatly comforted by this meeting and took it as an omen from Providence that our destinies would change for the better. I had every reason to convince myself of this happy opinion because of the improved trend that our affairs appeared to take all of a sudden.

First of all Lucilio carefully examined my eyes and, having told me that they were covered by a cataract, said that within a few months they would be ready for an operation which he had no doubt would be entirely successful. This put new heart into me. What a great gift is sight! No one can truly appreciate it save he who has once lost it. Then the doctor asked me all about myself, my family and how matters stood and, once I had explained everything to him, gave me hope that he would be able to bring Acquilina and my sons to England where he hoped to be able to set me up in some way that would be more useful for the future and less expensive for the present. He had a wide clientele among the aristocracy and could use his influence among them. The remonstrances that had been made in Parliament about the decisions of the Congress of Verona were, I believe, inspired by him.

I wanted to refuse because of the great expense involved, since my purse was far from prepared for it and then, I must confess, I was almost ashamed of showing any great eagerness to have my family about me lest it seem to belittle the devotion of the Pisana. Once when we were alone together for a moment, I conveyed my scruples to the doctor.

'No, no,' he replied sorrowfully. 'Your own people are necessary to you; believe me, they will be of great service to the Countess Pisana also.'

I wanted him to explain this enigma, but he avoided it, saying that caring for a blind man must certainly be a very heavy burden for a lady accustomed to Venetian comfort, and that the help of another woman would considerably lighten it.

'Tell me the truth, Lucilio,' I said. 'Does the Pisana's health too come into your considerations?'

'It does, yes . . . because it could easily be affected.'

'But now, at the moment, you find it good?'

'Can one ever say if health is good or bad? Nature has her own secrets and it is not even given to doctors to guess them. You see, I have grown old in the profession, but only yesterday I left a sick man who seemed to be recovering, yet the same evening I found him dead. These are blows that Nature gives to those who want to pry into and violate her mysterious virginity. Believe me, Carlo, science is still a virgin; up till now, we have only stroked her cheek.'

'Don't you believe even in science? What then do you believe in?'

'I believe in the future of science, that is if some comet or the cooling of the earth's crust does not come to destroy the work of centuries. I believe in the enthusiasm of the soul that, breaking out when it will into social life, will anticipate by some millennium the triumph of science, as the calculating mathematician is sometimes forestalled in his discoveries by the bold hypotheses of a poet!'

'Therefore, Lucilio, you still follow the dream of your youth and believe in rekindling that vast enthusiasm by secret intrigues and obscure machinations . . . ?'

'No, do not condemn even in jest those things that you do not understand. I am not pursuing a phantom; I satisfy a need. Carlo, intrigues are not always secret nor machinations obscure. . . . Touch this scar . . .' and he bared his chest near his throat. 'That I got at Novara. It was useless, but the scar remains.'

'Look what I got at Rieti,' I replied, rolling back my sleeve and showing my arm.

Lucilio threw his arms around my neck with an emotion I would never have expected of him.

'Blessed be those souls,' he said, 'who see the truth and follow it. even when not driven on by some irresistible force! Blessed be those for whom sacrifice has no pleasure, yet they too offer it, noble and voluntary victims. They are the really great!'

'Don't flatter me,' I said. 'I went to Naples, one might say, for my own self-respect and I ought to feel remorse at having sacrificed the interests of my family to my own petty pride.'

'No, I swear to you, you have not sacrificed anything. Your family will rejoin you here. You will see again the lovely light of day and the features of your loved ones. It is true that the sun of London is not that of Venice, but the melancholy of its tints is in perfect accord with the tear-filled eyes of exiles.'

'Can you give me some hope that the Pisana will by then be perfectly well?'

'Perfectly,' replied the doctor with a tremor in his voice.

I trembled all over; I seemed to hear in that word a death sentence, but he went on, speaking with so much calm about the Pisana's illness and the course it was likely to take and the most suitable treatment and the infallible cure, that the memory of that funereal 'perfectly' quite passed out of my mind.

Lucilio did everything he could to be of use; thenceforward thanks to his spontaneous help, we no longer lacked anything and I became ashamed of living in this way on alms, but he said his duties towards his future kinswoman demanded it and he would not forego his right to be of use to her for anything in the world.

'What do you mean?' the Pisana said to him. 'Are you still obsessed with the idea of marrying my sister? Can't you see that she is even older in soul than in body and, above all, a nun to her finger-tips?'

'I am incorrigible,' replied the doctor. 'What I attempted at twenty and did not accomplish, I tried at thirty, at forty, at fifty and I will try again at sixty, which is not so far off. I want my life to be an effort, but a strong, persistent effort; in everything I am made this way, and may others imitate me! It is by hammering that one drives in the nail.'

'But one cannot overcome the obstinacy of a nun.'

'Very well, then, we will speak of it no longer; let us rather talk of the Signora Acquilina and her two children, who should soon be arriving. Have you any news of their journey?'

'I had a letter yesterday from Brussels,' I broke in. 'Bruto is coming with them, wooden leg and all. I really do not know how to thank you for the great expense to which you have been put.'

'Thank me? . . . But surely you know that a hundred pounds means no more to me than writing another prescription? I prolong for a couple of days the aristocratic gout of some noble lord and get enough out of it to enable all of you to travel all over Europe. Do you know Lord Byron, the poet? . . . He wanted to give me ten thousand guineas if I could succeed in lengthening by a single inch his right foot, which is clubbed. Even though I had some pretensions to success, by a certain method of my own, I had no need of money at that time and did not want to waste my time stretching the legs of the House of Lords. I laughed in the great poet's face and told him that they had greater need of me in the hospital.'

'And he?'

'Oh, he revenged himself on me in the neatest sonnet ever written in English. I can assure you that, beneath that tempestuous mask of a Manfred or a Don Juan, a pure flame is hidden that must break forth sooner or later. Byron is a great man; there is more in him than books and verses. He will end his life as a great poet should.'

'God forbid!' I exclaimed. 'Poetry is the realization of all spiritual happiness, the only one that is true and complete . . .'

'Well said,' replied Lucilio, repeating my words in an undertone, while I felt proud of such an honour. 'Poetry is the real happiness of the spirit. Beyond it there are distractions but no content.'

'Am I then a poetess, since I am content?' asked the Pisana in a gay but feeble voice.

'You are Corinna, you are Sappho,' exclaimed Lucilio. 'But you are not satisfied with mouthing odes but create them by your actions. You give poetry its most worthy semblance, action. Achilles and Rinaldo before becoming poets were heroes.'

The Pisana began to laugh but with a sincerity that excluded any suspicion of false modesty.

'I am a very pallid Corinna and a very bony Sappho!' she said, still laughing. 'I seem to have become like an Englishwoman, who resemble mares, but at least I have gained in aristocratic ideas.'

'You have gained in everything,' said Lucilio, growing more and more fervent. 'Your soul shows through the pallor of your face; it rejuvenates you and prevents you from ever becoming old! . . . Whoever swore you were only twenty-five would surely be believed.'

'Yes, indeed, now that the poor old rector who baptized me is dead. You know it is very melancholy to find one's life more and more encircled and overshadowed by graves! Already the first rank has almost all gone. Now it is we who are in the first rank.'

'But we will not shrink from the ordeal, you may be sure. Neither you nor I nor Carlo have the urge to live on. We have three very different natures, but we are marvellously in accord in this, to be obedient and resigned to the dictates of nature. Even though my own temperament commands me to spend freely and make the most pitiless use of life. I want to suck out of it all its juices, like the wine lees which, once the wine has been pressed, is again pressed to extract the oil.'

'And you have gained something from it?'

'Enough. To have made all my talents bear fruit and to have given a good example to those who come after.'

I nodded in approval. That theory of the good example has always been present in my thoughts and I put more trust in it than in books. The Pisana remarked that in all her doings she had never thought of the glory of finding imitators, but that she was devoted with all her soul to the sentiment that inspired them.

'At least you have not given your own spirit to others to waste it away,' said Lucilio sadly.

I felt for that strong and tenacious spirit that for forty years had nurtured a wound and had scorned to think of healing or of forgetting. It was the boundless pride of one who wishes to feel pain in order to show himself capable of enduring it and to be able to mock at it as a betrayal and a baseness. The doctor, honoured by the dukes and peers of London, had not repudiated the humble sawbones of Fossalta; he did not admit having ever been little but claimed to have always been in some way great, and his iron old age extended its hand to fervent youth, to lift it upward to the reward of all pain, to the unbreakable force of a conscience sure of itself.

In the few days that preceded the arrival of our travellers, the Pisana became more reserved towards me than usual; but from time to time some strange whim of tenderness broke through, only to be followed by a thousand rebuffs as if to prove to me that it was only a whim, almost a joke.

'Poor Carlo!' she said once. 'What would have happened to you if pity had not induced me to give you a little help! It was lucky that the importunities of my aged husband made me long to leave Venice. I have tried to be of some use to you and now you will soon have the joy of embracing your dear ones again!'

She had never spoken to me with such bluntness and showed few traces of generosity in enumerating to me almost all the benefits that I owed solely to her pity. I suffered bitterly and convinced myself that no trace of love remained for me in her soul and that the very heroism of her pity was only a whim or a caprice.

A few days later Acquilina arrived in London with my sons and Bruto Provedoni. At last I could clasp my sons to my heart, kiss their fresh round cheeks and refresh my spirit in the pure sentiments of their youthful hearts. Acquilina, who like a brave and loving mother, had done her best to educate them, had her share in my caresses and I responded eagerly to the friendly greetings of Bruto. But I could not see their faces! . . . Then for the first time I felt rising in me a feeling of foolish rage against fate and it seemed to me that the force of my will should have been sufficient to rekindle the light in my eyes, so intense and burning was it. Lucilio put a little balm on my wound by assuring me that in a short while he would try the operation and so, reserving until then the pleasures of sight, he allowed me to enjoy all the others that my unfortunate condition permitted.

For the whole of that day and the next there were unending questions, demands, recollections of this or that person, of the smallest detail of events however transitory and inconclusive. Of Alfonso Frumier they knew nothing, of Agostino they had said at Venice that he was thirsty for ribbons and decorations and had enough on him to deck a little altar; he had also an abundance of sons, to one of whom he had allotted the future position of Minister, to others those of general, of patriarch, of Pope. His Excellency Navagero was much as usual, neither dead nor alive, always with Clara at his bedside, when it was not time to repeat the Hours or her evening prayer. Then, even had he been dying she would have done nothing. Old Venchieredo had died at last, leaving to his son an inheritance so involved that he, with his headstrong and thoughtless nature, had not the slightest hope of untangling it. It was rumoured that Raimondo might have married the eldest daughter of Alfonso Frumier who, however, had been unwilling to be liberal about the dowry. For the rest, things were much as usual; the country was indifferent, some persons occupied in amusing themselves, others allured by easy money; there was no commerce, no life. The political trials had caused great uneasiness in the noble families, but the common people had paid no attention to them. They still complained about conscription, but their trouble had been somewhat blunted by habit, especially since to become a soldier meant to eat well and smoke excellent cigars at the expense of those who muddled along with their polenta and only smoked with streaming eyes around the chimney place.

'And at Cordovado?' I asked.

At Cordovado there was even less news than elsewhere, if one excepts the madness of the Spaccafumo, who believed that he was being assailed by ghosts and raged about beating to right and left with his hands. This mania of his caused him to fall into the Lemene where one morning they found him drowned. But it was believed that the numerous glasses of brandy that he had swallowed were at least as much to blame as the ghosts. So ended a man who might have been a hero, if . . . but I must ask your pardon. After that 'if' I would have to relate to you all the whys of our history from the fourteenth century onwards. Better to leave it as it is. The Count Rinaldo had had another section of the Castle of Fratta demolished, and Luciano and Bradamante had buried the Signor Captain without too many tears because of the income of seven hundred lire that they had inherited from him.

I heard a light footfall in the room; it was the Pisana who for some days past had scarcely spoken to me. I felt the lack of her voice, but by remaining reserved towards her I felt I was revenging myself for the time when she had spoken to me so cruelly. Lucilio that day had asked her several questions about her health, to which she had replied in monosyllables and in a voice even weaker than usual.

She went out again, perhaps hurt by my manner. Acquilina followed her leaving Lucilio and me alone.

'Tell me,' began the doctor in a tone that foreboded a serious conversation. 'Tell me what right you have to play the tyrant with the Pisana?'

'So you have noticed?' I replied. 'Then you will also have noticed the unusual coldness she is showing towards me! . . . I know that I am much in her debt and I shall never forget it; I wish my blood were enough to prove my gratitude; I would spill it for her to the last drop. But sometimes I cannot prevent some touch of pride. You know that lately she has been singing all tones to me and saying that it was only to escape her marital importunities that she went to Naples and that I owe all the help of which she has been so generous only to a feeling of pity?'

'Then you suspect she no longer has that love for you that she had earlier?'

'I am certain of it. I am as sure of it as that I am alive. Even though I am blind, I can none the less see. I know the Pisana's nature as well as I know my own and I know she is not capable of submitting herself to certain conditions once some inner uneasiness forces her to violate them. I speak thus frankly to you because you are a physiologist and can sympathize with human weakness, especially when mingled with so great a measure of nobility. I repeat, our living together like brother and sister for these last two years has convinced me that the Pisana has forgotten the past and I do not find it hard to believe her when she says that pity alone is responsible for so many miracles of affection and devotion. In any case, her nature is too extreme to obey any premeditated maxims of continence.'

'Carlo, don't be led away by rash judgements. These unusual temperaments are just those that elude the general rules. Mistrust your judgement, I tell you; the eyes of the body sometimes reason better than those of the soul, and if you could see . . .'

'What need have I to see? . . . Don't you know that I still love her, that I have always loved her? . . . Didn't I tell you the other day the story of my marriage? . . . Only too well has she sworn to make me feel how much I have lost by being excluded from that inmost part of her heart where she had always received me! . . . Only too well is she punishing by her pity a love that has been too docile and too persistent. It is a terrible punishment, a refined cruelty, an added vengeance.'

'Be quiet, Carlo, every word is a sacrilege.'

'A truth, you mean.'

'A sacrilege, I repeat. Do you know what the Pisana was doing for you when I met her, pale, exhausted and in rags in the streets of London?'

'Well . . . what? . . .'

'She was holding out her hand to the passers-by! . . . She was begging, Carlo, she was begging to keep you alive!'

'Heavens! It is not true! It is impossible!'

'So impossible that I was just about to give her some coin or other when . . . How can I tell you what I felt when I recognized her? . . . How can I tell you her dismay . . . and mine?'

'Enough! Enough! For pity's sake Lucilio; I feel as if I am going mad when I look back at what we have been through . . .'

'Yet you would still doubt her love? . . . It is a love without bounds and without comparison, a love which has kept her alive and will be the cause of her death!'

'Have pity on me! . . . Don't say that!'

'I speak as a doctor and I am telling you the truth. She loves you and has forced herself not to reveal it to you. This continual effort, even more than the privations, the sorrows and the vigils, has destroyed her health. . . . Carlo, open your eyes to so much heroism and worship the virtues of a woman whom you should not dare to distrust! . . . Worship, I tell you, this virgin force of nature that exalts the disordered ardours of a soul to the sublimity of a miracle and keeps it there suspended by its own force like an eagle above the clouds.'

I was indeed overwhelmed by the sublimity of that virtue that I could scarcely have dared to hope for from a human soul. Who would have thought the Pisana capable of this modest reserve, of this humble and concealed self-denial and of this holy deception carried so far as almost to seem true, just in order not to disturb the concord of a family created, one might say, by herself? . . . How false had been my judgement on that spirit, changeable perhaps in her lesser feelings, but constant and indomitable in her greater ones as perhaps no other had ever been! . . . The increase of reserve in her manner after the announcement of the imminent arrival of Acquilina, her flashes of tenderness suddenly restrained, her recent melancholy and her voluntary estrangement from me, all combined to persuade me of the truth of what Lucilio had said. For two years I had been mistaken in my judgement, but my very error was a proof of the extraordinary tact and perseverance with which she had kept up her heroic decision.

'Lucilio,' I replied in a voice so moved that I had difficulty in speaking clearly, 'do with me what you will. Tell me, teach me, a way to save her. My life and the lives of all my family would all scarcely be enough to recompense such sacrifices! The least that I can do is to offer her what life still remains to me!'

'Let us think it over, Carlo. I agree with you. The health of all my illustrious clients, believe me, gives me less concern than a single regret, a sigh or a complaint from the Pisana. She has the right to live out her days fully and happily and to die at last from excess of joy.'

'Don't speak of dying, for pity's sake, don't speak of it!'

'Might it not be that for certain souls, rare and privileged, death might be a reward? None the less, let us reason as we would do for others. The only way I can see is to arrange for her to be where there is need for patience and sacrifice. Send her back to her husband; by his bedside she will recover the strength to live and perhaps the air of her own country will assist in the restoration of her health.'

'Send her back to Venice, you say? . . . But why, Lucilio, why? . . . Must I send her away, drive her from me, now that I seem to have no more need of her help?'

'Not at all, you must go back with her. And she must go on living with your family, in that intimacy of love without which natures such as hers cannot exist. When the excess of her spirit finds other activities in which to develop, other miracles to attempt, other deeds to accomplish, the past will lose every torment for her and her unattainable desires will find ease in a sweet and contented melancholy. You will have once again a friend and a magnificent friend.'

'God grant it, Lucilio! Let us leave for Venice to-morrow!'

'You forget two things. The first is that I have promised to give you back your sight; the second is that you have no way of returning to Venice without peril. But while I take it on myself to find you such means, the cataracts will be maturing and I promise you that you will see the pale sun of Christmas.'

'Can't we hasten things? . . . Not for my eyes, Lucilio, but for her, only for her! . . . Perhaps you could try the operation even now?'

'Very fine, Carlo! You would like to be completely blind, so as to pay a great debt of gratitude with your eyes? . . . Be more humble, my friend. Two eyes are not enough; it is better to keep them and you can pay later and pay far more with your glances. You have a credit on Turkey which, supported by private efforts will never get you anything. Would you like me to sell it to some Englishman?' . . . England has now some claim to the good graces of the Ottoman Porte, since it is ships from London, Liverpool and Corfu that are helping the most holy work of martyring poor Greece. England is a loving mother, above all in making others pay her sons what is due to them; in that she is a real treasure. For a credit of a thousand pounds she would have no remorse in setting the four quarters of the world in flames. Leave it to me; let me unravel this skein.'

'You needn't waste words in convincing me of that. I will give you the papers tomorrow. Bruto has them with him; I certainly could not find a better agent.'

'Till tomorrow then. We are agreed. I will look into the matter. A couple of weeks from now the operation; then the usual forty days' rest and you can start for Venice. It will not be difficult to get you a passport.'

The day drew near when Lucilio was to use all the resources of his skill to restore my sight. He did not speak to me again of the Pisana, while she went on avoiding me, however much I tried to placate her with the most tender words. Acquilina was even jealous, but, remembering all that the Pisana had done for me, she had not the heart to complain. Lucilio's silence foreboded nothing good and the rare words of comfort that he gave me I attributed not so much to his sincerity as to his desire to keep me calm for the day of the great experiment. I was happy when I was able to say: it will be the day after tomorrow. My heart beat at the thought that it would be tomorrow and when I could say: it is today, I was seized with such impatience that I thought I should die if I had to endure another twenty-four hours' waiting. Lucilio set about his task with every care. It was a question not only of a patient, but also of a friend; if a miracle could have been expected, it would certainly have been from him and he surely did not lack the trust of his patient. When he said to me: 'It is over', they had already shaded the light from the doors and windows so that the sudden shock should not harm me. None the less, I seemed to see vaguely and indeed did see a faint uncertain gleam and gave such a cry that Bruto and Acquilina, who were supporting me, were shaken. There was a faint cry in reply from the Pisana, who feared that some accident had happened, but Lucilio reassured her, saying banteringly: 'I bet the rascal has already seen something; but I advise you not to remove the bandages that I am putting on his eyes and above all, keep the shutters closed tight. The operation has gone off so well that I foresee that the six weeks of convalescence may be shortened to four.'

'Thank you, thank you, my friend! Hasten it as much as you can!' I exclaimed, covering his hands with kisses.

Even more than having restored my sight, I was thanking him for the hope he had given me of being able to do something for the Pisana earlier than I had thought.

When they had all followed the doctor out of the room to thank him for his great service or perhaps to find out how much they should believe of what he had said in my presence, the Pisana came softly up to me and I felt her warm breath on my cheek.

'Pisana,' I murmured, 'how wonderful was your love and your pity!'

She ran off, brushing against the furniture, and a sob broke from her. My wife, coming in again, met her in the doorway. . . .

'What do you think of our invalid?' she asked her.

'I hope everything will go well,' she replied with a supreme effort. But she could control herself no longer and ran away once more to lock herself in her own room before Acquilina should have time to notice her confusion. Then I understood more than ever the strength and nobility of her soul and from her room, which was on the other side of the house, I seemed to hear her weeping and each sob was like a stab in my breast. For all that day I thought no more of my sight, and those who were looking after me angered and irritated me. There were other things than two stupid eyes! . . .

Lucilio came to see me often, but it was seldom that we were alone and it seemed to me that he avoided any confidences. None the less, I often asked him about the Pisana's health and whether the prospect of returning to Venice had had the good effect that we had hoped. The doctor replied in vague terms without saying yes or no and she, when she came into my room, scarcely opened her mouth; I noticed that my sons were not so noisy as usual, as if her sadness had imposed some restraint on them. When Lucilio brought me the passport obtained through the Austrian Embassy, I asked her if our plan pleased her.

'Ah, my Venice!' she answered. 'You ask if I would like to see it . . . ? After Paradise, that is my only wish.'

'Very well,' I said. 'Doctor, when will you allow me to open the window, throw away these bandages and go?'

'The day after tomorrow,' replied Lucilio, 'but as to making a journey, you will have to wait another day or two; you must not risk exposing yourself suddenly to the midday sun.'

I managed to endure those two days, determined not to delay my departure for a moment once my eyes were completely cured. But the Pisana in the meantime came into my room less than ever and they told me that she spent almost all her time in her own. At last Lucilio came to take the wrappings from my face and remove the tapes that were over my eyes; the windows were still covered and a soft diffused light, like twilight, gently caressed my eyes. If the spectacle of the dawn, that is renewed every twenty-four hours, is so enchanting, you can imagine how wonderful was that dawn that followed a night of almost two years! . . . To find once more those everyday pleasures of which we take so little heed when we have them with us every moment and only appreciate their value when they are denied us; to revive with present use the memory of those feelings that had already begun to fade away like a tradition that with the passing of time has become a fable; to be satiated once more in the contemplation of all that is beautiful and sublime in the world and to interpret from its results on those dear to us a language forgotten by us, are such pleasures that one could almost wish to have been blind in order to reacquire sight. Certainly I think of that moment as among the happiest in my life. But immediately afterwards I had to endure a very painful one.

The Pisana had come too to be present at the final phase of the miracle; after the first sweet shock of the light on my eyes, when I began to distinguish persons and things around me, the first face on which my gaze centred was hers. How well she had merited such a preference! Neither friends, nor relatives, nor children, nor wife, nor even the doctor who had restored my sight deserved so much of my gratitude. But how changed I found her! . . . Pale, transparent as alabaster, with drawn features like one of the sorrowing Madonnas of Fra Angelico, and bowed like one who has borne on her back so heavy a burden that she can no longer rise upright. Her eyes had become extraordinarily large and the upper part shadowed by the eyelids shone through like a light behind a coloured crystal; the bluish hue of melancholy and the red of weeping were blended in the white as in the glowing splendour of an opal. She was an unearthly creature; she seemed of no age. One could only say that she was nearer to Heaven than to earth.

I am weak by nature and have never concealed it. My breast swelled with a deep and sudden anguish and I burst into a flood of tears. They all thought I was weeping for joy; Lucilio alone perhaps thought otherwise. I wept, indeed, because my eyes confirmed the terrible significance I had given to her silence of those past few days. I saw that the Pisana was no longer of this world; Venice, as she herself had said, was only her second wish; her first had been for Paradise.

As this sad thought filled my breast with bitter sobs, she moved away from Acquilina's shoulder, on which she had been leaning, and I saw her stumble from the room. I begged those who remained to leave me with my sorrow, since excess of feeling had exhausted me. Once they had gone, the gusts of weeping seized me again more violently than ever and Lucilio thought it was better to wait until weariness should bring about a truce. Later, when tears and sobs allowed me to speak, what words, what promises, what prayers did I not use to beg him to save for me a life a thousand times more precious than my own! I implored him as devout persons implore God and I had such need of hope that I would have denied reason and overthrown the order of the world to keep at least an illusion of it. The pitiful cunning of hope persuaded me that he who had rekindled for me the torch of light would be able to restore health and life to the Pisana.

'Lucilio,' I exclaimed, 'you can do anything you will. Even as a small child, I always regarded you as a supernatural and almost omnipotent being. You demand of nature the most incredible efforts. Search, study, try; there was never a cause more just, an enterprise more exalted and noble to merit the prodigies of your genius. Save her! In pity, save her!'

'So you have guessed everything,' replied Lucilio after a moment's pause. 'Her soul is no longer with us: her body still lives, but not even I know why. Save her, you tell me, save her! . . . Who can tell if wise nature is not already saving her by gathering her into her womb? . . . Much can be tried against the maladies of the flesh and the blood, but the spirit, Carlo! Where are the physicians who can heal the spirit, where are the instruments that can cut out the cancered part to prolong the life of that which is healthy, when an irresistible force absorbs it little by little into what Dante calls the sea of being? . . . Carlo, you are not a boy, nor a charlatan; you would not wish to be deceived, however much your present weakness endears to you these false and fugitive illusions as against the inexorable reality. I have tried till now to fortify you against every possible contingency; but I hope that you will talk with the Pisana and that her words, her manner, her looks will persuade you better than my reasoning. I do not want to say that we have already reached such a pitch of desperation and of danger. If she could get to Venice and find peace there in the life she knows . . .'

'Tell me the truth, Lucilio, is there any hope? You are not saying this now to comfort and delude me?'

'I am so far from wanting to delude you that up till now I have let you believe the worst. Even now I do not give you much hope, save that which wise nature always allows us until she puts to an end, perhaps also wisely, the mysterious motions of life. Meanwhile, I give you this advice, which may well seem strange to you: spend as much of your time as you can with the Pisana and trust yourself to her example. I promise you that she will end by dissuading you from any action of despair and my trust in her seals the sincerity of all that I have been saying to you.'

'Thank you,' I said, gripping him by the hand. 'Certainly from her cannot come examples, or from you counsels, that are unworthy.'

So ended that conversation, which was indeed memorable for me as it perhaps decided the future course of my whole life. I was still dismayed and perplexed enough; but Lucilio's strength of mind had to some extent restrained me and therefore I was willing to believe him right in trying to bring me closer to the Pisana and to repair the ills involuntarily committed, by adapting my conduct to her wishes and so give her the highest testimony I could of love and devotion. But at first these attempts brought considerable discouragement. The poor Pisana did all that she could to avoid me and it seemed that, feeling herself about to abandon me, she did not want to find a pleasure in my company that would later prove a sharper anguish in the moment of separation.

However, undeterred by her rebuffs and continuing to show her as discreetly as I could my gratitude and deep sorrow at not having shown it before more profoundly, I ended by overcoming that persistent stubbornness and by restoring our former intimacy. What torment it was for me to see reviving in her eyes the flame of life while at the same time watching the continual decline of her strength until her tired and wasted body could scarcely support her! What a terrible spectacle was that joy with which she welcomed my return to my former tenderness and the reckless resignation that made her shrug her shoulders and smile when her future was hinted at! One day I spoke to Lucilio, who had assured me that, if things went on in this way, we should next week be able to risk the journey to Venice. That evening I found myself alone with the Pisana, for Lucilio had taken my wife and sons to see I know not what marvel of London. She was paler, but in better spirits than usual; I hoped always that with her strange temperament, health could revive suddenly in disregard of the common rules of other beings and that the evil would not be irreparable after that rebirth of her gaiety of manner.

'Pisana,' I said to her, 'next month we may be in Venice. Doesn't the mere thought do you good?'

She smiled, raising her eyes, but did not reply.

'Don't you think,' I went on, 'that your native air and the peace that we shall enjoy when we are all quietly united there will end by curing you of your melancholy?'

'My melancholy, Carlo?' she replied. 'What makes you think that I am melancholy? . . . You must have known that I have never had true joy, natural and continuous, only brief flashes, fugitive gleams and nothing more. I have always been a variable creature, but more often silent and frowning. Only now there smiles on me a true period of serenity and peace; I have never before felt so calm and content. I think that I have played my part and I hope for a little applause.'

'Pisana, Pisana, don't talk like that! . . . You deserve far greater applause than we can give you and you shall have it. We shall go back to Venice; there . . .'

'Oh, Carlo, don't talk to me of Venice! My country is far nearer, or more distant if you will, but one gets there by a far more rapid voyage. Up there, up there, Carlo! You see, poor Clara, if nothing else, has made me believe and hope in the mercy of God. I have never managed to get into my head her theory of sin, but for the rest I believe and expect not to be punished too severely for the little evil that, without wishing it, I have committed. The little good that I have been able to do, I have done; it is just that some reward should not be too long delayed; I want to receive it at once and to abandon you for a short time with a smile on my lips and, grant me also that hope, with your forbearance.'

'Can't you see, Pisana, that you are tearing my soul by those words and that you are creating once more that blindness with which in these last few years I have looked at your apparent coldness? . . . Vile, ungrateful assassin that I am, I paid no heed to all your sacrifices and forced myself to believe in your indifference, perhaps in order to settle my account cheaply with you, so that I should not know of your devotion and of the wonderful way in which you showed it to me with that seal of sublime delicacy which you alone know how to place upon your sacrifices and make them appear ordinary actions without merit. Oh, curse me, Pisana! . . . Curse the first moment that you knew me and that has led you to squander as much heroism upon me as would have sufficed to reward the virtue of a saint or the pains of a martyr! . . . Curse my stupid pride, my ungenerous suspicion and the vile egoism in which I have lived for these two years. . . May the penalty of so much infamy fall upon my head! I have deserved it, I implore it, I desire it! Until I shall have paid with tears of blood for all my crimes against you, all the pain, all the humiliation I have caused you, I will no longer have either peace or the courage to lift up my head and call myself a man! . . .'

'Are you raving, Carlo? . . . What are you doing now, what are you thinking? Do you no longer know the Pisana, or do you think that she is still pretending in order to be thought contented or to rid herself of the complaints of others? . . . No, Carlo, I swear to you! . . . The question of living or dying in no way comes into my happiness. I do not conceal from you that I think my last hour to be very near; but am I the less happy for that? . . . Quite the opposite, Carlo. Your tenderness, your trust were the final blessing I was waiting for; and you have given them back to me. I bless you for it! . . . One single word of gratitude from you, one single loving glance, would pay for two lives even longer than mine and filled threefold with privations and sacrifices! . . . You have suspected me, you say, you have imposed on me pain and suffering? . . . But when, Carlo, when? I sinned, and you pardoned me; I abandoned you and you never uttered a complaint; I returned to you and you welcomed me with open arms and with honey on your lips! . . . You are the most noble, most trusting and generous being that ever was. . . If I had eternity before me to be passed in continual drudgery, not even consoled by your presence, only to spare you a tear, a single sigh, I would not hesitate a moment. I would resign myself, joyful and content, at the mere thought that all my days, all my affections, would be consecrated to your good. You alone, Carlo, have not cast out my soul. From your love alone, so noble and constant, I have drawn the courage to look into my heart and say: "I cannot be so despicable if such a heart continues to love me". Oh Carlo, forgive me! . . . Forgive me in pity if I have not loved you as you deserved.'

'Pisana, your words shame me; I have not the heart to look you in the face and to ask your forgiveness! . . . How can I remember without anguish all those moments in which one word of mine of love, one meek and humble glance of mine, would have, if not rewarded, at least convinced you of my gratitude? Instead I surrounded myself with evil suspicions and punished with reserve and silence the most noble and perhaps most costly sacrifice that a woman has ever made, that . . . yes, I want to say it, Pisana, that of your love! . . . And if I believed that you no longer loved me, why then did I treat you like a slave, dragging you through the world bound miserably to my miserable state? . . . Oh yes, Pisana! I was a vile tyrant and a merciless executioner! . . .'

'And I repeat to you that either you do not remember well or after so many years you still do not know the Pisana. Don't you understand that all those things that you call pain, suffering and sacrifice were ineffable pleasures to me, filled with a bliss the sweeter as it was more noble and sublime? Don't you understand that my strange and variable nature perhaps led me to tire of the more common pleasures and to search in another sphere, even at the risk of destroying myself, delights that had no comparison in my past life? Did you not sense the first symptom of that, I would almost call it madness, in my incredible and tyrannical caprice of marrying you to Acquilina? . . . I entreat you on my knees, Carlo! . . . Forgive me for having loved you in my way, for having sacrificed you to an incomprehensible whim, for having sought in your life for nothing more than an occasion to satisfy my fantasies! . . . You could not understand me, you should have hated me, and instead you bore with me! . . . When in these last years I found such sweetness in helping you and in hiding my love from you, giving you to understand that only pity and necessity moved me, should I not have known that I was tormenting you by my behaviour and that I was taking the greatest value from the few services I was able to render you? . . . Notwithstanding, I went on making a parade of my cruel delicacy and persisted in that silence of virtuous vanity in which your marriage had been only the first step. Can't you understand that in all this I sought my own pleasure first of all and at any cost? You see, you see, Carlo, how bad and selfish I was? Should I not have done better to trust myself to your generosity, so much greater and more tried than mine, and say to you: "I have erred, Carlo, I have erred from wilfulness and from caprice." But I mistrusted you, Carlo! I confess it with all the humility of a true penitent! . . . Your great and noble love did not deserve so sorry a reward; but a sincere confession will once more reinstate me in your eyes. You will still love me, yes, you will always love me, and my memory, sanctified by death, will live eternally amongst your sweetest and saddest thoughts.'

'Death? Do not say that word or I, not content merely to follow you, will precede you.'

'Carlo, Carlo, for pity's sake do not lay on my heart so great a burden of remorse! Deliver these last days of mine from the only fear that might embitter them. . . . Look, learn from me. . . . A hundred times I could have, should have, killed myself . . . and instead . . . I am dying! . . .'

'No, you must not die. . . . Pisana, Pisana, I swear you must not die!'

'It is true; I shall not really die if you live, if you honour my memory by making of value these few sacrifices that, however badly, I have made for you! . . . You will think of Acquilina, whom I first of all entrusted to you, of the sons that you have engendered and to whom you are bound by sacred and inviolable duties, to your country, to my country, Carlo, for which my heart has always beaten and for which, wherever the will of God may take me, I will not cease to pray and to hope! . . .

'Carlo, Carlo, I entreat you! Live so that your life will be worthy of being imitated by those who come after you. Then I shall at least be able to say in dying that my advice left an inheritance of great and noble actions! . . . Nothing else I ask of you, nothing else I desire, since the moment of my departure will be at the same time the happiest of my life. For the rest, all the little good that I have been able to do, I have tried to do well: I die content, I die smiling, because I go to wait for you! . . .'

'Here I am, here I am, Pisana. You shall not wait a single moment! I am here with you!'

'And if I told you that those would be the only hard words I have ever heard from you and that they humiliate me in my own eyes and take from me that swift reward with which I was leaving, happy and content? . . . Oh, Carlo, if you still love me, you would not want to see me die with fear and remorse! You know that when I want a thing, I want it, I lay claim to it, at all costs. Well, then, I do not want my death, so easy and sweet for me, to become the despair of a whole family nor to take from a whole country and from humanity all the good that you could, you must, still do . . . Carlo, are you strong and brave? Have you faith in virtue and justice? Swear to me, then, that you will not be base, that you will not abandon your post, that, miserable or happy, accompanied or alone, you will fight for virtue and for justice to the very end!'

'Pisana, what are you asking me? How shall I believe in virtue and in justice when I shall not have you at my side and when a life like yours receives so miserable a reward?'

'A life like mine is so enviable that any man would be blessed if he could have one like it! A life that begins with love and ends with forgiveness, with peace, with hope to raise itself to a love that has no end, so much more than I have deserved that I thank God as for a gracious gift. One happiness alone I still lack, but it is one that I am sure to obtain since it is in your power to concede it to me. Swear to me, Carlo, swear to me what I have asked of you. It is impossible that you should deny me the one favour that I ask of you, imploring you by all that you hold most sacred and dear in all the world, by the memory of the eternity of our love!'

'Oh, Pisana, I have never broken an oath!'

'Just because of that I entreat you; don't you see? The happiness of my last moments now depends upon your will, upon your lips!'

'Then it is really necessary. . . . Is that your irrevocable decree?'

'Yes, Carlo, irrevocable! As the gift that I have made you of myself, as the oath that I now renew that you are the most noble and generous being that has ever put on mortal form! . . .'

'You esteem me far more than I am worth: you ask me for what I cannot do . . .'

'Anything, you can do anything . . . if you still love me! Swear to me that you will live, for the good of the family that I imposed upon you, for the honour of the country that we have loved together and will always love!'

'Is it your wish, Pisana? . . . Very well, I swear! . . . I swear it by that desire I have to follow you, I swear it by the invincible hope that nature herself will soon relieve me of my oath!'

'Thank you, thank you, Carlo! . . . Now I am happy; I can return worthily to God.'

'But one thing also I ask of you, Pisana; not to harbour any longer these gloomy thoughts that make you die before your time; make use of the happiness that is reborn within you to revive your health and re-animate your courage, to preserve yourself, in short for us, for us who love you so much.'

'You ask for more than I can grant you! . . . Carlo, look me in the face. Do you see this smile of happiness, these tears of joy that flood my eyes? Well, do you believe that I, poor drunkard of love, could resign myself to leave you, to abandon you for ever, and never see you again, either on earth or in Heaven, if a hope, sure, deep and invincible, did not assure me that we shall meet again, that we shall be united and contented a thousand times more than we have ever been for all eternity?'

'Pisana, yes, I believe you! I can see your soul shining through your eyes! . . . Stay with us, stay, for pity's sake, stay!'

'Do you believe that if I should stay I should ever again enjoy the pure ineffable pleasure of this past hour? . . . Oh, no, Carlo! Every other joy would be colourless and ignoble to me now. Let me go, let me go! Adore with me the clemency of God that surrounds with the most splendid colours the sun that sets! . . . Thank Him for allowing us in this world to have a foretaste of the next, almost an infallible pledge that the promises instilled in our hearts are neither lacking nor false! . . . Good-bye, Carlo, good-bye! . . . Let us part now, when our hearts are strong and prepared! . . . We shall meet again, perhaps many times, perhaps once only! . . . But a last time we shall surely meet again, never to part. I go to wait for you, to learn to love you truly as you deserve! . . . Good-bye, good-bye!'

She fled from my arms and I had not the force to hold her back. I wept, I wept as if she were really dead, as if that 'good-bye' had been her last word. Wherever my thoughts wandered, I saw nothing around me save darkness and desolation. That soul so great and sublime shone so brightly that, as she fled, all the splendours of this world seemed as shadows and every affection lost strength and warmth in comparison with hers. When a little later, Lucilio, Acquilina and the others returned, I had only strength to make a gesture towards the door through which the Pisana had disappeared and burst once more into tears.

After about an hour, during which he had advised the others to leave me alone, Lucilio returned to tell me that the Pisana had been overcome by a sudden exhaustion but had come to herself once more after drinking a cordial and had then sunk into a sweet sleep. He advised us to leave her in peace and let nature work unassisted, since there are no restoratives more powerful than hers. He would come again to see if his skill could afford any help and continue the improvement obtained by those hours of rest.

This was followed by a respite of several days, during which the gay serenity of the Pisana was never clouded for an instant.

When she could have me near her and make me repeat softly that I would keep my promises, a heavenly smile lighted up her face; I had never seen her so contented, not even in the moments of her greatest joy. So, little by little, I watched die down in a joyful and serene calm that fiery soul that I had always seen before in so high spirited a tempest of passions; I saw her purer nature rise to the surface and shine with a light ever clearer and more tranquil, and saw vanish all those earthly emotions that had troubled her from time to time; I saw how much a single affection, full and constant, was able to do despite her false and corrupted upbringing; I saw the swift passions that had disturbed her spirit become completely still and death approach, beautiful, as a friend smiling to the kiss of her smiling lips.

The delirium of the death agony was for her a dream of enchanting visions; up till then I had always believed that the noble words put into the mouths of the dying were artificial lies, but I was convinced then that holy souls turning back for a moment from the supreme instant to cast a last glance upon life, express the greatest and most noble sentiments, as if to make of them a viaticum for the great voyage towards God. She mentioned Italy many times, clasping my hand and murmuring words of courage and of faith. 'Your sons, your sons,' she said to me, 'Carlo, I see them and they are happier than we were! . . . But in this world, in this world! . . . Beyond this world we shall be even more blessed, since it is we who have prepared their happiness.' At other times she would fall into uncertain mutterings in which I seemed to understand that she was thinking of Naples and of the glorious and terrible days passed there twenty-four years before. After invoking these distant memories, she clasped her hands and said with an imploring glance: 'Forgive, forgive!'

When the Pisana came to herself once more, Acquilina asked her if she wanted a priest to be called since religion might even more assure the marvellous tranquillity of her spirit.

'Yes, yes,' she replied, smiling sadly, 'it would give my sister such pain to know that I died without a priest.'

'Don't speak of death!' said Acquilina. 'The comforts of religion aid us to live according to the Lord's will.'

I dried my eyes furtively and, in looking away, saw Bruto and the two boys who were watching in wonder and almost in envy, this noble death. Peace and greatness breathed around her bed and I too ended by believing that it was only a matter of a few years' separation, that I was not present at a scene of despair but only at a sad but friendly leavetaking. Lucilio came in, felt her pulse, and smiled at the dying woman as if he would say: you will leave us soon, but in peace. He too believed. At last the priest came and remained with the Pisana for some time. She was without cynical disdain but also without affected devotion. Content as she was in herself, it was not difficult to convince her to be at peace with God and the first of the funeral rites, that is carried out with so gloomy and terrifying a ceremony at the bedside of the dying, in no way changed her serene expression.

Then she turned to talk to us, to thank Lucilio for his care, Acquilina and Bruto for their friendship and to bless my sons, telling them to obey and imitate their parents. Then she took me by the hand and asked me not to leave her bedside again even to take a cup of cordial that was on the sideboard, and which Acquilina held to her lips. She thanked her with a smile, whispering in my ear: 'Love her, Carlo, love her! It was I who gave her to you!' I had not the breath to reply, but nodded, nor have I ever forgotten that promise as Acquilina herself could bear witness, however much some differences of opinion may from time to time have embittered us.

The Pisana's breathing began to grow more laboured; she gripped my hand ever more tightly, smiling from time to time at each of us, but when she turned to me her gaze was longer and more intense. If she broke off to look at Acquilina it was as if to ask forgiveness for these last tokens of love. She sometimes tried to speak, but her voice was beginning to weaken; I felt myself growing weaker in sympathy with her till suddenly by a fresh glance she gave me renewed courage to remember what I had promised her.

'I am here,' she said suddenly in a voice stronger than before, and tried to lift herself on her pillows, but fell back once more, exhausted but not cast down at her own weakness. 'I am here!' she murmured once more and then, turning to me, said: 'Remember, I shall wait for you!'

I felt a quiver pass across my heart; it was her soul that once more greeted mine in passing. She still gripped my hand, her lips smiled and her eyes remained open; but the Pisana had already gone to prove the truth of her eternal hopes. No one moved; all remained there in silence, to watch the serenity of that death. Lucilio told me afterwards that he too had wept but almost for joy; I did not see him then and indeed I saw nothing for the rest of that day. I did not move, I did not weep, I did not speak until they took the Pisana's hand from mine to lay her on the bier. Then I myself arranged her clothes around her, I myself placed her in her last bed, and at the last kiss that I placed upon her lips it seemed to me that my soul would have flown away with hers.

For many days I hardly knew whether I was alive or dead, but it was a suspension of life, and not despair; little by little my thoughts freed themselves from that lethargy until at last I regained full consciousness of myself and of the memory of what had been, and to have once more the strength to obey the last wishes of the Pisana. From then on my character took on a gravity and austerity that it had never had before and I instilled those examples of virtue and fortitude into the upbringing of my sons. When Acquilina reproved me gently for risking them to a pitiless and tempestuous destiny, it was enough for me to recall to her the death of the Pisana for her to withdraw and say that I was right! Indeed one should take no heed either of perils or of sacrifices to merit such a death.

A few days before we were due to leave London came the news that His Excellency Navagero had passed to a better world, leaving the Pisana his sole heir, and should she die intestate, all his property was to go towards the founding of a hospital which should bear her name. He possessed a clear couple of millions and had lived all his last years in feigned poverty in order to accumulate this vast sum for the end for which he intended it.

I suffered greatly at having to leave England where in a country graveyard so great a part of me remained; but the Pisana had commanded me to think of my sons and we left. Spiro and Aglaura had asked me to see to some of their affairs that had remained in abeyance in Venice and therefore I went there, determined to settle down. Bruto, after a trip to the Friuli to set his affairs in order, was to join us and so I sadly arranged my winter quarters for my old age. I also suffered much at having to part from Lucilio, but when he took leave of me he said: 'I will come to die amongst you!' I knew that he would not break his word.

We reached Venice on 15 September 1823. I passed the first night in that well-remembered little room where I had lived through such happy and carefree days, kissing with tears and sobs two locks of hair. One I had torn from the tresses of the Pisana as a little girl, the other I had cut reverently from the pale brow of the Pisana dead.

EPILOGUE

THE reasons for which Venice fell are well known and those very reasons made it impossible for her to rise again to her former commercial activity. Destiny has the major blame for that, for the torpor of the government and the flaccidity of the people both derived from the closing of those seaways on which the activities of the one and of the other had borne good fruit in the past. The Venetians continued to be bold and excellent merchants while it was possible for them to sell the goods of distant countries at greater profit than their competitors; they retained their warlike manners and their power since that vast and daring commerce required a vigorous guardianship. Once that initiative ceased, there ceased also the call of their ancient and glorious traditions.

Venice continued to live by habit, *per accidente* as the Doge Renier had said; none the less three centuries of slow decadence, honoured and almost happy, had given another proof of her ancient power and of the virtues created in her government and her people from the times of their glorious activity. If the Republic of St Mark had taken part vigorously in the life of the *terraferma*, then perhaps after the decline of her commerce she would have found fresh fields for her activities. But in the Italian provinces she appeared more of a merchant than a governor; they were not an integral part of her, but colonies destined to nourish the reigning patricians, a means of supplying wealth. Whether by habit or respect, other governments left the Venetians to enjoy their commercial prosperity in peace and, little by little, all need for armed protection ceased and, content to cancel a stave on the credit side of their ledgers, the Venetians trusted solely in their own prudence and the discretion of others for the assurance of their dominion.

After those first revolutions that took from her every support in the *terraferma* and closed to her more than ever the now unfamiliar seaways, Venice remained, so to speak, at death's door. When, later, peace returned and the sea was no longer blockaded, her resources were so miserable that they could no longer compete with those of other ports which had grown strong during her inactivity. Trieste entered the contest boldly, backed up by the trade of Vienna and with the aid of a government that either despaired of, or did not care about, restoring Venice to the former field of her triumphs. Venice remained shut within herself, melancholy and sorrowing, like a dethroned prince who resigns himself to die of hunger rather than deign to stretch out a hand.

When I returned to Venice that torpor of inertia and of shame was at its height. There was no commerce, no wealthy land-holding, no arts, no sciences, no glory, no activity of any sort. Venice seemed dead and certainly there was a suspension of life.

My first thought was to arouse once more some sort of activity in those rusting and stagnant forces. Little could be attempted since there was practically nothing available; but he who begins well is already half way. To revive, even to create, a spirit of co-operation would be the first step and I was encouraged by the power of England, at which I still marvelled. But even giants are born as babies. I became cautious in order not to involve in sudden downfall the good will I began quietly to accumulate.

A first company founded by me for trade in dried fruit, nut galls, oil and other materials from the ports of Greece and the Levant had some success. It showed, if no more, that we had emerged from that deep somnolence. Other companies were formed and competition, increasing our activities, enlarged our enterprises and enabled us to take greater risks in the hope of greater profit.

When a stone is thrown no one knows where it may fall, and if the prosperity of Venice was still insufficient to entice foreigners to settle there with their capital, at least there was as much as was needful to stir up the energies of her own countrymen. It was not much but I hoped for more.

Meanwhile, grave matters were disturbing me within the city itself. About this time the cholera, which had penetrated Italy for the first time with all the horror that accompanies contagious maladies, had thrown all Venice into the greatest consternation. It swept the world of many persons who did not even realize how they had been taken. One of the first to go was Agostino Frumier, who left behind him a crowd of children and was greatly afflicted at having to descend below the earth without the Chamberlain's keys that had so long been his ambition. In the general mortality his brother lost the old Correggiarice who died, I believe, more from fear than from real illness, and he returned to an everyday world so unfamiliar that he wondered at not finding his head in a wig and at no longer seeing the Doge and the great cloaks of the Most Excellent Procurators. They used to say in Venice: 'Look at the Cavalier

Frumier just out of college'. He was then about sixty-five and the Signora Correggiarice had already passed seventy when she had finally decided to die. To find a constancy like that, one would have had to go back to the earliest times of the human race when there was only one man and one woman.

In that outbreak of pestilence I believe that Doretta also died. After a life filled with degradation and wandering, she had returned to Venice to a shameful old age. I learnt from Signora Clara that she had disappeared that summer from the hospital. I had come across her several times but had pretended not to recognize her, since her sordid appearance filled me with disgust and it seemed to me a sort of sacrilege to associate the memory of Leopardo with this disgusting creature. However, her end helped to convince me that a supreme justice controls the events of this world and that, though there are indeed many and painful exceptions, the general rule that evil attracts evil is true.

We had scarcely recovered from the terror of that pestilence when one evening, about the middle of November as I recall, Dr Vianello was announced. I had always kept up a desultory correspondence with Lucilio; but after '31 when he had paid a brief visit to Italy, only to return almost at once, our letters had grown more and more infrequent. At that time we had had no news of him for more than a year. I found him bent, pale and his sparse remaining hair quite white; but his eyes were still the same as ever. His strong and upright spirit still gave warmth to his words and one could still divine the force that lurked in that dried and wizened little body.

'I told you I would come to die amongst you!' he said to me. 'Very well, I am here to keep my word. I am seventy-two, but that would be of little importance were it not for an irritating chest complaint presented to me by the London climate. We have much to do, we children of the sun, to defend ourselves; the fogs destroy us . . .'

'I hope you are joking,' I replied, 'and just as you cured my sight, I swear to you that I will cure your chest.'

'I repeat that I have come to keep my word. We know one another and have no need to exchange pleasantries or lies. We know how much can be hoped for from life and how much good or evil may be expected from death. You know that I speak as I think and that if I say I shall die in peace, then I shall die in peace. . . . I will admit to you, however, that it pains me not to be able to see the end; but that, after all, is a misfortune that has touched ten generations before me, so that I have no right to complain . . .'

'Would you like to see Clara again?' I asked him, 'or have you forgotten all about her?'

'Oh no,' he replied, 'I have every intention of seeing her, to contemplate once more the diverse ends of a single passion in differently educated temperaments. To learn as much as one can should be the supreme law of existence. This inextinguishable thirst to know does not depend on any apparent motive of individual reason. It may well derive from the necessity of a vaster order that is prolonged beyond death.'

'Tell me, Lucilio, how is it that I have never heard you either wondering or indignant at the incredible change in Clara towards you? It is a long time now since I have wanted to ask you that. It seems to me even more remarkable than the constancy of your love.'

'Why is it that I did not marvel and was not indignant? Clara's soul was prone to sublime illusions and I could not wonder that she sought to escape by that way, the more so since I, my mind disturbed by quite different thoughts, had allowed myself to fall into a foolish certainty. Women often fly off from lower motives; then it is easy enough to get them back again and it is a misfortune common enough and a danger most generally feared. I, who felt myself sure on that account, did not think of the other. Woe to you, woe when they fly from you for higher reasons! To follow them is useless, to call them back is vain; there is no pleasure so great as that of sacrifice, there is no reason that can conquer faith, no pity that can divert from the absolute consideration of things eternal! . . . And women, you know, have a greater facility than we to live, if I may so put it, beyond life. It seems that they have more clearly than we the presentiment of a future life. As for being angry with Clara, well, in the first place, if you will excuse my saying so, anger is a schoolboy's sentiment; I have never felt any anger against her, because hers was not injustice but hallucination; she thought to love me better in this way and to procure for me not a worldly and transient pleasure but a celestial and eternal satisfaction. Imagine to yourself! I might even be grateful for it!'

Lucilio and Clara saw one another almost every evening that winter, and the company in the Fratta household had often reason to be scandalized at the outbursts of the old doctor. Augusto Cisterna used to say that he should be excused because of his old age, but Clara carried her tolerance still further, saying that he had always been mad but that God would forgive him because of his good intentions. She was very careful not to raise her eyes in front of the doctor, perhaps because she had so vowed on leaving the convent; but otherwise, so great was the simplicity of her faith and the ingenuousness of her manner, that Lucilio smiled at her more in admiration than in scorn.

Amongst those who had been very pleased to see Doctor Vianello again was, though you will scarcely believe it, Count Rinaldo. From his daily incubation among the books in the library something was about to be born; a tremendous tome on the trade of Venice, from Attila up to Charles V, in which the boldness of the hypotheses, the erudition of his sources and critical acumen were intermingled wonderfully, as Lucilio told me at the time. Lucilio seemed greatly astonished at finding so great a treasure of learning and such a fervent love of his country in that dirty and grumbling little manikin, Count Rinaldo, but at the same time guessed the reason for this phenomenon.

'You see,' he said, 'how in times of error and national sloth, the minds of those who see justly and far ahead and the energies of those who are not content to rot, are exploited! . . . Their love and their work are lavished on digging up old inscriptions and broken stones, and these they love and study. It is the almost universal destiny of our writers.'

Had Lucilio stayed longer with us, his conversation and his ideas would have been of great value to us. But towards the beginning of spring, his malady took a turn for the worse and his premonitions that he was to die were fulfilled. He breathed his last looking me proudly in the face as if forbidding me to accompany him; Clara was in the next room praying for him and the last words of the dying man were: 'Thank her!' I did thank her, but for what was far from clear.

However much she had prayed for him, she had not consented to console the dying man with her presence; but since she had made a peculiar study of thwarting her own wishes, I think I can say that she would have liked to have done so, and that she offered this sacrifice also for the greater good of his soul.

As I go on with my story, I often think of the daisy, that modest little flower of the golden heart and the white petals with which young girls try to foretell their love. One by one they tear off the petals till only the last remains; and so it is with us, with the companions with whom we set out along the paths of life; one falls today, another tomorrow, and at last we find ourselves alone and melancholy in the desert of old age. After Lucilio's death came that of Spiro, which redoubled my sorrow.

In the two or three years that followed misfortune struck more directly at us; one by one Acquilina's brothers died, leaving only Bruto who supported the weight of his years cheerfully enough and only complained that destiny had given him Venice as a residence since the great frequency of bridges was very inconvenient for his wooden leg.

So we went on slowly declining into old age, while the country found once more its youth and what followed then was a sufficient proof that all those years were neither dead nor sleeping, as the pessimists had clacked to us. From nothing, nothing is born; it is an unanswerable axiom.

About 1840, feeling my age and once again having trouble with my eyes, I took stock of my resources and found I had increased my substance to such an extent that it could provide me with enough to live on when invested in the funds. Also the Internunciature at Constantinople advised me that the Ottoman government had finally recognized my father's credit in part and that, if not the greater amount for which the heirs of the Grand Vizier of that time were considered responsible, at least a considerable sum would be paid me.

I had never really believed that anything would come of that credit. Therefore the eighty thousand piastres that were handed over to me came as a very welcome gift, and as to the heirs of the Grand Vizier, I left them in peace, since I had been told that they were all poor and obscure persons. With this sum and the thirty thousand ducats that I had received from the final settlement of my affairs, I had quite a nice little balance with which I bought a fine property near the Provedoni house at Cordovado.

A little later Pope Gregory XVI died and was succeeded on the pontifical throne by Giovanni Mastai Ferretti under the name of Pius IX. Who, on reading this name, does not hear singing once more in his mind a lovely melody that echoes in the brain long after it has been heard? . . . Pius IX was above all priest and Pope, but they tried to transform him into a sort of Julius II, pontifex and soldier; it was like glimpsing through a cloud some symbol, some figure that whoever has once glimpsed, immediately recognizes but is quite unable to make it seen by others.

Clara was one of those most enthusiastic for the new pontiff; she spoke of him as a prophet and her conversation seemed almost scandalous, since it could hardly have been imagined that the old bigot, the Abbess Emerita of St Theresa, would have applauded with all her heart a Pope who paid more attention to politics than to his sacerdotal duties; or at least so they believed then. But they were perhaps unaware of why Clara had been made a bigot and a nun and on what conditions she had been obliged to observe her vows to God. I did not then know for sure; but from some half word was able to guess it.

Amid all these commotions money got tighter than ever and it was then that the Count Rinaldo sent an urgent order to his bailiff at the Castle of Fratta to send him some money at all costs, and the poor peasant extricated himself by selling the remainder of the castle and sending the price to his master. With this little sum the Count wanted to found a patriotic newspaper in I know not which city of the *terraferma*, but the money slipped through his fingers and Clara remained without her coffee and he with little bread, but the one praying and the other reading and building castles in the air, they defended themselves valiantly against hunger. Sometimes I had the Christian charity to ask him to lunch; but he was so absent-minded that, although he often had a two days' hunger gnawing at his stomach, he would forget the time and come only for dessert. However, once they got moving, his jaws displayed a good enough memory of his fasts and a discreet desire not to suffer from them again for a considerable time.

Meanwhile, street demonstrations all over Italy were getting more open and warlike; from France, changed unexpectedly into a Republic, blew a wind filled with hope. Revolution threatened Vienna and came to a climax at Venice in the way we all know. However old I might be, half blind and father of a family, I still went out on to the Piazza with the others. I threw aside my seventy years and felt gayer and younger than I had half a century before when I had made my first political appearance as Secretary of the Municipality.

The National Guard was then being formed and they wanted to make me Colonel of the Second Legion. Without consulting either my eyes or my legs I accepted wholeheartedly, recalled all my antiquated knowledge of military tactics, and made a few good and willing youths draw up in file and wheel to right and left. Only in the evenings, when I returned about midnight, after submitting to the finest scolding that a good husband might expect, did I feel the weight of my years.

Later, when the Neapolitan levies entered Venice under the command of my old acquaintance, General Pepe, an officer came to ask for me. It was Alessandro Giorgi, who had returned from South America, old, bronzed, crippled and Marshal and Duke of Rio-Vedras. With his great ungainly body swathed in a pompous scarlet cloak covered with gold and ribbons he seemed, at the least, like some grotesque ancestor of Queen Pomare. But the heart that beat beneath that indescribable uniform was always the same, that of a boy and a soldier. On seeing him, I could do no less than make a comparison between him and the Partistagno; both of more or less similar temperament, both had taken up the same career. But what a difference in the end! So much can counsels, examples, company and circumstances react upon these pliable and ingenuous temperaments; they become, according to chance, either cut-throats or heroes.

'My dear Carlino,' he said, after embracing me so warmly that some of his orders got hooked in the buttonholes of my coat, 'as you see, I have left everything flat, my Dukedom, the army and America, to return to Venice!'

'I never doubted it,' I said. 'How many times when I heard an unfamiliar step on the stair I have said to myself: can it be Alessandro?'

'As for me, if I had not this cursed gout, I would be ready to dance a tarantella! . . . Why, Bruto, my brother! . . . Here is another of us ballerinos! . . . I swear on the Gospels if it had not been for your wooden leg, I would scarcely have recognized you.'

These exclamations were provoked by the appearance of Bruto, who in his uniform as a civic cannoneer, cut a strange enough figure worthy of matching the American Duke and Marshal. . . . But however comic they appeared, they gave a good example of military discipline to certain youths who aspired to be Admirals and Generals. Alessandro, despite his dukedom and marshalate, had been satisfied with the rank of Colonel, and Bruto had returned to his cannon as if he had only left it the day before. His limping gait and bantering manner even among the shells and rockets kept up the spirits of his younger companions.

Everyone at that time was a soldier, even Count Rinaldo who many times, as I saw for myself, mounted guard before the Doge's Palace with such gravity that he seemed like one of those silent sentinels who adorn some great spectacle. But one poor fellow who did not come in time to mount guard was Alfonso Frumier. Fallen from heaven to earth after the death of his lady, he had no longer been able to follow the thread of his ideas and however much he tried was never able to succeed until one day his servant came to tell him that they were shouting 'Long live San Marco!' on the Piazza, that this was the Republic and a thousand other things, each stranger than the last. The old gentleman struck himself a great blow on the forehead with his hand. 'Here we are!' he seemed to say to himself and then, with eyes starting out of his head and limbs convulsed and trembling:

'Quick, quick!' he stammered. . . . 'Bring me my toga . . . give me my wig. . . . Long live San Marco! . . . My toga . . . my wig, I tell you! . . . Quickly! . . . I must be in time!'

It seemed to the servant that his master could scarcely utter those last words and that he was swaying on his legs; he put out an arm to support him, but Alfonso crashed to the floor, dead from excess of joy. I still remember that I wept when I heard of this moving scene, which explained nobly enough the semi-century of torpor of that good cavalier.

I heard, too, at that time of Doctor Ormenta. He had fled to the *terraferma* and had died there of fright after a partisan skirmish. It in no way helped him to have worn in his youth the cloak of St Anthony, though he was accepted into the Camposanto.

The winter of 1848 was, however, gloomy and pregnant with foreboding. I no longer believed either in France or England and the rout at Novara, rather than an unexpected setback, was the sorrowful confirmation of long fears. One fought now for honour rather than for victory, though no one said as much for fear of lessening the courage of others.

After the public misfortunes came our private griefs. One day they came to tell me that Colonel Giorgi and Corporal Provedoni had been wounded on the bridge by a shell and had been taken to the military hospital whence, because of the serious nature of their wounds, they could not be moved. I rushed there, more dead than alive, and found them lying on two palliasses one next to the other; they were talking of their early years, of their former wars and of their mutual hopes, like two friends before falling asleep. But they were breathing with difficulty because their chests were torn by terrible wounds.

'It is strange,' whispered Alessandro, 'I feel as if I were in Brazil.'

'And I at Cordovado in the Square of the Madonna,' replied Bruto.

It was the beginning of the death agony, a sweet delirium such as nature only grants to her elect to make their passage from this earth smooth and easy.

'Console yourselves,' I said, scarcely holding back my tears, 'You are in the arms of a friend.'

'Ah, Carlino,' Alessandro murmured. 'Good-bye, Carlino! If you ever want anything for yourself, you have only to ask. The Emperor of Brazil is my friend.'

Bruto clasped my hand, since he was still in his right senses, but a little later he too fell into delirium and both revealed in these last flights of their imagination so much goodness of heart and greatness of feeling that I wept hot tears of despair at not being able to hold back their spirits from ascending to the heavens. They came to themselves only for a moment to salute first me and then each other, to smile and then to die.

Acquilina, who came a little later, found me weeping and kneeling between two corpses.

The same day, in the camp of the besiegers near Mestre, General Partistagno died. Only a few miles away were his many sons, but none of them was willing to come to gladden his last moments.

After having closed the eyes of two such friends, I felt that it was no longer a sin to wish for death also and turned my thoughts to the Pisana, who was perhaps watching me from the heavens above, asking her if it were not time for me to come to rejoin her. But a still, small voice in my heart replied no, and indeed there were still more sad offices for me to carry out. A few days later Count Rinaldo was struck by the cholera that had again begun its ravages, especially amongst those who were starving. The bombardment had concentrated the people in the wards of the city that were most distant from the *terraferma* and it was a solemn sight to see the grim patience with which they endured so many and such deadly scourges. The poor Count was already at his last gasp when I reached his bedside; his sister, bent by age and privations, watched beside him with that imperturbable courage that never abandons those who truly believe.

'Carlino,' the dying man said. 'I asked them to fetch you because of the extremity in which I find myself and the recollection that parts of my life work are in danger of remaining unfinished. Therefore I put my trust in you and want you to promise me to have it printed in forty sections with the same paper and format as the first!'

'I promise you,' I replied almost with a sob.

'I will leave the corrections to you,' murmured the dying man 'and also . . . if you think necessary . . . any changes . . .'

He was unable to say more and died with his eyes fixed on me, once more confiding to me with his last glance that sole fruit of his life. I undertook to see that due funeral honours were accorded him, and took the Signora Clara into my house since she, more than ever afflicted by rheumatism, was scarcely able to move about by herself. But the satisfaction of giving her the most constant and loving care possible was not to last for long. She too died on the day of the August Madonna, thanking the Mother of God who had called her to herself on the day of Her Assumption and blessing God that the vows she had made fifty years before for the salvation of the Republic had received so fair a reward in the sunset of her life. I thought then of Lucilio and perhaps she too took thought of him with a smile of hope, since she had much faith in her own prayers and a thousand times more in the clemency of God.

On 21 August the capitulation was signed. Venice retired from the Italian battlefields as Dante said: '*A guisa di leon quando si posa*'.

Acquilina and I remained alone, weighed down, distressed, silent, like two tree-trunks struck by lightning in a desert. But life in Venice became every day more hateful and insupportable, so that by common accord we moved to the Friuli, to the little district of Cordovado. There we lived a couple of years in the religion of our sorrows; at last she too, poor woman, was mercifully visited by death. And I remained, I remained to meditate and fully to understand the terrible meaning of that fearful word: alone.

Alone? . . . Ah no, I was not alone! . . . I may have believed it for a moment, but recovered myself and blessed in my anguish that Holy Providence that, to him who has sought for the good and avoided the evil, concedes another and supreme comfort, peace of mind and the sweet but melancholy company of memories.

It was four years after my return to Cordovado that I found the courage to visit Fratta. I went there with the grandchildren of old Andreini, he too the father of many sons, on the eightieth anniversary of my entry into the castle, when I arrived there from Venice in a basket.

After lunch I went out alone, to see once more at least the site where that famous castle had once been. Not a trace remained: only a few stones amongst which two goats were browsing and near by a young girl singing to herself, who watched me with curiosity and ceased her weaving. I recognized the shape of the courtyard and in the middle the stone under which I had buried the Captain's old hunting dog. Perhaps it was the sole monument to my memories that had remained intact; but no, I deceive myself. In those beloved places I could still remember those happy years of infancy and youth: the bushes, the fishpond, the meadows, the air and the sky took me back to live once more in that distant past. At the corner of the moat there still stood in my imagination the great black tower where so many times I had admired Germano winding up the clock; I saw once more the long corridors through which Martino led me by the hand when it was time for me to go to bed, and his hermit-like little room where the swallows would no longer hang their nests. I seemed to see passing before me on the unpaved road Monsignor with his breviary under his arm, or the grandiose family coach with the Count, the Countess and the Chancellor inside, or Marchetto's old horse on whose back I used to climb. I saw arriving one by one the after-lunch visitors, Monsignor di Sant'Andrea, Giulio del Ponte, the Chaplain, the Rector, the handsome Partistagno, Lucilio; I heard their voices sounding in the dining-room around the card tables and Clara skimming through some stave of Ariosto under the willows in the garden. Then followed the noisy invitations of my childish companions, but I did not reply to them and withdrew into myself, alone or happy to play with the Pisana on the edge of the fishpond.

With what devout sadness, with what delicate tenderness, did I dwell on this memory that still surpassed all the others and gave to them increased sweetness and melancholy. . . . Oh, Pisana,

Pisana! How I wept that day! And how I bless you and bless God that the tears of eighty years are not all of grief.

After nightfall I left those ruins; the little birds in the near by poplars were still twittering before going to rest as in the evenings of my childhood. They are still twittering, but how many generations had succeeded one another since then in the simple families of the birds! . . . Men see nature always the same, since they will not deign to look at her minutely, but as we change so she changes also and while our black hair turns white millions of existences have completed their turn. I left that world of old to return to that of today . . . the past is sweet for me, but the present for me, as for all others, must be still sweeter.

* * * * *

On Sundays, when I go in my carriage (ah me, I too now feel the scirocco of Monsignor) to the spring of Venchieredo or to Fratta, a cloud of melancholy gathers on my brow, but I soon brush it away and return to my usual gaiety. Misfortunes no longer matter so much when one is on the edge of the tomb; and, without believing anything, without claiming anything, it is enough for me to be sure that there, on the other side, no worse destiny and no chastisement awaits me! Take heed to give yourself such an assurance and you will be able to die smiling.

Yes, to die smiling! That is not the aim, but it is the proof that life was not ill spent, that it was not an evil either for ourselves or for others! Now that you have gained a familiarity with me, my masters and friends, now that you have listened patiently through all the long confessions of Carlo Altoviti, will you grant me your absolution? I hope so. Certainly I began writing them with this illusion and you will not deny some of your pity to an old man since you have been courteous enough to bear him long and indulgent company. Give your blessing, if no more, to the times in which I have lived. You will have seen how I found the old and the young in my childhood and how I leave them now. It is a quite new world, a mixture of feelings and old loves that moves beneath the uniform veneer of modern society; perhaps caricature and romance have been the losers, but history has gained. If, as I have already said elsewhere, we should not claim to measure with our lives the life of nations, if we should be content to gather that good which we can, as the reaper places contentedly in the evening his sheaves cut during the day, if we should be humble and prudent enough to cede the continuation of our work to our sons and grandsons, our own souls made young once more, so that day by day all that has grown weak is lost and what has become discoloured by age becomes once more enriched, if we should be educated to believe in goodness and eternal justice, there would no longer be so many differences of opinion about life!

I am neither a theologian, nor a learned man, nor a philosopher, and yet I want to give my opinion like the traveller who, however ignorant, can rightly judge whether the land that he has passed through be poor or rich, unpleasant or beautiful. I have lived eighty-three years, my sons, therefore I have a right to give mine.

Life is what our nature makes it, that is to say our nature and our upbringing; as physical fact that is a necessity, as a moral fact it is the office of justice. Who by his own temperament will be in all matters just towards himself, towards others, towards all humanity, he will be the most innocent, useful and noble man who has ever passed through this world. His life will be a benefit to himself and to all and will leave an honoured and profound mark upon the history of his country. That is the archetype of a real and perfect man. What matters it if others live afflicted and unhappy? They are the degenerates, the strayed, the guilty. Let them be inspired by that example of triumphant humanity and they will find that peace that nature promises to every little part of her vast design. Happiness is in our consciences; bear that well in mind. The certain proof of our spiritual life, wherever it may be, resides in justice.

Oh light, eternal and divine, I entrust to your imperishable rays my life, which is about to be extinguished! . . . So is the rush-light extinguished before the sun, so the firefly loses itself in the mist. The calm of my soul is for ever undisturbed, like the calm of a sea where there are no winds; I march towards death as towards a mystery, obscure and inscrutable, yet deprived for me of menaces and fears. Oh, if my assurance should be false, if nature should be pleased to mock, to contradict herself! I cannot believe it since in all the universe I have not yet found a principle that both chills and warms, that both denies and affirms. A shudder tells me of the immensity of the peril; but would our minds be so blind as not even to have the involuntary prudence of our nerves? . . .

No, I feel it within me, I have said it with unbroken faith, I repeat it now with firm hope! The peace of old age is a calm gulf that opens little by little into that ocean, immense, boundless and infinitely calm, of eternity. I see no more my enemies on the face of the earth; I see no longer my friends who have left me one by one, concealing themselves behind the shadows of death. . . I have measured with brief days the past of a great people and that universal law that brings the fruit to its maturity and guides the sun in its round, assures me that my hope will survive to become certainty and triumph. What can I ask more? . . . Nothing, my brothers! . . . I bend my brow, more content than resigned, upon the pillow of the tomb and enjoy seeing widen ever more before me, step by step, those ideal horizons, even as those of earth begin to vanish before my dimming eyes.

Oh souls of faith and love, living or dead, I feel that all my kinship with you is not ended! . . . I feel that your spirits are fluttering around me as if inviting mine to join them again. . . . Oh first and only love of my life, oh, my Pisana, you still think, you breathe in me and around me! I see you in the sunset, clothed in the purple cloak of a heroine, vanishing among the flames of the west and a flash of light from your pure brow leaves a long furrow in the air as if to point my way to me. I glimpse you, celestial and compassionate, in the dying rays of the moon, I speak to you as to a living and breathing woman in the mid hours of the day. Oh, you are still with me, you will always be with me; since your death had really the semblance of a sublime resurrection to a higher and more serene life! We have hoped and loved together, together we must find one another there, where are gathered the loves of past humanity and its hopes for the future. Without you, what am I? . . . For you, for you alone, my heart forgets its every anguish and is filled with a sweet sadness lightened by hope.